Praise for Debra Clopton and her novels

"[A] moving romance about loss and the knowledge that only God knows the future."
—*RT Book Reviews* on *Cowboy for Keeps*

"Debra Clopton writes a terrific story with a great mix of humor and tenderness."
—*RT Book Reviews*

"A touching story about accepting that God knows what's best, even when it's beyond human understanding."
—*RT Book Reviews* on *Her Forever Cowboy*

Praise for Leann Harris and her novels

"A great story of God's healing power and ability to expose the silver lining of even the darkest cloud."
—*RT Book Reviews* on *Second Chance Ranch*

"The kids will capture readers' hearts in this tale that reminds us that prayers are always answered, just perhaps not in the way we anticipate."
—*RT Book Reviews* on *A Rancher for Their Mom*

"Harris' characters are easy to connect with, and her novel highlights the healing power of animals."
—*RT Book Reviews* on *Redemption Ranch*

Award-winning author **Debra Clopton** lives in Texas with her husband, Chuck—whom she met on a blind date. She enjoys touching readers' hearts, making them laugh and entertaining them with her stories—sometimes using the real-life escapades that happen on her ranch. She likes to travel and loves spending time with her family, including her beautiful baby granddaughters. Visit her at debraclopton.com.

Leann Harris has always had stories in her head. Once her youngest child went to school, she began putting those stories on a page. She is active in her local RWA chapter and ACFW chapters. She's a teacher of the deaf (high school), a master composter and avid gardener, and teaches writing at her local community college. Her website is leannharris.com.

Cowboy for Keeps

Debra Clopton

&

Second Chance Ranch

Leann Harris

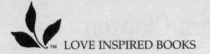 LOVE INSPIRED BOOKS

Recycling programs
for this product may
not exist in your area.

ISBN-13: 978-1-335-00666-0

Cowboy for Keeps and Second Chance Ranch

Copyright © 2017 by Harlequin Books S.A.

The publisher acknowledges the copyright holders
of the individual works as follows:

Cowboy for Keeps
Copyright © 2010 by Debra Clopton

Second Chance Ranch
Copyright © 2011 by Barbara M. Harrison

www.Harlequin.com

Printed in U.S.A.

CONTENTS

COWBOY FOR KEEPS

Debra Clopton

This book is dedicated to Chuck Parks. My life changed the day God sent you to my front door— what a wonderful beginning that blind date turned out to be! I love you, Chuck…you are my very own God-loving, honorable *cowboy for keeps* ☺

And Jesus answered and said unto him,
If a man love me, he will keep my words.
—*John* 14:23

Chapter One

"Are you sure this is what you want to do? I just can't believe it."

Amanda Hathaway met her boss's sympathetic, if somewhat startled, gaze. It wasn't what she wanted, it was her only option. "Yes. It is, Joyce. I've given it a lot of thought and I want—I *need*—to move strictly to adult cases." Adults, not children. Not the kids she'd loved working with—felt called to work with.

"But you've always loved working with children," Joyce Canton said as if reading her mind. "And you have such a gift. Don't you want to think this through?"

Amanda took a deep breath, her chest constricted with the strain she was feeling. "I have, Joyce. This is not easy for me. But I don't have the heart for it anymore."

"I can't believe that."

"Being around…" The words trailed off because she couldn't voice the words that being around children right now made her feel ill. What good would she do as a physical therapist when she couldn't look at her patients without crying or feeling hollow? "It's tearing me up inside" was all she could manage. She had to change her life. And she had to do it now.

"He was a jerk, Amanda."

Joyce's words emerged in a growl of disgust, one completely the opposite of her normally professional demeanor. Amanda blinked hard as her eyes began to burn. She looked away, willing herself to keep her composure. God had a plan. He did; she just didn't understand it. And that didn't make what she was feeling any less heartbreaking.

"You can't let what *he* said and did have this kind of power over you," Joyce continued. "If I were a man I'd go over there and I'd punch him."

Any other time Amanda might have smiled at her boss's show of affection, but today she just couldn't summon one. Her fiancé—no, her *ex*-fiancé's decision ate at her. "He only expressed his true feelings," she managed, willing herself to truly understand him. Anger wasn't going to help her in this situation. Anger very seldom did help, but in this instance it would simply exaggerate her already shot emotions. "He can't be faulted for being honest."

"Honest. *Honest!* The man knew the facts and asked you to marry him. Then out of the blue he drops this bomb on you. How could he ask you to marry him and then break it off because you can't—"

Joyce didn't finish the sentence as her voice broke. Her eyes welled with tears. She snatched a tissue from the box on the desk and dabbed her eyes. Amanda had experienced the same anger and disbelief when Jonathan had made his revelation three endless weeks ago. But then, reality sank in and she knew that deep down she'd been expecting the breakup all along. And how could she blame him? How could anyone blame a man for realizing he couldn't marry a woman who was unable to give him children? She couldn't, and that was where the anger had dispelled. She was twenty-four years old with no hope of ever carrying a child. Her chest constricted again.

She still wasn't sure why she'd started dating Jonathan in the first place. She'd told herself she wouldn't date. Not dating held less risk for her. But then, Jonathan had asked her out for lunch—and when she'd said no, he'd kept coming back. She'd finally agreed. She revealed the cold hard facts of her situation to him on their second date. She hadn't expected to hear from him after that, but he'd assured her that her infertility didn't matter to him. After a whirlwind few weeks, he'd told her he loved her and said adopting children would be totally fine with him. Deep down in her heart, Amanda had known there would be few men in the world who would take on marrying a woman who'd not only lost the ability to carry children, but who had also lost a leg. *Two strikes against you,* the tiny voice in her head chanted. That voice was not good and she knew it, but it wouldn't hush.

"He lied to you, Amanda. What kind of man would do that?"

Focusing on the reality of the situation, Amanda shook her head. "He probably was being honest with himself." Amanda knew it was true. "He made the right choice for himself…and for that I'm grateful—otherwise it would have been wrong for me in the end, too. And besides, you and I both know I rushed into this."

"I really can't believe you are defending him. Although I do agree that it was a rushed relationship. I think you were settling if you ask me. He came along and asked and you jumped at the chance."

Amanda felt a twinge of agreement with that statement. Was that what she'd done? "I learned a long time ago that there are some things you have no control over. That God is in control of our lives and he has a plan." She just hadn't expected it to hurt so much—after all, she'd already faced this reality once in her life at the age of fourteen when the doctors had explained to her that they'd had to give her a complete hysterectomy while they repaired all the internal damage she'd sustained in the accident that had almost killed her. She was blessed to be alive and she'd thought she'd come to peace about her life and her circumstance. But she'd been wrong. After Jonathan ended their relationship, her emotions had spiraled into a tailspin. She'd been struggling for the last month to cope—not sleeping and turning down each job Joyce had offered her.

It didn't make sense. She had a full life. Her career as a physical therapist specializing in children's needs had been borne from that accident. Because she knew she couldn't have children of her own and because she'd had to be fitted with a prosthetic leg at such a young age, she'd been drawn to help kids.

She was good with children, especially those in need of prosthetics. She understood how they felt, and could relate to the many emotions they experienced because of the loss of a limb.

And it made her feel good because she had also been an inspiration to them when they realized life hadn't ended. She'd helped them see that their dreams could still become reality wearing an artificial limb.

That wasn't true for her anymore. Coming face-to-face with Jonathan's choice, she'd also realized that she'd been living a lie.

She couldn't have children of her own. She could never know what it felt like to feel that tiny, precious life growing inside of her. Suddenly it was unbearable.

With shaking fingers Amanda slid the folder of what was supposed to be her new assignment across the desk. "I want—" she paused, digging deep "—I *need* to move to adult cases only."

Amanda couldn't withstand the sympathy in Joyce's gaze any longer. Pushing out of the chair, she moved to stand beside the large window overlooking the busy streets of San Antonio. The thunderstorm that had been hanging over the city all morning had finally given in and was raging full force. She could relate as a violent streak of lightning flashed across the sky. An explosion of thunder immediately followed. She took a shaky breath and reminded herself that she'd overcome so much in her life. She'd thought she'd had it all under control. What a lie that had been. "Jenny told me she had to back out of that long-term job in the hill country. The one with the man in the plane crash."

Joyce didn't look pleased. "She did, but you don't want that. It's—" Joyce stopped speaking and sank into her seat behind her desk as Amanda turned from the window. "It's a tiny town almost a hundred miles from any town of any real size. You don't want to go there."

But she did. "That's exactly what I want." She felt ill but knew this was what she had to do.

"No, it isn't. This is a three-month on-site assignment. You don't—"

"I do." She moved to stand across the desk from her boss. How could she make Joyce understand that she was trapped in a dark hole and the idea of this job seemed like a crack of light showing her the way of escape? A lifeline had been revealed. "I have to do this job. It's exactly what I need."

"But," Joyce started. They held gazes for a long moment and Amanda was almost certain that Joyce could see into Amanda's damaged heart.

"Give me the chance," she urged her. "You know I can do the job."

Another long moment passed. "They want someone with more experience."

"I have enough experience."

"You know…" Joyce murmured thoughtfully as she tapped her fingers on her chair arm. "You actually might be perfect for this job. The other brothers said they thought their brother was depressed. You could help with that. You know about that journey."

Yes, she did. It was what she was fighting off from happening to her again. This job gave Amanda a ray of hope. Her heart kicked up and the constriction eased when Joyce reached for a file on the top of the stack on her desk. A file labeled *Wyatt Turner*.

"I was going to have to turn this job down because Jenny couldn't do it. You know how I hate to pass up jobs. But are you sure this is what you want? I'm comfortable with the idea of you doing the job. I just want to know your state of mind is okay."

The very idea of spending three months in a tiny town away from everything was what Amanda needed. Her eyes hurt with unshed tears of relief. "I'm sure." She hadn't been able to pray since Jonathan broke off their engagement, but she found herself praying now that she would get to do this job.

"Wyatt Turner is a man of means," Joyce said at last. "He can afford to hire a full-time PT to help him all day if he chooses, and so he's doing it. You will be coming up with not only his daily therapy, but also helping out with other things he might need—acting as his personal assistant or cooking if he wants you to. It's an odd job, but the pay is excellent and I promised his two brothers that I'd find the perfect person or I would turn the job down."

"No need for that. It sounds wonderful—"

Joyce held up a hand. "Not so fast. The brothers said Wyatt is impatient with his injuries and will probably not be the easiest person to work with. Being a high achiever and fairly powerful man in his own right, he'll probably be demanding. Are you absolutely certain you can handle this job?"

"I can handle it."

"Why don't you take his file and read over it carefully before you commit to this?"

Amanda didn't need to look over the file. She knew she was capable of getting this man back on his feet. He might be demanding and he might take her for granted. But she could help him and he would help her by getting her away from San Antonio.

"I can do this job." She met Joyce's gaze with determined eyes.

Joyce studied her hard, clearly weighing the decision on all sides. "Then it's yours," she said at last. "I'll let Wyatt's brothers know you'll be there on Monday."

Amanda's heart clamored with the first real excitement she'd felt since Jonathan's words had slammed a hole in it. "Thank you," she managed.

"Honey, I'm praying while you're there you'll realize that none of what Jonathan said is true."

Amanda knew it wasn't that easy to fix the emptiness that filled her. It was far more than Jonathan's words that were affecting her. It was as if they'd released long-dormant emotions she hadn't been able to experience as a young girl when she'd been told there were no children of her own in her future. Her being so young, the loss of a leg had been more devastating than the nebulous idea of being barren. But it was different when a man told a grown woman he couldn't marry her because he wanted children she couldn't give him. It had opened a wound she hadn't realized was there.

She pushed that thought aside and focused on the positive moment now. "I just need to get away and get my head on straight," she said, but she was afraid even that wouldn't fix the emptiness and the loss that now gripped her heart fresh and new. "Please don't worry. I can do this job."

"Then it's yours. I hear Mule Hollow, Texas, is a lovely little town even if it is off the beaten path. You do realize what town this is?"

With memories and intentions tangling in her mind, she hadn't even given the name of the town any consideration. Now she shook her head.

"It's the one that advertised for women to come marry their lonesome cowboys a couple of years ago," Joyce said. "There are cowboys, new wives and babies there now, from what I can find out. But you should know that Mr. Turner's ranch is located several miles away, so you may not be that involved in anything going on in town."

"I can handle it." Amanda needed air and room to breathe and think. "I'll be fine." She didn't want to think about anything right now, not the heartache that was eating at her over her life or the losses she'd suffered. Or Jonathan. She just needed to get away and focus on work. And maybe somewhere during that time this utter sense of emptiness and worthlessness would loosen its hold around her heart.

Maybe in that small town, on that big ranch and in that open space she could find her footing again.

Wyatt Turner shot his brothers, Cole and Seth, a scowl. "It's my body that's broken, not my mind." The wheelchair he'd been sentenced to for the next few weeks felt like cement blocks chained around his waist. Three weeks ago he'd awakened in the hospital lucky to be alive—especially with both legs still attached. Ever since that moment, he'd been fighting to find some kind of balance with the anger he was feeling.

Four days ago he'd been flown in by helicopter to the ranch he and his brothers owned, and he'd been mothered and worried over by his brothers, their wives and the ladies of Mule Hollow—who'd decided that food was the answer to his problems—to the point that he was about sick. He loved them all, but enough was enough. He just wanted to be left alone.

Needed to be alone.

Because of this, his brothers were getting the brunt of his bad temper.

A month ago he'd had the world by its tail. He'd had everything in control. He'd managed to match his younger brothers up with good wives and he'd been able to rest easy that he'd done his parents proud in his family responsibilities. His brothers were happy and that had made him happy. But then he'd crashed his plane and turned his world upside down. The stupidity of his actions ate at him as much as the consequences did.

Looking at him with the patience of Job, his middle brother, Seth, spoke up. "We aren't so sure your mind is working. The fun-loving brother we know and enjoy is sitting in this dark house looking like he hasn't showered in days."

"Seth—" Wyatt bit the word out but Cole, his youngest brother, butted in.

"We love you, bro, and you know you have to snap out of this. You're not going to be in that chair for long."

"Look, you two, go to work and leave me alone. I'm not joking." He had lost his sense of humor three weeks ago.

Cole held up his hands and gave a lopsided grin that usually made anyone and everyone smile along with him. "We're goin'," he said. "No call to get so riled up. That temper's one of the reasons we're worried about you."

Wyatt hiked a brow as a shooting pain ripped through his left hip and tore through his lower spine. He gripped the arm of the wheelchair with his hands and willed his expression to remain pain-free. "I'm only skimming the surface here," he said, trying not to clench his teeth. "You need to stop worrying about me. I'm an adult." Who'd made a bad error in judgment.

"Cole, let's give him some space." Seth headed toward the door. "But Wyatt, whatever you do, don't run Amanda Hathaway off. Yes, you want to be alone, but remember you need her. And the agency said she was the perfect person for the job."

"Yeah, so give her a chance," Cole drawled. "Don't forget Mule Hollow is a long way from the nearest rehab center. It wasn't easy to find a physical therapist willing to come all the way out here to live for three months."

"*And* you can't do therapy on your own," Seth added somberly. "Not this time. Not even you, Wyatt."

He got that loud and clear.

"As stubborn as you are," Cole prompted when Wyatt remained silent, "and as driven, there is no doubt in our minds that you'll be back up globe-trotting in record time. With the right physical therapy program. So stop worrying—and we know you are. You can't hide it from us. Just like you can't hide the fact that you're in a heap of pain right now."

"I'm fine," Wyatt snapped as his gut tightened at the denial as the spasm began to ease up a bit. They came and went at their leisure and he'd begun to wonder if this was what a woman felt like when she went into labor… if so, it was a miracle there were children born. "Look," he said. "I don't need you two knuckleheads trying to run my life—"

"*Oh, man,* you did *not* just say that!" Cole hooted, his eyes dancing as he stared at Wyatt in disbelief. "You, the master of interference—"

"Not that the two of us are complaining," Seth interjected with a grin. "You found us both our wives and we are eternally grateful. But you aren't yourself these days, Wyatt. Not since the accident. We've got to help you get out of this funk you're in from being out of control of everything."

Seth's somber, determined gaze locked with Wyatt's. He knew Seth couldn't be budged when he had that look—it was chock-full of Turner stubbornness. It was true he was in a "funk," but it was only to be expected. He was letting down his clients and his firm because he'd been careless...and careless was unacceptable in his book.

"I should have gone back to Dallas so y'all wouldn't worry—"

"No, you shouldn't have," Seth countered emphatically. "We love you and want what's best for you. Therapy out here on the land you love is the best way to get you healed up."

"That's all we care about," Cole added, all laughter and teasing gone. That in itself told Wyatt how concerned they were for him. "You just need someone to help you get the full range of movement back into that hip and arm. Then you'll be your old overachieving self again. If it were either one of us in your position, this is what you'd be doing for us and you know it."

It was true. He'd have meddled in their lives until he got what was best for them. "I'll be fine," he grunted, not liking losing control of his life like he had. It was not a feeling he'd ever experienced before, and he wasn't dealing well.

"Yeah, you will be after the PT arrives. *Now* we'll go to work." Seth walked out the door.

Cole sauntered after him, but stopped in the doorway. "Hang tough, big bro."

Through the window, Wyatt watched them leave. Their boots thumped loudly as they hurried across the rough wooden porch and down the two steps to the old stone sidewalk that led to where they'd parked the ranch truck earlier. He reminded himself that his little brothers were only looking out for him because they loved him. Still, having the control taken away from him fisted him up inside. Giving control of his life over to anyone wasn't something he did...but it seemed he had no choice. If he wanted his life back he was going to have to trust this Amanda Hathaway.

Seth and Cole wouldn't have hired someone who wasn't capable, he assured himself an hour later as a red SUV pulled over the cattle guard.

Feeling suffocated inside, he'd moved his wheelchair out onto the porch. He waited as a woman got out of the vehicle. She was young, about twenty. No, she'd have to be around twenty-four or -five to have a degree in physical therapy *and* have any kind of experience at all. They'd said she was good at her job…hard to believe if she was as young as he suspected.

She seemed ill at ease as she tucked a strand of fine brown hair behind her ear and looked his way. Being ill at ease didn't give him any more confidence in her than her young age.

Wyatt's eyes narrowed as she walked up the path. Surely this wasn't the woman he was supposed to put his confidence in? If he was going to have someone living on the premises for the next two or three months, invading his privacy and telling him what to do, he expected someone who looked as if they could do the job they were hired to do. His ire escalated with each step she took toward him.

She was medium height with a slight build—no way could she help him get in and out of the wheelchair. She came to a halt at the foot of the steps. Up close it was worse. She had the fresh face of a kid, made more so by the splash of freckles and large doe eyes that looked up at him with what he could only call fear. *Seth and Cole were dead meat!*

"Who are you?" he demanded before she had time to say anything.

"I—well, I'm Amanda. Amanda Hathaway."

This was a joke. It had to be. He was notorious for pulling jokes on his brothers. This would be just like the two of them to get him back for stunts he'd pulled. But he knew it wasn't true. Even they wouldn't pull a stunt like this now.

Nope. This was the woman he was supposed to give control over to—the woman he was supposed to trust with his future.

He didn't think so.

Despite what his little brothers thought, he could still make decisions on his own and that started with telling Amanda Hathaway she wasn't staying.

Chapter Two

Wyatt Turner didn't look right in the wheelchair.

It was the first thought that had hit Amanda when she'd spotted him sitting on the porch. Her confidence had faltered as she'd driven the three hours to Mule Hollow—not surprising since she hadn't been feeling like herself. Seeing Mr. Turner did nothing to help matters.

He was an extremely physically fit man with a broad chest and the lean build of someone used to working out. A man who took care of himself—though she'd already assumed that about him. Joyce had said he was a high achiever, driven to be the best. If that was true, keeping physically fit would fit the profile.

He was handsome—or would be if he didn't look so angry. He had black, wavy hair and bold features including a strong jaw, which at the moment was dark with a five o'clock shadow. It wasn't, however, his look and build that had her smoothing her hand across her flyaway brown hair in a display of nerves. No, it was his eyes. Hard, intense cobalt-blue, they narrowed and grew cold as they studied her. These were the all-seeing eyes of a man who read people for a living.

He probably hid his thoughts well. He looked as if he only let a person, or a jury, see what he chose to let them see.

Amanda stilled her nerves. She didn't have to look close to see he was not happy to be in a wheelchair. He was probably not used to needing someone else.

Despite her resolve that she could handle this job, Amanda's heart fluttered with worry and she wondered if she'd made a mistake in coming.

No mistake.

This man's intensity might serve to be her saving grace. If he was as demanding as she assumed he would be, that meant all her time would be consumed.

And all-consuming was exactly what she needed right now.

"I'm sorry I'm running a bit late. I'd hoped to be here before lunch but traffic on I-35 was killer."

"How old are you?"

His question caught her off guard, halting her rambling. "I'm twenty-four."

"How long have you been a physical therapist?"

Okay, so he had a right to know these things. But still, he hadn't even said hello. "Two years. I graduated high school early and started college two years early. I have experience, Mr. Turner, if that's what you're worried about." The realization that he might not have wanted her here hit her.

"You graduated two years early?"

She heard the astonishment in his voice.

"How did that happen?"

"I had an accident and almost died when I was fourteen. I wasn't able to attend class." It shouldn't have been any big deal, but the fact that he had yet to be cordial at all set everything on end. She assumed he was going to make her stand in the sun until he was satisfied with her answers. She lifted her chin, shifted her weight to her good leg and smiled. "I was hit by a drunk driver. I was training to be a cross-country runner on the freshman cross-country team and was out running near our house. I... Like I said, I nearly died. My parents homeschooled me after that. It was work-at-my-own-pace. I decided I liked to move quickly."

She saw the flicker of surprise in his dark eyes—good, she'd meant to get a reaction out of him. He knew about nearly dying and surely would relate to that. It was easy to see he was spoiling for a fight. Anger wasn't uncommon in his situation. She suspected he was probably stunned to find out that he wasn't invincible. Overachievers often thought they were untouchable. That they had everything under control and nothing could go wrong. She had news for him—it happened to the best of them. Including herself.

Life was not controllable. At least not completely.

"Look, I'm sorry, but this isn't going to work."

"What do you mean this isn't going to work?" Surely he didn't mean what she thought he meant.

His face hardened more—if that were even possible—and his jaw jutted. "Just what I said, Ms. Hathaway. My brothers and your employers all knew I expected a fully capable, highly trained physical therapist for this job. I'm sorry you've been brought all the way out here, but I don't have the luxury of time and can't waste what I do have."

"Mr. Turner, I might be young, but I'm capable of doing this job. I wouldn't have come if I hadn't been. You've read my résumé, I'm sure."

"Actually, no. My brothers handled these arrangements."

"Well, then, you also should know that the majority of my work has been done with children and teens. But that doesn't discredit me from being qualified to handle your case." Nor did her lack of a leg, but obviously his brothers had chosen not to tell him that, and they must have had their reasons, so she didn't say anything.

"That doesn't change anything." His expression was blank. "I'll make sure you're paid for your time coming out here. This is not going to work."

Amanda watched in shock as he pressed the forward button on his wheelchair with the fingers of the arm not in a sling and guided it toward the open doorway.

"The agency I work for doesn't have another therapist open for this job." She hoped something would change his mind; obviously it wouldn't be anything about herself that would do it. "Being all the way out here is going to cause a big problem when it comes to finding a good therapist. I'm good. Are you sure you don't want to reconsider?" She hadn't expected that she'd get turned away.

He halted at the door and shot her a glare—that look took her faltering thoughts from stunned disbelief to complete peevishness! *The man is really being unreasonable.* Of course she had no clue what was going on in his head, she reminded herself. For all she knew, he might be like this all the time. Boy, would that be an unpleasant way to go through life. However, looking at him, something told her he wasn't. Something told her he was struggling. And she saw pain in his eyes right then, even as she watched him. He winced slightly, favoring his left side where she knew his hip and lower back injury needed her attention.

"I'm sure," he said, his words almost a grunt, but he held on and almost covered up the fact that he was having a spasm.

Even in pain he was stubborn, though Amanda had no doubt about his sincerity. She could see that changing his mind wasn't something he did. She knew from his profile that he was probably also used to getting his own way, doing things his way and more than likely able to buy anything he needed in order to make it happen. This could very well be doomed from the start—begging him to keep her on was not an option that would work for either of them, no matter how much she wanted to stay.

"Then I guess that does it." Disheartened in so many ways, she fought to think rationally—something she'd been having a bit of a problem with lately. Her stomach decided to step in and help her out by letting out a long, drawn-out roar. It broke the uncomfortable silence that stretched between her and Wyatt. That was one way to end their meeting: food. It might help her refocus. She'd been stuck in traffic and running late, so she hadn't taken time to stop for lunch. "Is there somewhere in town I can get a bite to eat?" she asked, fighting to keep her tone neutral.

He'd entered the house and turned the chair—probably so that he could slam the door in her face! His brows locked in consternation as he stared at her through the screen. For a minute she wondered if he'd expected her to beg him for the job. She needed this job to take her mind off her own troubles, but she would never beg. He had to realize he needed her. Surely she knew how badly his injuries needed attention before they began to worsen. That would start to happen while he looked for someone to replace her. Time was of the essence, she wanted to say—but he was a smart man and he knew this.

"Sam's is the only diner in town. You can't miss it."

She held his gaze and almost challenged him...any other time she might have, but not today. "Thanks," she said, turning to go. She'd eat and then she'd call Joyce. If anyone was going to fix this it would be up to her boss. With her back held straight she retraced her steps to her vehicle. In her heart of hearts she hoped Wyatt would reconsider and stop her before she drove away...but she knew he wouldn't.

Wyatt Turner was not a man who changed his mind. He also wasn't the only person who was good at reading people. It was a trait she'd learned after the accident, watching nurses and doctors and her parents when they gave her hard information. It had come in handy in her profession as she evaluated her clients' needs and signs of pain.

It was a shame that it did her absolutely no good now...then again, maybe she wasn't as good at it as she'd thought she was. She'd read Jonathan about as wrong as possible.

Or maybe she really hadn't. Maybe she'd only imagined in their relationship what she'd wanted to see there.

She got into her car, pulled the strap of the seat belt securely about her and stole a glance toward the house. He was watching her...and he was rubbing his hip since he thought she wasn't looking. So be it. She started the SUV and drove away. She watched the house disappear in her rearview mirror and felt more lost than she had in ages. What was she going to do?

The feelings she'd been able to set aside as she'd headed toward this job crowded back in around her.

In the early days, working with kids gave her something to focus on other than herself. Now she didn't even have that comfort any longer. God had a plan for her life. She clung to that belief, but right now it was giving her little comfort.

As she turned onto the blacktop, her thoughts turned to Wyatt Turner and she found herself wondering if that was how he felt. If so, he had her sympathy. Even if he had just fired her.

Wyatt needed out of this wheelchair.

He needed out before he went crazy. It had to happen and it had to happen sooner rather than later.

It *would* happen—he'd make it happen as quick as possible. Something about Amanda Hathaway bothered him. She would only have slowed down his progress.

Letting her go had been his only option. Still, he hadn't liked doing what he'd done.

She wasn't up for the job, it was obvious. It niggled at him that he'd judged her by her appearance, but he didn't have time to go soft. He hadn't gotten where he was in life by going soft. The facts were that she wasn't strong enough—she was small and young. There was no way she'd be able to handle strenuous training like he expected and needed. And she'd worked with children! Of all things. What had Cole and Seth been thinking?

They'd wanted to remind him about how important his physical therapy was and yet they'd gone and pulled a sorry stunt like this.

His doctors had assured him he could make a full recovery, but only with hard, diligent work. There wasn't

an ounce of quit in him—never had been, but this physical disablement had thrown his world upside down.
Every time his hip and back seized up he felt weak…if
he let his guard down. If he didn't work absolutely as
hard as he was supposed to there was a chance he would
always have a limp and lower back pain.

He'd admit that deep inside he was scared. If he let up,
if he messed up in the least little bit he wouldn't come
out of this as strong and healthy as he'd been before
he'd botched things up with his stupid error in judgment
when he'd decided to fly his plane in unsafe conditions.

That was the scariest thing—how weak he felt. As
if to show him who was boss, pain shot through his left
hip once more and attacked his lower back with a vengeance. This time it was so strong he groaned before he
could stop it. Perspiration beaded across his forehead
as he grimaced against the pain. He closed his eyes, he
counted to ten, willing his muscles to relax. Tensing up
made the spasm worse—not a good thing.

Sucking in a heavy breath, he tried to relax and let the
pain pass. *What if I can't make it back to the way I was?*
The question sliced through him like a knife to a wound.

It had been three endless weeks since he'd crash-
landed his twin engine plane in a pasture during a storm.
It had happened not long after he'd left Mule Hollow and
was headed back to Dallas. He'd taken time he didn't
have to fly home to congratulate Cole on his wedding
engagement. Since he was responsible for matching up
Cole and Susan, he'd wanted to make the quick day trip
and share in the joy of the moment. If he'd listened to
his gut—which was usually right—and stayed the night,
taken time to really enjoy the moment with them, he'd
have been all right. But enjoying the moment wasn't

something he did. Instead he'd rushed off in the middle of dangerous winds and a severe thunderstorm. He'd been arrogant enough to believe he could handle the storm. What an inane bit of stupidity.

When had he decided he could control everything?

He hadn't closed the door after watching Amanda drive away and now he stared across the land that had been in his family for over a hundred and fifty years. It was in this place his roots ran deep and was from his ancestors' example that he'd become the man he was.

Being used to control was a good thing, he reminded himself. It had driven him to where he was in his career as an attorney. It would get him through this. Taking another deep breath, he began to relax as his mind cleared and the pain began to recede.

Good blood ran through his veins. Hardworking, upstanding—well, upstanding except for his good ole great-great-great-great-great-grandpa Oakley—him being upstanding was questionable. By and large the Turner men and women were tough. Generations past had stared across this land that stagecoaches had crossed on their way to this old stagecoach stop. Like this house, his ancestors had stood the test of time and so would he.

His brothers had been right in bringing him home.

This place had always been good for his soul.

Two months. He would get better and he'd get to work. He would not let himself get waylaid by debilitating, unproductive thoughts again. He hadn't been feeling like doing anything except sitting in this chair and feeling sorry for himself. It wasn't something he understood or wanted, but that was what had been happening. He wasn't sleeping and his attitude stank. But lately he hadn't been able to do anything about it. Cole and Seth had known and they'd taken action when he wouldn't. Their action had helped him—jolted him enough to fight…and fight was what he needed.

Action: that was what he needed.

He needed a therapist capable of helping him achieve his goal. The soft, sweet-faced Amanda Hathaway hadn't been up for the challenge.

Still, even he couldn't help admiring the way she'd walked away with her head held high.

Chapter Three

As dismal as Amanda felt, the sight of Mule Hollow perked her up the instant it peeked over the horizon. Why, it was darling! So cute with its bright stores, welcoming flowerpots along plank sidewalks and window boxes. Driving down Main Street, she began to smile. It was a wonderful feeling.

There was a pink two-story hair salon called Heavenly Inspirations, a bright yellow feed store with peacock-blue trim, a real estate office painted A&M maroon—which she was a big fan of—and beside it was Sam's Diner painted a bright grass-green.

Amanda pulled into the parking space and got out. More stores just as brightly painted stood all along Main Street. The dress store and candy store across the street were memorable as well as the community center a few doors down the wooden sidewalk. She watched a cowboy clomp into the feed store down the way and felt very nostalgic. She half expected to see a horse tied to a hitching post. This was smiletown if ever there was one. Just lovely.

There was a really huge older home that anchored the

town at one end. It had a green roof with turrets on each corner and a sign that read Adela's Apartments. Amanda studied the structure with interest. What would it be like to just walk in there and rent an apartment? Start over?

Crazy. She was thinking crazy and she knew it. It had been one thing to pretend she was running away from her life when she was coming here for a job, but this—this was simply a daydream, and it was too much. She was not the kind of person who ran away. At least not for good. She would get her head on straight. She would.

Yet it was as if Wyatt Turner's stormy scowl had burned its way into her head.

She wondered if he'd slammed the door after she left. Something about the man intrigued her, despite his easy dismissal of her. Maybe it was simply that she hated to see anyone in pain. Maybe it wasn't the man himself that kept her attention but the fact that she knew she could help him.

She could help him if he'd only give her the chance.

The man had to want her help. There was no getting around that. She couldn't force anyone to accept her. Especially a man like him! She bit her lip and stared at the rooster weather vane sitting on the top of one of Adela's turrets. No seesawing or riding the fence for him. Jonathan came to mind and she cringed. Jonathan had probably known his mind long before he'd finally spoken it. Maybe if he'd have cut her loose early like Wyatt had she wouldn't be hurting so much right now.

At least Wyatt had been honest with how he felt. For that she admired him—even if he *did* need her.

A squeaking door sounded behind her. "Norma Sue, are you or are you not going to come out tonight and see my moon lily?" a woman said.

"I told you I would, but you were too busy running your mouth in there to hear me."

Amanda turned. Two women were coming out of the diner. They looked up from their conversation and stopped short when they spotted her.

"Hello there," the one who'd just been accused of running her mouth said. She had bright red hair and was wearing a daffodil-yellow capri set.

"Hello," Amanda said.

"Honey, you look a bit dazed. Are you all right?" the woman called Norma Sue asked. She was a robust, strong-looking woman with wiry gray curls and a big wide smile that spread all the way across her face. "Being dazed is understandable when folks first look at all these wild colors. It tends to make people's heads spin."

"Now, Norma Sue, we don't know that this is her first time to see Mule Hollow—"

"Esther Mae." Norma Sue stared in disbelief at her friend. "Have you ever seen her before?"

"Well, no—" The redhead looked at Amanda sheepishly.

"Then there you go. She's as new to Mule Hollow as that calf I had born this morning." She directed her hazel eyes back at Amanda. "Tell *her* this is your first time to our little metropolis, isn't it?"

Amanda smiled, liking these two on the spot. "First time."

"See, I knew it was!"

"I'm Amanda Hathaway." She held up her right hand like she was swearing in at court and said, "And yes, I am new in town and I love it. I was just admiring the colors."

Both ladies grinned as she let her hand fall.

"It does attract folks—kind of like red flowers attract hummingbirds. I'm Esther Mae Wilcox, by the way, and this is Norma Sue Jenkins." She leaned forward slightly as if telling a secret. "She's my sidekick."

"Ha! Don't believe a word of it," Norma Sue huffed. "She's *my* sidekick."

It was easy to visualize these two getting into all kinds of trouble.

"What brings you to town?" Esther Mae asked. "Are you here looking for a cowboy?"

The statement took Amanda by surprise, even though she knew the background of the town. She said the first thing that came to mind. "I don't know, do you have some for sale?"

"We don't sale 'um, but we sure do give them away at the altar," Esther Mae volleyed back.

"To the right women," Norma Sue added. "You need one, don't you? I don't see a ring on your hand."

Amanda glanced at her finger where three weeks earlier there had been a ring. She blinked hard and stilled the sudden rolling of her stomach.

"Honey, you okay?" Esther Mae asked.

"Y-yes, I'm fine." Meeting two sets of curious eyes, she pushed the jab of pain back into the corner of her heart where she'd barricaded it. "Um, how exactly do you get these cowboys to the altar?" she asked, a little too brightly. A vivid picture of Norma Sue behind them with a shotgun popped into her mind. "And is it legal?"

That got her chuckles from both women.

Norma Sue's grin was wide. "Oh, the preacher makes it legal and the cowboys usually go willingly after a spell. Ain't that right, Esther Mae?"

Esther Mae was watching her intently and Amanda feared she might have seen more than she'd needed anyone to see.

"Esther Mae, did you hear me?"

"Of course I did," she said, her cinnamon brows puckered above alert green eyes. "So are you really telling us you haven't heard about us?"

"No, I was teasing. I've heard a little about Mule Hollow." It hit her that she had been teasing—it seemed like forever since she'd done that. She glanced at her ring finger, as empty as her heart felt. As her life was now. And yet she'd just teased these ladies spontaneously.

It was a good sign that maybe the entire trip out here hadn't been a waste. "And no, I'm not looking to marry one of your cowboys. I came here from San Antonio for a job I was supposed to start today."

"A *job?*" Esther Mae cooed. "What job?"

Amanda's stomach growled loudly, reminding her why she'd come to town. She slapped a hand over it.

"Whoa, girl, that's not good." Norma Sue grabbed her by the arm. "C'mon, Esther Mae, we've got to get this young'un inside the diner and fill that stomach up with some of Sam's good cooking."

Esther Mae scooted to the door. "While you eat, you can tell us what job brought you to our neck of the woods."

And just like that Amanda found herself being escorted into the diner by her new best buds. One thing was certain, this trip had been anything but boring. She might be headed home in an hour, but today—though disappointing in that she'd been dismissed basically on sight—she felt better.

"So you know about our little advertisements for wives?" Norma Sue asked.

"Yes, I don't think many people, at least here in Texas, haven't heard about it. My boss reminded me. I had forgotten about it when I first got my assignment, but I read a few of Molly Jacob's columns back when they started." Molly was a local newspaper reporter who'd begun writing a column about the goings-on of the little town that advertised for wives and it had been syndicated across the country. She enjoyed reading, but the column had taken a backseat to her always-full work schedule, training for the marathons she loved to run and…then, the connection she'd finally found with Jonathan. As soon as the thoughts of him came she pushed them away, refusing to go there.

"Then you know gals like you come from all over to marry our men. See, look over there." Norma Sue pointed across the diner to a table where four cowboys were hunched over plates of food.

Esther Mae had slid into a booth and patted the seat beside her. "We've married off over a dozen couples with several engagements pending right now. And babies are arriving now, too. It is so exciting."

Amanda sat down and inhaled the scent of food wafting through the air.

"Our church is busier than one of those tacky Las Vegas drive-through chapels." Norma Sue grunted as she took the seat across from her. "Of course we just lost our preacher so we've got to find a new one to carry on the ceremonies."

"Oh, *brother,* you two again!" A little man came out from the kitchen and headed to their booth. "I can't get rid of you gals no matter how hard I try." He settled teasing eyes on Amanda. "Hangin' out with these two'll get you inta trouble, little lady. Just so you know." He held out his hand. "I'm Sam. Welcome to my place. These two git my Adela into more trouble than you can shake a stick at."

Amanda introduced herself as she grabbed his hand and gave a firm squeeze, nowhere *near* the iron grip he attacked her with, but still, she gave as good as she could.

He grinned. "Fer a tiny woman, that's some shake ya got thar."

She flexed her hand. "You aren't so bad yourself. My daddy always did say a person's heart was measured by the firmness of their handshake. You must have a giant heart."

That won her a big grin; his weathered face creased with a mischievous look. "Ain't nobody 'sposed to know about my big heart. So let's keep that one quiet. If these two or a couple of others, who shall remain nameless at the moment, were ta suspect I had a big heart, they'd thank I was a pushover and then I wouldn't never be able to get my bluff in on 'em."

Norma Sue rolled her eyes. "Don't believe none of it. If it wasn't for me and Esther Mae and his two 'nameless friends' keeping him in line, the man would be bored out of his brain."

"Ha! I wish," he grunted. "So, what brangs you ta Mule Hollow? And why in the world are you brangin' these two back into my establishment when I jest got rid of them?"

Amanda laughed—it felt good. "Honestly, Sam, I just met them outside and they dragged me in here."

As they all chuckled with her she thought they reminded her of her cantankerous grandparents who lived on a farm in West Texas.

"We thought she was here looking for a cowboy," Esther Mae told Sam. "We were just telling her about what nice ones we have around here."

Norma Sue nodded toward the window. "There are two of our success stories about to come through the door right now. That taller one is Seth Turner. He got married a couple of months ago. The other one is his younger brother, Cole. Cole is having a wedding in about four weeks—had to be put off because his big brother got injured in a plane crash."

The door swung open and the men burst inside like cowboys looking for trouble. Instantly she saw the resemblance to their brother. Their expressions were serious as they scanned the room, but nowhere near the intensity of Wyatt's.

Esther Mae nudged Amanda in the ribs. "Those two Turner men are handsome, but you should see that big brother of theirs!"

"He's something worth seein', all right," Norma Sue whispered, leaning forward over the table.

She didn't have to be told that these were the brothers who'd hired her. They'd stopped just inside the door and their searching gazes locked on to her almost instantly.

Norma Sue looked from them to Amanda as the cowboys advanced toward them. "Hey, boys," she drawled. "Y'all look like you're lookin' for somebody."

Both men swept their Stetsons from their heads. The taller one with the more serious eyes that reminded Amanda of Wyatt's tugged at his collar. "Are you Amanda Hathaway?"

Amanda nodded as suddenly all eyes turned on her.

"We've come to apologize and ask you to reconsider."

"Seth, what in the world do you want Amanda to reconsider?" Esther Mae asked.

Norma Sue's eyes widened. "*You're* Wyatt's new physical therapist! Aren't you? The one that was arriving this morning?"

"Of course," Esther Mae snapped. "I don't know what I was thinking."

"Was," Amanda corrected. "He fired me on the spot." She cringed, not having meant to blurt it out that way.

"No, he did not," Esther Mae gasped.

"I'm afraid so," Amanda said, more evenly. "So unless he changes his mind, I'll be leaving after I eat. I can't help anyone who doesn't want me to." It was true. But as she looked around at the faces of her new friends, her heart tugged and she wished things had worked out differently.

"I'll be." Sam rubbed his jaw. "Ain't this here a bunch of interestin' information."

"It sure is," Norma Sue drawled. "What you boys got to say about this?" she said at the two men who'd been patiently standing by.

"First, we should introduce ourselves. I'm Cole and this is my brother Seth. We have most definitely come to hire you back. The ball's in your court, just name your price."

"Well," Esther Mae harrumphed. "This is getting better by the moment."

Amanda hadn't expected this, but it didn't matter. She shook her head. "Like I said, I can't help someone who doesn't even want to give me a chance. Believe me, it won't work for me and it won't work for your brother."

"He's not against you," Seth said. "He's got a lot on

his plate. Don't get me wrong, he's going to be a bear to work with, but he needs you and he knows it now."

"What do you say?" Cole asked, giving her a wink and a lopsided grin.

They were cute and they obviously cared a lot about their brother. But that still wouldn't make this work. There was only one thing that might. "The only way I'd take the job back is if Wyatt asked me himself."

"That-a-girl." Sam chuckled. "Hold your own. When my Adela gets back home from her sister's, she's gonna want to hear all about this."

"That's what he thought." Seth reached into his shirt pocket and pulled out a folded piece of paper. "I think this should do it." He handed a yellow paper to her.

She eyed the page as she took it. It was from a yellow legal pad, and when Amanda opened it there was one sentence scrawled in a bold masculine print across the middle of the page.

If you are up for the challenge, come back and prove it. Wyatt Turner.

Her lip twitched and she held back a smile. No way had she expected an apology. What really startled her was that he'd written exactly what she'd needed…a challenge. She and Wyatt Turner needed the same thing.

Folding the paper again, she looked at the brothers. Giving them an encouraging smile, she took a settling breath. "Okay. I'll stay. I need to eat and then I'll head back out there. Will you please tell your brother that I said I was up for the challenge. But—*is he?*"

Chapter Four

He was waiting on the porch when Amanda got out of her car. In some ways he reminded her of George Strait with his dark hair and square chin. And despite the intensity of his eyes, she thought there was a hint of mischievousness lurking there as he watched her walk up the path. In doing her job, no matter what personal crisis she had going on in her own life, she must be positive and figure out the best way to bring her patient around. Not just physically but also emotionally—she had to be positive and engaging in a way he would respond to.

Somewhere in the background a cow mooed—well, several cows mooed, sounding as if they were heralding her arrival. She halted in front of Wyatt and gave him her best grin. "I'm here for my challenge." His gaze flickered down her as if assessing her once more and wondering if he'd gone crazy asking her back. The distrust was there as clear as day. Determination sprang through her like a runner out of the starting blocks. She hiked a brow when he said nothing, deciding a little challenge of her own was in order.

"I guess I am, too," he drawled in a voice she bet jurors found almost hypnotizing in a courtroom.

She had to give him credit, though: his tone was civil for the first time since she'd met him. They could build on that.

"I promise you won't be sorry. I'll get results."

"I'll make sure you do."

His words were meant as a warning, but they made her smile widen. "I think we are going to have some fun, Mr. Turner."

The scowl of earlier returned. "I'm not interested in fun. I want out of this chair and on my own two feet and I want it yesterday."

She chuckled—not a good thing but unstoppable. He was actually very cute in his state of *irked.* "Then you shall be. *Will* and *want* work together to make things happen. I can just look at you and know you're going to push your limits every time I ask you to do an exercise. So for now, put your scowl away and relax. I promise you, it's going to be all right." She sounded like she was talking to one of her kids. Not dissimilar—teens were just as anxious to be up and about as Wyatt. His impatience was nothing new to her and that was a good thing.

"I know with the pain you're in you might be worrying whether you'll ever return to your normal lifestyle. Stop worrying, you'll be back if you do as I ask."

"You always this sure of yourself?"

"In this case, *your* case, yes, I am." Their gazes held and she wanted so badly to tell him again not to worry. But she saw the skepticism alive and well in that look.

She wouldn't say more for now. He'd think she was patronizing him if she kept on. She'd been watching him for pain and didn't think it was too bad at the moment, but it was there. With a strained back, cracked hip, along with the tendon and ligature trauma his hip had gone through, the spasms would come and go with a vengeance. Not to mention the constant pain from the damage to his shoulder. She could help with all of that.

Later. "So I guess I'll put my things up and get settled. Seth and Cole told me the temporary trailer was set up and ready for me. Is it out back somewhere?"

"By the barn. I'll show you," he said, his words clipped.

"That would be great." She turned and headed back to her car, not even considering telling him that she could find it on her own. The last thing he needed was to be treated like he was helpless. There was a ramp that had been built off the side of the old porch and the ground was level all about the house. That top-of-the-line motorized wheelchair would have no trouble maneuvering the landscape. The man exuded energy, even in a wheelchair. It was a miracle that he was alive, though. During the small-engine airplane crash he'd pulled and stressed nearly every muscle, tendon and ligature on the left side of his body. Even the fact that he had no broken bones other than a hairline crack in his hip was yet another miracle. She suspected surviving sitting still on a porch might kill him, though. She completely understood how he was feeling.

Running with the rising sun was more her style. She wondered if he'd run in the mornings prior to the crash. She had a feeling he was a runner, too. One who liked to run outside. Then again, he might be a treadmill runner—too white-collar to run outside...not that that was a bad thing. She just preferred to do her running outside.

"Did you bring much?"

"I have a car full of things. Not all luggage, though."
She laughed. "Most of it I'll be setting up in the therapy room. But all I want now are my suitcases." They'd
made it to the SUV and he waited, watching her as she
opened the glass window and then lowered the tailgate
of the SUV. For some reason his watchful eyes made
her self-conscious. She tucked her hair behind her ears
before she reached for the first suitcase and hefted it to
the ground.

Without speaking, he reached with his good arm and
took some of the weight from her by grabbing the bottom of the case. "Thanks," she said, knowing that every
little thing he did that was positive would help him move
forward.

"You're welcome," he said as she grabbed the slightly
smaller one. He helped with that one, too. She'd loaded
it all up herself and was quite capable of removing all
the luggage herself but still she appreciated the fact that
Wyatt Turner was—behind his poor manners earlier—a
gentleman. This was instinctive on his part. She wondered if his mother had drilled the manners into him as
he grew up.

"You're looking at me like I've surprised you," he
said as she shut the tailgate.

Grinning, she stepped out of the way as she lifted
it. The movement brought her closer to him than she'd
been. "I guess I'm a bit shocked you're a gentleman,"
she answered truthfully. *He'd asked.*

His lip actually twitched! "My mom would have
skinned me and my brothers alive if we weren't."

Bingo. "I thought so."

"You're thinking, otherwise I wouldn't be?"

"It crossed my mind when you booted me off your

property," she said drily. "And that was after I'd driven three hours to get here—with no lunch!" She looked at him ruefully as she extended the pull arm of the large suitcase and set the overnight bag on top of the big one, fastening them together for transport.

His eyes crinkled around the edges. "I'd apologize…"

"But…" she drawled slowly. "You wouldn't mean it." She knew it was true.

"I did what I thought best at the time."

"That's exactly what I thought you did. And that's why I'm just teasing you." She winked at him, picked up the smallest suitcase with the hand on the same side as her prosthetic. The action balanced out the weight as she grabbed the handle of the other case and started rolling it behind her across the lawn.

The thing about Wyatt was exactly that—he did what he thought he needed to do. After Seth and Cole had left the diner to return her message to Wyatt, the ladies had told her that he'd pulled out all the stops when it came to finding wives for his two brothers. He'd seen women he thought fit them and made certain they came in contact with each other. It was really sweet! The man was a romantic—who would have thunk it?

It did her broken heart good to know there were men like him in the world looking out for those they loved. It was a very admirable quality in a man. But even if she hadn't known all of that, she'd already figured out that he was an honorable man just by the way his brothers talked about him.

"You could roll that second one," he said, driving up beside her. "Or better yet I could carry it."

She glanced at him. "You don't need to carry it. You're absolutely right—I could roll it if I wanted to."

"But you won't."

"I wouldn't get any kind of workout from rolling it, and besides—" She'd almost said it helped her keep her balance. Instead she said, "I'd be a bit of a hypocrite if I harp on my patients about keeping their strength and agility up and I wasn't practicing it myself."

"True," he mused.

They walked around the old homestead in silence. The large travel trailer came into view and the size startled her.

It was sitting out under a giant oak tree, not far from the low-slung barn. It was huge compared to some she stayed in while on-site. But then again, looking at Wyatt, she wouldn't put it past the man to have had a double-wide mobile home sitting back here for her. There was just something about him—even if she hadn't read his profile and didn't know that the man was worth a bundle—she'd still have the feeling that only the best was good enough for those around him.

"I hope this will do," he said. "Cole and Seth assured me that your boss said a small one was all you needed."

"I don't call this small. Believe me, this is more than enough." She smiled. "I'll feel like a queen in there compared to the tiny place I had on the last job. Don't get me wrong, though, it was great. It was one of those little round jobs that had only room for a bed, a small television and a table for my books. I have to admit taking a shower in a three-by-three space also occupied by the sink and toilet was a bit of a chore, though."

He looked aghast. "How long did you do that?"

"Six weeks. I wish it had been longer, but the insurance ran out…" She'd hated leaving. Shawn, the teen, needed more help with his new prosthesis. She was still in contact with him, checking on his progress—or at least she had been until three weeks ago. Joyce was checking on him now and told her he was getting along pretty well, doing everything she'd instructed him to do. She had confidence that he would be fine. He was a totally determined teenager. Just like she'd been. It was the younger kids she'd worried the most about. They needed services longer to acclimate to their prosthetics and she'd hoped—at least she had before she'd walked away—that someday she could do something to help them more. Now she wasn't sure if she could ever go back to working with young patients.

"You obviously like what you do to put up with that sort of thing that long."

Wyatt's words broke into the wandering thoughts. "Oh, I *love* my job." Even now, moving from children to adults, she did love it. "Not many people can say they are blessed to be where they are in life. I can. Tiny shower stalls and all." She didn't add that she'd had to give up the part that she'd once loved the most. No one needed to know that, and that fact still didn't change her love of her profession. It just altered her reality.

His expression grew troubled. "I know what you mean," he said, almost under his breath as he looked away, out toward the pastures that stretched from the barn endlessly. Two football-goal-size lines formed between his brows, and his expression darkened. That scowl told her she'd somehow just shot down the little progress they'd just made. The man had actually lightened up for a few moments. It was a glimpse, but nonetheless a start.

Deciding that for now she'd said enough, she opened the door to the trailer and stepped up on the single step.

"Thank you for this." She'd wondered what was roaming around in his head. Something was troubling Wyatt. Maybe it was worry about his injuries. Maybe something more. Helping him with his pain and getting him up and about would help him physically. And mentally, too. "I'll unpack and get settled. Is there anything you need me to do this evening? I could give you a therapeutic massage to help with that pain." Therapist plus general factotum was an odd arrangement for her but she was looking forward to it.

He didn't look at her. "No, we'll get everything figured out tomorrow." Unsmiling, he drove his wheelchair back toward the house without further elaboration.

Watching him, Amanda felt his pain. Still, she knew he was going to be all right physically with time.

She wondered if he realized that. He'd almost lost his life in that plane crash. There might be more going on in his head than anyone realized. She said a prayer for him as he rounded the corner and disappeared.

He'd seemed all alone in that moment. As alone as she was. *Don't let your thoughts go there.* Right. She was here to work, and to get her mind off her own troubles. The last thing she needed to do was empathize so strongly with her client that she let it bring her down. He was counting on her and she wouldn't fail him.

Glancing about the land that surrounded her, she breathed deeply. It was hot and dry, the reports of drought were increasing and the cool wind that had suddenly started blowing in across the dry grass was a pleasant surprise. Tomorrow she would run and gain every feel-good endorphin that running would give her.

Tomorrow she would begin to prove to Wyatt that he'd been right to hire her.

She realized that she wanted to make him smile—just as she always did her kids. A real smile. Not just a twitch of his lips, but a full-out smile.

And she would. The thought energized her and it gave her yet another purpose for being here.

Tomorrow *would* be a good day.

Bam! Bam-bam-bam.

Amanda woke with a jolt as the entire trailer shuddered. She sat up in bed, glanced at the alarm clock. It was four in the morning and something was ramming her house! *Bam!* It started over. The entire travel trailer shook like she'd just been hit by a earthquake. Scrambling for her yellow flowered housecoat, she yanked it on then glanced out the window above the bed. In the moonlight she saw…hogs?!

Hogs! She was surrounded by wild boars with long, ugly tusks. *"Fifteen,"* she gasped, counting the animals. They were everywhere. Big ones and small ones and every size in between. What was she supposed to do? Did she need to try to wake Wyatt?

She slipped on her sock and then pulled her leg on in a movement that had become as natural as standing. Heading to the door, she peered out the window. There was a light on inside the house. Was Wyatt up? Did he know these animals were out here? Another slammed into the trailer, making her cringe at the thought of dents. Nibbling her lip, she tried to figure out what she needed to do. The porch light came on and she wasn't sure how that would help since Wyatt was in a wheelchair, but at least she wasn't alone out here anymore. Maybe he would call his brothers.

Reaching for her warm-up pants, she pulled them

on, not exactly sure what she expected to do. She heard someone yell something. She swung back the curtain and saw Wyatt driving his chair out onto the back porch. No! What was he thinking? Her shoe was already on her prosthetic, so she quickly put on her other one and reached for the doorknob. Wyatt was now at the edge of the porch and it was easy to see even from this distance that he was not happy.

Her heart was pounding and her temper soared. The hard-headed, injured man was outside with a herd of wild hogs!

Didn't wild hogs tear people up with their horrible tusks? A vivid memory of *Old Yeller* came to mind. The man had lost his ever-lovin' mind and was going to get himself hurt if she didn't do something. Surely he would go back inside.

Nope. Not him. She was fumbling for the door as she watched, in horror, him drive his chair right to the edge of the porch—what she remotely planned to do was a mystery to her. She couldn't just let her patient get mowed over by a bunch of hogs, though.

"Wyatt," she called through the cracked door. "What are you doing?" This was something that was completely off the chart on what she'd ever been prepared to handle.

"*Close* that door, Amanda."

His command cracked through the night like thunder, sending the hogs scattering in a wild frenzy of movement. And of all the rotten luck, one big, giant shadow headed straight for Wyatt!

Amanda flung open the door and stepped to the ground. "Run," she screamed, taking a step and realizing she couldn't move fast enough because of the ruts the animals had plowed into the ground—

"Get back!" Wyatt yelled at the top of his lungs just as the animal veered away from him and—to her great relief—raced toward open pasture.

Amanda's heart thundered.

"What were you thinking coming out of that trailer?" Wyatt demanded, his eyes glittering in the moonlight. "Do you know what those animals can do to you?"

"Me! *Me!*" Amanda would have flown across the land between them, she was so hot, but had to settle for making slow progress to keep steady. It was amazing, the small amount of time the hogs had been there, how destructive they'd been with their rooting. Mounds of dirt and holes turned the land into a hazard. Because her prosthetic was stiff, a misstep on uneven ground could throw her entire balance off. Still, she kept on talking. "You're the one who wheeled himself out into the direct path of those…those creatures." She shuddered, pointing the direction the ugly, hairy hogs had gone. "That hog was coming straight for you."

"I was fine. I've been around hogs all my life. I know how to deal with them. But you coming outside while they were out here was not acceptable. You could have fallen and that hog would have gutted you."

She gasped, halting in front of him. "Gutted me. And you're telling me you would have been okay? I don't think so."

Wyatt's eyes flashed dangerously. "I would have been fine."

They glared at each other, seconds ticked by and slowly sanity seeped back to Amanda. What was she doing? She was behaving very unprofessionally. She'd just basically told him that he was an invalid and that was unforgivable. He had every right to be angry at her.

"I'm sorry," she said quietly. "I'm way out of line. My only excuse is that I was really scared."

It was the truth. "I mean, I've never seen hogs that size. And when that one headed toward you all I could think of was *Old Yeller*—"

"I should have known," he groaned.

"Well, it was scary. The hogs killed that poor dog."

"Amanda, you're here to help me get back on my feet. You are not here to get yourself hurt. Stay inside at night no matter what. Do you understand me?"

Loud and clear. "You are absolutely right. I'm going back to get a little more shut-eye right now." She held her fuzzy housecoat closer around her.

Wyatt's eyes glinted a hard warning. "Don't come outside again if you see hogs."

Just as mad as he was, she locked gazes with him. "I reacted without thinking to what I saw. Maybe it's you who needs to think about staying inside."

Wyatt's glare iced over. "I'm not kidding, Amanda."

And he thought she was? Hardly. "That makes two of us. Sleep well, Wyatt, because work begins at eight-thirty." Turning, she started carefully across the yard. The last thing she needed was for Wyatt to see her fall. From the standpoint of her pride, that wouldn't be good. And now wouldn't exactly be the opportune moment for him to realize she had only one leg. Maybe she should have told him earlier. But right now certainly wasn't a good time to reveal it…no telling how mad he'd be. Knowing Wyatt, he'd fire her all over again and this time she'd be gone for good.

Chapter Five

Wyatt sat on the back porch long after Amanda weaved her way back to the trailer. She was plucky, that was for certain—plucky enough to get herself into trouble. When she was safely back inside he breathed a sigh of relief. If that wild boar had headed her way, he'd have been hard-put to do anything to help her. He'd almost died of fright when she'd come outside yelling for him to get back.

What had he been thinking? He knew he'd put her in danger by his decision to come outside to run off the hogs. It would have been okay had he been standing and able to handle himself. With this hip injury he was useless. Of course he hadn't expected her to come outside, either. But that was beside the point—he shouldn't have come out here, plain and simple. He'd put them both in danger.

Disgusted, he spun the chair and drove back inside, letting the door slam behind him. He didn't even pretend that he was going to go back to sleep. He knew he wouldn't—he hadn't been sleeping ever since the crash. Instead he put on a pot of coffee and headed to the shower—and the ordeal that it represented to him. Standing for any length of time was hard. Getting dressed or undressed was trouble, too, often sending his back into spasms. Hopefully therapy would help.

Twenty minutes later, in pain, he poured himself a cup of coffee and headed to his desk, but he couldn't concentrate on the transcripts he was trying to go over.

Back before he'd crashed the plane, if he'd been disturbed about something when he was here, he'd have saddled a horse and gone for a ride across the pasture, even in the moonlight. Something about being in the saddle always helped ease his mind. He'd spent more time on horseback growing up than Cole and Seth put together. Then again, he'd helped out on the ranch from the day he'd turned eight. There was always something that could be done at almost any age and his dad had instilled a great work ethic in all of them. Those had been good days spent with his dad and his granddad, too. It was hard to realize how long it had been since both of them had passed away. First his granddad when a tractor had overturned on the side of a hill he was mowing. And then later his dad and mom when their plane had gone down over Missouri. He'd spent long hours in the saddle during those days. He'd been eighteen when his parents had died. When he'd become the head of the family. Being in the saddle had helped. In college he'd started running to do his thinking. He'd taken up flying then, too, much to his brothers' surprise. As odd as it seemed, being in the pilot's seat had helped him feel connected to his mom and dad. Now, all he could do was sit in this chair and stare out across the land.

The spasm grabbed him suddenly. As if he were being twisted apart by two different forces, the excruciating pain snarled through him, through his leg and upper body while the spasm tightened and jerked. Sweat popped across his forehead and despite trying not to, he groaned. Never in his life had he felt this weak. This out of control.

This scared.

There, he admitted it. The doctors had assured him he would recover, but he wanted out of this chair—the need to be out of it consumed him. The fear that it was all a lie worried him. He gripped the chair arms and fought off a wave of nausea as a flashback of waking up in the plane wreckage overcame him…the caustic smell of burning gas and oil hit him anew. He'd awakened to find himself trapped. He'd tried to move but couldn't, his legs were pinned. Blood had been everywhere and then the pain…even now he couldn't forget it. What he was feeling now was nothing. Needing to be free of the flashback, he forced memories away and drove his wheelchair to the kitchen. With an unsteady hand, he poured himself another cup of coffee, watching the pot shake as he did so.

Think of something good. His sister-in-law, Melody, had come over and made certain he could reach the things he needed. That had been sweet of her. Seth had a great woman in his life. That was a very good thing.

He took a drink of the hot brew and felt the burn all the way to the pit of his stomach. *You are alive.*

The thought hovered about him in the silent kitchen.

It was a good thought. God had kept him alive in the wreckage of that tiny plane. Unlike his parents, his life had been spared. It was a miracle that he'd lived. He knew this. He should be grateful.

Instead he continued to feel at loose ends. Lost.

Wyatt had always known where he was going. What he wanted out of life and who he was as a man.

The truth was…something had changed in that wreckage. He'd lost something of himself and he wasn't sure how to get it back.

The alarm blasted at 7:30 a.m. Amanda woke from a dead sleep, cracked one eye open and glared at the clock. Normally she was a morning person, but not today. She groped for the alarm, shut it off and pushed herself up on her elbows then dropped onto her back. *Had she really had an encounter with wild hogs?*

Yup, it wasn't a nightmare. Wyatt had actually put himself in danger. The memory of that hog heading toward him flooded back to her, sending terror racing through her once more. Obstinate man!

No wonder she was so tired—being scared witless by ugly hogs and an irritating man would do that. And then to jump on her the way he had—the nerve of the man!

Yes, no doubt at all that they were going to grate on each other's nerves. She could see it coming as plain as day. Sighing, she sat up, threw her covers aside and rubbed the end of her leg. It was a habit she'd started right after she'd first lost her leg all those years ago. Her leg was gone but she still felt it. She'd gotten used to it now but still, the habit of rubbing the scar remained. Kind of like saying, "I haven't forgotten you." The kids liked the idea and had found comfort in knowing it was okay to miss the limb they'd lost. She yawned then stretched. Hopefully there would be no more hog incidents and she could get a good night's sleep tonight. She needed to not get too tired or she really would have a hard time dealing with Wyatt.

Wyatt. It was time to get up and get busy.

Thirty minutes later, after she'd showered and dressed, she felt wide-awake and ready to tackle her first day of work. She made her way across the shredded yard. It was amazing how bad it looked.

She found herself glancing toward the direction in which they'd vanished, making certain they didn't come charging out of the woods after her. She shivered. She'd lost her mind last night.

At the front door, she knocked. She'd begun to think he was asleep when he swung it open.

"Good morning," she said. He, too, looked as if he'd just showered. The hair at the back of his neck curled up slightly with dampness. Wyatt had great hair—not that it mattered to her, but he did have that run-your-fingers-through-his-hair sort of vibe going on.

Instead of returning her greeting, he gave her a quick nod and pointed to the phone earpiece he was wearing. "Yes," he said to the person on the other end as he whirled the wheelchair around and headed back down the hall, deep in conversation.

"Okey-dokey," she grunted under her breath. Entering the ancient building, she watched him disappear through the second doorway on the right. She peeked around the first doorway and saw that both openings led into the large living room/kitchen combo. Since he was on the phone, she decided to look at the wall of old photos in the hallway. There were many, many of them.

"I see you found the wall."

"Yes." She looked over her shoulder to where he'd reappeared in the doorway. She'd been so intent on the pictures that she hadn't realized his conversation had ended. "These are wonderful. I feel like I'm in a museum." Would he hold the hog incident against her?

"It is in a way. Those are all authentic. We don't know who many of them are, but Melody is trying to figure that out. Being a history teacher, she's really interested in discovering who everyone is."

"That's awesome. I'm afraid my family knows nothing of its history past my great-grandfather." Obviously they were going to ignore the hog incident and move forward. He looked tired and she wondered if he'd slept much. It dawned on her that he might have been up before the hog attack.

His gaze ran down the length of the photos. "If it hadn't been for the fact that I was born into a family whose history had been so documented because of this place then I probably wouldn't know anything, either. I'm proud of it, though. This ranch represents a lot of hard work and dedication."

He was halfway through this conversation when it dawned on her that they were actually carrying on a decent conversation. She wanted it to keep on; maybe talking about family was a way to pull him out. "So what exactly do you know about your family?"

He shifted in the chair. "This ranch has our roots in it six generations back."

"Really?"

His lip hitched on one side. "My great-great-great-great-great-grandpa Oakley won this stagecoach house in a poker game."

She laughed. "Get-out-a-here! A poker game."

"That's right. Ole Oakley was a card. He didn't have the best reputation around and was a horse trader, too. Word is you never knew if you were getting a stolen horse or not. But he could spin a tall tale and convince anyone to do what he wanted. He was also a man with a perfect poker face. Thus the winning of this place. Can you imagine throwing away your livelihood in one roll of the dice?"

"No, I can't," she said.

"Pretty sorry, if you ask me."

"I agree. So he won this and then what?" She was totally interested in this conversation but she was also thankful for the opportunity to visit with Wyatt.

"He moved his wife and son here and they ran the stop for years. There were only seventy acres with the stagecoach house, but Oakley's son, Mason, married a girl whose family owned the rest. Through the years each generation has added land as it came available."

Wyatt's phone rang and he answered it. Obviously it was his office again. She wondered how much work he was still doing. She lingered in the hall a few more minutes and then gave up hope that he would hang up anytime soon. She walked into the living room/kitchen. Their gazes met as he pointed to the coffeepot. She shook her head, which he barely acknowledged as his full attention was drawn to the phone conversation. Finally, after a lot of talk that sounded like something out of an episode of *Law and Order,* he hung up. But from what she'd gathered he was about to receive a ton of casework to review.

"So it sounds like you're working hard." She tried to hold back the censure in her voice but it was impossible. He was, after all, the high achiever who probably thought the office wouldn't continue to function without him.

"Consulting on a case with a junior partner."

"I hope that doesn't get in the way of our therapy."

"Nothing will get in the way of that," he assured her, his jaw tightening as he spoke. "Nothing is more important than me getting out of this chair and back on my feet."

They stared at each other across the old wooden kitchen table as a heavy silence cloaked the space between them. "Good." She was used to having confrontations with her clients over cell phone usage during workouts—texting their friends or surfing the Web. She was used to them being fresh-faced teens or younger, not a handsome man with challenge in his gaze. Telling him how to behave felt totally uncomfortable, since there was no obvious doubt that he didn't appreciate her interference. "I guess we should get started," she said, attempting to diffuse the tension between them. This was her job and she needed to do it. "Where is the room we'll be using for the therapy?"

"Across the hall." He led the way into what had probably been a bedroom but now held an assortment of workout equipment.

"You have a regular fitness center in here."

He stopped his chair in the center of the room. "I wasn't sure what we would need, so I had everything brought in."

Was that embarrassment she was seeing?

There was a bench press, a state-of-the-art universal machine, a treadmill that looked like it could do everything for you—even walk for you. There was a massage table center stage and a rolling cart with towels and room for anything she'd brought. "The table is great." She moved over to it. "This is where we need to start this morning. I'm going to evaluate your situation and then we'll get started with your treatment. How does that therapeutic massage sound this morning?"

His forehead crinkled—cutely. "Now *that* I can get excited about."

"If you'll get up here, we'll get started." A beeping sound came from another room in the house and then the distinct sound of a fax working as pages came through.

"Let me check that."

He was gone before she could say anything. She had the distinct feeling she was going to have to compete with his office. She wasn't going to jump to conclusions just yet because he'd sounded so determined yesterday.

She had the massage table prepped when he came back ten minutes later.

"Do I need to help you?" She got a quick shake of the head in answer and watched as he stood. Putting all his weight on the one leg, he balanced on his good leg. His face told more than he probably wanted it to about the pain he was experiencing.

She knew it was hard for a man like him to ask for help, so she held back but still took a step forward. There was nothing weak-looking about him. He had on gym shorts and his well-developed calves had a good dusting of dark hair and were tanned enough for her to pretty much know he jogged outside—if he was a jogger like she suspected he was.

She started to ask him, but he turned too quickly, winched in pain and lost his balance. If he'd had the use of his left arm, he would have reached out for the table to help him regain his balance, but he didn't. One minute he was standing, the next he was toppling. Once again, Amanda reacted on instinct. Heart pumping, she scooted into the line of what seemed like a toppling oak tree and wrapped her arm around his waist. "Here we go," she gasped, looking up at him. Relieved she'd gotten to him.

His good arm curled about her shoulders for support. "Don't hurt yourself," he grunted.

"I won't." Amanda concentrated on her own balance and not on the fact that Wyatt's arm was around her and hers around him. He smelled great—

"Nothing like being a klutz," he ground out.

Amanda laughed. Poor man was so out of his comfort zone needing help. Especially help from a woman. She squeezed his waist encouragingly. "I feel your pain," she told him as she met his eyes. Their faces were so close. Her nerves jangled like alarms, and looking at him, she felt breathless. Goodness. She couldn't look away as his gaze dropped from her eyes to her lips then shot back up to hold hers. Her breath caught. She was close enough to see the iridescent blue flecks encircling his darker blue irises.

They both reacted at the same time. He dropped his arm, but she was already moving away. Putting the table between them, she gave a weak smile. "You're not a klutz." A hunk, no doubt about it, but not a klutz. "You're doing great."

He scowled. "I've managed until now to not fall on my face. And I don't need to break your back or your leg in the process of doing it now." And just like that he slammed a door between them as he sat down on the edge of the massage table.

"You didn't," she snapped. Flustered from the encounter and not exactly sure how to deal with it, Amanda set to work evaluating his shoulder. What was she doing— she'd just been dumped by her fiancé, and yet here she was noticing how amazingly attractive her new client was. It was disturbing on so many levels and very much unlike her.

"So what's the verdict?" Wyatt asked finally when it looked like he wasn't going to speak. Amanda had clammed up after he'd almost crushed her—and what was with him? He'd found himself almost drowning in her eyes when he'd looked down at her. He'd forgotten himself for a minute. But he wouldn't have lost his balance if his hip hadn't seized up on him. That was all it took to remind him Amanda was going to help him walk again. And that was the only thing he needed to be thinking about where she was concerned.

Only problem he found with that line of thinking: doing it. Not easy with her poking and prodding his shoulder with gentle, efficient fingers. *Twelve years.*

Their age difference wouldn't have seemed so vast a difference before the plane crash. But right now, it was generations. He'd never been one to date women more than a couple of years younger than him. He'd always found women his own age to be more in touch with life as he enjoyed it.

"Lift your arm, please," she asked, breaking the silence. Holding her hand out, she waited for him to do as she asked.

He raised his arm but couldn't get it as high as her hand, which was about midway between his elbow and shoulder.

"Fine. On a scale of one to ten, what's the pain?"

"About a seven," he managed.

"On the conservative side?" she asked with a knowing look. One that said she knew exactly how bad he hurt.

He nodded, letting her know she was right as he let his arm down. His shoulder throbbed.

After a few more questions and then some evaluation of his hip and back she finally moved away, giving him some much-needed space. The woman was all business and he liked the way she worked. Her serious expression belied her attractiveness as she asked questions and jotted notes. Impressive.

"Just as I'd thought from reviewing your charts," she said. "We'll start with some simple, isolation exercises to help the rotator cuff. It will show steady improvement as we go and you really shouldn't need that sling for long. The doctors put you in it just so you wouldn't strain it any more before we could get started working. That might help you sleep better."

He rubbed his jaw. His shoulder wasn't what was keeping him awake at night or pushing him to find ways to keep his mind occupied. Bad dreams were doing a bang-up job of that all on their own. "That'd be good," he said, and though he knew it wasn't going to help him sleep, he was ready to ditch the sling and not put it back on. "You can burn it right now and I won't complain."

She smiled and her doe eyes twinkled. "I'll give you that honor if you'd like. You just have to promise me you won't overuse your arm or I'll have to make you wear the sling again."

"Scout's honor I'll behave."

"Good. With the hip and back it'll take more time, but the good news is you'll be up and out of that chair in less than two weeks. Then the real work will begin. You have nothing to be worried about, though, you will mend."

He let her words sink in. The doctors had said the same thing, but he hadn't believed them. Not with the pain he was experiencing. "You're sure?" He felt vulnerable voicing the question but the fact that Amanda had been through what she'd been through made him pretty sure she understood his hesitancy in believing.

Amanda crossed her arms, leaned her head to the side and gave him an assuring look. "I'm sure. You just have to give it your all. That hip is going to complain, but I'll help with those spasms and every day it will get better."

Only time would tell whether his putting his trust in Amanda was well-founded—but he did feel encouraged. And that was a good feeling. "Then let's get busy. Results are what I'm interested in. I'd like to make that two into one."

"Realistically, I don't see that happening." She gave him a frank look, her lips curved upward gently. "But for some reason I get the feeling that when you set your mind to something you make it happen."

Thoughts of the crash flashed across his mind. He rubbed his temple but it didn't ease the throbbing behind his eyes. "Yeah, that's me. I get it done."

Chapter Six

"So how are y'all getting along?" Seth asked Wyatt on the second day after Amanda's arrival. He'd insisted on bringing the tractor over to smooth out the ground destroyed by the hogs.

Fighting a spasm shooting through him from his hip, Wyatt hid a grimace from Seth. "We get along fine."

Seth didn't look impressed by his answer. "Fine? I don't like the sound of that. Are you still giving her a hard time?"

"We'll be fine, Seth. Stop worrying. If she doesn't get herself killed acting impulsively like she did last night."

"What did she do?"

"She came out of her trailer when all the hogs were in the yard."

Seth looked alarmed. "Why would she do a fool thing like that? She could have fallen—" He clamped his mouth shut midsentence and frowned. "Did she tell you about her accident?"

"You mean being hit by a drunk driver?" Wyatt asked, wondering what was wrong with Seth.

"Yeah," Seth said. "What did she say?"

"That she was hurt badly—almost killed—and had to be homeschooled."

"Did she say what her injuries were?"

"No. I didn't ask her to elaborate. I'm sure if she'd wanted to talk about it she would have told me. That must have been horribly traumatic for a kid her age." He knew what he was going through with his nightmares. "Why, did you read about it in her file?"

Seth looked angry. "Yeah. She didn't have any business out there with those hogs."

Wyatt felt remorse. "I can't let her take all the blame. I was on the porch and one of them headed my way. She thought I was about to be run over by the thing and I guess she thought she could save me."

"What were you thinking? You're in a wheelchair, Wyatt. And she could have really been hurt. That's a little different than when you, me and Cole used to hunt those things. What were you planning to do? Play chicken with them? Wrestle them with one arm?"

Maybe he shouldn't have admitted his guilt and avoided this dose of reality. He hadn't had a clue what he was going to do once he got out there... "I'd have handled it," he snapped. "The important thing was that Amanda came charging out there in the middle of them and could have been injured—she could have gotten knocked down. At least they were too busy trying to get away to hurt her. Still, the crazy one that was coming at me could have turned on her."

"So I guess you jumped her pretty bad?"

"Not too bad. But she doesn't take criticism too well."

"Ha!" Seth laughed. "You and her have something in common."

Wyatt shot him a scowl.

"It's true and you know it."

"She's not happy that I'm working, either."

"She *tell* you that?"

"She might as well have. It was written all over her face the moment she found out."

A wide grin spread across Seth's face along with a teasing glint that could only be described as a Turner trait through and through. "Why does this woman bug you so much? You are irritated about everything having to do with her."

Wyatt prickled. "Hey, you and Cole were the ones that hired her. I still don't know what you two knuckleheads were thinking. She's too young. And for the most part, she's only worked with kids. She is totally not right for this job. The hog incident proved that. And yet she's here. Why is that?"

"Because, big bro, we had hired someone else who had to back out for family reasons. Amanda was—well, bluntly, she was a last resort. But her boss assured us that she was far more capable than the other physical therapist to handle your case. So we took her. You're just going to have to straighten up and fly right. It's going to be great."

Yeah, right. He'd believe that when he saw it. "And she doesn't bug me. It's not personal. She just isn't right for the job." Well it was a little personal. But he sure wasn't opening his big mouth again and saying that.

Seth gave him a look of complete disbelief. "You are so bothered by this woman that it isn't even funny. All those other excuses aside, I'm curious if it has anything to do with the fact that you find her attractive. She's pretty, got grit and enough determination that I figured you'd like her."

"She's *twelve* years younger than me—"

"So. You're not in high school anymore. It doesn't matter."

Wyatt disagreed. Yeah, sure, no doubt about it—he did find his physical therapist attractive. "Twelve years is too big a difference to me. I'm not looking to date Amanda anyway. She's here for a job and all I want right now is to get mobile. That's more important than a date."

For some reason, Seth's grin told him he wasn't buying any of that. Too bad. "Stop grinning, brother, and get back on that tractor and smooth out this ground."

"She seems to get along really well… I mean, you know, since being in such bad shape."

"She does. That drunk driver almost killed her and had no injuries. It's criminal."

Wyatt had been careless in flying his plane when he shouldn't have. "I'm grateful that my plane crash didn't harm anyone other than me," he said remorsefully. "I wouldn't have been able to live with that. What if I'd killed someone?" The idea made him ill. His gut clenched and his back started tightening up. He knew any minute it would seize up and put him in a world of pain.

"I hadn't thought of that," Seth said, all humor evaporated. "Wyatt, it's not the same thing. You didn't knowingly have that crash and you weren't drinking and flying. I hope you don't hold that against yourself. It was an accident. That's all. Just like Mom and Dad's crash."

Wyatt grimaced against the pain shooting through him and fought to hide it. "I knew better than to go up in the middle of a storm like that. That makes me liable in my book. It was a straightforward act of negligence.

It's different than Dad. His crash was on a clear day. He did nothing stupid."

Seth looked away, studying the ground as he thought of a comeback. Wyatt knew that deep down Seth had to agree. Seth was too responsible, too black and white where right and wrong were concerned not to see it Wyatt's way. It was only his protective instincts for Wyatt that had him making excuses.

"You can agree with me," Wyatt said. "You know good and well that you tried to talk me out of it. I should have listened."

Seth took a deep breath, thumbed his Stetson back off his forehead and looked at him with worried eyes. "Come on, Wyatt, maybe that's all well and true. But you have to snap out of this mode of thinking. It's eating you up. You can't keep second-guessing your decision. You took off in the middle of that storm—you'd done it before with no problems. You're one of the best twin-engine pilots around. You've never had an incident before—and that time when you had engine malfunctions you got that plane back to the airstrip on a wing and a prayer, basically. This happened because it happened. Period. Let it go and get on with it."

Wyatt closed his eyes against the pain ripping through him and the images of being trapped started playing across his mind. Not good. He opened his eyes to meet Seth's studying him with concern. "I'm fine, Seth. Stop worrying."

"You aren't and we both know it. I'm going to smooth out this ground, then head back home. My advice to you is to lighten up. Stop thinking about how you lost control—you and I both have a problem with control. God is in control even when we think we're the ones doing the driving. God has a plan. You can't see what that is right now, but believe me, He can. I learned that the hard way. Just go with the flow and get yourself well. Stop looking back and blaming yourself and thank God that you didn't hurt anyone else in that crash. And by all means do what your pretty physical therapist is telling you to do so you'll get back to being yourself."

Wyatt wasn't sure if he'd ever get back to being himself. What Seth said was true. He'd found out in that crash just how easily and quickly control could be lost.

Seth started to walk away toward the tractor but stopped. "There was only one perfect man and his name was Jesus. You're human, Wyatt. Always have been, always will be. Humans all make mistakes, so give yourself a break, won't ya? Cole won't get married until you're able to stand up and be his best man. He's counting on you to be there for him body and spirit."

Wyatt watched Seth head across the yard toward the tractor. Catching Seth's grin as he climbed up into the seat, Wyatt was reminded of how strong Seth had been during the deaths of their parents. The serious one, Seth had always been steady and true. Sometimes too serious, but always the one with wisdom beyond his years. Wyatt knew Seth's advice was as true now as it always was, but right now, with the things going on in his head, taking that advice wasn't as cut-and-dried as it should be.

"Hey, big brother, while you're working on standing up, forget about those twelve years and get to know Amanda. She seems like the kind of gal who might be great for you."

"Mow, Seth." That advice he wouldn't take. Right now the last thing he needed to be thinking about was a woman.

Seth plopped into the seat. "Hey, I'm goin', but I'm just sayin'—"

"And I'm just sayin' *mow.*" Wyatt thought about Amanda and knew that if she heard what Seth was saying she'd probably laugh her way off the property and back to San Antonio…and well-warranted on her part.

"So, why don't you work with kids anymore? Did you get tired of it?"

The question took Amanda by surprise. She was standing in the kitchen taking a chicken casserole out of the oven. Earlier that day, Seth's wife, Melody, and Cole's fiancée, Susan, had stopped by to meet her. They'd come bearing food and warm welcomes. Melody was a history teacher and Susan was a veterinarian. They hadn't stayed long but she'd enjoyed meeting them. Wyatt visited with them some, but after they left he'd immediately gone back to being about as communicative as a rock for the rest of therapy. And now he wanted to ask her *this?* Of all things to want to talk about.

She set the hot dish on the burner to cool and then removed her oven mitts as she debated exactly how to answer his question. "No. I didn't get tired of it. I just needed a change."

She reached inside the cabinet and pulled out a plate for him and one for herself—to take back to her trailer like she'd been doing since she arrived. She could feel his blue eyes on her and had to make herself not feel self-conscious. The fact that she found him attractive bothered her. It didn't help matters at all. Call her daft and it would fit.

"I thought you told me the other day that you loved your work."

The man remembered way too much of their conversation in detail. "I did." She weighed her options. She wasn't going to tell him about not being able to have children, but she needed to tell him something. "Look, I was supposed to get married and my fiancé decided he didn't want to. That tends to make you need a change of scenery. I decided coming here to Mule Hollow for a few months was a good idea." There, that was about the best answer she could stand to give. It was the truth, too. Just not all the details.

She dished the chicken and rice onto his plate, glancing at him when he didn't say anything. He had an intense expression on his face as he watched her.

"That had to be rough." His voice gentled.

His compassion was unexpected. "Yes," she said, inhaling slowly, trying to steady her rattled nerves. "It was. But it is what it is. I'm better off knowing up front."

"True, but that doesn't make it hurt less."

She stared at him briefly, startled all the more. With shaking hands, she dished her own meal onto the plate then grabbed the foil, ripped a piece off and covered her food with it. She needed to go home—to her trailer across the yard. "But I have my work and that's a good thing," she finally said, hoping he didn't ask too many more questions. Hoping he let it go at that. She wasn't ready for questions.

Not from him, anyway.

Wyatt studied Amanda and wondered what she was hiding. He'd been thinking about their conversation a lot, though he'd tried not to.

"So you're here to work. To escape?" What was he doing?

She set his plate on the table beside the glass of tea

and the neatly folded napkin. She'd taken care with the place setting and now she straightened the napkin—despite that it didn't need it. She was upset, nervous. He waited to see what else she said. Nervous people talked if you kept quiet and gave them room.

"I guess I could deny it but there isn't really any reason to. Yes. I'm here to work and forget and..." She took a step back and smiled, though it didn't reach her eyes. No, her eyes were too bright. "Well, anyway, here's your supper. I'm going to head over to my house." She turned away and grabbed her plate. She was almost in tears.

Wyatt had the impulse to ask her to stay and talk more—but it was clear talking about it upset her, so he didn't. She wasn't ready. And this was more personal than he wanted to get....

But how had a man hurt her like that?

He forced himself to move his chair up to the table. "Thanks for the supper," he said, clamping down on his natural instinct to dig deeper. Now wasn't the time... and it wasn't his business anyway.

She barely looked at him. "You're welcome. Call if you need anything."

He watched her go. Her shiny dark hair swung in time to her step as she moved. Why had her fiancé dumped her? It didn't matter really, because she was better off without him if he didn't love her. It was evident that she'd loved him, though—still did, from the way she'd reacted. Her emotion had been real. Her heartache was evident; Wyatt didn't like seeing her pain. But she was right—her work would help her escape. To cope, at least, just as his was helping him.

Chapter Seven

Amanda hurried out of Wyatt's as though the house was on fire. She shouldn't have talked about Jonathan. She hadn't planned on telling anyone—especially Wyatt. And now she'd gone and opened up to him like that, when keeping her mouth shut would have been the better way.

Anxious, she sank into the kitchen chair of her travel trailer and felt the walls closing in on her. She'd laid her Bible beside her bed when she'd unpacked, but she hadn't opened it. Now she reached for it, feeling an urgent need.

But, like all the other times she'd tried to read since the breakup, she couldn't do it. It felt like there was a barrier between her and the words written on the page. Oh, she could scan them, but it was as if someone was speaking and she was inside a soundproof room, hearing nothing. She closed the book and, needing space, she went outside.

She walked to the rear of the trailer, not wanting Wyatt to see her pacing. She'd seen what looked like a low wall near the wood's edge and she was pleasantly surprised to find an archway with an iron gate. The hinges squeaked as she pulled the gate open, and with a feeling of excitement she found stone steps leading down the hill.

How old were the wall and steps?

She could hear rushing water and she carefully followed the steps downward toward the sound. Through the trees she saw the river—it was as restless-looking as she felt as it swept by in a swirling mass. At the base of the steps she found a large rock that jutted out over the water. She went to the rock and stared down at the turbulent water.

Though the water swirled and rolled, it was a peaceful place. And it was absolutely beautiful. Huge oak trees lined the banks behind her. In front of her, the rock she stood on connected to a long formation that caused the river to narrow. It was a great place. She moved down the wide rock and found a place to sit. Surely she could think here.

She'd allowed herself to cross that line, thinking about Jonathan. He'd realized there was so much more out there that he could have without her. How could she blame him when even she knew he was right? Sucking in a shaky breath, she felt a tear roll down her cheek and brushed it aside. *Dear Lord, help me get through this.* The prayer came to her, a plea more than a prayer. And all she could do was hope God would answer her.

Wyatt was on the phone when Amanda poked her head through the door the next morning. She still couldn't believe she'd told him about Jonathan. She knew Wyatt probably hadn't missed how upset she'd been. Or that she hadn't turned her light off much that night…he hadn't turned his off until early morning.

She needed work today—not conversation. One look at his face told her he was in extreme pain.

"Looks like you really need me today." She felt for him as she headed toward the therapy room. "Let's get you on the table and after we ease up some of that agony you're in, we'll work on the ligature of that hip. Then, if you're up to it, we'll get started on your arm."

"Give me a minute," he said, distracted. "I need to make another call." He was already dialing the number when she turned back to glare at him from the doorway.

He looked worn-out on top of being in pain, and she was in no mood to let things slide. "You're hurting and you need to relax. Period."

His expression darkened. "I said I'll hang up in a minute. This is important."

Amanda slammed her fists to her hips. "Right now your well-being is the most important thing in your life. And the *only* thing I'm interested in. This work you're doing isn't my priority. How many cases are you working on, anyway? You can't tell me all these phone calls and all that paperwork is just one case."

He didn't answer, just stared at her like she'd lost it. Maybe she had, because she just kept right on going. "Are you consulting on the cases of the entire law firm? Don't these people know you need time off to heal?"

He looked perplexed. "I'm working because I want to. And because these are my cases that have had to be borne on someone else's shoulders. I need to see them through."

"Well, I need to see your therapy through. So hang that phone up right now."

He was in shock. His expression was one she'd seen on her teenage patients when she'd threatened to take away their phones. It was a combination of disbelief and irritation. "I'm not joking, Wyatt. As your physical therapist I'm telling you that you need to put your health first and get in here on this table."

Not looking happy at all, he set the phone down and drove his wheelchair past her into the PT room.

Amanda prayed for patience as she followed him. She never expected this to be easy, and in reality she'd had far worse rebellion from some kids who took their pain and loss out on her. She'd eventually helped them and she would do the same with Wyatt. Yesterday she'd let him see her get emotional, personal. That had been a mistake.

She waited as he removed his shirt and got settled on the table. His muscles rippled as he did so, drawing her attention. The man was something—even with the fresh scars on his back. He didn't say a word and she was fine with that. She needed to keep this strictly business. Her mind couldn't dwell on his muscles in any way, shape or form other than the ones she was here to fix.

She got to work, focused on it and, like she had the other times when she'd given him his massage, she refrained from asking him anything about his accident. She figured if he wanted to talk about it he would. The red scars ran down his back on his left side, and there were also some on his arm and chest.

From the heating unit she took heated pads and applied them to his back and hip then covered them with warm towels.

"Just relax and let the heat loosen you up," she said, then went to the small desk and opened his chart. One thing she was glad about was that he hadn't pursued his line of questioning today.

She'd had a rough night after telling him about Jonathan. Sleep hadn't helped—what little she'd had was restless. She'd awakened more tired, it seemed, than when she'd closed her eyes.

Her gaze wandered back to where Wyatt lay covered in towels with his head down staring at the floor through the hole in the table.

"Your place is beautiful," she said, suddenly needing conversation. "I found the stone stairway yesterday evening."

"You went down by the river?"

"Yes. It was almost like being swept back in time sitting down there. I wonder how old that stairway is?"

"At least a hundred and fifty years—like the house. I think it was all done at the same time."

"Amazing." When he said nothing she filled in. "Those who passed this way over the years must have felt a sense of peace when they arrived here." She'd felt it briefly. Very briefly.

"That's what I always thought."

She didn't have anything to fill the silence with this time.

Wyatt shifted on the table. "I've always loved it here."

That she'd gathered from others' conversations. "Why did you move away?" The personal question was out before she realized it. But she was curious and she did need something to take her mind off her own troubles. Seconds clicked by as if he, too, was unsure about wanting to continue conversing.

"I've always wanted to be a lawyer," he offered finally.

"Oh." She searched for something to ask. Why had she initiated the conversation?

"Are you always so bossy?"

She was grateful for the unexpected question even if it was grunted. "My momma says yes."

He raised his head from the table and looked at her. "I have a feeling she's right."

She could see it in his eyes that he was still in pain and she wasn't sure whether he was talking to distract himself from it. But he didn't need to be looking at her. "Put that head back down. You still have five minutes."

He ignored her. "So what was this sorry guy's problem?"

This was not the conversation she wanted to have. "He wasn't sorry."

"What?" Wyatt pushed up from the table with his good arm. "If that's the case, then what did you do?"

She crossed to him and started hastily removing the heating pads. "Nothing. Can we not talk about this?" Why had she said that? It would only spike his curiosity further.

She pushed him down and started working on his back. "So are wild hogs the norm around here? Am I going to have to dodge them?" She hadn't begun her early morning jogs, but knew it was time. She needed the release jogging gave her. But the wild hog incident had put a damper on that and…in actuality she just hadn't been able to make herself get out of bed like she usually did. She knew getting back into it would help her feel better…. She just wasn't sure about jogging alone in the pastures at the crack of dawn.

"Seth has trappers come periodically to keep them down. Most every rancher has problems with them. So you might run into them, but not likely in the daytime. Why, are you planning on starting to trap them?"

"*Hardly.* I really don't want to have anything to do with those mean-looking things."

"Good. They might be back during the night at some point and if so, no matter what, you need to stay inside. But you probably won't see any during daylight hours."

"You're sure?" She didn't want to specifically mention that she was going to be running early in the morning and that they scared her a little. Okay, a lot. She was a coward. She *was* running tomorrow. Pigs or no pigs, she was going to pull herself out of this state of lethargy. She knew it was all the oppressed emotions dragging her down. She'd hoped work would help, but so far nothing had helped. Not even God.

"You're loosening up. Is the pain ebbing?" She was glad to feel him relax with each motion of her hands.

"It's a dull ache right now."

"You'll be glad to know that we're stepping it up today. We're going to push harder and then we'll get cracking on standing up. You're in great shape, so that's going to work to your advantage." No doubt about it, Wyatt was in *excellent* shape.

"Hey!" he yelped when she hit a sore spot.

"Sorry!" *Focus, Amanda! Focus!* "I thought I had that worked out of there."

"That's okay." He grunted and shifted uncomfortably. "Just wasn't expecting it."

"So are you a runner?" She asked the first thing that came to mind, venturing another personal question. When he was talking he seemed to loosen up quicker.

"Before the plane crash, I jogged every day. Plus, I worked out at the gym. It helped with my mental acuity. It's good to know all that work wasn't for nothing."

So he was a jogger just like she'd thought. "Getting

in shape is never for nothing. Have you run any marathons?"

"I did the Alcatraz Iron Man Triathlon last year. That was my first venture into competitive running."

"Your first venture!" Amanda said in disbelief. "You tackled a swim from Alcatraz, topped it off with biking and running for your *first* venture. I am in awe."

"Don't be," he drawled, glancing over his shoulder at her. "I came in middle of the pack in my age group."

The way he said that said it all. He'd gone out to come in first on his very first marathon race. The man had high expectations for himself. To him, middle of the pack was as bad as coming in last. It was all or nothing for Wyatt Turner.

"I'm still impressed."

He grunted. "I'm not."

She worked in silence for the next few minutes. He seemed content to relax and let her work.

Finally she asked him to flip to his back and she placed her fingers beneath his ankle again. "Lift, please. Good. Now, this time I'm going to rotate it. How does that feel?"

"Tight."

"In other words, it still hurts."

"That is correct," he said, tense.

She smiled at the lawyerly way he'd answered. Not a yes, but: *that is correct.* "It is getting better. But during the next few weeks pushing your limits will mean pain," she warned. "It's the only way to gain full range of motion."

He didn't hesitate at that, but gave her a boyish grin. "If it takes you beating me up every day in order for me to gain back my 'full range of motion,' then have at it, Doc. You have my full cooperation."

Startled by his smile, Amanda felt lighter suddenly. But *full cooperation*. She'd believe that when she saw it.

Chapter Eight

Amanda decided to drive into town during her break that afternoon and check out some of the shops. It was a beautiful Saturday and she felt a little lighter after her morning session with Wyatt. They'd made progress in more ways than one this morning. Her heart had been lifted during their conversation. She knew she made him feel some relief, also, by the time she'd left. Not just physically but mentally. That may have come strictly from the fact that he was about to start putting some weight on his hip. Forward motion for him was all he cared about. She knew the lightness in her heart that had hit her when he'd smiled at her had come from the fact that she loved to see her patients feeling better.

The memory of that boyish grin replayed across her mind all afternoon, though. Each time it did she found herself smiling. Just like she was doing now.

She parked in front of Heavenly Inspirations hair salon. The bright pink building could be seen all the way from the crossroads, a beacon for the town. The pink car sitting in front of it did the same. It was one of those Elvis Cadillacs, the kind from the 1950s with the shark-tail fenders. Who did it belong to? No telling, since there seemed to be a good amount of folks in town today.

Cars lined the street and a chattering group was heading into the diner that very minute. And at Pete's, the feed store directly across from the salon, there were three trucks backed up. Cowboys were loading big sacks of feed into the beds. As she was standing there, she noticed a sign on the window of the salon. There was going to be a roping event at the Matlock Ranch Arena the following Saturday. Amanda was thinking that this sounded like fun when the salon door was flung open and a small woman with a head of very blond hair stepped outside.

"Hey there! I'm Lacy Matlock." She held out her hand and smiled. Her hair was about three inches long all over her head and looked like she'd just stepped out of a wind tunnel. It was tousled this way and that way and looked really cute on the perky gal whose blue, blue eyes were twinkling with warmth. "You're Amanda, the one working out at Wyatt's, aren't you?"

"Yes." Amanda shook Lacy's hand. "How did you know?"

"Norma Sue and Esther Mae described you to me perfectly and when I saw you through the window, I knew it had to be you."

Amanda couldn't help smiling at the bubbly blonde. She was the kind of person who made you feel good just by being near them. She was animated with joy and energy, smiling and waving her orange-tipped fingernails about as she talked. "Should I ask how they described me or should I be afraid?"

"Oh, it's all good. Believe me, those two liked you

the minute they saw you. Which only got better when they found out you were here to take care of their boy."

"Their boy?"

"They claim Wyatt, Cole and Seth. They *claim* all the cowboys within the seventy-mile radius around Mule Hollow, but those Turner men practically grew up at their houses. They were real close with Wyatt's parents."

"Oh, I see. That explains why they were so excited that I was here to take care of Wyatt."

"Yep. They have been so worried about Wyatt. And they have been talking nonstop since you arrived. How are you doing? Are y'all getting along all right?"

How did she answer that? "We're getting used to each other." That was the truth.

Lacy's expression grew compassionate. "He's been through a lot, I'm guessing he's still having a hard time dealing with the situation. Even with the blessing of being alive, men don't enjoy being tied down. My Clint would be like a penned-up bull if he couldn't get out and tend to his ranch." She patted her small rounded stomach. "And I'm sure our baby will be the same way."

"I'm sure you are really excited about the baby even if he or she is a ball of energy."

"Oh, yeah, that is for certain. We have wanted a baby for a long time. God finally said the timing was right and here we are, waiting for the happy day. I'm loving every minute of it."

Amanda decided to open up a bit but didn't feel right saying too much. "Wyatt is having a hard time. But each day he's getting further along."

Lacy checked her watch. "Are y'all going to try and get out some? He's not even been to church since he was injured. We'd love to have y'all come tomorrow. Or even if Wyatt doesn't want to get out, we'd love to see you."

"You know, I hadn't thought about going to church just yet, but that is actually a wonderful idea. It would get Wyatt out of the house and get him around people who care for him." She hadn't thought of it because she was still trying to deal with her own faith issues.

"And God will be pleased to see y'all there as much as we will be."

"I think that's a great idea, Lacy." It would be good for him…and for her.

"Well, I need to run, I've got a color client under the dryer and her time is almost up…" She hesitated before turning back to the door. "Amanda, I normally wouldn't say this, but you're right, coming to church will be good for him. I think Wyatt is angry with himself and I just think he needs some peace. Connecting with God and fellowshipping with his church family will help him."

That struck Amanda hard—almost as if Lacy had hit her with a rock, because that was exactly what was wrong with Wyatt—not to mention that *she* needed peace, too…but this was about Wyatt. She'd known something had him hiding in his work. *And* something had him moody—he just didn't strike her as the kind of man who would normally be moody. He'd almost died and he was stuck in a wheelchair. That was enough to make anyone moody. But she was curious as to what Lacy's thoughts were. "Why do you think that?"

Lacy shrugged. "It's just, I was with my husband, who is a first responder on our volunteer fire department, so I was there when they pulled him out. He was barely conscious. I mean, it was a miracle that he wasn't harmed worse. A miracle and good flying skills. He

landed that plane in the middle of a horrible storm in a
very bad area. It wasn't as if he were in open pasture but
rather a tree-covered spot near some of the hills we have
in Texas Hill Country. God had to have had His hand on
that plane. I think maybe that is what could be worrying Wyatt. He kept mumbling that he'd been stupid and
arrogant—I don't even know if he remembers that he
said that. When we all got to him, he was in such bad
shape. He'd lost a good bit of blood." Lacy stopped
speaking suddenly and looked uncomfortable. "I'm
sorry. I know it's hard to believe since I'm the town
hairstylist and salons are the gossip mills of small towns,
but I really don't do this normally. It's just I get the sense
that maybe you need to know this. Come tomorrow if
you can. Everyone would love to meet you. And just give
me a call if you need anything."

Amanda watched as Lacy practically flew back into
her salon. She'd spent less than fifteen minutes talking
and she felt as if she'd known Lacy all her life. There
was something about her that made a person know she
genuinely cared.

Amanda liked that. She liked feeling like she was
among folks who looked out for each other. She stared
down the sidewalk at the tiny town and, as she had that
first day, she wondered what it would be like to just
move here. Would that be considered running away from
her problems?

"Tomorrow is Sunday and I thought we'd go to
church," Amanda said when they'd started their afternoon session. Once again, Wyatt had been buried in research when she'd arrived.

Now he shot her a scowl. "I'm not going to church. No way."

So much for full cooperation—of course she'd seen that already. *"Yes way."*

He'd been okay during the therapy after she'd been firm, but he hadn't been very talkative that afternoon. Again she wasn't happy about his workload but had decided to hold her tongue. For now, anyway. She processed the information Lacy had given her. "When was the last time you got out of this house?"

"I haven't left since they brought me home and I'm not going to church in that *chair.*"

So that was it. "It will do you good."

"Forget it, Amanda."

"Look." She could be just as stubborn as he could be. "This is part of therapy. Getting out and about will be good for you. You have gotten too tied to these four walls surrounding you. And way too connected to your phone."

He glared at her, his dark brows crinkled and almost touching in the middle. "I'm not going out in that stinkin' chair. Get it out of your head."

His words hit Amanda wrong. She fought down her temper. Did he not know how blessed he was? Did he think he was too good to be seen in a wheelchair? Irritated beyond words, she glared right back at him. "I don't know if you've noticed," she gritted through clenched teeth. "No, you probably haven't since you've been too busy feeling sorry for yourself. But there is an abundance of people who live *every* single day of their lives in wheelchairs. For them there is no hope of ever getting out of 'that chair,' as you so callously call it." She shook her head and willed herself to remain calm. Irrational behavior never helped anything. "Instead of feeling sorry for themselves, they enjoy life…thankful that they have 'that chair,' which enables them to not be shut in. And so can you. Why do you continue to be so obstinate? Why are you being so hard on yourself?" She couldn't jump him about being too prideful to use the chair. This went deeper than that and she knew it.

Instead of answering, he drove his chair to the window and stared out across the pasture.

"Don't you know how fortunate you are? You came through that plane crash alive. I understand it must have been a harrowing experience, but God brought you through it. What you have wrong with you can be fixed. I've tried and tried to get that through to you. You are about to be on a walker. And then a cane. But this is about more than walking, isn't it?" Instinct told her that Lacy was right. Wyatt was hiding something deeper. She could relate to that in more ways than he could imagine. Crazy as it sounded, she wished she could tell him her problem. But this was about him, not her, and it didn't seem right.

"Why are you so angry?" She asked the question half expecting him to scoff and tell her it was none of her business. Instead he swung his chair around to face her.

"Look, I took my life for granted, all right?" He rubbed his temple as if he had a headache.

"How did you do that?" It was the only question to ask to such an observation.

"I climbed into that plane never even imagining that it would crash. When I woke—" He stopped speaking and she stilled her fingers working out a knot tightening up along his spine. "When I woke trapped inside, with the smell of gas all around me, I felt stupid. I was going to die because I'd been incompetent. That isn't acceptable to me."

That couldn't be it. "You're this angry about being stuck in this wheelchair because you feel stupid?" This seemed totally out of character for him. She hadn't tagged him as being so shallow.

"No. Because like you just pointed out, I'm an arrogant fool."

"Hey, that's not what I meant at all!"

"Isn't it? It's the truth."

He was an overachiever. "Do you think you're a superhero? You're being unreasonably hard on yourself. You got in an airplane and it crashed. It happens. That's just like me getting in my car and being involved in that car crash—I didn't do it on purpose. I didn't drink and drive. *That* would be stupid. Was stupid, irresponsible and criminal."

He went very still. "You're right. But even if I weren't guilty of drinking…" His words were quiet. "I did know there was risk in taking off in that storm. All I can think about is what if I had harmed someone because I chose to fly my plane in unsafe conditions. I do corporate law for the most part, but I also handle cases every year where someone was injured from acts of neglect. It turns my stomach that I could have been in that category. At the very least I was neglectful of my own safety. My grandfather died that way. He basically made a decision to mow on a hill that any beginner would have known was too steep. But he did it anyway and his tractor rolled on top of him. All my life that's bothered me and here I went and decided to fly my plane into a storm because I believed I could fly through anything. God and everyone else has got to be thinking I'm an idiot. But that's not what bothers me. It's the carelessness of it. It's un-forgivable."

There was a lot here. Amanda searched for words. "Everything is forgivable," she said. "I—I learned that when the drunk driver that had almost killed me came and begged me for forgiveness. I couldn't do it at first. But then, my dad helped me realize it was what God expected of me. He forgives us so we have to forgive others. It was tough at first. But that was the first step in my recovery. I've helped my young patients get through some of the same pain by helping them take that step. You need to do that. You need to forgive yourself." She walked over to stand beside him. She wanted to reach out and touch him but didn't.

He didn't look as if anything she'd said had made a difference. She pushed on. "You hold yourself up to too high a standard and you're right, that is pretty arrogant on your part. I hate to say this, but you don't have a clue what your grandfather was thinking." Maybe she was stepping over the line here, but she felt it needed to be said. Bluntness might be the only thing that got through to him.

He didn't say anything for a heartbeat. "You don't hold back, do you?"

"Not very often," she said, more gently. She wanted to help him. "I deal with people's physical impairments every day. Many times it's the things going on in their heads after an injury that play a role in their healing. My kids—I mean many of my patients—see counsel-ors simultaneously. Normally, I leave this sort of thing for them."

"I don't know, you're giving this thick-headed fool sound advice. At least you are stating the facts."

"You deal in facts. I was probably out of line."

He lifted his hand and placed it on her arm. The contact was warm.

"You weren't out of line. I needed a kick in the pants. It's at least something for me to think about. New perspectives and all."

Her gaze was stuck on his hand on her arm. She forced herself to raise her head. "I hope if you think it's good advice, you'll take some of it. You aren't the type of man who would knowingly put yourself or someone else at risk. For some reason you were meant to be in this wheelchair in this moment in time."

"I don't know if I believe that."

He'd almost opened up a bit, but now he was shutting down again. Amanda pushed. "I don't begin to understand the mind of God. Believe me, I'm the worst—" She stopped herself. She could not go where she'd almost gone. "I believe that God has a reason and a purpose for everything. Whether you agree with him or not." If he only knew how hard it was for her to believe what she was saying. "Even you being in this wheelchair, at this time and place. Maybe it's so you'll go to church in this chair, and get over your pride—"

He shot her an icy glare. "Pride—" The phone rang and he reached for it. "I'm expecting a conference call. I'm not going to church."

And that was that. She watched him drive into the other room, frustration settling over her. He'd iced over like a freeze pop when she'd blurted out *pride.* Any moron would know you don't call someone on their pride unless you're prepared for them to cut you off instantly out of exactly that emotion.

She might not ever get him to listen to her now.

Chapter Nine

In the predawn hours of Sunday morning Wyatt gave up trying to sleep. He sat up, ignoring all the parts of him that protested with shooting pain. It wasn't his shoulder, his hip or his back or nightmares that kept him up for most of the night. It was Amanda.

She'd heaped the guilt on the day before. *Pride.* She'd thought he was too proud to be seen in the wheelchair. He hadn't needed her to point out to him that there were people who couldn't get out of their chairs. She'd acted like he didn't know this… He knew better than anyone that he could have very easily been one of them.

He carefully swung his legs over the edge of the bed, stood for a minute before easing into the wheelchair. He could feel the progress they'd made, feel the strength coming back to him and knew the pain was ebbing, also. Still, he despised the wheelchair more every day even knowing soon he wouldn't have to use it anymore.

He'd been whining.

He shouldn't have been startled by her boldness when she'd tried to put him in his place for it.

Whining. The thought hit him and it wasn't pleasant. The idea was so far removed from what he'd ever thought he'd do in the face of adversity that he wanted to shove it away and deny it.

Uncomfortable with the idea, he drove the chair to the kitchen and made himself a pot of coffee. By the time he poured himself a cup, he wasn't feeling any better about himself. He was still sitting at the front windows as the sun's morning light began to seep through the darkness. The last thing he was expecting to see as the thin sliver of pink crept over the treetops was Amanda. But there she was rounding the end of the house *jogging* down the road. But it was the prosthetic leg that caused him to almost drop his coffee.

She had on a blue top and gray running shorts that completely exposed the prosthetic leg made specially shaped for running. Her leg was missing from about five inches above the knee, and the prosthetic slipped over her thigh. The reality of what the drunk driver had done to her hit him like a punch in the gut, knocked the breath out of him. No wonder she'd given him a dressing-down over his attitude about the wheelchair. He felt sick. Even though he'd been in the process of taking a good hard look at himself, it didn't matter. Now he felt embarrassed by his entire attitude.

Here he was temporarily in a wheelchair with a clean bill of health ahead of him, according to Amanda and the doctors, and still he was whining.

Some man he turned out to be.

His disgust couldn't be measured, it was so great.

Amanda had lost her entire leg and hadn't said anything. No, on the contrary. She had taken what life had thrown at her and she'd triumphed over it. She'd become a physical therapist—working with kids who needed her attention and upbeat attitude. And on top of that she was running.

It was amazing.

He remembered her asking about his running and wondered why she'd chosen not to mention it then. Why had she not told him about her leg? *You fired her, you jerk, for being too small and too young.* She probably was afraid he'd fire her again if he knew about her leg. Remorse sank over him like a black cloud. She would have been right. For certain, he wouldn't have thought she was strong enough if he'd known this. He knew differently now, though. Amanda Hathaway was stronger than she looked…inside and outside.

Feeling like a fool, he watched her cross over the cattle guard and head down the gravel road dissecting the pastures. She followed the curved road across the prairie with such grace and fluidity that he found watching her hypnotizing.

Transfixed, he watched until she disappeared over the horizon where the trees peeked over the edge. He was profoundly and humbly changed as he sat there watching the spot where she'd disappeared.

Amanda had faced death and lost a limb and yet she'd overcome it. Instead of floundering as he'd been doing, she'd flourished.

Wyatt took a long draw on his coffee, then he turned his chair around and headed toward his bedroom.

Amanda pushed hard as she ran. Sleeplessness had driven her from her bed and out into the morning light with a vengeance. She'd given Wyatt all that advice the day before and felt like a hypocrite.

Why was it that depression and doubts always surged

back just after progress was made? It was as if the devil were reaching out and pulling her back into the hole.

God had a reason and a purpose for everything.

Boy, she'd been real quick to spout that advice off to Wyatt. Even telling him that him being in that wheelchair at this time was His purpose—what had she been thinking? She didn't know God's reasoning. She kept trying to figure out her own way and couldn't do it, but she was sure full of advice for Wyatt.

So what had she been doing lecturing Wyatt on his attitude toward wheelchairs?

Needing to clear her head, she'd taken action, dressed in her running clothes, pulled on her running prosthetic and headed out into the gravel roads with the welcoming spirit she'd had all her life toward jogging. When she ran she was strong. She felt happy. She felt like anything was possible. And usually she felt at peace—that hadn't been the case for weeks. But still, she'd needed it these days more than ever.

"God never promised that life would always be easy," she said, out loud now. "He did promise that He would be with His people always and that He would help them. He will help Wyatt. And He will help me."

He would. It just seemed like…she couldn't find peace about it. Why was that? She felt such betrayal over what Jonathan had done, and she felt betrayed by God, too. This was where the turmoil lay.

She watched the sun rise as she ran down the gravel road that seemed to head straight for the glowing ball lifting upward. She asked God to give her the peace she needed.…

If only she could get Jonathan and the life she'd envisioned with him off her mind. And the children. Her purpose seemed so far away from her now she couldn't get her heart back into it.

She'd thought getting here to Mule Hollow and throwing herself into this job with a demanding client would be her saving grace. But this morning, the loss she felt inside was so great she could hardly stand it. All she could think about was never giving birth to her own children. Or having a husband.

"You *will* marry one day," she said, rather loudly. There was no one around to hear her and she needed to hear the words. "You will find a good man who won't think you aren't worth marrying because you can't carry his children..." Her voice broke and she stumbled to a stop; hands on her knees, she bent forward and blinked back the surge of tears that had risen suddenly. How was she supposed to help Wyatt when she couldn't help herself? Nothing she'd said the day before had gotten through to him.

The cattle kept on chewing as they studied her. It was like they were waiting for her to continue. *Focus.*

Amanda blinked hard and thought of Wyatt. She was here to help him. "Suck it up and focus on what God has for you to do." Resuming her jogging, she evaluated her plan. Help him get on his feet. Help him get back to his life. Help him move past the things eating at him and holding him back. This job was about him, not her.

"You can help him."

And today that started with getting him to church. Getting him out of that house and back in the midst of people. She already knew that the folks of Mule Hollow would eagerly welcome him. She'd worry about herself later.

All she had to do was get him out of the house.

The last thing she expected an hour later, after she'd showered and dressed for church, was to round the corner to find Wyatt sitting on the porch with his Bible in his lap, also dressed for church.

She'd worried when she came back from jogging that he had seen her leg. She'd been so focused on running at the time that she'd overlooked the fact that he would be awake when she returned. But as she'd jogged past the house she'd decided if he was outside then it was meant to be. She was going to have to tell him anyway. It was time. He'd either respect her for the PT that she was or he'd give her the boot.

But finding him ready for church, in starched jeans and a crisp white shirt, threw her.

She halted at the bottom of the steps. "Hi. Don't you look nice." She didn't want to jump to conclusions, but her heart was pounding with hope.

His gaze was serious as he gave her a slow smile. "Thought I'd hitch a ride with you this morning, if that's all right."

A smile as wide as the Guadalupe River cracked across her face. "I think that would simply be wonderful."

The Mule Hollow Church of Faith was a sweet little number on the outskirts of town. The rural church made Amanda think of weddings and picnics on the lawn. The classic white-washed chapel with a tall steeple looked well maintained and inviting. It fit the country, down-home town perfectly and she could easily see happy couples standing together at the front of the church saying their vows before God and all of their friends and family. It would have been a lovely place for— *Hold it!*

Amanda's thoughts came to a screeching halt. She was done imagining weddings. This was a good day and she didn't plan to spoil it. Wyatt had agreed to come to church with her and that had made her day brighter than she'd ever expected.

"I love it," she said, glancing at Wyatt. "Is this where you went to church growing up?"

"All my life. See that second window? I threw a baseball through that when I was nine. I thought my mother was going to kill me. She'd already told me that I needed to stop throwing the ball to Cole so close to the church because he might miss one. And he did. The ball tipped his glove and crashed through the window."

Amanda could just see them standing there. She knew without being told that Cole had idolized his big brother and Wyatt had probably taken his role as older brother seriously, even at that young age.

"You didn't listen," she guessed. His look said he'd been in hot water.

"You better believe I did the *next* time, though. I had to save up my own money to repay my parents for repairing the window. Plus, every Saturday for a month I had to weed the flower beds. I hated weeding then and more than ever now."

She laughed. "Your parents knew that, didn't they?"

"Oh, yeah. They got my attention."

Amanda laughed as she got out of the SUV. No sooner had she gotten the wheelchair unloaded from the chair rack on the back of the vehicle than they were spotted. Then surrounded. Poor Wyatt had more help getting out of the vehicle than he wanted, but he was pretty good at hiding his feelings. She, however, could tell that all the attention bothered him. She still didn't have a clue what had changed his mind, but she was glad they were here.

Norma Sue was the first to come barreling across the lawn with her husband, Roy Don, in tow. Wyatt filled her in on that tidbit as they came. The same with Esther Mae and her husband, Hank.

"It's a pure miracle that you got this man out of his house," Norma Sue said, practically tackling Wyatt to give him a hardy hug.

Esther Mae was right behind her. "We are so glad you came," she said, pushing Norma Sue out of the way and getting her own hug. She had on a lime-green hat with red daisies clustered all about its brim, and when she engulfed Wyatt the brim whacked him in the nose.

"Like your hat, Esther Mae." He chuckled, meeting Amanda's gaze over Esther's shoulder. It looked as if his head was going to get squeezed right off.

"Don't smother him, Esther Mae," Norma Sue huffed.

"I'm not doing anything you didn't do," she snapped, finishing off with one more squeeze that caused the hem of her dress to dance right along with the daisies. "When do you get out of that?" she asked as she pulled away and straightened her hat.

It wasn't exactly the question Amanda had hoped Wyatt would get the minute he ventured out. She was afraid it wouldn't help the situation, but to her pleasant surprise, Wyatt didn't seem bothered. Instead he gave Esther Mae a gentle, almost flirtatious smile that had Amanda enjoying his interaction with the two older ladies.

"This next week is the goal, so says my boss." He gave Amanda a warm glance.

The charm in that glance and the way his voice dipped

low on the last words sent a shiver of attraction racing
through Amanda. Her heart lifted even more. Wyatt's
sudden turnaround had given her own hard morning a
turnaround. To her surprise, the sting of tears ambushed
her. She looked down quickly and blinked them away.
She'd been doing so well. Why now? Why were these
emotions raging forward now, here? She could not cry
in front of all these people.

Especially Wyatt.

She couldn't answer questions about what was wrong
with her and she certainly didn't want Wyatt asking her
what was wrong. Was it that her emotions were just so
close to the surface that being happy for Wyatt's attitude adjustment was enough to set them off? That was
all she could figure.

Wyatt caught sight of her staring and hiked a brow,
ever so subtly. Immediately she realized that she'd been
staring at him. She yanked her eyes from him and focused on what Norma Sue was saying.

"...your parents loved each other, too, and don't you
ever forget it." Norma Sue patted his shoulder. "They'd
be mighty proud of you."

Amanda couldn't help but look at him. His jaw jerked
ever so slightly and he tensed up on his left side. As
quick as that, he was suddenly in jeopardy of pushing
himself into a spasm...all because something about that
statement bothered him.

"Me and Esther Mae are singing the special in the
choir this morning, so we have to head on in, too. See
y'all later."

Esther Mae gaped at him, her big green eyes wide.
"I still can't get over how great you look, Wyatt. Why,
you're the picture of health." She grinned. "I think

Amanda must be good for you." With that she spun and hurried after Norma Sue into the church.

Amanda's cheeks warmed.

"You know Esther Mae is right," Roy Don said, turning his attention on Wyatt as the ladies walked off. "If you were sitting in the pew and I didn't know any better I'd never a thought you couldn't walk—not saying you can't. But you know what I mean. It's a pure act of God Himself that you're sitting here. There's no doubt about it."

"Ain't that the truth," Hank agreed. "God don't just let everybody fall out of the sky and live to tell about it."

Wyatt's eyes darkened and he didn't look happy at all. Amanda braced for stormy weather.

"Well, fellas," he drawled. "You two sure know how to make a man feel good."

Both older men grinned. "We're glad we could help," Roy Don said. "Your daddy would want us to keep you knowing from where your blessings come."

"Yes, sir, he would," Wyatt said gruffly as they followed their wives into the church.

Amanda looked down at Wyatt as they went up the ramp. "Have you already thought about that?"

"You mean about how my dad would want me to know that God saved me for something?"

"Yes."

"Every single day since the crash," he said quietly, then drove through the doorway.

Chapter Ten

Babies. Meeting Lacy the day before should have prepared her for seeing other women who were expecting,
but it didn't. There were pregnant women everywhere!
Lacy gave both of them a big hug the minute they entered, then introduced Amanda to her husband, Clint.
Obviously Clint and Wyatt knew each other well because they launched into a conversation immediately
while Lacy began introducing her to the women as they
passed by heading for their pews.

Thankfully there was so much going on that no one
seemed to notice that she didn't ask the usual questions
like "When are you due?" or "Is it going to be a boy or
a girl?" She was able to smile, and she tried really hard
to mean it. Meeting Lacy the day before she'd been able
to focus on their conversation and not Lacy's pregnant
state, but today it wasn't so easy. They were all so happy.
She understood their joy completely.

She was relieved when Seth motioned to them from
his pew to come join them.

"I never expected to turn around and see y'all here,"
he said, his disbelief apparent.

"Thought I'd see if I could shake things up a bit." Wyatt gave him a handshake.

Seth bent forward and grinned. "It's good to see you haven't lost your touch."

Amanda crowded into a pew next to Seth while Wyatt parked himself at the end of the pew. Melody, Susan and Cole all greeted them just as a cowboy stepped up to the mic and got the music started. From the choir Norma Sue and Esther Mae—surrounded by cowboys—smiled and she got the uncomfortable feeling they were grinning too big as their eyes kept going from her to Wyatt.

No sooner, it seemed, was the music over than the visiting preacher stood up and gave a sermon that ended almost before it had begun. The man told a joke—and not even a very good one—then he talked about an article he'd read in a popular magazine about some folks who'd done a good deed. Then it was over.

"We didn't pay him fer *that,* did we?" A tall, skinny, older man boomed in disgust as they were leaving. His thin face was rippled with frown lines.

Melody whispered to Amanda, "That's Applegate Thornton. He's hard of hearing and ornery but a total marshmallow. He's always looking out for Mule Hollow. I knew he wasn't going to be happy about this."

Seth stopped to talk. "Applegate, there's no need for you to get upset about this. I'm sure there are plenty of churches across the country who might like a five-minute sermon. We just aren't one of them."

"That's the surefire truth," a plump, balding man standing next to Applegate grumbled. "App, ole hypocrite, ya know good and well you got your moments when that'd be fine by you, too."

Melody leaned in close. "And that is Stanley Orr, Applegate's GBFF."

"What does that stand for?" she whispered. She could text message with the best of them, but those initials didn't compute to her.

Melody chuckled. "That stands for grumpy best friend forever. *Remember* I teach middle school."

Amanda bit back a laugh, totally picturing the two as "grumpy best friends forever"! While she and Melody were whispering, Applegate gave his GBFF a glare that would fry bacon it was so hot and a comeback—

"I ain't no *hypocrite!* Shor I might want ta go fishin' early ever once in a while, but I still expect a message. Even if it is a short one. That right thar was a touchy-feely piece of hogwash. That's what that was."

Amanda had to agree. There hadn't been one sincere thing in the sermon that spoke of being a word from God. But she wasn't worried about that, she was worried about the two old men as Seth, Cole and even Wyatt began to try to calm them down. "Are they okay?" she asked softly.

"Yes," Susan said, sidestepping the guys to stand beside Amanda and Melody. "They just get excited and they talk to each other like that all the time."

"They like to harass each other." Melody shook her head. "They can get pretty funny sometimes."

From behind her she heard Wyatt chuckle. It was a low rumble that made her want to smile. The sound of him chuckling and to see the way he'd relaxed were total reassurance that she'd done the right thing in trying to convince him to come to church. She still wasn't sure what had changed his mind, but she was giving all the credit to God.

"You hang around long enough and you'll see App and Stanley a lot. They're down at Sam's every morning playing checkers. They pretty much keep everyone in line and they can come up with some of the funniest things."

"Whatever you say. I'd have to see it to believe it," Amanda said. Her gaze was drawn to Wyatt. He was smiling and at ease as he got involved with the conversation. It was wonderful to see him this way. She was so glad he'd chosen to come with her.

Where had the man who'd been so adamant about not going to church in a wheelchair gone? This guy was the life of the party—and totally unknown to her.

"You've helped him already," Melody said about thirty minutes later.

She and Wyatt had gone back to Seth and Melody's for lunch along with Cole and Susan. She was in the kitchen with Melody and Susan helping get lunch ready to serve.

Melody was a pretty brunette with violet eyes whose color and intelligence were accentuated by her purple glasses. Amanda could totally see her as the middle school history teacher that she was. "The fact that you got him to come to church in the wheelchair was amazing."

"And he actually smiled a couple of times," Susan said as she chopped tomatoes up for the salad. She was tall, blonde and beautiful—not at all what Amanda pictured as the local veterinarian when they'd met. But she was, and according to Wyatt her work was well-respected.

Amanda liked both women a lot. She still had a hard

time looking at them and believing that one was married to a Turner brother and the other was about to be married to a Turner brother all because Wyatt had set them up. Wyatt Turner did not look like a cupid or a matchmaker. And he most definitely didn't look like a romantic, but that was exactly what he was in her eyes. She wondered why he didn't have a special woman in his life. Or maybe he did back in Dallas. What did she know?

Remembering the sound of his husky chuckle caused her pulse to skitter just thinking about it. That was a dangerous thing and she knew it. Today had been an awakening on many levels and she was seeing danger signals. The more he came out of his shell the more trouble she could have with these unwanted feelings of attraction.

"I've only been here this past week and a half, but I think he's doing better because he sees we are making progress." Eleven days she'd known Wyatt. It seemed longer. "I'm surprising him tomorrow with a walker."

"Oh, Seth is going to be ecstatic," Melody gasped.

"Cole, too. Oh, Amanda, you are amazing," Susan said. "I'm telling you, getting him out of that chair is going to bring out a whole new side to him. If you think the change over the last few days is something, this is going to blow you away."

Amanda could believe that. She already was, truth be told.

Chapter Eleven

Wyatt studied Amanda as she drove them back home. He was glad he'd gone to church. But he'd been thinking about Amanda most of the time. Maybe what she said about God having a reason for placing him in this chair was true. Maybe. But how did she view the fact that she'd lost her leg? Had this been the reason her fiancé had broken off their engagement? The idea had hit him not long after she'd jogged past him. It had plagued him all through church, when he had to pretend to everyone that he was great—he was great from the standpoint of what she'd done for his physical therapy. But from the standpoint of how he'd behaved from day one of meeting Amanda until now, he was about as shamed as a man could get. And he had been trying to figure out the best way of going about giving her an apology.

"Why didn't you tell me about your leg?" Not exactly tactful but it got things moving. It wasn't as if he could get any more sorry than she probably already thought he was.

She turned her head. "You saw me this morning?"

"If you don't want to talk about it I understand...."

He paused and decided to open up and lay it on the line. "But, look, I owe you. I needed everything you threw at me yesterday. And today was good for me. I'm glad you opened my eyes and got me there in this wheelchair. It was a good perspective for me to see. I don't know why you haven't told me about your leg, but I can make an educated guess."

She looked at him apologetically. "I meant to tell you. But you'd already fired me once for looking too young. I didn't think my having only one leg would give you any confidence in me."

They crossed the cattle guard and stopped in front of the house. She didn't have to say that she'd thought he'd look at her handicap as a negative. He felt sick. "Honestly, I probably would have done that then. But now that I've seen you in action, I'm sorry. I shouldn't have been thinking that either way. But I can't change it. All I can do is tell you I'm sorry now."

"I feel like I should have said something. Don't apologize."

He touched her arm. "Amanda, I'm about to get out of this chair because of you and I'm grateful for all you're doing for me—I owe you that since I haven't been the best patient. You weren't the only one. My brothers knew, besides. It was on your résumé."

She looked as if she hated admitting this even more. "Yes. But I assumed they were waiting on me."

"I said something to them. They told me they didn't want to give me any other reason not to let you stay. So they kept quiet. They laughed and said it was my fault for being so pigheaded. I have to agree."

"I've had tougher, believe me."

It was his turn to be skeptical. "No kidding?"

"Kids can be tough when they are adjusting to loss of a limb. I understood." She turned the ignition off and their eyes held.

The silence cocooned them in the vehicle and Wyatt felt transfixed by the understanding and forgiveness in her eyes. "You're a good woman, Amanda." He was startled when her eyes suddenly grew bright with tears. He reacted by reaching to touch her arm again, but she blinked hard, opened her door and was gone. He got out slowly and waited while she unloaded the motorized wheelchair from the ramp. He told himself to remember this was strictly a business relationship and he would not cross the line.

"I think you'll be happy to know that this is your last ride in this thing," she said, too brightly. "You are moving on to the next step as soon as you drive into the house. Starting then, you will be on your walker."

"That's great." He figured he should have been elated. But all he could think about as he drove up the ramp and into the house was Amanda and what she was hiding behind that too-bright smile of hers. Why had she almost cried when he told her she was a good woman? Did she think she wasn't?

Did she think the engagement ending meant she wasn't a good woman? Questions swirled in his brain.

Had she been told she wasn't?

He wheeled the chair around, ready to ask and find out. *Strictly business, cowboy,* the voice in his head warned.

She glanced at him and immediately disappeared inside the workout room. When she returned a few moments later she carried the walker over and set it down in front of him.

"Let's try this out."

He stared up at her, contemplating the right move.

"Well, don't look so excited," she said. Her serious eyes seemed to beseech him not to continue with where his thoughts were going…he'd seen that look before. From people who'd sworn to tell the truth and had just realized they were about to be asked questions that would pry into an area of their life they didn't want to talk about.

"It's time to stand up, Wyatt. Stand up and let's park that scooter."

"You're right." She didn't want to talk about her personal life and had come here for a job to escape talking and thinking about her breakup. Wyatt reminded himself that he was her work. Not her friend or her keeper. He was her client.

And he'd do well to remember that.

There was an uneasy tension between them. It ran just beneath the surface of their cordiality, as if she was afraid if he studied her hard enough he'd see all the way through her.

It made her uncomfortable.

"That's as far as it will go," Wyatt said on Thursday morning. It had been four days since he'd started using the walker.

She smiled encouragement. "Don't worry, you're coming along great. Okay, stand and do the weights." She watched him stand up. He was growing stronger by the day. She handed him the five-pound weights he would use to strengthen the rotator cuff and stabilize it.

"How did you sleep last night?" she asked, watching as he held the weight in his hand, kept his arm close to his body, elbow tucked in at his side, and then swept the weight out and away from his body. She touched his elbow to make sure he kept it motionless. "That's good." She watched him do his repetitions. "Sleep?" she asked when he'd set the weights down and turned toward her. Weariness met her eyes as she looked up at him.

"Rough," he admitted. "But that's nothing new. This thing is just uncomfortable as all get-out at night."

"Are you placing the pillows like I showed you?"

"Yes, it's helped some." He was staring down at her, searching her eyes. It felt personal. She was so close to him that she felt the heat of his arm against hers. Her mouth went dry and her pulse quickened. This was trouble. He was her patient—racing pulses were totally off-limits. Bottomless stomachs and breathlessness were, too. She backed up—so quickly she ran into the weight rack. It wobbled and she stumbled as she reached down to steady it, but Wyatt's hand closed securely around her arm.

"Easy there. We don't need you falling and hurting yourself." His blue eyes bored into hers before dropping to her mouth. "We would be in a mess, both hobbling around here."

Her skin burned—of course it did—where his fingers closed around her arm. She couldn't have formed a coherent sentence to save her life. All she could do was nod up at him.

"You don't sleep much yourself." His voice was as smooth as his hand was steady. His gaze lifted back to hers.

"What do you mean?"

"The jogging at sunrise, that's what."

She smiled tightly. "It's something I love to do. No big deal."

"No big deal. You and I both know you running is a big deal for you—and impressive. You're gone hours."

He'd really been watching her. The thought pleased her more than she could have known. "Why have you been paying so much attention?"

His lips curved gently and he dipped his chin as if talking to a child. "Amanda, I pay attention because you're alone in my pasture in the wee hours of the morning. I worry about you. I like to know you get back safely."

"I'm safe." Amanda took a breath and tried to calm the butterflies rolling around in her stomach as disappointment washed over her—he was concerned because she was on his property.

For a moment she'd thought—*hold it, sister, just one minute there*—what had she thought? That he was watching out of concern for her because he *cared?*

The very idea sent her into a tailspin. Yes, she was attracted to Wyatt like she'd never been attracted to anyone…not even Jonathan. But she'd just been engaged—dumped didn't matter—she'd been engaged and now she was seriously having thoughts of another man this soon after thinking she'd been in love. What kind of woman did that make her?

No, Wyatt was wonderful, handsome, built like a dream and deserved better than she could give him— so why was she even thinking about that? Besides, she knew now that she could never risk being rejected again. She needed to keep her head on straight and remember this was a patient/client relationship and would never be anything more.

"You're doing good with this exercise," she said. "You're building strength, and you should be feeling relief soon. Like I tell my kids, no matter what you do, keeping good muscle tone is the secret key."

"I'm not complaining." He continued with his exercise, slowly going through different sets of exercises she'd shown him.

"So the kids you worked with were mostly amputees like you?" Wyatt asked after a few repetitions.

"Yes. I loved working—I mean, I used to enjoy working with the kids because they'd been through so much and it was an awesome feeling to be able to ease some of their fears of the unknown and also prepare them for life after their loss."

"I bet that was rewarding." He paused and studied her.

What did she say to that? It had been rewarding until the reality hit her that she could never have her own children. "It was. I didn't like it when insurance coverage ran out and I had to leave before I felt like they were ready."

He set the weights down and eased into the cane-backed chair at the table. "Did that happen a lot?"

She huffed with frustration. "Too often. Amputees—uninsured and insured alike—have a hard time with the expense of prosthetics. I've always wished I could do more. But I haven't figured out how to do that. I could only give them as much help as I could in the time I was there and leave them with an in-depth plan of action for when I was gone. That and my phone number in case they had any questions. It seems to work fairly well."

"You sound really dedicated. I'm amazed you decided to move to working with adults. Sounds like those kids really need you out there showing them the way."

Why had she even let this conversation get started?

Her mouth was dry as she tried to look unshaken by his words.

"There was a lot of stress. I've been comfortable with the decision I made."

His gaze seemed to sharpen as he studied her with piercing eyes.

"What are you not saying?"

She stood up and glanced at her watch. The session was over. "I'm not saying anything except that you did a great job today and should be proud. You did great on your walking exercises, too. Keep it up and before you know it I'll be handing you a cane."

The expression on his face told her that he wasn't fooled by her. "Sounds like a plan," he said, much to her relief.

She would eventually grow more at ease talking about this. Surely the pain she felt about losing her ability to carry a child would ease. At least to where she could function and have a conversation about it.

"My back and hip are feeling better every day, I have to admit," Wyatt said a week later. He was practically giving himself a pep talk! She was proud of him.

"And you are using a cane. Don't forget that."

"That is correct," he said in that way of his as he held up the cane. "Thanks to you, I'm almost a brand-new man."

His smile was a dazzler and sent butterflies fluttering inside Amanda. "That's good to hear," she croaked, trying to ignore the growing attraction and feelings toward him. "H-how about your shoulder? Start your exercise and tell me how it feels today." She zeroed in on his shoulder and avoided his gaze. He placed his pointer finger and index finger on the wall like she'd shown him. Starting at shoulder level, he slowly walked them upward along the wall. His shoulder extension was improving incrementally.

She watched as he did the exercise again. She still couldn't believe the change in him since Sunday a week ago. "Good," she said. "This time continue higher if you can."

He nodded and concentrated hard on extending his arm higher.

Ever since he'd found out about her amputation, he'd been different. He worked hard, complained less and was easier to get along with. He'd told her what she'd said had done him good. That he'd needed to hear it. But she could also tell that he felt remorse about her leg as if he felt guilty he'd complained.

They'd been working hard. Wyatt wanted to be ready for Cole's wedding, but it also seemed that he worked hard to please her—or maybe to make her feel better. It was almost as if he didn't want her to feel like he was taking her for granted. Why she got that feeling she wasn't sure—maybe it was because he'd been so careful to thank her. So careful not to complain.

Even so, that hadn't stopped him from trying to find out more about her. As if he wanted her to talk about Jonathan…as if he thought talking might help her. And it had almost worked several times—he was an expert at leading the conversation toward her. She could see where this uncanny ability of his would come in handy in his career choice. But she had been equally determined to not go there if at all possible. She was struggling as it was with finding her footing, and so she'd led all conversations right back to something general.

Each time, he'd backed off with a small smile. A smile that told her he knew she was evading him. It was a challenge not to let herself spill her every troubled heartache to him.

"You've been working overtime," he said, drawing her thoughts back to the moment. "But I've been behaving and doing just what the doctor ordered."

She gave him a thumbs-up. "Yes, you have. Now let's see you walk across the room with just this cane. Take it slow. We are pressing things a bit, but I know you can do it."

He started walking, his steps halting.

"When will I stop dragging this foot?"

"We'll have you with a normal gait soon. But not before the wedding, I'm afraid. You'll be able to stand and walk, but you won't be at a hundred percent. Right now, you just concentrate on your steps. How does your back feel?"

He made it slowly, carefully across the room and sank heavily down into the chair beside her.

"How can that exhaust me?" he growled, his brows dipping in consternation. His shoulder rested against hers and it took all her willpower not to lean into him. Especially when he was staring at her, so close she could see the tiny light blue specks that dotted the dark blue of his eyes. Her stomach fluttered again and she breathed steady, trying to make herself get straight.

Her defenses were down today. The emotions that she'd locked inside her heart threatened to overwhelm her suddenly. She'd dreamed of children all night long— children she would never give birth to. She'd awakened near tears and longing for comfort...all she could think about was how it would be to feel Wyatt's arms around her. It grew harder each day she spent around him. And now this—she didn't need to go there.

"Talking does help, you know."

Amanda hadn't meant to get lost in her thoughts. She shook her head, so tempted to talk to him that she didn't trust herself. "Not for me. I'm sorry, Wyatt, I need to go."

She hurried to the door.

"Amanda!" Wyatt's call followed her but she didn't look back. No, she was too intent on putting as much space between them as possible.

As she fled the stagecoach house, the need to talk to him was like nothing she'd ever experienced before. As gruff and ill-tempered as Wyatt had been, she knew that he would listen to her with a compassionate ear.

If she threw herself into his arms—which she might have done seconds later if she hadn't fled the premises— he would hold her and comfort her, because that was the kind of man he was.

Once at the trailer, she slammed the door and locked it. As if that would keep her from turning around and going back!

Closing her eyes, she inhaled slowly, trying to calm her racing heart.

She was mixed up about her entire state of mind. She needed to talk to someone. Her gaze landed on the Bible as if drawn there, like it had been the last time she'd come up with no answers. She felt a need to try reaching out to God once more. She needed to know what her purpose was. Surely He had a plan for her and all the things that she'd been through. There had to be reasons for the way her life was turning out.

What are Your plans for me? There had to be a reason she was left to feel such emptiness.

Her knees were weak as she stared at the Bible.

She'd been reading it and searching it and nothing had helped yet. It was as if God was trying to get her attention, but she simply couldn't find what He was trying to get her to see.

What kind of person had she become?

God didn't want her to feel this way. Her mind knew this. Her heart knew this. But deep inside none of that helped.

So why did she think Wyatt could make anything better?

Chapter Twelve

"You raised all of this?" Amanda asked Melody a couple of days after her meltdown. Melody had called and asked if she would like to see her vegetable garden and then go with her into town to help plan the wedding with some of the other ladies. Amanda jumped at the chance to get out of the house, though she worried it might trigger another meltdown. But she needed out and away from Wyatt. They were dancing around each other like two eighth graders at their first dance. She continued to want to find comfort in his arms, but she wasn't kidding herself, either. She knew there was more to it than that.

Melody smiled and pushed her purple glasses firmly into place in front of her shining violet eyes. "I can't take all the credit. Poor Seth." She shook her head in sympathy for him. "I worked him to death getting him to help me prepare the soil out here."

"It's *huge*." Amanda laughed in amazement. "This is half a football field! You could feed an army."

Melody put her hands on her hips and proudly surveyed her living masterpiece. "It's only about a half acre. I still have tomatoes, though the drought has made it tough this month. August is dry anyway, but without rain it's a chore. I had corn but now I'm doing peas and beans. Over there I've got watermelons and cantaloupe. And all kinds of peppers—I honestly don't know what I'm going to do with all the salsa I'm going to make." She handed Amanda a basket. "Come on. Pick all you want. Seth and I have to go out to the other ranch the family owns on Friday and I'm not sure how much of this will still be alive when I get back. But this might be my last time for a little while to go with him since I'll be starting back to school next week."

"Do you need me to do something while you're gone?" Amanda asked, picking a tomato.

"Well, the ranch hands are supposed to water, but I just worry that it won't be done like I want it done." They were walking down opposite sides of the row of tomatoes. Melody looked around a huge plant with a sheepish look on her face. "I really don't mean that to sound rude. It's just they are cowboys, not farmers. Even if my Seth was in charge of it I would be worried. They're thinking about cattle."

Amanda plucked a plump, juicy tomato. The color was deep orange and she knew from the ones she'd eaten at Melody's it would taste just as great as it looked. "I've got time on my hands during the day. I'd love to come and take care of this for you." Boy, would she.

"Are you sure?"

"Yes," Amanda said. "I don't know much about gardens, but I really want to do this. I'm close and there's no need for you to make your cowboys be farmers."

"Is Wyatt driving you that crazy?"

"No. Well, a little. But not in a bad way. I mean…" Amanda couldn't blame this all on Wyatt. "I have some things on my mind. Things that happened before I came here. I really could use something to occupy my mind and hands."

Melody stopped picking tomatoes and real concern etched her face. "Is it something I can help with?"

"No—"

"Is it another man?"

Amanda shook her head too vehemently.

"It *is*," Melody gasped, her eyes tender. "You have a boyfriend?"

"No," Amanda said. "I *had* a fiancé." There, she'd been honest about it. What did it matter anyway? Really. She needed to move on and she saw in telling Wyatt that it was okay.

"You were getting married. Does Wyatt know this?"

"I told him the other day."

"I'm glad you were able to confide that in him. I don't mean to pry, but how are you?"

"I'm *better* than I was. I've struggled, but I am thankful that it ended before we said our vows."

"That is a blessing. You need the man God has waiting for you. I know this has to hurt, but God will send the right man—maybe sooner than you want." She smiled sheepishly. "Who knows what the future holds? Look at the witness your life is since losing your leg. That is testimony to your strength right there."

Amanda went back to picking vegetables. "That's what I want it to be." They'd reached only halfway down the row but already her basket was overflowing with tomatoes. "I can't carry anything else in this basket." She laughed, staring at the abundance of those left. This garden would keep the entire town supplied. Why in the world had Melody planted so many plants? "What's going to happen to all of these?"

"Oh, don't worry about that. I've invited the ladies from No Place Like Home out to pick whatever they want. That's the women's shelter that Dottie and Brady Cannon run. Brady is our Sheriff."

"I didn't know there was a women's shelter here."

"It's been here for a couple of years. You know the candy store in town? That's run by the ladies. Dottie teaches them candy making and how to run a business while they are at the shelter. It is really a wonderful ministry."

"It sounds like it."

"And Wyatt wouldn't tell you this, but he does all the legal stuff for the ladies if they need it. And he does it for free."

"He does?" She hadn't meant to sound so shocked. And she really wasn't; she'd already figured out that he was a good man.

Melody's eyes twinkled with merriment. "He truly is a nice guy. We weren't just saying that. He does stuff like that all the time."

"I've figured that out about him. He's been out of his element."

"Like we told you the other day, we were all so worried about him after the crash. I don't know if you've caught on to the fact that he thinks he is everyone's keeper. You see, Seth told me that after their parents died, even though Wyatt was only a senior in high school he took on the role of being the head of the house. He feels responsible for Seth and Cole. Even so, they want him to think about himself now. They'd hoped that he would come back here someday and settle down. He got Cole home, now they'd like him here, too. But that may never happen."

Amanda listened with interest. They'd walked back to the front of the garden and Melody set her basket down and she did the same. She took a small basket when Melody handed it to her.

"Let's grab some peppers before the poor bushes fall over under the weight."

Amanda was thinking about Wyatt as they walked over to the peppers. Her perspective of Wyatt was very muddled. What she'd just learned explained more about his frame of mind. He'd taken on responsibilities of a grown man at an early age. He was probably an over-achiever prior to that, but the responsibility of his brothers and the ranch had probably made him more so. No wonder he'd been so hard on himself. He'd not been irresponsible ever, it seemed. Not until he got into that plane and took off in that storm.

She was only twenty-four, but she knew that what she'd gone through at fourteen had aged her beyond her years. Her respect for Wyatt went up knowing this about him. There was absolutely no denying that he was one of the good guys. One of the really good men of Mule Hollow.

"You know, some woman is going to really be blessed when Wyatt falls in love with her," Melody said. Her pretty eyes blinked innocently from behind her glasses.

Amanda felt uncomfortable suddenly at what Melody was hinting. "So, there isn't anyone special in his life right now?" Amanda had no business asking, but the question just kind of came out.

Melody shook her head as she twisted a red bell pepper from the bush. "Never has been, according to Seth.

Wyatt works. He dates, don't get me wrong, but he's not been interested in marriage. That's one of the things that has been so curious about him being so determined to find Cole and Seth wives. He just felt like that was his responsibility, to get them married and happy. Funny how he associates happiness with marriage. I think deep down inside he wants the same thing for himself. He just hadn't slowed down from his career long enough to remember that there is life beyond the law practice."

"That is for certain. The man never stops. He brought the practice home with him." She and Melody paused on that, perplexed.

Melody shook her head. "Cole and Susan had decided to go ahead with the wedding Saturday after next since Wyatt is on a cane now. They are so happy and anxious to be married. Cole is going to go by today and tell Wyatt. We're hoping that as soon as they're married that maybe Wyatt will be next."

Amanda wasn't sure what to make of Melody's wistful smile. "Maybe so," she said. "I'm sure back in Dallas there are plenty of women who would want that spot in his heart. And fit into his lifestyle."

"Like I said, we're praying he'll fall in love with a Mule Hollow girl."

"Well, good luck with that." Amanda hated to discourage Melody, but she didn't see that happening ever. Wyatt Turner might be a cowboy at heart, but she didn't see a country girl fitting into his life at all. His heart was in Dallas. Why else would he be consulting on all these cases?

He obviously couldn't wait to get back to it...and besides, though they didn't know it, she knew clearly that she wasn't the right woman for any man.

* * *

Wyatt stared at the floor through the face-hole in the massage table and tried hard to keep his mouth shut. It was obvious Amanda had no desire whatsoever to talk about herself. It was driving him crazy. The last few days had been like a bad rodeo. He'd try to talk to her and she'd shut him out. He felt like he'd been bucked off straight out of the chute at every turn.

Not only was he concerned about her, but he was finding himself more and more attracted to her. It was so bad lately that even when he was supposed to be working he was thinking about her.

And he couldn't stop wondering about that deep sadness he'd kept glimpsing. What made her sad? Had she loved this man so much she couldn't forget him? Couldn't move forward? What was it?

Staring at the floor, he fought wanting to press her. If he started questioning her he was afraid it would come out sounding like an interrogation.

Amanda Hathaway was a mystery to him. He didn't like mysteries until they were solved.

What he knew was that he'd misjudged her in the worst way the day she'd arrived. She'd told him she was good and that she'd have him back to new if he only trusted her. She was holding up her end of the challenge with ease. Even with her disability.

Yes, he was attracted to her, but more important he respected her—and it took a lot to win his respect. And she was completely immune to him in every way.

It was downright depressing.

Oh, she'd had him thinking a few days ago when she'd stumbled over the weight rack that maybe she was attracted to him. When he'd touched her he'd *almost* made a fool of himself and tried to kiss her. No way did he need to start thinking about that again. It was ridiculous. He was a thirty-six-year-old man and she had him feeling like a mixed-up schoolboy.

"You need to relax," she demanded, pressing hard on the muscles lining his spine. "You're so knotted up that you're going to seize up on me."

"This is as good as it gets," he growled. If she thought he was going to relax today, she was dreaming.

"In that case, I'm just spinning my wheels."

He felt her draw back from him and then her footsteps headed away from him. He yanked his head up, staring over his shoulder as she disappeared down the hall. "Hey, you're not through."

"I am today," she called from the kitchen.

Using his good arm he eased up to a sitting position and then got off the table, wincing when he moved too quickly. This was getting old despite the progress he'd made. He didn't feel a hundred years old anymore, but he was still pushing eighty.

"Why did you walk off like that?" he demanded as he eased into the kitchen. "You are real good at walking away."

She was chopping up peppers and her back was to him. Her short hair swung about her ears to the very aggressive rhythm of the knife. At his accusation she glared at him.

He'd been surprised to find out that she was a good cook. She'd been thrilled with all the things she'd been getting from Melody's garden earlier that week and he'd been benefiting from it. Her early morning omelets made his mouth water. But good cook or professional cook, she was being far too scary with that knife at the moment.

What was she thinking? Her gaze shot back to her task. Angry, he stalked over—as best he could given his gait—and leaned against the counter next to the eggs and mixing bowl she'd set out. His hip ached and his back throbbed, but none of that bothered him more than the fact that she was hiding something important from him and he wanted to know what it was. Maybe it was the lawyer in him that wanted to always dig deep to find the truth, and the why of what made people do things. Until you knew the whole story, you couldn't find the right solution.

But he knew that wasn't it where Amanda was concerned. It was the man in him that simply wanted to know what was bothering the woman he was beginning to care about. The knowledge had its problems, but at the moment he wasn't thinking about them.

"You're going to cut your fingers off if you keep that up."

"I can handle this," she snapped.

That did it. "Not on my watch." He reached for the knife. "Give me the knife."

"No." Icy eyes glared at him, but she stopped chopping. A good thing.

"I said—hand over the knife. I'm not playing with you, Amanda. I'm in the mood for breakfast at Sam's this morning."

"Well, I'm not."

"Doesn't matter. I am and you're going to drive me. It's your *job*. Or did you forget?" He wasn't playing fair, but he didn't care.

She stared at him like he had just lost his mind. Maybe he had. All he knew was he was taking her out to breakfast—in a weird roundabout way.

"I'm not going to be good company."

"Fine. There will be plenty of good company to be had even if you choose to sit in the corner and pout. Now hand over the knife."

Pout! Wyatt thought she was pouting. She handed him the knife. She'd been struggling to not fall for Wyatt but it was happening despite everything she was doing.

"Thank you very much." He took the knife and dropped it into the sink. "Let's go."

She had no choice but to follow him out to the SUV.

The whole way into town, the tension between them escalated...even though they didn't say much. Maddening as it was, he seemed relaxed, which made her all the more tense. She was trying to keep her distance from him, but with every piece of new information about him everyone was so keen on throwing her way it was almost impossible. And then there was the issue of him pressing her to find out what was bothering her. The man was relentless.

"You're in for a treat if you haven't had Sam's breakfast."

He didn't sound mad or upset, even though he'd forced her to come along. He sounded like he was looking forward to spending time with her—dangerous.

Maybe if he'd been talking to her, she wouldn't have been *thinking* about how good he looked...or how he'd gotten under her skin in the few short weeks since she'd known him.

What she needed was for him to go back to being Mr. Ill-Tempered and make it impossible to like him, or worse, for her to...to be thinking fairy-tale thoughts about what falling in love with him would be like.

"I'm not much of a breakfast eater," she said, fighting to fill the holes that were being blown into the barrier around her heart. But oh, what did Wyatt do? He grinned! And it was no small grin. No, this was a wickedly fun grin, that sent mischief to his eyes and an electric shock to her like she'd been hit with a Taser.

"You are determined to be miserable, aren't you?" he asked, still smiling. Totally enjoying himself!

"I'm only telling the truth," she snapped. *Now* she sounded like a child pouting!

The amused twinkle in his eyes said he thought the same thing as he opened the door and got out.

With his weak arm, a bad hip, a bad back and a cane to maneuver with, he needed to be more careful. *"Wait!"* she exclaimed. Jumping from the SUV, she hurried around to help him, fearful that he might fall—and she'd have to catch him!

He was standing beside the open door watching her, still grinning. "You could have hurt yourself," she snapped, closing the door with a snap.

"I figured that was the way to get you out of the truck for breakfast."

She shot daggers at him. "You are not playing fair."

"Never said anything about playing fair. One thing you need to know about me is I do what I need to do."

"Okay, okay, I'll eat breakfast. But I'm warning you, buster, I can play dirty, too."

That got her a deep, baritone laugh that made her knees weak. As she followed him up the steps she had a feeling she was in for a rough ride. This Wyatt Turner, the playful one, might possibly be irresistible.

Chapter Thirteen

"Stanley, would ya look at that," Applegate said, jumping his red checker as he scrunched busy eyebrows together and stared at Amanda and Wyatt entering the diner.

They were sitting at the front window table with a checkerboard between them. There was a five-pound bag of sunflower seeds sitting beside them and on the floor at Stanley's feet was a brass spittoon.

Staring wide-eyed at them, Stanley spit in rapid-fire succession and the shells hit the spittoon's mouth dead center. "Wyatt, yor walkin'. That's a real sight fer sore eyes. I almost didn't turn around and look cuz I figured ole App was tryin' ta pull a slick one on me."

"Are you saying App here cheats?" Wyatt asked as he walked slowly toward them.

Stanley tugged at his ear. "Naw, he don't. But if he wants ta beat me, he's gonna have ta start."

Applegate frowned and cut his eyes at his buddy. "Don't believe it. I beat him plenty. Might be doin' it right now if he don't watch out."

Despite her qualms about coming, Amanda had to

smile at the two friends. She was distracted, though, by the breakfast scents emanating from the kitchen. Goodness, but the place smelled great.

"Well, look what the cat dragged up." Sam hustled out of the kitchen. "It's about time you came in and brought this little gal with you. Leave them two ornery coots alone and let's get this little gal a booth."

Applegate grinned, his lean face a cascade of wrinkles. "Y'all jest have a seat over thar while I beat the socks off of Stanley here."

Sam was waiting at the booth all the way across the diner from App and Stanley, and Wyatt led the way to it.

"This is great, Sam." Wyatt remained standing while she took her seat. There was absolutely nothing romantic about eating breakfast in an old-fashioned diner with three old men watching, but Amanda still got butterflies as Wyatt slid carefully into the seat across from her.

She had to get over this. She had to—had to—had to!

"How you doin', Amanda? Keepin' this fella straight?" Sam set two mugs on the table in front of them.

"I'm trying." She nodded when Sam lifted the pot so she could indicate whether she wanted him to fill her mug.

Applegate grunted loudly from across the room. "That ain't never been an easy task."

Amanda thought he had a problem with his hearing.

"It's good to see you out of that wheelchair. That jest didn't look right."

"It shor didn't," Stanley boomed, spitting a sunflower seed into the spittoon. "Growing up, this fella never stopped. Always workin' with his grandpa or his daddy. Or later, with them brothers and on that ranch. Your folks would be proud of you, son."

"Thank you, sir. That means a lot to me."

Knowing what she did about him now, Amanda knew this did mean the world to Wyatt. It was apparent that everything he'd done had been to make them proud and to fill the gap their deaths had made in his brothers' lives.

"Now, though, you need ta get yourself home where you belong." Sam set the pot on the burner and Applegate's face fell into a river of wrinkles. "It jest ain't right, you bein' away like you are. Yor a Turner. Turner men belong here."

Wyatt shrugged his good shoulder. "I've been through this with y'all a hundred times. I'm good at what I do. I'm happy in Dallas."

Sam, Applegate and Stanley all shook their heads. Amanda watched, fascinated. These men were serious. They wanted Wyatt home as much as Seth and Cole. *Everyone* wanted him home. But it was obvious that Wyatt didn't want it.

"What would y'all like ta eat?" Sam grumbled. "Ain't no way yor gettin' my kinda cookin' over yonder in that city."

Stanley jumped a checker and grinned at Applegate's scowl. "Yeah, you used ta tell Sam he was the best cook in the world when you was knee-high to a grasshopper and yor grandpa would sit you up thar on that bar stool on a stack of *The Farmers' Almanacs*."

"Sam's food *is* the best. I never disputed that. Why do you think I made my lovely physical therapist bring me here as soon as I got this cane? I want my usual, Sam. How about you, Amanda?"

He'd called her *lovely*. Of course he was teasing the older men, but his eyes warmed her blood as they settled on her. Electricity seemed to hum in the air. She grabbed the plastic menu from beside the silver napkin holder and stared at the breakfast menu. A visual of Wyatt as a child sitting at the bar with his grandpa played across her mind's eye. He would have been a cute little kid. Inquisitive and probably bossy. No probably about it, he would have been bossy. He'd have been a take-the-world-by-the-horns child straight from the womb, she was pretty certain. His children would no doubt be the same.

She met his gaze and he had a mischievous light in his eyes as he watched her. Almost as if he could read her thoughts. The man would probably have been a great poker player—they did say he took after his many-greats Grandpa Oakley who'd won the stagecoach house in a poker game. "I'll have the Texas French Toast," she blurted, only because it was the first thing on the menu. Wyatt's grin lifted crookedly—and she was certain he was looking inside her head and figuring everything out. She swallowed the lump that lodged in her throat and found herself unable to look away.

"How did you do that?" Applegate snapped, his voice breaking the spell like a bullhorn.

Amanda cut her eyes to the checker players and saw he was glaring at the board.

Stanley looked smugly at her. "I pert near get him every time. And he never learns. He was too busy watching you two make goo-goo eyes at each other to see he'd left me a three-jump opening."

"Goo-goo eyes!" Amanda exclaimed before she caught herself. "I was not doing any such thing."

"Yup. That's what I saw. And I'm glad ta see it."

She stared at Applegate and slammed her mouth shut or she might have said something she would regret. She regretted this breakfast, that was a given. And Wyatt wasn't helping. Oh, no, he was laughing. His shoulders were hunched over he was laughing so hard. *Shaking.* His shoulders were shaking with his laughter. This was ridiculous.

"I do not, have never and will not ever make goo-goo eyes at my patients."

"Well, we certainly hope not." Stanley chuckled right along with Wyatt. "If ya did that, then what would be special about you and our boy here ogling each other? Nothin', that's what."

Amanda was going to be sick. She hadn't meant to get this sort of talk started. She hadn't meant to stare at Wyatt like a lovesick puppy right here in front of everyone. But who would have thought three crusty old men—two who were sitting across the room—would start talking about goo-goo eyes. Wyatt didn't look any happier than she was.

"Hey, fellas, hold off on marrying me and Amanda off. For one, she's way too young for me. For two, I'm not on the market and for three, Amanda doesn't like me much."

Amanda couldn't believe he'd just come out and said that in front of everyone. Too young. That one really got her. The man thought she was too young. There were only twelve years' difference in them. "I like you," she hissed, leaning toward him across the table. "Just not like that. Besides, fellas, I'm not looking for a husband right now."

Sam came out and set her steaming plate of French toast down in front of her. He grinned as he slid Wyatt's bacon and eggs in front of him. "And why not?" Sam looked insulted on Wyatt's behalf.

"Yeah," Stanley joined in. He had abandoned the

checker game and was digging a handful of sunflower seeds. "He's handsome, funny—"

"And," App broke in, "he's got a highfalutin job and owns a bunch of land."

At that Wyatt almost choked on his bacon. Sam slapped him on the back and scowled at her. "Yeah, he's a real fine catch. What do you mean too old? He ain't old."

Amanda got tickled despite her horror at the situation. "I didn't say he was too old. He said I was too young. But he is right, there is too big a difference in our ages."

"Hogwash!" Applegate grunted. "Thar's plenty of folks married with that many of years between them. It ain't like y'alls in school anymore. Them years don't matter a lick after you get past yor teens."

Amanda could only see this conversation going downhill from here. She dug into her toast—not that she was the least bit hungry anymore—and kept her head down. If they didn't get out of here soon she feared the fellas would grab the visiting preacher and have them hitched before the lunch rush came through the doors.

"Fellas, stop," Wyatt commanded. "Let Amanda eat her breakfast in peace. My brother is getting married soon. It's his wedding y'all need to be concentrating on."

Stanley's hand holding his black checker hovered in midair. "The ladies have that'un under control. Seth was in here with Susan about an hour ago. Them two is so in love they didn't even *try* to hide thar goo-goo eyes."

"Yup," Applegate barked. "Only thang holdin' them up is you gettin' well enough to walk down the aisle."

Wyatt's expression darkened and Amanda couldn't miss the muscle jerk in his jaw. "I told them not to wait on me when I was in the hospital. Now that I'm on this cane, there's going to be a wedding soon. I can promise you that."

All three men grinned from ear to ear.

Sam filled Wyatt's coffee cup up. "Now that right thar sounds like you, son. That's always been yor strong point, takin' charge and pushin' forward. We was plenty worried when all you wanted ta do was sit in that house out thar and mope."

"Mope. I was doing no such thing."

Applegate grunted and Stanley spit sunflowers.

"Suit yourself." Applegate lined his black checkers up on the board. "But when a man is so knotted up with anger that he don't get out of the house, that thar is moping."

Stanley stood up. "We've got to get over to play practice. Y'all should come out to the theater sometime. We do the lights and the sound. It would be a good date fer y'all."

"We might do that." Wyatt took a swig of coffee and met her gaze over the rim of his cup. She'd pretty much decided to keep her mouth shut on this entire conversation. Beside that, she was interested in what they were revealing about Wyatt despite the talk about them…but she even found that fascinating—not that she'd let them know it. No, she'd realized that there were some things you kept to yourself in Mule Hollow.

A little while later, they eased out of the diner to the booming encouragement for Wyatt to take Amanda out on a real date. Wyatt didn't say anything until they were in the SUV.

"Well, that didn't exactly go the way I'd planned."

Amanda laughed so hard her shoulders shook as she drove the vehicle toward home. "It was totally unexpected for me, too." Boy, was that the understatement of the year. She'd relaxed some during all of the conversation, though, and that was a good thing. Now, however, alone with him again, she started tensing up.

He adjusted his arm, looking for a more comfortable position, and he watched her as he did it. She didn't look at him but knew he was because she could feel his gaze on her.

"At the meeting with the ladies I went to with Melody the other day, it seemed like the wedding plans were set."

"Yes. Seth told me that Chance has that weekend off, so he'll be coming to do the service. With the PBR it runs a pretty hectic schedule, so it's a good time."

Amanda knew that PBR stood for Pro Bull Riding organization and had been fascinated at the planning meeting when she'd learned that Chance was a preacher. He was Wyatt's cousin on his dad's side and had been raised up with them half their life, whenever his dad hadn't been able to take him on the rodeo circuit during the school year. "That's something I never thought about as a career, but it is wonderful." She really thought so. What a great witness.

"Chance is a great guy. He has a heart of gold and a mission to preach God's word to those bull riders."

Amanda liked that. She'd been sharing her witness with the kids when she worked with them. She wasn't sure what she was doing now. Running?

"I need to check on Melody's garden. Would you like to ride over there with me?" She was asking for trouble by spending more time with Wyatt, but she suddenly didn't want to go back to that tiny trailer at the stagecoach house.

"Sure. Maybe you'll finally tell me why you don't want to talk about your jogging?"

And there it was. Right back to square one. "It's no big deal. I like to run, okay? I just didn't tell you."

"But why? We both know your running is a big deal. I looked it up. A runner with a leg missing above the knee has a much harder time running with a prosthetic. You make it look easy. You run like a deer."

Not only had he been watching her every morning, he'd done research on her condition. Amanda's heart fluttered at the thought. She pulled to a stop beside the green garden. It was surrounded by a tall fence, which Melody had told her was to keep the deer out. The old fence had been described as having some of the original wood from the stagecoach house. Amanda liked the look of the garden, but it wasn't the garden she was thinking about as she climbed from the SUV.

"Yes, I was fourteen at the time of the accident. And all I wanted to do was keep running." She stared across the hood at Wyatt. The man was persistent. And the sun gleaming off his dark hair made him look all too dashing—she'd never in her life used that word before, but it just fit. She could imagine him dressed in his tuxedo for a big benefit ball. He would fit perfectly into that scenario. The wealthy rancher/lawyer—that was the image of him she needed to focus on. That was the life she could never fit into.

And she also couldn't stop thinking about him as a child sitting on the bar stool at Sam's... Wyatt's son would do that one day—that was, when Wyatt brought him to the ranch on weekend visits.

"My parents said I loved to run from the moment I started walking. I decided I wanted to do marathons. So that was why I was on the side of the road the day that man drove over me."

"That's tough to hear every time you say it. It must be even harder to have to repeat to nosey people like me."

It touched her that he would care. "I'm dealing with it. Be careful here," she said, hoping to divert the conversation, but also concerned that Wyatt might hurt himself. "Concentrate on your balance. Use your stomach muscles to stabilize your back."

He was standing close to her, looking down at her with serious eyes. She suddenly felt panic rising, but she couldn't move. She had that overwhelming urge to take a step and wrap her arms around him. To feel the solid strength of his arms about her.

Wyatt shifted to lean against the gate post, and before she realized what he was doing he'd set his cane aside and lifted his hand to her cheek. The feel of his touch should have made her run all the way home, but she couldn't move. She couldn't breathe. She could only think about his touch and the gentle look that came into his eyes as he stared down at her.

"Amanda, I wish you would tell me what is really bothering you. My gut tells me there's more to you giving up working with kids and coming all the way out here. What are you running from?"

Chapter Fourteen

What was he doing? He was stepping over a boundary he hadn't wanted to cross. But Amanda brought something out in him he wasn't used to feeling. He'd been unable to stop himself from touching her. Her deer-in-the-headlights look the instant his fingertips touched her was expected, but he didn't like it. He'd told himself not to do it. But he hadn't been able to stop himself. It had taken everything in him not to demand she tell him earlier. All morning he'd been building up to finding out what was bothering her…or what she was hiding—if she was. "I have to tell you that I think you are an amazing woman."

She shook her head and her eyes slid away from his. Did she not see that? Was that why she downplayed the fact that she was a runner? He had the sudden need to pull her into his arms.

He tucked his fingers into his pockets instead and forced them to stay there.

"Come on, Amanda, I know we've had our issues, but I really am a good listener. If you need a friend right now I'm here. Did this guy hurt you? Do something you haven't said?" She wanted to tell him, he sensed that she did with every fiber of his being. *Come on, Amanda. Talk to me.*

"Why are you so certain?"

She was still fighting it. "Because too much points to something being wrong. You love kids and yet you've given that up. Yes, you've been through a hard breakup, but most people would find comfort in doing what they love. You said you loved working with kids…so why aren't you? And why do your beautiful eyes get the saddest expression at times? I saw it at church the other day."

She looked shocked, and he wasn't sure if it was because he'd noticed so much about her or because he'd called her eyes beautiful. But as quick as she looked shocked, the sadness flooded her eyes.

He couldn't help himself. "What is it, Amanda?" He reached for her. To his surprise, she came into his arms and buried her head against his shoulders. Her tremble vibrated through him and he tightened his arms about her. Feelings of protectiveness like nothing he'd ever felt before surged over him. Amanda was right up there as being one of the bravest—if not *the* bravest—people he'd ever known. So what had her so shaken?

"I'm sorry," she mumbled against his shoulder. She was so tense that he began rubbing the muscles between her shoulder blades in a gentle circular motion.

"Talk to me." He was treading on quicksand. Amanda was in his arms, and he was going to have a hard time letting her go when she decided to back away from him.

But she didn't move away. She took a deep breath and looked up at him.

She glanced out past the tomato bushes before pinning him with surprisingly clear eyes. Too clear, maybe.

"When Jonathan broke up with me, it was because…" Amanda shook her head. "I can't… I can't talk about it."

Wyatt tried to follow what she was trying to tell him. She'd said she couldn't blame Jonathan for calling off the engagement. That he'd made the right decision for both of them. That it was better to know it up front than later on. Wyatt agreed on all counts. She *was* better off without the guy. Still, he found no place in his heart for understanding the man. You did not tell a woman you loved her and then call it off. When a real man said those words, he meant them. There was no turning back. Wyatt had never found anyone who'd ever tempted him to even think about it.

But he'd never met anyone like Amanda. The thought should have thrown him, but it didn't. Amanda was a woman well worth loving. Did she not feel like she was? Was that the problem?

"You're hurting," Amanda said. "What am I thinking? I've had you trapped here. Let's get you back to the house."

"I'd rather you talk to me." She was closing him out.

"There are just some things I can't put words to, Wyatt."

"Try. It might help."

Instead of answering him she walked away. His hip and back strained as he pushed himself to cross the ground to catch her. "Amanda, I know you and I got off on the wrong foot. I was an idiot, but I hope you consider me a friend."

She turned back to him, her beautiful aquamarine eyes glistening with unshed tears. "Thank you, Wyatt. I like the idea of you being my friend. But—"

Wyatt's heart clutched, and he wanted to pull her back

into his arms and comfort her. "You are a remarkable woman, Amanda. I hope you know that."

"I can't do this, Wyatt. What I'm dealing with is something I have to deal with on my own."

She walked around to the truck and got in. Her statement only caused more questions. He should back off. Give her what she wanted.

It was none of his business.

But, staring at her through the windshield, he knew he wasn't going to be able to do that.

Amanda couldn't forget the feel of being in Wyatt's arms a few minutes earlier in the garden. Or that she'd almost told him everything! It had been only by sheer willpower that she'd stopped herself before revealing how totally empty she felt inside. Knowing Wyatt, he wouldn't have understood that at all.

He'd have tried to comfort her. As he'd done so sweetly before. She'd been grateful for his concern, but she didn't want his sympathy.

As it was, she was having a hard time figuring out how to handle this new relationship they'd begun. He'd wanted to be her friend. And he'd said such nice things about her—she felt awkward believing that he thought she was remarkable. And yet he'd said so.

As she waited for him to stretch out on the table, she tried not to think about how nice it had felt to be in his arms. It had been just as comforting as she'd suspected it would be…even if she'd thrown herself at him. But it had been so much more.

Unbidden, she suddenly wondered how there couldn't be a woman in Wyatt's life. Melody and his brothers had said no, but maybe there was someone they didn't know about. He could have a whole little black book or he could as easily be free and unencumbered.

Just like she was—free as a bird to date whomever she wanted.

That thought had her staring down at her bare ring finger. When she'd talked to Wyatt earlier, she'd realized that she had absolutely no feelings for Jonathan. Hadn't for a while.

There was no lingering sadness at the idea of Jonathan's ring not being there. The only sadness—the deep, neverending sadness—was the reason his ring wasn't on her finger.

I want children of my own. His words seeped through her soul like unshed tears filling her up on the inside.

She'd told herself there was no reason to dwell on it. God had a plan for her life and it wasn't to have children. She would find a way to come to terms with that. Just as she'd found a way to come to terms with the fact that she had only one leg.

Someday she'd understand what His plan was where children were concerned. She just had to deal with the ups and downs she faced until that time came. And right now she had to figure out what to talk to Wyatt about.

"Do you compete in marathons?"

His question was like a gift, as if he knew she needed help. "I do two or three a year, but nothing major. My priority has been my work. After I realized that it gave me a purpose when I lost my leg, I backed off from the running."

"But the running is also a way to reach and inspire people." He glanced over his shoulder at her.

"Oh, I believe so, too. It's just that I was so busy with my work with the kids that I didn't have the time to train as heavily as I needed to. I enjoyed helping kids gain confidence after losing their limbs. There is nothing like watching a kid walk for the first time after…" She faltered, realizing she'd started talking about her work as if it was as natural as breathing. She remembered how rewarding her work had been. Only twenty minutes earlier she'd been in tears thinking about it.

"I can see where that would be rewarding. It's worthwhile. It means something, Amanda."

"I know it does." But that didn't mean she could go back to it.

"Do you think you'll be able to go back to working with kids later on?" he asked gently.

He was reading her mind. "I don't think so," she said.

"Why?" He looked over his shoulder again. His eyes sharp. Digging. "Why is that? I have a feeling you were great with kids. You said you loved it."

"I have my reasons. How does this feel?" She pressed a knot too hard to distract him. He jerked.

"Hurts," he gritted. "If I didn't know better I'd say you did that on purpose."

"Well, I did, but only because I need to in order to make it better. You know that."

She was testy. But this was not what she wanted to talk about. How in the world had she let this conversation go to this?

"Why can't you go back to doing what you love? What is it that you aren't telling me?"

That did it! The man was entirely too inquisitive. Maybe it was because he was a lawyer. "Wyatt, I'm not on the stand. I've made it clear that I don't want to talk about this."

His brows dipped. "When a client goes on the defensive like that it's not a good thing."

Amanda's brows did some major dipping of their own. "See, that's where you are obviously confused. I am not your client. You are mine." With that she turned and marched out the door.

Unprofessional—you bet.

But she didn't care anymore. The man needed to back off. And he needed to do it now.

Chapter Fifteen

"You look beautiful!" Amanda stood inside Ashby's Treasures, the dress store beside Lacy's Heavenly Inspirations. It was a cute boutique store that carried a little bit of everything—even bridal dresses! When Susan had called and asked Amanda to come see her dress, she'd been honored to be included. She'd also been glad to get away for a little while.

The dress was white with beading along the edge of the bodice and along the bottom.

To go with the dress, Lacy had swept Susan's blond hair into a soft style that exposed her neckline. Amanda thought all brides were beautiful, but she didn't think she'd ever seen a happier one.

Amanda hadn't known exactly how she would handle seeing a bride, but she'd felt as if she would be fine. It had been a shock to realize how little it bothered her not to be marrying Jonathan.

She wasn't certain that she'd even loved Jonathan. He had been convenient—was that the right word? It made her sound so horrible. But the truth hurt sometimes, and she was afraid that she'd convinced herself that she was in love with him because he was willing to marry her even though she was damaged. She hated that word, but what else was she? She couldn't have children. That couldn't be fixed. *Damaged* seemed an appropriate word choice. She needed to face reality and move on.

"Susan, I think everything works great together," Lacy said from where she was standing beside the mirror. "Amanda and Ashby, what do y'all think?"

"You're beautiful, Susan," Amanda said. "And I love the hair the way you did it, Lacy."

Ashby was smoothing Susan's train out. "I think it's perfect. This dress was meant for you."

Susan was studying her slim, elegant reflection in the mirror. "I love it. I'm so excited I don't know what to do." She met Amanda's gaze in the mirror. "I can't thank you enough for coming here and helping Wyatt. If it weren't for you he would be miserable and I wouldn't be standing here yet."

"He's doing great. His arm is doing well. I told him yesterday that he could start using it. He tried to hide it but he was really happy about that." She had gotten secretly tickled at the macho way he took the news. He'd clearly wanted to jump up and down and do flips, but instead he'd nodded and just flexed his arm. Of course he'd thanked her—carefully. They were both treading on eggshells around each other. He at least was taking her hint and not asking her personal questions for now, and for that she was thankful.

"So what are you going to do when this job is over?" Susan asked.

"She's going to stay in Mule Hollow," Lacy chimed in.

Ashby smiled. "You can't go wrong moving here. I love it."

"I've thought about it. I really have." That got big smiles from both of them. "From the first moment I drove into town and saw Adela's Apartments. I've thought about it. But I can't."

"Why not?" Lacy crossed the room to be closer. "You like it here, don't you?"

"Yes, she does," Susan answered for her. "I can tell. And Wyatt would be happy if you did that."

"Wyatt will be in Dallas. Besides, there is nothing going on between us that he would care one way or the other if I stayed or not. Besides, my job would make moving here impossible." That might not have been true, and she knew it.

Susan and Lacy looked at each other and shook their heads as if she was totally missing the big picture. She wasn't—they just didn't have all the facts.

"Wyatt will be back and forth." Susan reached for the hook at the neck of the gown. Amanda moved to help her. "Thank you," she said, then continued talking. "We are hoping someday soon he'll decide to come home for good and help with the ranches. Until then, if you were in town that would give him more reasons for coming home."

Amanda laughed nervously. "Y'all, I'm his physical therapist. Not his girlfriend. And like I said, my job could make the move impossible."

"You could be. And nothing is impossible," Lacy said, not giving up.

"*Lacy,* I could not be. Besides that, I would never fit into his lifestyle in Dallas. I'm not a black-tie-event type person and he reeks of it. I'm also—"

"That is a no-brainer," Lacy said, rolling her blue eyes. "You can fit in anywhere."

"That's true," Susan added, heading toward the dressing room. Ashby followed and held the dressing room door open for her. Susan paused. "Why would you even think you wouldn't fit in?"

"I don't want to fit in. I'm a simple girl. I like blue jeans and running shoes. I don't like dressing up and mingling."

"So does this mean you aren't coming to my wedding?"

"Of course I'm coming. I wouldn't miss it for the world."

"That's what I hoped you'd say. See you in a minute and then we can all go to lunch."

"Are you all right?" Lacy asked when they were alone.

"Sure. Why?"

Lacy studied her. "Because you look so sad."

"I just had something on my mind, but I'm good."

"Are you sure? I'm a good listener." Her eyes sparkled with compassion.

Amanda shook her head; she just couldn't talk about it. "I'm fine. Really."

"I don't believe you, but I'm not going to press you. If you need to talk, I'm here. Oh, and don't try to get out of coming Friday night to Susan's party at my house, either. I'll come chuck you in my car and haul you there kicking and screaming if I have to."

Amanda laughed. "I'd like a ride in that car." Lacy was the owner of the ancient Cadillac convertible. They matched since they both looked like fun.

Lacy grinned. "Then you'll have one. I love my car. It's different and makes me happy."

"I think it matches you," Amanda said. "You are unique. I love that about you."

"Well, thank you! When my baby is born, the one thing I want him or her to know is that God loves people who aren't afraid to be the way He made them. I love that in my job I get to witness to people every day. And hopefully make folks smile—even if it is just because I talk too much."

"There is way more to you than that! I like that you are sure of who you are and what you're here to do." Amanda knew Lacy witnessed in everything she did, so that was no surprise. It made Amanda feel like she was failing the Lord even more than she'd already been feeling. She'd walked away from her kids and now, since being here with Wyatt, had she done anything that could possibly be called a witness?

"Don't keep patting me on the back," Lacy said, waving her pink-tipped fingernails. "Believe me, God has His hands full keeping me in line. That's what's so great about Mule Hollow. I just love all the friends I've made since being here. We keep each other straight and help out and pray for each other. We have each other's backs. How about you, Amanda? Does someone have your back?"

Amanda hesitated and Lacy winked at her. "You should really think about staying. I'm serious. Logistically, it might make your job harder—but something could probably be figured out about that. Believe me, though, if you pray about it and God leads you to hang out with us, then you should stay."

Amanda sighed. It was tempting. It really, really was.

"But just so you know, you've been given a reprieve on the matchmaking efforts of Norma, Esther and Adela. They have been so distracted by trying to find preachers to come in on Sunday that they haven't had the time they usually do to try and get something going with you and Wyatt."

"They know I'm leaving and that wouldn't work."

Lacy laughed. "Girlfriend, don't you know that those three don't know anything of the kind? They know God has put you and Wyatt here right now. And they know that you are single and so is he. And they also know that there've been sparks flying between y'all from day one. To them that's like waving a red flag."

Amanda hated that they were having a hard time finding a preacher, but she was glad they had something distracting them. The last thing she needed right now was a posse after her in full pursuit!

Wyatt had made a huge mistake. He'd pushed Amanda too hard and now she'd withdrawn from him. She did her job, but if he so much as looked like he was going to get personal with her, she clammed up. He'd been praying for guidance and hoped that she might talk with Lacy or Susan. All he knew was she needed to talk to someone.

"So did you have a good time with Susan and Lacy yesterday?" Wyatt asked when she came in the next morning.

"Yes, I did. It was a good trip."

She looked more at ease than she had the last couple of days, and that made him happy. He couldn't stop thinking about her. Couldn't stop wanting to give her a reason to smile. He'd been praying lately—something he'd let slide over time—that God would help her with the struggle she was having. He wished she would feel comfortable enough to confide in him. He'd started to care about Amanda, and he couldn't even pinpoint when it had happened. It had just happened.

When it came to Amanda, his unsureness was a new experience for him. Even different from the lack of confidence he'd felt about his recovery when she'd arrived. For a man who'd had all the confidence in the world just a couple of months earlier, his world had been shaken up on all corners.

"Susan and Cole are going to be happy." *That* he was confident of.

"You made a good match, Mr. Turner."

He was pleased by her teasing tone and the sparkle in her soft eyes. It was starting off like a good day. "I just saw the obvious and acted on it."

She tilted her head to the side. "And what was the obvious?"

"There was just an electricity in the air when they set eyes on each other. And then later at the reception Susan seemed to make something in Cole come alive that I hadn't seen since his fiancée died."

"I didn't know about that." Amanda's heart hurt for Cole.

"He had a hard time. But he went on with his life at the same time. He was even his happy-go-lucky self at times, but it took time. When he saw Susan, I just had a gut feeling that something could come of it."

"Well, I think that's great. Susan was so happy yesterday. She looked beautiful in her dress. Which brings us to your therapy. I want us to head outside today. We need to try different surfaces to build your balance. Are you up for that?"

The phone rang and he started to reach for it but stopped. This was important. And he wanted to continue his conversation with Amanda. Nothing was urgent that was happening in the office. He also knew from the

tiny movement of Amanda's jaw and the slight quirk at
the edge of her lips that she was fighting patience with
him and his work. "I'm up for it," he said, standing up
slowly and feeling his hip strain. It was getting better,
and walking always seemed to help it. "Is now a good
time for you?"

Amanda didn't try to hide her pleasure at him choosing therapy over work. Only she was wrong, it was therapy with *her* he'd just chosen over the call.

Wyatt had a good heart. An unselfish heart that was
easy to see and she liked that. Amanda and Wyatt were
walking down the gravel road with cattle grazing on either side of them. She was amazed at his perception and
intuition in intervening in his brothers' lives in order
to help them find the loves of their lives. One day he
would find the love of his life and the lucky lady would
be getting a jewel. But today, she was walking with him
in the pasture.

If she moved to Mule Hollow, would he come home
more? Would he come home to see her? Lacy and Susan
had her thinking.

Pushing the thought away, she watched him walk. His
gait was improving, but there was still a way to go. The
hitch in his hip movement remained very pronounced.
She'd hoped to have him in better shape for the wedding just because she knew he would like to walk down
the aisle as normally as possible. "Your persistence is
paying off."

"Thanks to you. Lucky me to have you in my corner."

Amanda's heart skipped a few beats as she met his
serious eyes. It would be so easy to let her emotions
lead her right now. But emotions were deceiving. She'd

learned that with Jonathan. "You would have done great with anyone."

His brows dipped. "I don't think so. You taught me more about courage and real strength than anyone else could have because of what you've been through and how you handled it."

Others she'd seen had been through much more than she had. "There are kids out there who have been through far more than me. Kids who don't have the money to have the best prosthetics or the money to continue therapy that will enable them to walk without limps. But they keep on working at it even after I'm pulled off the job. Those are the ones who have really been through it."

"See, that's what I love about you," Wyatt said. "You will not let anyone feel bad for you. You are determined to keep your chin up and think positive. And to think of others."

That's what I love about you. Amanda's heart had stopped at the words. Oh, she knew it wasn't true. She knew it was just quirky word choice. Still...

She pushed her hair behind her ear and concentrated on the road. There were rough spots along this stretch and while she was watching his gait she could very easily forget to think about her own. "You give me too much credit."

"You give yourself too little."

She smiled at that. "You have an argument for everything."

His lips curved up slowly. "I am what I am."

"That is the understatement of the decade."

"You are as much an avoider of questions as I am at pushing them."

Amanda stopped walking and he did, too. A swallow flew by being chased by another. They dipped and dived—much like the conversation. Wyatt wasn't going to let her get away with forgetting that she hadn't told him everything. And maybe she really didn't want to.

"I've realized I didn't love Jonathan," she said unexpectedly.

"Really." His surprise couldn't be disguised, but to his credit his expression remained neutral.

"We should start back before you overdo it and your back starts to tighten up." She began walking slowly back the way they'd come. Wyatt fell into step beside her, his gait slow but steady. She gave him a sideways glance, knowing she had to look as embarrassed as she felt. "I think I let my emotions convince me that I was in love with him. It had taken me so long to decide to go out—I had pretty much convinced myself that no man would ever want me. And here, on my first venture out, I'd found one. It's embarrassing."

Wyatt's hand on her arm stopped her. "Amanda, why would you not think someone would want you? You are a special woman."

His eyes glittered with anger. Amanda went breathless, she was so startled. She hadn't meant to say what she'd said. She'd been talking about her being barren— he wouldn't know that. How careless of her. She'd let her guard down.

"I don't like what I'm hearing. Amanda, any man would be blessed to have you fall in love with him."

What about you? She was treading on dangerous ground—stupid ground was what it was. Looking into his eyes in that moment, she didn't care.

When Wyatt leaned in and kissed her, Amanda's heart stopped.

Wyatt tugged her close. Dropping his cane, he wrapped both arms around her and sent her world spinning out of control as he deepened his kiss.

Amanda knew she was never, ever, ever going to be the same after this moment.

She was falling in love with Wyatt.

I want children of my own. Jonathan's words hit her.

"Stop." Her voice didn't sound like herself as she pushed Wyatt away. "This is a bad idea."

Wyatt let her go and, to her surprise, he looked as dazed as she felt.

"You might be right. I shouldn't have done that."

She reached for his cane, trying not to let his agreement cut her to the core. But it did. Straightening, she handed the cane to him. "We should get back. Your hip is going to need attention after this long walk."

"Amanda. It's nothing personal," he said quietly.

She felt ill. "You're right, Wyatt. This is business. And only business. We should never have crossed the line. Now, let's get back. You have a bachelor party to go to in a couple of hours and your hip needs some rest."

He didn't say anything as they walked back toward the stagecoach house. Amanda had the sinking feeling that she should have kept right on driving after he'd fired her that first day.

It would have saved her a lot of pain.

Chapter Sixteen

"What's going on between you and Amanda?" Cole straightened his tie and turned to Wyatt. "Is this straight?"

Cole, Seth, Wyatt and their cousin Chance were waiting inside the back room of the sanctuary before the wedding started. Wyatt had been asked that same question several times the night before at the bachelor party. Even Chance had asked him what was wrong thirty minutes after he'd arrived yesterday. For a man who'd been known to have inherited his poker face from his great-great-great-great-great-grandpa Oakley—the best poker player in seven counties—Wyatt wasn't holding up so well. Try as he might, he couldn't hide the fact that he'd made a huge error in judgment. The guilt of that error must have been written all over him because it was obvious he wasn't fooling anyone.

"Cole, I told you last night at your party that nothing was wrong. This is your wedding day. You're supposed to be thinking about Susan walking up that aisle, not about your big brother. I'm flattered and all, but come on, bro, give a man a break. Susan wouldn't be too happy if she knew."

"He's right, you know," Seth said, slapping him on the back. "Little brother, this is a great day. Don't think about anything but you and her. I'll get big brother straightened out while you're on your honeymoon."

Cole chuckled. "Thanks. It's the greatest day, but it wouldn't be happening if it weren't for you, Wyatt, so its only fitting that I be thinking about you, too."

Cole's grin was as big as Wyatt had ever seen it.

"All I did was act on a hunch. You did the rest."

Seth thumbed his black hat off his forehead and settled speculative eyes on Chance. "You might want to get Wyatt to act on a hunch for you. After all, you aren't getting any younger, you know," Seth teased.

Dark-headed like the rest of them, Chance had the Turner look of lean jawline and crooked grin, only his eyes weren't shades of blue but as green as clover.

He just shook his head. "I haven't found a woman yet who was willing to put up with my schedule, and I'm not planning to stop my work." They all knew that was how he felt. Chance took his work very seriously. "I love preaching to those cowboys before they ride. I've got Christian cowboys and unbelievers alike coming to services. God's put me where He has and until He tells me different I'll be standing right outside the turnout gate every Sunday when my cowboys ride." He turned serious green eyes on Wyatt. "How about you? When are you going to settle down? I'm prepared to be a bachelor for the rest of my life if that's what God has planned for me."

Wyatt respected Chance and his uncommon faith. Any man who thought God didn't save the roughest of the bunch could just look at his cousin and they would know the redemptive power of God's grace. Chance had dedicated his life to serving the Lord. He did so among the men he'd competed with and counted as friends for years.

As for Wyatt, he hadn't really thought about his marrying status until lately. He'd been so intent on getting his brothers married off so the Turner name could be carried on. And just because he felt responsible for them. He'd known his parents would want them to be happy and he'd been determined to see that done.

Prior to the plane crash he'd been satisfied with his life tenfold. Now, he wasn't sure of anything except that he'd caused Amanda pain.

Yesterday he'd not been able to stop himself from kissing her. She'd made that statement about not thinking a man would want her—how could she think that? It had to have come from the breakup...*and her lack of a leg?* Maybe. The idea stunned him. How had Jonathan been so cruel? How had *he* been so cruel? He'd kissed her before he'd thought things through. He wasn't ready to settle down. His life was in Dallas and Amanda's life was wherever the next job took her. Even if he was ready to settle down, the logistics wouldn't work. He'd cared for her for a while now, and he wanted the best for her. She deserved the best. Not another man messing with her heart.

What was best for her was for him not to think about how she'd felt in his arms. Or how one touch of her lips... Wyatt stopped right there and pushed thoughts of kissing Amanda out of his mind. This was Cole's wedding. He needed to focus on Cole and Susan.

He did not need his brothers and his cousin asking

him what was going on in his brain because he was too distracted to keep up with where their conversation had gone while he had Amanda on his mind.

"Okay, it's time, ladies," Norma Sue commanded, entering the dressing room. She and Esther Mae were the wedding planners and were taking their positions seriously. Amanda had shown up early when she'd driven Wyatt to the church, and Melody and Susan had drawn her into the dressing room with them and Lacy. Melody was the maid of honor and Lacy was the bridesmaid. Amanda was hired to help and was having trouble. Had been since the kiss.

"It sure is," Esther Mae said, hustling in behind Norma Sue. She had on a purple dress topped off with a purple-and-white hat with a riot of morning glories encircling the rim. "You should see those men. I tell you, they marched out there in those black, Western suits and those black Stetsons and I thought I was going to pass slap out right there in the doorway."

Norma Sue had traded in her overalls for a pink striped dress without a hat. She ducked her chin and looked down her nose at her friend. "That would have been a catastrophe in more ways than one. We'd a had to just roll you out of the way and gone on with this wedding. After the plane crash we are not letting anything get in the way of marrying off these two."

"Norma Sue," Susan said. "We would not have rolled Esther Mae out of the way."

"Now, Susan," Lacy said, smoothing her pale blue dress down. "We would have had to because if we didn't we wouldn't have been able to get the door open to get you inside."

Esther Mae harrumphed. "I didn't pass out, so hush, Norma Sue, and let's get these gals lined up and ready so Adela can start playing the wedding march."

"Amanda, you got the train?" Norma Sue opened the door.

"Yes, ma'am. I do." Amanda carefully gathered up the short train and smiled at Susan, who suddenly looked nervous.

"I'm so excited I can hardly breathe." She placed a hand on her stomach and took a deep breath, meeting Amanda's gaze with bright eyes.

"Oh, that's a good thing," Esther Mae called, waving them toward the door like she was directing traffic. "Just don't pass out or Norma Sue might send someone up that aisle for you…" She paused her traffic signals and grinned at Amanda. "We could always send Amanda in to marry Wyatt and then when you wake up we could continue with your ceremony."

All attention was suddenly riveted to Amanda. Lacy hooted behind her flower bouquet while everyone else laughed.

Norma Sue hiked a brow. "We could do that even if Susan keeps her wits about her."

"Y'all are crazy." Amanda laughed—it was the only thing to do. They never stopped. She wondered if Wyatt was getting harassment on his end. How embarrassing that would be. "Susan is the only bride in town today, so come on and let's get her in there before the groom passes out."

Or before poor Wyatt's hip and back gave out on him from having to stand for so long. He'd made great progress, but standing in one spot for long periods of time wasn't good for him.

As they all finally exited the annex building and started down the sidewalk, Amanda felt a surge of anticipation that rippled through her and settled in the pit of her stomach. Wyatt had looked fantastic in his suit. As they stepped up onto the church's porch, Amanda's knees felt weak thinking about him. Would she ever have a wedding?

"Amanda," Esther Mae said, "spread that out here and then you come stand by the door with me and Norma Sue while the vows are exchanged."

Lacy looked over her shoulder at her and winked. "Yeah, that way when Susan and Cole both pass out they can send you right on in as the pinch hitter."

Amanda laughed again. But the next second Norma Sue tapped lightly on the door and Applegate stuck his head in and gave a frown.

"It's about time," he snapped. His voice cracked like a cannon over the soft music Adela was playing and the entire church of folks turned to look at them. "We about figured we had a runaway bride on the loose."

Chuckles erupted through the sanctuary.

"Not hardly," Norma Sue grunted. "I'd tell you to give the signal so we can get these two lovebirds married off finally, but you done alerted the whole place, so move out of the way. We're coming through."

Adela switched music and Norma Sue practically shoved Lacy over the threshold. The wedding was on.

But from the back of the bride Amanda had had eyes for only one person the moment Applegate had swung the doors open. Wyatt, broad-shouldered and taller by an inch than the others, locked his gaze on to her, too. For the life of her, Amanda couldn't look away.

Norma Sue patted Amanda's hands, reminding her

to let go of the train, as she leaned in close. "Uh-huh. That man can't take his eyes off of you."

"I think it's romantic," Esther Mae hissed in her other ear as the three of them scooted over to stand at the back of the church so they could see over everyone's heads.

Amanda looked from one beaming grin to the other as Adela ended the wedding march and everyone sat down. She felt the posse suddenly closing in on her as Esther Mae nudged her and Norma Sue leaned in again.

"That's a good man right yonder."

Amanda could have kissed Wyatt right then and there because he wasn't looking at her. His attention was focused on Cole and Susan as they took hands—just as it should be.

If he'd have been looking at her again she wouldn't have had any kind of chance to stop the matchmaking plans spinning around in the posse's heads.

Thankfully, his attention was exactly where it should have been. It was her *own* that was misbehaving.

Wyatt knew. He listened to the vows that Chance spoke to Susan and Cole and his gaze kept locking on Amanda. She was standing in between Norma Sue and Esther Mae, and he caught her looking to him as frequently.

"To have and to hold from this day forward." When Chance spoke those vows, Wyatt knew Amanda was the woman he wanted to marry. How he knew it—when he hadn't even realized he loved her—was a mystery to him. But just as he'd known when he met Melody and then Susan that they were the women for his brothers, he knew it with everything in him that Amanda Hathaway was the woman for him.

He'd never felt the protectiveness that he felt with her. She was somewhat lost right now, and though he'd been deeply troubled when she'd come along, she'd helped him. She'd put away her own problems and pulled him back from the dark emotions he'd been trapped in. He hadn't thought of his own problem since the morning he'd seen her running. The morning after she'd stood up to him and pointed out what blessings God had bestowed on him. The morning after she'd said all that and not pointed out anything about her own lost leg or the things she'd had to suffer through. She'd told him what he needed to hear and she'd done it without any self-pity whatsoever. He loved and admired that.

He loved what she stood for. He loved how she stood her ground with him. But most of all he loved her spirit. She'd chosen to look at what God had in store for her and to move forward with a purpose.

And now, though he knew something was eating at her, he loved the way she was fighting it…and he knew she was. She would have confided in him, or someone else, if it weren't true.

She was alone and he wanted her to know he was there for her…wanted her to know that she could lean on him.

For the rest of their lives.

He hadn't given marriage a thought before now, but he knew he was going to marry Amanda.

The wedding was beautiful. Chance gave a traditional ceremony, which was Amanda's favorite ceremony and what she'd wanted for her own wedding.

Wyatt was in great spirits as they drove to the wedding reception. He seemed more at ease and relaxed than he ever had, and she attributed it to the fact that he'd accomplished what he'd set out to do when he'd decided it was time to marry off his brothers. Again she was struck by what a romantic he was. Home and hearth meant everything to him.

She'd struggled the entire service not to stare, but she'd known he was watching her. Even with Esther Mae and Norma Sue flanking her, he'd repeatedly found her gaze across the sanctuary. And each time her heart squeezed and her stomach filled with butterflies. Oh, how she wished...

She couldn't let herself finish that wistful thought. Life and love with Wyatt was not a possibility.

"You did a good thing," she said as she parked in front of the community center.

He surprised her by reaching for her hand. "Are you all right?"

Her skin burned where he touched her and she wanted to pull away but couldn't. "Yes, I'm fine."

"I hope so. The ceremony didn't bring back bad memories or hurtful ones?" His thumb was making gentle circles on the back of her hand.

"No." She could hardly speak. All she could think about was the feel of his hand on hers. The tender way he was looking at her and the overwhelming need to be in his arms. Being with Wyatt had helped her in so many ways. "I actually thanked God for not letting the marriage with Jonathan go through. I didn't love him and I know that completely and clearly now."

Wyatt's eyes darkened. "I'm glad. You deserve a man who is going to love you with all his heart and give you all the good things you deserve."

Amanda's heart dropped. He was squeezing her hand

ever so gently, his voice carrying on its husky tone something that confused her. "I'm not going to ever marry." She hadn't meant to say that.

People walked by, laughing and talking as they headed into the reception. But neither of them made a move for the door.

"Why do you say that?"

"Because I have my reasons, Wyatt."

"And what are those reasons? And don't say you can't tell me, Amanda. You need to tell someone what it is that you are dealing with alone. Don't you know I care for you and that with all that you've done for me, I wouldn't do anything to harm you? God put you in my life to change me. And He has. In more ways than you know right now. But I believe He put me in your life to help you. Please talk to me. It's time!"

"We need to go to the reception."

He shook his head. "We need to get to the bottom of this."

"Wyatt, why does it matter to you?"

"Because I care, Amanda—you'd be surprised how much."

Amanda's heart began pounding at his words. "Wyatt—" she said, but lost all train of thought when he touched her cheek.

"Trust me, Amanda. I'm here for you."

"I have nothing to offer y—a man." The words came out before she could stop them. Wyatt's eyes sharpened and his hand stilled. She looked down, her gaze falling on the hand he still held. She loved Wyatt. She knew it, knew it wasn't anything like what she'd thought she felt for Jonathan. She knew she loved this tender man and that there was absolutely nothing she could do about it.

"You said that before. What makes you say that? You have everything to offer."

She took a deep breath; her insides were churning. "I lost more than my leg when I was hit... I lost my ability to have children."

Her words knocked the breath out of him.

"What? Why didn't you tell me?"

"Hey, you two," Seth called from the door. "Cole wants y'all in the picture with them cutting the cake, pronto."

Wyatt scowled.

Amanda grabbed the door handle with shaking hands. "We need to go inside so you can be in the pictures with Cole and Susan," she said, pushing her car door open. "Your family is waiting."

"I want to talk about this," Wyatt growled, grabbing her arm.

"No, Wyatt. This isn't fair. Cole and Susan have waited for you long enough and you know you wouldn't miss this for the world."

He let out an exasperated breath. "You're right. But this is important, Amanda, and we will talk. You can bet on that."

Amanda got out of the car, closed her eyes, praying for help... It seemed hopeless, though.

Chapter Seventeen

⤚❦⤙

He was tired of smiling. Wyatt had smiled for the camera over and over again so that when Cole and Susan looked back over their wedding pictures he wouldn't look angry. He'd already caused them to wait this long to get married, he didn't want to be responsible for ruining their wedding pictures for all of eternity.

But the conversation with Amanda kept playing over and over in his mind. She couldn't have children. She loved children. The thought of it broke his heart.

He couldn't imagine all that Amanda had lived through. Why had she been able to work with kids for so long and now she didn't want to? Couldn't.

Moving to the corner of the room, he leaned against the wall and watched her serving cake with Adela. The reception was a success. Cole and Susan were happy and everyone was having a blast. Norma Sue and Esther Mae worked beside Amanda and Adela serving cake and punch as though it was a free-for-all. It even seemed that Amanda was having a great time as she placed sliced cake onto plates. She smiled at everyone and even laughed when cowboy after cowboy made some comment—flirting with her, no doubt. It hadn't escaped his notice that she had an ever-growing army of admirers. He wondered if any of them could see past her smile to the heartache she was hiding.

One thing about Amanda, she seemed to be able to shut her own needs away and focus on the needs of those around her. Watching her, he wasn't sure if that was a good thing or not.

He wanted to storm across the room, take her in his arms and tell her that he loved her. That it didn't matter if she couldn't have children—was this the reason Jonathan had broken off their engagement? *Had he known when he asked her and then changed his mind?*

The questions wrestled for answers—answers Wyatt would uncover as soon as he and Amanda were alone.

It was late when they finally headed home. The sun was low in the sky and the roads to the stagecoach house glistened white as Amanda followed them toward home. Home. She'd begun to think of this as home in the short few weeks that she'd been here. She knew it was because of Wyatt. She loved him and couldn't imagine leaving here. But she would.

She'd made so many friends, even tonight she'd made more. For a town that only a few years ago had been dying, it was full of life now. Bustling with life. She felt good just having been in the middle of such a positive atmosphere tonight, even after practically breaking down in the car with Wyatt.

Working with Adela had been part of that. "I loved working with Adela tonight," she said, needing something to fill the silence as she drove. "She is a delight."

Wyatt had watched her all night. She knew that their

conversation was inevitable. She'd expected him to practically interrogate her the minute the SUV's doors were
closed. But he'd been quiet, lost in thought. It was plain
to see, by the distracted look she'd come to recognize
in his eyes, that his mind was working overtime. Dread
filled her. She'd wanted to tell him for so long about not
being able to have children and now…now she'd told
him. What was he thinking?

"I'm so sorry, Amanda. Talk to me. Tell me what
happened."

His words were a low rumble in the darkness. They
reached out to her, urging her to open up.

Amanda took a shallow breath, feeling as if she were
treading on quicksand. It was time. "It just recently hit
me what I've lost…."

Wyatt stilled his heart as her words flowed, as rough
as the cattle guard she drove the SUV over. He was glad
they were home. This hadn't been a conversation to have
while driving. He'd meant to wait.

She pulled to a stop in front of the house and cut the
engine. He waited for her to continue.

"I've dedicated my life to helping kids. Felt like it was
my calling. My purpose. Over the years I came to realize that at fourteen I didn't understand how the complete
hysterectomy would affect me." Her words were stronger
than he'd thought they would be. "I didn't realize how I
would one day long…" her voice cracked "…for a baby."

Wyatt could see where at fourteen the loss of her
leg would have been the focus of her young life. A kid
wouldn't understand that she might one day long for a
baby. A kid might only think about having to face life
without the leg she'd had before she'd gone into sur-
gery. A woman of twenty-four who saw other women

all around her who were expecting children would understand only too well what she'd lost...especially one whose fiancé had broken off their engagement. He had to ask. "Did you start struggling with this prior to Jonathan breaking the engagement?"

She nodded. "Some. I'd been thinking about it since I was about twenty. But I'd been counting my blessings. Focusing on them and letting God get me through it. But it was getting worse each year. And then, well, I realized the truth."

"And what is that?"

She bit her lip, crossed her arms as if to protect herself. "I'm a woman with one leg and no ability to give a man children. I'm not the prize—" She halted as if unable to continue.

She didn't need to finish her statement. Her view of what that truth was showed in her expression.

"You know that's not right," he said softly, touching her cheek.

"What man would want me under those conditions? I'm not one to beat around the bush or want sympathy. This is fact. I didn't date because of that."

This was something new. "You didn't date?"

She shook her head. "I couldn't handle thinking about someone confirming what I had realized."

Then she'd decided to date Jonathan the jerk. Wyatt shifted in his seat to face her more fully. Amanda needed to talk about this and maybe she needed him to ask frank questions. "What made you change your mind and start dating Jonathan?"

"It just happened. He..." She sighed. "He was nice and he was persistent. I told him on our second date and he was okay with it."

"But he wasn't."

She looked down at her hands folded tightly in her lap. "No. He wasn't."

Wyatt would have decked the guy if he'd been standing there. How could the man do that? "You are better off without him." She looked pained as she closed her eyes, shaking her head. Wyatt's heart clenched. "Do you still *love* him?" Surely not. She'd said once she was over him, but was she? "You are better off without him."

"No. I don't love him. I can just understand—"

"Stop defending him, Amanda. The man saw a pretty, sweet woman and chased her down. As far as I'm concerned he was looking out for only himself the whole time. He told you what you wanted to hear at the time because it suited him." Anger boiled inside of Wyatt. He sucked in a hard breath and counted to ten as he slowly exhaled. He didn't need to upset Amanda any more. The look on her face told him it was too late. "Is this why you don't work with kids?"

Her eyes darkened with sadness and she nodded.

"Amanda, you can't have children, but you have so much to offer a baby. And all those kids whose lives you've touched. Anyone can look at you and how you've lived your life and know that God is using you. Your life is a testimony. It has been to me. And there is no telling how many others—kids and adults alike—who you've inspired firsthand. God has a plan for you. He wants to prosper you and not to harm you." Wyatt couldn't remember the last time he'd quoted scripture but it felt right to do it now.

Tears formed in her beautiful aquamarine eyes. "They have touched my life…but, Wyatt, I can't do it anymore."

He didn't understand. "Why?"

"When I'm around kids now—" She brushed a tear away and it was all he could do not to reach for her. "It started with Jonathan. It hit me then with full force how big the hole inside me is." She paused, closing her eyes briefly. "I'm dealing with it in my way—here."

"Amanda, there are babies who need adopting. You can do that."

"It's not that…" She faltered as if she almost couldn't get the words out. "It's in here." She flattened her hand to the center of her chest. "I feel so empty. So broken— like I have a hole inside me that can't be filled. Nothing makes it better. No scripture. No prayer. It's just there. And I feel—" she sighed "—worthless."

"Amanda, no—"

She kept on going. "I can't look at kids now without aching so badly inside that I feel as if I'll be sick. It's a horrible thing. It's something I have to deal with." She shifted her shoulders back and lifted her chin. "And I will." She reached for the door handle. "I'm tired, Wyatt. I think I'll head in. Are you okay? Do you need me to help you get inside?"

She was almost bubbly again—clearly a veil over her pain. Wyatt shook his head. "I'm good, Amanda. You go on in and get some sleep. It'll make you feel better."

She didn't look at him as she climbed from the SUV and headed across the yard. She worried him. There was so much he wanted to say and so much he didn't know *how* to say. It felt strange to be in a situation where he didn't have the words. *I love you* were the words that came raging to the forefront of his heart and soul…but was that what she needed to hear right now? She'd heard those words once and they'd been taken back. They'd led or added to the feelings of unworthiness she said she was feeling.

Worthless! She was a jewel.

He just had to find a way to show her.

After Amanda disappeared around the edge of the house, Wyatt got out of the SUV and slammed the door. He winced from the pain that shot through his shoulder. He'd come a long way, but there was still a long haul ahead. Right now the pain didn't compare to what he was feeling for Amanda. Or what she was feeling herself.

She'd come here to help him heal when she had far deeper hidden scars than anyone could know and certainly see.

Grief was a complex emotion. He and his brothers had lived it when their parents had died tragically. It was a death of flesh and blood. A tangible loss that everyone in the community saw and felt. Amanda's grief was different. It was almost intangible—who would know if she didn't tell? Who would comfort her if she didn't expose it? And if she didn't tell anyone, she suffered alone.

Did she not know how precious she was?

This wasn't what he'd expected. She was a fighter, and so he wouldn't have thought that this could kick the wind out of her the way it had. He'd almost told her he loved her but held back. His gut told him now wasn't the time. He'd been messing up ever since Amanda walked into his life. The last thing he wanted to do was speak too soon. He had to help her first…and then pray she felt the same way about him. He had to have a plan before he did anything stupid. But what?

He needed to ride.

Needed to move.

Restless winds rolled across the pasture as unease and uncertainty clashed inside of him. *What did he need to do for Amanda?*

The sun was settling over the trees. Cole and Susan had planned the afternoon wedding and reception so they could make the long drive to the airport in Ranger. Wyatt glanced into the SUV and saw the key still in the ignition. Walking around to the driver's side, he pulled open the door and slid carefully into the seat.

He needed time to think. He needed to ride. Needed the calm he felt when he was around his horses—

Five minutes later, he pulled into the yard of the main house where Seth and Melody lived. He knew they were probably still in town cleaning up after the reception. Driving to the barn, he eased on the brake and got out of the vehicle. His hip and back tightened up but didn't spasm. His shoulder hadn't complained too much, either. It didn't matter as he made his way into the barn.

Why had God not helped Amanda? She'd said nothing had helped her. No scripture. No prayer. Why had God not given her something to ease her pain?

He stopped in front of the black gelding. "Hello, Soot," Wyatt said, rubbing the horse's neck. "How about a ride?"

"Do you think that's a good idea?"

The question startled Wyatt and he looked over his shoulder. Chance was standing in the doorway.

"I don't really care at the moment. What are you doing here? I figured you'd still be in town."

His cousin shrugged and strode over to prop a boot on the bottom rung of the stall. He patted Soot's neck. "When you were troubled about something, riding always did help you think, didn't it?"

"Same as you."

Chance gave him a Turner grin. "Yup. There's peace out there on those plains."

"I'd almost forgotten how much."

"Do you need to talk?" Chance turned his head and stared at him from beneath the brim of his hat. His serious green eyes bored all the way through Wyatt.

"Nope. I'm fine." It wasn't true and he knew it. But this was a private matter.

"Give me a break. You looked like a cowboy about to get on the rankest bull of the draw and you aren't prepared."

"That bad, huh?"

"Worse. I saw the way you couldn't take your eyes off Amanda all evening. What's going on?"

Maybe counsel from a man of God might help him help Amanda. Wyatt gave in. "This is just between you and me," he clarified.

"This is between you, me and *God*."

Wyatt proceeded to tell him about Amanda's problem. About how she couldn't have children and how she was in a crisis with it now. "She's run here to Mule Hollow trying to find some peace and answers, I think. She's just treading water, hoping God will take away the pain and grief she's feeling, but she's hurting, Chance. And tonight she told me how empty and worthless she feels. That's not good. I don't know what to do for her. She's a remarkable woman. I've never known someone with the heart that she has. She's spent her life inspiring people with the way she's handled losing her leg. She let God take that bad situation and make it good. But this is really hurting her. How can I help her? She is not worthless because she can't bear children."

Chance had been watching him closely. "Man, that's a tough one. First, you can start by doing what you are doing…loving her."

"Is it that obvious?"

Chance placed a hand on his shoulder. "I see it. But I also hear it and see evidence in the concern you're showing her. God puts people into our lives when we need them. It seems to me He's placed you and Amanda in each other's paths at this specific time because it's the right time. Be patient and be there for her like she's been there for you. You're almost back to being yourself because of her care. You can do the same for her. Help her know that this emptiness she's feeling can be filled with God's grace if she'd let it. He's the ultimate comforter and loves her. He'll use this for good, too, if she can let Him. You need to pray about it and then follow God's lead. God doesn't steer us wrong if we can hear His voice when He speaks."

Wyatt stared out into the near darkness, his heart heavy. "But what if I don't feel like I'm hearing God these days?"

"Then wait. Pray and study God's word while you wait, and be patient with yourself. You'll grow during that time. Meanwhile, Amanda needs to know that she isn't less of a woman and that God has made her the way she is for a reason. His love for her is abundant, and though her fiancé forsook her, God never will. *Sometimes* He's quiet because it draws us to seek Him more. He hasn't forsaken you, either, Wyatt. In trials and tribulations God pulls us back to Him. He wants us to rely on Him and not ourselves."

Wyatt closed his eyes and thought about that. It was

so simple. So obvious. "That's me." Unable to be still, he walked toward the outside.

Chance fell into step beside him. "It's all of us sometime or other."

"Yeah, but I've been doing it for so long I didn't see anything wrong with it. I'd begun to think I was invincible. That all I've accomplished was by my own merit and not God's." That was what had been eating at him with crashing the plane. "How can I fix that?" He stopped outside.

Chance smiled easily. "Simple, Wyatt. You've acknowledged it, now just ask God to forgive you and start fresh. The Bible says that when we confess our sins, God forgets it as far as the east is from the west. You believe that, don't you?"

He nodded. "What if I'm not the one to help her? Maybe she should talk to you. You're the preacher."

"He sent you. You're the right man for the job. Go back and talk to her. God will lead you." Chance laid his hand on Wyatt's shoulder. "I'll pray for you both."

"Thanks. I'll need it."

With that said, Chance walked back toward the house, pure cowboy swagger. If God put people into our lives when we needed them, Wyatt knew there was no mistake in the timing of Chance showing up in the barn. Amanda would be glad to know God had kept him off the horse, he thought as he climbed back into her SUV.

He paused at the cattle guard and stared at the sunset's lingering glow, bowed his head and asked God to forgive him. He prayed God would show him the way to help Amanda…and also the way to win her heart.

Chapter Eighteen

Amanda was waiting on the front porch when she saw headlights winding toward her across the dark pasture. She'd started feeling guilty for not having made certain that Wyatt had gotten inside safely. Yes, he was getting around better and better, but still, he was her patient and she should have walked him to his door. Instead she'd let her emotions—her personal life—interfere with her work.

The last thing she'd expected to find when she'd come to check on him was that her SUV would be gone.

What was he thinking? She headed toward him the minute he pulled to a stop. She had every intention of setting him straight on the issue of driving, but the minute he closed the door she could see something was wrong. He looked nervous in the moonlight.

It was a look she'd never seen on him before.

"Wyatt, is something wrong?" She stopped at the edge of the stagecoach house. He walked steadily toward her and stopped only inches from her. Amanda automatically reached out and touched his arm. As if her touch would calm him. The last thing she needed to do was reach out to Wyatt. But it was becoming an impossibility. He knew everything about her. Her darkest fears and her deepest sorrows. They were connected, and despite everything she'd told him, she'd realized when she'd walked away from him that talking to him had helped her. "Why did you take the car? You aren't ready to drive."

"It doesn't matter. I needed to think. I'm not sure how to approach this, but I can't let you go to sleep tonight without telling you how beautiful you are inside and out." His eyes burned fierce in the starlight. "God did not make a mistake when He made you, or when He allowed everything in your life to happen to you. I've prayed all the way back from the barn for God to lead me on this. I've told myself now isn't the time, but here it is, Amanda."

Holding her captive with his gaze, he stepped up and took her face between his hands. Their warmth seeped into her. "I love you. I love you just the way you are and can only pray that you might someday fall in love with me and let me show you how wonderful you are."

Amanda had gone still when he'd touched her and now on the "I love you" part, joy filled her… Her heart lifted in her chest with a lightness she had never felt. But then reality hit her like an arrow to a balloon.

"No." She took a step back.

"Yes." Wyatt held on, stepping with her. "I'm just giving you warning that I do love you. It may scare you. It may terrify you, and after all you've been through, you have every right to feel that way. But, Amanda Hathaway, I'm a very patient man when I need to be. And I'm very determined, as you well know. So hold on to your

hat because I want you for keeps. And I'm going to ac-
tively seek to win your heart from this moment forward."

Amanda didn't know what to say. "I'm not going
there, Wyatt. I can't—"

"What, risking your heart on someone who truly does
love you? Here in Mule Hollow we call that chicken. And
there is nothing about you that is chicken."

"Wyatt—" She broke from his tender hands, backing
away, only to back straight into the logs of the stagecoach house. Trapped, she was forced to look into his
eyes, her heart breaking. "I have nothing to offer you.
Nothing. Don't you get that?" She looked down at the
ground. Didn't he see the truth?

Wyatt took her face in between his hands once more
and tilted her head. He stared deeply into her eyes. "I've
realized ever so slowly, getting to know you, and as I
fell for you, that you hold the key to every dream and
aspiration I will ever have. God didn't put us into each
other's lives for no reason, Amanda. You are all that I
could ever want, and I thank God for sending you into
my life when He did."

Amanda felt tears rising as her heart swelled. Her
spirit felt buffeted by strong winds, one moment elation,
the next desolation. She wanted to run and she wanted
to cling to Wyatt and ask him to repeat everything he'd
just said. Her locked knees let her do neither one.

Then without warning, Wyatt lowered his head to
hers and kissed her. Long and slow. Her insides burned
with longing of hopes and dreams long lost.

"I want to marry you," he whispered against her lips.

She gasped. "Don't—"

He pulled back; his arms that had wrapped around
her and drawn her into the shelter of his body held her

tightly against him. His heart pounded against hers…and she wondered if he could hear the thunder of her blood.

"I love you, Amanda. And I wasn't lying when I said I'm patient. I'm just letting you know this is where I stand and I'm praying you fall in love with me."

She swallowed the words she so wanted to say to him. *I love you, too.* "It would never work."

"Why?"

"Because I can't give you children. You need a little boy who looks like you to sit at Sam's beside you on the bar stool ordering the best food in the world."

"I can have a son with you who can do that if he wants to."

"No—"

"Yes. Amanda, you are a whole and complete woman. God is in you and that makes you whole. The emptiness you feel can be filled with the grace and peace of God if you'll just let it. I did that tonight. I let go of all the anger I'd been feeling—most of it you'd already helped me let go of by just being here and working with me and inspiring me. But I let it go and am going to rethink my life goals. I'm just trying to get you to see that you have to do the same. Face that you are who you are and you are beautiful in every way. Nothing about you is lacking in my eyes or God's. A child out there somewhere desperately needs you to love him or her, or for that matter, a houseful of them. And in my mind I'm the man who God wants to stand there beside you loving them. Please tell me there is a possibility that you could love me back."

Amanda couldn't speak. He had just offered her the world. God was offering her the delights of her heart.

"Just so you know, I've made another decision tonight. This place where we are standing has been home to six generations of my family. The Turners belong here, Amanda. I want to raise my children—our children— here on Turner land. I'm going to open a small law office in town where I can practice and also do some consulting work for my firm. *And* I thought, if you do fall in love with me and become my wife, that you could head up a pro bono division working to get amputees the therapy they need for the time that they need it."

Amanda felt a trail of tears spill out of her eyes. He'd thought of all of this. "Oh, Wyatt. You make it all seem so easy."

He smiled that crooked, wonderful, curl-her-toes smile. "All you have to do is say that you love me."

Amanda's heart felt like it might burst. She hesitated for a moment, inhaled deeply and then wrapped her arms around his neck. She couldn't stop herself. For a woman who'd had to fight for every step forward since she was fourteen, all the fight drained from her and she simply did and said what was in her heart.... "I love you."

Wyatt closed his eyes and lifted his face toward heaven. "Thank You, God. Thank You." And then he kissed her.

And Amanda felt God's smile and it filled every dark spot inside of her with hope and light, and she felt whole.

It was the most wonderful feeling she'd ever experienced.

Epilogue

"You boys want a barbecue plate?" Applegate asked, waving a sausage link from behind a long table that he, Sam and Stanley were manning.

Wyatt stood in the yard of the stagecoach house, where tents had been set up for his wedding to Amanda. They'd thrown a regular party to celebrate. Across the way, he caught Amanda smiling at him. She looked beautiful in her white dress, and to him she was the most radiant woman God had ever created. There was no other like her.

"Save one for me, will you?" he said, inching toward her.

"Will do. Chance, how 'bout you?"

"Thanks, App. I'd appreciate it if you'd store a plate back for me, too."

App's bushy brows crinkled like a caterpillar inching across the floor. "You ever thank about movin' home, Chance? That rodeo'ns got ta be gettin' old. We need a good preacher. Jest ask Wyatt, he knows what kind a lazy preachin' we been hearin' since Pastor Allen had ta retar."

Chance grimaced. "I'm sorry y'all are havin' a hard time, sir. But until the good Lord brings me back, I'll be out there on the circuit. I'll keep praying that the Lord sends the right man to y'all. He's got him out there, you can be assured of that. It'll just be in His timing that he gets here. Be patient and give the ones that come a prayerful consideration."

App grunted, fiddling with his hearing aid. "It ain't as easy as you thank."

Wyatt felt for the town. He knew Applegate wanted what was best for the town. He was grumpy because he missed Pastor Allen, who'd been there for a while but had to leave when his wife became ill and needed to be closer to the doctors who were taking care of her. Change was hard. While he wasn't sure if all the pastors who'd come in were as bad as the one that he'd heard that first Sunday he'd gone to church, they hadn't been right, either. "When the right man shows up, God will lead y'all and you'll know," he offered, and Chance agreed. Honestly, he'd like it if Chance felt called to Mule Hollow, but Wyatt didn't see that happening anytime soon. Chance *was* doing what he was called to do.

Stanley, who'd been busy cutting up brisket on the table behind App, brought a new trayful to App's table. "The question is will we survive till he gets here!" Stanley boomed over the music.

"You'll survive," Wyatt said, distracted by his bride as she started his way.

"God's timing is perfect, I'm proof of that," he said. He left the others to their discussion and met Amanda in the center of the tent. She walked into his open arms. "Have I told you how blessed I feel today?" he asked, kissing her temple and holding her tightly.

"Me, too," she whispered against his ear. "God is good, isn't He?"

Wyatt leaned his head back, feeling humbled by God's goodness. "God is great. He sent me you, and I can't wait to see the plans He has for us as a family."

* * * * *

Dear Reader,

As always, I'm thrilled when you decide to spend time with me and the gang in Mule Hollow! Thank you so much for letting me entertain you for a few hours. I've loved coming up with all the different men in the MEN OF MULE HOLLOW series, and I knew when I introduced the Turner men in the first book, *Lone Star Cinderella,* that I was going to have fun telling their stories. Creating Wyatt was a challenge, and I couldn't wait to write his story.

You see, I'm a bit like Wyatt when it comes to being an overachiever…and being stubborn. I think I'm Superwoman and I hold myself up to an unrealistic level just as Wyatt sort of thought he was a superman. God had to show me this past year that sometimes I can rely on myself too much when what I need to do is rely on Him. I wanted to create a character who had to be taught this same lesson, and so I took Wyatt out of his comfort zone and threw him into uncharted waters when he found himself helpless. God says that when we are weak He is strong. I have found this is true, and Wyatt also found this is true. If you are trying to handle too much by yourself I pray that you will reevaluate, relax and let God help you and give you strength. He is waiting. And in doing this you will give Him the glory He deserves since it is He and not ourselves who deserves our high praise!

I love to hear from readers! You can reach me at debraclopton.com. I hope until I see you again that you live, laugh and do give God the glory.

Debra Clopton

QUESTIONS FOR DISCUSSION

1. Did you enjoy this story? If so, what aspect drew you to it?

2. Wyatt is an overachiever. Do you know someone in your life who is this way or are you this way yourself? Discuss the good aspects or drawbacks that you see.

3. Amanda shows real courage in the way she accepts the loss of her leg. Her father was the person who helped her realize she still had things to be thankful for, which helped her move forward with her life. Do you know someone who has done this?

4. It is through her disability that Amanda realizes her purpose in life. What is her purpose?

5. There are many people who have lived through tragedy, heartache and other problems to realize that they can use their experience to help others. Have you done this or do you know someone who has done this?

6. How have they touched your life or those around them?

7. Do you believe that God puts people in your life when you need them? How has He done this?

8. God says He will make good from bad situations for those who love him. I personally have seen Him

do this in my own life over and over again. Can you give your testimony to the readers' group about how He has done this in your life?

9. Wyatt is really hard on himself. Why is that? What lessons did he need to learn?

10. In 2 *Corinthians* 12:10, it says, "Therefore I take pleasure in infirmities, in reproaches, in necessities, in persecutions, in distresses for Christ's sake: for when I am weak, then am I strong." I love this verse from Paul. It is so wonderfully true if we think about it. When we are weak then we are strong because we must rely on Christ's strength. I have to remind myself of this almost daily when I begin to worry about something. How did Wyatt have to learn this?

11. The prior verse, 2 *Corinthians* 12:8–9, explains it: "For this thing I besought the Lord thrice, that it might depart from me. And He said unto me, My grace is sufficient for thee: for my strength is made perfect in weakness." How did both Wyatt and Amanda learn this?

12. The last of the verse Paul says, "Most gladly therefore will I rather glory in my infirmities, that the power of Christ may rest upon me." When Amanda lost her leg, she found the strength of these verses and used her life as a testament to God, letting Him rest upon her, and use her. Do you think she will be able to use her inability to have children as

a witness for God in the years ahead of her? How can she do this?

13. Amanda says she feels worthless and empty. Chance tells Wyatt to help her know that the emptiness she is feeling could be filled with God's grace if she would let it. God is the ultimate comforter and loves her and wants only the best for her. He also tells Wyatt that God would use Amanda's situation for good if she would let him. That promise is in *Romans* 8:28. "And we know that all things work together for good to them that love God, to them who are the called according to His purpose." Do you believe this is true? Can you see how God can fill any emptiness or sorrow that we might have and help us to help others in similar situations? Discuss this with the others in the group.

14. Amanda and Wyatt are really strong people. As a couple, how do you think they can touch lives and be a team for God?

SECOND CHANCE RANCH

Leann Harris

To the men and women of the US Military, all current and former members. Thank you for your service to this country.

Acknowledgments

I want to thank:

Brenda Rozinsky and Ariane Mele at Equest Therapeutic Horsemanship Ranch for their help.

Donald R. Cummings at Scottish Rite Hospital in Dallas for his generous time and explaining to me how prosthesis limbs work.

Theresa Zumwalt and Jane Graves for your insight with horses.

I pray also that the eyes of your heart may be enlightened in order that you may know the hope to which He has called you…
—*Ephesians* 1:18

Chapter One

Zachary McClure closed his eyes and breathed in the
calming and familiar smells of the barn—horses, grains,
leather and liniment. He hadn't smelled anything that
comforting in the past four years. Dust, diesel and fear
had filled his days in Iraq. Disinfectant, moans and sickness had filled his last year in the hospital. The smell
of horses took him back to pre-army days. That was
before—

He stopped the thought. He couldn't change the past.

"You all right?"

Zach opened his eyes and looked into his sister's concerned face. Beth had always looked up to him, but lately
they argued a lot. He hadn't wanted to come today, didn't
want to face the ghosts of his past and the limitations
of today, but she kept badgering him with phone calls
and coming by his apartment, telling him he needed to
start riding again. He tried sending her home, but somehow she got him to agree to come once here to the New
Hope Ranch.

"I am."

"C'mon. My friend Sophie is waiting for us." Beth

linked her arm with his and started moving forward. "You remember her? She was my roommate in college."

He definitely remembered Sophie Powell. The weekend Beth brought Sophie home he'd been thunderstruck by the coltish girl. She wasn't model-beautiful, but there'd been a beauty about her. It had been her eyes, piercing blue. And her smile set him back on his heels. She had a crooked nose with freckles scattered across it and her cheeks. But that only added to her beauty. "I remember," he muttered. *Only too well,* he silently added.

Beth leaned close and whispered, "I think she had a crush on you."

"What?" Zach's head jerked around and his gaze clashed with Beth's. Her grin told him she was teasing him. Yet, there was a twinkle in her eye that made him wonder *if* maybe it was true.

"And she's ex-army, too."

This had the smell of a setup.

They walked down through the walkway between the stable and the office. Children's voices filled the air with laughter and excitement.

When they emerged, he could see the two practice rings. In the far ring a horse with its rider and two spotters moved around the enclosure. On the far side of the rings stood bleachers where three people sat, watching. In front of the closest ring, a woman knelt before a horse. A young boy, maybe six or seven, stood beside her.

"Will he bite?" the boy asked, eyeing the reddish-brown horse.

"No, *she* won't. You should give it a try. Samantha, or as we call her, Sam, is very gentle."

Zach remembered that low, rich voice. Sophie's. He often wondered what had become of his sister's college roommate and had wanted to ask, but that would've given his sis ideas.

Sophie held an apple in her hand. "Put your hand out," she instructed, "and I'll give you the apple."

The boy frowned at Sophie, then at the apple.

"You sure? I saw the *b-i-g* teeth." The boy kept his hand clenched in a fist.

Zach felt a smile bubble up, but he knew Sophie wouldn't appreciate his reaction.

She nodded. "I'm sure. Sam's my friend. She can be your friend, too."

The boy glanced around and saw Zach and Beth.

Without thinking, Zach walked over to the pair and took the apple from Sophie's hand. Her startled gaze locked with his. The connection was instantaneous and well remembered. Silently, he asked her permission.

Her nod was almost imperceptible.

Zach hooked his cane over his left forearm and put the apple into his right hand.

"You need to make sure your hand is flat. It makes it easier for the horse to get the apple if your fingers are not in the way," he explained. "I'm sure Sam wouldn't want to bite your fingers, so you have to make it easy for her."

The boy's eyes widened.

Zach showed the boy how to hold the apple, then offered it to the horse. Sam opened her mouth and took the apple.

"Wow. Can I try?"

"Sure." He looked at Sophie.

She stood and walked over to the barrel by one of the wooden porch columns, opened it and pulled out another apple. She gave it to Zach.

"Open your hand," Zach instructed the boy. When he looked up, doubt colored the youngster's eyes.

"Would you like for me to help?"

He nodded his head. "'Kay."

Zach moved behind the boy. Zach wished he could've squatted, but the prosthesis wouldn't allow it. Instead he put the apple in the boy's outstretched hand. "Now, be sure your fingers are out straight."

Zach slipped his big hand under the boy's and they moved their hands to the horse's mouth. Sam's lips and teeth picked up the apple.

The boy giggled. "That tickles."

Sam chewed happily.

Zach grinned.

Sophie's eyes twinkled. The lady's impact on him hadn't diminished over the years.

She stepped to their side. "Would you like to ride Sam?" she asked the boy.

"Okay." He turned to Zach. "My name is Andy. I come here to ride. Mom says riding's goin' to help me. Is that so? What if I fall off the horse?"

He was way over his head here. Zach glanced at Sophie, hoping for some sort of direction.

"You don't have to worry about falling, Andy. You see all the other people around here walking beside the riders? That's to make sure no one falls."

Andy looked around. "Oh." He turned to Zach. "Are you here to help me? Will you walk beside me?"

The question took Zach by surprise.

"This is Zach's first time here," Sophie explained. She stood on the other side of Andy. "He doesn't know how to be a sidewalker."

A mulish frown settled on Andy's face, and he crossed

his arms over his chest. He looked at Zach. "Would you ride with me?"

Zach swallowed. "Well, Andy, I haven't been riding in a few years. Besides, my leg doesn't work as well as it used to."

Andy looked at Zach's legs, then at the cane hanging over Zach's arm. "Why?"

Suddenly the air filled with tension. He glanced at his sister, then Sophie. Did they think he'd go off on the kid? Zach leaned close and whispered, "I have a fake foot and calf."

"Calf?" Andy frowned.

Nodding, Zach pulled up his pant leg and showed the prosthesis on his right leg to Andy.

"That's cool. Can I touch it?"

"Maybe—" Sophie started.

"Sure."

The boy squatted and touched the artificial leg. His eyes widened. "Wow. How'd that happen?"

Sophie stepped in. "You want to ride, Andy?"

"Can Zach help? He can walk beside me."

"Sophie knows how this works. I don't." Zach turned to her. "What do you want me to do?"

The tension seeped out of her shoulders. "I'll lead Sam and you can walk on one side of Sam, and Beth on the other. Will that work for you, Andy?"

"Yes," he crowed, hopping to his feet. He patted Zach's arm. "It's okay about your leg. I've got Down's."

"Really?"

Andy nodded. "Mom says I'm extraspecial."

"She's right."

Sophie smiled at Zach. "Thanks," she mouthed.

Satisfaction spread through Zach's chest.

They walked to the mounting steps. Sophie got the horse into position. Andy scrambled up the steps.

"Put on your helmet, Andy," Sophie called out.

He raced back down the steps and over to the row of helmets sitting on a shelf at the end of the stalls. He grabbed a helmet and put it on. He raced back to the steps. Zach rested his cane against the side of the stable by the mounting steps.

"Let Zach help you get on the horse, Andy," Sophie instructed.

Whoa, he didn't know how he was to help. Glancing at his sister, he silently questioned her.

"Just support him as he slips his leg over the pad," she instructed, "then guide his foot into the stirrup."

Resting his hands around Andy's waist, Zach lifted the boy onto the saddle blanket. A smile curved Andy's mouth.

Beth helped Andy put his leg in the stirrup attached to the blanket.

"Now, just hold his leg to make sure he doesn't slip," Beth instructed her brother. Beth had been here before and worked as a sidewalker.

"What do you say, Andy?" Sophie asked from her place by Sam's head.

"Go forward," Andy crowed.

Sam started walking.

Zach grabbed the front of the saddle pad and his other hand rested on Andy's leg. Andy turned and smiled at Zach. His heart overturned. With the warm New Mexico sun on his back and the feel of the horse under his hand, Zach felt a peace in his soul—a peace he hadn't felt in a long, long time.

Oddly enough, Zach, Beth and Sophie worked in tandem, he on the left side of the horse, Beth on the right, and Sophie leading Sam.

After three times around the ring, Zach felt the strain in his arms and legs. He stumbled, and his artificial leg folded underneath him, and he fell to the ground.

Andy cried out in dismay. Beth raced to Zach's side. Sophie started to move away from Sam, but Zach waved her back.

"I'm okay."

All the activity in both rings stopped. One of the side-walkers from the next ring came to Zach's side. The man stopped and said, "How do you want to handle this?"

He would've rather faced a terrorist in the streets of Baghdad, instead of being facedown in the dirt in front of his sister and the woman he'd been attracted to. He rolled to his side and told the man how to help him stand. It was slow and awkward as he struggled to his feet. When he stood, Andy clapped.

"You need any more help?" the man asked Zach.

Zach shook his head. He limped over to a bench under the stable's awning, which sheltered the entrance to the stables. He'd been thrown by plenty of wild broncos and bulls in his rodeo days, but there'd been no shame in it. This time, he'd fallen flat on his face walking.

Walking.

What kind of man can't walk?

He closed his eyes and rested his head against one of the porch posts. He knew that coming here this morning was a mistake. He just didn't know how big a mistake it would be.

Sophie looked at Zach. Her heart had skipped a beat earlier when she glanced up and saw him standing above her. Beth had called Sophie at the beginning of this week begging for help with Zach. Beth and Sophie had kept in contact since their college days when they roomed together and Sophie was more than happy to offer her friend a helping hand.

Zachary McClure still took her breath away. Tall, with wide shoulders and narrow hips, he cast a large shadow. Somehow, that handsome face seemed to have aged more than the few years since she'd last seen him. The weariness in his deep blue eyes matched the new lines bracketing his eyes and mouth.

"Is Zach feeling okay?" Andy asked, snapping her out of her memories.

Turning to Andy, Sophie saw the frown crossing his young face. "I think he's fine." She prayed he was.

For the next few minutes Sophie walked Sam, but Andy remained quiet. When she guided Sam toward the steps, she motioned for another sidewalker to help Andy dismount. The instant Andy's feet touched ground he raced to Zach's side.

"I'm sorry you fell," Andy whispered, tears in his voice.

Sophie's heart contracted.

Zach opened his eyes. Sophie felt Beth stop behind her. They both waited breathlessly for Zach's answer.

Reaching out, he ruffled the boy's hair. "I'm okay. Only my pride was damaged."

Andy nodded and moved closer. "I hate it when I trip and the other kids laugh." His lower lip trembled.

Zach slid his arm around Andy's shoulders and pulled him to his side. "I do, too. Makes me feel bad."

Andy nodded. "That's why my mom wanted me to come to ride on the horse. She said it would help me." He touched his stomach. "She said it would make my tummy stronger. Maybe it would help you, too."

Zach's brow arched and he glanced at Sophie as if accusing her of planning that little scene. He couldn't believe that, could he?

"Thanks, buddy."

The boy accepted the praise and leaned against Zach. "Will you be here next time I ride?" The youthful hope in Andy's expression pulled at Sophie's heart.

Zach rubbed his neck. "Well—"

She knelt by Andy's side. "Zach isn't trained for this. He only came today to see what we do here."

Andy faced Zach. "I'm learning. So can you."

Well, Andy certainly didn't beat around the bush.

Andy's mother walked up to the group. "Did you enjoy your ride?" After two sessions when Andy hadn't left his mother's side, she agreed to disappear until the session was over.

"I rode Sam," Andy explained, throwing out his chest. "And I met a new friend, Zach. He's got a fake leg. But he helped me get on Sam. You want to show my mom your funny foot and leg?"

Andy's mother's face lost all color. "I'm—"

Zach stood and smiled at the woman. "I'm glad I could help Andy."

"I asked him to help me again next time, but he told me no." Andy crossed his arms over his chest and stuck out his bottom lip.

Things were quickly getting out of control.

"Andy, Zach needs some practice himself," Sophie gently explained. "Why don't you come back next time and we'll see what we can work out."

Andy glared at the group. "I'd want Zach to help."

Andy's mother stepped in. "We need to get going. Why don't you put up your helmet?" She unbuckled the strap and Andy ran to put his helmet on the rack.

"Thank you," Andy's mother said. After shaking everyone's hand, she led her son down the breezeway to the parking lot behind the stable.

Zach sat back down and closed his eyes.

Sophie faced Beth. Before Sophie could say anything, Beth shook her head.

Sophie knew brother and sister needed time to themselves. She turned and headed toward Sam, who'd been left tied to the ring by the mounting steps and needed to be unsaddled.

Tears gathered in Sophie's eyes as she walked Sam back to her stall. She knew the battle that raged inside Zach. She'd seen that clash countless times in each of the men she treated in Iraq as a medic. She helped soldiers, airmen and civilians survive their wounds. Now she wanted to help those brave men and women win the heart-and-soul skirmish to gain back their lives.

She stopped and pulled off the saddle blanket, resting it on the half wall of the stall.

"I want to save as many as I can," she whispered into Sam's neck. And maybe, just maybe, she could atone for the one life she couldn't save.

Zach sat in the tack room. The humiliation this afternoon hadn't been any worse than when he fell off his horse at his parents' ranch in full view of his family and all the ranch hands. It was the first time he'd been on a horse since before the attack. He'd tried to ride away from the stable and his mount spooked and he fell off. Unfortunately, his prosthesis didn't come out of the stirrup and he'd been dragged around in front of the stable. When his brother, Ethan, caught the horse, he hit the release button, breaking the vacuum holding the prosthesis onto Zach's leg. His mother had cried, rushing to his side, and his father yelled for his brother to get the horse out of his sight. This afternoon wasn't that gut-wrenching, but had left a mighty bad taste in his mouth. Literally as well as figuratively.

The door to the tack room opened and an old man walked in. He nodded.

Zach acknowledged the greeting with his own nod.

The old guy went about putting up tack. "I saw you ride at the Frontier Days Rodeo in Ocate. It was a great win."

Zach remembered that rodeo held in the little town in northeastern New Mexico. It had been his first all-around championship. He'd been a senior in high school and full of himself. "Thanks."

"You've got a natural talent, Zach McClure."

"Had."

The old guy stopped. "I didn't know talent was in your foot."

The unexpected comeback stunned Zach. The old guy had a point. A smile curved Zach's lips. "I didn't know it, either."

The man walked over to where Zach sat. "When I was young and riding the circuit, I had more drive than sense. I got tossed off a bull. He was a nasty piece of work. Once he throwed me, he came back to stomp on my arm." He shook his head. "I never saw a clown move so fast as to get that bull's attention on him.

."It took me six months to heal. It took another six months for me to get my body back into shape. I kept falling off those mean critters until I built my body back up. I figure with you being in the hospital a while, you got the same problem." He started toward the door. "You might cut yourself some slack, son." He continued toward the door.

"You know my name. What's yours?" Zach called out.

"Ollie Morton. I'm foreman here."

"Thanks." Zach closed his eyes and shook his head. Was he feeling so sorry for himself that he couldn't see the obvious?

"Did Ollie hit it on the head, Lord?" Zach asked when Ollie had left. As he thought about the foreman's advice, Zach realized he may not have been thrown by a bull, but he might've stumbled onto the truth.

Sophie walked back from stabling Brownie, the small chestnut mare they used with the younger children.

Other riders were exiting the arena and the chatter of happy voices surrounded her. There would be no other lessons today and all the horses needed to be unsaddled, watered and fed.

There were two other hands to help with the horses, but they needed more help. Sophie's boss, Margaret, couldn't help anymore since her stroke six weeks ago, and Margaret's children wanted nothing to do with the facility.

Sophie worked for twenty minutes, putting the horses in the corral on the east side of the barn. Each of their stalls needed to be mucked out, and fresh water, feed and hay put in each one. The large metal building had two main halls that ran parallel. Stalls were on either side of the hall and an enclosed tack room stood at the far western end of the building closest to one set of large double doors. At the end of each hall was another set of double doors leading to the outside corrals.

She tried not to think, but went on automatic with the chores. She prayed under her breath, asking the Lord for wisdom and to comfort Zach's heart.

"Sophie, I've finished. So has Marty," David Somers called out. "You want me to put the horses back in their stalls?"

"No, go on. I'll see to it."

He nodded and disappeared.

Each of the horses had earned an extra treat and praise for their performance today. She wished Ollie was still here, but with her encouragement he'd gone to the hospital to see Margaret.

Sophie put new hay in Sam's stall and walked to the tack room to put up the lead ropes she used. Sitting on a bale of hay was Zach. In his hands he held one of the bridles. Those strong hands worked over the leather, cleaning it.

Sophie stopped and stared at him. "You're still here?"

"I am."

Now what? Zachary McClure had a way of rattling her that no other man had. She had no trouble dealing with the soldiers in her unit or her patients. None of them had this effect on her of making her stomach flip-flop. She tried to ignore the feeling.

Zach's hands stilled. "I've been thinking a lot about what happened this afternoon."

He hadn't been the only one. She'd played the scene over and over in her mind, wondering what she could've done differently. She knew that Beth had worked weeks to get Zach here, and then to have him trip in the middle of the ring… She'd wanted to run over to him and help him up, but she knew he wouldn't appreciate it. He'd been rodeoing since he was in middle school and had been on track for a championship rodeo buckle before he joined the army.

"This afternoon with Andy has been the best afternoon I've had in a long time." He closed his eyes, and a satisfied smile curved his mouth. "I wanted to get up on Sam myself and ride." His wistful smile nearly brought her to her knees. "It's a dream for me."

Sophie held her breath. There was hope here.

He opened his eyes and his gaze met hers. "Beth told me you wanted to start a program for wounded soldiers."

"That's true. One of the guys I treated when I was a medic in Baghdad was a double amputee, losing both his arms. But when I saw him riding at the stables near Walter Reed with such joy on his face, I knew what I wanted to do." There'd been a certainty in her heart she knew God had given her. "I knew Margaret had started a therapy group here. She and I talked about expanding the program to include vets, also. We wanted to approach the army to see if they would use our program for their wounded vets."

He nodded and went back to working the cloth over the bridle.

There was more she wanted to say to him, she knew, but she didn't know how to bridge that gap. "Want to help me bring in the horses for the night? Ollie's off visiting Margaret, the ranch owner who's in the hospital, and the rest of my help has left."

His head came up and she read hunger in his eyes. "Yeah, I'll help." He hung the bridle on a hook beside the other tack, placed the rag in the bin below and grabbed his cane.

As he walked to the door, Sophie saw flickers of the old Zach she knew. Her nerves danced with excitement and hope.

"Lead the way, Miss Sophie Powell."

"That's Lieutenant Powell."

"I outrank you. I was a captain."

"A smart officer listens to his subordinates who know more than he does." The instant the words left her mouth, she wanted to snatch them back.

His mouth curved into a smile. "You're right. A smart officer listens to his men."

"And you're going to listen to me?"

He nodded. "You're the expert."

"Smart move."

"Finally, after months of knocking my head against the wall." The corner of his mouth tilted up.

She knew about knocking one's head against the wall. She'd been an expert at that.

The day had cooled and the sweet smell of pine filled the air as they walked in silence to the corral behind the barn. Sophie's heart soared with hope—the hope Zach wanted to ride.

"How long have you been working here?" Zach asked.

"I mustered out nearly twenty months ago. I started riding here in high school." She didn't mention she'd wanted to feel closer to her brother, who died in a riding accident. "In college, I came whenever I was home. I knew Margaret had started working with Down's children when her first grandbaby was born with Down's." She rested her arms on the top rail of the fence. Too bad that daughter had moved to Oregon, leaving her brother and sister here who opposed using the ranch to help children with disabilities. "She and I talked about my dream of seeing if we could help the wounded vets. But just as we were going to present it to the army, she had a stroke."

Sam trotted to the fence and nudged Sophie's hand. She laughed and stroked the white blaze on her nose. "Oh, you're so spoiled."

The horse turned her head toward Zach, nudging his hand. He obliged Sam and patted her neck. "I felt like a fool out there today, eatin' dirt."

Sophie didn't respond.

"I know Beth's been after me for a while to start riding again." He continued to stroke Sam's neck. "She was right. I miss the horses. I miss the physical activities." He turned, facing her. "I'm not in good physical condition, which I've found out the hard way. But maybe I can be your first test case to show the army what equine therapy can do?"

Not sure she heard correctly, she turned toward him. "Really? You want to be my test case?"

"I do."

His words floored her.

"I also want to help around the stable, too. Maybe I could be a sidewalker for some of the kids you deal with."

"I know Andy would love that."

Zach grinned. "Yeah, you're right. He's a persistent little boy."

Here was the dream she had for the future, of helping vets overcome the physical wounds of war. Zachary McClure, ex–rodeo champ and army veteran, wanted to be her first client.

"You sure this is what you want to do?"

He nodded, a grin creasing his mouth. "I spent the afternoon wrestling with my pride, which took a beating.

I also questioned God. He and I talked, and it's what I want to do."

"All right. Let's do this."

Chapter Two

After they finished putting the horses in their stalls, they walked to the stable's office.

"When would you like to start?" Sophie asked, collapsing into her chair.

He settled in the chair beside the desk. "Work me around the other therapy sessions."

"How about tomorrow morning?"

Zach leaned back in his chair and laughed. "You're not going to let me chicken out, are you?"

Sophie felt the heat in her cheeks as she blushed. "That's what the army taught me. You get permission, you act."

"How long were you in theater?"

His question caught her by surprise. "I did a full tour there, plus my tour was extended twice. I was all over Iraq, but mostly around Baghdad and Fallujah."

He nodded. "Summer's a killer."

"You want to start tomorrow?" she pressed, refusing to be diverted.

"Fine. Tomorrow it is. What time?"

She glanced at the schedule. "8:00 a.m. We'll do it before any other appointments."

He studied her. "I'll be here."

Her tension melted away.

"You need a ride home?" Sophie asked going to the door.

"I'll just call for a taxi."

She shook her head. "No. I'll drive you home."

He opened his mouth, then closed it, stood and joined her at the door. "So you had a crush on me in college," he said, his voice full of mirth.

Sophie's hand froze on the key in the office door. Zach leaned his shoulder against the building, his body filling her vision. He arched his brow as he waited.

"Wh-what are you talking about?"

He lifted one shoulder. "The last thing Beth whispered in my ear before we emerged from the breezeway earlier today was that you had a crush on me while you were in college."

She was going to kill Beth. "I think maybe your sister tried to appeal to your masculine ego. If you knew that I found you attractive, you might be more willing to—"

"You think I'm handsome?"

He wanted to provoke her. She pulled the key from the door. "I'm going to plead the Fifth."

His satisfied grin told her that he understood she hadn't answered the question. He fell into step beside her.

One car stood in the parking lot. Hers. As they approached it, a truck pulled up in front of them.

Zach laughed. "My sister called in the cavalry."

"She called the army?" Sophie asked, totally confused.

"No. She called my brother, Ethan."

Ethan was Zach's older brother. When they were in college, Beth told her about the adventures of her two older brothers. They had tolerated a younger sister until she turned thirteen and started attracting male attention. Much to Beth's chagrin, her brothers decided to be her guardians and ran off more boys than Beth could count. It wasn't until she was at the University of New Mexico campus in Albuquerque that she had her first serious boyfriend.

The truck door opened and Ethan got out and came around the front of the truck. "Hey, bro, Beth sent me to pick you up. She said you were kinda prickly." Ethan grinned, wagging his brows. Sophie choked on a cough.

"So she chickened out, did she?" Zach remarked.

Ethan laughed. "No one said Bethie was stupid. A royal pain, yes, but she knows how to save her own skin."

A smile spread across Zach's face and he shook his head. "I assume you agree with her that I needed to get off my backside and start living again."

Ethan crossed his arms and leaned back against the front fender. "Couldn't have said it better myself."

The strong family resemblance between the brothers made one look twice. Ethan and Zach could've been twins. Zach was an inch or so shorter than his brother, and his eyes were blue while Ethan's were gray. But both men were handsome, with dark hair, strong cheeks and full mouths. Ethan grinned easily. Zach didn't.

Apparently, Beth wasn't the only McClure sibling who wanted to help Zach. Interesting.

"Well, I'm glad that you feel that way. I'm going to have my first session tomorrow morning at eight."

Ethan jerked up straight. "Really?"

"That's right, and I'll need someone to help in the session, won't I?" Zach directed the last question at Sophie.

"Huh, yes." Zach's question surprised her, but if he wanted his brother to be the sidewalker, she'd welcome the help. "Since both of you are horse people, I think that Ethan should do fine. I'll have another sidewalker here, but I'd love to have Ethan work with us."

Without any hesitation, Ethan answered, "I'll do whatever you need me to do."

"Then it's set."

"I'll see you all tomorrow."

It took a few moments for Zach to maneuver himself into the passenger side of the truck. He jerked the door closed, rolled the window down and rested his arm on it. "I'll see you tomorrow, Sophie."

"Be prepared to work, Zach."

"I'll be ready."

Alleluia, there was hope. "See you tomorrow."

She stood watching the truck disappear down the road. *Lord, I see the open door and I'll walk through it, but could it have been with someone else? Someone else who hadn't captured my heart and left it in jail.*

"Have I been that much of a pain?" Zach asked his brother.

"Well, let me put it this way. I've been tempted to punch you. My prayer life has certainly increased, little brother."

Zach knew his brother was at the end of his rope. He got called "little brother" only when he was in major trouble.

"I've been that much of a jerk?"

Ethan glanced at him. "Yeah."

This afternoon had torn away the apathy Zach had wrapped himself in. When he woke in Walter Reed Army Hospital and looked at what was left of his leg, he'd wanted to shout and throw things. He'd reached for the bedpan, but the guy in the next bed stopped him.

"Go ahead and throw it. It won't change anything."

When Zach looked over at the guy, he was minus both of his legs and his left hand and forearm.

After that warning from Bill Jensen, the two men became fast friends. Bill's wife and family had adopted him, and when Zach's mom came to D.C., she considered Bill another son.

There had been so many times after a therapy session when he'd question God about why this happened. Why him? What had he done? The night he read in the Book of Luke about Jesus's death on the cross, he realized that there was nothing He did to deserve such an awful death. What was his loss compared to Jesus's?

Zach had slowly worked through most of his anger. Bill had gone back to his job, teaching in a community college in Wichita Falls, Texas. But what was Zach going to do? Before, he'd planned on following the rodeo circuit, trying to earn a championship belt buckle.

"Today, being with the horses gave me hope. I want to ride again."

"About time."

"So you're ready to come with me each time I ride?" Zach asked.

"I am, and I'll spring for breakfast."

"I really must've been a pain if you're willing to pay for breakfast."

"And then some."

* * *

Sophie walked back to the guest cabin. She moved there after Margaret had her stroke. Margaret's son, Austin, had asked her to stay on the property while his mother recuperated. He wanted Sophie to take over the day-to-day running of the ranch since none of Margaret's kids wanted to divide their time between their jobs and their mother's ranch.

Austin complained about having to continue with the equine-therapy sessions, but several of the parents had bought package sessions for their children, and Austin didn't want to refund the money. The ranch foreman, Ollie Morton, had planned to retire at the end of the month but he agreed to stay until Margaret could hire a replacement.

Sophie let herself into the cabin. No welcoming aromas from a cooked dinner filled the air. The hum of the refrigerator cut off, leaving the house silent. Sophie loved being with the horses, but she needed a maid. Or someone to take care of the mundane things like fixing dinner and washing her clothes. In the army, she had three square meals a day and clean clothes.

She pulled a frozen dinner out of the freezer compartment and popped it into the microwave. What had the women a hundred years ago done after a long day of working on the farm? The phone rang the same instant the microwave dinged. She picked up the wall phone. "Hello."

"You're a miracle worker, Sophie," Beth gushed.

"I wish."

"You don't know how hard I had to argue with Zach this morning. I had almost given up when I told him that his heart wanted to be back on a horse. And then I prayed under my breath." She laughed. "I'm surprised I didn't have a wreck on the way to the stable. Every time I stopped at a light, I closed my eyes and prayed."

"Well, your prayers were answered."

"Oh, Sophie, I thought it was all over when Zach tripped. I wanted to die."

"I'm glad you were strong, Beth. He had to face the truth that he needs to rebuild his strength."

"You're right. I tell you the first time I saw him without his foot and on crutches, I wanted to break down and cry."

"He needs you to treat him as you always have—like a pain-in-the-neck big brother. He's the same man."

Beth remained quiet.

"He needs that consistency. He needs to know that the essence of the man Zach was is still there, and his family still sees the old Zach."

Sophie thought she'd gone too far, but she heard Beth sigh. "You're right. And he's coming tomorrow to ride."

Sophie heard the tears clogging Beth's throat.

"This afternoon when I walked into the tack room and saw him, I didn't know what to think. I know some demons were defeated in that room today."

"Mom and Dad are excited and want to come and help."

News in the McClure family traveled fast. She wished it were the same in her family. Her mother hadn't talked to her grandmother in over fifteen years, and they both lived in the same little town of twenty-four hundred people. "Let's give him a few times before he has an audience, okay? I don't know how things are going to go tomorrow, and I think if Zach doesn't have an audience, it will be easier."

"I hadn't thought about it. I'll call them."

"I do have a bone to pick with you, friend."

"Oh?"

"Why did you tell Zach I had a crush on him in college?" When he'd thrown that out at her, Sophie didn't know how to answer. Sure she'd been attracted to the handsome cowboy. His loose-hipped walk and cocky grin appealed to anyone with two X chromosomes. And she fell into that category.

"Hmm, I thought it would ease him into the situation. It certainly gave him something to think about besides his discomfort."

It had done that. "I think we have Andy to thank for our success. And your prayers."

"Will you let me know how the session goes tomorrow?" Beth asked.

"You're not coming with Zach?"

"No. I'll let Ethan do it instead of me. He'll be more help than I could be."

"Okay. I'll give you a call."

After hanging up, Sophie took her dinner out of the microwave. Settling at the kitchen table, she pulled her Bible toward her and opened it up to the book of Psalms. The twenty-third Psalm was her favorite. *The Lord is my shepherd, I shall not want.*

In high school, her best friend's family were shepherds. She'd had some wonderful insight as to how the author of the Psalm felt. Her friend explained how they were responsible to move the sheep from one pasture to the next where there was abundant grass. The sheep didn't move until the shepherd led them to another place.

"Okay, Lord, You've led me here. Help tomorrow to meet Zach's needs."

* * *

At seven the next morning Sophie walked out to the stable, heading for the office.

"Want some coffee?" she called out to Ollie who was inspecting all the horses' tack.

"Sure. Bring it black, none of that fancy stuff," Ollie answered.

"Fancy stuff?"

"Cream and sugar."

"And do you eat your steak still mooing?" she retorted.

"Is there any other way?"

Sophie grinned. She walked into the office and poured two mugs of coffee. Ollie always started a pot of coffee when he arrived at the ranch. She opened the mini-fridge, pulled out her favorite French vanilla creamer and poured it in her mug. When she carried the mugs outside and gave Ollie his coffee, he glanced at the brown coffee in her mug and shook his head.

"Sissy."

She shrugged her shoulder. Looking out over the rings, and hearing the morning sounds, Sophie knew this was where she belonged.

"You're going to miss this when you retire, Ollie." She took a sip of her coffee.

"Nope. I'm going to sleep in until seven and get up and spend hours reading the newspaper."

"Fibber."

He simply grinned.

"Will you help me this morning with the rider who's coming?"

"Sure. Who's comin'?"

"Zach McClure."

"Ah, the guy with the fake foot."

She winced. Ollie didn't pull any punches, but there was not a mean bone in his body. "He was a wonderful rider. Watching him ride…" She could still remember how awed she'd been watching him practice calf roping. "It's like he was born on a horse." She heard the wistfulness in her voice.

Ollie's mug stopped inches from his mouth.

Sophie realized her feelings colored her comments. "Zach's sister was my roommate in college," she hurried to explain. "I went home with her several times. She was with him yesterday."

Ollie took a swallow of his coffee. "I saw him when he was a teenager. He had a talent."

"Really?"

"Best I'd seen up 'til that time."

Then Ollie would understand. "He lost his foot when a roadside bomb caught his patrol in Baghdad." She looked down into her coffee. "I think that talent awoke yesterday. He's willing to work to get stronger."

Ollie nodded. "My son was in the First Gulf War. He needed help when he came home. I'll do it."

Those were the most words that Ollie had spoken since she knew him. And she never knew he had a son. Maybe Zach's rehab would touch more than Zach himself.

She heard a car pull into the parking lot. It was seven-thirty.

"Looks like your client is here," he murmured, looking down at his watch. "And I think he's eager."

She prayed Ollie was right.

Chapter Three

Ethan pulled the key out of the ignition. "You ready to do this?"

Zach had tossed and turned all night and finally gave up trying to sleep at five this morning. He spent the time praying and reading his Bible. For the first time in a long time he felt like himself. "I am."

They got out of the truck and walked toward the office. Some of the horses were in a corral on the other side of the stable.

"There's some good-looking horse flesh out there," Ethan commented.

From what Zach saw he had to agree with his brother. "I'll have to ask where they get their stock."

They emerged from the tunnel and saw Sophie and Ollie resting up against the hitching rail. The sun kissed Sophie's skin and her brown hair danced with red tones in the sunlight. The braided tresses nearly came to her waist. She'd been beautiful at eighteen, but now there was a maturity about this woman. That coltish girl had become a stunning woman.

"Good morning," Ethan called out, touching the brim of his cowboy hat.

"Good to see you this morning," Sophie replied, pushing off the rail. She introduced Ollie.

"We've met," Zach said, meeting Ollie's gaze.

Sophie looked from Zach to Ollie. Apparently the old guy hadn't told Sophie of their little chat. His opinion of the ranch foreman went up.

"You ready?"

"I am. And Ethan's up for the session."

"He couldn't keep me away," Ethan added.

Zach didn't know whether to be encouraged by his big brother's eagerness or insulted.

"Let me go get Prince Charming, and we'll start." Sophie put her mug on the apple barrel and turned to Ollie. "You want to go get the tack?"

Ethan straightened up, then glanced at his brother. He grinned. "Prince Charming?"

Ollie nodded. "He's the right size for a man of Zach's stature—sixteen hands." He nodded at Sophie. "She calls him Prince Charming." He shook his head. "What kind of name…" He headed for the tack room.

A whirlwind of feeling churned in Zach's stomach. He lifted his hat and wiped the sweat off his forehead. He wanted to ride so much he could taste it. He watched as Sophie pulled a halter out of one of the stalls, grabbed a lead rope and carrot from the pail on a bench in front of the stalls and walked to the corral beside the stable.

At the gate, she called out. A handsome black horse with a star on his nose and his left hind foot with a "white stocking" trotted up to her. She crooned to the magnificent gelding and offered the carrot.

The man in Zach reacted to her tender treatment of

the horse. He glanced at his brother and saw Ethan smiling at him.

As Prince Charming ate the carrot, Sophie rubbed his nose. When he finished the carrot, he nudged her hand. "No, I don't have another one. It's time to work, big boy."

The horse nodded and allowed Sophie to put the halter over his head and attach the lead rope. She opened the gate and led him to where Zach stood.

Ollie quickly put the saddle blanket and pad on Prince Charming's back. He handed Ethan one of the stirrups to attach to the pad.

"No saddle?" Ethan asked.

She shook her head. "I've been in constant contact with the folks running the rehab program outside of D.C. For the first few times, we want to have Zach ride without the saddle. It will exercise his muscles."

Doubt colored Zach's eyes. "I could've jumped up on his back in my rodeo days, but now—"

"That's why you should try the mounting block. You're going to be asking your body to do a lot of work today, Zach, which it hasn't done in a while. You've got to focus on the final goal."

His pride fought with his common sense. *Lord, this is hard to swallow.*

His gaze touched each person's face. He saw only support, but in Sophie's eyes, he saw something else. A promise. He reached out and stroked the horse's nose. "You going to be nice to a rusty cowpoke?"

Prince Charming nudged his hand. Zach patted the horse's neck. "I'll take that as a yes."

Taking a deep breath, Zach walked up the steps of the mounting block. Ollie and Ethan took their positions on either side of the horse. Zach handed his cane to Ethan, put his foot into the left-side stirrup, then threw his right leg over the horse's back. He tried a couple of times to get his prosthesis into the stirrup attached to the saddle blanket. Ollie helped. He pushed back his cowboy hat and a spark of admiration lit his eyes.

Using the mounting block wasn't as big a deal as Zach had thought it might be. He looked down into Sophie's face. She smiled. "You look good."

He felt good. The world lay at his feet. "Let's move."

"You want a helmet, Zach?" she asked. "It's just a precaution."

He was willing to go just so far. "I'm okay."

She didn't try to argue but led Prince Charming into the arena. She walked around the perimeter of the ring.

"Things look much better up here," Zach commented.

"Amen, brother," Ethan quietly said. A hint of moisture gathered in his eyes.

They walked around the arena for close to thirty minutes. Zach realized the muscles of his stomach and thighs were protesting.

"How are you feeling?" Sophie asked, looking over her shoulder.

He didn't want to admit weakness. "I'm okay."

She accepted his word and they worked for another ten minutes before she called a halt to the session. She led the horse toward the mounting block.

"I won't need that," Zach told her.

"Zach," Sophie said, touching his leg, "I don't recommend that."

"I can dismount by myself." *Pride cometh before a fall.* The verse ran through his head.

She looked to Ethan for help.

"Uh, maybe she's right, Zach."

There was no saddle horn for him to grab on to to keep his balance and he felt a cramp in his injured right leg. There were a lot of scars up and down that leg.

"Okay." The word tasted bitter in his mouth.

She walked the horse to the mounting block. Zach pushed up on his left leg and swung his right leg over the horse's rump. When his prosthesis hit the wood, it folded on him. He tumbled back off the horse. Ethan stepped up and caught him. His left foot remained in the stirrup. Prince Charming didn't dance or spook. He stood calmly. Ollie sprinted around the horse and disengaged Zach's foot.

Ethan pulled Zach backward so his feet could touch the ground. His right leg didn't hold. Ethan's arms clamped around Zach's chest, holding him upright. Zach's hat fell to the ground.

Zach struggled to make his right leg work. Quietly, Sophie handed him his cane. He grabbed the lifeline and used the cane for balance. After struggling for a moment, he found his balance. Ethan picked up Zach's hat.

"We probably worked too long," Sophie said.

Zach wanted to rail that Andy had more endurance than he did. He nodded. "Ethan, you want to drive me home?"

Sophie dropped the horse's leads. "Zach—"

He shook his head and started to walk away.

Prince Charming turned his head and caught Zach's attention. The horse bobbed his head.

"He's expecting a carrot," Ollie offered. He nodded toward a pail on the bench. Zach took two steps and looked inside. Carrots. He pulled one out and turned toward the horse. Prince Charming readily accepted the treat.

Sophie stood on the other side of Prince Charming,

gently rubbing his neck, her eyes dark with worry. He didn't—couldn't—acknowledge her.

With a final pat on Prince Charming's shoulder, Zach turned and walked toward the parking lot.

What made him think that he could be the man he used to be?

Sophie buried her face in Prince Charming's neck, taking comfort from the strength and smell of the horse.

"Give him a few minutes."

Her head jerked up and she found Ethan standing beside her. "We never scheduled another lesson," she said.

"I'll talk to him." Sadness and concern creased Ethan's face. "Seeing him on a horse was great. I'll have him call you to set up another appointment."

She nodded and watched as Ethan walked toward the parking lot.

"Lord, touch his heart," she whispered.

"Don't you worry, Miss Sophie. I saw a spark in that young man's eyes. Once he wrestles his pride down, you'll see him again."

She glanced over Prince Charming's neck to Ollie. "I pray you're right."

Over the next week, Sophie held on to Ollie's words. She heard nothing from Zach. She called Beth, asking about Zach.

"He's not taking my calls," Beth informed her. "If I was in town, I'd drive out to his apartment and face him down again." Beth did a lot of traveling for her job with a big department store headquartered in Santa Fe. "I told Ethan to talk to him, but I haven't heard back from him."

Sophie couldn't wait any longer. Andy's next session

was scheduled for tomorrow. "Give me your brother's address."

Beth gave her the street number of the new and trendy condominium and town house.

Sophie helped Ollie finish putting out feed for all the horses. She stopped by Prince Charming's stall.

"Hello, handsome."

The big horse stuck his head out of the top half of the door. He nudged her hand.

"You are so spoiled," she said, rubbing his nose. "I'm going to try to get Zach. You were great with him. Now he needs to understand that he needs you."

Prince Charming nodded.

"You like him? He's a real cowboy. Well, I like him, too. I'll see what I can do to bring him back."

Driving to Zach's place, she prayed for wisdom and the right words to touch the stubborn man.

The new complex of town houses stood on the eastern edge of the city, built at the foot of one of the mountains surrounding the city. She found the number of his town house and parked. She whispered the opening lines of the twenty-third Psalm as she exited her car and walked up to the door and knocked.

Nothing.

She knocked again. "Zach, it's Sophie."

After several more seconds, the door opened. He was unshaved, and his closed expression didn't give her any hope.

"I was hoping to talk to you."

He studied her. "Why?"

Well, at least he didn't shut the door in her face. "I wanted to talk about your next lesson."

He shrugged his shoulders and walked back into the living room.

She followed him, closing the door gently behind her.

"How have you been doing?"

He shrugged again, settling into a leather recliner in front of a sixty-inch plasma TV. A baseball game flickered on the screen.

She walked to the sofa. "I think we pushed your first time too far. We should've stopped earlier."

He didn't respond.

"Zach, talk to me."

He turned to her and nailed her with his blazing gaze. "What do you want me to say? Yeah, I didn't tell you the truth when you asked if I was tired. I'm less of a man now than I was when I blew you off when Beth came home during college."

It was a reaction, but not the one she hoped for. "What I see is a man who's trying to come back. What I see is a man who helped a young boy overcome his fear and enjoy his ride on a horse."

He turned away from her, staring down at the head of his cane.

"Zach, the man I met in college was full of himself and knew his strengths. One of those strengths was a faith in God and a determination to do the right thing." She pulled a pamphlet out of her purse and put it on the coffee table. "This is from NARHA."

He gave her a puzzled frown.

"North American Riding for the Handicapped Association. It talks about equine therapy and its benefits. What you expected from your body was unreasonable."

His head came up and he looked at the pamphlet.

"When I fought for the guys who were wounded on

the battlefield, I wanted to save them all. The ones who survived were blessings. You have a duty to those who didn't make it. You lost a foot, but I don't think you lost your soul. The Zach McClure I knew is still inside you. You just have a challenge you've never faced before."

She stood. "Andy's session is tomorrow morning at ten. He's told all his friends about you, and I've had two more mothers of Down's children call me, wanting to start with equine therapy." She started for the door. Pausing with her hand on the knob, she turned to him. "I will never leave a fallen comrade." With those final words she walked out the door.

I will never leave a fallen comrade. The words of the U.S. Military's Honor Ethos echoed in Zach's brain. How many times had he gone back to get a fellow wounded soldier? With the guys who were gravely wounded, their survival depended on their individual will to live.

He'd made it. The roadside bomb that wounded him had killed two members of his team. He didn't remember much after the bomb, except his good buddy calling for him to hold on and telling him that they'd get him help.

They kept him sedated until he woke up in Walter Reed Army Hospital.

He picked up his Bible and turned to Exodus. The story that always amazed him was Joshua's. This was a man who led Israel after Moses's death in their fight to conquer the Promised Land.

Zach turned over to the book of Joshua and read the first three chapters, where Joshua faced his first major obstacle—the Jordan River. Not just a normal river but a river ten times its usual size. That crossing was a major miracle.

He faced his own Jordan River.

God gave Joshua a plan, and if Zach didn't miss his guess, God just gave him a plan. And it started with showing up to help Andy.

Chapter Four

Zach took a deep breath and glanced at his brother, who sat behind the steering wheel of his truck. Zach chafed at having to be driven, but he didn't want his truck fitted with hand controls. He wanted to be able to build up the strength in his leg to be able to drive his own truck.

"You sure you don't want me to stay?" Ethan asked.

Ethan had quickly covered up his surprise this morning when Zach called, asking for a ride.

"I'm sure."

Ethan studied him. "I'll stop by after I finish the business at the bank."

Zach put on his straw hat. It was already warm beyond normal for an early spring morning. "I'm okay, Ethan." He clamped his hand on his brother's shoulder. "Thanks."

Ethan nodded.

Zach opened the truck door and carefully rested his feet on the ground. He used his cane for balance. Hopefully, he could permanently retire it in a few weeks with hard work and exercise.

He walked down the breezeway to the open rings. The first thing Zach saw was Andy. The boy sat on a bench by the helmets. He stared at the ground. Glancing up, he spotted Zach.

"You came," Andy yelled, launching himself off the bench.

Zach braced himself for Andy's hug. The boy stopped and looked up at Zach. He reached out and grasped the boy's hand. Andy snuggled close to Zach's side.

"I see your sidewalker is here."

Zach's head snapped up. Sophie stood before him, her blue eyes glistened with moisture, and he read approval and something else there. But before he could analyze it, Andy raced toward Sam.

"Hi, Sam." Andy stroked the horse's shoulder.

Sam turned her head toward the boy.

Pride for Andy's actions filled Zach. The boy overcame his fear. It was something Zach needed to do.

"Get your helmet, and I'll take Sam to the mounting ramp," Sophie instructed.

Andy dashed off.

A smile curved Sophie's mouth. "I'm glad you're here. Andy was disappointed when he didn't see you."

"What did you tell him?" He waited, curious for the answer.

"I told him that Sam was glad he was here."

"Is that all?" He moved toward her and lightly ran his hand over Sam's withers.

She held his gaze. "When he asked about you, I told him that things would be okay. I prayed. I know Andy is happy you're here and…"

Zach understood the unspoken part of her sentence. She was glad he was here, too.

"I got my helmet," Andy yelled, waving it above his head.

"We're coming," Sophie replied.

Suddenly Zach knew that his "Jordan" could be divided.

Andy cheerfully waved one last time at Zach as his mother pulled him down the walkway. "I had fun. I'll see you next time."

Another child called out Sophie's name as she rounded the corner. "Miss Sophie. I'm here." The little girl's braids bounced as she waved.

"Go put your things in the office." Each rider had a small cubbyhole on the inside wall of the office for their things. "I need to take Sam back to his stall." Sophie lightly patted the horse's withers.

Zach grasped Sam's leads. "I'll take care of Sam."

She hesitated. "You sure? I didn't expect you to work."

"I'm sure. I've been doing this kind of thing since I could walk." He paused. "I think before I could walk. I remember my mother talked about taking me out to the barn and something about a pen." That sounded bad to his ears.

She laughed.

"Take care of your other clients. I'll take care of Sam."

Her eyes danced with mirth and the corner of her mouth kicked up. "You've got a deal."

Satisfaction raced through him. As he watched Sophie walk toward her next client, Zach's heart lightened. He was where he belonged. Sophie somehow touched his heart in a way he didn't understand.

Sam nudged his arm.

"What? You want a carrot, or are you thinkin' the same thing I am?" Zach rubbed Sam's nose. The horse lipped his hand.

"A carrot is what you want?" Zach walked to the barrel where the treats were kept and pulled out a carrot. Sam took the offered treat. Zach glanced at his cane propped in the corner behind the mounting steps and decided he felt strong enough to leave it there.

Over the next hour, Zach plunged into the wonderful pattern of caring for a horse. After removing Sam's tack, he walked the horse down to the shower stall and hosed him off. Even this early in the spring, the day would be a scorcher and Sam deserved a cooling shower.

Sam also ate up the attention. She was a flirt.

"I see you found the shower," Ollie said, walking by.

"Sam worked hard and I thought she'd like a little refreshing."

Ollie pushed the straw hat back on his forehead. "I'm glad to see you here."

Ollie's words surprised him. "I couldn't disappoint Andy."

"You need a sidewalker, count me in."

Ollie's offer touched Zach.

"Thanks."

"No thanks necessary. It's my privilege." He nodded and walked down the row of stalls.

Shock and amazement held Zach motionless. Ollie obviously was a man of few words, but each one held power. Ollie believed in him, which humbled Zach.

Untying Sam's lead, he said, "C'mon, girl, let's go."

Sophie grabbed an apple out of the mini-fridge and walked out of the ranch office. There'd been no time to eat and this would be her lunch. Things had happened so quickly this morning that it reminded her of the mornings in the field hospital in Iraq when she went on autopilot.

Finally, things had settled down and no clients were scheduled for the next hour and she could think. She'd panicked when Andy and his mother had shown up and there was no Zach. Her heart had soared when Zach walked out of the breezeway.

Where was he now? She moved down the row of stalls and found him outside, looking at the horses in the corral.

"I was worried that you might have disappeared."

He turned to her and flashed a wide smile. "No, I haven't left."

She noted a hint of satisfaction in his voice. "You were great with Andy."

He took off his hat and ran his fingers through his hair. "I couldn't have disappointed him, but I'll admit I was nervous when I got here today."

He didn't know how much prayer went into today. "It did go well. Andy didn't tire as easily as he did last time. You didn't, either."

"You're right. My leg held up nicely. Of course I took my time with Sam. She didn't mind if I sat down and caught my breath." He shook his head. "It was a one-sided talk, but Sam didn't mind."

"So, you ready to ride a little today?"

He glanced around. "You've got time today?"

"We have an hour, and I have Ollie and another volunteer to be sidewalkers if you're willing."

He nodded. "Let's do it."

"If you want to get Prince Charming, I'll get his tack and meet you at the mounting steps."

Zach walked to Prince Charming's stall while Sophie grabbed the tack and blanket and walked to the mounting steps.

Ollie and Ethan stood with Zach. Zach held Prince Charming by his halter.

"I see we have a new sidewalker," Sophie greeted them as she walked to the group.

Ollie took the tack, and Sophie threw the blanket over Prince Charming's back. Quickly they got the horse ready for the ride. This time when Zach mounted the horse, things went smoothly.

Sophie led Prince Charming into the ring. She stopped and glanced over her shoulder at Zach. "When you're ready, tell Prince Charming."

He nodded. She could see the excitement in Zach's face.

Zach patted Prince Charming's shoulder. "Let's go."

Prince Charming started forward.

After their first time around the ring, Zach asked, "Why'd you name him Prince Charming?"

Ollie snorted.

"What's that mean?" Ethan asked.

"'Cause this guy was an unruly beast when we first got him."

"So how'd he get the name Prince Charming?" Zach asked.

Sophie shrugged, but didn't turn around. "Because he reminded me of the horse in the storybook I read as a girl. I thought there was a wonderful horse under all that bad behavior. I was right. I worked with him and earned his trust. Prince Charming is only used with adult patients." She glanced over at Ethan. "We all have our bad moments. The place where Margaret got Prince Charming was a ranch in southern Colorado. Something happened. I think the owner was some city dude and didn't know much about horses."

They worked for close to twenty minutes, making rounds of the corral.

"Let me know when you're tired."

"I think a couple more times around, then we can call a halt to it."

Both Ollie and Ethan nodded in approval.

With a final round of the corral, Sophie guided Prince Charming to the mounting stairs. She held her breath as Zach swung his prosthesis over Prince Charming's back. His artificial foot rested on the platform.

She held her breath and Ethan tensed, ready to dart forward and help his brother.

Zach continued to hold on to the saddle blanket and slipped his good leg out of the stirrup. He paused for a moment, getting his balance. Slowly he released the saddle blanket and stood.

Tears welled in Sophie's eyes. Zach took a step back, turned and smiled at her.

"I listened to my body this time."

"That's good." She forced the words around the lump in her throat.

He held on to the railing as he walked down the stairs. Prince Charming nodded his head, as if agreeing with Sophie.

"I think this guy needs a carrot."

Sophie grabbed a carrot and gave it to Zach. Prince Charming took the offered treat.

Zach's stomach rumbled. Prince Charming nudged Zach with his nose.

"I guess I'm hungry, too."

Ollie took the leads from Sophie. "I'll take care of Prince Charming while you folks get something to eat."

"If you got time, I'll take us to the burger stand down the road," Ethan said.

Sophie glanced at her watch. "Can you get me back in forty minutes?"

"I can."

When Sophie hesitated, Zach added, "Trust me when I say if Ethan said it, we can do it."

Zach's words sounded as if they came from experience. She should turn them down, but the success of the morning needed to be celebrated.

"Let's go."

They squeezed Sophie between Zach and Ethan. Zach rested his cane between his legs. The morning had gone better than anything he could've hoped for. Zach wanted to grin, feeling young and more like himself than he had in forever. *Thank You, Lord,* he thought.

"So how'd my little brother do this morning?" Ethan asked.

Sophie turned to Zach. "He did great. He made Andy's day."

The truck rattled down the dirt road. When the front passenger wheel hit a hole, Sophie was thrown against Zach. Before they could do anything, she bounced away.

Zach's mind registered that although Sophie worked hard, she was still a feminine woman.

And he a man.

He felt the pull of attraction to her. She stole a glance at him. Her cheeks flushed pink.

Would she be attracted to him as a man? He knew she wanted to help him and he volunteered to be her test case for the army, but did it go beyond that?

The balance of the eight-minute trip passed in silence.

Zach didn't see the mountains in the distance or the small
stream that ran alongside the road. Trees grew on the
other side of the bank, but didn't stop the glare of the
sun off the river. As the road curved around the hill, a
building came into view. Freddie's Burgers and Fries was
painted on the sign beside the restaurant. Beyond the restaurant was a gas station and mini-mart.

Ethan pulled the truck into the parking lot of the restaurant. They climbed out of the truck, and walked inside and placed their orders. The crowd had begun to thin
and they found a table in the corner of the dining room.

"I guess the food in here's good." Ethan looked around
at the cowboys and high school students.

A teenage boy brought the tray of burgers and onion
rings to the table.

Both Zach and Ethan reached for the onion rings. The
taste of batter and onion exploded on Zach's tongue. "Try
the onion rings," he encouraged Sophie.

"I think I'm in love," Ethan said after he swallowed
his bite.

She laughed at the brothers. "Beth said you guys were
a challenge."

"What?" Ethan grabbed another onion ring.

"I heard how you two bullied every boy that came
near Beth." She pulled an onion ring from the plastic
basket and took a bite.

Zach shook his head. "Beth had terrible taste in boy-
friends." He shrugged. "We couldn't leave her defense-
less."

Sophie snagged another onion ring. "That's not exactly how Beth tells it."

Both men laughed.

"Oh, I don't doubt that," Ethan replied. "She probably described us as Attila the Hun and his horde."

"That's not exactly how she described it."

As they ate their hamburgers, stories from Beth's dating flowed around the table. The more they talked, Zach noticed a longing that entered Sophie's eyes. More than once, she covered up by laughing at something he or Ethan said.

At the end of the meal, one onion ring remained in the basket. "Why don't you have that last onion ring, Sophie?"

She raised her hands. "They're good, but I'm full. Besides, I don't want any of the horses to pass out from my breath."

They piled back into the truck and drove back to the ranch.

"How are you feeling now, Zach?" Sophie asked.

His energy level seemed to be coming back, especially after the meal. "I'm good."

She nodded her approval.

The morning had gone smoothly. What was even better was that Sophie hadn't made a big deal out of his showing up. She acted as if she expected him to be there and he appreciated her attitude. "When do you think we can do another session?" he asked.

"I'd give your body a day's rest. We could try Friday." Her smile took some of the sting out of the words. "If you push too hard now, before your body's ready, we'll lose ground."

He didn't like the reality of it, but he knew Sophie was right. It had taken a couple of days for him to recover from his first session where he overdid things. "Okay."

They agreed to a Friday-morning ride before everyone else's appointment.

"I think Beth would like to help," Ethan informed them.

Zach shrugged.

The ranch parking lot came into view. Although he wanted to stay the afternoon, he knew that wisdom demanded he go home.

Ethan drove his truck to the entrance.

Zach opened the door and got out of the truck. Sophie followed.

She turned to him and he could see she was ready to argue.

"I'll see you O-eight-hundred on Friday."

The stiffness went out of her spine. He knew his words shocked her.

"I want to ride again, Sophie, but I know common sense when I hear it."

"You're an unusual man, Zach McClure."

"Why do you say that?" he asked.

"Because you're letting common sense rule over ego."

"No. I'm just a man who finally has a goal—to ride again. I don't need Prince Charming to scold me like Balaam's donkey scolded him."

She frowned.

"You remember that story in the Old Testament—Numbers, I believe, where the Balaam was asked to curse the children of Israel and his donkey avoided the avenging angel standing in the road?"

She studied him. "I do, but you wouldn't have beaten Prince Charming."

"True, but he would've sensed my weakness."

"Good thinking." She laughed and disappeared around the corner of the stables.

Zach slipped back into the truck.

"What were you two whispering about?" Ethan asked as they drove off.

"Sophie thinks I've got more sense than a donkey."

Ethan frowned. "What does that mean?"

Zach laughed.

Sophie walked into the ranch office and checked the afternoon schedule. The answering machine blinked. She hit the button to listen to the messages. Two of the messages were from new clients wanting information about riding lessons for their children.

The last message was from Beth who wanted to talk. Sophie called.

"Did he show up?" Beth asked breathlessly. "I called his house, but he didn't answer his phone. And he doesn't own a cell phone anymore. He threw it away when he moved to that apartment."

"He did? Why?"

"Because he didn't want to have to talk to us, and if he didn't have the cell phone, he couldn't answer our questions when he was out. He said it made him feel like a dog with a microchip."

"Everything's good, Beth. He showed up and helped with Andy." She explained how Zach had worked this morning, then rode again. "He stopped when he was tired."

"My prayers have been answered."

"Well, you need to keep praying. It's the first step and it's going to be a long road."

"It's a start, Sophie. I—" A quiet sob stopped her.

"He's coming on Friday morning for another lesson."

"Oh, Sophie, I'm out of town. I'm scheduled to go to New York on a buying trip for the store."

"Ollie will be here to help."

"Can I call Mom and Dad and tell them the good news? They are dying to know what's happening."

"Sure. Of course, if Ethan talked, it will be old news."

"Ethan's so tight-lipped, he wouldn't tell me if the house burned down. I'll call." She laughed. "You know, Sophie, I think you can handle Zach in a way none of the rest of us can."

"I'm not family. It's easier for a stranger to tell him the truth than his family. He knows I'm not trying to spare his feelings."

"Maybe. But I think it's more than that. Zach looks at you—"

"What are you talking about?"

"There's something more. I don't know how to describe it. I'll tell you this, I haven't seen that look in his eyes with any other girl."

Obviously her friend was giddy with excitement and didn't know what she was talking about. Sophie shook it off.

"I'll call you when I get back into town," Beth said.

The dial tone sounded in Sophie's ear. She pulled the handset away from her ear and stared at it.

Beth had hung up on her. Hung up.

Sophie put the phone back. What on earth was Beth trying to imply? Zach looked at her in a different way. And that "way" was boredom. Indifference. She was his sister's bothersome roommate.

"Miss Sophie, we're here," Penny Littledeer called out.

"I'm coming," Sophie called back as she raced out of the office, Beth's words ringing in her ears.

Chapter Five

Ethan's cell rang. He pulled it out of his shirt pocket and offered it to Zach. "Answer it. I'm driving."

Zach looked at the ID. Beth.

"I think you should talk to Beth." Zach tried to hand the phone back.

"No, no. You answer it."

Zach could let it go to voice mail, but it would only postpone the inquisition.

"Hello."

"Zach? Are you with Ethan?"

"I am. He's driving me home." He waited for his sister's reply. "I'll put you on speaker." He hit the button to allow Ethan to hear, too.

"Aren't you going to tell me about this morning?"

"What do you want to know?" Zach wouldn't make this easy for her.

"Stop stalling. How was your ride? Are you okay?"

He laughed and told her how the morning went.

"He did great," Ethan added.

The joy in Beth's voice told him of her delight and relief. Glancing at Ethan, he saw his brother's involvement in the conversation. It hit him then that both of his siblings had suffered with him as he struggled to find himself again. The realization of how selfish he'd been hit him hard. "My next lesson is Friday morning."

"I won't be there. I'll be in New York."

"Don't worry about it. Someone has to work." After they said their goodbyes, he hung up and handed the phone to Ethan.

Putting the phone back in his shirt pocket, Ethan laughed. "I'm amazed how our sis knows everything the instant it happens."

"It is one of the mysteries of the universe." It had been that way ever since Beth had turned thirteen. He and Ethan might have turned into guard dogs, but Beth returned the favor by monitoring their movements as teenage boys.

"Do you remember when Beth dragged Sophie home?" Ethan asked as he negotiated the truck onto the interstate.

Zach remembered. He'd come in from checking fences, wet and grumpy, and found his sister and her roommate in the kitchen giggling. Beth threw her arms around him, kissed him, then introduced Sophie. She stood by the refrigerator and looked like she'd been touched by the angels with the sun streaming through the windows causing red highlights to dance in her hair.

"Yeah, I remember that weekend. My horse stepped into a gopher hole and I had to walk miles to the barn in my new boots."

"And if I remember, you were wet."

"That was because Clancey was spooked by the iso- lated thunderstorm that broke over our head." A more sure-footed horse Zach had never had, so that accident had rattled him. There hadn't been another place to seek shelter on that stretch of desert where it rained.

"You had some bad luck that weekend."

There'd been all sorts of reasons why he'd been on the wrong side of annoyed. Aside from the fact it had rained on his new boots, he'd also managed to put a gash in the leather. But when he clapped eyes on Sophie, something in him shifted, tipping him off balance. There was a certain fragileness in her that hit him in the heart. It wasn't her frame or build, but there was something in her eyes that spoke of a longing.

And need.

But what shook him was his reaction to her. He wanted to wrap his arms around her and ask her why she looked so lonely, but sanity quickly returned and he knew he had to keep his distance. Ethan had been stupid enough to date one of Beth's friends. After two dates, things went south and Ethan didn't hear the end of it for a year after that. Ethan made sure Zach was as miserable as Beth made him.

Yet, when Zach decided he didn't want to act on his feelings, he regretted it.

"What I remember is you stomped around like a bull with a cocklebur in his hide that weekend and nothing made you happy."

"I ruined my new boots."

Ethan's laughter filled the cab. Zach shook his head, but he had to smile looking back at it. He hadn't handled things well that weekend. Added to the chaos was his reaction to Sophie.

Later that night as Zach got ready for bed, his thoughts continued to swirl around Sophie. He sat on the side of the bed and took off his artificial leg, placing it by the nightstand. His crutches leaned against the nightstand.

He took off the protective stocking that cushioned the end of his leg. In the hospital in D.C., seeing other patients, both male and female, without their limb wasn't uncommon. It didn't shock him anymore, but the first time his mother saw his leg, her eyes had filled with tears.

What would Sophie think? Would her reaction show her distaste and revulsion? Or would she cry like his mother? There'd been countless times in the hospital when family members would visit their loved ones and see them without their artificial limbs. The two main reactions to seeing the stumps were revulsion or pity. Neither reaction appealed to him.

He stretched out on the bed, picked up the remote and turned off the bedside lamp. Rolling to his side, he let his thoughts return to Sophie.

His conversation with Ethan brought up so many memories. After that first weekend when Sophie and Beth came home from college, he'd seen Sophie a couple of times after that. Once when he visited Beth at school, he'd offered to take both girls to dinner, but Sophie declined, claiming to have a test to study for.

After he'd graduated from college and been commissioned as an officer in the army, he went to UNM to say goodbye to Beth. There'd been a moment when he and Sophie had been waiting for his sister. Sophie had asked why he'd joined the army. He'd told her that both his father and grandfather had been in the army. It was a family tradition. What he hadn't mentioned was that the only way he could afford school was with the army's help. Those were lean years for the ranch.

His last trip to see Beth was when they attended her

college graduation. Sophie hadn't been there. Beth told the family that Sophie had signed up for the army and she'd already gone to basic training.

At that news, a small flare of hope had settled in Zach's chest. Maybe their paths could cross? If a person was stationed in Baghdad, the chances of running into old friends weren't good, but it did happen.

They hadn't met. Instead, he'd ended up going home early wounded. He couldn't stop wondering what her reaction would be if she saw him without his artificial leg? She'd been a medic and had seen worse things. She'd already proven that pity wasn't in her vocabulary.

He folded his hands behind his head. Sophie Powell was a lady with guts. And smarts.

It was something he admired. And was attracted to.

Sophie's stomach knotted. Doubts about whether or not Zach would show up plagued her. He said he'd come, but she worked with vets who said they wanted help, wanted to ride, but ended up not showing. She walked to Sam's stall. The horse came to the door and stuck her head out.

"Hello, you sweet thing." Sophie rubbed Sam's nose. "You ready to work today?"

"I am."

Sophie whirled and faced Zach.

Zach stepped to Sophie's side and lightly stroked the horse on her neck. "Sorry I startled you. I'm not late for Andy's ride, am I?"

"He only comes on Mondays and Wednesdays. But you can help me with a new student who signed up last week."

"A newbie like me."

"You can see how we start. This little girl had a stroke and her mom feels riding will help."

"Really?"

"You've been riding for years and didn't know how beneficial it was?"

His hand stopped stroking Sam's neck. "There's a lot of things I've forgotten. But I'm ready to relearn those things. And I believe I'll see them in a new light." He shook his head. "Who would've thought that mucking out a stable could hold such appeal for me?"

"And hope."

"Really?"

"Absolutely." The word rang down the aisle of stalls.

"If you're willing to work, I'm happy to have the help. Right now, I want you to take Sam to the mounting steps while I get the tack. Later I can show you some of the specialized tack we use."

"I'll meet you there."

"Good to have you on the team, Zach."

He paused, as if he savored the word. "Teamwork, huh?"

"That's it. Teamwork. And sometimes our path with a rider isn't a straight line. We might take two steps forward and one back. But we keep going."

He didn't say anything, but he needed to understand if he started this therapy it wasn't going to be easy or a straight shot, but he would improve.

"Teamwork it is."

She could breathe again and smiled at him. When he grinned back at her, suddenly her mind short-circuited and butterflies filled her stomach.

After several moments, Zach said, "Your new student is looking at us."

His words snapped her out of her stupor and she turned and raced away.

* * *

An hour later, Zach led Sam to her stall. Thoughts of a little girl sitting atop Sam, smiling and enjoying herself, filled his head.

"Sam, I'm impressed what a patient, wonderful lady you are."

The horse nodded.

The little girl fell in love with Sam and was eager to ride. Sophie had gently led Sam around the ring, talking to the little girl. It had been obvious when the rider tired and Sophie had ended the session. There'd been nothing but praise for the child.

"Your performance was great, Sam," Zach whispered to the horse as he put her into the stall. He went to work caring for the mare, talking to her, telling her what a good horse she was.

The morning passed quickly and Zach helped Sophie with two more riders. At noon, he walked into the office, needing a few moments to rest. His leg throbbed and he knew he couldn't go any farther. His cane rested in the corner of the office, but he was to the point where he didn't need it unless he was extremely tired. Pride led him to be stupid the last time. This time, he'd listen to his body.

Ollie motioned Zach to the back of the room to the table and chairs. "Sit yourself down, and rest a minute."

Zach joined the older man.

"You've been a great help this morning," Ollie said.

"There's a lot of work here."

Ollie rubbed his neck. "Yeah, since Margaret had her stroke, work's kinda built up." He stood up and poured himself a cup of coffee. "Want some?"

"Yes."

"I hope you like it black, because I don't do that fancy stuff that Sophie does."

"In the army you drink it black."

"A man after my own heart." He poured a second cup and brought it to the table.

Zach sipped the dark brew.

Ollie studied him. "You going to be hanging around here for a while?"

"Plan to. I want to work with Sophie to get a program for vets going." He needed to ask Sophie who she'd contacted at the army. He might have more connections she could use.

"Good. Sophie needs to have some help. Margaret's not in any shape to do it."

Zach took another gulp of his coffee, sensing Ollie had more to say, and the old cowpoke would take his time at getting there.

Ollie leaned back in his chair and took another gulp of his coffee. "We're going to need some more help here at the ranch."

"I see volunteers working."

"Yup." Ollie ran his hand over his face. "But what we need is someone who knows his way around horses, who can direct things when Sophie is tied up. Make no mistake, we can't do it without the volunteers, but I'd feel better with someone who knows his way around stock. You know horses and been with them a long time. This ranch could use your help."

"Are you going to quit, Ollie? Is that why you're looking for a replacement?"

Ollie leaned forward, nailing Zach with a hard stare. "I was set to quit, but Margaret had her stroke. I told Sophie I'd stay, but I hadn't counted on my doc telling me I've got cancer. I'm going to the hospital next week to get cut on."

"Does Sophie know about this?"

"I haven't told her and don't plan to. She's a strong lady but I ain't going to burden her with my news. But she's going to need someone to help her with her thoughts."

Zach knew Sophie's world was about to crash in on her. "I'm far from being up to speed."

"So? You got a brain and can see what needs to be done. You can tell the volunteers what to do. Guide them. As you build up your strength, you can do things yourself.

"Sophie needs someone here who knows horses. Someone to lean on. I plan to continue, but I heard that those treatments make you puke out your guts. There might be days I'm worthless. I don't want to do that to Sophie. She's working her heart out here. I think maybe if I'm here and you're here, we can keep going."

Questions whirled around in Zach's mind. "Is there any chance that the owner's children or friends might help? Wouldn't they want to keep the ranch going? Or is there someone else who might help? Sophie's family? Your family?"

"Sophie's family?" Ollie snorted. "I don't recall them ever being here or calling. Don't count on them. As for Margaret's kids, forget it. The two that are in town are as worthless as—" He swallowed the rest. "They don't like what Margaret's done. They'd be just as happy if we shut down the program.

"My son lives up in the Northwest. He has a lot on his plate." Ollie shook his head. "The way I see it, I think the good Lord above sent you to help Miss Sophie. And she's the one who can help you."

Zach wasn't sure he'd agree with Ollie's conclusions. Divine intervention?

The door to the office opened and Sophie walked in with three sack lunches. "I hope you two are hungry." Walking to the table, she held up the sacks. "I've got one turkey sandwich, one bologna and one peanut butter." Placing the sacks on the table, she looked from Zach to Ollie. "Anything wrong?"

"No," Ollie answered. "I'll take the bologna. You got Fritos in there, too?"

"I do. And a chocolate-chip cookie. I didn't bake it, but Andy's mother brought me some the other day." She handed Ollie the sack with the bologna. Turning to Zach, she asked, "Which one?"

"Give me the peanut butter."

Once they all started eating their sandwiches, Sophie looked from one man to the other. "What were you guys talking about?"

Ollie's request shook Zach to his core, and yet it reso- nated with him as nothing else had since he woke in the hospital. He was needed here. He wasn't up to the mark, but he could help and direct the other volunteers. "I was just talking to Ollie, asking him if he thought I might start coming every day to help around here."

Sophie put her sandwich on the brown paper sack. "Why would you want to do that, Zach?"

He caught Ollie's eye and the old man silently ques- tioned him.

"I thought that I might gain strength quicker if I was here every day, helping a little here and there. Also, I know the owner is in the hospital. I thought you might need another hand who's spent his fair share of time with horses.

"Besides, I'm going stir crazy in my place, looking at the walls. Being outside can only help me build up my strength. And we can work on your plan for soldiers."

Sophie's eyes widened and she sat back in her chair. The longer she remained quiet the more nervous Zach became.

"You sure you want to do this?" she asked.

He released the pent-up breath. "Yeah. I'm sure."

Her eyes twinkled and a smile curved her mouth that Zach felt all the way to his toes. She held out her hand. "Welcome to the New Hope Ranch, Zachary McClure."

He shook her hand.

Ollie held out his hand. "Welcome, son."

As they walked out of the office after lunch, Ollie stopped Zach.

"Thanks for keeping my secret."

"I think you should tell her about your situation."

"Maybe, in time."

Before Zach could question him further, Ethan showed up. "You ready to ride, little brother?"

"I'm ready," Zach replied. And he knew he was ready for this challenge.

Sophie walked into room 320 of All Saints Hospital, expecting to see Margaret Stillwell. However, the room stood empty. Panic seized her. Sophie hurried to the nurses' desk.

"Where's Margaret Stillwell? Her room's empty."

The nurse looked up from her charts. "They moved her this afternoon to a rehab hospital."

Sophie took a deep breath. *Thank You, Lord.* "What hospital?"

The nurse gave her the address of the rehab hospital.

It took Sophie ten minutes to get to the older hospital on the western edge of Albuquerque. Once inside the building, she found Margaret's room after stopping at the front desk.

Margaret lay in the bed, watching TV. The stroke had affected her speech and the left side of her body.

Sophie smiled down at her dear friend. Margaret had become a surrogate mother to her. And Sophie had been like the daughter who was close to her mother, talking daily about the running of the ranch. Margaret's other children didn't fit that bill.

Sophie laced her fingers with Margaret's and sat. "How are you feeling today?"

Margaret turned her head toward Sophie.

"I'll tell you I had quite a scare when I walked into All Saints and found your room empty." A tear slid down Sophie's cheek. "Are you comfortable here, Margaret?"

With her free hand, Sophie finger-combed the gray hair from her friend's face. "I want to tell you of an old friend who's working at the ranch. My ex-roommate's brother lost his right foot when he was in Baghdad. He was a championship rodeo rider, and you know what? He's going to be a great rider again when he builds himself back up. He's had a bad time, Margaret, but you know about that.

"Well, Zach's going to help me with our plans to start the therapy for the wounded vets. He's riding Prince Charming and helping around the ranch." Sophie thought she saw approval in her friend's eyes.

"I'll admit I'm grateful for his help. And—" Sophie wanted to tell someone of her feelings. "First time I saw him, he was wet, dripping from being caught in a rainstorm, and he was madder than a wet hen. But he took my breath away.

"Of course, he ignored me. I was his little sister's college roommate and off limits." Sophie shrugged. "He's still a hunk." A bark of laughter burst from her lips. "A hunk with an attitude.

"Well, I fell head over heels for him. I felt like a thirteen-year-old with her first crush. He yanked all the right chains." She stroked Margaret's hand. Margaret squeezed back, letting Sophie know she was listening. "Of course, Zach had no interest in me. I could've been part of the wallpaper. But I had all sorts of dreams about him."

A smile settled on Margaret's face.

"I'll tell you all the guys in my unit and the guys I treated would laugh themselves silly if they knew about my crush. I was known as the best medic they had, but don't mess with the lady. She ain't buying."

"What are you doing here?"

Sophie turned and came face-to-face with Austin Stillwell, Margaret's oldest son. "I'm visiting with your mother."

His eyes narrowed. "It's late for you to be visiting."

Looking at the wall clock, Sophie noted the time as seven fifty-five.

"I would've been here earlier, but I went to All Saints and discovered your mother had been moved here. I thought she might enjoy some conversation."

Austin didn't look any more pleased with her explanation than he did with her presence.

"How does the doctor say she is doing? When do they think she'll be able to come home?"

"The doctor doesn't see her coming home. Her therapy is going to be long and cos—complicated."

He almost said costly and Sophie knew that Austin's bottom line was money.

"Surely, she could be at her home and recuperate there?"

Austin straightened his spine as if he was lecturing a child. "We don't know how quickly she'll respond. But I know this—she will be in no condition to continue running the ranch."

"Between Ollie and myself, we have that covered so don't worry about it."

"I think you misunderstood what I said, Miss Powell. The horse-therapy thing needs to come to an end. Mother will not be able to participate in it."

She hadn't misunderstood. Sophie knew exactly what Austin was doing. He never liked having the ranch used for equine therapy. She'd heard him complain several times to his mother about "those kinds of people" using the ranch. Sophie also knew that Austin refused to have anything to do with his nephew who had Down's.

Sophie let go of Margaret's hand and stood. "I don't think Margaret would want the therapy program shut down."

"That's your interpretation of my mother's wishes. Mine is to shut it down."

This couldn't be happening. The kids who came to New Hope were making great strides. And more came daily. And what about her plans for the vets?

Tamping down the panic, her mind raced to think of a way to stop Austin.

"Well, I must warn you, if you shut things down, you will have to repay several of the parents for the therapy."

The little bombshell she tossed rocked Austin back on his heels.

"What are you talking about?"

"I'm saying that nearly half the parents of kids we having coming have paid for lessons through the end of May." Eight weeks. That's how long the ranch was obligated to run sessions.

She could see Austin calculating how much money he'd have to pay back.

"I'll talk it over with the lawyers and the others. I'll get back to you. But in the meantime, don't take on any more clients."

"We've just had three new inquiries about riding lessons. And you know your mother and I wanted the army to use the ranch for therapy for wounded soldiers."

His mouth tightened.

There was a noise from the bed. Sophie and Austin looked down at Margaret. She blinked and her mouth twitched.

"What is it, Margaret?" Sophie asked.

The older woman's gaze settled on her son.

"What, Mom? You want this army thing to go through?"

Margaret blinked twice.

"I think she's answering you, Austin."

"You're just hoping, Ms. Powell."

"No." Sophie turned to Margaret. "Blink once for no and twice for yes. This is your son, Austin."

Margaret blinked twice.

"Could be a twitch."

"And I'm Sophia Loren."

Margaret gave a single blink.

"Don't I wish," Sophie said under her breath. "I'm Sophie Powell, one of your workers at the ranch."

Margaret acknowledged her.

"You see there. Your mom wants me to continue."

"Finish out the contracts."

Sophie knew that she'd pushed Austin into a corner. She only prayed that she could get that army contract, then Austin might change his tune.

Leaning down, Sophie kissed Margaret's cheek. "Get well, friend. Things are going well. Don't worry. And I'll be praying for you."

As Sophie left the room, she stopped by Austin's side. "I think your mother will recover quicker if she knows her dream is well and helping kids. She also wanted the contract with the army. And if you don't believe me, check her office. Our proposal is there."

If looks could kill, Austin would've ended her life there in the hospital room.

As she drove home, Sophie sent up a silent prayer of thanks that they put their plans for the ranch in writing. They'd also put into writing that if at any time Margaret wanted to sell the ranch, Sophie had the first right to buy. When Margaret first suggested it, Sophie thought Margaret was ridiculous. Now, she knew Margaret had been following her heart, guided by a Higher Power.

Chapter Six

Sophie paused as she entered the last figure into the spreadsheet for payments received for lessons. Their balance sheet looked good, and Austin couldn't complain about the bottom line.

But he would. She hadn't heard from him since that night at the hospital two weeks ago, but she'd felt the pressure.

She rubbed the back of her neck to ease the tension. *I know, Lord, I need to trust in Your plans. I'm trying, but—*

Her world had been turned on its head.

Zach had shown up every day and worked around the ranch, keeping her off balance and fighting her feelings. Zach helped with caring for the horses and by acting as a sidewalker. He slowly built up his strength during his time at the ranch.

Sophie immediately felt the difference that Zach's presence made. She didn't have to cover everything or worry that the volunteers might not know what to do. Oddly enough, Ollie had called in sick and had been gone half a week. Zach filled that gap. Both Beth and

Ethan also showed up and helped, filling in and doing Ollie's chores. And since they'd grown up with horses, they were a blessing.

When Ollie returned the next Monday, he moved slowly and Sophie worried about her friend's health. Zach took up the slack.

Zach smiled often and Sophie felt her heart opening up to him. But when she caught herself hoping for more, she remembered one of the shrinks at Walter Reed had warned her not to become personally involved with patients because too many people misread gratitude for love. She'd watched doomed relationships with therapists and patients. And she'd made that mistake, too, misinterpreting gratitude for something deeper.

So here she was again, her heart leading her. Could she trust it? And what of Zach? When he smiled and gave her that killer grin of his, was there more to it than just pleasure that he was now gaining his life back? Or gratitude for someone helping him?

Added to the mix, she'd had four more parents call, asking to bring their children to the ranch for therapy.

"You look puzzled." Zach's voice broke into her thoughts.

She looked up from the desk in the office and saw him in the doorway. He looked more and more like his old self. He smiled more readily these days.

"I was thinking about Ollie. I'm worried about him. He doesn't seem up to speed. There are days he looks fine and other days—" She shook her head. Last week, she'd rounded the stables and caught him throwing up.

Zach settled in the chair by the side of the desk.

"Ollie's not a young man."

A small laugh erupted from her throat. "That man can

run me into the ground most days. But lately—do you think I'm looking for problems where there are none?"

"You've got a lot of things on your plate. Margaret, Ollie, me."

"Yeah, it seems that if I don't hold on to it, then it's going to change." Fear and uncertainty clawed at her. She hadn't said anything to anyone about her confrontation with Austin.

"You can't do that. Ask someone who's tried."

He'd hit the problem square on. "I hate it when people throw my words back in my face."

He grinned. "Stop worrying. It's my time to ride."

His upbeat words touched her, bringing a ray of hope to her heart.

"Let me close out this file and I'll be there."

Sophie quickly got out of her program and followed Zach out of the office. Who would've thought Zach would repeat her words back to her? Was she only seeing the problems and not the solution? She needed to trust God.

Lord, I'm confused and adrift here. Please be with me and give me wisdom, she prayed as she walked out of the office.

Sophie smiled at Zach as he sat in the saddle atop Prince Charming. He'd ridden Prince Charming around the ring several times. She saw glimpses of the old Zach in his eyes. His improvement had astounded her with its speed. But there was still more for him to do.

"You're looking good," Ethan called.

"Like an older brother who is a pain." Beth's smile radiated her pride.

Sophie stepped up to the ring's wooden rail. "You up for a new challenge?"

Zach stopped Prince Charming and rested his forearm on the saddle horn. "What do you have in mind?"

"How about saber practice? I hear you old-time cavalry guys love to practice charges."

Zach's spine straightened and his chest came up. "Yes, those of us who were in the mounted corp did that." His eyes narrowed, waiting.

She nodded. "You want to try doing that?"

He glanced around, looking for any target. "Sure, why not?"

"Okay, let me set it up." Moving toward Beth and Ethan, Sophie started issuing orders. "Ethan, I'll need you to put up all the horses in the back corral in their stalls. Ollie will help. Beth, in the tack room there's a hula hoop in the back corner behind the saddle blankets. Get that and bring it to that back corral."

Everyone started moving. It took ten minutes for them to rig up the arm and suspend the hula hoop on a rope from the arm of the inverted L-shaped pole at the entrance to the paddock beside the stables.

Zach rode out to the corral.

Sophie ran into the office and grabbed a plastic light saber in the corner that she'd picked up at the local warehouse club store. She handed it to Zach. It was orange and black.

"What do you want me to use this for?"

She heard Ethan snort behind her.

"Work with me here, Zach. I didn't have a real live saber, so I thought you could use this."

He frowned as he evaluated the toy. "You want me to use this?"

She thought this would be a great idea but he sounded like she wanted him to do backflips off the horse. "It's the best I could come up with at a moment's notice. I have the broken handle off a pitchfork if you want to use that, but I warn you the end is jagged."

Beth and Ethan stood to the side, waiting for Zach's answer. Ethan's mouth kept moving as he tried to bite back his grin. Ollie stood beside Sophie.

Zach studied his siblings, then stared down at the toy. He remained silent, fighting some sort of inner battle. Finally he said, "This will do."

The breath she'd been holding swished out.

"He's a smart man," Ollie said, his voice pitched low so only Sophie could hear.

She'd questioned herself on whether this would work, but Zach needed to be challenged. "When you want to bring a real saber, you're welcome, but I'd thought we'd start with this. Besides, the weight is better for your first try." She'd talked to the therapist, Captain Perry, at Brook Army Medical yesterday and asked for ideas to help Zach. The therapist told her about this setup for his patients to help with balance. The patient would have to balance himself on his legs and this would tell her if he had the strength.

Ethan grinned. "It looks good."

Zach ignored him and Beth elbowed Ethan.

"What?" Ethan complained.

Sophie disregarded Ethan's antics and focused on Zach. "They use this exercise at Brook Army as part of their soldiers' therapy."

"They use that?" Ethan asked.

Sophie turned and glared at Ethan. His grin disappeared.

"I don't know what sort of sword the army uses, but for now that will work," she said.

Zach studied the child's toy. "Starting small is probably a good idea."

Relief rushed through Sophie. Out of the corner of her eye, she saw Beth and Ethan smiling.

"The therapist was very high on this exercise. It helps with balance, control and having all your muscles work together."

"That's genius." Ethan turned to his brother. "Let's see if you can do it."

Zach couldn't resist the challenge from his brother.

"Are you daring me, big brother?"

Ethan laughed. "You got it."

Zach turned Prince Charming around and rode him around the enclosure. Once, twice.

Sophie pushed fear out of her mind, just as she had when going out to get a wounded soldier in Iraq. Instead she focused on the goal and prayed that Zach was up to this challenge. The fear that maybe she should've waited for another week to allow Zach to build up his muscles tried to creep into her head, but she ruthlessly pushed it aside. He was a soldier. He'd faced the enemy before.

"But never himself." The whispered words floated in her brain.

On the third time around the ring, he lifted the plastic saber and thrust it at the hula hoop.

He missed and his body tipped toward his right side.

She held her breath. *Oh, Lord, help.*

Zach fought for his balance. He pulled his right arm in and managed to settle himself in the center of the saddle.

He turned around and grinned at Sophie.

Suddenly she realized Zach had used his core muscles, abdominal muscles and thighs to right himself in the saddle.

Her eyes filled with moisture but she wouldn't cry. She looked over at Beth and Ethan. From the looks on their faces, they also realized how much Zach had recovered.

Zach guided Prince Charming around for a second pass at the target. Zach raised the saber and rode toward the hula hoop. As he passed it, he thrust with his right hand. He didn't get the sword through the hoop, but he kept his balance.

Zach rode around the ring again and tried for the third time. He made it.

Cheers went up from his siblings.

"That's the prettiest thing I've seen in a long time," the whispered words came from behind her.

Sophie glanced over her shoulder to meet Ollie's gaze.

"I couldn't agree more," she replied.

"You've done good, girl. That boy's on the mend."

She wanted to ask him how he felt, but Ollie moved away.

Zach made several more passes at the target and got the saber in two of the three times. As he guided Prince Charming to the gate, Sophie could see the pride and joy in his face.

"I like your friend's suggestion," Zach said.

"When he told me about that last night, I had my doubts, but he knew what he was talking about."

Zach patted Prince Charming on the neck. "And you did a great job, boy."

Prince Charming nodded his head.

Sophie heard a car in the parking lot. After the car stopped, and the doors opened, a little boy called out, "Hey, Miss Sophie. I'm here."

Sophie waved back. "I'm coming." Turning, she looked up at Zach. "You did great." She headed toward the stable office. She didn't need to worry about putting Prince Charming back in his stall. Zach would take care of things. That was one less thing she had to do.

Zach did more than just fill a need at the ranch. He gave her a glimpse of what might be to have him here at the ranch—working by her side as a permanent member of the staff.

Beth and Ethan followed Zach as he walked Prince Charming back to his stall.

Ethan clapped Zach on the back. He didn't say anything, but Zach knew his brother was proud. Things were beginning to come back into focus.

"I'd like to help with the chores, but Dad called before I got here. I've got to run some errands for him at the bank, and he wants it done this afternoon and doesn't want to wait until Monday."

"I understand."

"Dad also asked when he and Mom could come down and watch you ride."

Zach felt none of the panic that request would've brought a month ago, and he realized how far he'd come. *Thank You, Lord, for bringing Sophie into my life.*

Beth stood beside Ethan, her posture tight as if ready to leap in and smooth the situation.

"That's not a problem. Any day they want to drive down will be fine."

Beth relaxed. "They'll be excited."

With a final slap on Zach's back, Ethan walked away. When Beth started to follow, Zach put his hand on her arm, stopping her. "You have a few minutes?"

He waited.

"I have a meeting at three, but I've got time to talk," she said.

Zach tied Prince Charming to the ring by his stable and unsaddled him. He put it on the saddle rest in Prince Charming's stall.

Beth joined him with grooming the horse.

"This reminds me of when you and I had to work together for my 4-H project."

He remembered the time when he was helping her with that particular venture. Beth had been in the eighth grade and he was in high school.

"What do you know about Sophie's family?" Zach asked as he ran the curry brush over Prince Charming's neck.

She paused and looked over the horse's back. "What brought that on?"

"I'm curious about her family. I know that Mom and Dad have called daily, wanting to come and watch me, wanting progress reports. And I'll admit, it's driven me crazy, but I know they care. But since I've been working here, I've wondered about Sophie's family." Sophie had mentioned nothing of her family and he knew of no contact between them. He wondered at the silence.

"I can't tell you much. Sophie didn't talk about them much. They called a couple of times a year, but it was mostly her grandmother that she talked to. I got the feeling her mother and grandmother weren't on good terms.

"She sometimes talked about her brother, Matt." Beth continued to brush Prince Charming, but her strokes were automatic and her eyes took on a faraway look. "Oh, there was one time, her grandmother came to visit. Sophie was glad to see her and they spent the day together. But other than that, I can't recall her family ever visiting."

"And since Sophie didn't go to the graduation ceremony, you didn't see them at that time," he added.

"It surprised me when Sophie told me she'd signed up for the army and was leaving after her last final exam for boot camp." She shrugged. "When I asked her about graduation, she said it didn't matter."

That troubled Zach. His family had been a bulwark for him. He knew he could count on them no matter what happened. They were there cheering for him when he walked across the auditorium stage at Eastern New Mexico State. And they cheered when he got his commission in the army.

Even though his parents had a tough time dealing with his injuries, Zach never doubted for an instant that his parents loved him and supported him.

"Do you have any idea what the trouble between them was?"

"Yeah." She set the curry brush on the table beside the stall. Running her hands along the side of Prince Charming, Beth seemed to debate with herself. Finally, she said, "It all revolved around her brother's death. She never told me what it was, but I know that there was the problem."

"Are you sure?"

"I'm sure."

"You're sure of what?" Sophie asked, walking toward them.

Beth's face lost all color. Her hand stilled on Prince Charming's side.

"She's sure she can't stay the afternoon and help with the chores," Zach smoothly supplied.

Beth's head came up. "That's right. I have a meeting—" she glanced at her watch "—in less than forty minutes at headquarters. I think I'll have just enough time to drive downtown." She kissed Zach's cheek. "Good ride. And I think with a little practice, you'll get the hang of the saber thing."

She moved to Sophie and hugged her. "Thank you," she whispered. When Beth pulled back, her smile quivered. "Bye." Beth sprinted down the center of the stable and slipped out the open door beside the tack room.

"I was hoping you'd help with this new rider. One of my sidewalkers had a flat tire and won't be here for another hour. Could you help?"

"Sure. I'll put Prince Charming up and meet you at the mounting steps."

Over the next forty minutes, Zach walked beside the new rider. The little girl spent the first ten minutes crying, then suddenly like flipping a switch she decided she loved to ride and she wanted to be the horse's best friend.

When the sidewalker showed up, Zach let her take his place. His energy was spent.

Walking into the tack room, he sat on the stool by the front cabinet. A thousand different thoughts shot through his brain. Pride and excitement for his accomplishment flooded him. He had to laugh. Riding with a child's light saber was one of the best moments he'd had in a long time. He remembered doing that very exercise during his time in the mounted cavalry.

His smile slowly faded as he thought about Sophie. Ollie hadn't told her about his cancer. The man needed to level with her ASAP. Zach wanted to warn Sophie, but he'd made Ollie a promise. If Sophie looked close enough, she'd see something wasn't right with her old friend.

But the thing nagging at him the most was Sophie's mysterious relationship with her family. Something wasn't right. In all the time he'd been here, Sophie hadn't mentioned her parents. Not once. And he didn't think she'd gotten any calls or letters from them.

Why?

He felt a protectiveness rise up in him.

His stomach rumbled, reminding him he hadn't eaten before he rode. Zach walked to the office and got himself a bottle of water and one of the cookies Sophie kept in the cabinet above the mini-fridge.

By the time he finished off the third cookie, Ollie walked in.

"How are you feeling?" Zach asked the older man.

"Like I've been stomped by a bull." He raised his straw hat and ran his fingers through his steel-gray hair.

"Anything I can do for you?"

Ollie nodded toward the water. "Got another one of those?"

Zach grabbed another cold bottle of water and handed it to him. "Anything else I can do?"

"Nope, you're doing it by keeping things going here. Sophie's got enough to handle without me pouring more worry on it. I know that Margaret is out of the hospital, but she ain't come home. I'm expecting trouble from her kids."

"What kind of trouble?"

Ollie shrugged. "I think they might want us to stop giving lessons."

Zach looked out the window and saw Sophie as she walked Brownie around the ring with a young girl on the horse's back. The girl had a leg brace on her leg. Hinged at the knee, the brace had red-and-white stripes on it with blue stars.

"I think it might be time for Sophie and me to go out and have dinner."

"I like your thinkin', young man. And you can discuss more than ranching." The old man's eyebrows wiggled.

Was Zach that transparent?

"Take the worry off your face, boy. I was just teasin' ya."

Ollie may have said he was teasing, but Zach got the distinct feeling Ollie was all for some "sparking" between Sophie and him. "I'll be sure not to call dinner a date. I'll tell her that we can talk shop."

Ollie grinned. "Good idea."

"I still think you should tell Sophie what's going on with you."

All humor left Ollie's face. "Not now."

"She's stronger than you think. If she was an army medic, she can handle a lot. I shudder to think of the things she saw. I know in quiet moments, I see too much."

Ollie remained quiet for several moments. "I know she can, but why put that burden on her? I'll fight this myself and won't borrow her strength."

"Ollie, haven't you read in Ecclesiastes that a three-fold cord isn't quickly broken? With Sophie and my strength, we can help you."

Ollie put his water down and joined Zach at the window. "That may be, but I just can't tell her right now. Let's see how I'm doing after my next chemo."

Zach's first impulse was to argue with Ollie, but he would honor the older man's wishes. "It's your call."

Ollie nodded and walked out of the office. Zach followed. He had work to be done.

Chapter Seven

Sophie pulled the office door closed and put her key in the lock.

Friday night and what did she have planned? Going to the house and nuking another frozen dinner. Pretty pathetic. Wanting to avoid the empty house and kitchen, she decided to check the stock before she called it a night.

Walking into the stables, she heard Zach's voice.

"You did a nice job out there, boy. You would've made a great cavalry horse. I think the Union soldiers would've loved to have ridden you into any battle against the Indians out here."

"He's probably not going to answer you."

Zach turned and shrugged a sheepish smile on his lips.

"When I was in Iraq, our shrink kept a puppy that had wandered into camp one day. That little ball of fur got so many GIs to come in and just talk, vent their feelings or just relax. Amazing what an animal can do." She leaned her forearms against the half wall of the stall and studied Prince Charming. "I talk to my horses all the time. They know all my secrets." She turned her head. "You think Prince Charming knows what you're saying?"

"I don't know, but I've gotten a lot of head-bobbing and agreeing."

Sophie laughed. "And I'm sure he didn't talk back."

"You'd be surprised how much Prince Charming lets me know when he's not happy."

"That I don't doubt."

Zach patted Prince Charming on the neck. "Instead of me talking to this handsome devil, why don't I talk to you about how things are running?"

What was he asking? "Sure."

"I thought we might do it over dinner."

"If you're up to a frozen dinner, sure."

His laughter rolled through the stables. "If I want to talk, then I should spring for the food. How about we eat Mexican? You know any good places out here?"

"Yup."

"Okay, why don't I drive us there and we have dinner?"

Sophie's heart beat faster. "Okay. But let me follow you in my car, that way you won't have to come back here."

"No can do. I want to show you how much my leg has improved by showing off my driving skill. If you're in another car, you can't see that."

His request surprised her. "Okay. Let me finish looking at all the horses, then we can go."

Zach's satisfied smile made her wonder if this dinner was more than a business meeting. She could only hope.

Mama Juanita's Kitchen was a small house turned into a restaurant on the southeastern outskirts of Albuquerque. The large corner lot covered in gravel and dirt was filled with cars. An overflow of vehicles parked on the street and in the alley. Zach found a spot behind the house next to the big industrial trash bin.

The wonderful smell of chilies, beans and mouth-watering spices wafted out the front door. Sophie's stomach rumbled and her mouth watered. "I didn't realize how hungry I was."

"You've put in a long day." His stomach rumbled, too. "So have I. Those cookies I snatched out of the office weren't enough."

"Especially for a growing boy like you."

Zach grinned and wagged his brows.

They stopped by the greeter and before the woman could open her mouth, a voice from the back of the room called out. "Ah, *chica,* it is good to see you."

Sophie turned to the voice. Juanita Espinosa hurried to the front of the room and wrapped her arms around Sophie. Sophie towered over the short, round woman. With her salt-and-pepper hair pulled back into a bun and her ready smile, too many people thought Juanita was an easygoing happy woman who could be walked over. It didn't take them long to realize their mistake.

When Juanita let her go, she looked up at Zach.

"Who is this? Have you finally got a man in your life?" Juanita grinned.

Blood rushed to Sophie's cheeks. "Zach is helping out at the ranch while Margaret is gone."

"How is Margaret? I called the hospital, but they tell me she isn't there."

Juanita and Margaret had known each other for twenty years. Often, Margaret and Sophie would treat themselves and have dinner here. The three women would laugh and trade stories. Juanita and Margaret would often swap stories of their errant children and would ask to hear about Sophie's experiences in the army. In an odd sort of way, Sophie had become their adoptive child.

Sophie slipped her hands into the back pockets of her jeans. "Austin put her in an extended-stay home for therapy."

"That boy," Juanita exclaimed. "He needs someone to grab him by the ear and sit him down and give him a good talking-to. That daughter who is still here—" She shook her head. "The only good child she had moved to Oregon.

"Come. I've got a special seat for you at the back. I'll come and join you when I can."

They wound their way through the tables to the back corner. A lit candle provided most of the light for the table.

"Sit and I'll tell your waiter to bring you the special." She disappeared into the kitchen.

"I don't get a menu?" Zach asked.

"You can have one if you want one, but I'll guarantee you that you're going to want her special."

He leaned back and studied her. After a moment, he nodded. "I'll trust you."

Oddly enough, she knew he'd been trusting her for the past couple of weeks. His recovery had been near miraculous. "You won't be disappointed."

"I haven't been so far."

Her brows wrinkled. "Meaning?"

"You've been right about therapy and riding. If you say 'the special' is something I'll like, I'll believe you."

Suddenly dinner seemed like a date. And her stomach decided to keep tempo with the upbeat music playing in the background. Her brain went blank and her tongue seemed to swell.

A waiter showed up with two glasses of iced tea and a bowl of fried corn tortilla chips and salsa. She snatched up a chip, dipped it into the salsa and popped it into her mouth.

The chip went down the wrong way and she started to choke. Instantly, Zach's hand slapped her on the back. The chip dislodged and went down. She grabbed her tea and took a drink.

"Thanks," she croaked.

"No problem. Is the salsa that good?"

Smiling through her embarrassment, she nodded. "It is. It's just the chip went down the wrong way."

He picked up a chip and ran it through the salsa. He popped it into his mouth. "Excellent."

Sophie felt like an idiot. She couldn't eat a chip without choking.

"I want to thank you for the light saber today."

She latched onto the change in topic. "I couldn't think of anything else to use. It was better than the broken handle of the pitchfork."

"After I got over the shock, I liked the challenge. And I'm sure I'll hear from my parents about today's exercise."

"I hope you're not complaining about your caring family."

He paused with a chip in his hand. "No, I'm not."

"Good. Be grateful. They might've approached things wrong after you came home from the hospital—" his face took on a mulish quality "—but as I recall your parents have good hearts."

When he opened his mouth, she leaned forward and whispered, "Remember, I was your sister's roommate. She told me a lot of things that her brothers did."

He leaned back in his chair and his eyes narrowed. "What exactly did she tell you?"

She had him worried. Good. Of course some of the stories Beth shared, she had her part in the adventure. There was one time when the boys snuck out to go to a cave in the mountain above their ranch. Beth had followed and ended up falling and breaking her arm, and her brothers had carried her home.

"I think I'll keep those secrets. Remember, your parents had a couple of wild boys, but they loved them through it."

Before he could respond, the waiter appeared with two plates. On the plate was a chili relleno covered with a light green sauce. Refried beans and rice filled up the rest of the plate.

Sophie leaned over her plate and whispered, "Try it. The sauce is excellent."

He eyed her.

"Trust me."

Cutting the relleno, he forked a bite into his mouth. He smiled. "You're right again."

Her eyes locked with his and Sophie knew she'd lost her heart.

Zach wolfed down the relleno. Her little mention about knowing about his misadventures rattled him. And of course, those adventures fell into two categories— pre-teen and teen. What had Beth told her? There were lots of things that he didn't want his folks to know about what Ethan and he'd done. What he needed to do was find a way to talk about her family.

Leaning forward, he said, "Since you know about my

secrets, don't you think I'm entitled to know some of yours?"

Sophie put her fork down and picked up her iced tea. After a drink, she sat back. "Why would I want to tell you about my misadventures?"

"To humor me?"

Her gaze searched his. "Once when I was six and my brother was nine, he took my Barbie and hid it because I was using his favorite truck for Barbie's car. He took his car back and I got so mad. I threw his shoes at him. My aim wasn't good and I missed him and his shoe hit a vase in the living room and broke it. Mom thought Matt threw the shoe. He didn't rat me out and took the blame." She fell silent.

His hand covered hers and lightly squeezed.

Her gaze met his. "I still miss him. It was as if the light went out in our family when he died."

Zach heard the rumors on the rodeo circuit that Matt had been killed in some sort of riding accident, but he didn't know the details. Sophie had told Beth her brother died when she was twelve, but no one knew exactly what happened.

She shook her head as if shaking off the sad memories. "Thank you for filling the hole when my sidewalker was late."

With her change in subject, Zach knew the door had been closed and he wouldn't push her further. He sensed a wound or tenderness that Sophie let few people see. He knew that she wouldn't have shown that weakness in the army.

"I'm glad I had the energy to do it."

Juanita came to the table holding two plates. Sopaipillas. "I wanted to bring you the finishing touch of your dinner." She placed the puffy cinnamon-and-sugar-coated fried pastries on the table.

It had been close to ten years since he had a sopai-pilla. "This is a treat, Juanita. And the rest of the meal was excellent."

The older woman nodded her thanks. "You need to keep this one, Sophie. Manners are few and far between these days."

Sophie's smiled weakly. "He's a good worker."

Juanita settled in the empty chair at the table and chatted with Sophie for a few minutes. The tension in her shoulders eased. He didn't know that tension resulted in Juanita's matchmaking or his questions about her family. But his plan to learn more about this woman had run into a serious roadblock.

What was Sophie hiding? Because in his experience, people who shared nothing of themselves often hid wounds they didn't want anyone to see.

Zach parked his truck by the guesthouse. Sophie smiled as she watched him drive with his right leg.

"I'm impressed," she said after he shut off the engine.

"I've been practicing. When I go home after I finish here, I take my truck out to a dirt road by my condo and practice driving. It's a good thing that when I bought this baby I decided to get an automatic. When I was at Walter Reed, Dad wanted to have the truck fitted with hand controls, but I refused." He shrugged. "Maybe it was vanity, but I was going to drive this the regular way."

He certainly worked to strengthen his muscles. "It was a goal, and you worked to achieve it," Beth said. He worked like a man possessed.

She got out of the truck, ready to say good-night, but

he followed her up the walk and stepped onto the front porch. A cane-back rocker sat on the porch surrounded by two whiskey barrels filled with pansies and snapdragons. The crispness of the air made her aware of all her senses. The comforting smells of horse and hay danced in the wind. Suddenly, Zach stepped close, filling all her senses. His tall form hovered over her, and she could feel the heat of him. Dinner took on a new dimension. This felt like a date, and dates usually ended with a kiss.

Feeling self-consciousness and shy, she said, "I called the army representatives yesterday to see when they could come out and observe your training. The colonel in charge told me he'd give me a call in the next day or so."

His eyes grew dark with emotion. "Don't worry about it."

"I wish I could, but this is too important." Hugging her waist, her hands moved up and down her upper arms. "I've been praying the Lord would help us establish this therapy program, but there'd been so many roadblocks thrown in the way. First Margaret's stroke, then Ollie disappears and when he comes back, he seems off."

"But He sent me."

Sophie felt her mouth go slack.

"Uh, that came out wrong."

"You think?"

"What I meant was I was the perfect test case for the army. I've got connections I might be able to use to help you."

He had a point. The Lord couldn't have sent a better example. "Well, if you could talk to someone that would be great because the colonel I contacted didn't seem eager to come out here, and I don't understand that. Before, he seemed so interested to see what riding could do for the men."

Zach grinned back at her. He stepped closer and lightly brushed back a lock of hair that came loose from her braid. "Maybe his superior chewed him out that day. I know that's happened to me when I got chewed on. What you have to do is keep your head down and keep going."

Sophie saw his mouth moving, but she was concentrating on his fingers putting those stray tendrils behind her ears. "Uh-huh."

His gaze captured hers. "Give me his name, and I'll call." With each word, his mouth moved closer and closer until his lips brushed across hers.

Once.

Twice.

When she didn't object, his mouth settled firmly on hers and his arms slipped around her back, drawing her close to him. Her eyes fluttered closed. All the times she'd imagined Zach kissing her didn't hold a candle to the real thing. He curled her toes.

When he pulled back, his eyes were soft and his smile broad.

She needed to respond to him, but words failed her. The phone inside the house rang, saving her from having to say anything. She unlocked the door and rushed inside. Zach followed.

Snatching the phone off the kitchen wall, she blurted, "Hello."

"Sophie. This is Lynda McClure."

Zach's mother. Sophie's gaze flew to Zach's. "Hello, Mrs. McClure."

Zach's eyes widened.

"I was hoping we might have dinner with you tomorrow night. We heard from Beth about Zach's progress today and wanted to know more."

Sophie watched as Zach reacted as she talked. "You could talk with Zach and ask him questions."

"I intend to, but I think we'd get a better picture if we talked to you, a more unbiased observer," Lynda replied.

Zach held out his hand. Sophie shook her head.

"Hey, Mom," he called out.

"Is that Zach? He's there?"

Sophie surrendered the phone.

"Hello, Mom." As he listened, his brow rose. "I think that's a good idea. I'll ask her." He covered the mouth piece. "You want to have dinner with my folks?"

The situation could be a powder keg. "I won't talk to them without your approval. It's up to you. If you want me to talk to them, I'll do it."

He put the phone back to his ear. "Okay, Mom." His mother said something that made him frown. "Driving all that way is a lot to ask. Why don't we meet at some-place north of the city?"

Nodding, he listened. "That sounds great, Mom. We'll see you at seven." He hung up and turned to her. "I talked her out of dinner at the ranch. We'll meet them at my mother's favorite restaurant in Albuquerque." He stepped to her side. "You sure you don't mind?"

"No. I've always liked your parents."

"Good night, Sophie. Be prepared for an inquisition tomorrow night, but at least you can comfort yourself with the best steaks in Albuquerque."

She hoped it would be that easy.

It probably wouldn't be. She wasn't known for her daz-zling conversational skills or her wonderful speeches. But she could talk horses, how therapy worked, its benefits and Zach's progress. But she wouldn't mention what a marvelous kisser he was. That would certainly bring all the dinner conversation to a screeching halt.

Chapter Eight

$\sim$

As Sophie watched Zach drive out of the parking lot, she suddenly felt overwhelmed. She stumbled through the front door, locking it. Her head resting against the door, she wondered what was happening. Dinner with Zach's parents tomorrow night was simply business. They wanted to know about their son's progress. Nothing more.

Walking to the kitchen table, she collapsed into one of the chairs. So, why did she feel so confused? Zach's kiss.

Obviously, Zach had feelings for her as proven by what just happened, but where had those feelings sprung from? Gratitude. Simple gratitude to his therapist for his recovery. Nothing more.

She'd pushed him into riding again, forced him to face the life he'd left. She expected him to ride, to be the man he was before the blast. She didn't operate from pity. She demanded the best from him and didn't accept excuses.

He responded to that tough love with an eagerness that surprised her.

So had he misinterpreted his own feelings?

And what about her feelings? Zach tapped into the attraction she felt for him so long ago, but watching him struggle, and watching him interact with the kids and Ollie, she gained a respect for the man. She admired him. That was it. Nothing more.

Too bad that logic didn't feel right.

Unlocking the front door, she raced to the stable and walked to Prince Charming's stall.

"Well, boy. I've got a problem." He came to the half door and nudged her hand, wanting her to stroke his nose.

"What am I going to do?" She rested her head on his neck. "I don't know what Zach's feelings are, but I'm sure he can't identify his feelings any more than I can."

Sophie'd been burned before and now she needed to guard her heart. She'd been halfway through her first tour in Iraq when the army sent her back to D.C. to learn the latest updated field techniques for battlefield injuries. She met an army captain, Bryan Denison, who'd lost both of his legs, but was recuperating and doing equine therapy. Sophie fell in love with Bryan and thought he loved her, too. They'd spent the two weeks that she'd been in D.C. together. When she wasn't in class, she was at the stable or in the hospital with Bryan.

The day before she was to ship back to Iraq, she went to Bryan's room in the hospital to spend her last night before she deployed. When she walked into the room, Bryan had his arms around a woman, and he was kissing her. When they came up for air, he introduced his fiancée to her.

If she'd been hit by an eighteen-wheeler, Sophie couldn't have been more flattened. When she quickly excused herself and fled into the hall, Bryan followed her and told her he was sorry she'd misread his feelings. He gently explained he did have feelings for her, but they were feelings of gratitude and thankfulness.

One of the shrinks had seen the scene in the hallway. He'd taken her arm and escorted her to his office. There he told her that she had to be careful to separate professional and personal feelings and that if she didn't, this wouldn't be the only time her feelings would be misread by the patient or herself. Even friendship with a patient carried danger. It was a good thing to have friendship with a recovering patient, but any relationship that developed in this stressed situation could be misconstrued by either party. She needed to guard her heart and to be sure her patients didn't mistake their gratitude for love.

She'd learned a valuable lesson that day. Never mix the two.

This worried her about Zach. Was he mistaking gratitude for something else? She knew her feelings were the real thing, but she couldn't be sure his were.

When Zach arrived home, his answering-machine light blinked. Before he could check the messages, his phone rang. He answered.

"Son, you need to buy a cell phone," his mother exclaimed.

He readied himself for the third degree. "Okay."

"I hope you're not upset about me inviting Sophie to dinner. Beth couldn't stop talking about how much progress you're making. Why, even Ethan bragged about you and I thought you probably wouldn't want to talk about it, so I thought I could get answers from Sophie."

Oddly, Zach wasn't upset with his mother's tactics. "What Beth and Ethan said must've been spectacular to have you call Sophie."

"When Ethan told your father and me about that thing

with the hula hoop, I laughed. Your dad even commented
that it was a smart idea."

Zach stretched out in his big leather chair. He remembered seeing that red hoop waving in the breeze and it
made him smile. At first he thought Sophie had lost her
mind. What was he going to do with a light saber? he
wondered, but once he got over the foolish feelings, he
wanted to do the exercise they did in the mounted cavalry.

Her idea had been a stroke of genius.

"I'll say she surprised me."

"Well, you can fill in all the details at dinner tomorrow night."

"Be nice when you pump Sophie for all the details of
my progress," he teased.

His mother remained quiet. "Do you think I'd do that
to her?"

His conscience pricked him. "Yes, but that's why I
love you."

"Thank you."

"Then we'll see you around five?"

"See you tomorrow, son. And I am so grateful to the
Lord for the good things that are happening. Do you
know He's got a plan for you? It might not be the one
you thought it was, but He doesn't desert His children."

"I know, Mom." He hung up.

He knew God had a plan for him, but he still didn't
know what that plan was. He knew it had changed. And
suddenly, he thought about a future with a wife.

He dialed his sister and got Sophie's number at the
guesthouse. The phone rang several times and Zach
began to worry about Sophie's safety. On the sixth ring
she picked up.

"I was getting ready to drive back out to the ranch and check on you."

"Sorry, I was out checking the horses."

"Talking to Prince Charming?"

Her laughter made him smile. "Guilty as charged."

"That horse is the best listener in the business. You should just hang out a shingle, Horse Psychologist."

"That's an idea."

"The reason I called is I want to make sure you're okay with talking to my parents tomorrow night. I know Beth has been bragging about your genius. I think Ethan echoed Beth's excitement."

"I'm fine. Remember, I know your folks and how they feel about their children."

"You're not doing this because you feel backed into a corner, are you, because if you are, then we'll cancel the dinner."

"Zach, I'm okay with it."

"They'll have a thousand questions, want your evaluation of my progress, want an overview of what's happening. I guess they wouldn't believe me."

"I'm okay with it, Zach." She chuckled. "As I recall, your folks won't put any thumbscrews on me."

"Don't say I didn't warn you."

"I'll consider myself warned."

He wanted to continue talking to her. He felt like a teen with his first crush. "I thought we might try having dinner again. And not with my parents."

She remained quiet.

"On the drive to the restaurant we could plan a strategy on how to get the army contract."

"That's a plan."

He breathed a sigh of relief. "I'll see you tomorrow. And, Sophie, I had a good time tonight."

"I did, too."

After the goodbyes, she hung up.

Zach stared at the phone. Oddly enough, he knew his mother had done him a favor by asking for Sophie to come to dinner. The arguments he gave Sophie were the bald truth. He didn't want to field any of those questions his parents would have, and Sophie would handle them better than he could.

He found himself looking forward to driving out to the restaurant tomorrow night. His mind wandered back to the kiss he shared with Sophie.

The heart he thought had shriveled up and died suddenly made itself known. His high school girlfriend, he later learned, had only wanted his father's connections to the movers and shakers in Taos, only wanted to advance her career in public relations. And his college girlfriend had abandoned him the moment he was commissioned in the army. He didn't fit into her plans for advancement.

Walking into the bedroom, he sat on the bed and removed his prosthesis, setting it by the nightstand. His leg had healed nicely. Looking down at what was left of his leg came the nagging fear of what Sophie would think after seeing it. He wouldn't allow his parents to see the stump. Ethan had seen it, but that was because he helped Zach in the beginning with putting on the prosthesis.

The army shrinks told him how to deal with others' emotions and reactions, but it was his roommate in the hospital that had helped him the most. Talk to God was what Bill told him to do.

The urge to talk to his friend hit him. He picked up the phone and called Bill.

"Hey, friend, how are you doing?" Bill asked.

Zach told him about his weeks at the ranch.

"I wish I could've done that. I think it would've made my recovery easier."

"Check around you, Bill. You might have something there in Lubbock."

"I will. Is that the reason you called, friend? Wanted me to start equine therapy?"

Bill saw right through him. "No. I have a couple of questions. What was your wife's reaction to seeing you without your prosthesis?"

Bill laughed. "The only reason I can think you'd be asking me *that* particular question is you've found someone."

"I don't kiss and tell."

"Oh-ho. I'm right. Well, Terri's reaction was to thank God that I'm alive. She's grateful I lived. She's never been repulsed by the sight of my stumps."

The weight on Zach's shoulders lifted.

"My mother cried, but I knew she was glad I was alive. After my daughter's first look at it, she asked, 'Does it hurt?' When I told her sometimes, she nodded, accepted and went on. It didn't faze her."

"I can believe that. I've been working with a little boy who thinks my leg makes me special."

"Kids are great."

Too bad all folks didn't react the way Andy did.

"Since you're working with equine therapy, have you talked to anyone at Walter Reed? Folks might want to know about where you're working."

"No, but that's a good idea. Thanks."

"Zach, don't let that missing leg define your life. If it's the right lady, it won't bother her."

Bill's words rang through his head as he reached for his crutches. After he finished in the bathroom, he slid into bed.

Sophie knew who he was, and she'd been working with who he is now.

His feelings for Sophie made him want more. He'd see how she'd held up to his parents' inquisition tomorrow night. If she could handle them, then she probably could handle anything.

Hope filled his heart.

Sophie hurried and dressed. How she slept so late, she didn't know, but she needed to get to the stable.

"Okay, Lord, I know why," she said as she grabbed a muffin and banana from the kitchen counter. She hurried out the front door toward the ranch office. Ollie pulled up in his truck. He was running late, too.

"Morning," Sophie called out.

Ollie grunted a greeting.

He looked pale this morning. His gait wasn't as steady as it normally was.

She moved to his side. "Are you feeling all right this morning?"

"I'm okay."

She wanted to argue with him, but if he wanted to show up here, she wouldn't make a fuss. But something wasn't right with the man. He'd never been as sick as he had been these past few weeks. "I'm going to run interference for Zach tonight with his parents."

That got Ollie's attention. "What?"

"Zach's mom heard about our exercise yesterday and wants to know more about it. I'm to explain what is going on to them."

"Good for you. I think you've done something special for that boy."

Sophie wanted to laugh at Ollie's use of "that boy," but she guessed from Ollie's view, Zach was a boy. "It's as if God sent Zach here to heal and help us establish the program for vets."

"I think you're right."

They walked toward the office. "Would you like some coffee?"

"Sure, bring me a cup."

They split up and she went to the office and Ollie walked into the stable. She heard the horses greet him.

She quickly made coffee and checked the schedule for today. She ate her muffin and poured herself a cup of coffee, gulping it down before she poured herself a second cup and Ollie his first.

Taking the mugs outside, she found him working in the tack room. She left the mug there and walked down the hall to greet each of the horses. Sam and Prince Charming always loved a greeting and pat in the morning.

She put the halter on Sam and brought her to the mounting steps. Walking to the tack room, she heard someone retching.

Looking into the tack room, she didn't see Ollie.

Whoever was throwing up continued to be sick. Sophie walked out of the stable and saw Ollie bent over. He stood on the side of the stable.

Racing to his side, Sophie put her hand on Ollie's back.

He looked at her and she saw the bleakness in his eyes.

"Let me help you to the office."

He didn't object, and that frightened Sophie more than anything else.

Once he settled in a chair, Sophie caught another chair and pulled it up to Ollie.

"What's wrong? And don't tell me it's a stomach virus."

Ollie wouldn't look her in the eye.

She grabbed his hand and held it. "Ollie, you can tell me anything. You're as close as my dad to me."

His eyes met hers. "Don't say that, because you don't talk to your father."

She gasped; his words nearly knocked her out of her chair.

"I'm sorry, Sophie. That wasn't right of me."

She wouldn't duck the truth. "You're right. I need to call my parents, but that's not going to tell me what's wrong with you."

He scratched the back of his neck. "I'm sick. Got cancer."

Shock and grief ran through her. "When did you discover it?"

"Right after Margaret had her stroke, I had bad stomach pains for a couple of weeks. I went to the doctor, thinking I might need something for an ulcer. He ran some tests and told me it was cancer. They operated and took out a tumor. Now I've got those torture treatments. Makes me sick for days. I can't even enjoy coffee."

"Why didn't you tell me?"

"'Cause you got enough problems without worrying about me. I wasn't going to put you into that hole. You need to be thinkin' about those kids and not some old coot."

Tears gathered in her eyes. "That's where you're wrong. You're my friend. More like a family member who's there to help." Snatching the tissue from the box on the desk, she wiped her eyes. "You are part of this team, and we share. If nothing else, I can pray."

Ollie grasped Sophie's hand. "That's why I know God sent Zach here. He's helping keep things together. And you're helping him."

His words struck a chord in her heart. "You're right. I think the Lord knew what we needed." She bit her bottom lip, praying for the right words to say to her friend. "You work as much as you like, but if you feel after a treatment you can't, don't come in. Call. We have several more volunteers coming. They won't replace you, but Zach seems good at directing them."

Ollie started to stand, but his legs gave out on him.

"Would you like to use the sofa in the guesthouse to lie down and take a nap?"

He shook his head. "Naw. I just need a little time to get my stomach right."

Glancing at her watch, she knew she needed to get back outside and saddle Sam. "Take your time, Ollie."

Over the next hour and a half, Sophie didn't have time to dwell on the news Ollie just gave her. Between the volunteers that needed to be directed and the kids and parents, every moment was filled.

Zach worked along with her, but she caught him stealing glances at her.

Ollie appeared and moved slowly about. He didn't act as a sidewalker, but helped with the horses.

After she finished working with her third rider, Sophie slipped into the office, telling herself it was for a bottle of water. She opened the mini-fridge and stared at the bottles of water. Tears filled her eyes and she couldn't see anything in front of her.

Lord, Lord, why?

She didn't remember closing the fridge door, or when Zach came into the office, but somehow she felt her face pressed against Zach's chest.

"Shh, Sophie." He lightly ran his hand over her back.

"Ollie has cancer," she said between sobs.

"I know."

It took several moments for Zach's words to sink in. When they did, she pulled back and looked at him. "You know?"

His fingers wiped away the tears. "He told me."

She stepped away from him. "And you've been keeping that a secret?"

"Ollie asked me to. He's worried that with Margaret's illness, it would be too much for you to have to worry about."

Anger flared to life. "How dare you not tell me something that important."

"Ollie asked me not to tell you. I gave my word."

"I don't care. You should've told me," she spat back.

"My word is my bond. I told Ollie that you needed to know, but he didn't want to tell you."

She wanted to yell at him, to tell him he should've told her, no matter his promise. Her conscience pricked her, letting her know she was being unreasonable. She wasn't ready to be reasonable yet. The hurt was too fresh. Instead, she turned around and walked out of the office. The next rider was here.

Zach worked with Red, a six-year-old mare that the younger children rode. He sprayed her down after her session and led her back to her stall.

He worked, trying not to think of how mad Sophie had been. He knew she felt betrayed. He prayed she would realize no one had betrayed her, but Ollie simply wanted to spare her the additional worry about his cancer.

Since Red was finished for the day, she needed to be groomed and fed. After he brushed her and rubbed her down, he walked to the feed room. Sophie stopped him before the door.

"I'm sorry for yelling at you."

"I understand. I was a convenient target. You couldn't yell at Ollie."

She leaned against the wall. "Am I doing the right thing here, Zach? It seems that major obstacles are being thrown in my way. Should I just quit after we finish these sessions?"

He touched her chin. "You think Moses wanted to give up the first time he asked Pharaoh to let the children of Israel go? Or the second time? Or the third time? Things got worse before they got better.

"And what of all those soldiers you want to help heal from their injuries? And are you going to leave Andy high and dry?"

"You know how to play dirty, don't you?"

He grinned. "That's not playing dirty. It's telling you that you have a mission. Don't give up. I know you've worked hard to save soldiers in Iraq, and you told them to fight, not give up, because their survival depended on their will to live. That was the key—the will to live. You've got that will, Sophie. And—" his eyes danced with delight "—you've got that in spades."

He saw the resolve enter her beautiful blue eyes. "You're right. I shouldn't complain, because neither Margaret nor Ollie is giving up. I don't have the right to give up, either."

He gave her a thumbs-up.

"Thank you." She leaned up and gave him a quick kiss on the lips.

"Miss Sophie, I'm here." A little girl stood in the broad entranceway to the stable. Her eyes were big and she'd obviously seen the kiss Sophie gave him.

Sophie looked back at him.

Zach wanted to return Sophie's kiss, but with an audience, he knew he couldn't. "Your next rider's waiting for you."

Sophie gave his hand a final squeeze before walking toward the little girl.

Zach's heart had nearly failed when Sophie asked if she should give up, if she was on the wrong road. He knew things weighed heavily on her but he didn't realize how much. He knew—and his heart and spirit confirmed it—that she was on the right road.

That "feeling" had happened several times in Iraq, when everything looked right, but something inside him shouted no. Other times, others said they were going the wrong way on a patrol, but he'd kept going and as it turned out, they'd avoided a problem.

The day he'd been caught by the roadside bomb, his spirit had been unsettled. He radioed his base that they were going to retreat and go a different direction to patrol that part of the section of Mosel when the bomb went off. Obviously, the insurgents had been watching them. Listening to his gut had saved most of his men and saved the little boy who'd approached the patrol for the usual chocolate they gave the kids.

It'd been a hard lesson to learn, listening to his gut. But he learned it well. He didn't want Sophie to regret her decision not to go forward with her dream.

She was on the right road.

Chapter Nine

Sophie clutched her purse in her hands and glanced over at Zach who sat behind the steering wheel of his pickup. "What do you want me to tell your parents?"

"Tell them the truth." He lifted his right shoulder. "I've got nothing to hide."

"Then why did you need me?"

He stared out at the oncoming traffic. "Sometimes it's easier for a person who isn't a relative to tell parents news than it is for the son or daughter."

She couldn't argue that. She wished that someone would've talked to her parents after her brother's death.

"I want you to understand that I'll answer honestly and won't sugarcoat anything," she pressed, wanting him to recognize she'd give an honest evaluation.

"I wouldn't expect anything else."

She nodded and looked out the window. Ollie's news still weighed heavily on her heart. She kept offering up prayers for his recovery.

The sign for the Golden Door came into view. They quickly parked and went inside. Sophie had never been to the upscale steak place in the northwestern part of the

city. Once inside, it took a moment for her eyes to adjust
to the dim light. Soft music floated through the air and
the tables were set with crystal water glasses and table-
cloths. The detailed wood paneling reminded Sophie of
an old English pub.

Zach's parents waved at them from a corner table.
They moved across the wooden floor to the table. Both
his mother and father rose and hugged Zach. Lynda
McClure was a beautiful woman who stood only a
few inches shorter than her husband's towering form.
Lynda's blue eyes quickly scanned her son. Sophie caught
Zach's father checking out how his son looked. From the
slight nod of approval, Ken McClure approved of his
son's progress.

"You look wonderful," Lynda exclaimed, kissing her
son on the cheek.

"The work agrees with you." Zach's father patted him
on the back.

Lynda moved to Sophie and enveloped her in a big
hug. "It's good to see you," she whispered. When she
pulled back, Sophie could see the gratitude shining in
Lynda's eyes.

His father grabbed Sophie's hand and gave it a
squeeze. "Hello, young lady." He stepped back. "You've
become a beautiful young woman."

Sophie blushed.

As they settled around the table, the waitress came
and took their orders. When she left, Lynda said, "Tell
us how Zach's doing."

Before Sophie could answer, Beth and Ethan walked
into the restaurant. The hostess moved the group to a
bigger table and after their orders were taken, Sophie
answered Lynda's question.

Throughout the meal, Ethan and Beth added their comments on how Zach had improved. Both his parents asked thoughtful, probing questions.

Zach's siblings praised him on his riding and work around the ranch.

"Mom, you should've seen him with that plastic light saber," Beth added after describing what happened on the last riding session. "I didn't know whether to laugh or cry when Sophie walked out of the office with it." Beth turned to Zach. "The look on your face was priceless." She patted Zach's hand. "Once you got over your initial shock, you gave it a try. I was awed. And proud. And you know what, this morning I tried something similar using a broom handle, and I'm telling you, it's not easy."

Zach's dad laughed. "That's what you were doing this morning on your horse? I choked on my coffee as I was looking out the kitchen window."

Beth's cheeks turned beet-red.

"I thought you'd lost your mind and I called your mother, asking her what that was about. Had you lost your job or had some sort of trauma I didn't know about? She said no. I wasn't going to ask you what you were doing because I was afraid I might have to contact a head doctor for you."

His comment brought chuckles from all at the table.

"I knew Zach's progress had gotten to a place where he needed a challenge." Sophie took up the conversation, enjoying the back and forth of this wonderful family. "I have to admit it wasn't my idea. When I called down to Brook Army, the therapist there gave me the idea. The guy I talked to had several more ideas on how to help build up Zach's strength. But I also think Zach's work-ing around the ranch helping with the chores has built up his strength." Sophie smiled at Zach, wanting him to know how much she appreciated his actions.

He smiled back.

All four of the others at the table traded looks. She wondered if she had anything on her face.

"The kids love him," Sophie added, wanting to break the tension. "One of my little boys told his friends about Zach's fake foot. He's had to show it to several of the other kids."

Lynda's mouth opened and Ken's eyebrow shot up.

"We're going to have a sort of graduation a week from Wednesday." Sophie looked around the table. "You should come and see the kids. It's amazing."

"Thank you for the invitation. I'd like to attend." Lynda turned to her husband. "Wouldn't you?"

"I would."

Beth and Ethan also wanted to be there.

Sophie excused herself and walked to the restroom. She felt as if she'd run a marathon and wanted a moment alone. Stopping in front of the sink, Sophie stared into the mirror. She didn't have anything on her face, which she'd feared she might have. Opening her mouth, she checked her teeth to make sure nothing was stuck there.

Looked good.

So the reason Zach's parents were staring at her was something she said? Something she said to Zach?

Lord, I see the love Zach's parents have. I wish—

The restroom door opened and Lynda walked into the room.

"Have we overwhelmed you?" Lynda asked, walking to Sophie's side.

Sophie turned and faced the older woman. "No. I'm thankful that Zach has your support, but—"

"But we were making it easy for him not to challenge himself? Enablers?"

Lynda understood what she'd been doing.

"Yes."

"That's why I wanted to thank you. You've shaken us out of our despair and made us do some soul-searching. I've prayed, asking God to help all of us, and He sent you. Thank you."

That news unsettled Sophie. "Beth was instrumental. If she hadn't brought Zach, then none of this would've happened."

Lynda nodded. "My little girl is a wonder."

A longing sprang up in Sophie's heart, seeing the affection Lynda had for her daughter. If only her mother felt that way about her....

The door opened again and Beth slipped into the room. She looked from her mother to Sophie. "Everything okay?"

Lynda laughed and pulled her daughter into her arms.

Zach watched his mother disappear into the women's restroom after Sophie. Alarm bells went off in his head. None of the people at the table said anything, but after a few minutes of uncomfortable silence, Beth excused herself and left.

Ethan glanced at his sister's back. "I wonder if mother's grilling Sophie some more over details of your therapy." He leaned over his plate. "You think Beth went to referee the conversation?"

Ken took the final piece of bread and slathered it with butter. "You know better than that, son. Your mama wouldn't do anything like that."

"True," Ethan acknowledged. "Mom won't nail Sophie with questions, but she'll find out what she wants to know, no matter what."

Truer words were never spoken, Zach thought. His mother wasn't confrontational, but Lynda McClure knew how to get information from an individual and she knew how to get her way. His father often lamented about being nailed by her talent more than once. Each of Lynda's children had been on the wrong end of their momma's questioning.

Ken settled his forearms on the table. "I'm glad Sophie's challenged you, son." He directed his words at Zach. "And I'm proud of you for taking up the challenge. I see the man I knew."

His father's words settled in his heart, bringing Zach's chin up in pride. "Thank you. That's what Sophie wants to do for other vets. Help soldiers find out who they are. She cut me no slack and expected me to be honest with her."

Ken's mouth pressed into a line.

Seeing his father's reaction, Zach realized how his words sounded. "I didn't mean—"

Ken waved off his son's apology. "We needed to be honest with you, son. The problem was we didn't know how to act."

Ethan laughed. "Be careful what you wish for, little brother, because you might get an earful."

Both his dad and brother had nailed him. God had been dealing with his heart. His family hadn't known how to cope with what had happened. He didn't know how to, either, so he got mad. At that point he didn't know what his future held, but he knew now he needed to work and get stronger.

"You're right. Sometimes what we think we want isn't

really what we need. But you need to pray that we can get this program up and running for other wounded vets. I know it will make a difference."

Before Ken could respond, the ladies rejoined them at the table.

His mother had an angelic smile on her face. Sophie looked fine, no worse for wear, and Beth grinned. That made Zach nervous.

As they drove away from the restaurant, Zach stole a glance at Sophie, trying to gauge her reaction to the night. She seemed lost in thought.

"Your parents are great," she mumbled.

"You think so?"

Her head jerked around and Sophie realized she must've spoken aloud. "Yeah. I've always been impressed with your mom and dad."

"Sometimes they're a little overprotective."

"Well, they could've gone in the opposite direction and not cared." The instant the words were out of her mouth, she clamped her lips together. Apparently, she said something she hadn't meant to say.

He ignored her embarrassment. "You've got a point, but sometimes they can be suffocating. I know Beth wasn't happy with them when her first date showed up at the house and my parents spent close to thirty minutes grilling him." He shook his head. "I thought the boy would swallow his tongue before they allowed them to leave for the date."

"Beth knows that's love."

"That's not the reaction she had at the time." He laughed. "I think Beth's reaction scared the poor boy more than my parents did."

"I can imagine. I only saw Beth mad once in the years we roomed together. It's not something I want to see again."

"See, I have a point."

"You do, but that's not the way a girl wants her date to go."

"Are you speaking from personal experience?"

The truck cab fell silent. She shook her head and looked out the door window.

They could go in the opposite direction and not care.

The words echoed in his brain.

Her tension reached out to him, making him wonder if her parents were the ones who didn't care. From what Beth had told him, Sophie didn't have a relationship with her parents.

"Thanks for inviting Mom and Dad to the graduation. I know they've been dying to see me ride."

She latched onto the lifeline he threw her. "They need to see you ride. Your brother and sister see it often, and can tell your folks about your progress, but they need to see it for themselves. I've invited the army officers to the ceremony, too. I want them to come out and evaluate the program."

That was the first he'd heard about the army coming to visit. "I hope they plan to spend some time and walk around the ranch and see what you have to offer. Have you submitted the proposal to them?"

"A preliminary one. I need to submit the final draft to them by Monday."

"Would you like for me to look at it? I could glance over it and give you my feedback."

Her shoulders eased and leaned toward him. "That

sounds great. You can tell me if I'm missing any of the bells and whistles I need." Her face lit up with excitement.

"Hey, it's the least I can do. I spent enough time in my unit helping others write requests. Our unit commander said I had the gift of *request*. If I requested it, we got it."

That got her attention.

"If that's the case, by all means, come and look my proposal over."

"Since tomorrow is Sunday, would you like to do that after church? Or I could meet you at church, we could eat afterward, then evaluate the proposal." The words were out of his mouth before he thought.

"I'd like that. I go to New Life Center in south Albuquerque."

"I know where that is." It struck Zach that his church attendance had been sadly lacking. He turned off the main road to the dirt road that led to the ranch.

"Good. There are two services. I usually go to the early service at nine o'clock."

"I can meet you there."

"Wonderful. I really like the pastor. He's an ex-military man. I think you'll like him."

"I'll look forward to it."

He pulled his truck into the parking lot. "Thanks, again, for talking with my parents tonight. I see that they're adapting. They seem to be easier with things."

"True, and it could be you're easier with yourself."

He stopped the truck beside the house. Her words set him back on his heels. Was that what he was feeling tonight? "You think so?"

"It's what you think that's important."

"No, no, don't give me that psychobabble. I was asking your opinion. I got enough of that kinda talk in the hospital."

"I think the reason my answer annoys you is because it's the truth." She put up her hand to stop his objections. "I noticed that your parents did seem easier with you. And the other thing I've noticed is your attitude is different. You don't want to bite anyone's head off."

"I wasn't that bad."

Her brow lifted. "You've changed, Zach. You've been a blessing to me. There's a strength in you that you needed to tap into and you have."

Her words made him realize that he'd come a long way.

"I'll see you tomorrow." She had her hand on the door handle.

He grabbed her wrist, stopping her exit. "I'll walk you to the door."

"That's not necessary, Zach."

Releasing her hand, he turned off the engine. "I know, but my mother taught me manners, Sophie."

Her cheeks puffed out and she blew out air. He easily slipped out of the truck, walked around it and opened the door for her. She shook her head and allowed him to walk her to the door.

She kept her head down as she unlocked the door.

"Sophie."

She looked up. He could see uncertainty in her eyes. He slowly lowered his head, allowing her time to refuse the kiss. She raised her lips fractionally and waited.

Satisfaction unfurled inside him. He cupped her face and covered her mouth with his. He felt her surrender and she returned his kiss. He didn't press for more. Lifting his head, he smiled down at her.

"'Night."

She nodded and slipped inside the door.

As he headed home, Zach felt a hope bubbling up in his spirit. He was looking forward to church tomorrow.

Sophie sat at the kitchen table, her Bible open, a cup of hot chamomile tea beside the Bible. She couldn't sleep and after an hour of tossing and turning, she got up and brewed some more tea. There were too many thoughts and feelings shooting around inside that she couldn't sort out.

She'd tried talking herself out of what she was feeling, telling herself she was headed for nothing but pain. In college, she liked Zach from afar, never having to engage with him or talk to him. It had been infatuation.

These past few weeks, working side by side with him, she experienced firsthand how after Zach accepted the challenge of building up his strength again, he hadn't turned back. He worked at building up his muscles and stamina.

The kids loved him. Andy couldn't get enough of him, and Zach was like a big brother to all the kids.

He charmed every horse at the ranch.

He won over Ollie.

What chance did she stand against all that charm?

But the cherry on top was seeing how his family loved him and he loved them back. That was how a family should be. Not cold and distant and lost in grief.

Her eyes fell on 2 Corinthians 1:3–4.

...The God of all comfort, who comforts us in all our

troubles, so that we can comfort those in any trouble with the comfort we ourselves have received from God.

Zach could do that.

And she would, too.

Chapter Ten

The final amen resounded through the auditorium. As the last strains of the organ faded, Sophie saw her small group leader, Rita Wells, rush out of the pew across the aisle and hurry over to where Sophie and Zach stood.

"Are you coming to class this morning?" Rita asked, looking at Zach. Sunday School classes ran concurrently with the services. If you went to early service, then you went to Sunday School afterward and vice versa.

Rita was in her late twenties, the wife of the assistant pastor. She introduced herself before Sophie could open her mouth.

Zach shook Rita's hand.

Rita glanced from Sophie to Zach. "How do you know Sophie?" she asked Zach.

Sophie wanted to grab Zach's arm and rush out of the church before Rita could question him. Rita had a mothering instinct that wanted all the young professionals in the church to find a mate. Sophie had turned down three dates Rita tried to arrange. It wasn't that Sophie didn't appreciate Rita's effort, but Sophie wasn't ready to join the dating scene, even at church.

"Sophie was my sister's roommate in college," Zach explained. "And she is a fellow army vet."

Sophie explained to Rita about their plan for helping soldiers and that's what they were going to do now and why they would be missing class.

The news caught Rita by surprise. She looked from Zach to Sophie, then back again. "I'll be praying for your efforts, Sophie. You let me know if you need any help. I've got a lot of teens who need projects. Your plan for the equine therapy sounds like something we might like to do."

The tension eased from Sophie's shoulders. "Thanks, Rita." She didn't waste any time, but pulled Zach out into the parking lot. They made plans to buy burgers on the way to Sophie's house, then eat them in her kitchen.

Zach picked up the burgers while Sophie went home, changed into jeans and a T-shirt and pulled out drinks and paper plates. Zach arrived a few minutes later and when he walked in, he held up the bags. "Chow."

They eagerly started on the burgers and fries.

"I thought for a minute there after the service that Rita was going to ask me for my ID and see what my intentions were toward you. I wanted to tell her that you're an ex-soldier, and she didn't have to worry about any male's motives because you could take them out."

Sophie choked on her fry. "Why do you say that?"

He sat back in his seat and grinned. "A mama bear isn't as fierce as your Sunday School teacher. I believe she'd be looking out for your interests."

Sophie dipped her fry in the ketchup and popped it into her mouth. "Rita thinks it's part of her job as the wife of the youth pastor to take care of all of us singles. I've been her latest mission." She shrugged. "I can't tell you the number of dates she's tried to set me up with nice guys, but…"

"You go on any of those dates?"

"No."

He rested his elbows on the table and reached for the two-liter bottle of Dr Pepper. "Why not?"

"Because I'm not looking for a boyfriend." She didn't want to tell him that none of those men made her heart flutter like he did. "I've got my hands full with the ranch. I don't have any spare time with trying to get the army program started. Speaking of which—" She stood and walked into the living room where the printer sat. Grabbing the pages from the tray, she brought it back to the table. "Here's my proposal." She handed him the pages. "Tell me what you think." Her stomach clenched with nerves.

Zach took the proposal and began to read it.

Over the next hour, Zach and Sophie went over every page, discussing how to improve and implement the program. He spotted several things he thought to reword, but he was impressed with Sophie's work.

"With those few changes, I think you've got a winner."

"I'll follow up with my army contact, and tell him we've refined the proposal." She smiled and squeezed his hand.

He wanted to lean over and kiss her. He saw the same awareness in her.

"I have some more of those cookies that were in the office." She stood and walked to the counter, grabbed the tin and brought it back to the table. Opening the lid, she presented him with homemade peanut-butter cookies.

"Beth told you that these were my favorite, didn't she?" He grabbed two cookies.

"No, she didn't tell me that. Other secrets, but that wasn't one of them. She told me about you sneaking out with Ethan and both going to a party you were grounded from."

He shrugged. "Well, I've got stories, too. Did Beth tell you that she followed us, then came home and ratted us out to my parents?" He laughed. "I didn't think I'd get to go to my junior prom. Who'd want to go the prom with a guy who had to muck out stalls for a month? I did finally forgive Beth in time for her college graduation," he teased. "But I was disappointed that I didn't see you there after all the work you did to get that degree."

She broke off a piece of the cookie and put it into her mouth. "I needed to report for basic training. You know the army isn't concerned with individual soldiers' time schedules. The drill sergeant didn't care about my walking the stage to receive my diploma. I wasn't going to get a pass."

That was true. You bent around the army, not the other way around. But he knew there were other reasons why she didn't stay. "Why'd you join?"

"I find that question strange coming from a man who joined before I did."

"I joined because both my father and grandfather were in the army. Grandpa, Korea. Dad, Vietnam. It was a McClure thing. And the ranch was going through some tough times and I needed cash to finish school. The army provided it." He popped the rest of the peanut-butter cookie into his mouth.

"The ranch had problems?"

He gave a shout of laughter. "It's only a matter of time

before a ranch goes through tough times. When I was a senior in high school, there was a bad drought in the northern part of the state, even for New Mexico. Mom and Dad were already paying for Ethan's college. Don't get me wrong, Ethan worked, tried to pay for as much as he could, but they couldn't swing my college, too. The army was the answer."

She fiddled with the salt and pepper shakers on the table.

"Why'd you join?" Zach pushed.

"I joined for the same reason you did—I needed the money for medical school. I wanted to become a doctor."

Her answer caught him off guard. "So why aren't you in medical school?"

Folding her hands on the table before her, she seemed lost in memories. A bittersweet smile curved her mouth. "I wanted to be a doctor—an E.R. physician—to help save people. But you know how the army changes you. For me, being in the field as medic, I was able to save guys. But I found once I helped save them, they were off on their own." She stopped, staring down at her hands.

"It was equine therapy and the healing that goes on in those sessions that I wanted to do, to help soldiers."

He rested his hand over hers and squeezed.

"It's the best of all worlds, horses and helping others," he supplied.

Her head came up and her gaze locked with his. "You do understand," she said. Her gaze lost focus as if she were remembering something. "My family had horses. My brother Matt loved to ride. So did I. Since we lived in a small town, we kept our horses in the stables outside of town.

"It was a beautiful spring day and we were out on

Easter vacation. I'd gotten into trouble. I hadn't done chores around the house and sassed my mom back. I was grounded. I couldn't ride that week. Mom had gone into Albuquerque to buy some new Easter clothes and Dad was off selling insurance. I was feeling persecuted, like only a twelve-year-old girl can feel, and went to the stables. Matt followed. I had saddled my horse, Twinkle, and was on it when Matt found me. He was mad. We argued, and Matt tried to grab Twinkle; she reared. Matt stumbled back and tripped over a pitchfork." She went silent. Tracks of tears ran down her cheeks.

His other hand came up and he held both of her hands.

"One of the tines of the fork pierced his lung and caught his heart. He only lived for about a week after."

Zach saw the horror and guilt in her eyes and he realized the burning purpose of Sophie's life was to save others when she couldn't save her brother.

"I got to see him in intensive care. He was on a ventilator and couldn't talk. I told him I was so sorry. It was my fault. He shook his head, but I knew it was."

"Sophie."

She refused to look at him.

"Sophie, look at me."

She didn't.

His hand came up and he cupped her chin, raising her gaze to his.

"It was an accident. You didn't intend for your brother to die."

"If I hadn't been at the stables, if I hadn't disobeyed my parents, it wouldn't have happened." Her mouth trembled.

Lord, give me the right words. "Did you want your brother to die?"

She jerked back and glared at him. "Of course not."
When she tried to stand to flee, he grabbed her hand.

He stood and pulled her to him. "Did you plan on the
event?"

"Are you crazy?"

"It was an accident, Sophie. An awful, tragic accident."

Her eyes sought his, wanting to see the truth of his
words.

"You were twelve. Right?"

"Yes."

His hands brushed the hair back from her face. "A
twelve-year-old does lots of stupid things, believe me.
You want me to tell you the stupid things I did? That
Ethan did? Or Beth? It was an accident, Sophie. There
was no malice in your heart."

She collapsed into his chest and wrapped her arms
around his waist as the storm of tears broke.

He rubbed her back as her body shook. His heart
ached with hers. Her brother's death had scarred her. But
with her reaction, he sensed there was more to the story.

He prayed for Sophie's wounded soul and he prayed
God would give him the right words to help and comfort
her. He now understood the driving force behind this incredible woman.

Finally, she quieted in his arms. She felt so right in
his arms.

She hiccupped. A giggle escaped her mouth. She
looked up. "Thank you."

"There's nothing to thank me for. I should thank you
for kicking me out of my funk."

"It was your family that you should thank. They're
the ones who prayed for you."

She stepped out of his embrace, then wiped her face. "I must look a mess." She walked to the kitchen sink, grabbed a paper towel from the roll under the cabinet, and wet it. With both hands, she placed it over her eyes.

He wanted her to talk more about her family, to fill in the part he knew she left out. "You should see Beth when she cries." He shook his head. "It's not pretty."

She laughed. "She might have an ugly cry, but she didn't give up on you."

That brought a grin to his face. "I know. But sometimes family can't get past the obvious. My mother cried every time she looked at my empty pant leg. Dad ignored the situation. Ethan and Beth didn't know whether to beat me or cater to me. How'd your family react?"

Her shoulders hunched. "Not well."

From her tone, he knew she wouldn't say anything more about her brother's death. He wouldn't push.

She picked up the proposal. "I think I'll input these changes and then email it to Colonel Norton. I'll follow up with a call to him tomorrow."

He'd been dismissed. He could fight it, but he wouldn't push. She revealed more of herself than she probably had in years. Beth didn't know the circumstances surrounding Sophie's brother's death. "I'll let myself out. See you tomorrow morning."

She turned and disappeared down the hall. Zach walked out of the house and down the walk. He looked out into the corral behind the stable. Prince Charming and Sam were out. He walked to the fence. When Prince Charming saw him, the horse walked to where he stood.

"Hello, big boy." Zach patted the animal on his neck. "Are you having a fine time for yourself?" The horse nudged his hand.

"I don't have any treats."

Prince Charming stood in front of him. Zach's thoughts returned to Sophie and what she'd revealed. She was twelve when her brother was killed.

That had to have been a dark time for all her family. She still carried open wounds from her brother's death. Was that why Beth had never seen Sophie's parents visit her at college?

What would it have been like not to have your family surround you and support you?

He'd been around a lot of guys in college and the army who didn't have contact with their families for one reason or another, but he noticed that a break with their families caused a loneliness in that person's heart. Could that be what he saw in Sophie's heart? Loneliness and despair?

He wanted to find out.

Sophie finished typing in the changes that Zach had suggested, saved the file, then composed an email to Colonel Norton. She included a mention of the graduation ceremony that they would have on Wednesday and invited him to come and see what they were doing. She promised to call him tomorrow to confirm plans.

When she hit the send button, she collapsed back into her chair. After exiting her email, Sophie closed her eyes and remembered Zach's words.

It was an accident.

Matt's death was an accident.

How Zach got her to talk about that day, she didn't know. She'd never told anyone about that day. Her parents didn't want to know the details, and her grandmother simply held her and comforted her. She never asked what happened. The only person she told was the sheriff when he came and talked with her. But with Zach the words burst out.

If she hadn't wanted to ride that day...

If Matt hadn't tried to stop her...

If she hadn't sassed her mother...

Matt had finally convinced his parents to allow him to work at the stables at the edge of town to earn extra money caring for other people's horses. Sophie loved to go with Matt and watch him. She often helped with chores. Matt even paid her a couple of dollars from his salary.

She wanted to work there, too. Their mom didn't like Matt working there, thought such manual labor wasn't as dignified as their mother wanted her friends to think of the family of the insurance broker. Having horses was fine and caring for those horses was the right thing, but mucking out stalls for other people wasn't how the privileged did it. But Grandma and their father told Mom she was being ridiculous. And selfish.

Suffocating under the weight of her memories, Sophie walked out of the house to the corral. The horses had been a refuge after Matt's death. Her mother had become withdrawn, seeming to give up. Her father had buried himself in his work, becoming the leading salesman in the Southwest. For Sophie, horses brought her closer to Matt. Neither of her parents objected.

As she walked by the open door of the stables, she heard a man's voice humming.

Drawn by curiosity, she walked into the stables. The tack room door stood open and the hummed tune of "Amazing Grace" drifted out.

She stepped into the door and saw Zach working on bridles. "I thought you went home."

Zach looked up from the leather in his hands. "I wanted to check the tack before I went home. It gets so busy around here, I thought I might get ahead of the curve."

Nodding, she walked into the room and sat on the barrel beside the door. "I made the changes you suggested and emailed Colonel Norton."

His large hands worked the cloth over the leather.

"It should be an exciting event, the graduation. It's a perfect time to invite people to view the program." He stood and replaced the bridle on the hook on the wall. "It might be a good time to invite your parents to view what you've done."

She jerked as if poked by a stick. "What?"

He moved to her side. "I think your parents would be proud of what you're accomplished here. Just let Andy loose on them. He'll convince them that you are the best thing since sliced bread."

The statement was so over-the-top, she laughed. "You're right. I probably should let Andy loose on the colonel, too."

"Naw, you let me loose on the colonel. I'll convince him that the program will be a benefit for the vets."

"Or I could let Ethan and Beth loose on him."

Zach's laughter echoed in the room. Sophie joined him.

After several minutes, Sophie smiled. "You know what I miss the most about my brother? I miss his laughter. It was a thing of beauty. No matter if you were in a sour mood, Matt's laughter could lift you out of your funk. I know my mother couldn't scold him while she was laughing. Dad loved the laughter. When Matt died, it was as if the light went out of our family."

Zach scooped up her hand. "Your parents were the adults, Sophie."

"You know, Zach, the night Matt died, I went into the living room to tell my mother how sorry I was and I heard her tell Dad if it hadn't been for me, Matt would be alive."

Zach's heart bled. What a devastating thing for a young girl to hear out of her mother's mouth.

"Did you talk to your mother?"

Her gaze fell to their joined hands. "No, I ran back to my room. I couldn't talk to my mother."

"What did your father say?" Maybe it wasn't as bad as it seemed.

Her left shoulder lifted. "I didn't hear what he said. I locked myself in my room. Over the next few days, Mom never said anything to my face, but I saw the accusation in her eyes.

"When we stood over Matt's casket, I wanted to trade places with him." She lifted her head. "I tried to be the best I could, but... My grandmother took up the slack. She tried to comfort me. And my youth pastor was great. He helped me, and got the kids in the church youth group to rally around me. I know I was the subject of a lot of prayers."

He lifted his hand and ran his fingers over her cheek. He wanted to shake Sophie's mother for losing sight of the child she had left. "Perhaps you should try talking to your mother about what happened."

Pulling back she asked, "Why?"

"She might not know you heard. Grief clouded her judgment. It's not fair to hold something a person says when they're mired in grief." He gave her a self-deprecating smile. "I know. I've said some ugly things I had to go back and apologize for. *Repent* is the word your pastor would use. And you're one of the people I have to apologize to."

"You don't have to do that, Zach. I understand the emotional pain you were in."

His eyes locked with hers. He knew when her own words echoed through her heart. She nodded. "I understand your point."

"I knew I was a jerk, Sophie, when you had to come after me that first time, wallowing in self-pity. Maybe your mother doesn't know how she wounded you."

He could see her processing his words. After several long moments, she nodded.

"I see what you're saying. I'll consider it."

He brushed a kiss across her mouth. "You're an amazing woman, Sophie Powell."

"No, I'm not."

He slid his arm around her waist. "Let's go see Prince Charming. I think he might like a carrot."

The lightness of his tone allowed her to relax. "He is rather spoiled."

They walked down the center of the stable to the far barn doors which stood open. Zach grabbed a handful of carrots. Prince Charming and the other horses were out in the corral. Once the horses saw them, Prince Charming made a beeline toward them.

The gelding nodded and bumped Zach's hand.

Sophie laughed. "He's worse than a big puppy."

"He is." Zach fed Prince Charming the carrot.

Sam nudged Sophie. She took a carrot from Zach and fed it to Sam.

"I guess you didn't stop riding after Matt died," Zach said.

Sam munched happily. "It was my way to stay close to

Matt. And there were times when I was on a horse that I cried and prayed. God talked to me through the land and horses. I know I talked to Him."

Zach understood that. "Sometimes when I was on my mount, and looked into a sunrise or felt the breeze on my face, I heard the voice of God. There's nothing like it."

"Amen."

That night after Sophie finished her evening chores, she walked into the house realizing that Zach's words had echoed in her spirit all day. They followed her as she fed all the horses. With time and Zach's perspective, she could see her mother's grief had overwhelmed her. Maybe she hadn't wanted Sophie to die, but it had been a wounded heart speaking.

The only way she would know was to talk to them.

Picking up the phone, she dialed her parents' phone number. She ignored the impulse to hang up. On the fourth ring someone picked up.

"Hello."

"Hi, Dad." Her stomach danced with nerves.

"Sophie, this is unexpected."

Not a great starting-off point. "I was wondering how you and Mom are doing."

"We're fine. Cindy, pick up the extension," he called out.

Her mother came onto the line. "Hello."

"Hi, Mom." Her stomach jumped with nervousness.

"Sophie."

It wasn't a warm welcome, but Sophie had to admit her part in the rift between them. "I wanted to invite you two to the ranch a week from Wednesday to see what we're doing here. You know I told you about the equine therapy. We're going to have a graduation for the kids. I thought you might like to see what I'm doing."

Both her parents were quiet. Her heart pounded.

"You don't have to come if you don't want," Sophie hurriedly added.

"We'd love to," her father said. "Isn't that so, Cindy?"

"I'd like that."

Sophie's mouth trembled. "Good. I'll see you around two in the afternoon."

"We'll be there," her dad answered.

Sophie next dialed her grandma and asked her to attend the ceremony, too.

"I wouldn't miss it, sugar," her grandmother replied.

"Mom and Dad are going to be there, too," Sophie added.

"It's about time that daughter of mine woke up. Don't you worry your head, Sophie. I'll be nice to your mother."

Sophie had heard her mother and grandmother arguing several months after her brother's death about her mother ignoring her only living child.

"I know you will be, Grandma. I thought you should know."

"You mean *warn* me. You're a thoughtful child."

When she hung up, hope fluttered in Sophie's heart. A hope she hadn't experienced since Matt's death.

Chapter Eleven

The next week sped by for Sophie. Ollie appeared stronger and was at the ranch every day. Color had returned to his face and his normal reserved attitude came back. Zach's strength also increased each day. By the end of the week, he brought his saber with him to the ranch. He wanted to try the lunge exercise with the "real deal." Zach and Ollie had rigged a hoop in the practice ring before the stands.

Before he started his practice, Zach's parents, brother and sister arrived and scrambled into the bleachers. Apparently, Zach had told his parents what he intended to do. Sophie saw Lynda offer up a prayer.

Zach rode with an ease of a seasoned cowboy and cavalry officer. Sophie smiled with pride. Zach beamed, and Ollie nearly busted his buttons. The McClures went nuts in the stands, with clapping, whistling and stomping on the wooden risers.

"Look at that," Ethan shouted. "Do it again, Zach."

It didn't take any encouraging to get Zach to repeat the performance.

"I knew that boy was good when I first saw him those

years ago," Ollie said to Sophie as Zach made another pass at the target. "He's got his balance back."

Joy flooded her. "Alleluia," she whispered, watching the performance. Zach seemed more like the boy she knew those many years ago. He smiled and laughed. He made her heart do somersaults in her chest.

She could only gaze at him in wonder and amazement.

Zach finished his ride. The grin on his face made him look sixteen again. He rode to Ollie's side and handed him his saber and dismounted.

"You're looking good." A smile curved the older man's mouth.

Zach's family raced out of the bleachers.

"Wow," Sophie said, looking at Ollie. Turning, she addressed Zach. "That's some high praise you handed out to him."

Ollie blushed. "I call 'em like I see 'em."

Sophie smiled, wrapping her arm around Ollie's shoulders. "I was teasing."

Before she could add anything, Zach's family engulfed him. Every one of them took turns hugging him.

Sophie's heart ached at the beautiful picture before her. The bridges that had been damaged between parents and child seemed to be repaired.

Lynda scooped Sophie up in a hug. "Thank you for giving me back my son." When Lynda pulled back, her eyes danced with joy.

"I didn't do anything. Zach worked. It's him you need to congratulate. He's done the work."

The chatter had died and Sophie's words rang out. She turned to Zach. "It's true. You worked. It's your victory."

"True, but I had a hard taskmaster."

"Hopefully, the army will share your opinion. I think

when those officers come to review the program, you'll blow them away."

The sound of cars pulling up in the parking lot drifted in the air, followed by the sound of car doors slamming.

"I think my time's over," Zach announced. "I'll put Prince Charming away. Sophie, could you lock up my saber in the office?"

His parents left and Sophie took the sword from Ollie. They scattered, each to a different chore.

An hour later, after Andy's session, his mother arrived to pick him up. Sophie had to take a call in the office. After she finished, she went looking for Zach. She needed to huddle with him about the call she had just received from the colonel.

When Sophie walked into the stables, she heard Andy ask, "So how do you keep that fake foot on?"

"It's a neat way. A vacuum."

"You mean like my mom's? That machine she uses to clean the carpet?"

Sophie stopped, curious to see what Zach would say.

"It's like that in a way. My fake leg latches onto my real leg. Ever put your hand under the vacuum?"

She couldn't see Andy, but she could imagine his expression.

"My leg's the same. See this button?"

"Yeah."

"If you press it, it makes the fake leg let go of my real leg."

Sophie peered around the corner to see Andy's little head bent over Zach's leg.

"Can I press it?" Andy looked up. His mother stood behind Andy.

Zach looked at his mother. She nodded.

"Sure."

The little boy pressed the button and the artificial leg slipped off.

"Oh, that's cool. It'd be fun if I had one of those."

"It's nice I have this leg, but it would be easier if I had my real leg, like you. This—" he said, touching the artificial limb "—makes things harder."

"So why'd you get this if you liked your real leg?"

Andy's mom's eyes widened.

Zach put up his hand. "It was an accident when I was a soldier. But the doctors fixed me up. And that's why I've been riding, to help me."

Andy sat back on his haunches. "I'm sorry for your accident. But it's good you have that 'ficial leg. You can walk normal."

"That's true." Zach slipped his leg back into the prosthesis.

Sophie walked around the corner.

Andy glanced up. "You see Zach's leg? I've been asking him if I could see. He talked to my mama and she said it was 'kay."

Andy jumped to his feet. "I understand now why he had to have the 'ficial leg. I wanted one, but it's good I have my own real legs." He smiled at his mom. "Let's go. I can't wait to tell Dad about this."

Andy's mom stepped to Zach's side. "Thank you. He's been curious about why you had the leg, why he couldn't have one, too, and why you got it."

Zach shrugged. "It's not a problem. And I think I answered his questions."

She nodded and went after her son. She paused by Sophie. "I hope you don't mind that Andy wanted to see Zach's leg."

Still struggling for her emotional balance, Sophie smiled. "Of course not. I'm glad that Zach could answer Andy's questions."

"Mom," Andy yelled.

"I'm coming," she replied. "Thank you." She nodded toward Zach.

Sophie leaned against the hall wall. Bewildered, she didn't know what to say.

"You upset?" Zach asked. He watched her carefully, expecting—what? Anger? Reprimand?

"No. I'm not upset. Surprised, but not upset."

"Are you going to yell at me that I shouldn't have showed Andy my leg?"

She didn't know where he was going. "No. If Andy's mom talked to you about the situation, I'm okay with it. Were you okay with it?"

He readjusted the cushioning sock on his stump and then put his leg into the prosthesis. He stood, putting pressure on the leg. He then pushed his pant leg down over the leg. The low boots he wore had a lower heel than normal cowboy boots, but when his pant leg fell over the boot, she couldn't tell that his shoes were anything else but a true cowboy boot.

"She surprised me, but she told me of how Andy wanted a 'ficial leg, too, just like Zach. I think she wanted to die of embarrassment, but Andy wanted to see my leg." He shrugged. "Andy asked honestly, so I showed him."

She noted how carefully he watched her reaction.

"You handled it perfectly. Thanks for answering his questions."

He visibly relaxed as if he'd been expecting a stern lecture.

"I was coming to tell you that I got a call from the

colonel just a few minutes ago. He's bringing his team out next Monday to look over the ranch and talk to us."

"That's great news. I'll be sure to be here bright and early." He started down the center aisle of the stables. He stopped and turned. "You like country music?"

"Yes."

"I have tickets for a Reba McEntire and Tim McGraw concert in Santa Fe this Friday night. Would you like to go?"

Suddenly, Sophie felt sixteen and being asked out on her first date.

"We could do dinner and the show."

"What about the horses?"

Laughing, he quipped, "I don't have tickets for them."

Resting her hands on her hips, she glared at him.

"I'll get Ethan to come and help us settle the stock. Will that do?"

"It will. And yes, I'd love to go with you to the concert."

"It's a date." He turned and walked away, whistling.

Turning, Sophie came face-to-face with Ollie. He grinned. "Good choice."

Smiling, she shook her head. If she didn't know better, she'd have thought Ollie set up the whole deal.

After the last rider's mother picked her up, the volunteers and sidewalkers helped care for the horses, bedding them down for the night. Ollie and Zach worked along with the volunteers.

As Sophie put out hay, she heard Austin in the stables. "As you can see, the stable is in great shape. If you want, you could also buy the stock, too."

Sophie froze in the stall.

"I'd like to look at the horses you have."

Sophie walked out of the stall. Zach emerged from the tack room. Ollie walked in from the large open doors at the end of the stables.

Austin and the man with him stopped.

"What can I do for you, Austin?" Sophie asked. She felt Zach's and Ollie's support.

He glanced at Zach, then back over his shoulder at Ollie. "Nothing. I was showing Mr. Jamison around the ranch."

The man held out his hand. "Cole Jamison."

Sophie shook his hand. "Sophie Powell. I'm in charge of running the ranch until Margaret returns."

Jamison's brow shot up. "I thought you told me that your mother was selling the ranch."

Both Zach and Ollie straightened.

With a tight smile, Austin nodded. "Mother realizes she's not ever going to be able to return to the day-to-day running of the ranch and decided to sell it."

Zach moved behind her. Ollie stepped forward.

"When did she tell you that, Austin?" Sophie calmly asked.

Glaring daggers at her, he said, "I'll talk with you later, Ms. Powell, after I've finished giving Mr. Jamison his tour." With those words, Austin dismissed her and guided Mr. Jamison out of the stable.

Sophie drew in several deep breaths to prevent herself from running after Austin and saying something she would later regret.

"Who was that?" Zach's words came from behind her.

"That was Margaret's son."

"And he wants to sell the ranch?"

She spun and looked up at him. "That's what it appears to be."

"Doesn't he know about the program you're developing for the army? And what of his mother's wishes?"

"It won't matter to him," Ollie spat out. "He's a little worm. He's never wanted any of this. He didn't support the equine-therapy program. I heard him arguing with his mother about this. Margaret did it in spite of her son's opposition."

Zach sat on the barrel outside one of the stalls. "What does this do to our plans for the army?"

"Nothing," Sophie answered.

Both men looked at her.

"When Margaret and I decided to try to set up this program for the vets, Margaret realized that if something happened to her, she told me I had first right to buy this ranch."

Ollie grinned. "Ah, that's my Margaret."

Sophie hid her shock at Ollie's comment. Ollie and Margaret?

Zach stood. "If Margaret wanted to sell, could you buy the ranch?"

"Yes, I have that right, and I'm sure Austin doesn't know about that."

Ollie slapped his leg as a bark of laughter escaped. "It'll be a major sticking point to his plan to get rid of this place."

"Did you put it in writing?" Zach asked.

"Yes."

Zach's eyes crinkled at the corners as he grinned. "Aw, you're a smart girl."

"Well, I have to share that title with Margaret. We decided to put our agreement in writing, just in case something happened. And it did."

Sophie walked out of the stable and watched as Austin and Jamison walked to their cars. Sophie waved at Austin. "I need to talk to you," she called out.

Austin said something to the other man, and slapped him on the shoulder. Jamison got in his car and drove off. Austin waited until the other man was out of the parking lot before he walked toward Sophie.

"What can I do for you, Ms. Powell?"

"How's your mother?" Sophie asked.

"She's improving. Her speech is getting better. The doctors tell us they don't think she'll walk again. She won't ever be able to run a ranch again."

Hearing how poorly Margaret was doing, Sophie wanted to cry. "I'm sorry to hear that, but I do have to tell you that your mother gave me first right to buy this ranch."

Austin's dismissive attitude evaporated. "What?"

"Your mom told me if she decided to sell this ranch, I would have the first right to buy this place."

"I know nothing of this."

"Your mother conducted business and I'm sure you didn't know of most of the day-to-day items of business she dealt with."

He waved off her words. "You could say anything you like and it doesn't make it true."

"You're right, but we put our agreement in writing."

His eyes widened. "I'd like to see that."

"I'll find that agreement and I can fax you a copy of it. I also think that she left a copy of the agreement with her lawyer. He'll have a copy of it, too."

"I'll check out your story. I'll be back in contact with you." With those final chilly words, he stalked to his car, got in it and sped off.

Later that night, after Sophie faxed a copy of the agreement to Austin, she got a call from him.

"You've got until next Friday to come up with the money for the ranch." He named a sum.

"That is not fair market value," Sophie replied. "Did your mother okay that?"

"I've been appointed guardian over the estate. That's the price I want for the ranch."

Sophie heard what he left unsaid. That was the price that Jamison would pay.

"If you can't come up with the sum, I'll sell it to another bidder." He hung up.

Sophie stared at the phone as if it was a snake. What was she going to do? She thought she knew what God wanted her to do: run this ranch. Help others.

"Lord, with You everything is possible. I need Your help now."

Chapter Twelve

Sophie left the bank and walked to her truck. The loan application seemed to go smoothly. The bank wanted collateral. The contract with the army would provide that. The loan officer knew Margaret and her, and was reassured by the future income.

Thinking of her old friend, Sophie wanted to see Margaret, to touch base with her.

The private recovery hospital was near the bank. It took only a few minutes to drive to the facility. Margaret had come back from her physical-therapy session. When the attendant wheeled her into the room, Sophie noticed a sparkle in the older woman's eyes.

The man left Margaret in the wheelchair.

Sophie kissed Margaret on the cheek. "How are you doing?"

Margaret nodded. Speech was still hard for her.

Sophie pulled her chair next to Margaret and took her hand. "We miss you at the ranch, but the Lord sent Zach McClure." Sophie spent the next twenty minutes talking about what had happened at the ranch, how Zach came to the ranch and her deal with him.

"I think those army officials will be blown away with what we can do. You should see him, Margaret. He's physically stronger, but I see a smile on his face. And laughter. He started laughing again.

"I nearly passed out when I saw Zach showing Andy his prosthesis." She shook her head, a grin playing on her mouth. "But that action answered all of Andy's questions. Zach has a wonderful way with the kids." Looking down at Margaret's hands, she whispered, "I'm confused, old friend." She raised her head. "I think I'm falling in love. But I'm scared, Margaret."

"No," the older woman said.

"No, what?"

"Afraid. Trust—" She tapped her heart.

Sophie didn't know if she could trust her heart. "That's easier said than done."

Margaret squeezed her hand. "Ranch. Heard Austin sell."

Sophie wondered if Margaret knew about her son's actions. "Do you want to sell the ranch?"

The door to the room opened and Austin stood there.

"What are you doing here?" he demanded in his usual nasty tone.

Sophie leaned back in her seat. She wondered if Austin paid someone to report her appearances to him. "I came to see your mother. She's making good progress."

"She is, and she probably needs to rest now after her session."

Margaret shook her head. "Stop."

Austin came to her side. "Mother, you need your rest."

Sophie didn't want to upset her old friend or bring any more problems into the situation.

"I need to go." Sophie patted Margaret's hand. "You're looking good and you're in my prayers."

Margaret tried to smile, but her weak left side gave her smile a lopsided twist.

Sophie quickly left the room and started down the hall. Standing in front of the elevator doors, Sophie noticed Austin walking out of his mother's room toward her. He held up his hand, preventing her from getting on the elevator when the doors opened.

"Ms. Powell, I don't want you visiting my mother without me in the room." Hostility radiated off the man as heat came off the stove.

"Why is that?"

"Because I don't want you to say things that will upset her," he responded.

"Like the truth?"

"Maybe your version of the truth."

"Too late. She knows you want to sell the ranch."

Austin's lips compressed. "I don't want you around my mother."

"Why, Austin? Margaret and I are friends. We've been friends for a long time, since before I graduated from high school."

He stepped closer. "I know, and you've been trying to worm your way into her heart from the first. What's wrong with your relationship with your own mother that you have to find another?"

Sophie gasped.

The second elevator doors pinged opened and Ollie walked out. He looked at the two before him.

"Everything okay?" Ollie asked.

Sophie turned to her friend. "Yes. Margaret's doing well."

Ollie nodded, but he didn't move.

She walked into the elevator. As the door slid closed, she saw Austin glaring at her.

Zach parked his truck beside the guesthouse on the ranch. He felt like a raw sixteen-year-old on his first date. Things were moving so fast, he needed to hold on or he was going to be thrown off this pony.

He finally acknowledged his feelings for Sophie. If he was honest with himself, he'd had feelings for her for a long time. She was amazing. Watching all the people depending on her, he knew that she didn't shirk from any of the responsibilities.

But he knew she had a hole in her heart. He understood that. She had wounds. He did, too.

He knocked on her door.

"It's open," she called out.

He walked into the living room. He felt foolish for bringing her flowers, but if this was an official date, he wanted to do it right. He looked down at his clean, white Western shirt and his starched jeans. The creases were military sharp. He had on his winning buckle. It wasn't the "all-around" that he wanted, but it reflected his wins.

He tested his new boots. He'd talked to the army to see if he could get another prosthesis that he could put into a boot. Once that prosthesis was slipped into the flat of the boot, it would be next to impossible to get out, but it was worth it to be wearing real Western boots again. He had on his best Stetson, but took it off inside.

He heard a sound from the hall and turned. The breath left his chest. Sophie stood there in a peasant blouse and a tiered white skirt. A silver concha belt circled her small waist and a beautiful squash blossom silver necklace hung around her neck. On her left wrist she wore an engraved silver cuff bracelet.

Her long hair fell loose down her back and silver earrings dangled among the strands of reddish brown hair.

His mouth fell open.

She gave him a shy smile. "Too much?"

Words stuck in his throat. It was like Prince Charming kicked him in the chest.

"I thought I'd get in the spirit of the concert and go Western, but if it's too much—" She started to turn.

"No." His brain finally kicked into gear. "It's not too much." Swallowing, he stepped forward. "Don't change. You look great."

The blush on her cheeks faded. Her gaze ran over him from head to toe. "Apparently, I'm not the only one who got dressed up."

He grinned. "Yup. I decided to do it up good. It reminds me of my first dress-up dance. My jeans had so much starch they stood on their own."

Her laugh touched his heart.

"I'm surprised those jeans didn't crack when I sat in my truck to pick up my date." He looked down at the jeans he had on now. "These aren't that bad. Of course, my uniforms had their share of starch." He knew she'd understand that comparison.

He realized he still held the daisies and tiger lilies. Raising his hand, he offered them to her. When she smiled, Zach noticed a dimple on the right side of her mouth.

"Thank you."

Their hands touched and the electricity ran up his arm. She moved away and went into the kitchen. After opening several cabinets, she pulled out a tall plastic cup. "This will have to do. I'm sure Margaret has something up in the main house, but I don't think I'll find anything here in the guesthouse."

After fixing the flowers, she put them on the table.

"Let me get my purse and wrap and we can go."

She disappeared into the other room.

Suddenly, life was very sweet. *Thank You, Lord. I know my attitude stank, but You were there and didn't leave me to my own pity.*

Sophie appeared, a gold shawl covering her shoulders. "I'm ready."

"Then let's go and stomp our feet."

The concert had been great. Sophie hummed the last duet Reba and Tim sang. Zach joined in. His wonderful baritone filled the cab of the truck.

"I think you went into the wrong business," Sophie said after they finished.

"Naw, I wasn't interested in singing." He shot a glance at her. "But the choir director nabbed me when my voice changed. Of course, he had to wait because one day I could sing the notes and the next day, I could've been a tenor. I'm telling you, there's nothing worse than trying to be cool in front of all the girls at school and church and then having my voice be all over the map."

"Well, that's a good reason, but your voice changed a long time ago. I think your excuse has run its course."

"Ya think?"

She laughed. "It's a convenient excuse."

He pulled into the parking lot of a trendy restaurant that claimed to serve home cooking and old-fashioned fare like your grandma cooked. It stood on the corner of a square filled with restaurants, trendy shops and several coffeehouses.

Studying the restaurant, she said, "I've wanted to try the food here. I heard good things about it." The fantasy night continued. She waited for Zach to come around and open the door for her. She got out and waited for Zach to close the door. Zach slipped his arm through hers as he guided her inside.

They were quickly seated and continued to joke and tease during dinner. Once outside, Zach guided her past his truck to a trendy new coffeehouse down the street. Over their lattes and cappuccinos Zach asked about the loan and status of the army proposal.

"I think the bank was impressed that I could get that contract. I touched base with the colonel yesterday and everything's a go. But I wouldn't be surprised if they just show up another day. You know, one of those surprise inspections." She saw the understanding in his eyes.

"I've been there and I know the drill. I remember one day—"

"Zach," a booming voice called out. A tall man approached the small table. "It's so good to see you."

Zach stood and shook the man's hand. "Tyler. What are you doing here?"

The man stepped back and nodded to Sophie. He turned back to Zach. "I'm out. My unit came back to the States around Christmas."

Zach turned to Sophie. "This is Tyler Lynch. He was with a unit in northern Iraq. Our paths crossed when he was briefly assigned to my unit to see how to operate some new equipment we got from the States." He introduced Sophie and bragged about her service.

Tyler's attitude changed and the walls he'd put up

seemed to lower. She was a vet and he knew he could talk freely.

"Sit," Zach said.

Tyler waited for Sophie to okay the invite.

"Please join us."

The woman working behind the counter shouted a "Café Americano." Tyler jumped up and got his coffee. He rejoined them. "I missed this when I was in Iraq."

He sat and they quickly began to swap stories.

"So you were a medic?" Tyler asked.

"I was. Unfortunately, I saw more than my share of the war."

Tyler looked down at the tablecloth. "My unit adopted a stray puppy while we were there. We called her Dodger, because we found her under a piece of a blown-up car. I guess she was far enough from the explosion that the piece of fender knocked her out. I heard a whimper and thought we might have a child. Searching through the rumble, we found her. Our medic cleaned up the wounds on her side and she stayed in our tent until she was well."

His story touched Sophie's heart. She rested her right arm on the table. "What happened to Dodger?"

"I had to go through a lot of channels, but I brought her home with me."

Sophie clapped and met Zach's smiling eyes.

"Too bad you couldn't have taken your horse," Sophie teased.

Tyler looked from her to Zach. "Am I missing something?"

Zach explained what had happened to him.

"Man, I'm sorry to hear that." Tyler looked over Zach. "I never would've guessed it the way you walked across the floor and shook my hand."

"I think you're going to have to thank Sophie. She's the hard drill sergeant who whipped me into shape."

Tyler's body language changed and he focused his attention on Sophie. "Tell me about it."

They spent the next forty-five minutes talking to Tyler about what they wanted to do at the ranch.

"If you'd like, come to the ranch," Sophie offered, seeing the man's interest. "If you live close, we always need sidewalkers. Also, we have a little graduation on Wednesday for the kids in the program. You might enjoy seeing that."

"I might check that out." He stood. "It was nice meeting you, Sophie." Holding out his hand, he turned to Zach.

Zach grabbed Tyler's hand and stepped forward. With a slap on the back, he whispered something in Tyler's ear.

Sophie watched as Tyler threaded his way through the crowd and out the door. Zach sat down.

Toying with her paper cup, Sophie murmured, "I wonder what memories he's wrestling with."

"You saw that darkness in his eyes, too."

"Yes." Sophie's mind filled with her own visions of war—wounded men and women, blood, missing limbs, the cries of the wounded, the silent haunted eyes. The silent ones were the worst. She recognized that look anywhere. "What'd you say to him?"

Zach hesitated, then said, "I told him he wasn't alone."

"You think working with the horses might help him?"

"You've made a believer out of me. I think it will help him." His forehead wrinkled. "I found it interesting that he brought the dog back with him from Iraq."

They exited the shop and strolled back to his truck.

His fingers tucked a long strand of hair behind her ear. "You're amazing, Sophie Powell."

"Why do you say that?"

His lips tilted up at one corner. "Because you're ready to jump headlong into helping Tyler."

She slid into the truck. Zach closed the door and walked around the front and got into the driver's seat. As he pulled out into traffic, he glanced at her. "Nothing to say?"

"There's nothing to say. I recognize pain and want to help."

He fell silent as he drove her back home. She stewed over Zach's words. She recognized pain. It was an area she knew a lot about.

As he parked his truck beside her house, he grabbed her hand and brought it to his lips. "I didn't mean to make you uncomfortable."

"You didn't."

He nodded and released her hand. Sophie didn't wait for him to open her door. She slipped out of the truck and met him on the walk to the house.

He took her hand again and walked with her to the porch. "Talking with Tyler tonight, I saw his hurting and guilt."

She jerked around to face him. "Guilt?"

"Yeah, I saw it." He touched his chest. "I've also felt my own guilt."

What was he talking about?

"Guilt for living when others didn't," he explained. "I should've done a better job on that last patrol. When I was telling you you needed to forgive yourself for your brother's death, I had the head knowledge.

"Seeing Tyler tonight, I realize that those words have

to be more than something I throw out. I have to do it. I have to forgive myself." There was no joy in his smile, only sadness and pain. "Sophie, you need to cut yourself some slack. Forgive yourself."

Her heart pounding, she whispered, "It can't be that easy."

"You're wrong. When a person gets saved, that's the argument they use. It can't be that easy. It is." He grabbed her other hand and held it close to his chest. "Lord, help Sophie and me to forgive ourselves. You've forgiven us, now show us how easy it is. Amen."

When her eyes met his, she knew every word out of Zach's mouth was truth.

He kissed her forehead. "I'll talk to you tomorrow."

She watched him leave. On unsteady legs, she walked to the barn. Sam bobbed her head, drawing Sophie to her side.

"Is it that easy, Sam?" Sophie rubbed the white blaze on her nose. Closing her eyes, she whispered, "Lord, I give You the guilt I've been carrying. You forgave me, and I forgive myself."

Suddenly, Sophie felt a peace in her soul. The weight of guilt pressing on her heart wasn't there.

She opened her eyes and looked around, expecting a two-ton stone somewhere on the floor behind her. Everything was as it had been before, and yet the barn looked brighter. Sharper. More full of life.

Sam nodded her head.

"So you're agreeing with me that burden is gone?"

Sam butted her. Sophie held the mare's head and kissed her as tears slid down Sophie's cheeks.

Her steps back to the house were lighter. The world was new.

* * *

Zach woke early and ate, and read his Bible. He couldn't wait for church. Last night when he heard himself comforting Sophie, the words that tumbled out of his mouth shocked him. Every word he uttered was directed at himself.

He knew he'd been holding on to guilt. Last night, he gave that burden away. He'd tried to protect his men. He'd sensed the danger and tried to short-circuit it.

Always, he would grieve his friends' death, but peace had settled in his spirit.

Glancing down at the table, he saw the verse in Joshua 22:3–4 and it resonated in his heart.

For a long time now—to this very day—you have not deserted your brothers, but have carried out the mission the Lord your God gave you...now return to your homes....

He hadn't deserted his men and tried to save them all. Most of his men came home. He gave it his all and reading those verses gave him peace. "Lord, thank You for taking that burden from me and giving me a pardon."

His guilt was forgiven. It was no longer his.

He got it and he was ready to go to church and celebrate.

Chapter Thirteen

At nine in the morning on Monday, Colonel Norton arrived with two other officers. He introduced the two men with him, Major Simms and Captain Perry. All three men were with the Cavalry and out of Fort Sam Houston in San Antonio.

"I'm glad we finally meet face-to-face, Captain Perry," Sophie told him. "Your suggestions for therapy were excellent. And Zach here is living proof."

After introductions were made, Zach told the officers his story and showed them his leg. He then brought Prince Charming out of his stall, saddled him with a regular saddle and mounted the horse.

Sophie held back the tears of pride, knowing she didn't want to be seen as an emotional female in front of these men. She wanted their respect. Later, she'd have a good cry and offer her prayers of thanks to the Lord.

Zach went through several of the exercises he used. When he did his saber lunges, Sophie knew he impressed the captain.

"Attaboy," Ollie said under his breath as Zach rode around the ring again for another jab.

Sophie's eyes never left the colonel and major. Their expressions gave away none of their thoughts.

The sound of a car arriving floated in the air. A door slammed, followed by Andy's mom yelling, "Walk, son, don't run."

"Aw, Mom."

Zach made one more pass at the target.

"Wow," Andy cried. He ran to Sophie. "Did you see that?" As he walked to the corral fence, he said to Zach, "You're getting real good."

Zach stopped Prince Charming beside Andy. "I've been practicing."

"Me, too. I'm better, too."

Zach rested his forearm on the saddle horn. "You are, and there are some people here who'd like to see you ride."

Andy glanced at the officers sitting in the bleachers. "They have on fancy uniforms."

Sophie bit back her smile. "Okay, Andy, let's get you ready to ride."

The boy grinned.

The officers spent the day watching how things were handled. At one point, when a sidewalker didn't make it, the major took off his uniform coat and worked beside Zach. All three men were comfortable around horses and did their share. They talked to the parents and riders. Once during the day, Sophie saw Ollie bending the ear of the major.

At the close of the day, Sophie sat in the office and faced the men.

"Do you have any further questions for me?" she asked.

Major Simms studied her. "Do you plan on having a therapist here on-site?"

"I work in tandem with most of the kids' doctors and if they have therapists, I keep in contact with them."

"You realize that the men you'll be dealing with will need to have a therapist on-site."

Her stomach twisted into a knot. "That could be arranged."

Colonel Norton's laserlike eyes pinned her. "Are you the owner of the ranch?"

"Margaret Stillwell owns the ranch at the moment, but I'm in the process of buying it."

"Is the owner about?" he pressed.

Sophie felt Zach stiffen beside her. "No. Margaret had a stroke and that's why she needs to sell the ranch. But when we came up with this proposal, Margaret was healthy and wanted to expand the program to help vets. Zach is a perfect example of how horses can bridge a gap in therapy that sometimes a skilled therapist has difficulty."

The men looked at Zach.

"You've seen my leg. I fell flat on my face walking around the ring the first time. But the lure of riding again and being with horses was stronger than my pride."

"But you were raised around horses," Captain Perry countered.

"I was, but there's magic in a horse and each of you know that, being horse people. It's a win-win for the soldier."

"It really doesn't matter," Sophie added. "When I was in D.C. attending a workshop, I went out to the program that worked with the caisson horses used at Arlington National Cemetery. Some of the soldiers didn't have any experience with horses. Others did, but it didn't matter. It's how the patient feels on top of that magnificent animal. They're connected. They feel as if they have their power back. It helped every patient I saw. Double amputees, single, even one man who lost both legs and an arm."

The three officers sat back. Colonel Norton looked at his watch. "We've got a plane to catch." He rose and the others followed. "Thank you for letting us see the facility. We'll be in contact."

Sophie accompanied the officers to their car. As she watched them drive away, Zach rested his hand on her shoulder.

"Don't worry about it."

She turned to him. "How can I not? I think things went well until they asked about a therapist."

"That's something you can get." He pulled her into his arms.

"I hope you're right."

Laughter rumbled through his chest. "I am. Ask Beth and Ethan. I'm always right."

She raised her head. "Is that so?"

A self-satisfied smile curved his mouth. "It is."

Wednesday dawned bright and clear. Sophie's stomach jumped and twisted as if she'd swallowed a mouthful of grasshoppers. She walked to the refrigerator, grabbed the whole milk and poured herself a glass. When she was a kid, her mother would pour her a glass of milk and tell her milk was magic and would fix anything.

The milk was from the local dairy the next ranch over. The rich taste made Sophie smile. She drank the glass. Her stomach settled. "I hope you're here today, Mom. If you are, I'll have to thank you."

Sophie sat down at the kitchen table, opened her Bible and spent several minutes reading. She closed her Bible and bowed her head and prayed. "Lord, help us today. Let me walk with Your wisdom, because I know I'll need it."

Sitting back, she opened her eyes. It was time to face the day.

Zach looked out from the stable entrance to the stands, which were filled with parents—the riders' parents and his parents. He saw a couple come and talk to Sophie, then an elderly lady. Sophie hugged and kissed the old lady. By the time he got to her side, the group was gone. "Who was that?" he asked.

"My parents and grandmother."

His gaze snapped back to hers. "Your parents?"

A frown settled between her eyes. "You think I don't have parents?"

He realized his mistake too late. "No. I just haven't met them."

Her expression remained firm, then a smile broke across her face. "You know, you look kinda cute when you blush."

This conversation was a losing proposition for him. "I need to make sure all the horses are ready."

Her laughter followed him into the interior of the stable. As he walked to Prince Charming's stall, his mind went over the meeting he saw. Sophie politely greeted her parents, but she hugged her grandmother with an openness. That made sense from what she'd told him and what his sister said.

He quickly saddled Prince Charming and led the horse outside. Sophie stood in front of him directing the other volunteers.

"Are we ready?" Zach asked.

She didn't turn. "I think so. You want to take the riders down the path to the river?"

"You think the kids will make it that far?"

Glancing back over her shoulder, she said, "Yes."

They would do the graduation in two waves. There weren't enough horses to let all the kids ride at once. Also the volunteers would come in two waves.

Zach mounted Prince Charming. Every time he put his foot into the stirrup and hoisted himself into the saddle, he offered a prayer of thanks. He didn't think he'd ever take for granted being able to ride.

From his perch on top of Prince Charming, he saw Tyler, his army buddy from Iraq, in the audience. By his side sat a black dog. A mutt. The dog sat quietly, not being disturbed by the crowd. "Tyler's here."

Sophie looked into the audience. "I see him. And he has a dog?"

"Remember he told us about that dog."

"Yeah, I remember. Okay, let's go." Sophie walked to the mounting block. Andy scrambled up on Sam.

It took several minutes for the rest of the riders to mount, their sidewalkers beside each horse.

Sophie led Sam out into the ring. "I want to thank everyone for coming today. Each of the riders you see here has worked hard and improved their balance and strength. I want to thank the parents here today for working with us."

"Hey, Mom," Andy said, waving to his mother.

The crowd laughed.

"We're going to ride around the ring and then take the path to the pond beyond the last corral. You are welcome to walk down there with us, but if you don't want to walk down there, you're welcome to stay here."

Zach rode out and Sophie followed, leading Sam. All the other horses fell in line behind them. Zach rode out of the corral and started down the path. Pictures were snapped and parents called out to their children.

It was better than any championship rodeo buckle he could earn, Zach thought. And suddenly Zach knew God had shown him the new path his life was to take.

People milled about the tables set up under the trees at the far side of the rings. Several mothers had baked cookies and cupcakes. Ollie had brought a case of soft drinks. Andy's mom had a bowl of punch for the kids.

"Did you see me, Mom?" one of the little girls asked.

"I was good—"

"What a good job you did—"

Voices floated around Sophie. All the snatches of conversation she heard were positive.

Sophie's parents stopped before her.

"This is impressive," her dad said, looking around at the crowd. "You did this yourself?"

"No. Margaret and I worked together."

"Where is she?" her mother asked.

"Stop, Cindy," Sophie's grandmother scolded. "Don't you have anything nice to say to your daughter?"

Her mother's spine stiffened.

"Margaret had a stroke," Sophie quickly supplied, hoping to defuse the tension. "She's recovering. Weren't the kids great?"

"I was amazed," her grandmother said. "They all looked like they were enjoying themselves."

"Miss Sophie," Andy called out, running to her side.

"You see my mom and grandma waving at me? And Zach's parents? I told them not to worry about Zach's leg. It worked fine."

Sophie ruffled Andy's hair. He turned and looked up. "You know Miss Sophie?"

Sophie's father nodded. "I do. She's my daughter."

Pride laced her father's words. Sophie bit her lips to keep them from quivering.

"Really?" Andy looked from her father to Sophie.

"Yes. And this is Sophie's mother and grandmother."

Andy smiled at each woman. "Are you as proud of Miss Sophie as my mom is of me?"

"Andy, Andy," his mother called.

He ducked his head. "I gotta go." He waved and dashed off.

Sophie noticed that her parents didn't answer Andy's questions, but silence reigned.

Finally, her mother cleared her throat. "You have a lot of volunteers here."

"I do. I've been amazed by the number of people who donate their time to help with the kids. If I get the army contract, I know I'll have plenty of ex-military members who will help. And wasn't Zach amazing? He's Beth's brother."

Her father glanced over at Zach, who huddled with his family. "I don't understand. He rode at the front of the line."

"Dad, he was wounded in Iraq and lost the lower half of his right leg."

"Oh."

"Zach was my test case."

"I heard my name being used." Zach strode up to the group. His family surrounded him.

Sophie did the introductions. Sophie stepped back and listened in amazement as Zach's family sung her praises.

"It is amazing what she's done with Zach," Lynda gushed.

Sophie watched her parents' reaction to the McClures' praise and their glowing opinions of the work done at the ranch. Andy's praise, combined with the McClures', made her mother squirm. Her grandma caught Sophie's eye and winked.

One of the mothers pulled Sophie away from her family. That was the last time she was able to talk to them. Other people demanded her time. The volunteers and families thanked her.

She watched Zach talk to the veteran they'd met the other night. The dog beside him sat quietly. The dog's eyes moved over the crowd, but he didn't leave his master's side. No leash kept the dog in place. Sophie wanted to join the conversation, but knew Zach and Tyler needed time to talk.

"Guide Zach's words, Lord," she whispered. Although Tyler had all his limbs, he wasn't whole. There were wounds in his spirit that needed healing. That's what she wanted to do, help the healing.

She might be in this place because of the guilt she'd carried from her youth, but freed from that weight, Sophie discovered this was what she wanted to do. She had a talent and a love for this work.

Late in the afternoon after all the families had cleared out, and her parents and Zach's parents had left, Sophie looked out at the empty yard.

"I think your graduation succeeded beyond your wildest dreams."

When Sophie turned, she saw the slight limp in Zach's gait. "You're tired."

"So are you."

"It's a good tired. Kinda like Moses at the end of that battle with—oh, some guys—the Israelites were still wandering around the desert. They were attacked and as long as Moses had his arms raised the Israelites were winning. When he put his arms down, they were losing. As I recall, he had to have assistance holding up his arms."

"I know the feeling. C'mon, I'll walk you back to the house then head on out."

"I wish Colonel Norton could've seen this."

Zach shrugged. "You know the army. They work on their schedule, but at least they made it here."

He slipped his arm around her shoulders. She felt his unsteady gait. As they reached the front walk of the house, a car pulled up. Austin got out. Over the years, Sophie watched Austin go from a tall, thin man to a man with a beer belly and a constant frown.

"You got the money for the ranch, Sophie?"

Not so much as a hello, how are you, Mom's doing better, but rather you got *the* money? "No. My loan hasn't come through yet. The army was here on Monday. We should have an answer any day."

"You've got until Friday or I'll assume you're not interested and I'll accept the other bid on the property."

"But—"

"I've honored your agreement with Mother. You've been given first opportunity. If you don't meet the deadline, it's not my fault." He got back into his car and drove away.

"Is that man always that abrasive?"

Sophie frowned. "I'm not the best judge of character when it comes to Austin. I know he's never liked this ranch and never felt comfortable here. I'm sure it's not a hard thing for him to sell this place."

They walked into the house.

"Sit and I'll get us something to drink."

Zach collapsed onto the sofa.

In the kitchen, Sophie poured them large glasses of iced tea. She needed to call the bank and check the status of the loan. Austin wanted this to be over.

Carrying the glasses of tea back into the living room, the blinking light on the answering machine caught her eye.

She handed Zach his tea and walked to the answering machine.

"Let me check this. It might be news on Margaret." She pushed the button to listen to the message.

"Ms. Powell, this is Colonel Norton. At this time we will not set up a program there in Albuquerque. Thank you for your work." The machine beeped.

Message number two. "Ms. Powell. This is Mr. Jenkins at First City National. We've considered your application for the loan to buy New Hope Ranch. Since you have no collateral, we will be unable to lend you the money at this time. If you have any questions, please call."

Sophie's legs turned to gelatin and she collapsed onto the chair.

Her eyes met Zach's. All her dreams and visions for the future evaporated in a moment of time. The glass of tea fell from her nerveless fingers.

"Oh, my." She stood and ran into the kitchen to get a

towel. She knelt over the wet place on the wooden floor and began to mop up the liquid.

Zach slipped his hand under her arm and drew her to her feet. Lifting her head, she looked at him.

"What am I going to do? I need that money. Even if the army doesn't use the ranch, what happens to the kids? And what happens to the horses?"

He pulled her against his chest, holding her.

Her brain shut down. As much as she wanted to find a way, nothing was coming.

Lord, why is this happening? I thought this was Your will.

She didn't cry and that worried Zach. He knew the devastating news set her back on her heels. He wasn't happy with what happened. There had to be a way around it.

There might not have been tears, but he felt her despair in the intensity of her hold. Her fingers dug into his back.

Resting his chin on her head, he said, "It's been a long day, Sophie. Let's go get something to eat, and afterward let's form a plan. There's been a frontal attack, so we need to counter with attack to the side or rear."

He immediately felt her body relax. She lifted her head and looked at him. "Really?"

"I've had plans go south too often while on patrol. You have to think on your feet. Let's come up with plan B. I mean, look at the success we had today. The kids were excited, their parents, your folks, my folks."

A spark of hope entered her eyes. "You're right. With all the excitement we had this afternoon, I think we have support from the riders and their parents." She released him and stepped back. "Let me get my purse."

He ran his thumb over her cheek. "Don't give up, Sophie."

Nodding, she disappeared into her room.

Now that he had her in the fighting mode, he needed a plan. He prayed all the way to the steak place for ideas on how to deal with the problem.

As they ate their dinner, life seemed to seep back into Sophie's eyes.

"The day was a rousing success." Zach cut off a piece of steak and popped it into his mouth. "I don't think any of those riders would willingly let go of their riding time. And the volunteers wouldn't quit. Even Ollie—"

"He'd planned on retiring."

Zach shook his head in amusement. "That old boy will die in the saddle. He won't quit, but likes telling himself that he's going to walk away."

His words brought a smile to her face. "Okay, you win on that one. They'd have to take him out, toes up." Hearing her words, she stopped.

His hand closed over hers. "You didn't mean anything. I know that and if Ollie would've heard, he knows it, too."

She nodded.

An idea took shape in his mind. "I have a friend in D.C. that I could talk with to see if we could get the decision reversed." Zach told of his friend who worked at the Pentagon. He worked for a brigadier general who used to be in the cavalry unit in San Antonio. "I'd like to find out the reason why we were turned down." He had other plans, but didn't want to discuss them with her.

"So that only leaves the loan," Sophie said.

"If we could get someone to back you, someone with land or other collateral, I think the bank would lend you the money. A cosigner. You can use my town house."

She shook her head. "No, I don't—"

"Zach, oh, Zach, it is you. I told Adam it was you."

They looked up and Zach saw his ex–college girl-friend, Donna Nance. Tall and blonde, the beauty looked as if she could be a model. He stood.

"It's good to see you again," she gushed, flashing him a thousand-watt smile. "What are you doing here? The last I heard was that you lost your leg in Iraq. When I talked to some friends, they said you weren't doing so well. Surely, that can't be true, looking at you." Her gaze took him in from head to foot. "I'll just have to tell those people spreading that nonsense around they're wrong."

Each word that Donna spoke, he felt his heart close up. She'd made it clear when he'd been commissioned and shipped out the first time that she wasn't waiting for him. He didn't argue. "It's true, Donna. I lost my leg."

She glanced at his legs. "Oh."

Out of the corner of his eye, he saw Sophie's fingers tightening around her knife handle.

"Donna, this is Sophie Powell. She runs an equine program that helped me walk again."

"How quaint."

Sophie's eyes narrowed and the knife wavered.

Ignoring Sophie, Donna turned to him. "You're riding again? Are you going to go back to rodeo and get that championship buckle that you planned to do after you finished with the army?" Her jab hit its mark.

Silence reigned.

"You should see Zach ride," Sophie said, breaking the tension. "He's amazing to watch. He also helps others who want to ride, young kids who've lost a leg or arm. It's amazing. We always need volunteers to come and be a sidewalker for the riders. If you'd like, we'd love to have you."

Donna stiffened. "That's wonderful." She turned back to him, her smile saccharin-sweet. "I have to get back to my date. He's a real estate broker here in town, but I wanted to say hi. It's good to see you." She nodded to Sophie and air-blew a kiss to Zach.

Easing back into his chair, Zach stared down into this plate.

"Who was that?"

Zach's head came up and he saw Sophie's puzzled expression. "A friend from college."

Sophie raised a brow. "A friend?"

"A girlfriend. When I was commissioned, Donna made it clear that our relationship was over. She wasn't the waiting type, or the type to carry on a long-distance romance. She wanted to date and have fun. If I wasn't there, well, that was too bad."

Sophie didn't reply. "She wasn't worthy of you, Zach."

Her answer touched a raw spot on his soul. He didn't want her pity. They quickly finished dinner and he drove her home.

Walking her to the door, he said, "We didn't figure out how you were going to get the money for the ranch."

"Don't worry about it, Zach. I'll think of something."

"Use my town house as collateral," he pressed again.

She shook her head. "I can't do that. Thank you for the offer." She squeezed his hand and walked inside her house.

Her refusal stung and somehow it felt connected to Donna's appearance. He didn't remember the drive to his town house but, as he sat on the couch in his living room, Donna's thoughtless words echoed in his head and heart. Who was he? Had he lost his dreams? What was he to do now?

He knew Donna was shallow, but having the homecoming queen on his arm helped his ego all those years ago. She'd stomped on that inflated ego when he left for the army. She was number one in her own eyes. He knew she wouldn't have stood by him after the accident in Iraq. But Sophie would've.

Sophie.

He remembered her reaction of her fingers clutching her knife in response to Donna's thoughtless words. Thinking back on it, he could smile at her reaction. He'd seen that protectiveness in her dealings with her clients, and he knew she'd been ready to go to bat for him. He recalled her helping Andy, trying to talk him into stroking Sam's nose or her laughing at the smile on a rider's face when they succeeded on a ride, or Sophie talking to Prince Charming about him. Even Ollie's cancer didn't stop her and she helped him in his struggle with chemotherapy.

She was a natural warrior. He would've loved to have seen her in action in Iraq. He knew she would've put everything on the line for those soldiers. And she still did.

And he knew why she fought so hard, but she didn't need to. Her brother's death wasn't her fault. Sophie's work awed him, and he prayed she'd realize that God had called her to this mission field. Wounded soldiers, whether in body or soul, needed help and he couldn't think of anyone better than Sophie. God had given her an amazing ability to work with those wounded hearts and bodies. He could vouch for that personally.

He needed her. If he was honest with himself, she'd

had his heart for a long time. He'd just been too stubborn to realize it.

Her dream was in danger of not coming to fruition, but if he could do something to make it come true, he would. Picking up the phone, he called a buddy who worked in the Pentagon.

"Hey, Zach, how are you? I heard about what happened in Iraq," Dale Grant said. He and Dale had met each other the summer between his junior and senior years in college. Dale had been Reserve Officer Training Corps, or ROTC as it's known, at the University of Texas, Austin, and they'd been in the same summer maneuvers. They'd kept in touch with each other over the years.

"I'm fine. Been working hard to get back into shape by riding."

"Riding?"

Zach had the opening he wanted. "Have you heard about equine therapy?"

"I've heard something about it. Why?"

Zach launched into his speech about the benefits of horseback riding and how it made a difference in his life and attitude. "And Sophie's worked wonders with this stubborn soldier."

"So your proposal was turned down?"

"It was, but I don't know why. Could you check?"

"I'll do it."

"Dale, I've got a deadline of Friday before the owner's son needs his money or sells the property. And if you need any allies, you might call over to Walter Reed. They have a program, or connections to a program, there."

"I'm on it."

Zach next called his parents and told them of the situation. "Got any ideas?"

"I'll check with my bank to see if we can come up with the money for that ranch. What's the asking price?"

Zach gave his father the amount needed.

"I've got some resources," his father told him. "Besides, I'll call some army buddies and get something going."

"Friday's the deadline, Dad. The owner's son doesn't want Sophie to have the ranch, so he's not giving her anything beyond what his mother originally promised Sophie."

"I got it."

His mother spoke next. She had to be on the extension. "This is a lot of work to do for your sister's roommate, Zach. Is there something more your dad and I should know?"

Suddenly, Zach's mood lifted. His mother wanted to match him up with a *nice* girl and had kept after him for the last ten years.

"Mom, I'll let you know when that time comes."

"Okay. A mother can hope."

He laughed. "Dad, when you find out something, let me know."

When he hung up, he rested his head on the back of the couch. He was in love.

Love.

He stood and walked to the window, staring out into the night. What did Sophie feel? He thought she returned the feelings, but doubt haunted him. Why would she want to tie herself to a man without a leg?

Love.

Did she love him? He felt she always held something of herself back. Why? Why wouldn't she use his town house for her loan? Was she afraid to love? Did her feelings have anything to do with pity?

"Lord, I don't know what she feels, but I love her." And no matter, he'd fight for her. He might not win, but it was the right thing to do.

Chapter Fourteen

Sophie sat at the kitchen table, her Bible open, and a cup sat beside the Bible. She hadn't been able to sleep. She'd poured over Ephesians and Psalms, reading, needing some direction for hours.

Everything had fallen through. Poof. Gone.

Even Zach. She'd watched in horror last night as that awful woman made it obvious that she was shocked that Zach looked whole. Sophie watched with outrage the woman's tactless comments and Zach's retreat. Doubts had jumped him.

"What am I going to do, Lord?" she whispered. She stood and walked to the window at the end of the dining kitchen. From there, she could see the stable and the corral behind the stable.

Wasn't this the dream God gave her? Then she needed to fight for it. The odds didn't look too good for the children of Israel when they moved against Jericho. Or David against Goliath. But God didn't fail them. If He was the same yesterday, today and forever, then why would she think He would fail her now?

With a firm resolve, she walked into the bedroom to get dressed. She wasn't going to give up now.

Sophie walked down to the stables, looking for Ollie. She found him talking to Prince Charming.

"How you feeling this morning?" she asked.

He whistled. "What are you dolled up for?"

"I got a call from the bank last night. They refused the loan, but I'm going down there, see if I can talk to them and arrange another form of collateral." She shrugged. "I don't know what, but I'm going to give it my best shot. Do you feel up to running the ranch with Zach?"

"I've got some savings. I'll gladly give it to ya. These kids need this therapy. And the wounded soldiers need it, too. If my son had had this…"

Ollie's offer made her heart swell in gratitude. "Thank you, old friend, but I'm not going to do that to you. I'll get the money somehow. Will you take care of things?"

"You bet. And I know Zach will take up what I can't. Besides, all those volunteers can pitch in."

Standing on her tiptoes, she brushed a kiss on his cheek. Ollie blushed.

"Go on."

Sophie laughed and raced to her car.

Zach arrived at the ranch ten minutes after Sophie drove out. Ollie told Zach where Sophie was.

"What's she goin' do, if they don't give her the loan?" Ollie asked.

"I've called a friend I know in the Pentagon. If we can get the contract, then I think we can turn things around. But I have another idea. Every parent here, if they knew about the situation, might donate to help keep the ranch open."

Cocking his head, Ollie nodded. "I like your thinking. We're going to wrestle down that bull, no matter what."

"I'm glad we're on the same page."

Around nine-thirty, Zach's new cell phone rang. He'd gotten the thing the day of graduation and knew he needed to give his parents and Sophie the number, but with all that had happened, it had slipped his mind. Pulling it out of his shirt pocket, he noted the call was his friend in D.C.

"Hey, Dale, you've got news for me?" Zach asked.

"I need you to fly to D.C., Zach, ASAP. I've got a couple of people we need to see. Can you get here by five this afternoon?"

"I can. I'll see you then." Closing the phone, Zach looked up and saw Ollie. "You heard?"

"Some."

"I've got to fly to Washington to talk to the powers that be. We've got a shot."

"Go."

"If you call Beth and Ethan, they can make the rest of the calls to the parents." Zach reached into his pocket and pulled out a tablet. "Let me give you their numbers. And my new cell-phone number. You show that to Sophie when you see her."

Ollie took the paper and darted into the tack room for a pencil and scribbled the numbers down. "Don't worry. I've got it in hand."

Zach grinned. "We're going to do this." He took off, his mission clear.

* * *

Sophie sat in her car outside the bank. The loan officer was sympathetic but he wasn't going to give her the loan. No army contract, no money.

She rested her forehead on the steering wheel. Now what? An outrageous idea popped into her head, startling her. But the more she thought about it, the more the idea appealed to her. She started her car and headed south. Her hometown of Tijeras was southwest of the city, about a forty-five-minute drive.

She prayed every mile she drove for wisdom and the words to say to her parents.

Tijeras had changed. There was a new gas station/ convenience store just inside the city limits. Also a new fast-food fried-chicken restaurant stood across the street from the gas station. Down two blocks on Main Street a new Mexican food restaurant occupied the corner where McFarley's Ice Cream shop had stood.

Sophie turned down a side street, Locust, and pulled up to her parents' house. Her father had painted the porch. The cactus in the front yard had grown and sage bushes dotted the rocks and dirt in the yard. She pulled into the driveway. Her father's car stood outside the garage. He worked out of his home office. He was the insurance salesman/adjuster for several counties. She walked up to the side door. It stood open, but the screen door was locked. Music floated outside.

She knocked.

Her mother appeared, dressed in jeans and a paint-splattered smock over her T-shirt.

"Hi, Mom."

Cindy stood frozen for a moment.

"Can I come in?"

The words broke into her fog. "Sure." She moved to the door and unlatched the hook from the eye.

Sophie climbed the two steps to the door and walked inside.

"What are you doing here?" Cindy asked.

It wasn't a good beginning. Sophie knew she could make chitchat, but she'd never done small talk with her mother, was never ever able to tell her mother about her school days or about having a boyfriend, or going to her high school prom. "I need your help."

"Jim," her mother called out. "Come to the kitchen." While they waited for her father, Cindy asked, "You want some coffee?"

"No thanks, Mom."

Her father appeared in the doorway. "Sophie, what are you doing here?"

"I wanted to talk to you and Mom about the ranch. The bank won't give me a loan to buy the place." She explained the situation. "I know you have that big parcel of land just outside of Santa Fe. I know you want to build on it, but I was hoping maybe to use it as collateral for the loan."

Her parents looked at her as if she were speaking Chinese.

Suddenly, her mother stood, the chair tipping back and falling to the floor.

"How dare you. You know how I feel about horses and you want us to throw away our retirement on a horse ranch? No."

"Now, Cindy—" her father began.

Turning on him, she yelled, "Don't 'now, Cindy' me. How could you even think I'd want to have anything to do with horses after what happened?" She rounded on

Sophie. "I don't know why you thought we'd give you money for that."

Sophie stood. "The ranch helps a lot of people overcome handicaps. I know it's what I'm to do."

"And you don't care about my feelings?" Cindy demanded.

Sophie glanced at her father. He sat there, immobile. There was no hope here. "I'm sorry I asked," Sophie said.

She turned to go.

"You should've known," her mother cried.

Pausing at the door, Sophie glanced over her shoulder. "You're right. I should've known, but I thought after so many years…" She shrugged. "I'm sorry, Mom, that it wasn't me who died that day. I've regretted my actions every moment since then. And there's not been a moment when I haven't tried to make up for it. But Zach finally made me see that Matt's death was an accident. I pray you can see that, too." She pushed open the door and walked to her car.

Numbness settled on Sophie until she reached her grandmother's house on the opposite side of town. She sat in her car, frozen, until her grandmother noticed her in the car. The older woman coaxed her inside and sat her on the sofa. After several questions, Sophie told her what had just happened with her mother.

"I thought, Grandma, if I tried hard enough maybe Mom would love me. And maybe Dad would speak up for me. If I tried to save others, give my life to make up for what I did, maybe—" She shook her head. "I was wrong."

Her grandmother wrapped her arms around Sophie. "I love you, child. And I think your mother loves you in her own way. It was easier for her to live in her grief than go on. I was never so proud as I was when I saw those kids riding yesterday." Her grandmother cupped Sophie's face. "It's going to be okay."

Sophie laid her head on her grandmother's shoulder and tried to shut out the pain.

When Sophie pulled into the parking lot of the ranch, she saw an ambulance by the stable. Quickly parking, she ran to the ambulance. She saw an unconscious Ollie on the gurney.

"What happened?"

The paramedic turned to her. "He was found unconscious on the floor. Are you related to him?"

"No, but he's a longtime employee and friend. He's on chemo for cancer."

The paramedic nodded. "Thanks for the heads-up." He climbed in the back and started to close the door.

"What hospital?"

"ABQ General." He closed the door and the ambulance took off.

Sophie looked around at the volunteers. "Anyone know what happened?"

One of the teen volunteers said, "I walked into the stable and found him on the floor by the tack room. When I couldn't wake him, I called 911."

Scanning the crowd, Sophie asked, "Where's Zach?"

"You know, I haven't seen him, but I got here about three."

"Has anyone seen Zach?" Sophie scanned the faces of the volunteers, but no one had seen him.

"Let me change and let's cancel all lessons and feed the horses."

The five volunteers standing in the parking lot scattered.

Sophie raced into her house. As she changed she wondered where Zach was and what had happened.

The doors to ICU closed. She walked into the waiting room for another chance to hold Ollie's hand for five minutes in the next hour. He looked old and frail, not like the hard-as-nails foreman she knew.

She dialed Zach's home phone number, but only got his answering machine. She called Beth. "Have you heard from your brother?"

"Zach? No. Why?"

"He's vanished. He wasn't at the ranch today, and he's not in his apartment. Did he ever get a cell phone like we begged him? I know he said he would, but I haven't heard anything."

"He talked about getting one, but I don't know if he did. He hasn't called me, so I don't know where he is. Call my parents. They might know."

"Is there—"

"I've got to go, friend. That's the last call for my plane."

The phone went dead.

Sophie stared at the useless instrument. She wasn't going to call Zach's parents. She'd sound like a desperate woman. Maybe he didn't want to hear from her after meeting his ex-girlfriend last night.

Lord, I thought he'd healed. Was I wrong? What's happened? They're all gone. Zach, Ollie, my parents, Margaret. There's no one.

Despair overwhelmed her. After she saw Ollie one more time, held his hand and prayed, she drove home. Her heart led her to the stable. Horses had always been a comfort for her. She found Prince Charming in his stall.

He bobbed his head, greeting her. In the corner, opposite the stall, rested a cane. Zach's cane, which he kept here for times when he was exhausted and his leg was bothering him.

Resting her head on Prince Charming's dark neck, the fear and despair overwhelmed her.

"Oh, Prince Charming, what am I going to do? It's all vanished overnight."

Prince Charming stood quietly. Well, at least she had her horses for now.

And God was there in the silence and grief.

Sophie woke up and looked around her. The morning light streamed through the crack in the walls of the stall. Straw under her hands and a saddle blanket under her cheek confused her. Prince Charming nosed her.

Prince Charming? Straw?

Suddenly the memories flooded back. She'd fallen asleep in Prince Charming's stall. He nosed her again.

"Thanks for the wake-up call, boy," she said climbing to her feet. She picked straw out of her hair. Letting herself out of the stall, she walked to the office and splashed water on her face. Looking into the mirror, she saw the circles under her eyes.

She moved out of the bathroom and grabbed the phone. She called the hospital, asking for Intensive Care. Sophie discovered that Ollie had awakened and been moved to a private room.

"Thank You, Lord," she whispered, hanging up the phone.

She needed to rush up to the house, change and snatch an apple before she started with the horses. Racing back to Prince Charming's stall, she grabbed her purse and started toward the house.

The sound of tires on the gravel drew her attention to the road. Zach's truck drove up. He stopped by her car and he got out, but there was another passenger in the front seat. The stranger opened the passenger door and joined Zach beside the car. Whoever he was, he was an army major.

"I've got good news for you, Sophie," Zach began.

"So you decided to show up?"

"What are you talking about?"

"Where were you yesterday? Ollie's in the hospital. When I came home, I found the paramedics loading him into an ambulance and all the volunteers shaken up, telling me how they found him."

Zach's face lost its color. "How is he?"

"He's out of intensive care. The hospital is optimistic."

Out of the corner of her eye, she saw the major who watched her outburst.

"This is Major Dale Grant. I was in Washington yesterday, trying to get approval for us to run a program here." Zach ran his fingers through his hair. "Dale and I wanted you to know the good news. We got the contract. He also wanted to see the ranch for himself after hearing my glowing reviews. He and I go back a long way. He's also a horseman."

She stood there frozen, feeling overjoyed and excited that their dream was coming true. And—stupid. Stupid and petty for her comments.

The major stepped close, offering his hand.

She shook it, her face blazing with color. "I'm sorry, sir, for my outburst. My only excuse is it's been a terrible thirty-six hours." She glanced at Zach, her heart in her throat. "I couldn't get the loan, so your efforts might be in vain."

Before he could respond, another car drove up. It was her father's car. What was happening? Sophie wondered. Much to her amazement, her parents stepped out of the front seat, and her grandmother out of the backseat.

Cindy McClure walked up to Sophie. Her mother smiled, but her lips trembled. "After you left yesterday, I thought about what you said. I never wanted you to die instead of your brother. Forgive me."

Sophie couldn't believe her ears. She wondered if she was still asleep in Prince Charming's stall.

Cindy glanced at her mother. "When Mom came to the house yesterday, we decided that there have been too many times when hurt feelings have kept us apart. And we also decided to put that property up for you as collateral. Your father called his banker last night and we were given the loan."

Tears silently flowed down Sophie's cheeks. "Oh, Mother." Sophie slipped into her mother's arms. She felt her father wrap his arms around both of them. The wall surrounding her heart just shattered. The love and approval she'd longed for from her parents was just given.

After a moment, Jim released them and Sophie turned to the major. "It looks like that program will be implemented." She glanced at Zach. He stood there watching. There was something in his eyes that told her of his feelings. She wanted to ask him—

Before she could say anything, more cars drove into the parking lot—a half dozen to a dozen. Doors slammed, and Beth appeared among the parents and kids who were part of the therapy program. Excitement raced through the air.

Andy's mom appeared. She looked around, then turned back to Sophie. "Yesterday Zach told me about what happened."

She glanced over her shoulder to where Zach stood. He shrugged his shoulders and smiled as if to say, you should have trusted me.

Andy's mom continued, "I told him I wanted to help, so he and I called a lot of people. I told my church and we collected money. All the other students and parents gave, too. We've collected close to five thousand dollars for you to use as a down payment on the ranch." She handed Sophie a check.

Sophie's hands shook as she looked down at the check. She felt Zach move beside her.

"You have a lot of grateful parents."

She nodded through her tears.

A tug on her jeans brought her gaze down.

"I helped, too," Andy added. "I stacked the money." His chest puffed out.

"Thank you." She turned to the crowd, fighting the tears and overwhelmed with gratitude. "I want to thank everyone for your generous hearts. This tells me that this ranch is as important to you as it is to me."

"We love you, Miss Sophie," Andy called out.

Everyone clapped.

Another car drove up and parked. Austin Stillwell got out. The crowd quieted.

Austin walked to where Sophie stood. "We need to talk."

Before Sophie could respond, Zach said, "I think whatever you have to say to Sophie you can say in front of her family and the people she serves."

Zach stepped closer and Sophie took courage from his presence.

Austin's mouth flattened with rage. His eyes narrowed as he focused on Sophie. "Do you have my money?"

"I do. We can go to the bank and have the check cut. Name the time."

He didn't look happy. "One o'clock this afternoon at First National." He whirled and strode to his car.

As he drove off, boos and hisses followed him.

Sophie turned to the crowd. "Thank you for all your work. Your support means so much to me. For today, lessons are cancelled."

Laughter filled the air.

Before the crowd could disperse, Zach raised his hands. "Wait."

People stopped and turned back to him and Sophie. No one said a word.

Zach offered up a prayer for wisdom. Last night, once they got the approval, Zach knew what he wanted to do the instant he got back home. Sophie's initial reaction threw him, dampening his hopes for their future. But he knew he had to gamble, take the risk of showing his heart to her. He had to take a leap of faith. He'd planned on talking to her in private, but something told him *now* was the right time and place,

Zach caught Sophie's hands. "I want to tell you what an amazing woman you are. Your vision has set me on the right road, but it's also become my vision. This is what I want to do to show others how to overcome whatever life throws at them. You have a strength and courage that awes and humbles me. You saw me as the man God wanted me to be and I want to be involved with this therapy program—"

She opened her mouth to respond, but his finger came up and he lightly pressed it to her lips.

"The position I want, Sophie, is as your husband. I love you and have loved you since I stomped into my parents' kitchen wet and disgruntled all those years ago. You took my breath away and still do. I hope you'll take pity on this beat-up cowboy and say yes. I've found my true purpose in this life and my true love."

Not a sound came from the gathered crowd.

"What do you say, Miss Sophie?" Andy asked, breaking the silence. "I like him. Besides, he's got a neat leg that makes him special."

The crowd laughed.

"He's right. I do have that extraspecial leg," Zach whispered.

Joy welled up in her eyes and her smile reflected it. "Yes."

The cheers surrounded them, but her eyes never left Zach's face. Pulling her into his arms, he sealed the deal with a kiss.

Epilogue

Sun filtered through the windows as Sophie sat at the kitchen table. Her mother and grandmother fussed over her hair, putting yellow and white daisies into the curls pinned on the back of her head. Her father stood on the porch, talking to Ollie. The last two weeks were like a dream—she'd talked with her parents, telling them all about the things in her heart, her dreams, her time in college and Iraq. Both her father and mother had listened and questioned her about a dozen different things. And they made sure she knew how proud they were of her. They even shared memories of Matt.

Both her parents had come to the ranch and trained to be sidewalkers. She'd even seen her mother smile at one of the little girls who had Down's. Molly adored her mother. Her mother blossomed giving to others. Sophie discovered her mother's marvelous talent for organization, taking the volunteer lists and perfecting a new schedule. Her father helped with the veterans. They had two soldiers in the program and would get another couple next week. Her grandma had accompanied her mother several times and worked in the office.

Zach's parents also visited frequently, helped with chores and started training another horse to be used by the soldiers.

"That's it," her mother declared, patting Sophie on the shoulder. "You look wonderful."

Sophie looked down at the white lace top and white tiered Western skirt and turquoise-and-coral Western belt. Her new boots had an edge of turquoise around the tops and the tips of the boot. She stood and hugged her mother. "I'm glad you're here."

"I'm glad, too," Cindy whispered.

Her grandmother beamed at Sophie over Cindy's shoulder.

Her dad opened the front door. "You ladies ready?" he called.

"We are."

When Sophie appeared on the porch, only her father stood there. He offered his arm. Her mother and grandmother walked ahead of them.

People filled the bleachers and spilled out between the rings and the shade trees beyond. Tables stood behind the group, filled with a wedding cake, buñuelos, fruits and punch. She saw Zach standing under the trees, Ethan and Prince Charming with a silver-concha studded halter beside him.

Zach. He looked like her dream in a white Western shirt, starched jeans and boots.

Sophie and her father stopped at the entrance to the stable. Beth held Sam's reins, daisies and pink cornflowers woven into her halter. Beth handed Sophie her bouquet, which was composed of the same flowers and flowing ribbons.

"You ready for this?" Beth teased. "You ready to hitch yourself to that ornery brother of mine?"

Sophie looked at her intended. "I've been ready for this since I saw him standing in your parents' kitchen, mad as all get-out that he'd ruined his new boots."

Beth laughed. She led Sam out into the sunlight. She stopped by Andy. "You ready for your part?"

"Yes."

Guitars began the wedding march.

Andy proudly walked down to Zach, waving at his mother and friends in the audience. Zach pulled the young man to his side. Prince Charming nudged Zach on the shoulder. Zach glanced at the horse, then his brother. Ethan laughed.

Beth walked down the path, leading Sam. The gathered crowd rose as Sophie and her father walked to Zach and the preacher.

Zach's heart skipped a beat when Sophie came into view. The sunlight danced off her hair, giving her a heavenly look. She was so beautiful, inside and out. He never would've imagined the changes to his life, and never would've thought of this turn. *Lord, thank You. She is a woman of great virtue.*

He didn't know how he'd been blessed with her. Out of horror came joy and hope.

Sophie stopped beside him. Her feelings of joy and gratefulness were clearly reflected in her eyes. He returned her sentiments. Her father kissed Sophie's cheek, gave her hand to Zach and stepped back.

Zach squeezed her hand and she squeezed back, sealing their joy.

The preacher—their preacher—opened his Bible, and

a butterfly landed on the daisy in Sophie's hair. The photographer captured the picture.

"I think we've been sent a blessing from above," Zach murmured.

"Amen," Sophie answered.

* * * * *

Dear Reader,

When I read in our local newspaper about an equine therapy ranch in the area, I was hooked. They worked with children, but wanted to work with wounded veterans. Since then, I learned about NARHA and their national website (www.pathintl.org).

On their website I found an article about how horses are being used to help the wounded veterans. "I Will Never Leave a Fallen Comrade" was the title of an article from the 2006 Fall edition of *NARHA's Strides*. The work they do is amazing and inspiring.

Both Sophie and Zach are ex-soldiers who love horses. They are two wounded souls who have to learn how to trust God again when the plans for their lives have been blown up. It is a journey of faith. It is a journey of hope. I pray you enjoyed their journey.

Leann Harris

QUESTIONS FOR DISCUSSION

1. When we first meet Zach, he has yet to deal with the reality of his life. Do you think his actions were justified?

2. Do you think Sophie's tough-love approach to Zach was the right way to go? What about how his parents dealt with him?

3. Ever had a time when you didn't know how to handle the situation like Zach's parents? What did you do when you felt helpless?

4. Was Sophie's reaction to Zach's interest in her valid? Do you think her doubting his feelings were justified?

5. When Sophie brought the light saber to the exercise ring, were you surprised? Have you heard of the unit in the army that is old-fashioned cavalry?

6. Have you ever doubted the direction of your life as both Sophie and Zach did? How did you deal with it?

7. Was Ollie's desire to keep his illness from Sophie the right thing to do? Should he have leveled with her?

8. Margaret's son was jealous of Sophie's relationship with his mother. Why do you think he felt that way? Was it reasonable?

9. Were you surprised with how much equine therapy is used? Is it a smart thing to do?

10. Sophie overheard her parents' grieving over her brother's death. She thought they blamed her. She blamed herself. Was her reaction over-the-top? Was she justified in her feelings?

11. What did you think of Sophie's mother's handling of her son's death? Her father? Have you known a relative or friend who got stuck over an incident and can't go beyond that? How did you handle that?

12. How do you feel about Sophie's refusal to use Zach's town house for collateral?

13. Were you surprised by Sophie's parents' reaction to her asking for the collateral to buy the ranch?

14. What was your reaction to Zach's meeting his old girlfriend and her reaction to seeing him?

15. What do you think of Zach's solution to the bank's refusal to give Sophie the loan?

Get 2 Free Books,
Plus 2 Free Gifts—
just for trying the Reader Service!

Love Inspired®

Save $1.00

on the purchase of any
Love Inspired® book.

Available wherever books are sold, including
most bookstores, supermarkets, drugstores
and discount stores.

Save $1.00

on the purchase of any Love Inspired® book.

Coupon valid until July 31, 2018.
Redeemable at participating retail outlets in the U.S. and Canada only.
Limit one coupon per customer.

52615199

5 65373 00076 2   (8100)0 12313

THE LYNCH MOB WAS ON ITS WAY!

The crowd's angry bellow made the hairs on Smoke Jensen's neck rise and vibrate.

They were coming for him.

How many were there? Would they be able to get in? Smoke had been scared many times before in his life . . . but nothing compared to what he experienced now.

He was absolutely paralyzed . . . he was so helpless, so vulnerable. Death rode the mob like a single steed, a hound out of hell, and it made Smoke think about his own fragile mortality. How easily they could take him!

NO! He had to find a way out of this! Somehow he had to escape . . . and if he couldn't escape, he had to take as many of the mob with him as he could . . .

TODAY WAS A GOOD DAY TO DIE!

WILLIAM W. JOHNSTONE
CUNNING OF THE
MOUNTAIN
MAN

ZEBRA BOOKS
KENSINGTON PUBLISHING CORP.

ZEBRA BOOKS are published by

Kensington Publishing Corp.
850 Third Avenue
New York, NY 10022

Third Printing: July 1996

Printed in the United States of America

One

Sound came to him first. It might be the buzz of an insect, only faint and teasingly erratic. Feeling slowly returned in the form of a throbbing stab of pain in his head. Light registered in a dimly perceived slash of pale gray rectangle, intersected by dark lines. Last to return was memory. Fragile and incomplete, it at least gave him a name, an identity. Jensen. Smoke Jensen.

For many, that name conjured images of a larger-than-life hero, as featured in over a hundred penny dreadfuls and dime novels. Legend had indeed drawn Smoke Jensen larger than his six-foot-two, although broad shoulders, a thick, muscular neck, big hands, and tree-trunk legs left him lacking in nothing when it came to physical prowess. He could truly be considered of heroic proportions.

In the opinion of others, Smoke Jensen was a killer and an outlaw. Some claimed he had killed three hundred men, not counting Indians and Mexicans. The truth was closer to a third of that. And, there was no back-down in Smoke Jensen. He had shot it out with the fastest, fought the toughest, outrode the swiftest. Now he found himself helpless as a kitten.

With an effort that nearly failed to overcome the pulses

of misery-laden blackness, Smoke Jensen forced himself up on his elbows. The back of his head felt like he had been kicked by a mule. Where was he? With the fuzziness of a swimmer emerging from murky water, his vision managed to focus on the gray smudge above his head.

A window . . . a barred window. How had he gotten here?

Slowly, scraps of memory began to solidify. "Yes," said Smoke Jensen in a whisper to himself. "I am—or was—in Socorro, New Mexico."

He had been on his way back to the Sugarloaf from selling a string of horses to the Arizona Rangers. They had been fine animals, big-chested and full of stamina. The Rangers wanted some sturdy, mountain-bred mounts for the detachment patrolling the areas around Flagstaff, Globe, and Show Low. Smoke's animals, raised in a high valley deep in the Rockies, answered their needs perfectly. The sale had been arranged through an old friend, Jeff York, now a Ranger captain. His recollection gave Smoke a sensation of warmth and contentment. Even though he was in jail, the money he had received would be safe. It had been forwarded to Big Rock, Colorado, by telegraph bank draft.

None of this told him why he had awakened with a gut-wrenching headache in a jail cell.

A new scrap of memory made itself known. He had three hands along. Where were they? Sitting up proved even more agonizing than rising to his elbows. For a moment the brick walls and bars swam in giddy disorder. Gradually the surge of nausea receded, and his eyes cleared. Full lips in a grim slash, Smoke Jensen examined his surroundings.

He soon discovered that outside of himself—and two drunks sleeping it off in adjacent cells—the jail was empty. The snores of one of the inebriates had provided the insect noises he had first heard. Again he asked himself what had gotten him in jail. Another wave of discomfort sent a big hand to the back of his head.

Gingerly, Smoke Jensen inspected the lump he found there. It was the size of a goose egg and crusted with dried blood. At least it indicated that he didn't have a hangover. Smoke then tried to focus his thoughts on the past few hours. All his effort produced another blank. Suddenly, a door of flat iron straps banged open down the corridor from Smoke's cell. Two men entered, both with empty holsters. Obviously the jailers, Smoke reasoned. At least now he would have some answers.

In the lead came a slob whose belly slopped over a wide, thick leather belt to the point of obscuring his groin. He waddled on hamlike thighs and oddly skinny, undersized calves. His face was a bloated moon, with large, jiggly jowls; the lard of his cheeks all but buried his small, pig eyes. He carried a ring of keys and a ladle.

Behind him came a smaller man lugging a heavy kettle, filled with steaming liquid. Shorter by a head than the fat one, by comparison he managed to look frail and undernourished. His protuberant buck teeth and thin, pencil-line mustache, over an almost lipless mouth, gave him a rodent appearance. In a giddy moment, Smoke Jensen thought the man would be more suited to be jailer in Raton, New Mexico. Their presence roused one of the drunks.

"Hey, Ferdie, what you got for breakfast?"

Ferdinand "Ferdie" Biggs worked his small, wet, red mouth and spoke in a surprisingly high, waspish tone. "Ain't gonna be any breakfast for you, Eckers. I ain't gonna have you go an' puke it up . . . an' me have to clean up the cell! Got some coffee, though, if you can call this crap coffee."

"How 'bout me, Ferdie Biggs?" whined the other boozer. "You know I don't spew up what I eat after a good drunk."

"It's a waste of the county's money feedin' you, Smithers. If you want som'thin' to fill your belly, suck yer thumb."

Smithers's face flushed, and he gripped the bars of his cell door as though he might rip them out. "Damn you, Biggs. If you didn't have these bars to protect you, I'd beat the livin' hell out of you."

"Says you," Biggs responded. By then he and his companion had reached the neighboring cells. Biggs turned and dipped the ladle into the light brown liquid and poured a tin cup half-full. "Since you gave me so much lip, you get only half a cup, Smithers."

"I'm ravin' hungry," Smithers protested.

Biggs gave him a cold, hard stare. "You want to be wearin' this?" Smithers subsided, and Biggs shoved the cup through the access slot cut in the bars above the lock case. He served Eckers next. Three steps brought him to the cell occupied by Smoke Jensen. He paused there, his small mouth working in a habitual chewing motion.

When he took in Smoke's shaky condition, Biggs produced a wide grin that revealed crooked, yellowed teeth.

"You're gonna hang, Jensen. You killed Mr. Tucker in cold blood, and they're gonna string you up for it."

Smoke nodded dumbly. Murder called for a hanging, he silently agreed.

Who is Mr. Tucker?

Martha Tucker sat on the old horsehide sofa in the parlor. Head bowed, hands covering her face, she sobbed out her wretchedness. Larry gone, dead, murdered they had told her. She vaguely recalled hearing the name Smoke Jensen, who the sheriff had informed her had killed Lawrence Tucker. Only her abysmal grief kept her from now recalling who or what Smoke Jensen was. What was she going to do?

What about the children? What about the ranch? Could she legally claim it? Most states, like her native Ohio, considered women mere chattel—property like a man's house, horse, or furniture. At least New Mexico was still a territory and under federal law. That might offer some hope. Martha's shoulders shook with greater violence as each pointed question came to her. For that matter, would the hands stay on with Larry gone? She knew with bitter certainty that no one who considered himself a "real" man would willingly work for a woman. Martha broke off her lamentations at the sound of soft, hesitant footsteps on the large, hooked rug in the center of the parlor floor.

She dabbed at her eyes with a damp kerchief and looked up to see her eldest child, Jimmy. At thirteen, albeit small for his age, he had that gangly, stretched-out appearance of the onset of puberty. His cottony hair had a shaggy look to it; Larry was going to take him into town Saturday for a visit to the barber. Oh, God, who would do it now?

"Mother . . . Mommy? Please—please, don't cry so. Rose and Tommy are real scared." The freckles scattered across his nose and high cheekbones stood out against the pallor of his usually lightly tanned face.

For his part, Jimmy had never seen his mother like this. Her ash-blond hair was always meticulously in place, except for a stray strand that would escape to hang down in a curl on her forehead when she baked. She was so young, and the most beautiful woman Jimmy had ever seen. His heart ached for her, so much so that it pushed aside the deep grief he felt for his father's death.

"Jimmy . . ." Anguish crumpled Martha's face. "Oh, my dearest child, what are we . . . what *can* we do?"

At only thirteen, Jimmy Tucker lacked any wise adult suggestions to offer. All he could do was at last give vent to the sorrow that ate at him, and let large, silent tears course down his boyish cheeks.

Quint Stalker sat his horse in the saddle notch of a low ridge. A big man, with thick, broad shoulders, short neck, and a large head, Stalker held a pair of field glasses to his eyes; bushy, black brows seemed to sprout from above the hooded lenses. Down below, to Quint Stalker's rear, in a cactus-bristling gulch, waited the seven men who would be going with him. His attention centered on a small, flat-roofed structure with a tall, tin stove pipe towering above its pole roof at the bottom of the slope.

Old Zeke Dillon had run the trading post beyond the crest for most of his life, Quint reflected. You'd think a feller in his late sixties would be glad to get away from all that hard work and take some good money along, too. But not Zeke.

Bullheaded, was Zeke. A stubborn, old coot who insisted on hanging onto his quarter-section homestead until he dropped dead behind the plank counter of his mercantile, where he traded goods for turquoise and blankets with the Hopi and Zuni. Well, today he'd get an offer he could not turn down.

It just happened that Zeke Dillon's trading post occupied ground far more valuable than he knew. But Quint Stalker's bosses knew. That's why they had sent Quint to obtain title to the 160 acres of sand and prickly pear, roadrunners and cactus wrens. Quint lowered the field glasses, satisfied that Zeke, and no one else, occupied the pole-roofed building half a mile from his present position. He raised a gloved hand and signaled his men.

Twenty minutes later, Quint and his henchmen rode up to the front of the trading post. Dust hazed the air around them for a while, before an oven-breath of breeze hustled it away. Quint Stalker and three of his men had dismounted by the time Zeke Dillon came to the door. He stood there, squinted a moment in hopes of recognizing the visitors, and rubbed wet hands on a stained white apron.

"Howdy, boys. Step down and bide a spell. There's

cool water an' lemonade inside, whiskey, too, if you ain't Injun."

"Whiskey and lemonade sound good, old-timer," Quint Stalker responded.

Zeke brightened. "Like in one o' them fancy cocktails I been hearin' about out San Francisco way, eh?"

With a nod, Quint shoved past the old man. "Sort of, old-timer." Inside, he let his eyes adjust to the dimness, his sun-burnished skin grateful for the coolness. Then he turned on Zeke Dillon. "Business first, then we'll get to the pleasure."

"How's that?"

"Before we leave here this afternoon, you're gonna sell us your trading post."

"Nope. Never on yer life. I've done turned down better offers than the likes of you can make."

Suddenly a .44 Merwin and Hulbert appeared in Quint Stalker's hand. "What if I were to say you'd sign a bill of sale and take what we offer, or I'll blow your damned brains out?"

Zeke Dillon swallowed hard, blinked, gulped again, and kept his eyes fixed on the gray lead blobs that showed in the open chambers of the cylinder. Tears of regret and humiliation filled his eyes. Not ten years ago, he'd have beaten this two-bit gunney to the draw, and seen him laid out cold on the floor with a bullet in his heart. But not now. Not ever again. With a soft, choked-off sob, Zeke said goodbye to his beloved way of life of the past fifty years.

Quint Stalker produced a filled-out bill of sale and a proper transfer of title form, and handed a steel-nibbed pen to the thoroughly intimidated old man. With a sinking heart, Zeke Dillon dipped the pen in an inkwell on the counter and affixed his signature to both. Then, sighing, he turned to Stalker.

"All right, you lowlife bastard. When do I get my money?"

"Right now," Quint Stalker replied evenly, as he shot Zeke Dillon through the heart.

Sheriff Jake Reno, of Socorro County, New Mexico, who looked every bit an older—but less sloppily fat—version of his chief jailer, stepped into the hall from an office above the Cattlemen's Union Bank in Socorro. He gleefully counted the large sheaf of bills, using a splayed, wet thumb. Nice doing business with fellers like that, he concluded.

All he had to do is see that one Mr. Smoke Jensen gets hanged all right and proper, and he'd get another payment of the same amount. Not bad for a couple of day's work. Given the sheriff's nature, he didn't even bother to wonder why it was that these "business men," as they called themselves, were so set on disposing of Smoke Jensen.

God, the man was a legend in his own time, a dozen times over. Sheriff Reno knew *who* Smoke Jensen was, and a thousand dollars went a long way to insuring he didn't give a damn why those fancy-talking men—clearly the one with a dash in his name sounded like an Englishman—wanted Smoke Jensen sent off to his eternal reward; it was none of the sheriff's business. Time, Sheriff Reno decided, to celebrate his good fortune.

Down on the street, he walked the short block and a

half to the Hang Dog Saloon. The building front featured a large, scalloped marquee, heavy with red and gold paint, lettered in bold black. It had a big, ornately bordered oval painting in the middle, which showed a dog, hanging upside down, one foot caught by a strand of barbed wire. It served as a point of amusement for some of the town wags. For others, more involved with the war against the "wicked wire," it represented a political statement. For still others, the sign pointed out man's indifference to cruelty to animals.

Sheriff Reno entered through tall, glass-filled wooden doors. The bevel-edged panels sported a cheery, six-wide border of mixed red, green, and black checks. He waved to several cronies and headed directly to the bar, where he greeted the proprietor and bartender, Morton Plummer.

"Howdy, Mort. A shot and a beer."

"Sort of early for you, ain't it, Sheriff?"

Reno gave Plummer a frown. "I'm in a mood to celebrate."

"Celebrate what, Jake?" Morton Plummer asked as he poured a shot of rye.

"I got me a notorious killer locked up in my jail. And enough evidence to hang him for the murder of one of our more prominent citizens."

"I heard something about that," Mort offered, a bit more coolly than usual. "D'you really believe a gunfighter as famous as Smoke Jensen would do something so dumb as let himself get knocked out right beside a man he'd just killed?"

Jake Reno's face pinched and his eyes narrowed. "Who told you that, Mort?"

"Hal Eckers was in for his usual morning bracer a while ago. Said he was locked up acrost from Smoke Jensen most of the night. Ferdie Biggs was shootin' his mouth off about the killin'."

An angry scowl replaced the closed expression on the face of Sheriff Reno. "Damn that Ferdie. Don't he know that even a drunk like Eckers remembers what he hears. Especial, about someone as famous as Smoke Jensen. Might be some smart-ass lawyer"—he pronounced it *liar*—"got ahold of that and could twist it to get Jensen off."

Reno downed his shot and sucked the top third off his schooner of beer. What he had just said set him to thinking. To aid the process, he signaled for another shot of rye. With that one safely cozied down with the other to warm his belly, he saw the problem with clarity. It might be he could use some insurance to see that he collected that other five hundred dollars. Slurping up the last of his beer, Jake Reno signaled Mort Plummer for refills and sauntered down the mahogany to where Payne Finney stood doing serious damage to a bottle of Waterfill-Frazier.

"Is Quint Stalker in town?"

Payne Finney gave the sheriff a cold, gimlet stare. "I wouldn't know."

"I find that odd, considerin' you're his—ah—foreman, so's to speak."

"I've got me a terrible mem'ry, when it comes to talkin' with lawdogs."

Sheriff Reno gave a friendly pat to Finney's shoulder. "Come now, Finney, we're workin' on the same side, as of . . . uh . . ." He consulted the big, white face with the black Roman numerals in the hexagonal, wooden case of the Regulator pendulum clock over the bar. "Ten minutes ago."

Finney's cool gaze turned to fishy disbelief. "That so, huh? Name me some names."

Jake Reno bent close to Payne Finney's ear and lowered his voice. The names came out in the softest of whispers. Finney heard them well enough and nodded.

"I guess you wouldn't know them, if you weren't mixed up in it. What is it you want?"

Sheriff Reno spoke in a hearty fashion after gulping his whiskey. "Thing is, of late, I've come to not trust the justice system to always function in the desired way."

"That a fact, Sheriff?" Finney shot back, toying with the lawman. "And you such a fine, upstanding pillar of the law. Now, what is it you don't trust about the way justice is done in the Territory?"

"Well, there's more of these smooth-talking lawyers comin' out here from back East. They got silver tongues that all too often win freedom for men who should damnwell hang."

"You may have a point," Finney allowed cautiously.

"Of course, I do. An' it's time something was done about it."

"Such as what?"

"Well, you take that jasper I've got locked up right now. Think how it would distress that poor Widow Tucker if some oily haired, silver-tongued devil twisted the facts an' got him off scot-free? It'd vex her mightily, you can be sure."

"What are you suggesting?" Finney pressed, certain he would enjoy the answer.

"Depends on whether you think you're the man to be up to it. For my part, I'd sleep a lot better knowin' some alternative means had been thought up to see that Smoke Jensen gets the rope he deserves."

Two

Ranch hands, local idlers, and a scattering of strangers crowded into the two saloons closest to the Socorro jail by midafternoon. Talk centered on only one topic—the killer the sheriff had locked up in the hoosegow.

"That back-shooter's needin' some frontier justice, you ask me," a florid-faced, paunchy man in a brocaded red vest and striped pants declared hotly from the front of the bar in the Hang Dog Saloon.

"Damn right, Hub," the man on his left agreed.

Several angry, whiskey-tinged voices rose in furtherance of this outcome. Payne Finney kept the fires stoked as he flitted from group to group in the barroom. "This Smoke Jensen is a crazy man. He's killed more'n three hunnard men, shot most in the back, like poor Lawrence Tucker."

Finney added to his lies as he joined a trio of wranglers at the back end of the bar. "Remember when it was in the papers how he killed Rebel Tyree?" He put an elbow to the ribs of one cowhand and winked. "In the back. Not like the paper said, but in the back."

"Hell, I didn't even know you could read, Payne."

"Shut up, Tom. You never got past the fourth grade,

nohow. I tell you, this Jensen is as bloodthirsty as Billy Bonney."

"Bite yer tongue, Finney," Tom snapped. "Billy Bonney is much favored in these parts. He done right by avengin' Mr. Tunstill."

Payne Finney gave Tom Granger a fish eye. "And who's gonna avenge Mr. Lawrence Tucker?"

"Why, the law'll see to that."

"An' pigs fly, Tom. You can take my word for it, somethin' ought to be done."

"You talkin' lynch law, Payne?" The question came from a big, quiet man standing at a table in the middle of the room.

Turning to him, Payne Finney blinked. Maybe, he considered, he'd pushed it a bit too far. Gotta give them the idea they thunked it up on their own. That's what Quint Stalker had taught him. Payne silently wished that Stalker was there with him now. He had no desire to get on the wrong side of Clay Unger, this big, soft-spoken man who had a reputation with a gun that even Quint Stalker respected. He raised both hands, open, palms up, in a deprecating gesture.

"Now, Clay, I was just sayin' what if . . . ? You know a lot more about how the law works than I do—no offense," Payne hastened to add. "But from what little I do know, it seems any man with a bit of money can get off scot-free."

"And you were only speculating out loud as to, what if it happened to Smoke Jensen?"

"Yeah . . . that's about it."

Clay Unger raised a huge hand and pointed his trigger finger at Payne Finney. It aimed right between his eyes.

"Don't you think the time to worry about that is *after* it's happened?"

"Ummm. Ah—I suppose you're right, there, Clay."

Finney made his way hastily to the doors and raised puffs of dust from his bootheels as he ankled down the street to Donahue's. There he set to embellishing his tales of Smoke Jensen's bloody career. His words fell on curious ears and fertile minds. He bought a round of drinks and, when he left an hour later, he felt confident the seeds of his plan would germinate.

After Clay Unger and his friends had left the Hang Dog, two hard-faced, squint-eyed wranglers at the bar took up Payne Finney's theme. They quickly found ready agreement among the other occupants.

"What would it take to get that feller out of the jail and swing him from a rope, Ralph?"

Through a snicker, Ralph answered, "If you mean co—oper—ation, not a whole lot. Ol' Ferdie over there surely enjoys a good hangin'. Especially one where the boy's neck don't break like it oughtta. Ferdie likes to see 'em twitch and gag. Might be, he'd even hand that Jensen over to us."

" 'Us,' Ralph?" a more sober imbiber asked pointedly.

Ralph's mouth worked, trying to come up with words his limited intellect denied him. "I was just talkin'—ah—sorta hy-hypo—awh, talkin' like let's pretend."

"You mean hypothetically?" Ralph's detractor prodded.

"Yeah . . . that's it. Heard the word onest, about a thang like this."

Right then the batwings, inset from the tall, glass-paneled front doors swung inward, and Payne Finney strode in. "What's that yer talkin' about, Ralph?"

Puppy-dog eagerness lighted Ralph's face. "Good to see you, Payne. I was jist sayin' that it should be easy to get that Jensen outta the jail and string him up."

Finney crossed to the bar and gave Ralph a firm clap on one shoulder. "Words to my likin', Ralph. Tell me more."

Seated in a far corner, at a round table, three men did not share the bloodthirsty excitement. They cast worried gazes around the saloon, marked the men who seemed most enthused by the prospect of a lynching. Ripley Banning ran short, thick fingers, creased and cracked by hard work and callus, through his carroty hair. His light complexion flushed pink as he leaned forward and spoke quietly to his companions.

"I don't like the sound of this one bit." He cut seagreen eyes to Tyrell Hardy on his right.

Ty Hardy flashed a nervous grin, and stretched his lean, lanky body in the confines of the captain's chair. "Nor me, Rip. Ain't a hell of a lot three of us can do about it, though."

From his right, Walt Reardon added a soft question. "How's that, Ty? Seems a determined show of force could defuse this right fast."

Tyrell Hardy cut his pale blue eyes to Walt Reardon. He knew the older man to be a reformed gunfighter. Walt's fulsome mane of curly black hair, and heavy, bushy brows, gave his face a mean look to those who did not know him. And, truth to tell, Ty admitted, the potential for violence remained not too far under the surface. He flashed a fleeting smile and shook his head, which set his longish, nearly white hair to swaying.

"You've got a good point, Walt. But, given the odds, I'd allow as how one of us might get killed, if we mixed in."

"There's someone sure's hell gonna get killed, if this gets ugly," Rip Banning riposted. "What'er you sayin', Walt?"

Walt's dark brown eyes glowed with inner fire, and his tanned, leather face worked in a way that set his brush of mustache to waggling. "Might be that we should keep ourselves aware of what's going on. If this gets out of hand, a sudden surprise could go a long way to puttin' an end to it."

Martha Tucker went about her daily tasks mechanically. All of the spirit, the verve of life, had fled from her. She cooked for her children and herself, but hardly touched the food, didn't taste what she did consume. She had sat in stricken immobility for more than two hours, after word had been brought of Lawrence's death. Now, anger began to boil up to replace the grief.

It allowed her to set herself to doing something her late husband had often done to burn off anger he dare not let explode. Her hair awry, her face shiny in the afternoon light, an axe in both hands, Martha set about splitting firewood for the kitchen stove. With each solid smack, a small grunt escaped her lips, carrying with it a fleck of her outrage.

She cared not that at least a full week's supply already had been stacked under the lean-to that abutted the house, beside the kitchen door. Neither did Martha have the words or knowledge to call her strenuous activity therapy; neither she, nor anyone in her world, knew the word catharsis. She merely accepted that with each yielding of a billet of piñon, she felt a scrap of the burden lift, if only for a moment.

"Mother," Jimmy Tucker called from the corner of the house.

He had to call twice more, before his voice cut into Martha's consciousness.

"What is it, son?"

Jimmy's bare feet set up puffs of dust as he scampered to his mother's side. "There's a man coming, Maw."

Cold fear stabbed at Martha's breast. "Who . . . is it?"

"I dunno. He don't . . . look mean."

"Go in the house, Jimmy, and get me the rifle. Then round up your sister and brother and go to the root cellar."

"Think it's Apaches?"

"Not around here, son. I don't know what to think."

Jimmy's eyes narrowed. "I had better stay with you, Maw."

"No, Jimmy. It's best you are safe . . . just in case."

"If it's that Smoke Jensen, I'll shoot his eyes out," Jimmy said tightly.

A new fear washed over Martha. "You hush that kind of talk, you hear? If I had time, I'd wash your mouth with soap."

Almost a whine, Jimmy's voice came out painfully. "I didn't cuss, Maw."

In spite of the potential danger of the moment, Martha could not suppress a flicker of smile. Since the first time, at age four, that Jimmy had used the *S*–word, a bar of lye soap had been the answer, rather than his father's razor strap. Oh, how Jimmy hated it.

"Go along, son, do as I say," Martha relented with a pat on the top of Jimmy's head, something else he had come to find uncomfortable of late.

In less than a minute, Jimmy returned with the big old Spencer rifle that had belonged to his father. One pocket of his corduroy trousers, cut off and frayed below the knees, bulged with bright brass cartridges. Martha took the weapon from her son and loaded a round. She held it, muzzle pointed to the ground, when the stranger rode around into the barnyard two minutes later.

"Howdy there," he sang out. "I'm friendly. Come to give you the news from town."

"And what might that be?" Martha challenged.

"Well, ma'am, it looks like it's makin' up for a hangin' for that Smoke Jensen feller. Folks is mighty riled about what happened to your husband."

Unaccountably, the words burst out before she had time to consider them. "Is it certain that he is the guilty party?"

The young rangler did a double take. "Pardon, ma'am? I figgered you'd consider that good news."

Committed already, her second question boiled out over the first. "They've held a trial so soon?"

A sheepish expression remolded the cowboy's face. "In a way. Sort of, I mean, ma'am. In the—in the saloons. The boys ain't happy, an' they're fixin' to string that feller up."

"Good lord, that's—*barbaric*."

Self-confidence recovered, the ranch hand responded

laconically. "There's some who might consider what he done to your husband to be that, too, ma'am."

"You're not a part of this?"

"No, ma'am. I just rode out to bring you the word."

"Then—then ride fast, find the sheriff, and have him bring an end to it. I don't want another monstrous crime to happen on top of the first."

"You don't mind my sayin' it, that's a mighty odd attitude, ma'am."

"No, it's not. Now you get back to town fast and get the sheriff."

"I say now's the time, boys!" Payne Finney shouted over the buzz of angry conversation in the Hang Dog. "Somebody go out and get a rope. Do it quick, while we still got the chance."

"Damn right!"

"I'll go over to Rutherford's, they got some good half-inch manila."

"No, a lariat will do," Forrest Gore sniggered. "Cut into his neck some that way."

"We'd best be making time, then," another man suggested. "Who all is with us?"

Twenty-five voices shouted allegiance.

"I'll go wind up the fellers at Donahue's," Finney informed them. "Take about half an hour, I'd say. Then we do it."

Covered by the shouts of approval, Ty Hardy leaned toward his companions. "Oh-oh, it looks like the boil's comin' to a head."

"Best we think fast about some way to lance it," Walt Reardon prompted.

"Yeah, an' quick," Rip Banning urged.

Long, gold shafts of late afternoon sunlight slanted into the office above the Cattlemen's Union Bank. Dust motes rose as a strong breeze battered the desert-shrunken window sashes and found the way inside. Crystal decanters sat squat on a mahogany sideboard; glasses had been positioned precisely in front of the three very different men who sat around the rectangular table.

Seated at one end, head cocked to the side, listening to the growing uproar from the saloons down the street, Geoffrey Benton-Howell pursed his thin lips in appreciation. Tufts of gray hair sprouted at each temple, creating a halo effect in the sunbeams, the rest of the tight helmet remained a lustrous medium brown. Long, pale, aristocratic fingers curled around the crystal glass, and he raised it to his lips.

Smacking them in appreciation, he spoke into what had become a long silence. "It appears that our designs prosper." Geoffrey's accent, although modulated by years in the American West, retained a flavor of the Midlands of England. "Miguel, you were wise indeed to suggest we take the sheriff into our confidence. It sounds to me that he is an inventive fellow."

Miguel Selleres glowed in the warm light of this praise. "*Gracias, Don* Geoffrey. *Mi amigos,* I would safely suggest that we have killed two birds, so to speak, with a single stone."

Although not quite as much the dandy as Benton-Howell, Selleres dressed expensively and had the air of a Mexican grandee. Short of stature, at five feet and six inches, he had the grace and build of a matador. Age had not told on him, though already in his mid-forties; he seemed every bit at home in this rough frontier town as in the salon of a stately hacienda. One side of his short-waisted, deep russet coat bulged with the .45 Mendoza copy of the Colt Peacemaker, which he wore concealed.

"*Señor* Selleres," the third man at the table said, pronouncing the name in the Spanish manner; *Say-yer-res.* "What, exactly, are you getting at?"

"May I answer that, Miguel?" Benton-Howell interrupted when he saw his partner's danger signal, a writhing of his pencil-line mustache.

"Go right ahead, *Señor* Geoffrey," Selleres grunted, containing his anger.

"What he's getting at, Dalton, is that Tucker is out of our way, with the perfect man to pin it on."

"Umm. You do make things so much clearer, Geoff," Dalton Wade said with a lip curl, to make clear his attitude toward Miguel Selleres.

Miguel Selleres cut his jet-black eyes from one partner to the other. He saw affability in the expensive clothing and impeccable manners of Geoffrey Benton-Howell, whom he had referred to as *Sir* Geoffrey. His obvious affluence radiated security to their ambitious goals.

Across the table from him sat a man Miguel thought ill-suited to their company. Although he masked it with sugared words and no overt insult, Dalton Wade's intense dislike of anyone or anything Mexican radiated from his

pig face in waves of almost physical force. His swelling
paunch matched his heavy jowls, and emphasized his
porcine appearance. Wade dressed in the tacky manner
of a local banker—which he was—in a rumpled suit of
dark blue with too wide pinstripes. Miguel Selleres felt
a genuine wave of revulsion rise within himself. Like a
seller of secondhand buggies, Miguel thought with a conscious effort to throttle his rising gorge. It further angered him to acknowledge that he was the youngest of
this unholy trio.

"In light of our obvious success, I'd suggest that you
contact Quint Stalker and ensure that he moves with dis-
patch on the properties we desire," Selleres aimed at
Wade.

"It has already been done," Wade snapped, barely in
the boundaries of civility.

Benton-Howell stepped in to keep the peace. "Let me
expand on that. As we speak, Stalker and some of his
men should be acquiring the trading post at Twin Mesas.
When that is accomplished, they will move on to the
next, and the next. So there is little left we must address
today. However, I have come upon a third benefit we can
count as ours in this affair."

"Oh, really? What's that?" Dalton Wade remained
cool, even to the man to whom he was beholden for
being included in the grand design.

"Why, the most obvious of all, gentlemen. I propose
a toast to us—the men who are about to put an end to
Smoke Jensen."

Three

Sheriff Jake Reno eased his belly through the doorway to his office in the Socorro jail. His small, dusty boots made a soft pattering on the floorboards, as he crossed to a tiny cubicle set in the wall that divided the office from the cellblock. He poked his head in the open doorway and grunted at a snoozing Ferdie Biggs.

"Open up, Ferdie. I want to talk with that back-shooter."

A line of drool glistened on Ferdie's ratlike face. It flashed as he wobbled the sleep out of his head and came to his boots. "Sure 'nuff, Boss. You gonna give him what for?"

"Do you mean beat hell out of him? No. No entertainment for you this afternoon, Ferdie. I only want to talk to him."

Disappointment drooped Ferdie Biggs's face. He reached for a ring of keys and unlocked the laced strap iron door that opened the cellblock for the sheriff. Reno stalked along the corridor, until he reached the cell that held Smoke Jensen.

Smoke reclined on his bunk, head propped up by both forearms. He didn't even open an eye at the sound of the lawman's approach. Heedless of possible damage to the weapon, Reno banged a couple of bars with the barrel of his Merwin and Hulbert. When the bell tone faded, Smoke opened one eye.

"What?" he asked with flat, hard menace.

"I come to get a confession out of you, Jensen."

"Fat chance. I didn't do anything."

"Sure of that, are you?" Reno probed.

"Yes. I'm sure I didn't back-shoot that man."

"You don't sound all that positive to me."

"Sheriff, I'm not sure about what exactly happened to me, how I got here, or when, but I *do* know that I have never deliberately back-shot a man in my life."

"Smoke Jensen, gunfighter and outlaw and he's never shot a man in the back before? I find that hard to believe. You're pretending, Jensen. I know it and so do you."

"Humor me, Sheriff. Tell me about it."

Taken aback, Sheriff Jake Reno gulped a deep breath. "All right. If it will help you see the light and give me a confession. It happened last night, about ten-thirty. Some shots were heard by customers in the Hang Dog Saloon. They rushed out to find out what was going on. In the alley at the edge of town, they came upon a body lying on the ground, and you.

"You were cold as a blowed-out lamp. The body was dead," Reno explained further.

"Mr. Tucker?"

Reno brightened. "Then you do admit knowing him?"

"No. Your jailer gave me the name early this morning."

"That idiot. Handed you a way out on a platter, didn't he? I'll fix his wagon later. Yes, it was Mr. Lawrence Tucker, a highly popular and respected local rancher.

He'd been shot. You were laying not far from him, with a .45 in your hand."

"I don't carry a .45," Smoke began to protest.

"You had it in your hand, damnit," Reno snapped. Then he drew a deep breath to regain his composure. "It had been fired twice. There were two bullet holes in Mr. Tucker's back. End of case."

"That's ridiculous, Sheriff."

"Oh, yeah?"

"Yes. I normally carry a .44. Two of them, in fact."

"Don't matter, Jensen. No .44s were found anywhere around you, or on Mr. Tucker, and no double rig. Your cartridge belt had a pocket for only one iron, and that .45 fit in it like in a glove."

"Did you or anyone recognize the gun and belt, Sheriff? Ever see it before?"

But Reno had already turned away. Over a shoulder he softly purred his last words for Smoke Jensen. "I'd like to stay and chat, Jensen, but I have important business outside town. You all just sit tight, an' we'll get you hanged all legal and proper."

Hank Yates turned from the batwings of the Hang Dog Saloon. "He's ridin' out of town now."

A wide grin turned the cruel, thin line of Payne Finney's mouth into something close to happy. Leave it to Jake Reno to cover himself. "Good. Now, boys, we can really get to work. Some of you go out the back way and wait in the alley between here an' the saddler's. The rest come with me. Spread out across the street and hold yer place, while I go get the fellers from Donahue's."

"You really think we can just walk down there and take Jensen out?" Yates asked, doubtful.

Finney started for the door as he spoke. "Matter of fact, I know we can."

With a surge of action, the men in the saloon obeyed Finney's commands. For a moment, their alcoholic confusion marred any smooth departure, as men bumped into one another aimed in opposite directions. They ironed it out quickly enough and left the barroom almost empty. All except for three men at the corner table they had occupied since the establishment opened.

"I think we'd best stay here awhile," Walt Reardon suggested.

"We've gotta do something to help," Rip Banning urged, his face nearly the color of his flaming hair.

"We will. In due time."

"Dangit, Walt, every second means more danger."

"Relax, Rip. Those boys have got to get all fired up with more whiskey and brave words, before they do anything drastic. Believe me, I know. I've been on the receiving end of more'n one lynch mob."

Neither Ty nor Rip wanted to dispute Walt over that. Rip eased back in his chair and stared balefully at the front doors. Ty examined his empty beer schooner. Walt eyed the Regulator clock on the wall above the bar. Sound exploded inside the barroom, as boot heels drummed on the planks of the porch outside.

Two rough-looking characters burst in, demanding bottles of whiskey. They took no note of the trio in the corner. After they left, Walt and the other two waited out ten long, tense minutes. Then Walt eased his six-gun from leather and put the hammer on half-cock. He rotated the cylinder to the empty chamber and inserted another cartridge. Then he closed the loading gate and returned his weapon to the holster.

"Rip, you go fetch our gear, an' go saddle up the horses."

Rip nodded and departed. Then Walt turned to Tyrell Hardy. "Ty, why don't you slip out the back door and go to the hotel. Bring our long guns back with you."

"Sure, Walt, right away." Ty Hardy was gone faster than his words.

Smoke Jensen heard the ruckus coming from the saloons and correctly interpreted its meaning. He needed to find some way out of this, before they drank enough liquid courage to come and do what they wanted to do. He had to think. He had to find out what had happened after the middle of the previous afternoon, when he and his hands arrived in Socorro.

"We checked into a hotel," Smoke muttered softly to himself. "Got our gear settled in the rooms, then stopped off at a saloon for a drink before supper." It felt like invisible hands were ringing his mind like a washcloth. "What did we eat? Where?"

The silence of the jail and in his mind mocked him. Smoke came up on his boots and paced the small space allowed in his tiny cell. "Something Mexican," he spoke to the wall. "Stringy beef, cooked in tomatoes, onions, and chili peppers. *Bisték ranchero,* that's it."

A loud shout interrupted his train of thought. One voice rose above the others, clear though distant; the cadence that of someone making a speech. It floated on the hot Socorro air through the small window high in his cell.

"I knew Lawrence Tucker for fifteen years. From when he first moved to these parts. He was a good man. Tough as nails when he had to be, but a good father and husband. Know his wife, too. An' those kids, why they're the most polite, hard-working, reverent younguns you'd ever want to know."

"Yeah, that's right," another voice joined the first. "Larry smoked cigars, like y'all know. Right fancy ones, from a place called Havana. Now, I'll tell you what. I'll buy a box of those special cigars for the first man who fits a rope around the neck of Smoke Jensen!"

Loud cheering rose like a tidal wave. Smoke Jensen stared unbelievingly at the stone wall and gritted his teeth. The testimonials went on, and Smoke could visualize the bottles being passed from hand to hand. In his mind he could see the faces, flushed with whiskey and blood-lust, growing shiny with sweat, as the crowd became a mob.

"In the fifteen years Lawrence Tucker has been here," the first orator went on, "he never done a mean or vicious thing. Oh, he shot him a few Apaches, and potted a couple of lobo wolves who wandered down from the San Cristobals, but he never traded shots with another man, white or Mezkin. Didn't hardly ever even raise his voice. Yet, he was respected, and his hands obeyed him. If it wasn't for havin' to tend the stock and protect the ranch, they'd be here now, you can count on that. And they'd be shoutin' loudest of any to hang that back-shooting sumbitch higher than Haymen."

More cheers. The whiskey, and the rhetoric, were doing their job.

Smoke Jensen climbed on the edge of the bunk and stretched to see beyond the walls of his prison. It did him little good. He found that his cell fronted on the brick wall of a two-story bakery. It had been the source of the tormenting aromas since his awakening. So far he had received not one scrap of food—only that swill laughingly called coffee, shortly after first light.

Never one to worship food, Smoke's belly cramped constantly now at the yeasty scent of baking bread and sugary accompaniment of pies and cakes. No doubt, the sadistic Biggs had placed him in this cell deliberately, and denied him anything to eat. For a moment it had taken his mind off his very real danger.

More shouts from the distant street soon reminded him. "What're we waitin' for?"

"The fellers at Donahue's are fixin' to join us," Payne Finney bellowed. "Y'all stay here, I'll hurry them on."

Smoke Jensen knew he had to do something before they got the sand to carry out their threats. To do that, he needed help. The question of getting it still nagged him. What *had* happened to the hands he had with him?

Three men sat on their lathered horses under a gnarled, aged paloverde tree that topped a large, red-orange mound overlooking the Tucker ranch. The one in the middle pulled a dust-blurred, black Montana Peak Stetson from his balding head, and mopped his brow with a blue gingham bandanna. He puckered thick lips and spat a stream of tobacco juice that struck an industrious dung beetle, which agitatedly rolled his latest prize back toward the hole it called home.

"That woman down there," he said to his companions. "She's got lots of grit. Say that for her. Wonder what the Big Boss will have to come up with to get her off that place?"

A soft grunt came from the thick-necked man on his right. "I say we jist ride down there, give her what her old man got, an' take over the spread."

Contempt curled the bald man's lips. "Idiot! You'd kill a woman? That's why you take orders from me, and I take 'em from Quint Stalker. It's gotta be all proper and legal, idjit."

"Didn't used to be that way," the bellicose one complained.

"Right you are. But ever since ol' Lew Wallace was territorial governor, we've had an extra large helpin' of law and order."

"You tell me? I done three years, breakin' rocks, because of him."

"Then don't open that grub hole of yours and spout such stupid ideas, or you'll do more than that."

"Sure, Rufe, sure. But I still say it would be the easiest way."

"All we're here to do is drop in and scare her a little."

"Then why don't we get on with it?"

They came down in a thunder of hooves. Dust boiled from under their horses, which rutched and groaned at the effort, adding to the eerie howls made by the men who rode them. Quint Stalker had sent only three men because it was such an easy assignment. In less than two minutes, the overconfident hard cases learned how badly their boss had read the situation.

A skinny, undersized boy with snowy hair popped up out of a haystack and slid down its side, yelling as he went. "Mom! Mom! Hey, they're comin' again!" The callused soles of his bare feet pounded clouds from the dry soil.

He cut left and right, zigzagging toward the house. A woman's figure appeared in one window. Rufe and his henchmen had no time to take note of that. With a whoop, the bald one bore down on the lad and bowled him over with the churning shoulder of his mount. A wild squawk burst from Jimmy Tucker, as he went tail over top and rolled like a ball. He bit down hard, teeth grinding, and cast a prayerful glance toward his mother.

In a flash, that became the last bit of scaring they did.

A puff of smoke preceded the crack of a .56 caliber slug that cut the hat from bald Rufe's head. He let out a squall of his own and grabbed uselessly at the flying Montana Peak, then set to cursing. Another bullet forced his companions to veer to the side and put some distance between them.

"Git back here! It's only a damn woman," Rufe bellowed.

Martha Tucker refined her aim some, her left elbow braced on the windowsill, tapered fingers holding the forestock. Calmly she squeezed off another shot from the Spencer. Her third round smacked meatily into Rufe's right shoulder, and exploded terrible pain through his chest. It also convinced him that this was no simple damn woman.

He'd had enough. He, too, reined to his left and put

spurs to the flanks of his horse. Another shot sounded behind him and sped all three on their way.

It started with a sound like an avalanche. A low, primal growl that swelled as it advanced, metamorphosing into the roar of a tidal bore, bent on smashing up an estuary and inundating everything along the river. Although coming from a distance, the angry bellow echoed from the brick wall of the bakery. It made the hairs on the nape of Smoke Jensen's neck rise and vibrate.

They were coming.

How many? Would they get in? Smoke Jensen had been scared in his life many times before. Yet nothing compared to what he experienced now—not the grizzly that had nearly taken off his face before he killed it with a Greenriver knife . . . not the dozen Blackfeet warriors who had surrounded him, alone in camp, with Preacher out running traps . . . not when he faced down a dozen hardened killers in the street of Banning. None of them compared. This absolutely paralyzed him for the moment. He was so helpless, vulnerable. Death rode the mob like a single steed, a hound out of Hell, and it made Smoke reexamine his own fragile mortality. How easily they could take him.

NO! He could find a way to get out of this. Somehow, he could hold off the mob. Think, damnit!

The rattle, squeak, and clang of the cellblock door interrupted Smoke Jensen's fevered speculation as it slammed open. He left the window at once, pressed his cheek to the corridor bars, and looked along the narrow walkway. Waddling toward him, Smoke saw the fat figure of Ferdie Biggs. The keys jangled musically in one pudgy paw.

"Turn around and back up against the bars, Jensen."

"You're taking me out of here?"

"Yep. Jist do as I say."

Smoke turned around and put his hands through the space between two bars. Biggs reached him a moment later, puffing and gasping. Cold bands of steel closed around the wrists of Smoke Jensen. A key turned in the small locks.

"Now step back. All the way to the wall."

"Am I being taken to some safer place?" Smoke asked, his expectations rising.

"Get back, I said." Biggs snarled the words as he reached behind his back and drew a .44 Smith and Wesson from his waistband. He stepped to the door and turned a large key in the lockcase. The bar gave noisily, and the jailer swung the barrier wide. He motioned to Smoke with the muzzle of the Smith, and a nasty smirk spread on his moon face. "Naw. I'm gonna give you over to those good ol' boys out there."

Four

Ferdie Biggs prodded Smoke Jensen ahead of him along the cellblock corridor. At the lattice-work door he passed on through without closing it. He had done the same with the cell, the keys hanging in the lock. The sudden rush of adrenaline had cleared the fuzziness from Smoke's head. He realized that for all of Biggs's slovenly appearance and illiterate speech, he was at least clever enough to lay the groundwork for it to appear the mob had overwhelmed him and broke into the jail.

"You're not smart enough to fake a forced entry, Ferdie," Smoke taunted him. "You're going to get caught."

Biggs gave him a rough shove that propelled Smoke across the room to the sheriff's desk. The narrow edge of the top dug into his thighs. Bright pinpoints of pain further cleared Smoke's thinking. He was ready, then, when Biggs barked his next command.

"Turn around, I wanna have some fun, bust you up some, before I let the boys in."

Smoke turned and kept swinging his right leg. The toe of his boot connected with the hand that held the six-gun and knocked it flying. It discharged a round that cut a hot trail past Smoke's rib cage, and smashed a blue granite coffeepot on a small, Acme two-burner wood stove in the corner. Biggs bellowed in pain and surprise, a moment before Smoke reversed the leg and planted his boot heel in the jailer's doughy middle.

Ferdie Biggs bent double, the air *whoosh*ing out from his lungs. Meanwhile Smoke Jensen recovered his balance and used his other foot to plant a solid kick to the side of Ferdie Biggs's head. From where it made contact came a ripe melon *plop!,* and Ferdie went to his knees.

"The keys, Ferdie," Smoke rasped out. "Give me the keys to these handcuffs."

"Ain't . . . gonna . . . do it."

Smoke kicked him again, a sharp boot toe in the chest. Ferdie gulped and sputtered, one hand clawed at his throat in an effort to suck in air. He turned deep-set, piggish eyes on Smoke Jensen in pleading. Smoke belted him again, from the side. A thin wail came from far down Ferdie's throat—he'd been able to gulp some breath.

"I keep kicking until I get the keys."

Smoke's hard, flat, unemotional voice reached Ferdie in a way nothing else might. One trembling hand delved into a side pocket of his vest. Shakily, he withdrew a single key on a small ring. He dropped it twice, while he knee-walked to where Smoke Jensen stood beside the desk.

"Now, reach around behind me and unlock these manacles." Smoke shoved the tip of one boot up in Ferdie's crotch. "Try anything, and you'll sing soprano for the rest of your life."

Sobbing for breath, and in desperation, Ferdie complied. It took three fumbling attempts to undo the first lock. Then Smoke took the key from Ferdie's trembling fingers and shoved the bleeding, glazed-eyed jailer back against the wall that contained a gun rack. Smoke freed his other wrist, then snapped the cuffs on Ferdie.

"Is there a back way out of here?"

Before Ferdie could answer, a loud pounding began on the closed and barred front door. "C'mon, Ferdie, open up!" a man bellowed.

"Bring him out! Bring him out! Bring him out!" the mob chanted in the background.

"Don't be a fool, Ferdie. He ain't worth gettin' hurt over."

"Your 'good ol' boys' don't seem to like you much, Ferdie," Smoke taunted. "Answer me. Is there a back way out?"

"N-no. Usedta be, but the sheriff had it bricked up."

"How brilliant of him. Nothing for it but to face them down."

Ferdie Biggs blinked incredulously. "How you gonna do that, all alone?"

"I won't be alone," Smoke advised him as he reached to the gun rack. "I'll have Mr. L. C. Smith with me."

He selected a short-barrel, 10-gauge L. C. Smith Wells Fargo gun and opened the breech. From a drawer at the bottom of the rack, he took six brass buckshot casings. Two he inserted into the shotgun. A loud crash sounded from the direction of the front door. Ferdie Biggs cringed.

"They shouldn' do that. It was all set—" He snapped

rubbery lips tightly closed, and lost his porcine appearance as he realized he had said too much.

"Set up or not, it isn't going the way they expected, is it?"

A rhythmic banging sounded as four men rammed a heavy wooden bench against the outer face of the door. Ferdie worked his thick lips.

"Oh, hell. Sheriff's gonna have my butt, if that door gets broke."

"The thing you should be worried about is that I've got your butt right *now*."

Ferdie Biggs looked at Smoke Jensen with sudden, shocked realization. "You ain't gonna shoot me, are you?"

"Not unless I have to." The door vibrated with renewed intensity, and Smoke cut his eyes to it. He saw signs of strain on the oak bar.

"Get something heavier," came advice from the mob.

"Hell, get some dynamite."

That sent Ferdie Biggs on a staggered course to the shuttered window. He shouted through the thick wooden covers and closed the lower sash. "Oh, Jeeezus, don't do that. I'm still in here."

"Who cares?" a laughing voice told Ferdie.

"Great friends you've got." Smoke Jensen added a cold, death-rattle laugh to increase the effect of his words.

From a drawer in the sheriff's desk, Smoke took a very familiar pair of cartridge belts. One had the pocket slung low, for a right-hand draw. The other rode high on the left, with the butt of a .44 pointing forward, canted at a sharp angle.

Smoke cut his eyes to a thoroughly shaken Ferdie. "And here the sheriff told me they found no sign of my own guns. Now they show up in his desk. Wonder how that happened?"

"Don't ask me. All I saw was that old .45."

Smoke hastily strapped himself into the dual rigs. His hand had barely left the last buckle, when the door gave a hollow *boom* and the cross-bar splintered apart and fell to the floor. Another *slam* and the thick oak portal swung inward. Three men spilled into the room. The one in the lead held a rope, already tied into a hangman's knot.

To his left stood another, who looked to Smoke Jensen to be a saddle tramp. His wooden expression showed not the slightest glimmer of intelligence. The rifle he held at hip level commanded all the respect he needed. To the other side, Smoke saw a pigeon-breasted fellow, who could have been the grocery clerk at the general mercantile. Indeed, the fan of a feather duster projected from a hip pocket.

Triumph shone on their faces for only a second, until they took in the scattergun competently held in the hands of Smoke Jensen. Payne Finney reacted first. He let go of the noose and dived for the six-gun in its right-hand pocket.

"For godsake, shoot him, Gore," he yelled.

"You shoot him, Payne," came a wailed reply.

Smoke Jensen had only one chance. He swung the barrels of the L. C. Smith into position between the two gunmen, so that the shot column split its deadly load into two bodies. The deafening roar filled the room. A scream of pain came from the suddenly animated man named Gore. A cloud of gray-white powder smoke obscured the view for a moment. Smoke Jensen had already moved and gazed beyond the huge puffball.

His finger had already found the second trigger; Smoke guided the shotgun unerringly to the next largest threat. When that man made no move to carry on the fight, he sought out the two he had shot. Both lay on the floor.

Payne Finney had taken the most of the 00 pellets, and bled profusely from five wounds. Gore had at least three pellets in his side and right forearm. He lay silent and still now. Shock had knocked him unconscious. A third man, who had been unlucky enough to be in the open space between Finney and Gore, was also down, his kneecap shot away. He writhed and whined in agony. Smoke's keen sight also took in something else.

Sputtering trails of sparks arched over the heads of the mob, who stood stunned on the stoop and in the street. Instinctively, Smoke dived away from the open door, expecting a shattering blast of dynamite. Instead, the red cylinders fell among the members of the lynch mob and went off with thunderous, though relatively harmless roars. Starbursts of red, white, and green fountained up to sting and burn the blood-hungry crowd. Immediately, three six-guns opened up from behind the startled men of Socorro. Yells of consternation rose among the would-be hangmen.

More shots put wings to the feet of the least hearty of them. Movement away from the jail became epidemic when Smoke Jensen stepped into the doorway, shotgun ready. Laughing, yelling, and shooting, Smoke Jensen's three missing ranch hands, Banning, Hardy, and Reardon, dusted some boot heels with lead to speed the lynchers on their way.

"Hey, Walt," Ty Hardy shouted over the tumult. "I told you those Mezkin fireworks I bought in Ary-zona would come in handy."

Walt Reardon looked upon Smoke Jensen with a near-worshipful expression. "Kid foolishness I called them. Reckon I was wrong. Smoke, good to see you."

"Alive, you mean," Smoke returned dryly.

Reardon brushed that aside. "What the hell happened? You disappeared, and the next thing we know, folks are sayin' you killed a man; back-shot him—which means it sure as the devil weren't you."

"What took you so long?" Smoke smiled to take the sting out of his words.

"We had to have a plan. You should have seen them. Half a hunnerd at least." Reardon tipped back the brim of his hat and wiped a sweaty brow. "What now?"

"I suggest we leave the lovely town of Socorro for better parts," Smoke advised.

"Suits," Reardon agreed. "We—ah—took the precaution to get your horse saddled and ready. It's down the block."

All four started that way. Behind them, Ferdie Biggs tottered out onto the stoop. "What about me? What's gonna happen to me?"

Smoke Jensen swiveled his head and gave Ferdie Biggs a deathly grin. "You'll have quite a story to tell the sheriff now, won't you, Ferdie?"

* * *

Through no fault of their own, Geoffrey Benton-Howell, Miguel Selleres, and Dalton Wade erroneously toasted the demise of Smoke Jensen when they heard the commotion coming from the jail. Beaming heartily, Benton-Howell refilled their glasses and raised his again.

"And here's to our prospects of becoming very wealthy men."

"Here, here!" Dalton Wade responded.

"I think it is fortuitous that our man found Quint Stalker so quickly," Miguel Selleres remarked. "Now that he is rounding up his men, we can put our next phase in operation."

"I'd like to see Smoke Jensen swinging from a tree." Bitterness rang in Wade's words.

Benton-Howell gave him a hard look. "It would be more politic for us to remain here, out of the sight of others. If you would be so kind, why is it you have such a hatred for Smoke Jensen?"

Dalton Wade considered a moment before answering. "Three close friends are in their graves because of that damned Smoke Jensen."

Geoffrey Benton-Howell said, "They were all good friends?"

"Yes, they were. Two of them were doing quite well, running a small town up in Montana with iron fists. Some of their henchmen stepped on the toes of someone related to Smoke Jensen. Jensen took exception to it. When Jensen finished, fifteen men were dead, another twenty-seven wounded. Among them, my friends."

"What about the third?" Benton-Howell asked.

"Jeremy and I were very close friends. He fancied

himself a good hand with a gun. Fast, exceptionally fast in fact. But . . . not fast enough. He braced Smoke Jensen one day. Jensen was actually a bit slower on the draw, but oh, so much more accurate. Jeremy didn't have a chance."

"I see. So all along this has been personal with you, not just a means to an end. For my part, and Don Miguel's, when our involvement in this is known, we'll be considered clever heroes to many people. It will make what comes after . . . ah . . . more palatable to them." His smile turned nasty. "From now on, events are going to turn rather rough. It's necessary that they are blamed on a mythical Smoke Jensen gang, seeking retribution for his death."

Benton-Howell poured more brandy, and his laughter filled the room.

Sheriff Jake Reno rode into a town oddly quiet for the scene of a lynching. Socorro slumbered under the hot New Mexico sun. A deep uneasiness grew when he saw no signs of a dead Smoke Jensen hanging from any tree on the northern edge of town. He found the jail door open, as expected, though no sign of Ferdie Biggs. He dismounted and entered.

Ferdie Biggs lay slumped on the daybed used by the night duty jailer. He had a fist-sized lump on the side of his head—bandaged in yards of gauze—a fat, swollen lip, and more tape and bandage around his ribs.

"What the hell happened to you?" Reno blurted.

"Smoke Jensen's what happened. He kicked the crap out of me and escaped. Had three fellers with him, outside the jail when the mob came. Set off some kind of explosives, shot up the place, and they all got away."

Rage burned in the sheriff's chest as he saw his five-hundred-dollar bonus flying away. He crossed to where Biggs lay and grabbed a double handful of shirt, yanking the slovenly jailer upright. "Goddamnit, can't you do anything right?"

"Ow! Oh, damn, I hurt! I meant what I said, Jensen *kicked* me."

"I suppose because he was in handcuffs?" Reno said scornfully.

Ferdie gulped. "Yep. I had him cuffed, right enough."

"But you got too close. Pushed your luck, right?"

"Uh-huh. I wanted to punch him up a little, have some fun before they hung him. Next thing I knew, he was usin' them of his boots on me."

"Idiot. Get that lard butt of yours out there and round up some men to form a posse. We're going after Jensen." Sheriff Reno's decision came automatically, without a thought of consulting the men who had bought his co-operation.

There'd be hell to pay when they found out his means of disposing of Smoke Jensen had failed, he reckoned. Best to put that off for a while. Chances were he'd run Jensen to ground easily, and come back to collect his five hundred. Sure, Reno's growing self-confidence told him, Smoke Jensen or no, the man was on the run in strange territory. It would be easy.

It would take all of the cunning of the last mountain man to evade the posse Smoke knew would be sent to pursue him and his hands. Ten miles out of town, Smoke had called a halt and sincerely thanked his men for the rescue. He saw clearly now, that they had laid low in order not to become ensnared in whatever skullduggery had put him in line for a lynching. He also explained the options open to them.

". . . so that's about it. You can all take off for the Sugarloaf, or take your chances with me."

"What do you reckon to do?" Walt Reardon asked.

"I'm going to find out who killed Tucker, and why. That should clear my name in these parts."

Reardon, used to being a wanted man, nodded soberly. "Might be a big undertakin'. I allow as how you could use some help."

"Same for me," Ty Hardy chimed in.

"I'll stick it out with you, Smoke," Rip Banning added.

"It can get rough. There's a chance some of us will draw a bullet."

"Way I see it, Smoke, that's an everyday experience. Long as it's not a stacked deck, count me in for the game."

Smoke Jensen looked hard at Walt Reardon, appreciating his staunch support and his knowledge. Smile lines crinkled around Smoke's slate-gray eyes, and he nodded curtly. "Best I could come up with is to head for the nearest mountains. Wear the posse down, confuse them. Sooner or later they'll give up and go home."

Walt grinned. "Now, that shines. I 'member the time me an' old Frisco Johnny Blue did just that up in Dakota Territory. Worked fine as frog hair. Is there . . . ah . . .

somethin' else we could be doin', while givin' that posse the slip?"

"Maybe. I'll think on it. Now, let's put some distance between us and them. Next stop's the Cibola Range."

Five

Sheriff Jake Reno trotted his blotched gray along the main trail leading north out of Socorro. The posse had covered eight miles at a fast trot, then slowed the pace to look for tracks. They found them easily. Reno held them to a leisurely pace from then on.

"My guess is they'll be cuttin' west soon," he advised the man on his left.

"Why's that?" the uncomfortable store clerk asked.

"Smoke Jensen's got him a rep'tation of bein' a mountain man. The last mountain man. I reckon he'd feel more at home in the hills. Too open to keep on north toward the Rockies. Those three saddle bums is wanted for jail break, along with Jensen, an' you can add murder on Jensen's head. No, they won't want to run into a lot of folks."

Snorting doubt through a nose made red by whiskey, the clerk issued his own opinion. "If he wanted mountains, there's plenty around Socorro."

"But too close to town for his likin'. Smoke Jensen's nothin' if he ain't clever. If he was to sneak around outside town, we could keep resupplied forever and wear him down. Now, you be for keepin' a close eye out for where they turn off."

They almost missed it, as it was. A bare, wide slab of rock led into the bed of an intermittent stream, presently made liquid by heavy rains in the mountains. A fresh scrape, made by the iron shoe of a heavy horse, told the story to the sheriff's favorite scout. He waved the posse down as they approached.

"They went into the water."

"Not too smart under the best of conditions," Jake Reno opined.

"It will run dry in an hour or two," the scout suggested.

"Or it'll come a flash flood gushin' down on us. We'll ride the banks, let them take the risk. Jensen and his trash friends'll come out sooner than later, I figger."

Five miles to the west, the posse came upon the spot where four horses began to walk on wet sand. Sheriff Reno halted the men and tipped back the wide brim of his hat. A blue gingham bandanna mopped at the sweat that streaked down his temples and brow.

"Yep. They're headin' into the Cibolas. Eb, you an' Sam head back for town. Get us some pack animals and lots of grub. This is gonna be a long hunt."

"Like I said, boys. This ain't like the High Lonesome, but at least it's mountains." Smoke Jensen dismounted and continued to speak his observations aloud. "I'd say the sheriff is a good ten miles behind. Time to fix up something for him to remember us by."

"How's that?"

"Walt, you were with the Sugarloaf back when those

Eastern dudes tried to attack the place. Perhaps you could enlighten young Rip here."

"Sure, Smoke." Walt proceeded to tell Ripley Banning about the deadfalls, pits, and the great star-shaped log obstacles that had so befuddled the army of Eastern thugs, who had been sicked on the Sugarloaf hands only a year past. Rip started to grin early on, and his eyes danced with mischief by the time the tale had been told.

"Considerin' your fondness for ornery tricks, Walt, it couldn't be that maybe you thought up some of those nasty traps?"

Walt Reardon pulled a face. "Rip, you wound me. Though I confess, it was my idea to gather up them yeller jacket nests in the night whilst they was restin', and flang gunnysacks full in among the sleepin' outlaws." He clapped his hands in approval. "They folks danced around right smartly."

Under the direction of Smoke and Walt, several large snares and a deadfall were rigged on the trail they left. "We'll cut south a ways now," Smoke suggested. "If I was making a way through these hills, I reckon I'd pick me a way through that pair of peaks yonder. Looks like a natural pass to me."

"You've got a hell of an eye, Smoke," said Walt admiringly.

Sheriff Jake Reno heard a faint *twang,* a second before a leafy sapling made a swishing rush through the air and cleaned two possemen off their mounts. One's boot heel caught in the stirrup, and the frightened horse he had been riding set off at a brisk run along the trail. The man's screams echoed off the high sandstone walls that surrounded them.

Not for long, though, as his head plocked against a boulder at the side of the narrow passageway, and he lost consciousness. Wide-eyed and pale, the sneering clerk lost some of his cockiness. He cut his eyes to the sheriff and worked a mouth that made no sound for a moment.

"What was that?"

"A trap, you dummy. Nobody move an inch, hear?"

The sheriff's advice proved wise indeed. The riders cut their eyes around the terrain and located two more of Smoke Jensen's surprises; a deadfall and another swing trap. Reno ordered the men to dismount and search on foot. That worked well enough, until a second *swoosh* of leaves and a startled scream froze them in place.

Jake Reno found himself looking up at a man suspended some ten feet off the ground, his ankles securely held in a rope snare. "Just like a damn rabbit," the lawman grumbled. "Some of you get him down. We'll stick to the center of the trail. Walk your mounts. And . . . keep a sharp eye, or you'll be swingin' up there next . . . or worse."

Smoke Jensen stood looking south at the summit of a natural pass through the Cibola Range, and studied the land beyond. "I figure that bought us a good three hours. It appears to me there's a small box canyon about a half hour's ride along this trail. We'll camp there for the night."

From that point on, Smoke and his wranglers took care to hide their tracks. Walt Reardon took the rear slot with a large clump of sagebrush, which he used to wipe out their prints on soft ground. They reached the overgrown entrance to the side canyon in twenty minutes. Smoke went ahead and made sure they could navigate the narrow passage without leaving obvious signs of their presence. At the back of the small gorge, they found a rock basin of water, cool and clear. Called a tank in these parts, from the original Spanish designation of *tanque,* these natural water reservoirs had saved many a life on the barren deserts of the Southwest.

Some, like this one, were even big enough to swim in. Of course, Smoke advised his ranch hands, that would have to wait until they and the horses had drunk their fill, and used all they needed for cooking.

"Though I don't mind leavin' behind some dirt for the good Sheriff Reno to swallow," he concluded with a chuckle.

Ty Hardy and Walt Reardon set about locating pine cones and dry wood to make a nearly smokeless fire. Smoke figured they had a good three hours in which to prepare food for that night and the next morning. Once well-accustomed to the outlaw life, Walt Reardon had prepared well, stuffing their saddlebags with coffee beans, flour, sugar, salt, side pork, and dry beans. Smoke got right down to mixing dough for skillet bread. Resembling a giant biscuit, baked over coals in a cast-iron skillet, and sealed with the lid of a Dutch oven, it was served in pie wedges. Not as tasty as the flaky biscuits Smoke's lovely wife, Sally, made, but it would serve, and could be eaten hot or cold. Rip Banning watched intently, until Smoke sent him for water for the Dutch oven to soak beans. Rip returned with a broad, boyish grin.

"Found me a bee tree. It's jam packed with honey. Reckon it'll go good on that skillet bread."

Smoke cocked an eye on him. "How you reckon on getting that honey without having an argument with the bees?"

"Why, I'll just smoke . . . uh . . . dumb of me, huh? Can't drowse 'em out with a big ol' puff of pearly white that'd let the sheriff know where we'd gone."

"You're learnin'. We'll just have to forego the honey tonight. And," Smoke continued, "I'm appointin' you to make sure all fires are well out before sundown."

"Make the lesson stick, huh?"

"You got the right of it, Rip."

Walt returned from his last trip for wood with four plump squirrels. Excitement filled Rip Banning. "We're gonna feast. How'd you git 'em without firing a shot, Walt?"

Walt made light of it, but could not avoid a tiny brag. "I come up on them, frolickin' on the ground. So I just locked eyes and mesemer . . . mesariz . . ."

"Mesmerized," Smoke provided.

"Yeah, that's right. I done stared them down."

Rip nodded with youthful enthusiasm, then produced a frown over his green eyes. "Squirrels are hard to dress out."

Walt gestured with his russet-furred contribution to dinner. "That's why you're cleaning all of 'em."

"Awh, Walt—"

"You fixin' to sink a tooth into one of 'em, you can do the honors."

They tasted delicious, roasted over the fire, helped along with skillet bread, thick beans, wild onions, and watercress from the tank. Half an hour before sundown, Rip poured water on the fire, raked the ashes, and distributed the stones that had formed the fire ring. With muttered good nights, Smoke and the two older hands rolled up in their blankets and fell into deep sleep. Rip, being youngest, had the first watch. He would wake Walt for second shift, who in turn would roll out Ty Hardy. Smoke took the last trick, usually the most likely for a surprise attack.

Setting down the empty tin cup, Sheriff Jake Reno wiped a drop of coffee off one thick lip and rested the hand on the swell of his belly. He was beginning to suspect that they had taken the wrong trail. This one led nowhere, if he recollected correctly. It would take them half a day to cross south over the ridges between them and the pass that led to the great inner valley of the Cibola Range. There they could get reinforcements and resupply at Datil, or further on at Horse Springs.

Provided, of course, that Smoke Jensen didn't get there first and tie up with some local guns. That could get nasty. The heavy breakfast the sheriff had eaten rumbled in his gut. Oh, lord, all he needed was to work up a burnin' stomach. Those damned traps set out by Jensen had cost them half a day. Just thinking about them put him in a stew.

"Herkermer, I want you to round up a dozen of the

boys and take the shortest route to Cristoforo Pass. I got me a feelin' we're in the wrong part of the Cibolas."

"The trail led us northwest," Herkermer protested. "Besides, the shortest way is the longest. All them ridges to climb."

"You'll pick up speed goin' down the other sides," Reno snapped back.

"What'll you be doing in the meantime?"

"Look, Herkermer, I'm runnin' this posse, not you. We'll be havin' a look-see at this trail; the canyons yonder link up, make for hard goin', but a body can get through. We have to be certain which way Jensen went. Then we'll join you in Datil. I've a hunch Jensen is makin' for the main part of the range."

"He'd sure have to know a hell of a lot about the country for him to figger that out," Payne Finney said obstinately, the pain in his side making him more irritable than usual.

"What's to say he don't have a map, you ninny? Those buckshot holes is makin' you dizzy-headed. Truth to tell, you ain't in fit condition to ride with us. I think I'm goin' to send you back to Socorro with a message for some certain gentlemen."

"Our mutual employers, you mean," Payne prompted nastily. "Suits me. I ain't feelin' all that whippy, no how."

"You tell 'em where we are and what we're doin'," came the sheriff's command.

You're splittin' the posse, an' makin' a fool of yerself, Payne Finney thought silently. He knew only too well how damned dangerous Smoke Jensen could be. *Goddamn you, Smoke Jensen,* Payne Finney vowed to himself, *I'm gonna fix your clock sure as shootin'.*

* * *

Geoffrey Benton-Howell and his partners already knew of the fiasco in the jail. Miguel Selleres and Dalton Wade fumed, while Geoffrey Benton-Howell tried to calm his partners and get some positive thoughts out of them about a bit of news just delivered. The bearer of the good tidings, Axel Gundersen, watched the two would-be tycoons vent their spleens with mild amusement. At last, he spoke into the silence after their tirade.

"*Ja,* sure, Sir Geoffrey, it's exactly like I say. The gold is there, true enough, *hufda.* Make no mistake about that. Some of it is exposed on the surface. The problem is getting it out."

Miguel Selleres rounded on him. "*Hijo de la chingada!* Make sense, *Señor!* Didn't you just say that gold was to be found on the surface? What's to make it difficult getting it out?"

Gundersen drew a straight face and called on his ample knowledge of English idiom. "About eight hundred angry White Mountain Apache warriors, *ja* sure."

"Ah . . . ummm, yes, Miguel. There is a small difficulty to get around the Apaches."

"What's the problem in that?" Dalton Wade snapped.

"The gold is on their land," Geoffrey Benton-Howell reminded his listeners.

"Land they've got no goddamned right to," Wade thundered. "What do those stupid savages know about gold?"

Benton-Howell tried a soft approach. "That we white men desperately want the yellow rocks, as they call the gold. That we go absolutely mad over possessing it."

Wade's lip curled downward in a parody of a pout. "There you go. To those stinking Apaches, they are just rocks. If people can't appreciate what they have on their land, it should be taken from them."

"Which we are in the process of doing. Here, take some brandy and relax. Well, Gunderson, you've done a fine job. Your compensation will be in keeping with your achievements."

"*Ja,* sure, I expected no less. Now all you need to do is follow through with the politicians."

During the lonely hours of his watch, Smoke Jensen had thought through the situation in which he found himself. The previous day had been given over to surviving long enough to examine conditions and options. He announced the result of his deliberations over breakfast the next morning.

"We're going to split up."

"We done anything that don't suit you?" Walt Reardon asked cautiously.

"No, nothing like that. We can stick together and run that posse ragged, but in a way, that's spinnin' a wagon wheel over a gorge. Someone needs to get word to the Sugarloaf. Ty, I'm going to leave that up to you."

"I'd rather ride beside you, Smoke."

"I know you would. But Sally has to hear about this from someone on our side. Besides, it might be we'll need help from the other hands, before this is over. Or from Monte Carson. He knows you, so does Sally. Walt, I want you and Rip to head back to Arizona. Contact Jeff York, the Ranger captain we sold those horses to.

Tell him what's going on, and ask if he knows what's behind it."

"Want us to bring him here?"

"Out of his jurisdiction, Walt. But if he offers, carry him along."

"I've got the feeling there's gonna be hell to pay 'fore long."

Smoke came to his boots, put a hand on Walt's shoulder. "You're right. And I aim to see the ones payin' it are Sheriff Reno and his posse. I'm headin' on. Lead your horses up the trail a ways in the direction you're going, then wipe out every sign of this camp."

Walt nodded curtly. "Keep a wall to your back, Smoke."

"I will, whenever I can, Walt."

"Hell, this ain't gettin' us anywhere, Sheriff," a disgruntled posseman complained.

Jake Reno considered that a moment. "You're right, Jim. We ain't seen a sign of them in hours. Might be we're following the wrong trail. What we need to do is fan out, follow ev'ry game and people path heading south. I know it in my bones that Smoke Jensen is headed toward Horse Springs. There's a telegraph there, and he can get help if he wants it."

"What would any wanted man go into a town for?" Jim asked.

"It's not like he really kilt—" Reno realized what he was about to say and bit off the words.

Two of the citizens of Socorro exchanged nervous glances. Doubt wrinkled the brows of several others.

"Now, I want you to keep this in mind. This whole affair has gone too damn far. Check out everything that moves, and if you see Jensen, shoot to kill."

Six

Smoke Jensen ghosted through the trees in a low ground mist that had drifted in around three in the morning. Only his wranglers had left the northern slopes of the Cibola Range. Smoke had kept his place, expecting to catch Sheriff Jake Reno off guard. And he had.

A crackle of brush made Smoke Jensen cut his eyes to the left. Only a second passed before he heard soft, murmured words from that direction. His keen vision marked the shapes of two heads, close together. The sheriff had been smart enough to put out pickets, but he hadn't been too smart about who he had assigned the duty, Smoke reckoned. The mountain man had exchanged boots for moccasins earlier, and now moved with utter silence.

Half a dozen carefully placed strides brought him up behind the unwary pair. One of the possemen had just fished the makin's out of a vest pocket. When he started to roll a quirley, Smoke Jensen reached out with two big, hard hands to the off sides of the duo's heads, and slammed them together. He made quick work of binding their hands and feet with short lengths cut from a rope he had taken off another unattentive sentry earlier.

Smoke stuffed the neckerchiefs of the unconscious

men into their mouths. Satisfied with his work, he moved on. A surprisingly short distance inward of the camp, he came upon a line of picketed horses. A reassuring pat on the muzzles of the critters gained their silence, while Smoke undid their reins from the tightly stretched lariat that served as an anchor. A sudden, cold thought speared at him. This was entirely too easy.

"I figgered you'd come lookin' for us. So, I left you a few tidbits to whet your appetite," said Sheriff Reno, as he clicked back the hammer of his Smith and Wesson .44 American.

Smoke Jensen turned his way and made a draw in one smooth motion. Jake Reno had never seen anything like it. One second he was looking at Smoke Jensen's back, a split-second later, Jensen faced him, the black hole of a .44 muzzle settling in on the lawman's belly. Without conscious direction, Reno's body took over, flexed at the knees, and he flew backward into the sharp thorns of a clump of blackberry bushes. Smoke's .44 roared and spat fire, before Reno could even think to trigger his.

Hot lead cut a shallow trail across the upper curve of the sheriff's buttocks. With wild squalls, the horses took off at a run, and so did Smoke Jensen.

"Goddamnit, he's shot me! Smoke Jensen's shot me," Jake Reno roared, more angry than hurt.

Bent double, the famous gunfighter streaked along, parallel to the camp and at a right angle to the direction taken by the frightened critters. From behind, Smoke heard new, painful yelps from the sheriff, who was learning why any man with good sense sent his woman and kids out to pick berries.

Sleepy cries of alarm rose from the disturbed camp.

Men began to curse hotly, when they realized what the sound of pounding hooves meant. Smoke Jensen ignored them and forced his way through the underbrush to where he had left his mount. He'd give them some time to settle down, he reasoned, then hit again about midnight.

Five of Quint Stalker's gang, who had ridden with the posse, paused at the dark entrance to a side canyon. Not even the full moonlight could penetrate the gorge. Under the frosty starlight, they cut uncertain glances at one another.

"Don't know why the hell the sheriff wants us checkin' this out in the middle of the night," one complained.

"Says he's got a hunch. You ask me, it's a little in-digestion proddin' his belly."

"Or his sore butt stingin'," another opined.

At the rear of the loose formation, the last man saw a brief flicker of movement right before his eyes. Then he let out a short, startled yelp, as the loop tightened and pinned his arms to his sides above the elbows. The others turned in time to see him disappear from the saddle.

"What the hell!" the nominal leader exploded. "Hub! Where the hell are you?"

But Hub wasn't saying anything. He was too busy sucking on the barrel of a .44 in the hand of Smoke Jensen. Smoke gave an unseen nod of satisfaction and bent low to whisper in Hub's ear.

"You want to stay alive, you keep real quiet." Smoke removed the steel tube from Hub's mouth at the man's energetic nod of agreement. "I'm going to tie your legs together and string you up in that tree."

"You said I could live," Hub blurted in confusion and fear.

"Upside down, idiot. And you will live, if you give me five minutes to get clear of this place. Then you can yell your fool head off."

Hub Peters had no problem believing everything Smoke Jensen told him. He felt the rope circle his ankles and the tension increase. The tight band around his chest eased off, and he swung free of the ground. His fear somewhat abated, he could again hear his companions.

"D'you see that? Where in hell did he go?"

"I don't know, but it's some more bad news from Smoke Jensen, count on it."

"We goin' in after Hub?"

"You crazy?" the leader challenged. "Want to wind up disappearin' before yer friends' eyes?"

"What about Hub?"

"Nice friends you have, Hub. If I was you, I'd light me a shuck for some place far, far away from them." Smoke's soft chuckle faded off into the distance.

Silently, Hub Peters agreed with Smoke Jensen.

Had they been looking in the right direction, the men of the posse would have seen a telltale spurt of gray-white powder smoke, some three seconds before the blue granite coffeepot gave off a metallic clang and leaped from the fire. Boiling liquid flew everywhere, then the sound of the shot came. Three hard cases—brought by the sheriff to keep the townies in line—squawked in alarm as the hot brew scalded their flesh.

They tore at their shirts and trousers in an effort to

escape their torment, unmindful of the danger. Most of the others had already bellied down in the dirt.

"Over there!" came a frightened cry as another blossom of gray rose from the hillside.

This time, one of Quint Stalker's gunnies went down with a bullet through his right thigh. He flopped and cursed and moaned in the dust, while his companions skittered off to find better cover. One outlaw hanger-on with better foresight had brought a long-range Express rifle. He unlimbered it from its scabbard, adjusted the sight, and took aim. After levering three rounds through the Winchester, he had to acknowledge that only a fool would have stuck around after the second shot. He'd wasted the ammunition.

When the sniper fire did not resume after five minutes, the possemen picked up the remains of their breakfast and fell into their routine. A crack-whisper of sound above their heads turned faces upward, to receive a shower of shredded leaves. Right on the tail of the high round, another snapped into camp and split the cross-tree of a pack saddle.

Once more, everyone dove for cover. One pudgy townsman didn't take as much care as his comrades, and paid for it with the heel of one boot. The howl he put up might have convinced someone his foot had been shot off.

"Goddamn you, Smoke Jensen!" Sheriff Jake Reno roared, shaking a fist above the boulder behind which he sheltered. A .45-70-500 Express bullet whipped past his knuckles, close enough to feel its heat. He gave a little yelp and hunkered down.

This time no one moved for fifteen minutes. Two of

Stalker's hard cases came out in the open first. "We'd best go look for a trail," one opined.

"What for? It'd only lead to an ambush," the other outlaw complained.

"Damn you, men, you're my deputies now, and you'll do as I say," Reno raved. "Get on your horses and go out there and hunt down Smoke Jensen."

"*Temp-orary* deputies, Sheriff," the reluctant one reminded Reno. "And, right about now, I'm figgerin' that short time has runned out."

"You're not leaving," an unbelieving Sheriff Reno gasped.

"Reckon to. I sure ain't gonna stand around and git shot at by a man who don't miss lest he wants to."

"You're cowards, that's what you are."

Eyes narrowed with sudden anger, the hard case faced off with the sheriff. "Now, I don't 'zactly take kindly to that, Sheriff. Y'all want to back up them bad-mouthin' words with gunplay?"

Ooops! Sheriff Reno suddenly realized he had gone too far. "Ah—ummm, no, not at all. I spoke out of hand, gentlemen. Go if you want. Besides, I need someone to take a message to our mutual friend."

"You mean Quint?"

Sheriff Reno winced. "Uh . . . tell him what's going on, and have him send some more men."

"Don't reckon he'll be able to do that. We've got other irons in the fire."

"Damnit, man, nothin's more important than stopping Smoke Jensen. Just carry the message, and I'll be satisfied."

"Sure 'nuff, Sheriff," the grinning hard case responded as he headed for his horse.

He made it three-quarters of the way there, before a bullet from Smoke Jensen took him in the meaty point of his left shoulder. Little pig squeals came from skinned-back lips, along with bloody froth from a punctured lung as he went to the ground.

"Oh. Sweet . . . Jesus!" Sheriff Reno shouted to the sky. And to those around him it sounded like a prayer.

Smile lines crinkled around Smoke Jensen's gray eyes, and the corners of his mouth twitched. After this, those townies would be afraid to drink anywhere in the mountains. Of course, it would be hard on anyone who happened on the stream before it washed clear.

He'd left the carcasses out to bloat and ripen in the sun for two days. They had become so potent, that Smoke needed to cover his face with a wet kerchief to cut down the stench. Even then, it near to gagged him when he rigged the rope that held them in the water. He made sure it was easy to see.

A final look around the clearing by the stream, and he got ready to leave. Carefully, Smoke wiped out any sign of his presence as he departed. Within a minute, only the muted echo of a soft guffaw remained of the last mountain man.

"What's that awful smell?" a townsman asked of Sheriff Reno.

"Smells like skunk. Mighty ripe skunk," the lawman replied.

"It's coming from the crick," one of Quint Stalker's outlaws advised.

"Skunks don't take baths," another contradicted.

"Hey, there's a rope hangin' down over the water," another shop clerk deputy declared. "Somethin's on the end of it."

Three of Stalker's men rode over to investigate. One dismounted and bent over the bank. He turned back quickly enough, his face a study in queasiness.

" 'Fore God, I hate that Smoke Jensen. He's put three rotten skunks in the water."

"Three skunks?" the sheriff echoed.

"Three *rotten* skunks. Flesh all but washed off of 'em, guts all strung out."

Gagging, retching sounds came from a trio of townies. Faces sickly green, they wobbled off into the meadow to void their stomachs. One finished before the others and turned back to the sheriff, who sat his horse with a puzzled expression.

"We—we drank from that crick not half a mile back. Filled our canteens, too."

A couple of Stalker's hard cases began to puke up their guts. Those affected wasted no time in remounting. They put heels to the flanks of their animals and fogged off down the trail in the direction of Socorro. Sheriff Jake Reno remained gape-mouthed for a moment, the slight wound on his hindside stinging from the sweat that ran down his back, then bellowed in rage. "Goddamn you, Smoke Jensen! I'm gonna kill you, you hear me? I'm gonna kill you dead, dead, dead, Smoke Jensen!"

* * *

While Smoke Jensen frazzled the nerves of the posse, five hard-faced men paid a visit to the Widow Tucker and her three small children. Their leader, Forrest Gore, had been barely able to stay in the saddle on the long ride out from Socorro. Jimmy Tucker saw them first, and the smooth, hard-callused soles of his bare feet raised clouds as he darted from the barn to the rear of the house.

"Some more bad guys comin', Maw," he shouted as he banged through the back door.

Martha Tucker looked up from the pie crust she had been rolling out, and wiped a stray lock of hair from her damp forehead with the back of one hand. The effort left a white streak. "You know what to do, Jimmy."

"Yes, ma'am," the boy replied.

He stepped to the kitchen door, put his little fingers between full lips, and blew out a shrill whistle. Rose and Tommy Tucker came scampering from where they had been playing under a huge alamogordo. A stray breeze rattled the heart-shaped, pale green leaves of the old cottonwood as they deserted it.

"Into the loft," their mother instructed.

Without a protest or question, the smaller children climbed the ladder to where all three youngsters slept. Rose covered her head with a goose-down quilt. Big-eyed, Tommy watched what went on downstairs.

"Hello the house," Forrest Gore called in a bored tone. "We mean you no harm. They's five of us. May we come up and take water for our horses?"

"You can go to the barn for that," Martha said from the protection of a shuttered window.

"Thank ye, kindly. Though it's scant hospitable of ye."

"Hospitality is somewhat short around here of late. If yer of a mind to be friendly, when you come back, I'll have my son set out a jug of spring water for your own thirst, and a pan of spoon bread."

"Now, that's a whole lot nicer. We're beholden."

When the five returned, Jimmy had placed the offered refreshments on the small front porch and withdrawn behind the door. The hard-faced men ate hungrily of the slightly sweet bread, and drank down the water to the last drop. When the last crumb of spoon bread had been disposed of, Forrest Gore glanced up to the window; he knew he was being watched.

"Mighty tasty. Say, be you Miz Tucker?"

"I am." Curt answers had become stock in trade for Martha Tucker.

"Then I have a message for you. You've forty-eight hours to pack up and get off the place."

"I thought I'd made it plain enough before. We are not leaving."

"Oh, but you got to now, Miz Tucker. Ya see, yer late husband, rest his soul, sold the ranch the day he was murdered by that back-shootin' scum, Smoke Jensen. No doubt he was killed for the money he carried."

"I don't believe you." Martha Tucker had opened the door and stepped across the threshold.

" 'Fraid you're gonna have to, Miz Tucker," Forrest Gore replied with a polite tip of his hat in acknowledgement.

"Not without proof. Lawrence didn't take the title deed with him to town. He couldn't have sold, and he didn't have any intention of doing so. Now please leave."

"Sorry you see it that way, Miz Tucker. But we got our orders. Forty-eight hours, not a second more. Pack what you can, and get out. The new owner will be movin' in direc'ly."

"We won't budge until I see the bill of sale and a transfer of title."

Gore's face stiffened woodenly and his eyes slitted. "That's mighty uppity lawyer talk, comin' from a woman. A woman's place is to do as she's told. Might be your health would remain a whole lot better, if you'd do just that."

"Meaning what?" Frost edged her words.

"Your husband's done already got hisself killed over this place. Could be it might happen to you next."

"Jimmy." Tension crackled in the single word, as Martha reached back through the open door.

Her son handed her a Greener shotgun, which she leveled on the center of Forrest Gore's chest. Deftly, she eared back both hammers. "Get the hell off our land. And tell whoever sent you that next time, I'll shoot first and ask questions after. My oldest son's a crack shot, too. So there'll be plenty of empty saddles."

Gore blanched white in mingled fear and rage. "You'll wish you'd done what's right . . . while you still had the chance." He mounted with his gaze fixed on the barrels of the scattergun. Nothing worser than a woman with a gun, he reminded himself in a sudden sweat. Astride his horse he cut his eyes to his men. "Let's ride."

Smoke Jensen knew a man could not drive a bear. Not even a big old brown, if one could be found in these desert mountains. But antelope and deer could be herded, if a fellow took his time about it. Through all the days of his travels in the Cibola Range, Smoke had often cut sign of deer. Now he set out seriously to locate a suitable gathering.

His search took only three hours in the early morning. He counted some thirty adult animals, a dozen yearlings, and a scattering of fawns. They would do well for what he had in mind. Slowly he closed on the herd, got them ambling the way he wanted.

It took all the skill Smoke Jensen possessed not to spook the deer and set them off in a wild stampede. A little nudge here, another there, then ease off for a while. So long as they only felt a bit uncomfortable grazing where they stood, they would remain tractable. By noon he had them out of the small gorge where he had found them.

"Easy goes," he reminded his mount and himself.

By putting more pressure on the herd leader, he got them lined out up a sloping game trail toward the crest. That, Smoke knew, overlooked the main trail. And that's where he wanted them any time now. The wary animals heard the approach of other humans before Smoke did. He nudged the creatures out into a line near the top of the ridge, then left the rest in the hands of Lady Luck.

With a whoop, Smoke set the deer into a panicked run. They boiled over the rim and thundered down the reverse slope. Alerted by the pound of many small hooves, the posse halted and looked upward. Dust boiled up through the piñon boughs, and a forest of antlers jinked one way, then the other.

Before they could recover their wits, the outlaws and

townsmen who made up Sheriff Reno's posse became
inundated by the frightened animals. The stricken beasts
bowled several men off their horses, set other mounts
into terrorized flight. Four townies wailed in helpless
alarm, and abandoned the search for Smoke Jensen right
there and now.

"Aaaawh . . . shiiiii-it!" Sheriff Reno howled in frustration, as a huge stag fixed his antlers on the lawman's
cavorting pony and made a spraddle-legged advance.

Seven

Sheriff Jake Reno's eyes bulged, unable to cut away from that magnificent twelve-point rack. Somehow, he knew Smoke Jensen had been behind the appearance of the deer. The grand stag pawed the ground again and snorted, hindquarters flexed for a lunge. Sensing the menace, Sheriff Reno's mount reared, forehooves lashing in defensive fury. It spilled the lawman out of the saddle.

He landed heavily on the sorest part of his posterior, and howled like a banshee. Alarmed, the stag lurched to one side and joined its harem in wild flight. An echo of mocking laughter bounded down from above. Sheriff Reno looked around to find that fully half of the remaining posse had deserted him. That left him with little choice.

He pulled in his horns.

Only eleven men remained with the posse when the corrupt lawman gave up his search for Smoke Jensen and turned back toward Socorro. Smoke watched them go. Faint signs of amusement lightened Smoke's face as he gazed down a long slope at the retreating backs. One leg cocked over the pommel of his saddle, he reached into a shirt pocket for a slender, rock-hard cigar, and struck a lucifer on the silver chasing of his saddlehorn.

A thin, blue-white stream of aromatic smoke wreathed the head of Smoke Jensen as he puffed contentedly. Walt Reardon had thoughtfully provided the cigars among the other supplies the hands had obtained when they planned to get Smoke out of the Socorro jail. These were of Italian origin and strong enough to stagger a bull buffalo.

Not exactly Smoke's brand of choice, it would have to do, he reckoned. And he would have to make tracks soon. South and west would best suit. That would put him closer to Arizona, when Ty Hardy and Walt Reardon brought word from Jeff York.

Smoke Jensen had met Jeff York a number of years ago. The young Arizona Ranger had been working undercover against the gang and outlaw stronghold of Rex Davidson, same as Smoke. When each learned the identity of the other, they joined their lots to bring down the walls of every building in Davidson's outlaw town of Dead River, and exterminate the vermin that lived there. As he rode down out of the northern reaches of the Cibola Range, Smoke Jensen recalled that day, long past . . .

Their pockets bulging with extra cartridges, York carrying a Henry and Smoke carrying the sawed-off express gun, they looked at each other.

"You ready to strike up the band, Ranger?"

"Damn right!" York said with a grin.

"Let's do it."

The men slipped the thongs off their six-guns and eased them out of leather a time or two, making certain the oiled interiors of the holsters were free.

York eased back the hammer on his Henry, and Smoke jacked back the hammers on the express gun.

They stepped inside the noisy and beer-stinking saloon. The piano player noticed them first. He stopped playing and singing and stared at them, his face chalk-white. Then he scrambled under the lip of the piano.

"Well, well!" an outlaw said, laughing. "Would you boys just take a look at Shirley. [Smoke had been using the outrageous moniker of Shirley DeBeers, a sissyfied portrait painter, for his penetration of the outlaw stronghold.] *He's done shaven offen his beard and taken to packin' iron. Boy, you bes' git shut of them guns, 'fore you hurt yourself."*

Gridley stood up from a table where he'd been drinking and playing poker—and losing. "Or I decide to take 'em off you and shove 'em up your butt, lead and all, pretty-boy. Matter of fact, I think I'll jist do that, right now."

"The name isn't pretty-boy, Gridley," Smoke informed him.

"Oh, yeah? Well, mayhaps you right. I'll jist call you shit! How about that?"

"Why don't you call him by his real name?" York said, a smile on his lips.

"And what might that be, punk?" Gridley sneered the question. "Alice?"

"First off," York said, "I'll tell you I'm an Arizona Ranger. Note the badges we're wearing? And his name, you blow-holes, is Smoke Jensen!"

The name dropped like a bomb. The outlaws in the room sat stunned, their eyes finally observing the gold badges on the chests of the men.

Smoke and York both knew one thing for an ironclad fact: The men in the room might all be scoundrels and thieves and murderers, and some might be bullies and cowards, but when it came down to it, they were going to fight.

"Then draw, you son of a bitch!" Gridley hollered, his hands dropping to his guns.

Smoke pulled the trigger on the express gun. From a distance of no more than twenty feet, the buckshot almost tore the outlaw in two.

York leveled the Henry and dusted an outlaw from side to side. Dropping to one knee, he levered the empty out and a fresh round in, and shot a fat punk in the belly.

Shifting the sawed-off shotgun, Smoke blew the head off another outlaw. The force of the buckshot lifted the headless outlaw out of one boot and flung him to the sawdust-covered floor.

York and his Henry had put half a dozen outlaws on the floor, dead, dying, or badly hurt.

The huge saloon was filled with gunsmoke, the crying and moaning of the wounded, and the stink of relaxed bladders from the dead. Dark gray smoke from the black powder cartridges stung the eyes and obscured the vision of all in the room . . .

Oh, that had been a high old time all right, Smoke reflected. But it hadn't ended there. Smoke had gone on back East to reclaim his beloved wife, Sally, who was busy being delivered of twins in the home of her parents in Keene, New Hampshire. Jeff York and Louis Longmont had accompanied him. And a good thing, too. Rex Davidson and his demented followers had carried the fight to Smoke. And it finally ended in the streets of Keene, with Rex Davidson's guts spilled on the ground.

The twins, Louis Arthur and Denise Nichole, were near to full grown now. They lived and studied in Europe. But that was another story, Smoke reminded himself as he gazed upon a smoky smudge on the horizon, far out on a wide mountain vale, vast enough to be called a plain.

Smoke Jensen rode into Horse Springs quietly. He attracted little attention from the locals, mostly simple farmers of Mexican origin. *Ollas de los Caballos,* the place had been called before the white man came. Near the center of town was a rock basin, fed by cold, crystal-clear, deep mountain springs. This natural formation provided drinking water for everyone in town. Fortunately for the farmers, a wide, shallow stream also meandered through the valley and allowed for irrigation of crops of corn, beans, squash, chili peppers, and other staples.

Smoke splashed through it at a rail-guarded ford and saw at once that it also accommodated as a place of entertainment. Small, brown-skinned boys, naked as the day they had been born, frolicked in the water, the sun striking highlights off their wet skin. Clearly, they lacked any knowledge of the body taboo that afflicted most whites Smoke knew. For, when they took notice of the stranger among them, they broke off their play to stand facing him, giggle like a flock of magpies, and make shy, though friendly waves of their hands.

Returning their greetings, Smoke rode on to the center of town. On the Plaza de Armas, he located what passed for a hotel in Horse Springs. *POSADA DEL NORTE*—Inn of the North—had been hand-lettered in red, now faded pink, and outlined in white and green over the arch in an adobe block wall that guarded the building front.

He dismounted and walked his horse through the tall, double-hung, plank gates into a tree-shaded courtyard. A barefoot little lad, who most likely would have preferred to be out at the creek with his friends, took the reins and led Smoke's big-chested roan toward a stable. Smoke entered a high-ceilinged remarkably cool hallway. To his right, a sign, likewise in Spanish, with black letters on white tile, advised; *OFICINA*.

Smoke stepped through into the office and had to work mightily to conceal his reaction. Behind a small counter he saw one of the most strikingly beautiful young women he had ever encountered. Her skin, which showed in a generous, square-cut yolk, a graceful stalk of neck and intriguing, heart-shaped face, was flawless. A light cast of olive added a healthy glow to the faintest of *cafe au lait* complexions. Her dress had puffy sleeves, with lace at the edges, and around the open bodice, also in tiers over her ample bosom, and in ruffled falls down to a narrow waist. There, what could be seen of the skirt flared in horizontal gathers that reminded Smoke of a cascade.

Her youthful lips had been touched with a light application of ruby rouge, and were full and promised mysteries unknown to other women. For a moment, raw desire flamed in the last mountain man. Then, reason—

and his unwavering dedication to his lovely and beloved Sally—prevailed. Those sweet lips twitched in a teasing smile as the vision behind the registration desk acknowledged his admiring stare.

"Yes, *Señor?* Do you desire a room for the night?"

Her voice, Smoke Jensen thought, sounded like little tinkling bells in a field of daisies. "Uh . . . ummm, yes. For a week, at least."

"We are happy to be able to accommodate you, *Señor.* If you will please to sign the book?" When Smoke had done so, she continued her familiar routine of hospitality. "The rooms down here are much cooler, but the second floor offers privacy."

Accustomed to the refreshingly cool summer days in the High Lonesome, Smoke Jensen opted for a first-floor room. The beautiful desk clerk nodded approvingly and selected a key. She turned back to Smoke and extended a hand comprised of a small, childlike palm and slender, graceful fingers.

"When Felipe returns with your saddlebags, he will show you to your room."

"I think I can manage on my own."

Her smile could charm the birds from the trees. "It is a courtesy of the Posada del Norte. We wish that our guests feel they are our special friends."

"I'm sure they do. I know that I—ah—ummm—do." Silently, Smoke cursed himself for sounding like an adolescent boy in the presence of his first real woman. He was spared further awkwardness by the return of the little boy, Felipe.

"Come with me, *Señor,*" the youngster said with a dignity beyond his nine or ten years.

After Felipe had unlocked the door to No. 12 with a flourish and ushered him inside, Smoke pressed a silver dime into the boy's warm, moist palm. Although fond of children, Smoke Jensen preferred to watch them from a distance; he recalled his first impression of this little lad and curiosity prompted him to speak.

"Do you work here every day?"

"Oh, *sí, Señor,* after school is over at *media dia.* It is my father's *posada.*"

"Wouldn't you rather be out swimming with your friends at the creek?"

An impish grin lighted Felipe's face. "After my early chores, I get to go for a while. Until the people come for rooms, and my father rings the bell to call me back. Sometimes . . . when I'm supposed to be cleaning the stable, I slip away and also go on adventures."

Smoke had to smile. "You remind me of my sons when they were your age."

Felipe blinked at him. "Did you run a *posada?* And were your sons Mexican?"

A chuckle rumbled in Smoke's chest. "No to both questions. But they were every bit as ornery as you. Now, get along with you."

After Smoke had settled in, he strolled out to the central courtyard. The corridor that served the second floor overhung the edges of the patio, to form alcoves where tables were being set for the evening meal. More pretty Mexican girls draped snowy linen cloths at just the proper angle, while others put in place napkins, eating utensils, and terracotta cups and goblets. Next came clay pitchers that beaded on the outside from the chill spring water they held, and bowls of fiery Southwestern salsa picante. Experience in Arizona, Texas, and Mexico had taught Smoke that prudent use of the condiment added a pleasant flavor to a man's food.

Beyond the alfresco dining arrangements, a fountain splashed musically in the center of the courtyard. Desert greenery had been arranged in profusion, in rock gardens that broke up the open space and gave an illusion of privacy. On the fourth side of the patio, opposite his room, Smoke found a small cantina. Tiny round tables extended onto the flagstone flooring outside its door. Smoke entered and ordered a beer.

It came in a large, cool, dark brown bottle. Smoke flipped the hinged metal contraption that held a ceramic stopper in place, and a loud *pop* sounded. Hops-scented blue smoke rose from the interior. Smoke took his first swallow straight from the bottle, then poured the remainder into a schooner offered by the *cantinero.*

"You are new in town," the tavern keeper observed.

"Yep. Just rode in today."

"If you have been on the trail a while, *Señor,* perhaps you are hungry for word of what is happening in the world. I will bring you a newspaper."

"Thank you," Smoke responded, surprised and pleased by this shower of conviviality.

It turned out to be a week-old copy of the Albuquerque *Territorial Sentinel.* Most of the front page articles had to do with the financial panic back East, and events in and around the largest city in the territory. Smoke read on. The second page provided at least part of the answer to his dilemma, although he did not realize it at the time.

SURVEYORS
TO LAY OUT
WESTWARD ROUTE

Bold black letters spelled out the caption of the story. Smoke Jensen scanned it with mild interest. It revealed that survey crews would soon arrive to begin laying out the right of way for a new spur of the Southern Pacific Railroad. It would pass through Socorro and head westward to connect with Springerville, Arizona, Winslow, and the copper smelters being built south and west of Show Low.

Interesting, Smoke considered. If one had stock in the railroad, or the right copper works. But it didn't seem nearly as relevant as the small article on the third page, which featured an artist's sketch of Smoke's own likeness, and a story about the supposed murder of Mr. Lawrence Tucker.

From it, he gleaned that Tucker had been a long and respected resident of the Socorro area, with a large ranch on the eastern slopes of the Cibola foothills. He was survived by a wife, Martha, and three children, boys aged thirteen and seven and a girl nine. Tucker had been outspoken about the prospects of dry land farming, and used the techniques of the Mexican and Indian farmers, long time residents of the area. He also advocated the protection of those fields by the use of barbed wire.

Not a very popular position for a rancher to take,

Smoke mused. It had been enough to get more than half a hundred men killed over the past decade. Maybe Mr. Tucker had enemies no one knew of? Maybe someone, like Sheriff Reno, knew only too damn well who those enemies might be? Smoke put his speculations aside, along with the paper, and finished his beer. Leaving money on the mahogany for the barkeep, he left to stroll the streets and get a feel for the town.

It might be well to have a hidey-hole. The inn seemed a good one. Although, Smoke allowed, with his face in the newspapers, and no doubt on wanted posters by now, it would be better to lay low in Arizona, until he could piece together more information. He had done well to scatter that posse. And it might be necessary to go back and scatter another, if he were to have that time of peace.

Early on the afternoon of the third day in Horse Springs, Smoke began to feel uneasy. A week had gone by since they had ridden out of Socorro. By now he should have heard from Walt Reardon and Ty Hardy. He would give them a couple of more days and then head west. With that settled, he turned in through the open doorway of a squat, square building with a white-painted, stuccoed exterior.

The odor of stale beer and whiskey fumes tingled his nose. No matter where in the world, or what it was called, Smoke mused, a saloon was a saloon. A chubby, musta-chioed Mexican stood behind the bar, a once-white apron tight around his appreciable girth. Two white-haired, re-tired caballeros sat at a table, drinking tequila and playing dominoes. Smoke Jensen relaxed in this congenial atmosphere and eased up to the bar.

"Do you have any rye?" he asked.

"Bourbon or tequila."

"Beer then."

A large, foam-capped schooner appeared before him a few seconds later. The glass felt pleasantly cool to the touch. Smoke had grown to understand the inestimable value of the icy deep rock springs that had named the town. Smoke drank deeply of the cold beer, and a rumble from his stomach reminded him that he hadn't eaten since early that morning. He'd finish this and find a place to have a meal.

"Jeremy, you don't have the sense God gave a goose." The loud voice drew Smoke's attention to the entrance.

"There you go again, Zack, bad-mouthin' me. I tell you, that feller made it sound so downright good, I jist had to trade horses with him."

"Only it done turned out that he had *two* gray horses, the other one all swaybacked and spavined. Which he hung around your dumb neck."

"Awh, Zack, tain't fair you go bully-raggin' me about that all the time. Hell, cousin, it happened a month ago! That's old news."

"It's an old bunko game, too," Zack replied dryly.

Smoke Jensen marked them to be local range riders. But with a few differences, that could make them dangerous. For instance, the way they wore their six-guns, slung low on their legs, holsters tied down with a leather thong. The safety loops had been slipped free of the hammers. The weapons were clean and lightly oiled, all the cartridges in their loops shiny bright. No doubt, they fancied themselves good with their guns, Smoke surmised. They had silver conchos around the sweat bands of their hats, sewn on their vests, and down the outside seam of their left trouser legs.

A regretful sigh broke from Smoke's lips. Almost a uniform in the Southwest for young, tough-guy punks. Smoke faced the bar, head lowered, and tried not to draw their attention. The one called Zack looked hard at the big-shouldered man at the bar and turned away. Smoke finished his beer, the taste nowhere near as pleasant as it had been, and pushed off from the bar.

Outside, he headed toward an eatery he had seen earlier. He had noticed a sign, hand-lettered on a chalkboard, that advertised HOY CARNITAS. His limited Spanish told him that meant they were serving carnitas today. He had become acquainted with the savory dish while in Mexico to help two of his old gunfighter friends, Miguel Martine and Esteban Carbone. Thought of the succulent cubes of pork shoulder, deep fried over an open, smokey fire, brightened Smoke's outlook considerably.

He had finished off a huge platter of the "little meats," with plenty of tortillas and condiments, and another beer, when he looked up from wiping the grease from his face and saw the same pair of salty young studs again. They stood in the middle of the street, hands on the butts of their six-guns, eyes fixed on the doorway of the bean emporium.

At first, Smoke didn't know if they had gotten so drunk that they couldn't figure how to get in the eatery. But when he rose from his table, paid the tab, and stepped out under the palm frond *palapa* that shaded the front, he soon learned that not to be the case.

"B'god, yer right, Zack. It's him, all right."

"Yeah, Smoke Jensen," Zack sighed out. "An' we've got us a tidy little re-ward comin', Jeremy."

Eight

Seems these boys had read the same newspaper he had seen, Smoke surmised. The reward was something new. Too bad about that. He spoke to them through a sigh.

"Don't believe everything you read, fellers."

"We believe this right enough. You're Smoke Jensen, and they's a thousand dollars on yer head."

"Not by the law. So there's no guarantee you'd *get* the reward, if you lived to collect it."

"What you mean by that?"

Smoke sighed again. "If I *am* Smoke Jensen, there's not the likes of you two who can take me. Not in a face-on fight."

"I ain't no back-shooter, an' I think we can," Zack blurted.

Smoke let Zack and Jeremy get their hands on their irons, before he hauled his .44 clear of leather. Jeremy's eyes widened; it caused him to falter, and he didn't have his weapon leveled when he pulled the trigger.

A spout of muddy street fountained up a yard in front of Jeremy's boot toe. Although a hard, violent man when he need be, Smoke Jensen took pity on the young gunny. He shot him in the hip. Jeremy went down with a yowl, the streamlined Merwin and Hulbert flew from his hand, and he clutched his wound with desperation. Smoke shifted his attention to Zack.

Zack's jaw sagged in disbelief. He hadn't even seen Jensen draw, and already the gunfighter had let 'er bang. Shot Jeremy, too, and he was rattlesnake fast. His consternation held Zack for a fraction of a second, during which he saw eternity beckoning to him from the black muzzle of Smoke Jensen's Colt.

"Nooooo!" he wailed and tried feverishly to trigger a round.

For this one, Smoke Jensen had no mercy. He had taken note earlier of the notches carved in the walnut grip of Zack's six-gun. That told a lot about Zack. No real gunhawk notched his grips to keep score. Killing men was not a game. They didn't give prizes for the one with the most chips whittled out. The only thing that came from winning was the chance to live a little longer. Smoke Jensen knew that well. He'd been taught by an expert. So, he let fly with a .44 slug that punched a new belly button in Zack's vulnerable flesh.

Shock, and the impact, knocked Zack off his boots. He hit hard on his butt in the middle of the street. He had somehow managed to hold onto his Smith American, and let roar a .44 round that cracked past the left shoulder of Smoke Jensen. New pain exploded in the right side of Zack's shoulder, as Smoke answered in kind with his Peacemaker.

"Damn you to hell, Smoke Jensen." Bitter pain tears welled up in Zack's eyes and Smoke Jensen seemed to waver before him like a cattail in a stiff breeze. Supported on one elbow, he tried again to raise his weapon into position. His hand would not obey. It drooped at the wrist, the barrel of the Smith and Wesson canted toward the ground.

"Y-you done killt me, Jensen," he gasped past the agony that broiled his body.

"It was your choice, Zack."

"I—I know." Zack sucked in a deep breath and new energy surged through him.

His gun hand responded this time, and he willed his finger to squeeze the trigger. The loud bang that followed came before his hammer had fallen. Zack couldn't figure that one out. He understood better an instant later, when incredible anguish blossomed in his chest and a huge, black cavern opened up to engulf him.

"You di'n't have to kill him," Jeremy sobbed from his place on the ground.

"The way I see it, he pushed, I pushed back." Smoke made a tight-lipped answer.

Despite his misery, Jeremy had managed to work free his sheath knife. He held it now by the blade. A quick flick of his right arm as Smoke Jensen turned in his direction, and the wicked blade sped on its way. It caught Smoke low. The tip slid through the thick leather of his cartridge belt and penetrated a stinging inch into meat. Smoke's .44 blasted reflexively.

From less than three feet away, hot lead punched a thumb-sized hole between Jeremy's eyebrows, mushroomed, and blew off the back of his head. Smoke eased up, let his shoulders sag. A sudden voice from behind him charged Smoke with new energy.

"*¡Tien cuidado, Señor!* They have a frien'." Black pencil line of mustache writhing on his brown upper lip, the owner and cook of the cafe where Smoke had eaten, stood in the doorway. He pointed a trembling finger toward the balcony of the saloon across the street. Smoke followed the gesture and saw a man kneeling behind the big wooden sign, a rifle to his shoulder.

Fool, Smoke thought. If he thinks that sign will stop a bullet, he's in for a surprise. The Winchester cracked once, and cut the hat from Smoke's head as he returned the favor. Two fast shots from the pistol in the hand of Smoke Jensen put a small figure-eight hole in the sign and the chest of the sniper. With a clatter, the hidden assassin sprawled backward on the floor planks of the balcony.

In the silence that followed, Smoke Jensen surveyed the carnage he had created. Damnit, he didn't need to be caught knee-deep in corpses. This spelled more complications than he wanted to think about. He reloaded swiftly.

"No question of it, I'm in more trouble than before," he muttered to himself. To the Mexican cook, he added, "The law will be coming soon. Tell them the man who did this is long gone."

The smiling man shrugged. "There is very little law in this town, *Señor.* Only the *alcalde*—the mayor—who is also the *jefe*—the marshal, an' also the *juez . . . el magistrado, ¿comprende?"*

"I reckon I do. You're saying you have a one-man city administration?"

"Seguro, sí." In his excitement over the confrontation in the street, the man had forgotten most of his English.

"Where do I find this feller?"

A broad, warm smile bloomed on the man's face. He

tapped his chest with a brown, chili-stained finger. "It is I, *Señor.*"

That made matters considerably less complicated for Smoke Jensen. Smoke recounted where he had first seen the would-be hard cases, and gave his opinion of what had sparked the attempt on his life. The mayor-police-chief-judge, his name turned out to be Raphael Figuroa, didn't even ask if they had the right man. He looked at the human garbage in the street and shrugged.

"They are no loss. This is not the first time they have provoked trouble. Usually with tragic consequences for the other party. This is the first time they have been on the receiving end. You are free to go, or stay as long as you wish, *Señor.*"

"I'm fixin' to pull out tomorrow morning," Smoke informed him. He did not give a destination.

Forty-six miles into Arizona, Smoke Jensen discovered why he had not been joined by his companions. Walt and Ty waited for him in Show Low, along with Jeff York. Smoke and the Arizona Ranger had a rousing, back-pounding reunion, and the four men retired to the saloon made famous by the poker game that had given the new name to what had once been Copper Gulch.

A drifter had played cards all through one night with the local gambler and owner of the town. His luck had run well and, on the turn of a card in a game of Low Ball, he had won title to Copper Gulch, which he promptly renamed Show Low in honor of his accomplishment. Or so the story goes.

"What's this about you being wanted for killing a man,

Smoke?" Jeff inquired, his pale bluish gray eyes alight with interest. "Don't sound like the Smoke Jensen I know."

"It's a long story, Jeff. Just yesterday, I found out there's a price on my head. A big one." Smoke went on to explain what he faced. He concluded with, "So with a reward out, I had to figure that sheriff would be out hunting me again, and decided Arizona would be a safer place to stay while I worked it all out."

Jeff York sat in silence a moment before responding to all Smoke had told him. "I'll cover for you here in Arizona, of course. And I'd like to help. As much as I can."

"How's that? The governor got his hand cinched up to your belt?"

"Not so's it chafes. I was up this way to check out something when Walt and Ty came along. So far it's only rumors. Still an' all, the ones puttin' them around are considered reliable men. 'Pears there's some scallywags that have their eyes on a land grab on the White Mountain Apache reservation."

"Do tell," Smoke prompted.

"The word is that some high-rollers are fixin' to bring a number of the big tickets in Washington out to be wined and dined—and bribed—to get them to cut a big chunk out of the res for the benefit of those same local money men."

"Why in the world would anyone want to move in next door to the Apaches?"

Jeff gave Smoke a bleak smile. "Perhaps it's because Chief Cuchillo Negro and some of his braves have found gold on that land. And, of course, it might be that these good ol' boys has gotten a serious dose of religion, and only want to make better the lot of their less fortunate red brothers."

"I'll believe that when pigs fly," Smoke grunted.

Smoke Jensen had fought and killed any number of Indians over the years, and he was not considered one to stomp lace-edged hankies into the mud over the wretched plight of the Noble Red Men. Yet, he respected them as brave men and fierce fighters. The Apaches most of all. He acknowledged the Indians' right to a place in this world. After all, it was Indian land before the white man came to take it away from them. Indians and the white men had different ways, neither one better than the other, to Smoke's way of seeing things. Truth to tell, he sometimes thought the Indian way came out a bit on top. They sure had more respect for nature and the land. And they used to live in harmony with all its creatures.

It wasn't the coming of the white man that spoiled all that, Smoke acknowledged. It was too *many* of them coming, too fast and too soon. Set in their own ways, and pig-head stubborn against change, they never considered the differences beyond the Big Muddy. Civilization ended at the Mississippi, and white folks stupidly refused to admit that.

Sharing that all too human trait, most of the Indians would not make any effort to accommodate to white ways. They preferred to fight a losing battle to preserve their way of life. Those tribes lost, too. Now only the Apaches and a passel of Sioux and Cheyenne remained any sort of threat to the tens of thousands of white men overwhelming the vast frontier. Smoke Jensen shook his head, saddened by his sour reflections. "There's six more

Rangers headed this way. I'm supposed to direct it all, and also get a man inside this consortium," Jeff went on.

"You wouldn't be electin' me to that position, would you, Jeff?"

"No," Jeff York shrugged. As tall as Smoke and nearly as broad, that gesture moved a lot of hard-muscled flesh. His big hands spread on the table, and thick fingers reached for a fish-eye whiskey glass. "I reckoned to do that myself."

"I recall the last time I knew you went under cover."

York smiled at Smoke's remark. "We sure shot hell out of Rex Davidson's Dead River, didn't we."

"And you damned near got yourself killed, before you could get to the doin'," Smoke reminded him.

"Water under the bridge. We're still here, both of us. Now, maybe I had oughtta make myself useful," York changed the subject. "First off, I'll fill you in on who is who around Socorro."

"You Rangers keep an eye on folks from another territory?" Smoke asked.

"Good practice to know the influential folks. Also the bad hombres and riffraff—all part of the job."

"Then tell me about them," Smoke prompted.

"First off, there's the Culverts and the Mendozas. About the richest ranchers around. Old Myron Culvert's son is mayor." He went on to list the power structure of Socorro, New Mexico. Then Jeff's voice changed, took on a tightness. "Then there's some who are sort of on the edge. There's an Englishman, folks say he's a lord or something. They call him Sir Geoffrey Benton-Howell. He owns a couple of large ranches, two saloons, a women's millinery store, and a number of houses he rents out to the Mexican workers. He's partnered up with Miguel Selleres. Selleres looks like one of those bull-fighter fellers. Neat and trim, a handsome dog. But we've heard word he's got a mean streak."

"What about hard cases?"

"Comin' to that, Smoke. Big frog in the pond over that way is Quint Stalker. Supposed to be a gunfighter from Nevada."

"I've heard of him. He crossed my path one time. I should have killed him then."

"He's for sure bad news, then?"

"Bet on it, Jeff."

"All right. He's got a gang of maybe thirty fast guns. There's talk he takes his pay from Benton-Howell. If that's so, we could be in heavy trouble. The lord and Selleres have been buying up parcels of land in New Mexico and Arizona for some time now. Most of them are out in the middle of nowhere. With the money, land, and the guns to back them up, they could become a power to reckon with. Only, why pick such remote spots?"

Smoke recalled the article he had read about surveyors for the Southern Pacific. "Would those parcels be any-where near the proposed right of way of the new South-ern Pacific spur line?"

It was as though a lamp had been lit behind the eyes of Jeff York. "They sure would."

"Water and coaling stops make great places for towns to be built," Smoke pointed out. "The man or men who own one—or in this case, *all* of those—will get mighty rich."

"Where did you come up with that?"

"I read about it in the Albuquerque newspaper,"

Smoke told him. "I wonder now, if the railroad intends to cross land owned by the late Mr. Tucker?"

"I wouldn't doubt it any. I think you waiting out more developments here might be a mistake, Smoke."

"I'm way ahead of you. I reckon we should all head back to Socorro and dig into the affairs of Sir Geoffrey Benton-Howell."

"Maw, there's someone movin' around out there," Jimmy Tucker informed his mother from the small, circular window in the loft.

"Can you make out who?" Martha Tucker asked her son, as she climbed from the bed in the room off the central part of the house.

"No, ma'am." Jimmy had a cold chill down his spine, though, that told him the mysterious figures were up to no good. He had an itch, too, that made him want to snug the butt-plate of his little Stevens .30-30 up against his right shoulder.

Martha crossed the living-dining area of her home in darkness, every inch familiar to her. She took up the Greener and slung a leather bag of shot shells over one shoulder. She reached a window just as a yellow-orange brightness flared in the barnyard. Jimmy also saw it, and the mop of snowy hair fairly rose straight up on his head.

He propelled himself off the pallet that served as a bed and flew down the ladder, his bare feet flashing below the hem of his nightshirt. He, too, went unerringly to the gunrack on the near wall. Martha saw the movement and gasped. She almost blurted out a refusal, then drew her lips into a thin line.

"You be careful, son," she urged him.

"Yes, ma'am."

Jimmy took his rifle and a spare box of shells and went back to the loft. The window that overlooked the barnyard had been installed on a pivot, with latches to both sides. Jimmy undid them and turned the sash sideways. Slowly he eased the barrel of his Stevens out into the night. Then he remembered his father's training. He stuck a small finger in the loading gate and felt the base of a cartridge. Satisfied, he slowly worked the action, to keep as quiet as he could.

Three more torches burned now, and so far none of the nightriders had noticed anything happening in the house. At a muffled grunt of command, the torchbearers started toward the barn. By the light of the firebrands, Martha and Jimmy saw that they wore hoods that covered their entire heads. When they reached a point fifty feet from the barn, the shotgun boomed, with the bright crack of the Stevens right behind.

One arsonist yowled and pitched off his mount, one arm and shoulder peppered with No. 2 goose shot. Another grunted softly, swayed in his saddle a moment, then sank forward to lay along the neck of his horse. For some unexplainable reason, Jimmy Tucker found his breath awfully short and tears filled his eyes. He had to swallow hard to drive down the sour bile that rose in his throat.

He took one deep gulp of breath and levered another round into the .30-30. Good thing he did, because a second later two of the hooded thugs turned toward the house and fired at the ground-floor windows. Jimmy shot one of them through the shoulder, and heard a thin wail answer his defense. From downstairs, he heard his Maw's shotgun belch in anger.

"I'm hit! Oh, God, I'm hit, Smoke," one of the outlaws sobbed.

The use of that name had been a clever contribution by Quint Stalker. He figured it would direct any suspicion away from him, and particularly his bosses. Unseen by the hard cases in the yard, it had the intended effect, as Martha Tucker's face hardened and she swiftly reloaded the shotgun.

"Fire that barn, goddamnit! You boys, go after the corral. Turn out that livestock."

"We're bein' shot at," another thug complained.

"I'll take care of that," the leader responded.

He turned toward the house in time to catch the side edge of a column of shot in his left biceps and shoulder. Grunting, he fired his six-gun dry and wheeled away. Another man took his place and got blown out of the saddle for his determination.

Flames began to flicker in the barn.

Jimmy brushed more tears from his big, blue eyes and sighted in on another man with a torch. At the last moment, the outlaw darted forward and to his left, the .30-30 round shattered his hand. It sent the blazing torch flying from his grasp to land harmlessly on the ground. A dozen young heifers bellowed in terror from the corral, then made thunder with their hooves as others of the nightriders swung open the gate and ran them off.

"We've done enough for now. Let's pull out," came the command.

While they raced off into the darkness, mother and son discharged several rounds each to give wings to their flight. Several ranch hands, who had been held impotent at gunpoint, rushed out and began hurling buckets of water on the blazing barn. But Martha knew it would do no good. A fine, beautiful building, destroyed by that bastard Smoke Jensen.

Then a smile broke through her outrage. At least she'd gotten some pellets in him. He'd be bandaged up after this, and not so cocky anymore. Next time she saw him, she'd kill Smoke Jensen, she swore.

Nine

A hot, dry wind blew steadily across the mesa even at this early hour. A low pole frame sat well back from the rim, protected from the view of unwelcome eyes. It consisted of a lattice framework covered with the thick, green leaves of the agave, what the whites called the century plant. Already five of the lesser chiefs of the White Mountain Apaches had gathered. They waited in patient silence for the arrival of their principal chief, Cuchillo Negro—Black Knife.

Long before their composure had been well tested, ten of the best warriors among the Tinde approached soundlessly from as many directions. At last, when the sun rode high overhead, Cuchillo Negro appeared. With him was Ho-tan, his most trusted advisor. He greeted the assembled council in the harsh gutturals of their language.

"Why do the white men come into our land?" Broken Horn asked of the chief.

Cuchillo Negro considered the question in silence a long time before he made answer. "It is true that many *Pend-dik-olyeh* come to our mountains. Words spoken on the winds say that they covet what little they left to us."

"That could be true," Ho-tan mused aloud. "It is the best of any of our agencies."

"The whites, who are always greedy, must think it is too good for us," Spirit Walker observed with tart humor. "They seek to send us back to San Carlos."

Angry mutters rose over that. Black Knife silenced them with a stern look. The breeze fluttered the long, obsidian wings of his hair, held in place by a calico headband. He rose to his moccasins from where he squatted on a blanket.

"You are right to be angry, my brothers. But we must be cautious, while we go about finding out what is behind this."

"No," Bright Lance, one of the senior warriors growled. "I say we drive them off the agency. I say we follow those who survive and take the warpath to all whites."

"Like Geronimo?" Cuchillo Negro asked sarcastically.

They all knew the fate of the famed and feared warrior chief. He was said to be rotting in a stinking, white man's prison in a far-off land called Florida. Obsidian eyes cut from one face to another. Broken Horn rose to speak.

"I am of a mind with Bright Lance. For us to meekly let the whites push us out, to be returned to San Carlos, is to die. Sickness will waste away our women and children, and we will catch the mosquito fever and die slaving in bean fields. I hate bean fields."

A loud murmur of agreement ran through the assembled council. Cuchillo Negro made a quick evaluation of the change in heart. "No. We cannot do that. I, too, hate bean fields, my old friend," he admitted with warm humor in his voice. "We must not take the fight to the whites off the reservation. That will bring the pony soldiers as certainly as Father Sun follows the night."

Clever man that he had to be to have achieved his paramount position, Cuchillo Negro shifted gears and spoke in laudatory tones of conciliation. "Yet, our good brother, Bright Lance, has some wisdom in what he says. If we hope to keep in our beloved mountains, we must not anger the soldiers. We must not leave the agency to fight." A beaming smile lighted the face of Cuchillo Negro, and his eyes sparkled with mischief. "But Bright Lance speaks well when he says we must punish those who trespass on our land. For now, we must satisfy ourselves with that."

To his surprise and satisfaction, he had no trouble achieving a consensus. The war societies of the White Mountain Apaches would soon ride to take retribution on the interlopers.

Smoke Jensen raised a hand to signal a halt. Ahead, a huge dust cloud rose beyond a swell in the red-brown desert country. Smoke and Jeff studied it a moment.

"Think it could be a posse?" Jeff asked.

"Too much dust for men on horseback. I'd say it's a trail drive."

Jeff cut his eyes to his friend. "Here? Headed this way?"

Smoke broke a grin. "I didn't say it made sense. What say we slip over and get a look?"

Dismounted, Smoke Jensen and Jeff York advanced, crouched low to avoid showing on the skyline. Both men bellied down near the crest of the rise and removed their hats. Jeff put a brass-tubed spyglass to one eye, and Smoke studied the distance with a pair of field glasses.

In the lead were three men, coiled lariats held loosely in their right hands. Behind, blurred by the reddish haze, they made out the horns of some fifty head of cattle. Smoke and Jeff exchanged a glance.

"Looks like you were right," York acknowledged. "Only I can't figure why they're headed toward Arizona."

"Better crossing places into Mexico, I'd reckon." Smoke Jensen took another look at the slow-moving cattle. "The border is less settled in Arizona than New Mexico or Texas. Even I know that. If someone had cattle that didn't belong to him, and wanted to dispose of them at a profit, that would be the way to go about it."

Ranger York didn't buy it entirely. "You think these cattle have been rustled?"

Smoke turned his attention to the men bearing down on them. "From the looks of those boys out there, they aren't regular hands. Not by the way they're dressed, or the way they wear their guns."

Jeff York's eyebrows rose. "If we're fixin' to do anything, we'd better know how many they have on flank and drag first."

"My thinkin' exactly," Smoke agreed. "We'll split up for a while. You take Reardon, I'll take Hardy. Let's ride around this gather and see what we can."

They joined up half an hour later, behind the herd. Jeff York wore a scowl. "Those beeves are wearin' the Tucker brand. I recognized it right off."

"The same Tucker I'm supposed to have killed?"

"Right, Smoke. Only those drovers aren't the sort Lawrence Tucker would have hired. Funny thing is, none of their horses are wearing the Tucker brand."

"What say we swing in for a little talk?" Smoke's suggestion met with ready agreement.

One man rode around the herd, which had been turned in on itself for the night. Five more squatted around a hat-sized fire topped by a coffeepot. A larger blaze had been started to cook on. All six looked up as strangers rode toward the camp.

"Hello, the fire," Smoke hailed. "I thought I smelled coffee."

"Yep," came an answer from a thick-set man with small, piggish eyes. "But we didn't brew up any extra."

Smoke pulled a face. "Now, that's mighty inhospitable in these parts, Mister. Mind if we ride up a piece?"

The gunhawk's eyes shot anger at Smoke Jensen, which didn't match his words. "It's a free country."

Once in by the fire, Smoke and his companions dismounted. They made no move to tie the horses off to the picket line, dropping the reins to the ground. Smoke nodded to the cattle.

"You're a far piece from the Tucker spread," he observed.

The proddy one's eyes narrowed. "Who says we ride for that brand? Truth is, we bought these steers off him three days ago."

"That would be kind of hard, wouldn't it? Considering that he's been dead better than a week."

Smoke's words were all it took. Without knowing who they might be facing off against, the edgy rustler dropped his hand to the gun at his side. At once, the other four did the same. Smoke, Jeff, and Walt beat them all out. For a moment, they had a standoff.

Then the herd guard, a long, lean character with frizzy yellow hair, pounded toward them, his hand clawing at the butt of a Colt on his left hip. Six against four apparently seemed mighty good odds to the argumentative one. He canted the muzzle of his six-gun downward slightly. Smoke Jensen shot him through the chest, before his hammer could fall. Startled into panic, the cattle exploded in every direction. Jeff York put a bullet through the side of another rustler.

He went down with a soft grunt, but kept hold of his revolver, which he aimed at Jeff York a moment before Walt Reardon plunked a round into the gunhawk's forehead and ended his career. Ty Hardy had joined the dance. Hot lead from his .45 Colt snatched the hat off the head of another hard case, who had made a dash to his horse. Dazed by the close brush with a bullet, the rustler fell out of his saddle and rolled into some brush.

Half a dozen head of wall-eyed steers thundered over his body and trampled him into an unrecognizable mess. Smoke Jensen had not been standing still, both literally and figuratively. He had jumped to one side and went to a knee for his second round, which trashed the kneecap of another cow thief. Squalling, the man flopped to the ground, clawed at his waistband for a second six-gun, and hauled it clear.

Jeff York was busy with another gunny, and did not see the swing of the barrel to his midsection. Smoke Jensen did, and dumped the tough shooter into hell with a fast bullet that sliced through the left collarbone, lung, and the edge of his heart. A slug cracked past Smoke's ear, and he moved again.

Snatching at the horn of one steer, Smoke used the animal as cover and transportation. He heard fat splats as bullets smacked into the slab-sided creature. It bellowed in pain and stumbled. It had served its purpose, though. Smoke Jensen let go, and lowered his feet to the ground in a shuffling run. The maneuver had put him behind the last gunhawk.

Surprise registered as the man turned to find himself facing Smoke Jensen. He eared back the hammer and let fly wildly. Smoke, always calm and cool in the heat of battle, had better aim. His bullet found a home in the right shoulder of the hard case. The six-gun he had been holding flew high and came down hard. It discharged the last round of the brief, fierce fight. Slowly, he raised his good left arm.

"Okay, okay. Ease up. I'm done. I ain't never seed anyone so almighty fast. Who are you?"

"You wouldn't want to know," Smoke Jensen told him. "Sit down over there, and I'll patch you up while the rest round up these cattle."

Jeff, Walt, and Ty set off to gather in the stampeded beeves. It was a task that would take them the rest of daylight and part of the next day. From the moment Jeff York had revealed the identity of the owner of the cattle, Smoke Jensen had an idea start to grow. It would be, he decided by the time the shooting was over, a good gesture to return the cattle to the widow of Lawrence Tucker. It might even go some way toward convincing her that he had nothing to do with the death of her husband. A few answers from the survivor of the shoot-out might prove useful, he also decided. So, while he prodded the wound, cleaned it, and poured raw, stinging horse medicine in the hole, he probed for information as well.

"I don't know why I should tell you anything," came the surly answer. "I don't even know who you are."

"I'm the man who let you live, instead of killing you like the rest."

"You gonna give 'em proper Christian burial?"

"There isn't a proper minister among us, but we'll dig a shallow hole and put some rocks on top of them."

Smoke's harsh plans for the dead outlaws seemed to upset the wounded gunman. "You're gonna put my friends in the ground all together?"

"Unless you figure on digging separate graves. Now, where were you taking those cattle?"

"Far as I can tell, it's none of your business."

"They hang cattle rustlers." Smoke's voice had a heavy tone of doom.

Ty Hardy rode up then and waved his hat over his head. "Hey, Smoke, we got twenty-three head rounded up down by the creek."

"Good. Jeff can hold them. You and Walt find the others."

Icy fear touched the voice of the wounded outlaw. "He called you Smoke. What's your other name?"

"Jensen."

"Oh Jesus! Smoke Jensen. I heard you was fast, but that—that weren't human. You gonna kill me, Jensen?"

"If I had that in mind, you'd already be stretched out there with your friends. Let's get back to the point. What about those cows?"

"W-we were takin' them into Arizona, and then into Mexico. The boss had a buyer all lined up."

"This boss have a name?"

"Uh—sure . . . only, I'd get myself killed for sure if I gave it to you."

"Like I said, I could give you to Jeff York, he's an Arizona Ranger, and see you hang."

"Jeez, Mr. Jensen, I don't want to hang!"

"Then give."

His face a lined mask of conflicting terrors, he shook his head. "Quint Stalker. He ramrods the outfit."

"And Stalker works for Benton-Howell," Smoke related later to Jeff York.

A week and a half had passed since the morning when the terrible news of her husband's death had been brought to Martha Tucker. At the time, she believed that nothing could dampen the awful grief she felt. Then the pressure had begun to force her and the children off the land.

She could not believe Lawrence had actually sold the ranch. Adding strength to that conviction had been that none of those who came would reveal the name of the person to whom he supposedly sold. Then the veiled threats took on substance; shots in the night, the attempt to burn the barn, cattle rustled.

Oh, she had been frightened all right. Yet that only served to strengthen her determination. Now she didn't know what to make of this latest development. Part of her wanted to believe. Another portion of her mind urged caution. It could be some sort of trick. The two young men, one slightly older than the other, who stood before her, could be seeking to gain her trust, catch her off guard, drive them from the ranch entirely. She cut her sky blue eyes to her eldest son.

"I believe them, Momma," Jimmy responded, as though reading her thoughts.

The older man cleared his throat as though preparing to repeat his remarks. Martha spoke over them. "Tell me again how you came upon our cattle."

"Well, ma'am, we were ridin' this way from over in Arizona. We came upon these six men workin' some fifty or so head of cattle. One of the men with us, an Arizona Ranger, recognized your brand. Also that none of the drovers was the sort your hus—er—late husband would have hired."

"So we questioned them," Ty Hardy took up for Walt Reardon. "They lied to us, said they'd bought the cattle offin your husband only three days before that."

"How did you know that to be a lie?"

"We—ah—well, ma'am, we were over Socorro way when it happened, him gettin' shot." Ty Hardy looked uncomfortable with the situation.

"Are you men employed somewhere?" Martha asked, liking the cut of them, more than half-convinced they spoke the truth.

Walt Reardon took over. "Yes, ma'am. We are. Our boss was along with us. It was him said we should bring back your livestock."

Thinking to thank whichever of her neighbors had been so considerate, Martha asked, "Who is it you work for?"

"Well—ah—it's . . . Smoke Jensen," Walt reluctantly told her.

Fury burned in those cobalt eyes. "I don't believe it! Not that murdering, back-shooting bastard!" Face pinched with her outrage, she demanded further, "Were you with him last week when he tried to burn down our barn?"

"Ma'am, please listen to me. Mr. Smoke didn't kill your husband. He'd never shoot a man in the back, no-how. And he wasn't within thirty miles of this ranch any time last week. We was all up in the Cibola Range, dodging a posse," Ty Hardy pressed urgently.

"Smoke Jensen is the finest man I know," Walt Reardon added his endorsement. "He—he saved me from a life of crime and evil. I swear it, ma'am. I was a gunfighter an'—and an outlaw. Smoke Jensen reformed me, an' that's God's own truth."

Doubting, but moved, Martha asked, "How'd he do that?"

A rueful grin spread Walt's lips, and he flushed with embarrassed recollection. "First he beat the livin' hell out of me. Only that wasn't enough, so later on he shot me. Said he spared my life because he saw a glimmer of good in me. So, I'm askin' you, not to think harsh of Smoke Jensen. He could never kill a man in cold blood, believe me."

Flustered by this, Martha ran the back of one hand across her brow. "I'll consider what you've both said. The return of our cattle, I must say, adds credence to your story. I'll thank you for that again. And thank your Mr. Jensen for me, also. I'll have to think over what I have learned. Good day, gentlemen."

* * *

Sheriff Jake Reno wanted to hit the man more than he'd ever wanted to hit anyone. Mash those pursed, disapproving, aristocratic lips into bloody pulp. Who was this Fancy Dan to talk down to him. Hell, this limey-talkin' pig probably didn't even carry a gun. Fat lot he knew about facing down Smoke Jensen. The lawman turned his face away to hide the fury that burned there.

"You are to raise another posse and go back into those mountains and track down Smoke Jensen. Is that perfectly clear, Sheriff Reno?" Geoffrey Benton-Howell accentuated each word with a jab of an extended index finger.

"Who am I gonna get? Those that were with me have been talkin' around town. Not a soul will volunteer. They got the idee that Smoke Jensen is ten foot tall, can shoot a mile with his six-guns, and disappear in a cloud."

"Quint Stalker will provide you ample men, Sheriff."

Reno glowered at the expensively dressed Englishman. "Then why the hell don't he jist go out after Jensen hisself?"

"Because we want this done all legally and proper. You are a lawman. Stalker is . . . just my ranch foreman."

"He's a gunfighter and an outlaw, is more near the truth," Reno snapped.

To the lawman's surprise, Benton-Howell chuckled softly. "He is that all right." Then the ice returned to his voice. "And the reason he is not out openly hunting for

Smoke Jensen is because everyone else knows it, too. So, use his men, Sheriff Reno, and bring me back the head of Smoke Jensen."

Ten

At first, Giuseppi Boldoni could not believe his good fortune. Only a month after he, his wife, and three children had gotten off the boat from Napoli, he had become the proud owner of a truly magnificent tract of land in the Far West. Not even the richest vine grower of his native Calabria claimed so many hectares. The nice man who had sold him the land, Dalton Wade, had also made arrangements for two wagons and all of the equipment Giuseppi would need to build his home. He had picked it up in St. Louis. All paid for, part of the—what had *Signore* Wade called it?—the package, that was it.

What Giuseppi Boldoni learned when he arrived in the White Mountains gave his shrewd Italian mind much food for thought. Small wonder the land sale presentation had offered such generous terms. No one had told Giuseppi that his neighbors would all be red Indians. From the start, they had not gotten on all that well. Now, as he faced a dozen hard-faced Apaches, every one of them abristle with weapons, Giuseppi came to the conclusion that his neighbors were down right hostile.

"You will leave our land now," the big one in the middle demanded in mangled English, which Giuseppi understood only poorly. "Take what you can put in your rolling wikiups and go."

"Perche?"

"It is our land." It sounded enough like *porque,* so the leader answered the "why" in Spanish, and Giuseppi could make out most of the words.

"But I bought it," Giuseppi protested in Italian.

"It was not for sale," came the Spanish answer. "Go now." The eyes turned to chips of obsidian. "Or you die."

Giuseppi went. His wife and daughter in tears, his sons blinking unspoken questions at him, they loaded the wagons and drove off with only some clothing, food, and the rifle Giuseppi had purchased in St. Louis.

The two salty prospectors danced wildly in the icy, rushing water of the stream on the White Mountain reservation. They had actually found color. And not flake gold, either. Nuggets the size of a man's thumb! Some even bigger. The man who had hired them to search had promised them a share. But what counted was who's name was on the claim form.

"We done it, Burk. We sure-nuff did. They's plenty here to share," one bearded sourdough went on. "But what says we got to divvy up with that feller with the double last name?"

"Yer right, Fred. There ain't nothin' writ on paper to say we had us a deal. We done the work, took the risk, we should get the reward."

Neither Burk nor Fred got the prize they anticipated. What they got was their last reward. An Apache arrow cut deeply into Burk's back, quickly followed by another.

He hadn't even time for a scream, when the third fletched shaft was embedded in his left kidney. He sank to his knees in the stream, eyes glazing on the shocked expression of his partner.

Fred didn't fare any better. A ball from a big, old .64 caliber trade musket punched through his chest and shattered his right shoulder blade. Two arrows festooned his belly and he wobbled obscenely as he gasped for his last breath.

Cuchillo Negro and three Apache warriors appeared before Fred's dying eyes. "You steal the yellow rocks," the war chief stated flatly. "It is said they make you feel good. Let us see if you can eat them."

He motioned to two of his braves, who took Fred by the arms. Cuchillo Negro yanked on the small leather pouch around Fred's neck. He opened it and extracted two of the large nuggets. One by one he shoved them down Fred's throat. Three more followed, before the last caught and set the white prospector to choking.

"It is enough," Cuchillo Negro said in his own tongue. "Let him die like that."

Smoke Jensen and Jeff York were about to discover that Quint Stalker was nowhere to be found. To keep his face out of Socorro during this phase of the take-over, Benton-Howell had dispatched Stalker and three of the outlaw leader's men to the White Mountain reservation. Under a morning sun, already made hot by the sere desert terrain, they busily occupied themselves pounding claiming stakes into the ground.

Stalker knew enough of the general plan to understand

that this land would be taken from the Apaches and given over to white settlement. The first claims filed on it would be those of his bosses. A neat little scheme, he considered it, as he began to collect stones for a boundary marker.

"Sure's hell's lonely up here, Quint," Randy Sturgis announced. "I thought there was supposed to be 'Paches around."

"They're around," his boss replied. "Only we just don't see 'em. Apaches don't usual get seen unless they wants to."

"Gol-ly, Quint, what if they's warriors?"

Stalker paused to give Randy a cold grin. "Then, I'd reckon as how we'd already be missin' our hair."

Half an hour later, Quint Stalker rounded a bend in the creek with an armload of stones for the last marker. He came face-to-face with two startled Apache boys about thirteen or fourteen years of age. The rocks clattered to the ground, and the youths bolted like frightened deer. Quint knew he dare not let the boys get back to their village with news of the presence of white men. His hand found the butt of his Merwin and Hulbert, as he shouted a warning to his followers.

"Heads up, boys. We got us a couple of rabbit-sized bucks headed your way."

A pistol shot cracked loudly a moment later, followed by a thin wail. Quint pushed himself to a lumbering run and caught up to the surviving Apache boy in time to put a bullet through the youngster's right knee. Eyes wide with pain, the youth fell down, lips closed against any show of pain. Stalker shot him in the other leg.

"Never could abide a damn Apache brat."

"Why's that, Quint?"

"They turn into growed-up Apaches, Randy."

"I can fix that quick enough," Randy offered, and shot the boy in the groin.

Intense pain and the horror caused by the nature of the wound brought a howl of agony from the little lad. "He sure ain't gonna have any git of his own," Randy laughed.

"Awh, hell, finish him off," Marv Fletcher encouraged. "Plum cruel geldin' even an Injun."

Quint Stalker turned away indifferently. "You want to do it, go ahead. I'd as leave play with him a little more."

The fatal round sounded a second later. It presented another surprise to the outlaws. A high, thin gasp, followed by a sob, drew their attention to a clump of deer berries on the bank of the creek. Quint Stalker walked to the screen of vegetation and reached in. He yanked out an Apache girl, of an age with the dead boys, her slim forearm firmly in his big-handed grasp.

"Well, lookie here," Randy Sturgis gloated, advancing on the terrified child. "We got us some rec-re-a-tion."

"I get seconds," Marv Fletcher blurted.

Sky Flower had never known such intense pain in all her life. She knew, of course, what men and women did together. Had known for a long time. Only there was no pleasure for her in what was happening. Tears streamed from her eyes, and she felt like being sick.

Her thought became the deed. It earned her a fist to the jaw, when she vomited on the bared chest of the *Pen-*

dik-olye who rode her. With all the pain within her, she never noticed the new source.

"Little bitch, puked all over me," Randy complained.

"No more'n' you take a bath, we'd never notice, Randy," Quint Stalker jibed.

"Go to hell, Quint."

They had all visited her body twice. This one, called Randy by his fellows, had come back for a third encounter. It went on forever before the youthful white outlaw finished.

"Anybody else?"

"Naw," Stalker answered for the others. "Finish her off."

Sky Flower did not hear the gunshot that robbed her of her life.

Walt Reardon and Ty Hardy rode into the small valley with important news. They joined Smoke Jensen and Jeff York at a small, smokeless fire, and eagerly accepted tin cups of steaming coffee.

"The Widow Tucker was mighty grateful for the return of her cattle," Walt drawled.

"Walt told her we worked for you, Smoke. She flew off the handle at first, but calmed down some when Walt an' me explained how you had taken the stock from rustlers and sent us to bring them back."

Walt offered a new possibility. "Way I see it, she might even be willin' to consider the chance you didn't kill her husband."

Jeff York reacted to it first. "I think that's something worth looking into, Smoke."

"When I can prove who *did* kill her husband, then I'll be glad to talk to the woman," Smoke replied stubbornly.

"Wait a minute, now," Jeff urged. "You need a secure place to operate from, right? My reading of our Sheriff Jake Reno tells me that when brains were being passed out, he was behind the door. When we start stirring things up around Socorro, there's bound to be some real serious hunting around for you. The last place Reno would think to look for you, has to be the ranch of the man you're accused of murdering."

Jeff's words received careful consideration. "You may have a point, Jeff," Smoke allowed. "At least it might be worth looking into."

"If a lawman vouches for you, and a famous Arizona Ranger at that," Jeff added with a mischievous twinkle in his eyes, "it might get the widow to see you in a different light."

"You reckon to handle this yourself?"

"Why not, Smoke? It's the strongest card we've got to play right now."

Smoke Jensen took a final sip of coffee. "Walt and Ty are going to poke around a little, see if they can get a line on Stalker. I'm headed south of Socorro. We'll meet in San Antonio three days from now. Between now and then, Jeff, see what you can set up."

Martha Tucker studied the silver badge pinned on the vest of Jeff York. He wore clothes a cut above the average range hand, was well-spoken, and no doubt was who he claimed to be. Still, she considered his proposal outlandish.

"I'm not certain I'm ready for what you have told me, Ranger York."

"Mrs. Tucker, I've known Smoke Jensen for years. In all that time I've never known him to do a dishonorable thing. What motive would he have to kill a total stranger?"

"But he was found beside my husband's bod—body."

"Unconscious, as I understand it. Tell me everything you know about . . . what happened."

For the next ten minutes, Martha Tucker related all that she had been told about her husband's death. Jeff York listened with intense interest. When she had finished, Jeff pondered for a moment before speaking.

"Taken with what Smoke told me, there's no doubt that someone arranged things to make him look guilty. For one thing, your husband was shot with a .45. Smoke carries twin .44s. Always has."

Martha nodded. "Go on."

"Smoke was found with the single holster strapped around his waist. Yet, when he escaped from the jail, his own guns and their holsters were found in the sheriff's desk. How would you suppose they got there?"

"I have no idea." Martha sighed heavily. "It doesn't appear that the sheriff, or the man he sent out here to tell me about it, has been entirely honest with me."

Jeff grinned in anticipation of success. "Not in the least."

"But why would you come over here from Arizona to look into it?"

"Like I told you before, Mrs. Tucker, Smoke Jensen is my friend. We've fought together before. And he's always stood up for what's right. At least, couldn't you hear him out? Give him an opportunity to tell you what he knows."

Martha Tucker's face lightened, and a soft smile of acquiescence lifted the corners of her mouth. "Yes. I suppose it's the least I can do."

Cuchillo Negro's face darkened with the fury of his outrage. They had been running off the *Pen-dik-olye* for three suns now. But to come upon such a scene as this threatened to make him break his resolve to keep their actions on the reservation. Three children, killed without reason, the girl ravaged before she died. He looked up sharply as Tall Hat spoke.

"I know their village, their families."

"You will carry the message to them?"

"Yes. They will want to come and care for their children."

"We will find the white men who did this. Their end will not be easy," the war chief declared flatly.

He sent men out looking for signs. They soon found plenty in the cairns of stones and stakes that marked the boundary of a claim. At the direction of Cuchillo Negro, the warriors scattered these items over a wide area. Faint traces of shod hoofprints pointed the way the interlopers had left the creek bank.

"Follow the trail," Cuchillo Negro ordered two skilled trackers. "We will come along behind."

"If they leave the reservation?" Ho-tan asked.

Black Knife looked back at the ruined face of the little girl. "We will go after them."

The sign left by the white men meandered through the White Mountains, roughly eastward, and downhill toward the land of the Zuni and Tuwa people. Diligently, the Apaches followed. They came upon the site of a carefully disrupted night camp. When Cuchillo Negro saw it, he spoke his thoughts aloud.

"These men know us well. They took care to see that no sign of their camp could be noted. Your eyes are clever, *Waplanowi*. Now see if you can bring me to them before this day is over."

White Eagle beamed with pride at the chief's compliment. *"Zigosti* is wiser than I. He says their fire burned two sleeps ago. We will not find them before *nolcha* sleeps."

Cuchillo Negro frowned. "We travel together from now on. The *Pen-dik-olye* seem in no hurry. By tomorrow we might catch them."

Wink Winkler mopped his brow with a large bandanna. "I'm shore glad we're shut of them mountains. I began to see an Apache behind every tree."

"There ain't that many Apaches around these parts, Wink," Randy Sturgis replied. "Though I'll admit I'm glad they prob'ly not follow us into New Mexico."

The two hard cases sat on a red-orange mesa that overlooked the Rio San Francisco outside Apache Creek, New Mexico. Randy, who could read on only a third-grade level and had quit school at the age of ten, was fortunate not to know how the small community had acquired its name. If he had, he would not have been nearly so confident. Quint Stalker stood with them, giving his horse a blow and considering their remarkably good luck in escaping the Apaches, who had no doubt set out after them.

"We're not out of it yet, boys. We'd best put more miles between us and the White Mountains."

"Awh, we're safe enough here, Quint," Randy protested. "These critters is near to run into the ground. They gotta have a rest. Us, too. From up here, you can see for miles. No way any Injuns could sneak up on us."

Quint worried that around awhile, then nodded, his mind changed. "Right. We can rest the horses and catch our breath. But no fires after dark, hear? Be sure what you do build is small and smokeless."

For all their precautions, Quint Stalker and the three members of his gang learned the extent of their error in judgement shortly before midnight. A dozen Apache warriors rose up in the darkness and fired a shower of arrows into their camp. The first volley failed to find flesh, but awakened two of the targets.

"What the hell?" Randy Sturgis blurted. Then by weak starlight, he made out the familiar silhouette of an Apache. "Ohmygod! It's Apaches, Quint, it's Injuns!"

"I know that, damnit. Make a run for the horses."

"Injuns ain't supposed to fight at night," Randy wailed.

Quint Stalker's .44 Merwin and Hulbert barked and produced a flare of yellow-orange that illuminated more of the warriors. "Someone forgot to tell that to these bucks."

By then the other pair had been roused. They added to the volume of fire and momentarily held the Apaches in check. Another volley of arrows hissed and moaned through the air. Wink Winkler howled and came to his bare feet.

"My arm! There's an arrow shot clean through it."

Quint Stalker put a bullet in the chest of the Apache nearest him, snatched up his bridle, and ran for the horses. If they lived through this, he reckoned, they'd face a lot more hell, being barefoot and without saddles, food, or a change of clothing. Another Apache materialized out of the gloom at the picket line. Quint coolly pumped a .44 round through the warrior's heart. Low, menacing whoops and the soft rustle of moccasins added haste to his fumbling efforts to slip the headstall over the twitching ears of his horse, and shove the bit between fear-clamped teeth.

Randy Sturgis appeared at his side. "Wink's bad hurt. There's three Apaches jumped him."

"I'll fix your bridle, go back and help him."

Doubt and fear registered clearly in the dim light. "That's a hell of a lot of Injuns back there."

"Do it anyway. I never leave a man who ain't dead," Stalker snarled.

"Might be that's already the case," Randy opined.

Gunfire erupted from two locations on the small mesa, which disproved for the moment Randy's expectation. A hard shove from Quint Stalker sent him back to the melee. Halfway there, he encountered Wink Winkler and Vern Draper.

The arrow still protruded from both sides of Wink's left forearm. He had been cut across the chest and a chunk of meat was missing from his right shoulder, where a war hawk had bitten deeply. Vern cut wild, glazed eyes to Randy, and gestured over his shoulder.

"Damn near got myself punctured back there," he panted. "But I freed Randy from those devils."

"Let's make tracks," Randy urged.

Quickly they rejoined Quint Stalker. Bridles fitted in place, the outlaws made ready to mount. Randy and Vern lifted Wink astride his mount. Then Vern gave Randy a leg up. Quint Stalker got Vern Draper on his horse, then vaulted to the back of his own. By then the Apaches had maneuvered into position close enough to see their targets in the dark.

More arrows sung their deadly songs as the white men rode fearfully away toward the trail that led off the mesa. Cuchillo Negro raised his trade musket to his shoulder and squeezed off a round that ended the evil career of the first to violate little Sky Flower. The big .64 caliber ball drove a hand-width chunk of shattered spine through the lungs and heart of Randy Sturgis.

Back arched suddenly, Randy did a back flip over his mount's rump. He landed hard on the reddish soil of the nameless butte that overlooked the San Francisco River at Apache Creek.

Eleven

Five of Quint Stalker's ne'er-do-well hard cases lounged in front of the Tio Pepe cantina in the little town of San Antonio, New Mexico. They listlessly passed a bottle of tequila from hand to hand, drank, spat tobacco juice, or rolled smokes. One of them, Charlie Bascomb, perked up somewhat when a stranger rode into town on a big-chested roan.

"Hey, don't he look like that feller we's supposed to be huntin' down?" Bascomb asked his companions.

Weak-eyed Aaron Sneed squinted and dug a grimy knuckle into one pale blue orb. "Nuh-uh. Don't think so. Last I heard, he was supposed to be up north a ways, in the Cibolas."

"I for one," barrel-chested Buck Ropon declared, "am glad to hear that, Aaron. After I heard what happened to them boys that went along with the sheriff, I'm not so certain I want to tangle with the likes of Smoke Jensen."

"Turnin' yeller, Buck?" Charlie taunted. " 'Sides, them boys was alone most times. They's *five* of us. I say us five can take any Smoke Jensen, or the devil hisself if it came to that."

Unwittingly, Charlie Bascomb had cast their fate in a

direction none of them would have wanted, and which none of them later liked in the least.

After the stranger entered the general mercantile across the way, Charlie kept on worrying aloud. Like a big, old tabby will a little, bitty mouse, it finally wore down the caution so wisely held by Buck Ropon. Rising to his boots, Buck adjusted the drape of his cartridge belt across the solid slab of lard on his big belly, and nodded in the direction of the general store.

"I reckon you're gonna keep on about that until we know for certain, ain'tcha?" Buck Ropon groused.

Charlie screwed his mouth into a tight pucker. "Wouldn't do no harm to get a closer look."

"Are you crazy?" a heretofore silent member of the quintet demanded. "What if it *is* Smoke Jensen?"

Charlie grinned widely, his eyebrows and ears rising with the intensity of it all. "Why, then, we've got his butt and a thousand dollars reward!"

Inside the mercantile, Smoke Jensen ducked his head to miss the hanging display of No. 4 galvanized wash-tubs, buckets, washboards, and various pieces of harness. A wizened old man with a monk's fringe of white hair around a large expanse of bald pate glanced up through wire-rimmed half-glasses, and peered at his customer.

"What'll it be?"

"Howdy," Smoke addressed the man. "I could use some supplies. A slab of fatback, couple of pounds each of beans, flour, sugar, a pound of coffee beans, some 'taters."

"Yessir, right away." The merchant made no move to fill the order.

"Better throw in a can of baking powder, some dry onions, and a box of Winchester .45-70-500's if you've got them."

"Ummm. That's for that new Express Rifle, ain't it? I don't have any."

In a moment of inspiration, Smoke amended his list. "Then throw in a dozen sticks of dynamite. Sixty percent will do."

"Don't stock that, either. You'll have to go to the gunsmith. He's got a powder magazine out back of his place."

"Thank you. Uh . . . I'll take me a couple of sticks of this horehound candy," Smoke added as he reached for the jar.

"You got youngun's?" the seam-faced oldster asked suspiciously.

"No Smoke replied with a smile. Truth was, Smoke Jensen had always been partial to horehound candy.

The storekeeper took in the double-gun rig: the right one slung low, butt to the rear, the left set high, canted so as to present an easy reach for the front-facing grip. A gunfighter. That fact screamed at the merchant. Hastily, to cover the tremor in his hands, he set about packaging Smoke Jensen's supplies. Smoke, meanwhile, rolled the sweets in a sheet of waxed paper and twisted the ends closed. He stuck his prize in his right shirt pocket, under his fringed leather vest.

When the small stack of purchases had been tallied, Smoke paid for them and removed a rolled-up flour sack from a hip pocket. Slowly, carefully, he put each item inside and hefted the load.

The clerk had a dozen questions forming in his mind—but caution kept him silent. He stood behind the counter and watched his customer head for the door. Then he tilted his chin and shot a glance beyond the tall, powerfully built stranger. He saw the five hard cases in the street, facing his store. He gulped forcefully and licked dry lips with a suddenly arid tongue. How he wished he had taken seriously the suggestions of steel shutters for his windows.

Smoke Jensen stepped out onto the abbreviated boardwalk that extended porchlike around one side, and along the wider front of the general mercantile. It also fronted the next building on the main street. No doubt the structures had been built at the same time, by the same man. Blazing, afternoon sun came from the right angle to blind the eyes of Smoke Jensen to all but five pairs of legs, stuffed into an equal number of boots, arranged in a semicircle that curved out into the street and blocked all avenues of egress. All that left him was a fight, or a cowardly flight back through the store and out the rear. Through the distortion of heat waves, Smoke heard a hoarse whisper.

"It's him, right enough."

"What we gonna do?"

"Well, for one thing, we won't even have to shoot him. He's got the sun in his eyes. An' he ain't got nowhere to go to get away. Let's jist jump him, boys."

Smoke Jensen sat the sack of his supplies on a bench

in front of one big display window, his vision gradually clearing. He raised his left hand in a cautioning gesture.

"I think both your ideas are wrong," said Smoke blandly.

Suddenly, three of the men launched themselves at him. Smoke stepped in on one with groping arms. He grabbed a wrist and pivoted on powerful legs. His attacker spun away. When Smoke released him, he hurtled sideways into a shower of glass as a display window broke. He landed in the midst of a selection of bolts of cloth. Bleats of pain came from him, accompanied by the sustained tinkle of more falling shards. Smoke had already turned to face his next threat.

Two hard cases rammed into him at the same time. For all the tree-trunk strength of Smoke's legs, they bore him off his boots. Smoke managed to turn slightly in the air and take them with him. They toppled through the open space created by the shattered window.

"Ow! Gadang, I'm cut," one outlaw wailed, and released his hold on Smoke Jensen.

Immediately Smoke flexed his right knee and drove it into the belly of the hard case. Forcibly ejected from the display counter, he slammed painfully into a four-by-four upright of the awning over the boardwalk. His ribs could be heard breaking like dry sticks. A painful howl tore from his throat. Before Smoke could get to work on the other, hard hands clamped on his shoulders and strong arms yanked him into the store.

"You're gonna git yours, Jensen," Charlie Bascomb snarled.

"I'm gonna kill him!" the outlaw with the broken ribs shrieked. "Let me at him. I'll kill him." He stumbled through the door, fingers curled around the flashy pearl grips of his six-gun. "Get outta my way, Charlie!"

Charlie got; but before he could fully register what happened, Smoke Jensen had recovered from his man-handling, drew, and fired. Smoking lead pinwheeled the crazed gunman. He dumped over, arms flying wide. His released Colt sped from his hand and broke a glass display case. A wail of protest came from the merchant, now crouched behind his counter. He had cause for further complaint a moment later, when the thug in the window reared up and threw a wild shot at Smoke Jensen.

It spanged off the cast-iron side of a black, pot-bellied stove, richocheted through the ceiling, and left a crack behind. Because Smoke Jensen was no longer where he had been. He moved the instant he fired. Now he swung the hot muzzle of his .44 toward the offensive gunhawk.

Smoke's six-gun spoke, and a yelp of surprise and pain came as shards of wood from the window's inner framework showered the gunhawk's face. It was not enough to incapacitate him, Smoke soon learned. Two more rounds barked from the outlaw's .45, as the remaining pair of gunslicks charged through the open doorway.

Another hasty round clipped the thug in the shoulder, a moment before the last mountain man ducked behind a floor island to escape a murderous hail of lead from the newcomers. A soft grunt told him he had scored a hit. Bullets ripped and shredded a rack of black, weather-proofed dusters, searching blindly for Smoke. He easily kept ahead of their advance, then hunkered down and duck-walked back along the section the slugs had chewed through. At the end of the island, the wounded hard case in the window spotted him and blinked in surprise.

"Nobody could live through that," he declared in astonishment a second before he died, a bullet from Smoke Jensen turning his long, sharp nose into an inverted exclamation point.

Smoke immediately reholstered his expended six-gun and cross-drew his backup. A snigger came from Charlie Bascomb. "That's five, iffin' I count right, Jensen. We're comin' after you."

Could this one they called Charlie be so stupid as to not have seen his second six-gun? Or did he forget about it? Smoke let go of the questions as quickly as he had formed them. He ducked low and spotted the boots of his taunter. The big iron barked, and Charlie shrieked as he went to the floor. He found himself staring into the steely gray gaze of Smoke Jensen.

Without visible pause, Charlie began to roll toward the door. He blubbered and sobbed as he called entreaties to his remaining sidekicks. "Go after him, boys. He's right back o' them coats."

Only Smoke was not there any more. One outlaw ankled around the far end of the island to discover that fact. He stared disbelievingly, while his partner emptied another six-gun into the linen dusters and his companion. The thug died without Smoke firing a shot.

The man from the Sugarloaf made up for that quickly enough, though. The last of a trio of fast shots found meat. A grunt and curse preceded a stumbling bootwalk across the plank floor toward the back counter. Smoke had only a single round left. He edged along a wall of shelves loaded with boots and shoes, until he could see the counters at the rear of the store.

From his vantage point, the gunhawk saw Smoke first.

He tripped his trigger on a final round, and immediately abandoned it for a large knife. When the target jinked to Smoke's right, it threw his shot off. Smoke's last slug punched through the outer wall of the store. Only then did Smoke see that the knife was not the usual hog-sticker carried by frontier hard cases. In fact, it looked more like a ground-down sword, with a two-foot blade.

While that registered on Smoke, his adversary gave a roar and leaped at him. The blade swished through the air with a vicious sound. Smoke jumped back and to the side, away from the swing. He instantly stumbled, tripped, and fell into a double row of light farm implements. Their clutter muffled his muttered curse. A second later, the knife-wielder charged Smoke again.

His own coffin-handle Bowie, formidable under any other conditions, would be of little use against this on-slaught. Smoke Jensen knew that in an instant. He bought himself some time by a quick, prone scramble down the aisle. Not quite far enough, as the two-foot blade whirred through the air and clipped a heel from Smoke's boot. While his opponent remained off balance, Smoke thrust upright. He backed away further, both hands groping among the tools.

A snarl of triumph illuminated the contorted face of Buck Ropon. He rushed after Smoke Jensen with his altered sword raised high. He had just begun the down-swing—aimed to split Smoke's head from crown to chin—when Smoke's hands closed on the familiar per-pendicular handle of a scythe. He tightened his grip and jumped backward.

Swiftly, Smoke swung the keen-edged blade like the Grim Reaper. The long handle easily outdistanced the reach of Buck Ropon. The big, curved blade hissed through a short arc. Shock jolted up the handle to Smoke's arms when the edge made contact. With Smoke Jensen's enormous strength, it cut clean through. Buck Ropon had just been decapitated by a scythe.

His headless body did a grotesque quick-time dance, while twin streams of crimson fountained to the ceiling. The head, lips still skinned back in a snarl, hit and rolled on the floor. When the blood geysers diminished, the deflated corpse fell full-length. Smoke Jensen immediately recovered himself.

He set the scythe aside and started to reload both six-guns. Stunned into mindless shock, the merchant stumbled around his business, alternately sobbing and cursing. Bitterness colored his words when he was capable of comprehensible speech.

"Mein Gott! Mein Gott! Look at this. I'm ruined! Who will pay? Who will pay for all this damage?"

By then, Smoke Jensen had finished punching fresh cartridges into both weapons, loading six rounds in each. Seeming to ignore the distressed shopkeeper, he went from corpse to corpse, examining the contents of their pockets. He accumulated a considerable amount of paper currency and coins. Then, with the merchant looking on in horror, he stripped the boots from them and recovered even more.

It totaled about two hundred dollars and change. He handed it to the horrified man. "This should help. And that scythe is like brand new. All you need do is clean it up, and sell it to someone."

"Never! No one would want it. I'll never be able to sell it."

Smoke delved into one of his own pockets and brought out a three-dollar gold piece. "Then I'll buy it."

"That's it, *Mench?* You are going to hand me money and walk out of here like nothing happened?"

"You saw it all. You can tell the law what happened. They attacked me, right? I only protected myself."

"Wh-who . . . are you?"

"Smoke Jensen."

A sudden greenness crept into the existing pallor of the merchant's face. *"Ach du lieber Gott!"* he wailed, as he tottered toward the cash drawer with the money clutched in one hand.

Smoke Jensen retrieved his supplies and assessed his own damage. He found the worst that had happened was that his horehound candy sticks had been broken. He left San Antonio without a backward glance.

Smoke camped a hundred yards off the only road he figured Jeff and his hands would use coming to San Antonio through this sparsely settled country. Sure enough, early the next evening, while coffee brewed and he tended a hat-sized fire over which biscuits baked in a covered skillet, he heard the thunder of the hooves; he made it out to be three horses in a brisk canter. Smoke kept a careful eye to the north, as the sound grew louder. He had the polished metal shaving mirror from his personal kit cupped in one hand, and when the riders came close enough to recognize, he signaled them by a series of flashes.

"You could have took that damn thing out of my eyes a little sooner," Jeff York complained, as he rode up to where Smoke bent over to add more fatback to a second skillet.

"Wanted to make sure you knew it was me. Might have been you Arizona boys don't know that trick," Smoke teased.

"Hell, the Apaches have been usin' mirrors to signal with since the Spanish brought them way back. That smells good."

"Step down and pour coffee. You two as well. What's the news?"

"We can't find anything of Sheriff Reno or Quint Stalker, nor any of Stalker's hard cases," Jeff declared.

"Everything is set up with the widder for two nights from now," Walt added his good news.

Smoke nodded. "Small wonder you didn't see any of Stalker's men. I had a run-in with five of them yesterday in San Antonio. That's why I'm out here waiting for you."

Jeff snorted and ran a hand through his sandy blond locks. "Did you stick around to explain to the local law?"

Smoke gave him a blank look of innocence. "I didn't know there was any. Didn't overstay my welcome by finding out. Not when one of them got away. My guess, our friend Sheriff Reno is in charge around here anyway."

"Losing five of his prize possemen will sure enough make his day for him," Walt said drolly. "Uh . . . one thing we did find out, the sheriff is usin' Stalker's outlaws on the posse. There's some folk around Socorro don't take too fondly to that. Includin' the Widow Tucker."

"Then I am even more inclined to meet with the good woman." Smoke's eyes twinkled with suppressed merriment, as he continued, "I seem to recall you mentioned she was some looker, Walt. There any chance of you making a place for yourself?"

"You hurt me to the core, Smoke. You know I ride for the Sugarloaf an' no one else."

"Sometimes the heart has a way of changing the mind. Whatever," Smoke summed up, "eat hearty and sleep with a packed outfit. Tomorrow we ride to the Tucker ranch."

Twelve

Smoke Jensen stared down into the black pool in his coffee cup. It struck him powerfully to realize how long it had been since he had last drank strong, dark brew from a delicate china cup like this. Of course, it had been back home, on the Sugarloaf. For all her ability to rough it like a man, Sally Jensen insisted on her finery in the large, log building that housed the headquarters of Smoke's horse-breeding ranch. Only there, he noted, the tension didn't grow so thick it could be felt and tasted.

After Jeff York had made the introductions, Martha Tucker sat across from Smoke Jensen, at the core of that tension. From her viewpoint, Smoke allowed, she had ample cause to radiate so much distrust and suspicion. Might as well get on with it and see how much of that he could boil away. Sighing, Smoke cut his eyes to the woman across the table. His eyes locked with her sky blue ones. In a soft, steady voice, pitched low, Smoke described what he knew of events surrounding the death of Lawrence Tucker.

She listened, hands in her lap, palms up, like opening flowers. Her face remained impassive, until he recounted the discovery of their cattle on the trail outside of Datil. Suddenly strained muscles tightened her face into deep, shadowed lines. She drew a sharp breath, recalling when and how the livestock had been driven off the ranch.

"Those cattle were stolen more than a week ago," she stated in a hollow voice. "The men who did it called their leader Smoke."

Smoke Jensen looked sharply at her. "Someone was being cute. My guess, based on what the survivor of that encounter told us, is that Quint Stalker thought that one up." He sighed and paused. "It couldn't have been Stalker. He's not been seen around Socorro for a good two weeks."

"Where might he be?" Martha asked.

"We . . . don't know," Jeff York inserted.

"Wherever he is, he'll be up to no good, you can be sure of that."

Smoke first picked up on this change in Martha's attitude. "Pardon me, Mrs. Tucker, but could you tell us more about what has happened here, to you and your children? Jeff has filled me in on part of it, though surely not everything."

Smoke's prompting opened the flood gates. "First, a man came from town, Elert Cousins it was, to tell me tha—that Lawrence had been killed. He said the sheriff had caught the man who had done it. That it was . . ." Her voice faltered, lowered, "Smoke Jensen."

"And now, maybe you're not so sure?" Smoke urged.

"You can count on what Smoke told you," Jeff York jumped in. "Like I said before, Smoke is on the right side of the law, a straight shooter." A sudden pained expression of embarrassment twisted the Arizona Ranger's handsome features. "Sorry. Poor choice of words."

"I understand," Martha said softly. Then she continued

to recount the efforts to force her and the children to abandon the ranch. When she had ended her account, she added, "At first they claimed that you had taken the money and bill of sale when you killed Larry. After that, when I insisted on seeing the transfer of title and sale bill, they stopped even mentioning that.

"Lately, I've been giving it some thought," Martha continued. "Especially after talking with your hands, who were quite gentlemanly, though with a few rough edges. Then, Ranger York, who spoke on your behalf. I got to wondering how it could be that you were found unconscious, beside my hus—beside his body, and they didn't find the money and bill of sale on your person?"

Smoke Jensen studied her calm demeanor. Certainly a powerfully attractive woman. Her heart-shaped face revealed a firm, though not stern mouth, wide-set, clear, blue eyes, and a high brow. Her hands, worn by years at the washboard and cookstove, still retained a semblance of youthful elegance. Carried herself well, too. Even the hostility she had directed toward him at the outset had been muted by an inner disposition toward true justice, rather than revenge. Her children, quiet and polite, showed good upbringing. They had been clean and wore neat clothing. They had gone off to their loft beds shortly after Smoke and Jeff arrived.

Most of all, as he had just discovered, her mind worked rather well. No one else had come up with that particular question, let alone an explanation.

"Score one for the lady," Smoke announced to break his contemplation. "I asked the sheriff that very question when he came into my cell to—ah—arrange a confession. He didn't have an answer."

"Neither do I," Martha allowed. "That's what perplexes me."

Much as she disliked the direction of her thoughts, Martha Tucker had to admit that this trim-waisted, broad-shouldered man was far more handsome than either of his hands. His hair, cut a bit longish for current fashion, had a natural curl in the ends, that turned inward to brush at his earlobes. His eyes had turned a soft, comforting gray. Martha had no way of knowing that they could take on the color of glacial ice when angered. To her dismay, Martha Tucker found herself comparing him with her husband, with Smoke Jensen coming out ahead in most attributes. She chastised herself for the strong, though unwanted attraction she felt toward the rugged mountain man-gunfighter.

Although, to give herself credit, she also felt repelled by his reputation. There! She had said it all. Yet, he seemed sincere in what he said. What with Ranger York to vouch for him, what reason did she have to distrust Smoke Jensen? She suddenly realized that she had been asked a question, when Smoke repeated it.

"How do you mean, Miz Tucker?"

"Why, simply that there have been rumors about our Sheriff Reno. It's said that he's lazy, which I can vouch for. Also that to make work easy, he's sent more than one innocent man to the gallows."

"That's not true, ma'am," Jeff York interjected. "The law don't have anything to do with convictions and sentencing. That's up to the judge and jury."

Martha's eyes held a heretofore unseen twinkle. "Don't their decisions rely a great deal on a lawman's evidence and testimony?"

Jeff knew when he had been bested. A light pink flush colored his fair cheeks. "You got me there, ma'am."

"I see that I haven't been entirely clear. What I was getting at, is that Sheriff Reno is supposed to have created evidence out of whole cloth several times before, also withheld evidence or suppressed testimony that would have favored the accused person."

"Fits with the way he handled this case," Smoke Jensen provided. "Last thing I remember, I was wearing my own guns. Then they showed up in Reno's desk drawer. And I was supposed to be packin' some hand-me-down, castoff, conversion Remington. And if I had the money I was supposed to have taken, he would have bragged that up to me, too."

Martha, who had cast a nervous glance up at the loft, cut her eyes back to Smoke. "Of course, it would be argued that the sheriff, or that sticky-fingered jailer of his, could have relieved you of it while you were unconscious. For my part, I think there never was any money. Because I know that Larry had no intention of ever selling this ranch."

"So then, that's what led you to believe me?" Smoke prodded.

Martha took a deep breath, sighed it out. "Yes. At least enough to ask you, what do you intend to do about it?"

"I intend to find the one who did it and why. That'll clear my name."

"Then the next question has to be, what can I do to help?" It had taken Martha considerable effort to frame those words, yet the strain did not show on her lovely face.

Smoke and Jeff exchanged smiles. "Well, Miz Tucker,

I need a place to operate out of. Somewhere the sheriff and Quint Stalker's men would never believe me to be."

"I can let you and your two hands and Ranger York move onto the ranch. They've tried so hard to make me believe you are guilty, no one would ever suspect you to be here."

Smoke beamed at her. "We'll be settled in by morning. Then I'll come let you know where we set up."

"Why, in the bunkhouse, of course. I read somewhere that if one wanted to hide something important, the best place would be in plain sight."

"Poe, I think," Smoke offered. *The Purloined Letter.*"

More of her heavy mood sloughed off, and Martha clapped her hands together in delight. "I am impressed, Mr. Jensen. I never expected—"

"A gunfighter to be well read? I had a good teacher."

"Who was that, Mr. Jensen?"

"A man they called Preacher. He raised me up from about the age of your oldest. Taught me things that would astound a body. Some of 'em I never believed until I'd gotten around a bit. Walt and Ty are close at hand. We should be moved into the bunkhouse before midnight."

"Fine." Martha rose, extended a hand in courteous fashion. "Then I'll see you for breakfast at first light. We can start laying plans on how to expose the truth."

Geoffrey Benton-Howell set aside the sheet of thick, creamy, off-white linen stationery. He could not restrain the smile of triumph that lighted his face, all except his malevolent, deep-set, blue eyes. He rose to his highly polished boots from behind the cherry wood secretary desk, and crossed the room to the tall, drape-framed window that overlooked the main street of Socorro. Backlighted by the searing sun, he struck a familiar pose, proud of his lean, hard body for all his fifty-one years.

"They will be here, as expected. Train to Albuquerque, then on by carriage. I suggest we send one of ours. It will make a good impression. These politicians of yours seem to dote on such privileges."

Miguel Selleres took a deep sip from a glass of excellent port wine. "They are not *my* politicians, my friend. I am a citizen of Mexico."

"New Mexico, to be precise," Benton-Howell thrust a sharp barb. "The country of your adopted nationality lost this territory to the United States in the Treaty of Guadalupe Hidalgo. That was long before you were born."

"No, *amigo,* I was born in this part of Mexico in 1845, and to me and my family, the distinction of which country has claim to it on paper is not in dispute. It is a part of Mexico. It always will be. The day will come when we cast off the foreign occupation of our lands."

Lordy, Quint Stalker thought as he stared at Miguel Selleres in disbelief, this boy's wagon's got a busted wheel. One good thing—so far no one had asked him why they had come runnin' back to Socorro with their tails between their legs. A moment later Benton-Howell destroyed Stalker's sense of relief.

"They will be entertained as planned. Now, tell me, Stalker, what brings you so hastily back to Socorro?"

A pained expression preceded Stalker's words. "Truth to tell, Mr. Benton-Howell, the Apaches runned us clear the hell an' gone out of them mountains."

Benton-Howell's tone mirrored his disbelief. "A few scruffy savages with bows and arrows? Surely you had enough firepower?"

"Not for more 'an a dozen of them. Those Apaches is tough fighters, Sir Geoffrey." Try a little flattery, Stalker told himself.

"Perhaps your men have lost their *cojones, ¿es verdad?*" Miguel Selleres sneered.

"Don't you get on my case, *Señor.*" Quint pronounced it *sayn-yor.* "What is it your people call them?"

"Ah, yes," Selleres replied, recalling. *"La raza bronce que sabe morir.* The bronze race that knows how to die. But they *do* die."

"Eventual." To Benton-Howell, Stalker explained, "Oftentimes, their raiding parties are no more than five, six men. But they can tie up a platoon-sized army patrol for weeks at a time. All the while, they're killin', burnin', an' running off stock. Those stinkin' Injuns kilt one of my boys, stuck arrows in three more. We was lucky to get out of it with our hair."

"Yes, I can appreciate that. The fact remains that we must keep control of those claims. I want you to gather in all of your men and head back to the White Mountains. This time, make certain you can hold off every red nigger there, man or boy."

"Mr. Benton—Sir Geoffrey," Stalker protested through a series of gulps. "Thing is, we take in too many, and it attracts the attention of the soldier-boys an' the Arizona Rangers. We can't fight all of that at once. Besides, I need to leave a few men here, keep a lid on things."

"Very well, those who are out with Sheriff Reno on

the posse can remain here to handle local matters. Take the rest and leave by noon tomorrow."

Chastened, Quint Stalker came to his boots, his head hung, and started for the door. "Yes, sir, if that's what you want." At the door he asked, "Does that mean you're givin' up the hunt for Smoke Jensen?"

"Oh, no, my dear boy. Not at all. We have some other plans for your Mr. Smoke Jensen. Plans I'm sure he will find most unpleasant."

They had left the Tucker ranch after this admonition: "Jeff, I want you and Walt to ride into Socorro. Hang around the saloons, the barber shop, and livery. I'm sure you know why," he added, cutting his eyes to Jeff.

"Any lawman knows that's where you hear all the gossip," Jeff replied with a grin.

"Right. Go soak up all you can get on Quint Stalker, this Benton-Howell you mentioned in Show Low, and his partner, Selleres. Find out about the sheriff, too."

Jeff and Walt reached town as the swampers were dumping their mop buckets and tossing out the dirty sawdust from the previous day. Jeff, who sported a clean-shaven face and fresh haircut, opted for the livery. Walt ambled his mount down the street to the barbershop.

He entered and settled himself in a chair. "Trim and shave. Trim the mustache, too."

"Right away, sir," a mousey, pigeon-breasted individual with a pince-nez squeaked.

"Hear there's been some excitement in town since I left?" Walt probed gently.

"Oh, yes, yes indeed. Were you here when Mr. Lawrence Tucker was murdered?"

"Yep. Rode out the next day."

"Well, then, you don't know about the jailbreak!"

"What jailbreak?"

"Three desperadoes broke that Smoke Jensen out of the jail."

Walt noted that the barber—Tweedy was the name on the fancy diploma above the sideboard, bevel-edged mirror—omitted to mention the lynch mob in his colorful rendition of Smoke's escape. When he at last wound down, Walt remarked dryly, "That sounds like quite a tale, right enough. Are you sure those desperadoes weren't part of the Stalker gang?"

"Oh, no, not at all. Mr. Stalker lent his foreman and some of his hands to the posse the sheriff took out. He's got more out with him now."

"Then . . . this Jensen is still on the loose?"

"From what we've heard. Hold still now, I have to shear over your ears."

Scissorlike sounds came from the mechanical clippers in the hand of Tweedy. He shaped and trimmed in silence for a while, then bent Walt's head the other direction. "One more now, and we're almost through."

Two men entered and peered curiously at Walt. Under normal circumstances this constituted a serious insult to any man on the frontier. Well accustomed by his years on the dodge, Walt Reardon showed not a flicker of annoyance at the scrutiny. As it continued, though, another idea occurred to him.

"You—ah—lookin' for somebody you know, Mister?" he gravel-voiced at the nearer of the pair.

"No—no, just thought I'd seen you around."

"Maybe you have, but what business is it of yours?" Tweedy, a nervous, flighty type, dithered in agitation. "Now, now, gentlemen. I'm sure these fellows meant no disrespect, sir."

"I ain't heard from the other one yet," Walt growled.

A long second ticked by, then the smaller of the pair cut his eyes away from Walt Reardon's riveting stare. "No offense, Mister. We was lookin' for a friend."

"That's right," the other one blurted hastily, suddenly nervously conscious of the miles-long, gunfighter stare of Walt Reardon. "We expected him to be here ahead of us."

Walt sensed a pair of easy marks here, and produced a smile. "No offense taken, then. Tell you what. I'll buy you a drink when we get through."

"That's mighty white of you, Mister—ah?"

"Walt—" He cut it off, well aware that the name Reardon still meant gunfighter to many. "Kruger."

"I'm Sam Furgeson. This is Gus Ehrhardt. We'll just take you up on that drink, Walt. Say at the Hang Dog?"

"I know where it is. I'll be waitin' for you there."

Hands still shaking, barber Tweedy knicked Walt's left cheek with the straight razor. Wincing as though he had cut himself, the short, slender tonsorialist quickly dabbed with a towel and applied a piece of tissue paper to the tiny wound. "Sorry, there. Just a little slip."

"Make certain you don't slip like that when you get to my neck."

"Oh, no! Why, I'd never—" Tweedy caught a glimpse of those gunfighter eyes in the mirror, and choked off his protest.

* * *

Three riders, looking the part of ranch hands, rode into the livery stable shortly after Jeff York arrived there. Jeff knew they were not wranglers when they turned their mounts into nearby stalls and called to the old codger who ran the place to take care of them, then walked down the alternating stretches of boardwalk and hard-pounded pathway into the center of town. A lifetime of observation had told Jeff York that *real* cowboys would never walk anywhere. They would straddle their horses to go from one saloon to another, even if only two doors apart.

Jeff stood in the shade of the big livery barn and watched them ankle down the street. He marked the saloon they entered, then turned back to the liveryman. "They come in often?" he asked.

"Right as rain." He added a wink, a nod, and a sharp elbow in Jeff's ribs. "Some of Quint Stalker's randy crew. Real hard cases. Looks like they don't bother you none."

"Oh, they do. It's just I don't show it all that much," Jeff told him lightly.

"There's some things a feller could say about them, sure enough. The breed, if not them in partic'lar."

"Oh?" Jeff prompted gently.

"Them three do their best work on wimmin an' kids, way I hear it. Right tough hombres, when it comes to scarin' the bejazus outta some ten-year-old."

"Sounds like you don't hold them in great esteem?"

"Nawsir. They're lowlife trash, an' that's for sure."

Jeff gathered a few more tidbits and then made his way to the saloon the men had entered. The Blue Lantern turned out to be a dive. Hardly more than a road ranch, Jeff York evaluated it, as he pushed through the hanging glass bead curtain that screened the interior from passersby. He had barely turned left toward the bar, when one of the trio spun around, his fingers closed on the butt of a big Colt in a left-hand holster.

"You followin' us, Mister?" Apparently with odds of three to one, they had no qualms about bracing a full-grown man.

"No, not at all," Jeff responded in his calming voice. "I only got in town a bit ahead of you."

"An' waited all this time to come in here, huh?" The taunting tone turned to vicious challenge. "I say you're snoopin' around where you don't belong. You smell of lawdog to me. You want to prove otherwise, you'll have to do it with an iron in your hand."

Well, crap, Jeff York thought. Not in town a quarter hour, and already he had a gunfight on his hands.

Thirteen

In the split second that passed after Jeff York's recognition of the situation facing him, he made a quick decision to follow a maxim of Smoke Jensen. "Let speed work for you, but remain in control," the savvy gunfighter had advised Jeff during their sojourn in Mexico with Carbone and Martin. So, Jeff followed that suggestion now.

Jeff's Colt appeared in his hand in a blur. The sound of the hammer ratcheting back made a loud metallic clatter. Jaws sagged on the three gunnies, which drew their mouths into gaping ovals. They had not even made a move. The one with his hand on the grip of his six-gun released his hold instantly, his arm rising up and away from his body.

"Did any of you ever see a lawdog haul iron that fast?" Jeff asked in a sneer.

All three shook their heads in a negative gesture. Then the mouthy one recovered enough aplomb to get in a word or two. "Well, there is Elfego Baca."

"He don't count," one of his companions nervously blurted. "He's over Texas way right now. Besides, Baca's about half-outlaw anyway."

"Right. An' Sheriff Reno runned him out of town after

that dustup with McCarty an' his crew down in Frisco," the third hard case added.

"So what will it be, fellers?" Jeff demanded.

"Awh, hell, we was just a little proddy. We been out chasin' some jackass who killed a rancher here-about."

Jeff recalled that Stalker's men were serving with the posse. If he could completely defuse this situation, he might learn something useful, he surmised. "All right by me. I'm just gonna ease this hammer back down, and then I'll join you for a drink."

"Shore enough, Mister. Say, you got a name?"

"It's Jeff."

"Good enough for me." He made the introductions of his companions and the palpable tension in the room bled off in a relieved sigh from the bartender.

Walt Reardon had gone on ahead to the Hang Dog Saloon, where the two rough-edged ranglers from the barbershop joined him half an hour later. A short while before they arrived, a conversation at the bar drew his interest.

"Say, I sure wouldn't mind workin' for the B-Bar-H right about now," one obvious cowhand advised his friends.

"Why's that?" one of the latter asked.

"Ain't you heard, Yancy? That English feller that owns the place is fixin' to throw a real fiesta. Gonna be the get-together of the season, from what some of his hands have been sayin'."

"What's the occasion? He gettin' hitched?" another one asked.

"Maybe he found a place to sell beeves for more than twenty dollars a head," suggested a third with a snorting laugh.

"Way I got it, this here Benton-Howell is doin' it to honor some big shot politicians from Washington."

Mighty interesting, Walt thought to himself as he took another swig of beer. Might be we'll hear more about that, he speculated hopefully. The gossipy one continued.

"Gonna be in three days. Even the hands is invited. At least after the high mucky-mucks git their fill of vittles. They're roastin' a whole steer, doin' some *cabrito,* too. There'll be likker and music and dancing. Those are lucky boys to be workin' for that English dude."

Yancy had another question. "What's these politicians done to be honored for, Hank?"

Hank smirked. "Don't mean they done anything . . . yet. The way it is, politicians are always lookin' for a little somethin' extra, if you get my drift. So, it don't harm nothin' to have 'em in yer pocket, *before* you want a favor done."

Walt's new, slightly nervous friends banged through the door at that point, and the interesting revelations got tuned out.

Smoke Jensen spent the day in a fruitless search for any sign that could lead him to the men who had been pestering the Tucker family. From the confession he had gotten out of the wounded rustler, he knew that Quint Stalker and his gang were involved in that job. Could he be responsible for all the other harassment?

More than likely, Smoke considered as he headed his

big roan back to the ranch headquarters. Ty Hardy cut his trail some ten minutes later.

"What did you find?" Hardy asked Smoke.

"From the look on your face, the same as you."

Hardy grunted. "A whole lot of nothin'."

"Too much time has gone by. We can't sift any strange tracks from those of the hands. I've been hearin' about a lot of little incidents around the valley from Mar—ah—Miz Tucker. One of them is a trading post owner who got himself killed back a couple of weeks. From what I figure, it happened the same day I got away from that lynch mob. I know this might be just chasin' another whirlwind, but I'd like you to ride over that way and find out what you can."

The younger man nodded. "I can do that, Smoke. What was the man's name, and where do I find this trading post?"

"Ezekial Dillon. He ran his outpost at the far side of the valley, north and east of Socorro."

"I'll set off first thing in the morning."

When they returned to the barnyard, Jimmy Tucker met them with an enthusiastic welcome. "Mom says we got fried chicken, smashed taters an' gravy, an' cole slaw for supper. An' a pie. She also said that if it holds off hot like this after, Tommy an' me can go down to the crick for a swim. You want to come along?"

Grinning in recollection of his own sons' boyish exuberance, Smoke Jensen declined. Still close enough in age to be vulnerable to the call of such youthful enticements, Ty Hardy agreed to accompany the boys.

After a sumptuous spread of savory food, Smoke Jensen took his last cup of coffee out onto the porch and lit up a cigar. Pale, blue-white spirals rose from the glowing tip. The rich tobacco perfumed the air. Sniffing appreciatively, Martha Tucker joined him a short while later.

"My father smoked cigars. I always liked the aroma. I suppose that's one reason I married a cigar smoker," she informed Smoke in an unexpected burst of candor. "Have you been married long, Mr. Jensen?"

Smoke flushed slightly. "Many years," he answered. "How'd you reckon I was a married man?"

Martha did not need to think about her answer. "The way you are with the children; affectionate, but not overbearing. Also, I might add, the remarkable restraint you show in my presence." She blushed furiously.

Half-amused, and uncomfortably aware of her alluring presence, Smoke answered with some evasion. "Not long ago you believed I had murdered your husband. But, I'll thank you for considering a more noble motive. Yes, Sally has been my treasure for most of my grown life. We have a daughter of marrying age and three younger."

"You must miss them?"

"I do. This is a far piece from the High Lonesome," Smoke admitted.

"The High—? Oh, I understand," Martha went on quickly. "Your hands said your ranch was in the heart of the Rockies. It must be beautiful. So much variety, compared to the desert sameness everywhere one looks around here."

"You're right about that." Smoke took a long draw on the dark brown tobacco roll.

For all her determination, and her grief, Martha could not help herself, she realized. She found herself strongly attracted to the big, handsome, soft-spoken man from the mountains. He's as closedmouthed as he is strong, she mused, then put her thoughts to words.

"You're not very talkative, Mr. Jensen. Don't take that as a criticism. What I mean is, that you may not say a lot, but your words are filled with meaning. It takes a wise man to conduct himself like that."

"I'm flattered," Smoke said, finishing his coffee. He came to his boots. "I'll be headin' to the bunkhouse now. Ty's headin' out early in the morning, and I want a few words with him before he turns in. Provided, of course, your boys don't drown him down there at the creek."

Martha laughed with an ease that surprised her. "Good night, Mr. Jensen."

By nightfall, liquor had loosened plenty of tongues in the saloons of Socorro. Jeff York and Walt Reardon had each obtained several independent confirmations of the big fiesta to be held at the B-Bar-H. When they met in the *Comidas La Jolla* for a meal of *carne con chili verde,* they quickly discovered this.

"I'd say Smoke would be mighty interested," Walt opined after they had exchanged information.

"What I think he'd be most likely to want to know, is what's behind the festivities. I'm going to try to wangle you and me an invitation."

"You think you can do it?" Walt sounded doubtful.

"Should be easy. A rich, Arizona cattleman, interested in buying the seed bull I saw advertised at the feed mill. Inquiries to be addressed to Mr. Geoffrey Benton-Howell, of the B-Bar-H."

Walt Reardon gave him a blank look. "I'll be damned. I missed that one entire."

Jeff York gave him a friendly chuckle. "You've got to have a lawman's eye for small details, Walt. We'd best head for the Tucker place and fill in Smoke. Then I'll outfit myself in expensive clothes, do up a flash-roll of currency, and head for the office of Benton-Howell. Might be we'll find out what's behind all this without any effort at all."

Late the next afternoon, Geoffrey Benton-Howell effusively welcomed Steven J. York, of Flagstaff, Arizona, into his office. He ushered his visitor to a plush chair beside the huge cherrywood desk, and crossed to a sideboard where he poured brandy for two.

"This is the first personal inquiry I've received from such a distance," the Englishman informed Jeff in dulcet tones. "May I ask what excited you sufficiently about Herefordshire Grand Expositor to pay me this visit?"

Jeff York leaned back in the chair with a comfortable slouch, conveying his ease to an attentive Geoffrey Benton-Howell. "I know it's common practice, and I don't want you to take offense," he drawled. "But I've learned that in horse trading and cattle buying, it's best not to purchase sight unseen." He chuckled softly and sipped the brandy to soften the implication of distrust.

"A wise man, indeed," Benton-Howell responded as he clapped one big hand on a thigh. "Of course, before any transaction was completed, I would urge the buyer to make a personal inspection of Expositor. He's a fine Hereford bull, and I'm justifiably proud of him."

He studied his visitor, while the Arizona cattleman framed a response. Geoffrey saw a well-dressed man, turned out in dustless boots. A hand-tooled, concho-decorated cartridge belt, of Mexican origin no doubt, fitted snugly around a lean waist. A shaft of magenta sunlight put a soft glow to well-cared-for gun metal in the leather pocket. The suit had a flavor of Mexico in its cut, sort of the *haciendado* style favored by Miguel Selleres. The flat-crowned Cordovan sombrero clinched it for Benton-Howell. He bought the man as genuine.

"I've heard good things about crossing these new, short-horn, polled Herefords with range cattle. Improves the stock remarkably," Jeff spieled off from memory of conversations with the more progressive ranchers in Arizona Territory.

"More meat, more pounds, with less size. They're all the rage back East."

"Not many willin' to take the risk out here, I'll bet."

Benton-Howell nodded agreeably. "Not so far. Tunstil tried it, and some say that's what got him in the Lincoln County War. Some people are slow to accept any change. Take barbed wire."

Jeff made the expected nasty face at mention of the often lethal barriers. That encouraged Benton-Howell to risk planting yet another false lead to Smoke Jensen. "We had a fellow around here who loudly advocated the use of barbed wire. Said all the small Mexican farmers around Socorro needed it, to keep range cattle out of their fields. There's some say that's why a gunfighter named Smoke Jensen was hired to get rid of him."

"Smoke . . . Jensen? I've heard of him. Did this happen recently?"

"Only a couple of weeks ago. Rancher's name was Lawrence Tucker. He was thrown out of the Cattlemen's Association because of his stand on barbed wire." Benton-Howell chuckled lightly and took Jeff's glass for a refill. "Might be someone took the whole matter a bit more personally than others. For my own part, I say live and let live. God knows there's plenty of rocks around here. If the Mexicans want to protect their fields, let them busy themselves building stone walls. They've worked well enough in jolly old England, I dare say."

"Quite," Jeff responded, well aware of the irony of his sally. "Aah, thank you," he acknowledged the excellent brandy handed to him. "Now, when can I get to examine Expositor?"

"How long did you intend to stay in Socorro?" Benton-Howell inquired.

"Two or three days. As long as it took to see this championship animal of yours."

Benton-Howell thought for a long moment. "I'm having a rather gala soirée at the ranch two days hence. I would be honored, if you would attend. You can see Expositor, and I can introduce you to some gentlemen who might be of some benefit to you over in Arizona."

"Sounds good to me. I've always liked nice parties— enjoy good grub, good whiskey, and interesting company." Jeff was enjoying himself, playing the role to the hilt.

"You're staying at the hotel?" At Jeff's nod, Benton-Howell went on. "I'll have one of my hands meet you there tomorrow, escort you to the ranch."

"Much obliged, Mr. Benton-Howell. It's sure nice doin' business with a gentleman like yourself." Jeff finished off the brandy and rose to his boots to leave. "Oh, I have my foreman along with me. He's a better judge of prime cattle than I am. Would you mind, if I bring him along?"

"Oh, not at all. He'll be most welcome. Until tomorrow, then, Mr. York?"

"Hasta la vista."

Down on the street, as Jeff York strode away from the brick bank building, he congratulated himself on catching a mighty big fish. That, or he'd gotten himself into one damn dangerous situation.

Out at the Tucker ranch, Smoke Jensen made his own plans for the day of Benton-Howell's big fiesta. He wanted to be on hand to inspect the layout firsthand. To do so, he would have to make a scout of the place. And that night seemed ideally suited to his needs. He asked Martha Tucker for directions and rode out an hour before sundown.

While midnight beckoned with stygian darkness, Smoke Jensen crested a piñon-studded ridge and started down the back slope. Only the scant, frosty light of stars illuminated his surroundings. Well and good, Smoke thought to himself. If Benton-Howell had night riders posted, he had a better chance of eluding them this night. What he had in mind could all go up in a flash, if some nighthawk stumbled on him prematurely.

Might be he was overcautious, Smoke decided, as he descended the eastern grade that formed the bowl valley which housed the B-Bar-H. The thicket of trees grew denser the further he drifted toward the distant ranch house. He wanted to check out sites within long-rifle range of the area where the fiesta would be held, in the event he needed to make use of them.

Smoke had used this tactic with telling effect in earlier confrontations with some of the evil trash that infested the frontier. Not one to discard a useful strategy, he always considered employing it when presented the opportunity. Preacher had seen to it that a much younger Smoke Jensen had learned to be an effective fighter, even when entirely alone. Yet, he didn't like being out of contact with Jeff York. No idea what might develop there. He had to live with it, though.

The widespread nature of this sinister business made it necessary to go at it from more than one direction at a time. He recalled situations in the past when it would have been convenient to be able to divide himself in two or even three parts. A sudden flare of yellow light alerted Smoke that Benton-Howell had put out sentries.

Not very smart ones, at that. The flare of a match not only gave away the position of a guard, but destroyed his night vision long enough for him to lose his hair, if there were Indians about. One of the first lessons Preacher had taught him, Smoke thought grimly. Now he would have to find out how many there might be, and where.

Smoke combined his missions. He worked his way with great caution around the crescent face of the ridge through the long hours of early morning. A thin line of gray brightened the eastern horizon when he finished scouting the ranch. Another hour on foot took him away from the area far enough so that he could risk mounting and riding off toward the Tucker spread.

It would take some doing, but he could spoil Benton-

Howell's little party right easily. "And that's the way I like it," Smoke said aloud to himself.

"Viejo Dillon come to these mountains long time ago," the wrinkle-faced, Tuwa grandfather related to Ty Hardy, both men seated outside his summer brush lodge.

"I hear he was killed recently," Ty prodded.

A curt nod answered him. The old man looked off a moment, then spoke in his lilting manner. "It's supposed to look like a thief took things. But this one's eyes saw the men who came."

"Do you know them?" Ty hadn't thought of getting this much so fast.

"Oh, yes. Very bad men—*malos hombres.* The big one . . . their chief . . . this one has seen him before. He is called Stalker."

Ty's eyes widened, and he fought to keep his expression calm. "You are sure of this? Did you tell the law about it?"

The Tuwa shrugged. "Why do this? This Stalker and the *Jefe* Reno are like two beans in a pod, this one is thinking."

How many other unexposed secrets lay buried in this old gray head? And those of others like him. Ty had learned much about respect for Indians from Smoke Jensen. And, Ty considered, the old man sure had the sheriff down right.

"Thank you, Hears Wind. I will hold your words close to me."

"You tell the *Jefe* Reno?" Anxiety lighted the obsidian eyes.

"I don't think so. I work for another man. Smoke Jensen."

Hear Wind's expression changed to one of pleasure. "His name is known to our people. That one walks tall with honor. You are fortunate to be one of his warriors. Go with the sun at your back."

Ty Hardy left with the certain knowledge that he had learned something important, and also that he had been honored simply for being one of Smoke Jensen's hands. Powerful medicine, as the Injuns said.

Fourteen

Still done up as a wealthy rancher, Jeff York, along with Walt Reardon, arrived at the B-Bar-H mid-afternoon the next day. Not a lot of originality in that name, Jeff thought for the tenth time since discovering the notice of sale in the feed mill office. He was greeted by Geoffrey Benton-Howell in person; he had come out the day of their meeting to oversee final preparations.

"Glad you came," the Englishman remarked abruptly. "I'll introduce you to some of the other guests who journeyed out early. Then I'll show you Expositor."

"That's my main interest," Jeff replied.

On a wide, flagstone veranda, several portly men, dressed in the typical garb of Washington politicians, lounged in large wicker chairs. All had drinks in their hands, and it was obvious to Jeff York that these were not their first for the day.

Benton-Howell ushered Jeff and Walt from one to the next, making acquaintances. Uniformly, their handshakes were weak, soft, and insincere. Not a one of them has done a day's work in his life, thought the Arizona Ranger. A white-jacketed servant shoved a cut crystal glass of bourbon into Jeff's hand, and he took an obligatory pull.

After their first drinks had been drained, Walt ac-

knowledged a signal from Jeff and excused himself. He
wanted a good look around the ranch. Most of the next
half-hour conversation centered around competing ac-
counts of the importance of each man to the smooth
functioning of the federal government. Jeff York endured
it with less than complete patience. He felt genuine relief
and expectation, when Benton-Howell announced that he
intended to show off his prize stud bull.

"What do you think of them?" the corrupt rancher
asked, once he and Jeff were out of earshot of the guests.

"They're not long on sparkling conversation," Jeff replied cautiously.

"Boors, the lot of them. Boobies, too," Benton-Howell
snapped. "Although, quite necessary, if one is to operate
unhindered in your territory or mine. Well, then, here we
are," he concluded, directing Jeff into a small barn that
contained a single stall.

Expositor had a slat-level back, his face, neck, and
chest a creamy white mass of tight curly hair. The rest
of him, except for the tip of his tail, was a dark red-brown
with similar woolly appearance. The bull had one slab
side turned toward them, and he regarded them over a
front shoulder with a big, brown eye. Although a lawman,
rather than a stockman, Jeff considered him to be a magnificent animal, and said so.

"I thought you'd be impressed. He's barely four years
old, and he's already topped over three hundred heifers
and cows."

Jeff chuckled. "Wonder he isn't worn down to a nub-
bin'."

Geoffrey Benton-Howell had been away from England,
and on the frontier, long enough to understand. "Oh,

there's nothing wrong with his equipment. Far from it. If I had a cow in season, I'd show you."

They talked of the animal's performances for a while, then Jeff moved in close to look at the confirmation of the huge beast. "He's certainly blocky," Jeff observed.

"That's how you get the weight-to-size ratio to work out," Benton-Howell advised. "The bloodline came originally from Herefordshire." Benton-Howell pronounced the county name *Hair-ford-sure*. "They've revolutionized livestock raising back East. Even a man with a small farm can pasture thirty or forty head. Not like out here, where one needs a thousand acres for fifty head."

For a moment, Jeff began to doubt Benton-Howell's involvement in the murder of Lawrence Tucker, or anything else not above board. The man's expert knowledge of animal husbandry, and his obvious rapt interest in it, argued that it must be his main concern. Yet, why the obvious allusions to bribing or otherwise obtaining a favorable connection with the slippery striped-trouser crowd? Jeff would have to wait and see if something important came out at the fiesta the next day.

"What time does this shindig start tomorrow?"

"When the heat breaks over. About four o'clock, I would imagine," Jeff's host responded genially. Then he changed the subject. "Are you ready to buy Expositor right now?"

"He's a handsome critter, I'll allow. A lot bigger than I'd expected from the breed. I'd like to think on it awhile."

Benton-Howell clapped a hard hand on Jeff's firm shoulder. "Sleep on it, if you want. Enjoy what the ranch has for diversions tomorrow, and then give me your answer at the fiesta."

* * *

A festive atmosphere prevailed over the ranch headquarters the next morning from early on. Two huge,
stone-lined pits had been stoked with wood long before
dawn. With the contents reduced to glowing coals, half
a steer turned slowly over each of them. Whole goats
revolved on smaller spits on fires of their own. Ranch
hands worked clumsily at unfamiliar tasks, erecting
striped canvas awnings to provide shade and a pretense
of coolness, setting up tables under them and laying out
tableware and napkins. More guests began arriving
shortly after an early breakfast. Jeff York took careful
note of the occupants of each buggy, and consigned to
memory the name and position of each visitor.

"And this is Senator Claypoole," Benton-Howell introduced yet another to York. "He's on the committee for
Indian Affairs. Steven York from Arizona," he concluded.

Claypoole had a politician's, glad-hander shake, pale
blue eyes dancing with merriment. "A pleasure, sir. Are
you a cattle breeder, too?"

"No. I raise cattle for market."

"I see." The good senator cooled off, wondering why
a common rancher had been invited. "Sparse vegetation
over Arizona way, I'm told. How many hundred head can
you feed?"

"Not hundreds," Jeff exaggerated wildly, "thousands.
I run five thousand head this time of year. And I hold
most of the mountain pasture from Flagstaff to Globe in
the Tonto Range."

Claypoole warmed immediately. This was a big rancher. "I—ah—stand corrected. How do you manage such a vast area? Aren't the Indians a constant threat?"

Jeff gave him a warm smile. "Not really. If all the Indians killed in the dime novels had been for real, there wouldn't be an Apache left alive. I've found that the Eastern journalists tend to embellish the truth."

Another carriage, a mud-wagon stage coach hired for the occasion, rumbled in with more politicians. That ended the exchange between Jeff York and Senator Claypoole, much to Jeff's relief. Benton-Howell took him in tow and made him acquainted with the newcomers. From the corner of one eye, Jeff noted that Claypoole made directly for the heavily laden liquor table.

The heavy drinking began around ten-thirty. Jeff held onto a single tumbler of whiskey and took sparing sips from it. He began to wonder what Smoke Jensen had in mind for this gala party. Knowing the gunfighter as he did, Jeff could not see Smoke passing up such an opportunity.

Noontime came, and still no sign of the fine hand of Smoke Jensen. Many of the ranch hands drifted in during the next hour. They all had the look of second-rate gunhawks to Jeff. The rich aromas of cooking meat and pots of beans, field corn, and other delights filled the air. Jeff had emptied his glass and had turned back to the beverage table, when he found himself face-to-face with a man he knew only too well.

"What the hell you doin' here, Ranger?" Concho Jim Packard growled in a low, menacing voice.

"Excuse me? You've got me mixed up with someone else," Jeff tried hard to misdirect the desperado.

"Not a chance. No gawdamned Arizona Ranger kills

three of my best friends and I don't remember him."
Packard turned to search the crowd for his employer.
"Hey, Boss," he shouted over the buzz of conversation.
"You done brought a rattlesnake into your nest."

Geoffrey Benton-Howell came over at once. "What
are you talking about?"

"This one," Concho Jim snarled, pointing at Jeff.

"Why, Mr. York's my guest. He's come to buy Expositor," Benton-Howell spluttered.

"He has like hell! His name's York, right enough, but
it's Jeff York, Arizona Ranger," Concho Jim grated out.

Strong hands closed on Jeff York's arms before he
could react or try to make a break. Benton-Howell gave
him a disbelieving look, then cut his eyes to Concho Jim.
"You're sure of this?"

"Damn right I am. He got me locked up in the territorial
prison for six years, killed three of my partners, too."

Unseen, but witnessing it all, Walt Reardon made a
quick evaluation of the situation. Two guns against all
those present made for poor odds. Better that he get
away from here and find Smoke Jensen. He edged his
way out of the crowd and made for the livery barn and
his horse.

Frowning, Benton-Howell lowered his voice and addressed the gunhands holding Jeff. "Let's not make a
spectacle of this. Take him away quietly. Lock him in the
tool shed. We'll deal with our spy later, after our distin-
guished guests have eaten and drunk enough to forget
about it."

Careful to create the least disturbance possible, the
hard cases lifted Jeff York clear of the ground and carried
him to a shed out of the direct sight of the partying poli-

ticians. There they disarmed him and threw him inside.
A drop bar slammed down, and Jeff heard the snick of
a padlock.

By three o'clock that afternoon, most of the guests of
Geoffrey Benton-Howell had forgotten the small disturbance in the side yard of the ranch house. Great mounds
of barbecued beef and goat *(cabrito)* filled the serving
tables, where a splendid buffet had been laid out. Laughing and talking familiarly, as colleagues do, they lined
up to pile Benton-Howell's largess on their plates. Some
tapped a toe to unfamiliar strains of music.

Mariachi musicians played their bass, tenor, and alto
guitars, Jaliscan harp, and trumpets with gusto. Songs
such as *La Golandrina, Jalisco, Cielo de Sonora,* and
El Niño Perdido, won applause and praise from the visitors from Washington. Three white-aproned cooks toiled
over the pots of beans, bowls of salsa, skillets of rice,
platters of corn boiled in its shucks, and, of course, the
savory meat, as they ladled and served the festive
crowd. Beer, whiskey, and brandy had flowed freely
since mid-morning. It kept everyone in a jolly mood.

Yes, his fiesta was going exceedingly well, Geoffrey
Benton-Howell thought to himself as he gazed on this
industrious activity. It continued to go well until a whole
watermelon, taken from among half a dozen of its twins
in a tub of icy deep well water, exploded with a wild
crack, and showered everyone in the vicinity with sticky,
red pulp.

* * *

Smoke Jensen shifted his point of aim and destroyed a line of liquor-filled decanters in a shower of crystal shards that cut and stung the now terrified guests. He levered another .45-70-500 round into the chamber, and blasted a round into a large terracotta bowl of beans, showering more of the politicians with scalding *frijoles*. That made it time to move on to the next position.

Two hours earlier Smoke had met with Walt Reardon. The ex-gunfighter had come upon Smoke with the news of Jeff York's unmasking and capture. Quickly he panted out his account of events. He concluded with, "They put him in a little shed out of the way of the party."

"With the right distraction, do you think you could get in there and get Jeff out?"

Walt grinned. He had a fair idea of what Smoke Jensen considered the "right distraction."

"Damn right."

"Then, let's ride."

They made it back unseen to the ridge overlooking the B-Bar-H headquarters. Walt ambled his mount down a covered route back to the party. He soon found he had not been missed. No one, in fact, paid him the least attention. He took up a position close to the tool shed and waited for Smoke to join the dance.

Smoke Jensen had a clear field of fire over the whole ranch yard. He used it to good advantage, firing four more rounds, then reloading the Express rifle on the move to another choice location. Two of Benton-Howell's hard cases had more of their wits about them than the others. They grabbed up rifles and began firing back.

Their spent rounds kicked up turf a good two hundred yards short of Smoke's last position. Smoke knelt and shouldered the .45-70-500 Express, and squeezed off another shot. The bullet made a meaty smack when it plowed into the chest of one rifleman. The dead man's Winchester went flying, as he catapulted backward and flopped and twitched on the ground. His cohort made a hasty retreat. Then Smoke went to work on the nearest buffet table.

A stack of china plates became a mound of shards as Smoke's rifle spoke again. A short, stout congressman from Maine yelped, and popped up from the far side of the table like a jack-in-the-box. He lost his expensive bowler hat to Smoke's next round. With a banshee wail, the portly politician ran blindly away from the killing ground.

He crashed headlong into a Territorial Federal judge. They rebounded off one another, and the little man wound up on his butt. "I say, Judge, someone is trying to kill us," he bleated.

"Congressman Ives, you are an ass," the judge thundered. "If whoever is out there wanted to kill us, we'd be dead. Like that outlaw thug who returned fire. Now, get ahold of yourself, man, before someone thinks you're a coward."

When another watermelon showered those nearby with wet shrapnel, Walt Reardon considered the confusion to be at maximum. Lips set in a thin, grim line, he made his move. He approached the shed from the rear. Rounding one side Walt placed himself behind a guard posted by Benton-Howell. With a swift, sure move, Walt drew his six-gun and screwed the muzzle into the sentry's right ear.

"I'll have the key to that lock, if you don't mind," Walt growled.

"What the hell—!"

"Do it now, or I'll put your brains all on one side of your head."

"You son of a bitch, you don't have a chance," the gunhawk displayed the last of his rapidly waning bravado.

"I'm talking the outside," Walt snarled, and gave his Colt a nudge.

It took less than a second for the thoroughly cowed hard case to fish a brass key from his vest pocket. His hand trembled, when he raised it above his shoulder. Walt Reardon snatched the key with his left hand.

"Thanks, buddy," he told his prisoner a moment before he clubbed him senseless with the barrel of the Peacemaker.

Walt bent to the lock on the door of the shed, as Smoke shifted his aim to the house. Smoke had already scattered the striped-pants politicians in utter panic. Some had fled to the carriages that had brought them, and driven off in reckless abandon. Others dived into corrals, Smoke noted with amusement, where fresh, still-warm cow pies awaited them.

Now the last mountain man listened to the satisfying tinkle of glass, as he shot out windows and trashed the interior of one room after another. A sudden gout of black soot from a chimney told Smoke a ricochet had hit a stove pipe. Half a dozen females—painted ladies provided by Benton-Howell to entertain the politicians— came shrieking out every door visible from Smoke's position.

While he kept up this long-range destruction, Smoke kept an eye on an unpainted shed, its boards faded gray by the intense New Mexico sun and desiccating effects of the desert. It was there, Walt Reardon had told him, that Geoffrey Benton-Howell had confined Jeff York. Smoke saw the guard stiffen, and a hand appear with a six-gun poked in the hapless fellow's ear. Good work, Smoke mentally complimented Walt. Now it's time to make a stir down there.

When Walt opened the door and Jeff came stumbling out into the light, Smoke shifted his aim once more. Two of the outlaw trash Benton-Howell hired walked rapidly toward Walt, each with a hand on a gun. The third mother of pearl button on one hard case centered on the top of the front post of Smoke's Express rifle. The weapon slammed reassuringly into his shoulder, and a cloud of powder smoke obscured the view. A stiff northwesterly breeze cleared it away in time for Smoke Jensen to see the impact.

Shirt fabric, blood, and tissue flew from the front of the gunhawk's chest in a crimson cloud. It slammed him off his boots, and he hit the ground first with the back of his head. No headache for him, Smoke thought. He shifted his sights to the second saddle tramp in time to see him jackknife over his cartridge belt and pitch head-long into hell. Smoke cut his eyes to where he had last seen Jeff and Walt.

A thread of blue-white smoke streamed from the muzzle of Walt's six-gun. He and Jeff advanced on their challengers, and Jeff stooped to retrieve both of their weapons. Smoke took advantage of the lull to shove more fat rounds in the loading gate of the Winchester Express. Time to move, he decided.

From his fourth location, Smoke had a clear view of the other side of the headquarters house. The windows quickly disappeared in a series of tinkling, sun ray-sparkling showers. Faintly, Smoke Jensen made out the rage-ragged bellow of Benton-Howell.

"Goddamn you, Smoke Jensen!"

At least he knew who had paid him a visit, Smoke allowed with a smile. From his final position, where he had left his roan stallion tied off to a ground anchor, Smoke Jensen gave covering fire, while Walt Reardon and Jeff York burned ground out of the B-Bar-H compound. Smoke chuckled as he mounted and set off obliquely to join them, well out of range and sight of the terrorized mass of milling men below.

"Smoke Jensen?" The name echoed through the raddled politicos after Geoffrey Benton-Howell's furious bellow.

Livid with outrage, their host stomped around the flagstone veranda of his house, looking bleakly at the broken windows, shredded curtains, the bullet holes in the interior walls. He cursed blackly and balled his fists in impotent wrath.

"Everything is under control, gentlemen. Don't let this act of a mad man interrupt our celebration today. Come, fill your plates, get something to drink. You there, strike up the music." Then Benton-Howell turned away and hid his bitter anger from the still-shaken politicians. "I know it was him," he shouted to the skies as though challenging the Almighty. "It was Smoke Jensen. Somehow . . . he's . . . found . . . out."

Most of those present had no idea of what he meant. Miguel Selleres, who had taken a slight nick in the left shoulder, knew only too well. He hastened to the side of his co-conspirator. "Softly, *amigo,* softly! It would not do to bring up such unpleasant matters in the presence of our guests. You have suffered enough loss today."

"How do you mean?" Benton-Howell demanded.

"When the shooting stopped, all but two of your working hands rolled their blankets and departed. They don't like being shot at."

Benton-Howell blanched. "Damn them! Cowards, the lot. Oh, well, they were only fit for nursing cows anyway."

"One does not run a ranch without someone to nurse the cows, *¿como no?*" Selleres softened his chiding tone to add, "I can lend you some men, until you can hire more. Or clear up this difficulty with Smoke Jensen."

"Thank you, my friend." Benton-Howell clapped Selleres on his uninjured shoulder. "Now, I want the—ah—other hands to assemble outside the bunkhouse. Tell those hired guns of Quint Stalker's to hunt down Smoke Jensen and *kill* him, or don't come back for their pay!"

Fifteen

Much to his discomfort, Forrest Gore had to deliver orders to the hard cases hired on to do Benton-Howell's dirty work. With the boss gone, leadership devolved on Payne Finney, who had sent him out to take over the boys in the field. Finney was making slow progress in his recovery from the pellet wounds given him by Smoke Jensen. If he could speak honestly, Finney would prefer to have nothing further to do with Smoke Jensen. Absolute candor would reveal that he feared the man terribly.

With good cause, too, Payne Finney told himself as he sat in the study of the B-Bar-H, covering ground already talked out with Geoffrey Benton-Howell. He had never seen a man so skillful that he could divide a shot column between two targets. Benton-Howell's next words jolted him.

"I don't care if you have to use a buggy. I want you out there looking for Smoke Jensen." Half of the influential men he had gathered at the ranch had failed to return after the shooting ended. It put a damper on the conviviality of those who remained. He hadn't even been able to broach the subject of cutting away a portion of the White Mountain Apache reservation.

"I take my orders from Quint, the same as all the

others," Payne began to protest. "I'm still weak from being shot. I doubt the men would do what I told them."

Benton-Howell's fist hit the tabletop like a rifle shot. "They had damned well better! Stalker isn't here now. You give the orders; I'll see they are obeyed."

Payne Finney winced at the pain that shot from the knitting holes in his lower belly as he came to his boots. He accepted the finality of it with bitterness. "I'll do my best."

Half an hour later, Payne Finney rode out of the B-Bar-H on the seat of a buckboard. His face burned with the humiliation of being reduced to such a means of transportation, and for being talked down to like some lackey on the mighty lord's tenant farm. His saddle rested in the back, along with supplies he carried for the men searching for Smoke Jensen. His favorite horse trailed behind, reins tied to the tailgate. With effort, he banished his resentment and thought of other things.

If Finney had his way, Smoke Jensen would be run to ground in no more than two days. After all, the man was flesh and blood, not a ghost. He had to eat and sleep and eliminate like any other man. And Payne Finney had brought along the means of ensuring that Smoke Jensen would be found.

Seated right behind him, tongue lolling, was a big, dark brindle bloodhound. All they would have to do is find a single place Smoke Jensen had made camp, and put the beast on his trail. That's why Finney gave the ambitious estimate of two days. He raised himself slightly off the seat, and his right hand caressed the grip of his .44 Smith and Wesson American.

"Goodbye, Smoke Jensen, your butt is mine," he said

aloud to the twitching ears of the horses drawing the wagon.

Forrest Gore had his own ideas about finding Smoke Jensen. "It's goddamned impossible," he declared to the five men gathered around a small pond in the Cibola Range.

"Smoke Jensen camped here last night. We all know that," Gore lectured to his men. "Then he rode out to the west early this morning."

He was wrong, but he didn't know it yet. Ty Hardy had spent the night there, and ridden back to the Tucker Ranch shortly before first light. Two of the hard cases, suspecting that they chased the wrong will-o'-the-wisp, muttered behind gloved hands. A minute later, Smoke Jensen proved them right.

With startling effect, a bullet cracked over their heads and sent down a shower of leaves. Forrest Gore jumped upright and hugged the bole of a tree, putting its bulk between him and the direction from which the slug came. Then the sound of the shot rippled over the mountain slopes.

"We been set up," another gunhawk announced unnecessarily. "That's Smoke Jensen out there, and he's got us cold."

"I'm gettin' out of here," the fourth man announced.

"No! Wait," Forrest Gore urged. "Keep a sharp eye. When he fires again, we can spot where he is, split up, and close in on him."

Vern Draper snorted in derision. "By the time we get there, he'll be gone."

"Yeah, an' firin' at us from some other place," Pearly Cousins added.

Forrest Gore gave their words careful consideration. They had been hunting Smoke Jensen for the better part of two weeks now. With always the same results. The bastard was never seen, and they got shot at. Maybe it wasn't Smoke Jensen at all? With a troubled frown, Gore worked his idea over out loud.

"What if that's not Jensen at all? What if it's one of those hands of his, who broke up the lynch mob? It ain't possible that he was down in San Antonio and leadin' you fellers around by the nose up here in the Cibolas at the same time."

"I don't think it was him down there," Cousins opined.

"Who else could do in four of our guys, and send Charlie Bascomb runnin' with his tail 'twixt his legs?" Gore challenged. "I say we're lookin' in the wrong place. I say we leave whoever it is up here to hisself, and head south."

"You better clear that with Quint," Vern Draper suggested pointedly.

"Quint's busy elsewhere. Payne sent me out here to help you find Smoke Jensen. I think he's clean out of the area. So, we go where he is."

Another round from the Express rifle of Smoke Jensen convinced the others to follow the rather indistinct orders of Forrest Gore.

Later that day, Smoke Jensen met with Jeff York and the hands from the Sugarloaf. They sat around a table in the bunkhouse at the Tucker ranch, cleaning their weapons and drinking coffee. Smoke made an announcement that caught their immediate attention.

"Looks like the searchers are being pulled out of the mountains. I think it's time to pay another visit to the B-Bar-H."

Jeff produced a broad grin. "I sorta hoped you'd do that. I want to pay my respects to Sir Mucky-muck."

They rode out half an hour later. Ty and Walt went deeper into the Cibolas, to track and harass the hard cases with Gore. Also to determine where they might be headed. Smoke and Jeff covered ground at a steady pace.

An hour before nightfall, they reached the tall, stone columns with the proud sign above that declared this to be the B-Bar-H. Smoke studied the fancy letters a moment. Then he cut his eyes to Jeff.

"I think this is a good place to start," Smoke declared.

He loosed a rope from his saddle, and Jeff did the same. It took them only a minute to climb the stone pillars and affix their lariats to the edges of the sign. Back in the saddle, they made solid dallies around the horns, and walked away from the gateway. When the ropes went taut, the metal frame began to creak and groan. Smoke Jensen touched blunt spurs to the flanks of his roan stallion, and the animal set its haunches and strained forward.

Jeff York did the same, with immediate results. A loud crash signaled the fall of the wrought-iron letters. Badly bent and twisted, the B-Bar-H banner lay in a cloud of dust, blocking the entrance road. Smoke and Jeff retrieved their lassos and chuckled at their mischief, as they cantered off over the lush pasture grass. The rest of Smoke Jensen's plans contained nothing so lighthearted.

* * *

Geoffrey Benton-Howell had learned one thing from the attack on his headquarters. Smoke Jensen located the first night guard while a magenta band still lay on the mountains to the west. He signaled Jeff to ride on to their chosen spot, and put a gloved index finger to one eye to sign to keep a lookout for more sentries. Then he walked his roan right up to the guard.

"Who are you?" the surly hard case asked, a moment before Smoke Jensen drew with blinding speed and smacked the hapless man in the side of his head.

Well, perhaps they weren't all that much smarter than those he had encountered before. At least this one recognized a stranger when he saw one. Smoke dragged the unconscious outlaw from the saddle and trussed him up. He pulled the man's boots off and stuffed a smelly sock in a sagging mouth. Then, with the empty boots fastened in the stirrups, he smacked the rump of the gunhawk's mount and sent it off away from the house.

A short distance further, he found another one, similarly done up by Jeff York. Smoke smiled grimly and rode on. A roving patrol of two came into sight next. Smoke Jensen eased himself out of the saddle and slid through the tall grass. When the horsemen drew nearer, Smoke rose to the side of one silent as a wraith. Sudden movement showed him Jeff York likewise engaged.

One startled yelp came from an unhorsed hard case before Jeff had him on the ground and thoroughly throttled. Smoke's man made not a sound. Smoke came to his boots after tying the sentry, and waggled a finger at Jeff.

"Sloppy. He made a noise."

"Sorry, teacher," Jeff jibed back. "I'll do better next time."

"Might not be a next time before we're in position. I'd like to put them all down, before we start shooting."

"That'll take some time," Jeff observed.

"That's why we came early."

Smoke drifted off to recover his horse. Jeff York swore to himself that he had not even seen his friend start away. For a moment he had a flash of pity for the men they would encounter this night. Then he said softly to himself, "Nawh."

A quarter hour went by before Smoke found another night guard. The man sat with his back to a tree, eyes fixed on the higher ground away from the ranch house. Somewhat brighter than the others, Smoke reasoned. He had no reason to suspect someone coming from behind him. Too bad.

Easing up to the tree, Smoke bent around its rough bark and popped the unaware sentry on the head with a revolver barrel. It took only seconds to secure tight bonds. Then Smoke Jensen slipped on through the night. There would be a moon tonight. Smoke had taken that into consideration.

He and Jeff would fire and move, fire and move, until each had exhausted a full magazine load. Then time to leave, before the silver light of the late-rising half-moon made them too easy to see. All in all, he anticipated making life even more miserable for Geoffrey Benton-Howell.

* * *

Windows had been reglazed in most of the downstairs portion of the two-story frame house. Yellow lamplight spilled from one, as Smoke Jensen eased into a prone firing position on the slope above. He sighted in carefully, with the bright blue-white line of the burning wick resting on the top of his front sight. Slowly he drew a deep breath, let out half, and squeezed the trigger.

With a strong jolt, the steel butt-plate shoved his shoulder as the Winchester Express went off. While Smoke came to his boots, he listened for the tinkle of glass. It came seconds later, followed at once by sudden darkness within the house as the lamp exploded into fragments. An outraged voice wailed after it.

"Goddamnit! Jensen's back," Geoffrey Benton-Howell raged in the darkness.

While Smoke moved to his second location, Jeff let off a round from the opposite side of the house. Yells of consternation came from the bunkhouse, as the thin wall gave little resistance to a .44-40 slug. Grinning in the starlit night, Smoke dropped into a kneeling stance.

"Get in here, somebody! Damnit, this place is on fire," came a yelp from a now frightened Benton-Howell.

"*Tien paciencia, amigo,*" Miguel Selleres called out.

"Have patience, hell! I'll burn up in here."

An eerie new light glowed in the ruined window. It flickered and grew in intensity as Smoke Jensen sighted in once more, this time on the door across the room. He put a round about chest-high through the oak partition. A muffled scream came from the hall beyond. It served to notify Benton-Howell that he had a fat chance of getting out that way.

Smoke Jensen was already at a steady lope through

the trees, when the remaining glass in the sash tinkled and Geoffrey Benton-Howell dived through to escape the flames. Smoke stopped abruptly and fired a round into the pool of darkness directly below the window. A howl that blended into a string of curses told him he had come close, but not close enough. Jeff York shot twice this time, and dumped a man in the doorway of the bunkhouse with a bullet in one leg.

"Don't get overconfident, Jeff," Smoke whispered to himself.

From the position he had selected earlier, Smoke put a .45-70-500 round through a second floor window. At once, he heard the alarmed bellow of a man, nearly drowned out by the terrified shriek of a woman. His shoulder had begun to tingle. He knew from experience that it didn't take too many cartridges run through the big Winchester, to change that sensation to one of numbness. Three rounds left in the magazine tube.

Smoke wanted to make them count, so he swiftly changed positions. On an off chance, he put the next bullet through the outhouse at about what he estimated would be an inch or two above head high on an average man. He was rewarded with a howl of sheer terror as a man burst out the front of the chicksale, his trousers at half-mast. Legs churning, the Levis tripped the hard case and sent him sprawling. Two cartridges to go, then Smoke would meet Jeff where they had left their horses.

Unexpectedly a target presented itself in Smoke's field of fire. A huge man, barrel-chested, thick-shouldered, arms like most men's thighs, hands like hams, barreled around the corner of the house and snapped a Winchester to his shoulder. He fired blindly, the slug nowhere near

Smoke Jensen or Jeff York. Cursing, he worked the lever rapidly and expended all eleven .44-40 rounds.

Sprayed across the hillside, the next to the last found meat in horseflesh. Jeff York's mount squealed in pain and fright, reared, and fell over dead on its side. Anger clouded Smoke Jensen's face.

"Damn, I hate a man who'd needlessly kill a horse," Smoke grunted.

He took aim and, as the last bullet sped from the Winchester in the giant's hand, discharged a 500 grain slug that pinwheeled the shooter and burst his heart. Only twenty yards from his horse, Smoke put out another light in a downstairs window and hurried to the nervous roan.

Jeff York joined him a moment later, and began to strip the saddle off his dead mount. Smoke had the bridle and reins in one hand. "We'll double up," he informed Jeff.

"Make it easier to track and catch us," Jeff complained. "I'll walk out."

"No. I brought you here; I'll get you back. They aren't going anywhere for a while."

Jeff looked back toward the house. A bucket brigade had formed to douse the flames that roared from two rooms of the ranch house. With a whinny, a horse-drawn, two-wheel hand-pumper rolled up from a small carriage house next to the barn. A pair of hard cases ran with a canvas hose to the creek bank, and plunged the screened end into the water. At once four volunteers began to swing the walking arms up and down. An unsteady stream spurted from the nozzle.

"No, I guess you're right," he told Smoke.

Even so, Smoke Jensen wasted no time, nor spared

any caution in departing from the B-Bar-H. He left behind a cursing, shrieking, livid Geoffrey Benton-Howell.

After the large number of recent disasters, Benton-Howell had been forced to send for reinforcements. The nine men who had been patrolling the slope behind the house on the previous night had quit first thing after being found the next morning. Smoke Jensen had nearly succeeded in burning down his house. His study was a ruin. All meals were being prepared in the bunkhouse; the kitchen had burned out completely. Now he confronted one of the men he considered responsible for his current calamity.

Sheriff Jake Reno stood across the cherry wood desk in Benton-Howell's office above the bank. With him was the mayor of Socorro. Both wore sheepish expressions. Benton-Howell had poured copious amounts of his deep-seated vitriol over them. Only now had he begun to wind down.

"I didn't spend the money to get you two elected to hear a constant stream of reports of failure. I expected competence. I expected success. Now, I'm going to get it. I want your full cooperation. No complaints, no excuses, no lectures on why it can't be done. I'm putting out the word for every available gunhand in the Southwest, to come here to put an end to Smoke Jensen."

"I thought you wanted it all done legally," the sheriff protested.

"I wanted results!" Benton-Howell snapped.

Mayor Ruggles looked stricken. "You'll fill the streets of Socorro with saddle tramps and every two-bit gunslick around," he whined. "Think of the good people of the community."

"I am thinking of the good people—Miguel Selleres and myself."

"Why don't you simply offer a larger reward?" Jake Reno suggested.

Too tightfisted to raise the ante on Smoke Jensen's head, Geoffrey Benton-Howell spluttered a minute, then focused his disarrayed thoughts on a new proposition. "Without gunmen to collect it, that would only tie up more of my money. What's going to happen, is that the city is going to add a thousand dollars to the reward."

"What?" the mayor and sheriff echoed together.

"If you think it such a good idea for me to put out more funds for the purpose, then surely it behooves you to do it." To Mayor Ruggles he added, with a roguish wink, "Sort of putting your money where your mouth is, eh, old boy?"

In that quick, pointed thrust, Mayor Ruggles lost his head of steam. "If that's what you want, we'll see about it right away. Only let me appeal to you to keep the gun trash out of town."

"It's your posterior they'll be saving, as well as mine. You and Sheriff Eagle Eye here. Now, get out of here and run your errands like good little lads. I want fifty— no a *hundred* guns in here, and Smoke Jensen stretched over his saddle shortly thereafter."

Sixteen

Socorro became a busy place as the word went out for fast guns. Mayor Ruggles stewed and dithered, his anxious eyes scanning the rough-edged characters who swarmed the streets. The new posters came out with the wording: "$2000 Reward Offered for Capture Dead or Alive of the Killer of Lawrence Tucker." No mention was made of Smoke Jensen. It sounded good that way, all agreed.

Some of the gunfighters and wannabes who came to Socorro to search for the "killer," left suddenly when they learned the identity of the accused. Sheriff Jake Reno noted with some smugness that eleven no-reputation young pretenders departed in a group shortly after the mention of the name Smoke Jensen.

"Perhaps they decided that it was safer to travel in numbers," he confided to Morton Plummer at the Hang Dog shortly after they blew out of town.

"Considerin' who it is they were expected to run to ground, I'd say they're right smart fellers," Mort responded with a grin. He loved to tweak this pompous ass of a sheriff.

Reno scowled. "Watch that lip, Mort." He quickly downed his shot and beer and stormed out of the saloon.

Being on the payroll of Benton-Howell and Selleres had other drawbacks, Sheriff Jake Reno considered as he directed his boots toward the jail. Those politicos who remained behind had been frightened almost witless by that second visit from Smoke Jensen. Only an hour ago, Benton-Howell had summoned him to the office to demand that he put men on the ranch to keep the politicians there, until an agreement could be reached on his White Mountain project.

"Like he'd bought all my deputies, too," Reno complained aloud, as he hurried to round up men to guard the B-Bar-H.

He returned to the world around him in time to meet the cold, hard stare of one of a pair of gaunt- and narrow-faced men with the look of gunfighters about them. Their square chins jutted high in arrogance, and the mean curl of their lips had to come from hours of practice before a mirror. The one with black leather gloves folded over his cartridge belt spoke, revealing yellowed, crooked teeth.

"Sheriff. Just the man we wanted to see. How are we supposed to find this feller done killed your Mr. Tucker, if we don't know his name? Who is he, or do you know?"

"Oh, I know all right. The name is Smoke Jensen."

"Not *the* Smoke Jensen?" the sneering one blurted as his face grew pale.

"The only Smoke Jensen I know," Sheriff Reno replied, as he laughed inwardly at the discomfort his words sparked.

The sneer gone from his face, the gunhawk cut his eyes to his partner. They appeared to reach wordless agreement that concluded with a nod. "Do you happen to have any idea where he might be found?" The question seemed to lack conviction of being acted upon.

"Yep. He's hangin' out in the Cibolas, last I heard."

"Why ain't you got a posse out?" the taller of the two challenged.

"I already lost a dozen good men to that bastard. I don't reckon to reduce the whole population of Socorro to bring him outta there." It was a lie. Smoke Jensen had killed only three of the posse, wounded six or seven more. Also some twenty had quit all together. What Sheriff Reno wouldn't admit was that he couldn't get anyone to go after Smoke Jensen. Not even Quint Stalker's men.

"Bein' we're from Texas, which way is these Cibolas?"

Suspecting what would come next, Sheriff Reno waved his arm expansively. "All around here. To the east, north, and mostly to the west. That's where Smoke Jensen can be found, west of here, I'm certain of it."

"Thank you kindly, Sheriff," the tall one replied.

Together they crossed the boardwalk and mounted their horses, while Sheriff Reno watched in silence. They touched reins to necks and pointed the animals south. Face alight with quivering amusement, Sheriff Reno pointed out their error.

"West's that way, fellers."

"We know it," the second-string hard case with the black gloves replied in a low, gruff voice.

They barely cleared the business district of Socorro, down in its canyonlike draw, before they fogged out of town in a lather. Behind them, Sheriff Jake Reno bent double with a torrent of laughter that rose from deep within. He kept on until the tears ran, then laughed even more . . . until he counted score and realized that that made a record of twenty-two for one day, and left him with that many less to stand between him and Smoke Jensen.

Senator Claypoole examined the certificate authorizing him to draw on the Philadelphia mint for the sum of twenty thousand dollars in gold bullion. Carefully he folded it and placed it reverently in an inside coat pocket. He gave a beatific smile to Geoffrey Benton-Howell, and patted over the spot where he had deposited the draft.

"You are a gentleman and a scholar, Sir Geoffrey. Likewise a man of his word. Nice, anonymous gold has always appealed to me. It can be used anywhere."

Benton-Howell pushed back his castored desk chair and lit a fat cigar. The rich aroma of a Havana Corona-Corona filled the study at the B-Bar-H. "I dare say, if you fail to use your usual, impeccable, diplomatic skill in this, you might have need of somewhere else to spend that."

"I know. My colleagues and I shall invent some sort of reason why that land has to be separated from the reservation. Heaven forbid that we ever mention gold being found there. Too many others would want a piece of the pie, and spoil your project all together."

"You understand only too well, Chester. Now, then, I suggest a small tot of brandy to seal the bargain, and then I have others to see."

"Certainly."

Ten minutes later, Chester Claypoole had departed, and the leather chair opposite Benton-Howell had been occupied by His Honor, Judge Henry Thackery of the Federal District Court for the Territory of Arizona. His Honor didn't seem the least bit pleased. A heavy scowl furrowed his high, shiny forehead.

"You've handled this Smoke Jensen affair miserably, Geoff," he snapped, accustomed to being the ranking person in any gathering.

"I will admit to having erred slightly in regard to the security of my ranch headquarters," Benton-Howell answered with some asperity.

"It's a great deal more than that, Geoff. If it ever comes out that your man, Quint Stalker, arranged the scene of the crime to indicate the guilt of Smoke Jensen, you may find yourself seeking the life of a grandee down in Mexico, or even South America. Or worse still, standing on the gallows in Santa Fe. I certainly do not intend to be there beside you."

Benton-Howell fought to recover some of his sense of well-being. "And you shall not be, my friend. Judge, everything is arranged as you asked. Seven thousand, five hundred in gold coin, mostly fifties and twenties. It is right there in my safe. A like amount to be paid, whenever you are called upon to hear any challenge to our claim of the White Mountain reservation land."

Judge Thackery pondered a moment, pushed thin lips in and out to aid his musing. "That's satisfactory. However, Geoff, I must caution you. Smoke Jensen has to be dealt with swiftly and finally . . . or the consequences will fall on you."

Jeff York and Walt Reardon rode into Socorro with Smoke Jensen. They had come for supplies for the Tucker ranch. Martha's idea of hiding in plain sight seemed to have worked so far. Recently, Smoke began chafing at the inactivity, and expressed a willingness to test how anonymous he had become. Walt halted the buckboard at the rear loading dock of the general mercantile, and dismounted.

"Jeff and I are going to amble over and visit with Mort Plummer at the Hang Dog, while the order is filled."

"Fine with me. I'll meet you there when it's loaded," Smoke replied.

"We'll be waitin', Kirby," Jeff drawled, a light of mischief in his eyes.

Being a purloined letter did not include speaking Smoke's name in public. Jeff had wormed Smoke's given name out of him for just such events as this. From the pained expression on the face of the gunfighter, Jeff gathered that Kirby was not Smoke's favorite handle. Walt untied his saddle horse from the tailgate of the wagon, and stepped into a stirrup. Together, he and Jeff rode to the mouth of the alley and turned left on the main street.

Business was sparse in the saloon at this early hour. Only a handful of barflies lined the mahogany, shaky hands grasping the first eye-opener of the day. Walt and Jeff ordered beers and settled at a table near the banked and cold potbelly stove. Walt started a hand of patience.

"You ever play two-handed pitch?" he asked Jeff.

"Yeah. About as exciting as watching grass grow."

"Now, I don't know about that," Walt defended the game. "If it's four-point, a feller's got a whole lot of guessin' to do to figure out what his opponent is holdin'."

"For me, I like to have all the cards out. Seven players is my sort of game."

"What about that fancy game all the hoity-toity Eastern dudes play—whist?"

"Not for me," Jeff declined. "I'm a five-card-stud man myself."

Walt chuckled. "Now yer talkin'. I ain't had a good hand of poker for nigh onto six months. Nobody on the Sugarloaf will play with me anymore."

"You win too much?"

"You got it, Jeff. And honest, too. No dealing seconds or off the bottom, either. Never stacked a deck in my life."

Two young wranglers stomped into the saloon. They turned to the bar at once, and did not take notice of the pair in conversation at the table. Jeff York had a good look at them, though. He grew visibly tense and sat quite still.

When they had sipped off their first shots and chased them with beer, the tall, lanky blond turned from the bar and peered into the shadowed corner that contained Jeff York and Walt Reardon. His face took on an expression of extreme distaste.

"I'll be goll-damned, Sully. It's that no-account Ranger from back home."

"You're seein' things, Rip. We's in New Mexico now."

"Nawh, I'm right. Turn around an' see for yourself. I know an asshole, when I see one."

Walt Reardon cut his eyes to Jeff York's muscle-tightened face. Jeff knows this pair, that's a fact, he reasoned. This could get deadly in about a split second. He scooted back his chair, came to his boots, and started for the rear.

"Got to hit the outhouse," he announced to Jeff, but cut his eyes toward the location of the general store. Jeff nodded.

"Hey, Rip, you're right," Sully declared as he turned to look Jeff's way. "It's the same lawdog that locked us away in Yuma prison for three years. Like to have kilt me, heavin' all them big rocks onto the levee. Bit far from your stompin' grounds, ain'tcha, Ranger?"

"You're making a mistake, Sullivan," Jeff grated out.

"Nope. Way I sees it, it's you've made a big mistake. They's two of us . . . and this time our backs ain't turned."

Jeff rose slowly, shook his head in sad recollection. "Never could abide a liar, Sully. You two were facing me that day in Tombstone. Didn't either one of you clear leather before I had you cold. I did it then, I can do it now."

"You've got older now, slower, Sergeant York."

"No. It's Captain now, and I'm not getting older . . . only better."

Two more second-rate fast guns stepped through the batwings and took in the action. "Sully, Rip, you got some fun lined up?" the chubby one asked.

"That we have, Pete. Just funnin' with an old acquaintance from Arizona. Ain't that right, Ranger York?"

"Can we get a piece of him, too, Sully?" the skinny teen next to Pete asked eagerly.

"Sorry, Lenny. When I get through, I don't reckon there'll be enough left to go around," Sully refused the offer, a sneer aimed at Jeff York.

"You're forgetting the Ranger here has a friend along," Mort Plummer said from behind the bar. He hoped to delay the inevitable. To at least get the killing started out in the street, not in his bar.

"He run out at the git-go. Plumb yellow," Sully brayed.

"I don't think so," the bar owner countered. "I sort of recognize him from a while back. Never asked him personal, understand? But I figger him to be Walt Reardon, the gunfighter from Montana."

"No wonder he ran. I hear he lost his belly a long while ago."

"Not so's you'd notice," Walt Reardon announced, as he pushed his way between Pete and Lenny. He was followed a second later by Smoke Jensen.

"I'm gonna go get the rest," Lenny declared, as he moved his boots quickly through the door.

Mort Plummer chose that moment to avoid damage to his property. "Get out. The bar's closed."

Sully turned back to him. "I don't think so. Pour me another shot, and set up the boys, too, when they come."

"Get out of my saloon."

"You pushin' for a bullet all your own, barkeep?"

Mort Plummer tried to stare Sully down, but it was Smoke Jensen who answered. "You've got a nasty mouth. Too bad you don't have a brain to go with it."

Two of the town drunks, who blearily recognized Smoke Jensen from the day of the lynch mob, beat a hasty retreat. One literally dived through the space below the spring-hinged batwings. He collided with the legs of five proddy outlaw trash. Lenny led the way as they entered. Mort Plummer had gone white with fear. The hard case quintet spread out and faced off against three coldly professional guns. Eight to three. Pretty good odds, the way Sully figured it.

"You boys have no part of this," Jeff told the new-comers. "Walk out now, and no harm will come of it."

Sully's eyes never left Jeff. "You boys have a drink on me, then I'll open this dance."

"No. I will," Smoke Jensen contradicted. Smoke's .44 leaped into his hand, leveled at Sully's belt buckle, before the wannabe gunhawk's hand could even reach his. Smoke forced a sneer to his lips. "You're too easy."

The humiliation of having been tossed back, like an undersized fish, pushed Sully to unwise desperation. He foolishly completed his draw.

"Goddamn ya, I'll kill ya all."

Smoke Jensen didn't even bother with him. Jeff York had iron in motion, and completed the life of the petty outlaw with a round to the heart. Sullivan never even fired a shot. Three of the gang of outlaws-turned-bounty hunter had their own six-guns in play. Smoke shot one of them in the upper right chest, and put another down with a .44 slug in the thigh.

When that one went down, three of the remaining shooters pounded boots on the floor in an effort to widen the space between them all. Walt Reardon tracked one, and took him off his boots with a bullet in the side. Jeff accounted for another. But the third had disappeared. Sudden motion behind Smoke Jensen's back ripped a warning from Mort Plummer, who had ducked below the thick front of his bar and had seen the reflection in the mirror.

"Look out, Smoke!"

"Smoke Jensen!" Pete and Rip yelled at the same time.

"Oh, my God! I give up," Lenny wailed. "Don't shoot me, Mr. Jensen, please. Ranger," he appealed to Jeff, "I give up." He raised his arms skyward, the Smith American dangling from one finger by the trigger guard.

"Yeller belly," Rip growled at Lenny as he swung his six-gun on Smoke Jensen. "Kiss your butt good—"

Smoke Jensen drove the last word back down Rip's throat with a sizzling .44 slug. Mort Plummer moaned in anguish. Glass exploded outward in a musical shower from one of the paint-decorated front windows, as two of the remaining hard cases dived through it to escape certain death.

Pete found himself alone, facing the guns of Smoke Jensen, Jeff York, and Walt Reardon. Pete's momma had always considered him a bright little boy. He proved her right when his Colt thudded in the sawdust that covered the plank floor. He raised trembling hands above his head.

"All righty, I call it quits. After all, Sully said we was only funnin' with y'all."

Smoke cut his eyes to Jeff. "Do you want him, or shall I?"

"My pleasure," Jeff York announced as he reholstered his .45 Colt.

He took a pair of thin, pigskin leather gloves from his hip pocket and slid them on his hands, his eyes never off of Pete for a second. Slowly he advanced on the frightened two-bit gunhawk.

"Eight to three. Is that the way you boys usually play it? Now it's just one-on-one," Jeff taunted. "You got a choice. You can pick up that gun on the floor and try me . . . or you can use your fists."

"I ain't got no quarrel with you, Ranger. Ain't no fight in me," Pete pleaded.

"No backbone, either," Jeff retorted. "Do something, even if it's wrong. I'm getting tired of waiting."

Pete's eyes widened suddenly, then swiftly narrowed. He lunged at Jeff with a knife that seemed to spring from behind his back. Jeff popped Pete solidly in the mouth. Lips mashed and split, blood sprayed from Pete's face in a rosy halo.

Jeff sidestepped the blade and grabbed the wrist and upper arm of the knife hand. He brought it down, as he quickly raised a knee. The elbow broke with an audible pop. Pete went down, to howl his agony in a fetal position in the spit-and-beer-stained sawdust. Jeff silenced him with a solid kick to the head.

"Sneaky bastard, wasn't he?" Jeff rhetorically asked the silent room.

"The supplies are loaded," Smoke Jensen said dryly.

"Then I suppose we're through in town," Jeff said in an equal tone.

"You weren't never here, Mr. Jensen," Mort Plummer swore from behind his bar. "Wouldn't do to confuse our good sheriff as to who shot up my place."

"Take whatever you can find in their jeans to cover your loss," Smoke suggested.

"Right. And I've never seen you in my borned days. Good luck."

"We'll need that," Smoke advised him. "Used up a bit here today."

Seventeen

He didn't like going to Arizona to take charge of the turnover of the White Mountain land. He felt even worse when the lacquered carriage he rode in jolted to an unexpected halt.

"Woah up, Mabel, woah, Henry, hold in," the driver crooned to his team. "What the hell do we have here?" he asked next.

"Yes," Miguel Selleres called from the interior of the coach. "What do we have? Why did you stop out here in the middle of nowhere?"

"It's—it's . . . I think it's Quint Stalker and some of his boys."

"They are supposed to be in Arizona," Selleres shot back.

"Well, we're here," came the familiar voice of Quint Stalker, noticeably weakened.

Selleres poked a head out of the curtained window. Four men, without horses, all wounded, all dirty and powder-grimed, stood at the side of the road. Astonishment painted Selleres's face. He had never seen the proud, gamecock Stalker so bedraggled. "How did this happen?" Selleres demanded. "Why are you not in Arizona?"

"We were headed there," Stalker related glumly.

"Those damned Apaches waited around and hit us a second time. Killed all but us four. And we're all wearin' fresh wounds."

"You have had a hard time. There are some tanques not far ahead. Climb on the top and we'll ride there. After you've cleaned up, you can ride inside with me," Selleres told them grandly.

"Well, thanks so damned much, *Señor* Selleres," the aching Quint Stalker replied sarcastically. "Only we ain't gonna go back out there. No way, no how."

"Oh, I disagree, *Señor* Stalker."

His patience tried beyond any semblance of his usual cool nature, Miguel Selleres reached under his coat and drew out a Mendoza copy of the .45 Colt Peacemaker. Slowly he racked back the hammer, as he leveled the weapon on the tip of Quint Stalker's nose. "You will go back to that Apache reservation with me, or I will shoot you down for the cowardly dog you are."

Nervously, Quint cut his eyes to his three remaining men. Slowly he shrugged and outstretched both hands, palms up. "Who can argue with such logic?"

Martha Tucker looked at the mound of supplies being carted into the kitchen and the bunkhouse with eyes that shined. The ranch had run dangerously low of nearly everything in the three weeks since her husband's murder. She clapped her hands in delight, and made much of the small, tin cylinder cans of cinnamon, ground cloves, allspice, and black pepper.

"Now I can bake pies again! What would you like?" That she directed to Smoke Jensen.

"Anything would be fine. I'm pleased you approve of my shopping. It's not often I do such domestic chores."

"And I'll bet your Sally doesn't have to send along a list," Martha praised him delightedly.

Color rose in the cheeks of Smoke Jensen. "No, Mrs. Tucker, but then, Sally usually comes along with me. Watchin' her is how I learned to pick the best."

They had ambled off during this exchange. Horizontal purple bars filled the western quarter of the sky, layered with pink, orange, and pale blue. At this altitude, stars already twinkled faintly in the east. Martha Tucker led the way to a circular bench, built around the bole of a huge, old cottonwood. There she turned to face Smoke Jensen.

"I feel that Mr. Jensen and Mrs. Tucker are rather stiff after so much time. May I call you Smoke?"

"If you wish, Martha." Smoke produced a rueful grin. "You know, it's funny, but I've been thinking of you by your given name for several days now."

They sat, and each resisted the urge to take the other by the hand. "I don't wish to seem prying, but could you tell me about your life before now," Martha urged.

Smoke sat silent for a while, then sighed, and laced his fingers around his right knee, crossed over the left. "I ran away . . . ah, that's not quite true. My home ran away from me, when I was twelve. I wandered some, and wound up out on the plains. I was about to get my hair lifted by some Pawnee, when this woolly-looking critter out of hell rose up from the tall grass and shot two braves off their horses with a double-shot Hawken rifle. Dumped two more with another of the same, then banged away with a pair of pistols, which I later learned were sixty caliber Prentiss percussion guns, made in Waterbury, Connecticut. That's how I met Preacher."

Smoke went on to relate some of the milder adventures he had encountered as a youth in the keeping of Preacher. Martha listened with rapt attention. When words ran dry for Smoke, she told of her life back East, before she married Lawrence Tucker.

"We had a fine place, right outside Charleston, South Carolina. The War ruined all that, though. I was not yet eighteen, when I met Lawrence. He had come down with the occupation forces of Reconstruction. Like a proper young Southern lady, I hated all Yankees. Yet, Lawrence seemed somehow different.

"He had genuine concern for the well-being of white Southerners. He treated whites and darkies with the same reserve and respect. And I found out later that he didn't profit a penny's worth out of the false tax attachment schemes that deprived so many of their land and property."

"Given the circumstances, I'm surprised you ever got together," Smoke prompted.

"I had little choice. Lawrence and his staff occupied our plantation house. Daddy had lost a leg at Chancellorsville, and been invalided out of the service. Lawrence insisted from the first day his carpetbaggers moved into the main house, that rent be paid. Only, it was him paying that rent.

"He was young, and a lawyer. He'd only served the last year of the War with the Bluebellies." Smoke smiled at the use of that term, while Martha paused to order her recollections. "One night at the dinner table, he absolutely astonished the whole family by stating forcefully that the War had been fought for economic reasons and politics, and had nothing whatsoever to do with slavery."

"Not a popular opinion among our brethren to the north," Smoke observed.

"I'll say not. He and Daddy got along famously after that. One day, one of the vilest of carpetbaggers showed up with those falsified documents about back taxes on Crestmar. Lawrence produced a stack of paid receipts, and said those taxes were not due anymore." A tinkle of laughter brightened her recounter. "He even threatened to have the man run off the plantation by our darkies, who were working then for wages. They were armed with some shotguns and a few Enfield muskets left over from the War. We whites were not permitted to carry arms, even for self-protection, although General Grant said we could."

A profound change had come over Martha Tucker. She talked like a young girl, when she recalled her life in the South. Her mannerisms also revealed the stereotypical Southern belle. Smoke noted this with not a little discomfort. He saw it as though she were two different persons, the lighthearted one hidden under the burdens of the other. He wondered if it was good for her. To make matters worse, he received a strong impression that she was flirting with him.

"I've enjoyed this talk of old times, Martha. No offense, but right now, my stomach thinks my throat's been cut."

"Oh, my! What a ninny," Martha babbled, the Old South sloughing off her speech as she rose. "I'll see to supper right away. The children will be starved, too. And thank you for confiding in me about your past life."

Smoke Jensen heaved a long sigh of relief as Martha Tucker headed toward the kitchen. A soft chuckle came from the far side of the tree trunk, and Jeff York stepped into view. "That one's fallin' in love."

"You can go straight to hell, Jeff York," Smoke growled as he came to his boots.

Awakening at the palest of dawn light, Miguel Selleres drew a deep breath, redolent with sage and yucca blooms. He immediately understood why Benton-Howell coveted this land so much. Very like the valleys of the Sierra Madre Occidental, where he had grown up. A moment later he received a lesson in why it was not wise for white-eyes to desire this vista of piñon-shrouded mesas.

Some twenty-seven Apache warriors—in varying sizes from short and squat to tall and square, painted for war—rose up to fire a volley of arrows into the camp erected by the seven men who had accompanied Miguel Selleres and Quint Stalker's survivors. The whirring messengers of death had barely begun to descend on the unsuspecting white interlopers, when a ragged fusillade of rifle fire erupted, shattering the quiet of early morning.

With grim silence, the Apaches swarmed down into camp on the tail of their surprise opening. Shouts of confusion and alarm came from the sleep-dulled outlaws. Only their leader had the presence of mind to make a positive move. Miguel Selleres unlimbered his Mendoza .45, and shot the nearest Apache through the breastbone. He then came to his boots and made directly for his carriage.

Unlike most of its contemporaries, fashioned by the

skilled wainwrights of Durango, it did not have sides and a roof of thick oak planking. Sandwiched between layers of veneer, strong sheets of steel—fashioned from the boiler plates of a wrecked locomotive on the *Ferocarril de Zacatecas*—made it nearly impregnable. Even the curtained windows had bulletproof shutters. Miguel Selleres reached his goal, along with Quint Stalker, who knew about the construction of the coach. They entered, secured the doors and shutters, and began to pick targets among the attacking Indians.

Durango's coach makers had provided firing ports, not so much for fighting off Apaches, but for bandits. They well knew the requirements of the rich and powerful in their own country. The armored vehicle withstood assaults from arrow, lance, ball, and stone war club. Many who attacked it died for their efforts. A growing volume of firepower drove off the Apaches after a closely fought five minutes.

"Did you think to bring some water and grub?" Quint asked anxiously, when the shooting dwindled to long-range sniping.

"Under the seat. There's extra ammunition, *también.*"

"You think of everything, *Señor* Selleres."

"Not everything, or I would not be in here, with those cursed devils outside."

Quint Stalker actually cracked a smile, and his troubled countenance brightened. "That shines! I like a man with a sense of humor in tough situations."

"You flatter me. Help yourself to my humble repast."

Stalker dug into the wicker hamper inside the hinged rear seat. He pulled out a cloth bag of *machaca*—shredded dry beef, Mexican style—another of parched corn, a tin can of bean paste, and another of peaches. "We're gonna feast like kings," he exclaimed with delight.

"The men won't fare so well, unless they gather up what the *indios* failed to destroy. I suggest you order them to bring everything they can, and form defenses around my carriage. We could use two more guns in here. The rest can form barricades from rocks, saddles and . . ." Selleres winced, "dead horses."

Mid-morning came and the situation had changed little. It had grown blood-boiling hot inside the coach. Great wet patches showed under the arms of the occupants and along their spines. Several of the hard-bitten outlaws had managed to round up enough horses to harness the carriage and provide transportation for the survivors, if some rode double. Miguel Selleres noted that spirits had risen considerably. Then Fate struck them cruelly again.

This time, when the Apaches charged, the solid drum of shod hooves joined in the whisper rush of moccasin soles. A dozen Arizona Rangers, led by Tallpockets Granger, stormed the mesa top and the desperate hard cases who had been trapped there. A steady swath of bullets made a drum of the inside of the carriage.

Desperation added its own brand of discipline to the forlorn outlaw band. When the Apaches crashed into the improvised barricades, the white vermin reversed their rifles and used them for clubs. Winchesters bashed Apache heads, broke ribs, slowed the advance, and low-held six-guns blazed a clear path through the throng.

Miguel Selleres spotted it first. The reins of the team had been threaded through a narrow, hinged slot near the roof of the coach. Selleres handed them to one hard case and shouted through a riskily opened window.

"Get this team going. Surround the coach and ride for it. That's our only chance."

"That was damned Arizona Rangers out there fightin' alongside the Apaches," Quint Stalker observed in a wounded tone. "What they takin' the redskins' side for?"

Miguel Selleres gave him a droll look. "Perhaps our bought politicians have not been able to accomplish all they promised. Or they aren't honest."

"What's a honest politician?" Quint asked, never having known of one.

"One who, when he's been bought, stays bought by the same people," Selleres answered glibly.

"Oooh, hell, here they come again," Stalker groaned as he slammed the shutters tight.

At once the two outlaws at the lead team spurred their mounts and got the armored vehicle in motion. Firing to their sides, they fought clear of the horde that rushed at them. Driving blind, the border trash who held the reins expected at any instant for the carriage to turn over. Bouncing and swaying, he kept erect as the seconds, then the minutes passed.

"Ohmygod!" he gulped in a rush, as the coach canted downward onto the trail off the mesa.

"I think . . . we have . . . made it," Quint Stalker muttered in wonder.

"*¡Gracias a Dios!* I do believe we have," Miguel Selleres breathed out softly.

* * *

Tallpockets Granger watched the heavy carriage lumber down the steeply inclined trail and called in his detachment of Rangers. Most of the tough, Arizona-wise lawmen cautiously eyed the charged-up Apaches, who also broke off pursuit. An explosive situation could erupt at any second, Tallpockets knew, yet he had to fight an amused smirk as he made known his plan. Using the *Tinde* language, which he had learned as a child, he made a stunning announcement to Cuchillo Negro and his warriors.

"Black Knife, I want you and your braves to raise their right hands. Yeah, that's the one. Good. Now, do you swear to uphold the laws of the Territory of Arizona, obey the orders of the law chief over you, and keep the peace as directed? Answer, *enju.*"

"Wadest, what is this you are doing, *shee-kizzen?"* Cuchillo Negro asked, calling Tallpockets White Clay— the name he had earned as a boy when his father was agent to the White Mountain people—and calling him blood brother.

"Why, I'm making you my deputies, *shee-kizzen."*

Black Knife's reaction began as a grin, grew into a broad smile, and ended in a deep belly laugh. *"Enju-enju*—yes, yes," he responded. "I never believed I'd live to see this day."

Tallpockets, who at six-foot-five truly fit the name, pulled a perplexed expression. "General Crook organized two companies of Apache scouts for the Army, so why can't the Rangers take you on?"

"For what purpose?"

"To track down those white lice and squash them," the long-faced Tallpockets stated levelly, his one brown and one blue eye glinting with his anger. He had heard of what had been done to the Tinde children.

Tension evaporated as the rest of the Tinde offered their oaths and went among the Rangers clasping forearms in the Apache fashion. Tallpockets stood beside his blood brother and accepted the fealty of the warriors, all the while glancing at the fading streamer of dust that marked the course of the outlaws. At last his patience wore thin.

"Let's mount up and go after that slime."

Sir Geoffrey Benton-Howell received two pieces of extremely bad news at the same time. The rider from town brought him word of the shoot-out in the Hang Dog, and a telegram, sent in haste from Springerville, Arizona Territory. He listened in a growing storm of rage.

"It was Smoke Jensen, right enough. Enough folks recognized him while the shootin' was goin' on, and when he rode out of town. He was with a buckboard from the Tucker ranch."

"WHAT!" Benton-Howell bellowed.

"He was with some riders who drove a Tucker ranch buckboard."

"I heard what you said, fellow, I just could not believe it. We worked so hard to convince that foolish woman that Smoke Jensen had killed her husband. How could she do this?"

"He didn't kill Tucker?"

"Of course not, you lout," Benton-Howell snapped, his control rapidly slipping. "One of Quint Stalker's men, Forrest Gore, did the job, and bungled it mightily I might add. Wait here while I read this, then I will have some instructions for you."

Benton-Howell slit the yellow envelope and pulled the message form. His face went crimson with each word that leaped from the page. Miguel Selleres defeated and put to route by a band of Apaches and the Arizona Rangers? His mind refused to accept it. The Arizona Rangers? Impossible. That made it even more important to end this matter with the Tucker woman at once.

"Rocky, I want you to round up five or six men, and ride over to keep a watch on the Tucker ranch. Better take enough to send messages back, for that matter. What you will be looking for is the next time Smoke Jensen leaves there. You are to send word to me, and then go in and apprehend the widow and her children. We're going to make them disappear from the face of the earth, and then take that ranch."

Eighteen

Smoke Jensen turned away from the window that overlooked the dooryard of the Tucker ranch. "I'm not satisfied with the results of the visits to Benton-Howell's ranch. We need to take the fight to what's left of Stalker's men around Socorro. The four of us can get them mightily stirred up."

"How you figure to work it?" Jeff York asked.

"We'll split up, cover more area that way. You and Walt, Ty Hardy and I."

"Must you do this?" Martha Tucker asked with almost wifely concern as she entered the room.

"I'm afraid so. I don't figure this Englishman for being stupid. His partner's smart enough from what I've heard," Smoke explained. "They'll figure out sooner or later that the only place we can be is here. I want to keep the fighting away from you and your youngsters."

"I'm grateful for that, Smoke, but the risk . . . ?"

Smoke gave her a smile just short of indulgent. "I've taken risks before and come out all right." He didn't mention the scars that crisscrossed his body, or the eyes swollen shut and blackened by hard knuckles, the loose teeth and split lips. "We'll head out in half an hour," he told Jeff.

Not unexpectedly, Jimmy Tucker wanted to ride along. When the four gunfighters—Ty Hardy just a beginner— had mounted up, Jimmy came to them and blurted out his wishes. Smoke Jensen looked down at the lad long and hard.

"That's not possible, Jimmy. Although they're hardly the best of a sorry lot, it's no place for you to be. You're good enough with a gun to protect your mother and the other kids, so your place is to stay here and do just that."

Jimmy made a face like he might cry, then turned away. "Awh . . . hell, I never get to do anything," he muttered.

Smoke Jensen withheld his sympathetic chuckle until they had ridden away from the ranch headquarters. When he looked back at the crest of a low rise, Martha and Jimmy were waving at them with equal enthusiasm.

Forrest Gore slid the brass telescope closed and slipped it in the case hung from his saddle horn. "They're long gone, and nothing's stirring around the bunkhouse or corrals. You boys spread out, take your time, so's we can hit them from all sides at once. Today's washday, so the woman'll be out in the yard. If we cut her off from the house, we won't have any troubles at all."

For once it worked exactly like Gore wanted it. He and seven men swarmed down on the Tucker ranch, and caught Martha Tucker at the clothes line. Arms above her head, a sheet flapping in the breeze, she did not have a chance to reach for the rifle that leaned against one upright of the drying rack. Two men literally plucked her off the ground and rode away.

After her first, startled yelp, Martha shouted desperately, "Run, Jimmy!"

Only Jimmy Tucker did not obey. He dived for his own rifle and came up with the lever action cycling. The other five men, led by Forrest Gore, closed in on the children. A slug cracked over Gore's head, close enough to make him cringe. He still smarted from the pellet wounds given him by Smoke Jensen. Three of the Tucker hands got into the fight a moment later.

Outnumbered by the outlaws, one went down almost at once, as Marv Fletcher blasted him in the center of his chest. A second gunhand took a bullet in the leg and lay helplessly under the guns of the Stalker gang. The third hunkered down behind a large water tank and fired at those surrounding his friend.

After Vern Fletcher took a slug in his shoulder, Arlan Grubbs got around behind the wrangler and shot him in the back. Jimmy got off another round before the broad chest of a lathered horse knocked him off his bare feet.

Forrest Gore dismounted swiftly and wrestled the rifle from the boy's grasp. Then he backhanded Jimmy hard enough to loosen teeth. Quickly he tied the boy's hands and feet. With a grunt of effort, he booted the dazed lad onto the crupper of his saddle. Shrieks of fear from Rose and Tommy Tucker cut through the rumble of hooves. Dust swirled in the abandoned yard, as the outlaws rode off with their prisoners.

"What do we do with 'em?" a snaggle-toothed hard case asked.

"We're to take them to the B-Bar-H. Sir Geoffrey wants to entertain them for a while," Forrest Gore replied with a lustful leer.

* * *

Jeff York pointed ahead to what Smoke Jensen had already seen. "Someone's sure foggin' the road this way," the Arizona Ranger stated the obvious.

"Must have come from a long way off," Smoke stated flatly. "I've been watching the dust rise for a good twenty minutes."

"Carbone said you had the eyes of a *halcon*—a hawk," Jeff said softly. "Now I believe him. Who do you think it could be?"

Smoke studied the growing column of red-brown dust, and the thin line far behind. "Not someone we're going to enjoy meeting."

"Quint Stalker and his gang?" Jeff suggested.

"It could be, Jeff. Right funny if we set out hunting them and they find us first."

"I'd maybe see the fun in it, if we still had Walt and Ty along," came Jeff's glum reply.

Smoke looked around the barren desert terrain. "There's nowhere to hide out here."

"There'd be plenty, if you were an Apache."

Smoke cut his eyes sharply to Jeff. "Think like an Indian. That's a shinin' idea, Jeff. Let's get busy."

A quick coursing of the ground located a shallow gully. Smoke and Jeff rode into it and dismounted. At Smoke's direction, they stripped the saddlebags from their mounts and put the animals down on their sides. With stones from the bottom of the wash, they reinforced the lip of the draw in two places and set out rifles and ammunition.

"Nothing left to do but wait," Jeff spoke out of nervousness.

"Not for long, either." Smoke had already picked up the distant, growing rumble of wheels that moved fast and carried a heavy burden.

They had a good view down the reverse slope of the elongated ridge where they had found the gully. Only thing, the road curved out of sight against the swell of the land, a scant three hundred yards away. Outriders came into view first.

Smoke caught sight of the heads of their horses, then the forward-bent outlines of three men, riding abreast. Behind them came a six-up team, hauling a lumbering coach. The men to the rear of the carriage had their weapons out and ready, and kept casting glances behind them.

"Whoever it is, looks like they're in some sort of trouble."

"I reckon, Jeff. Only, which side do we pick?" At Jeff's droll expression, Smoke went on. "Reckon we let them get in close enough to see if we recognize any of them."

"Not too close, I hope," Jeff suggested. "I count nine men, plus whoever is in that coach."

"Funny there's no one up on that box to drive." Jeff nodded understanding at Smoke's observation.

By then the lead riders had come well within field glass range. Smoke studied the faces, and his full lips thinned into a grim line. He put the binoculars aside and levered a round into the chamber of his Winchester.

"One of them is Quint Stalker," Jeff advised a moment later.

"Well, we know which side we're on," Smoke tossed back as he made ready for a fight.

Quint Stalker had obtained a horse at the first homestead they came upon after escaping from the White Mountains. He used the simple expedient of stealing it. He had so far ridden two mounts into the ground, and the team hauling that armor-plated carriage had been replaced three times. The cause of their unseemly haste hovered tauntingly on the western horizon.

Contrary to the assurances of Miguel Selleres, the Apaches had continued in pursuit, and by all appearances, the Arizona Rangers rode with them. Try as he might, Quint Stalker could not visualize those two traditional enemies as allies. Yet they had joined against him and the eight men who remained. That conclusion had been reached in the moment Quint swerved his mount to the left to avoid a large rock in the trail.

That movement put the bullet meant for his heart in the eye of his horse, and killed the animal instantly. When the dead beast's foreknees hit the hard, red-brown soil, Quint Stalker catapulted out of the saddle. He hit hard, the air driven from his lungs, and rolled along in the sharp-edged gravel that lay in his path.

His chin took a lot of punishment, and wound up bleeding profusely when he sprawled to a halt. What the hell? Those Injuns couldn't have gotten ahead of them. After his ordeal, thoughts didn't stick too well in Quint's mind. He tried to see to his left, from where the shot came, only everything looked fuzzy. Then his blood turned to ice.

From behind, he heard the coach bearing down on him.

He'd be squashed into a red pulp by two dozen hooves. To say nothing of those wheels! Squalling, Quint lurched upward and threw himself to one side. He could see the hooves of the horses up close, and feel the heat of their bodies as they thundered past. The swaying carriage halted directly beside him.

"Get in here, you idiot!" Miguel Selleres growled from the open doorway.

Grateful for the protection of those armored walls, Quint Stalker did so with alacrity. Once secure, he found himself the target of unanswerable questions.

"What happened out there?"

Quint Stalker gaped at Miguel Selleres. "I . . . don't know. Someone shot my horse out from under me."

"Who? How many? I don't see anyone," Selleres rattled off, while squinting out the firing loop of one window. "It can't be *los indios,*" he added to himself.

"That's what I thought, and you're right. It can't be."

"Then who?"

Stalker's first attempt at an answer got drowned out by the loud slam of bullets into the side of the coach. In a brief lull, he tried again. "Smoke Jensen."

"*¡Bastante, no mas!*" Selleres barked. "We have enough men to finish him for all time."

He came to his feet and leaned over the seated outlaw. A hinged panel in the back of the coach opened, and Selleres shouted through it. "Get over there and find who's shooting at us."

At once the gunmen spread out, and jumped their horses toward the lip of the ravine. Withering fire challenged them, yet they pushed on. One hard case yowled and clutched at his arm, where a bloodstain began to spread. Another doubled over, lips to the neck of his mount, as though kissing it. The remainder drew off, seeking cover behind the carriage.

"*¡Cobardes! ¡Pendejos!* Get out there and kill those men! I see only two guns against you. *¡Adalante, pronto!*"

With obvious reluctance, the outlaws charged again. This time they fired steadily at the noted gun positions. Their heavy volume of fire forced Smoke and Jeff to pull down below the lip of the bank. Selleres watched with growing satisfaction. The riders reached the edge of the gully.

Then a gunhawk from Albuquerque threw up his hands and fell backward off his horse. Smoke Jensen had switched to his .44 and blasted upward into the man's face. Jeff York opened up also. Bullets gouged the ground and cracked through the air. Another gunhawk grunted in pain, as one of Smoke's slugs pierced his left leg, front to rear, right below the knee. Suddenly they had had enough.

Huddling behind the armored coach, they heard a muffled string of curses from inside. The shutters opened on one window, and they saw the face of Quint Stalker. "Get over there and finish it, you sonsabitches."

"Give us some covering fire, damn you," Charlie Bascomb snarled.

"Yeah—yeah, good idea. Spread out, hit them from two sides. We'll keep their heads down."

It worked even better than Miguel Selleres expected from the thoroughly demoralized gunmen. He and Quint Stalker opened fire first, the riders charged out from behind the carriage, and streaked for the arroyo ahead of and behind the position of the ambushers. Victory lay only fractions of a second away.

Then Selleres and Stalker learned how deceptive the desert terrain could be to eyes accustomed to a fifteen-mile horizon. Around the bend in the road that masked the back trail, swarmed some twenty Apache warriors and a dozen Arizona Rangers. Rapidly closing ground, they opened fire immediately. Miguel Selleres weighed the outcome quickly and accurately.

"Get us out of here," he snapped to the driver at his side.

Tallpockets Granger saw the coach stopped in the road ahead. A dead horse lay on its side behind the armor-plated vehicle. Someone had ambushed them. He knew that someone had to be Capt. Jeff York. At once he turned in the saddle, waved an arm over his head, and pointed forward.

"Unlimber your irons, boys. It looks like ol' Jeff's bit a bear in the butt."

They crashed into the nearer trio of outlaws with rifles and six-guns blazing. One man fell without a sound, shot through the head. Another took two bullets in his side and dropped from the saddle. The last threw up his hands. The Apaches accompanying the Rangers streamed on by, intent on taking on the child-killers beyond the coach. Suddenly the vehicle bolted forward, the horses straining to pull the heavy load.

Terror blanched the faces of the *Pen-dik-olye* as Cuchillo Negro and his warriors raced toward them. One had self-control enough to steady his mount and take careful aim. Smoke Jensen rose up slightly and put a slug through his chest. The gunhawk made a gurgling cry as he fell sideways off his saddle.

His companions started dying seconds later, hard and slowly, as the Apaches swarmed over them. It took some time to stop them. While the Rangers did what they could to drag the vengeful warriors off the outlaws, Tallpockets Granger pounded boots to the edge of the draw.

"Thought it might be you, Cap'n," he drawled through a grin. A nod toward Smoke. "Mr. Jensen, good to see you again. Them horses you brought us worked real good. Let us run the hell out of those *ladrónes."*

Smoke came up onto the level. "Glad you like them. What brings you over this way?"

"We decided to wipe out that Stalker gang once and for all. Besides, I sort of figgered ol' Jeff here might need some help."

"And the Apaches?" Jeff asked with a nod toward Cuchillo Negro.

"They're my deputies." At Jeff's astonished gape, he added, "We're after the same enemy, Cap'n."

Smoke clapped a hand on one shoulder of Granger. "Then they are as welcome as can be. Only thing that bothers me, is that coach got away. I thought we'd shot it to doll rags."

"Wouldn't have done no good," Tallpockets informed Smoke. "That belongs to Miguel Selleres. It's all made of boiler plate under thin wood."

"That ties everything together," Smoke allowed, after hearing an account of the battle in the White Mountains. "I think the time has come to move directly on Benton-Howell and his partner."

* * *

Tallpockets Granger volunteered his posse of deputy Arizona Rangers. That gave them an effective force of fifteen. To Smoke's surprise, the Apaches led by Cuchillo Negro offered to continue as deputies to Tallpockets. At the suggestion of Smoke Jensen, they rode first to the Tucker ranch to enlist any others who wanted to join the fight.

"A good place to start is in Socorro. We can clean out the trash that Benton-Howell has been gathering, then close in on the ranch," Smoke declared.

When they reached the Tucker ranch two hours later, a wounded hand, Sean Quade, gave them the bad news. "They killed Hub and Carter," he concluded, "and took Miz Tucker and the kids."

"Who?"

"Don't know all of them. Some of the trash that's been showin' up in town. Forrest Gore led them. I saw him clear."

"Which way did they go?" Smoke asked with winter in his voice.

Quade scratched an isolated circle of sandy hair that hung down his forehead. "Southwest, toward Socorro."

Shock at learning of the abduction had turned to cold, controlled anger in Smoke Jensen. "Then that's the way we're going. We'll send a doctor out to take care of that leg, Sean," Smoke advised the wounded man.

"Damned right," Jeff agreed.

"I'm goin', too," Sean Quade stated flatly.

Jeff York tried to reason with Quade. "You wouldn't be much use with a bullet in your leg."

"I can sit on my butt in a buckboard, and use a shotgun," Sean defended his decision.

"You've lost a lot of blood," Smoke Jensen told the man. "The ride in could knock you out, or worse."

Quade could not argue with that. "All right. I'll stay here and wait for the doc. Good luck . . . and keep your heads down."

Nineteen

Socorro literally burst at the seams with gunfighters and wannabes. From beyond rifle range, Smoke Jensen studied the crowded streets through field glasses. When he had worked out in his mind how it should be done, he turned to Cuchillo Negro and spoke, with Tallpockets translating.

"I want to save you as a nasty surprise for the gunhawks in there."

The Apache chief pulled his full lips into a grim smile. "These white men will have no heart for the fight when we attack."

"That's what I'm thinking. They won't think much of the rest of us riding in. We can take a few by surprise. But the best of them will fort up somewhere. When that happens, and we get bogged down, you hit them from the far side of town."

Cuchillo Negro cut his eyes to Tallpockets. "This one thinks like a *Tinde.*"

Tallpockets rendered it in English. Smoke nodded in acceptance of the compliment. "I learned most of my fighting skills from a man named Preacher."

Eyes widened, Cuchillo Negro grunted harshly. "My father knew such a man and spoke of him often. We

Tinde called him Gray Wolf. No other man could move so silently, or fight so ferociously. I do not say that lightly."

"He'd be proud to know you folks thought so highly of him," Smoke returned.

Black Knife smiled around his eyes. "Many *Chiricahua, Mescaleros,* and *Tinde* died before we learned to respect him."

That could go on Preacher's headstone, if he had one, Smoke thought. "They had plenty company," he told the Apache chief.

A second later, the Apaches left for their position. They seemed to dissolve into the empty terrain. One moment they were in plain view, the next, only faint puffs of dust showed where their horses had walked. And *they* had this great respect for his mentor. For perhaps the thousandth time, Smoke saw Preacher in yet a new light.

"We'll give them half an hour, then ride in," Smoke informed the others.

Two second-rate hard cases sat their horses at a point where wood rail fences and a cattle guard kept livestock from wandering the streets of Socorro. One of them jolted out of a doze at the sound of approaching riders. He tipped up the brim of his hat and peered into the wavery heat shimmer of midday.

"More guns on the way," he remarked to his companion. "You'd think we were going after an army."

"Hell, Mike, for twenty dollars a day I'd take on ol' Gen'ral Sherman hisself."

"No denyin' the money's good." Suddenly Mike's

spine stiffened him upright, and his hand went to his gun.

"Damn! That one in front's Smoke Jensen!"

"Yer seein' things," his partner contradicted. He just knew Smoke Jensen would never be within ten miles of Socorro.

Mike whipped his six-gun clear of leather. In the time it took for him to reach the hammer, his intended target had spoken and drawn his gun.

"Your friend's right, you know."

"Awh, hell."

The last thing Mike saw was the beginning of a spurt of smoke from the barrel of the .44 aimed at him. He died so quickly, he didn't fall off his horse. Smoke Jensen's second bullet hit the other would-be gunfighter somewhat lower. It ruined his liver and spine on the way out. He pitched to one side and landed with a heavy *plop*.

"So much for taking anyone by surprise," Smoke complained, as he and the Rangers rode past the dead men.

Halfway down the block, a trio of lean, gaunt-faced men stepped into the street to block the way. "That something personal between you an' Mike?" the one in the middle asked. Then he saw the silver badge on the vest of Jeff York. "Awh, damnitall," he bemoaned his fate as he drew against the Arizona Ranger.

Jeff shot him with the Winchester in his right hand. The other two scattered. They threw wild rounds behind them, as they made for the nearest saloon. Jeff grunted and put his free hand to his left shoulder. It came away bloody-fingered. Jeff brought the rifle to his right shoulder then, and took careful aim. His bullet shattered the offender's ankle and put him on the ground.

Smoke's second slug shattered a kerosene lamp beside the door through which the last gunman dodged. The Rangers spread out, weapons at the ready. Smoke and Jeff continued toward the barroom. Jeff York stuffed a neckerchief under his shirt front, to sop up the blood from the deep gouge cut in the meat of his shoulder point. Glass crunched under their boot soles, when they dismounted and stepped up on the boardwalk. Smoke and Jeff entered through the batwings together. They found themselves facing nine outlaw guns.

Five of those roared at once. Showers of splinters erupted from the door frame and lintel. One bullet went by so close to the ear of Smoke Jensen, that it made more of a hum than a crack. Smoke already had one of the shooters on the floor, doubled over the hole in his belly. Jeff York had a second gunhand down, crying really sincere tears over his ruined left hip. Then the remaining four six-guns exploded into life.

Smoke Jensen had dived to one side and flattened a felt-covered poker table, scattering chips, cards, and players in all directions. He did a forward roll before the table came to rest, then bounced to one knee, flame spitting from the muzzle of his six-gun. At short range, a .44 slug does truly awful damage to human flesh. Smoke's round hit a thick, hard-muscled belly, with a *splat* like a baseball bat striking a whole ham.

His target gave a hard grunt and looked down stupidly at the hole where his fifth shirt button used to be. "Jeez, Mister, who is it killed me?" he asked weakly.

"Smoke Jensen," the owner of the name told him.

Then Smoke was on the move again. He jumped over a man who had only then come off the sawdust from his upset chair. The move saved his life. The hard case they had chased into the saloon leveled a round at where Smoke had knelt. All it killed was a fly on the faded, pale green wall. The gunhawk gaped at his act of minor mayhem, and paid for it with his life as Jeff York shot him down.

One of his comrades in murder reeled backward into the bar, blood gushing from a neck wound he had received courtesy of Smoke Jensen. The bodies continued to pile up at an incredible rate, the bartender, Diego Sanchez, noted. He sat on the floor behind two full beer barrels, and watched the slaughter in reverse through the mirror. It was a technique barkeeps learned early on in their profession, or they didn't have long careers.

A stray slug shattered a decanter and sent shards of thick crystal shrapnel flying. They in turn broke half a dozen cheaper bottles, and inundated the bartender's apron with bourbon, rye, and tequila. Taking a bath in booze came with the territory also, Diego Sanchez knew from experience. *¡Por Dios!* His Conchita would make him sleep in the hammock between the palo verdes again.

Suddenly it got eerily silent in the saloon. Not a boot sole scraped the floor. No one could be heard breathing. No glass shards tinkled. Even the echoes of gunshots had died out. Slowly, Diego Sanchez sucked in air. He raised himself slowly until his eyeballs came above the top of the bar. Four men faced one another from opposite ends of the mahogany. Two he knew; Logan and Sloane, gunfighter trash that had drifted into town three days ago.

The other pair wore badges, a U.S. Marshal and an Arizona Ranger.

"It's your choice," the Marshal said tightly.

Jesus, Maria y Jóse, he was a big one. Diego moved back from the bar, until he pressed against the shelf behind.

"You ran that thing dry," Logan drawled nastily. "Now I'm gonna ventilate that tin star of yours."

"You know, I think you're right," Smoke Jensen told him, as he threw the .44 in the air and instantly snatched the second one from its left-hand holster. The hammer dropped on the primer before Logan could react and yank his trigger. Smoke caught the flying six-gun left-handed, at the same moment his bullet punched a hole through Logan's chest. The gun in the Ranger's hand blasted a second later and downed his man.

"Jesus, Smoke, I didn't think anyone could do that," Jeff York said in awed tones.

Smoke? Smoke Jensen? Diego Sanchez sucked in air and crossed himself. Then he slowly lowered his head below the bar. As though spoken from far away, his words reached the ears of Smoke Jensen.

"Vereso nada, Señor Jensen."

"He said, 'I saw nothing,' " Jeff translated.

"Yeah. I caught that. I think we're through here, Jeff." Then, with a chuckle, *"Adios, Señor cantinero."*

"Conosco nada, nada," came a weak reply.

Diego Sanchez might have been willing to see and know nothing, but that didn't go for the swarm of hard cases and two-bit gunslingers who thronged the streets of town. They damn well wanted to know what was going on in the *Cantina La Merced*. They didn't like what they found when the batwings swung outward. Smoke Jensen and Jeff York had reloaded, and met the gathered gun-slicks with six-guns roaring.

"This town is out of bounds for your kind from this minute on," Jeff York bellowed over the sound of gunmen panicking. Half a dozen of them were foolhardy enough to resist. Two of them died instantly. One of them shot the hat off Smoke Jensen's head and bought an early grave for his efforts.

"On the balcony over there, Smoke," Jeff shouted.

Smoke pivoted to his left and sent another wannabe gunfighter off to hell. The gunman staggered forward and tripped over the railing. He did a perfect roll in the air on the way down. The other lawmen had spread out along the main street, and began herding surprised hard cases off benches and out of saloons, prodding them to-ward the jail. By that time, Jeff had drilled a second resister in the shoulder.

"Jeff, drop!" Smoke shouted the warning as a gunhand popped up from behind a rail barrel and aimed at Jeff York's back.

Jeff went down, and the bullet fanned air where he had been standing. A fraction of a second later, a .44 slug from Smoke Jensen's iron flattened the back-shooter against the wall of the Mercy Cantina. The corpse left a long, red smear down the whitewashed stucco, as he slumped beside a cactus in a large terracotta pot.

Hot lead cracked through the air around Smoke then. He moved swiftly across the street, charging the shooter instead of fleeing. The mountain man's six-gun bucked one. The gunslinger stiffened, then his knees buckled. Smoke had already turned away.

None of the original, six foolish gunslingers remained on their feet. Smoke cut his eyes to Jeff and nodded down the block to where the volume of fire had increased noticeably. "I think Tallpockets and the boys could use some help," Smoke suggested.

"Then, let's go see," Jeff agreed, shoving fresh cartridges into his still-hot Colt.

Some twenty gunfighters and assorted saddle trash had banded together and taken over a bank building. Its thick fieldstone walls made it into a fortress. The structure stood alone, an island at an intersection, which allowed the Rangers to completely surround it. When Smoke Jensen and Jeff York arrived, the occupants hotly exchanged shots with those outside.

"I reckon they have the Tuckers in there," Smoke allowed.

"Won't they be in danger?" Jeff asked.

"Most likely they'll be somewhere safe. Probably in the cellar, if there is one. Dead hostages don't make good bargaining chips."

On the roof, the head and shoulders of a hard case appeared. He apparently wore all black, and had a full-flowing walrus mustache in matching color. He put a Ranger down with a bullet in the side. While he ducked down behind the stone verge and cycled the action of his rifle, Smoke Jensen didn't even break stride. His hand dropped smoothly to the .44 at his side, which came free of leather with a soft whisper. When his left boot sole next struck the street, the weapon barked in Smoke's hand.

Above, behind the low stone parapet, the gunman's hat took sudden flight, along with a gout of blood and brains. Jeff York stared at his friend in open amazement. Smoke pointed with the smoking barrel of his Peacemaker.

"There's a narrow crack right . . . there. I just waited until his black hat blotted out the light."

"That was one steady-handed shot," Jeff complimented. Smoke merely shrugged and sought another target. When the volume of fire increased even more, Jeff looked toward the north end of town. "Any time now," he observed.

"Them damn Rangers ain't even supposed to be over here," one lanky gunfighter from Arizona declared, as he fired an unaimed shot into the street. "They ain't got no juri—jures—they ain't the law in New Mexico!"

"You see that slowin' down the lead they're punching at us?" growled an exceptionally short, bushy-headed gunslick with thick, gold-rimmed glasses.

"Shut up, Bob," the Arizonan snapped.

Glass tinkled like chimes as more windows took fire from the Rangers. Gradually, over the roar of gunfire from both sides, the men inside the bank heard the rumble of hooves and thin, high-pitched yelps. Bob cut his eyes upward at the slender Arizonan.

"What the hell's that?"

"Sounds . . ." The gunfighter cocked his head and concentrated. "Sounds like Injuns."

"What Injuns would that be?" Bob challenged.

"By god, it sounds like Apaches. I've heard enough of them to last a lifetime."

"What are *they* doing over here?" Bob gulped. "Are they attacking the town?"

Arizona Slim edged to a window on the north side of the bank lobby and peered out. "No. Oh, hell no! I can't believe this. They—they've joined the damned Rangers. They're comin' after us!"

Outside, the Rangers checked their fire as the Apaches swarmed through their cordon and flung themselves directly at the shot-out windows of the bank. The Arizona lawmen began reloading, while the men led by Cuchillo Negro raced closer, firing bent low over the necks of their mounts. Three dived through shattered sashes with stone-headed war clubs held high.

Muffled gunshots came from inside, and the screams of dying men. A second wave hit the stone building, and a lance hurtled through an opening to pin Bob to a desktop; bloody froth accompanied his screech of agony. With the Apaches rampaging inside, the Arizona Rangers charged the building.

Once the lawmen got in close and mixed it up with the gunhawks, all resistance ended quickly. When the survivors had been rounded up and secured in manacles, Smoke Jensen and Jeff York made a thorough search of the cellar. They came up with no sign of the Tucker family. But Smoke did find Payne Finney, hiding in a coal bunker.

"The Tuckers? Where are they?" he demanded of the thoroughly demoralized Finney.

"They aren't here. Never have been. I don't know where Stalker told Gore to take them," Finney lied smoothly.

Smoke clasped Finney by one shoulder, his thumb boring into the entry wound from a .44-40 round. Finney squirmed and grunted. "You wouldn't figure to try to run a lie past me now, would you?" he asked Finney in a calm, level tone.

"No—no. I'm serious. I don't know where they took them. I've been here all the time."

"He's right," a surly member of the Stalker gang supported Finney. "He's been in town like the rest of us. We never heard anything about the Tuckers."

Smoke cut his eyes from Payne Finney to Jeff York. "Case of the right hand not lettin' the left know?" he asked.

"Could be. Where do we start from here?"

"Back at the ranch." Jeff groaned as Smoke went on. "The trackers I set out should have something by now. It's not your fault, Jeff. I figured, too, that they'd want to take 'em to some neutral ground to arrange terms."

Jeff brightened. "There's only one place makes sense. We can save a lot of time, if we ride direct for the B-Bar-H."

"That fits. But I want to hear what the trackers say first. And we do have these prisoners to take care of. After that, we'll ride."

Twenty

Half a dozen hard cases had ridden out of Socorro as the Rangers thundered into town. From a safe distance they had watched the roundup develop, heard the gunfire raise to a crescendo, and then watched in horror as a horde of Apaches swarmed into town. Then they lit out for the B-Bar-H.

They arrived on lathered, winded horses that trembled and walked weak-kneed to turns at the water trough. Charlie Bascomb, the nominal leader of the contingent that had escaped, reported to Quint Stalker and Geoffrey Benton-Howell. What he had to tell them did not get a warm reception.

"It's the truth, Sir Geoffrey. I tell ya, the Apaches sided with those Arizona lawmen. My guess is they'll be headed this way before long."

Quint Stalker swore and smacked a balled fist into the opposite palm. "That's the same lawmen that came after us. But they ain't got authority in New Mexico."

Frowning, Benton-Howell answered him, "I'm afraid they do. It's called hot pursuit. If you are right, then they can keep coming until you are caught."

"You ain't gonna let them, are you?" Stalker all but pleaded.

"Of course not. You've served me well and faithfully—ah—with a few recent exceptions. I think it expedient to bid my friends from Washington and Santa Fe a fond *adieu*. We can hold off any force here, until the governor learns of my plight. I'm sure he can get the interloping Arizona lawmen out of his territory."

"Hummm. That could be," Stalker caught at the thin strand of hope.

"Meanwhile, I want you to organize the men we have here. Fortify the headquarters, and prepare to stand off a siege."

"Do we got supplies for that?"

"Oh, my, yes. Ample food and ammunition, even some dynamite. Water might become a problem, if this becomes protracted."

Stalker raised a brow. He knew the absolute importance of water in a desert. "Like how long?"

"Four or five days. All of the wells are out in the open. A marksman's delight, don't you know?"

"What about the Tucker woman? Can't we use her and the brats to bargain with?"

Benton-Howell considered Stalker's words a moment. "That was my intention, if the situation required it. More to the point, I want her signature on a bill of sale. That must come first. I'm going to see her now. See to the preparations."

Martha Tucker looked up from her dark contemplations when Geoffrey Benton-Howell entered the small, bare pantry in which she had been confined. She had been separated from her children the moment they arrived at the ranch. That troubled her a good deal more than the constant insistence that she sign the ranch over to the Englishman. Jimmy would be all right, she felt certain, but little Rose and Tommy could be easily frightened. When her eyes fixed on her visitor's face, she noted at once that something seemed to have ruffled his usual icy composure.

"Mrs. Tucker, I'm afraid I really must insist on you signing the quit claim deed form I provided. Time is—ah—running short."

"For you or for me?"

"For both of us, I regret to say."

Again, Martha noted a flash of distress, and seized upon it at once. "What is it, Mr. Benton-Howell? Is Smoke Jensen closing in on you?"

Damn the woman, Benton-Howell thought furiously. Had she heard anything, even locked away here? He fought to retain his calm demeanor. "Smoke Jensen has nothing to do with the business between us. What I want is your ranch."

"Smoke Jensen has *everything* to do with it," Martha surprised herself by saying. "I see it now. You tried to frame Mr. Jensen for the murder of my husband."

"Damnit, madam, I'll not have that sort of talk from you. I had nothing whatever to do with that sorry incident." He omitted mentioning Miguel Selleres and Quint Stalker. "The matter is plain and clear. I—want—that—ranch."

"How much are you offering for it?"

Benton-Howell pinned her with icy eyes. "Your life, and the lives of your children."

"I have had better offers than that," Martha snapped.

"Which you chose to spurn. My patience is growing short. Perhaps I should have one of the youngsters brought here. I assure you my men have ways that are most persuasive when dealing with a child."

Martha paled, then red fury shot through her cheeks. "You'd not dare harm one of them."

"Ah, but I would, indeed. If my wishes are not acceded to. The form is on the counter there, and pen and ink. I recommend you sign now."

"Why do you want our ranch so badly?"

"That's none of your affair. Sign that paper, madam."

"Or else?"

Benton-Howell thought a moment. "That younger boy of yours, ah, Tommy I believe. Is he a good scholar?"

"He does very well in school."

A smirk twisted Benton-Howell's aristocratic visage into a mask of ugliness. "He wouldn't do so well missing a couple of fingers, would he?"

Outrage and horror choked Martha Tucker. She made no sound as she leaped to her feet. Her fingernails flashed like the talons of an eagle, as she raked them down the face of her tormentor. Benton-Howell cried out in an almost feminine shriek, and he pushed her roughly away. He stormed to the door and hurled his last threat over one shoulder.

"Sign it or suffer the consequences."

By late afternoon, half a dozen hard-faced men had ridden in and tied horses at the Socorro livery. Smoke Jensen observed to Jeff York that there must be an inexhaustible supply of second-rate gunhawks in New Mexico. They decided to delay their departure from town. One of the hands who had volunteered to help was sent back to the Tucker spread to make contact with the trackers, and bring their discoveries to Smoke. Now, with twenty gunmen locked in jail, more than half of them wounded, the town began to fill up with more of the same.

"By this time tomorrow, it'll be every bit as bad as it was when we rode in," Jeff stated in disgust, as he sipped at a beer in the Hang Dog.

"Too bad we couldn't keep the Apaches in town," Smoke observed.

"The good people of Socorro would have died of heart failure left and right. Some of my own men were concerned about how Black Knife's bucks would behave when they got the killin' hunger on them."

"They're damn good fighters," Smoke said tightly.

"They're that. They're also savages. No different from any other tribe. They got their ways; we've got ours. There isn't often that the two meet and work well together, like we did here yesterday."

Smoke lifted the corners of his mouth in a hint of a smile. "It worked well enough, I'd say. Of course, we had common cause. Some of those men you chased down were responsible for killing those Apache kids. I'll give you that if we go into their country next week, there's no guarantee they won't lift our hair. Like Preacher used to say, 'Injuns is changeable.' "

Boots clumped importantly on the porch outside. Sheriff Jake Reno bustled through the doorway and came directly to Jeff York. "I see you are still in town, Ranger. Maybe that's a good thing. There's more of that border trash drifting in every hour. I'm danged if I know what got them stirred up."

Jeff York put on a big grin and hooked a thumb in Smoke Jensen's direction. "Maybe it's that big reward you put out on my friend here."

Sheriff Reno turned to see whom the Arizona lawman meant. He came face-to-face with Smoke Jensen. His jaw sagged, and the color drained from his cheeks. He staggered back a few small steps. At first, no sound came. Then, a wheeze and squeak slid past rigid lips. A moment later, he found full voice, and bellowed, albeit with a quake.

"Goddamnit! It's Smoke Jensen!"

"In person, Sheriff. How's tricks?" Smoke asked with a mischievous twinkle in his eyes.

Sheriff Reno choked over the words that rushed to spew from his lips. He reached for his Smith American and handcuffs at the same time. "S—sta—stand ri-right there, Jensen. You're under arrest. Give up, or by God, I'm gonna gun you down right here."

Smoke Jensen backhanded Jake Reno so swiftly the sheriff never saw Smoke's big hand. The impact sounded like a shot. "You're not arresting anyone, Sheriff," Smoke told him in a flat, deadly tone.

No small man, Jake Reno balled huge, ham fists and swung at the taunting man before him. Smoke easily slipped the first blow and caught the second on the point of one shoulder. He brought his hands up and worked on the sheriff's soft middle. The fat yielded easily and, to his surprise, Smoke found a hard slab of muscle beneath. Reno grunted and punched Smoke in the face.

Smoke's head snapped back and heat flared in his eyes,

as he drove a hard left to the side of Reno's jaw. Jake Reno backpedaled rapidly until he struck the bar. Smoke followed with hard rights and lefts to the sheriff's ribs. He felt bone give under his pounding, and shifted to Reno's gut. Stale whiskey breath gusted from behind yellowed teeth.

A hard right from Smoke stopped that when it cracked three of Reno's teeth and mashed his lips. Blood flew through the room when Sheriff Reno shook his head violently in an effort to clear his fogged mind. He managed to get his guard up in time to parry two more solid swings, then Smoke broke through and did more damage to Reno's mouth.

Jake Reno sagged slowly, desperately seeking his second wind. It came gradually as his vision dimmed. With a blink of his eyes, he saw everything clearly again. He lunged awkwardly for Smoke Jensen and planted a left on the gunfighter's cheek. Smoke took it without a flinch. Smoke's own knuckles stung—he had not had time to put on his gloves before handing out this lesson in restraint. He ignored it and planted another fist in Reno's face.

Reno countered with a vicious kick aimed at Smoke's crotch. With a slight bob, Smoke slapped the booted foot away and then yanked upward on it. A startled *whoop* came from Jake Reno as he fell flat on his butt. Smoke closed in and stood over the seated man, to pound blow after blow onto the top of Reno's head. Reno began to gag and spit up blood. He must have bitten his tongue, Smoke considered.

With what would prove to be his final defiance, Jake Reno reached out with both arms and encircled Smoke

Jensen's legs. He hauled with rapidly dwindling strength. When he put a little shoulder in it, he dislodged Smoke's boots from the plank floor and toppled the mountain man.

Smoke recovered quickly though, and popped Reno on one ear with a stinging open palm. It had the effect of a gun going off beside the sheriff's head. Through the ringing, with eyes tearing, Jake Reno pawed uselessly at Smoke Jensen's torso while Smoke drove hard, punishing blows into already weakened ribs. Without warning, Jake Reno uttered a small, shrill cry, arched his back, and fell over backward. His head thudded in the sawdust.

Panting, blood dripping from the cut under his left eye, Smoke Jensen came slowly to his feet. He reached gratefully for the schooner of beer Jeff York offered him. He rinsed his mouth and spat pinkish foam into a brass gobboon.

"We've got enough evidence on the good sheriff to lock him up, don't we, Jeff?"

"I'd say so. It'll be up to the prosecutor if he's tried for anything."

"Then get this trash out of here. Put him in his own jail, and make sure he stays there."

"We found sign about three miles from the ranch," one of the trackers Smoke Jensen had sent out reported late the next day. "The Tuckers were taken to the B-Bar-H, sure enough. The closer they got, the less careful they were about covering their trail. An' something else, Mr. Jensen. That place is being turned into a fort. Armed riders everywhere, fence lines are being raised higher, the windows of the main house are boarded up."

Smoke considered this report while he sipped coffee. "Kevin, how many men do you figure are siding with Benton-Howell and Selleres?"

Kevin Noonan evaluated the quality of the gunmen they had seen. "I'd say twenty-five to thirty of them are average to good. They stay off the ridge lines, keep to the trees where they can, most don't smoke at night. There's another twenty or so who just don't measure up; trash with a gun strapped on. And there's more driftin' in all the time, five to ten a day."

Those numbers didn't appeal to Smoke Jensen. Even a poor shot could hit someone sometime. He simply didn't have enough men for a head-on fight. "It sounds like they're getting ready to stand off an army."

"Could be that this Englishman is trying to buy time," Walt Reardon suggested.

"For what purpose?" Jeff York asked.

Smoke Jensen picked it up from there. "He did have all those politicians out there for a big party. While you were there, did you gather that they were being paid for favors already done?"

"More like Benton-Howell was courting them," Jeff recalled. "It could be that they haven't come through so far."

"Yes. So he has to stall us, until whatever he is doing becomes legal," Smoke completed the thought. "Which means we should do a little pushing right soon. We have to force the issue *before* he can get whatever he's after out of the politicians."

"How soon?" Walt Reardon asked.

Smoke thought on it. "In a day or two. First we have to make Socorro unpopular with the sort Benton-Howell is attracting to town."

Walt Reardon lightly touched the grips of his six-gun. "We'd best do that before the place fills up again."

"Right about now should be a good time to start," Smoke announced, rising to his boots.

Orin Banning turned away from the lace curtains that covered the window of the parlor in Fanny Mae's Residence for Refined Young Women. "I never saw a town with so many badge-toters in it," he grumbled.

Beyond him, in the street, Arizona Rangers busily nailed up small, neat posters. One of the six men who had ridden with Banning to Socorro to answer the call put out by Benton-Howell made his way toward the brothel, eyes fixed on the industrious lawmen. After one had fastened a notice to a lamppost, he ripped it down and made his way quickly to the front door.

"Hey, Orin, lookie at this. We're being posted out of town."

"You mean *us?*" the would-be gang leader demanded.

"Well, yeah. Us an' everybody else. It says here that, 'Everyone not a resident of Socorro, New Mexico Territory or its environs'—whatever that means—'is hereby ordered to be out of town by noon Tuesday.' That's tomorrow."

"Who is going to be doin' the throwin'?"

"Them Rangers, I reckon. Oh, an' I heard a funny thing down at the Hang Dog. A feller said Smoke Jensen was in town."

Banning frowned. "Jensen would never mix into something like this. Thinks he's too damned good to work for another man."

"Maybe so, maybe not," the gunslick opined. "Anyway, what'er we gonna do?"

"For starters, we're not going to leave," Banning told him firmly.

By late afternoon, some of the least confident among the gunmen began to drift out of town. A few more joined them the next morning. Many hung around though, to see how this hand would be played. Some soon learned, when the Rangers—and some local residents who had been deputized—began to make sweeps of the streets.

"You ride for one of the ranches around here?" Tallpockets Granger asked a pair of wannabe gunhawks lounging outside the barbershop.

"Nope."

"Then fork them scruffy mounts of yours and blow on out of here."

"What if we don't want to?"

Tallpockets's eyes turned to ice. "Then you'll be in jail faster than you can whistle the first two bars of 'Dixie.' "

From down the block, a voice of authority made a hard demand. "Move along. You don't have business in this town anymore. I'd make it fast, if I was you."

Three Arizona Rangers filled an intersection off the main street and began to walk along the dirt track. Every time they looked at a man, the subject of their scrutiny shied his eyes away and silently mounted up to ride out.

Slowly, the crowd of low-grade gunfighters began to thin noticeably. Most of them knew who was hiring and how much would be paid, Smoke Jensen believed, and many even knew how to find the B-Bar-H. No doubt they'd be heading that way.

He had to admit to Jeff and Walt that there was little they could do about it. They had spoken on the matter only a minute before one of Granger's men approached. "There's some hard cases over at Fanny Mae's parlor house say they're comin' out shootin'. One of them with a big mouth told us that they'd take on all comers at that windmill in the center of town."

Jeff and Walt cut their eyes to Smoke. The legendary gunfighter quirked his lips in a hint of a smile, and hitched up his cartridge belt. "Then I guess we'd better get down to the *Plaza de Armas*. This might get interesting after all."

Twenty-one

Seven self-styled *pistoleros* stood spread out in the central plaza of Socorro. A wooden windmill squeaked and groaned above them, the blades turning listlessly. The pump below musically sloshed water into a cuplike, leather harness over its spout. From there it ran through a pipe to a large, square, wooden tank that provided water for any horses so inclined, the local stray dogs, cats, and birds. Water lily pads dotted the surface. From its pedestal opposite, a statue of an armored Spaniard, bearing a long, lancelike cross, wrapped in the *Chi-Rho* flag of the Church of Rome, looked down on it all. When Smoke Jensen, Jeff York, and Walt Reardon rounded the corner of the adobe block building that housed the Mercado Central, the one in the middle took two long strides ahead of his henchmen.

"Hold it right there," he demanded. "I hear you badge-pushers done run some friends of mine out of town. I'm here to tell you that you ain't runnin' me out."

"Carry you out, more likely," Smoke replied in a tired voice.

"You ain't man enough. Ain't got the guts. Uh—who might you be?"

"Capt. Jeff York, Arizona Rangers," Jeff introduced himself.

That didn't seem to faze Banning, but he paled slightly when Walt said, "Walt Reardon. No doubt you've heard of me."

"Y-yeah. Can't believe you've turned lawdog. How about you," he directed at Smoke.

"Smoke Jensen."

Right then Orin Banning did a right peculiar thing, considering he faced three of the best gunfighters on the frontier. He gave his sidemen the signal and went for his gun. Most of them didn't clear leather before Smoke, Jeff, and Walt fired their first rounds.

One of the outlaws went down gagging, a hand clutching his belly. Another spun sideways, then turned back to the action with a vengeance. He put a bullet through Walt's left arm a moment before he died of .44 caliber poisoning from the pistol in the hand of Smoke Jensen.

Bullets zipped through the small garden of the *Plaza de Armas* as Smoke sought another target. He soon found one. A hard case from the short-lived Banning gang crouched behind the edge of the pedestal of the unknown Spanish don. He rested the barrel of a Winchester on the smoothed surface of granite. Smoke put stone chips in the man's eyes with a quick round. The shooter fell back screaming. A hearty boom came from the barrel of the short-barreled L.C. Smith double ten that Walt Reardon had swung up from behind his back, after he emptied his six-gun.

The shot column of 00 Buck lifted a short, squat gunslick off his boots and planted him in the water tank. He went under without so much as a second splash. Walt cut his eyes to Smoke, then Jeff, to make sure of their where-abouts, then swung the shotgun toward a new target. The wound in his arm bled profusely. Smoke Jensen headed his way, when he saw Walt Reardon's knees start to buckle.

"Hang on, old friend," Smoke encouraged. "We've got to stop the bleeding."

"In the middle of a shoot-out?" Walt asked wonder-ingly.

"Damn betcha," said Smoke as he forced a grin.

Bullets cracked overhead and to both sides, as Smoke quickly bound Walt's arm. He helped Walt to the edge of the artificial pond created by the water tank, and eased the younger man to the ground.

"You can cover us from here." To Jeff, "Time to clean out the rest of this vermin."

"I'm with you," Jeff agreed.

They faced only three living enemies. Orin Banning would have been fortunate to have died first. That way he wouldn't have to see the destruction of his gang. Smoke gave that passing thought as he darted between the neatly trimmed clumps of hedge that defined walk-ways through the plaza. He saw a flicker of movement to his left and spun on one heel.

Gunfire had attracted more of the ne'er-do-wells, like vultures to carrion. The newcomer had only a brief in-stant to see the badge on the chest of Smoke Jensen before the famous gunfighter busted a cap and sent the gunhawk off to join Orin Banning's men in Hell.

"Awh, damn," Smoke grumbled, as two more took the dying one's place.

* * *

Wildcat Wally Holt could not remember a time when he didn't have a gun in the waistband of his trousers or on his hip. He'd killed his first man at the age of eleven; shot him in the back. He had killed a dozen more since. At nineteen, Wildcat Wally saw himself as one of the best gunfighters in New Mexico Territory. Why, he had even been so bold as to compare himself with Billy Bonny. In less than thirty seconds, he was about to learn that he had nowhere near the speed, accuracy, or determination of Billy the Kid, let alone the man he suddenly found himself facing.

"You gonna use that thing, or sit on it?" Smoke Jensen asked of him as the youthful tough skidded into the center of the gunfight on the plaza.

"Yeeeaaaaah!" Wildcat Wally roared as he drew his Colt.

Or at least he tried to draw it. Suddenly his right arm would not obey him. Immense pain radiated from his shoulder through his chest and neck. Wildcat Wally jolted backward a few wobbly steps, and again tried to raise his six-gun. Nothing happened. Swiftly he made a grab for the Peacemaker on his left hip. He had it clear of leather when some unseen force punched him solidly in the center of his body, right below his ribs. A splash of crimson droplets rose before his eyes, as they started dimming.

Wildcat Wally next discovered that he could not breathe. He willed himself to draw deeply, yet his chest never moved. Slowly he dropped to his knees, an unbelieving expression on his face.

He worked his mouth. "Wh—who are you, Marshal?"

"Smoke Jensen."

"Go—good. At least it took the best to do me in." So saying, Wildcat Wally Holt lost all his wildness and slipped into the long slumber of death.

"Smoke, behind you!" Walt Reardon shouted from the water tank.

A Winchester gave its familiar .44-40 bark and Smoke Jensen felt a tug and fiery burning sensation along the right side of his ribs. He had dodged and started to turn at Walt's shout, which had saved his life. Now he faced the back-shooter and watched fear drain the smirk of triumph off the coward's face. Blood ran freely down Smoke's right side as he raised his gun and put a .44 period right between the would-be killer's running lights. The back of his head left with the gunman's hat, and he did a high kick backward into oblivion.

"Thanks, Walt."

"Any time, Smoke."

Three more hard cases, lured by the sound of action, dashed onto the plaza, weapons at the ready. Walt cut the legs out from under one of them with a load of buckshot. The other two turned in his direction to see the double zeroes of the L.C. Smith pointed their way. They also saw Smoke Jensen off to the right. The wounded man managed to fish his six-gun out from under him, and died instantly from a gunshot wound delivered by Jeff York, whom they had not seen off to their left.

Made desperate by the sudden confrontation, the remaining pair swung weapons toward Smoke and Walt. The scattergun ripped one's chest apart. Smoke pumped a round into the last man, who draped himself over the back of a wooden bench. A dozen others, wishing to have no part of these deadly gunfighters, gave up a bad cause.

It was then that Orin Banning reared up from behind a low hedge and, screaming defiance, emptied his six-gun in wild, stray rounds that hit no one. He jammed the smoking weapon in his waistband and hauled another six-gun from his left-hand holster.

"Smoke Jensen, you baaastard!" he yelled as he opened fire.

Smoke dodged the first bullet, then returned fire. Banning grunted and staggered to one side. He got off another round, which plowed the ground between Smoke's legs. Then Smoke's second slug caught Banning full in the chest. That dropped him at last, amid the useless dregs of human garbage that had formed his gang. All at once the shooting stopped.

"Lay down your weapons and put hands in the air," Smoke Jensen demanded.

"What are you goin' to do to us?" one bleated.

"You're going to jail. When we have time to sort you all out, we'll send you home," Jeff York added.

A straggly parade of glum, disgruntled would-be gunhawks wound along the way to the jail. Inside, Ferdie Biggs had been talking with Sheriff Reno. When the prisoners trooped in, led by Jeff York, Ferdie cut his eyes to the disgraced sheriff. He received a slight nod in response.

"Lock 'em up yourself," he grumbled to Jeff York.

Jeff took the keys from Ferdie as the latter pushed past him. A moment later, Ferdie Biggs reached the office section. Smoke Jensen bent over a seated Walt Reardon. He changed the makeshift bandage and again insisted that Walt see a doctor. With Smoke's back turned, Ferdie had all the encouragement he needed. His six-gun had already cleared leather with a soft, wicked whisper.

Before Ferdie Biggs could ear back the hammer, Smoke Jensen turned in an eye blink, his right fist filled with a big .45 Colt. Transfixed by surprise, Ferdie stupidly tried to continue. Smoke shot him twice before Ferdie could squeeze his trigger.

Ferdie's legs reflexed violently and catapulted him over the former sheriff's desk. He sprawled on the floor behind, twitched and shuddered, then sighed out his life.

"Damn, how'd you know?" Walt Reardon gulped out.

"I saw your eyes narrow," Smoke answered.

"I was going to call a warning to you."

"Ferdie didn't give you enough time, Walt. But that squint did enough to tip me off."

"What now?"

"We drag that garbage out of here, and get on with it," Smoke answered with a glance at the corpse.

With their assorted wounds properly tended to, Smoke Jensen, Jeff York, and half of the Rangers with Tallpockets rode directly toward the B-Bar-H. Walt Reardon stayed behind to hold the jail. Even as they rode past the town limits, more fast-gun types drifted into Socorro.

"We're mighty short on numbers," Jeff observed tight-lipped.

"I thought about that before we left." Smoke flashed a white-toothed grin. "So I brought along enough dynamite to lower the odds a little."

Jeff let out a low whistle. "Reckon this is the last go-round."

"It had better be."

They rode on in silence for a while. By late afternoon they reached the boundary of Benton-Howell's ranch. Smoke noticed it first. The split-rail fences had been filled in with rocks and dirt, to form parapets; behind them stood some twenty rifle-toting gunhawks, lured by the high money paid and a chance to test themselves against Smoke Jensen. Smoke and his men reined in just out of range.

"We aren't going through there, even with dynamite," Jeff opined.

"Don't go off too sudden, Jeff. What we need to do is look around a little more. We'll ride around the whole spread, and see how much is done up like this."

They made it only halfway around the ten sections controlled by Benton-Howell by nightfall. So far it appeared that only a half-section, some three-hundred-twenty acres, had been sealed off. Not all the approaches were covered by so many men. Smoke had led them out of sight of those guarding the road and gate, when they had been able to cross over onto the ranch property. Well-accustomed to the rigors of man hunting, the rangers made a cold camp.

Smoke sat, chewing on a strip of jerky, and took council from the stars. After a while, he rose to his boots and walked over to where Jeff York had already bedded down for the night. He squatted beside his friend and spoke softly.

"I've made up my mind. Come first light, we'll ride back to the Tucker place and send for the rest of Tallpockets's men. Then I'm going to fix up something that will get us through all those defenses."

"What do you have in mind, Smoke?"

"The dynamite got me to thinking on it. That and the wide gaps along this side that aren't being watched. You'll see what I'm doing when we get to working on it."

Smoke Jensen had added to the mystery by instructing the young Ranger headed for Socorro, "Bring the wainwright from town out here, when you come back."

Now, two days later, with night on the sawtooth ridges to the east, the curious among the Arizona Rangers stood around, watching while the wagon builder rigged an unusual attachment to a buckboard which Smoke Jensen had purchased from Martha Tucker. One of the older—which meant a man in his late twenties—Rangers scratched at a growing bald spot in his sandy hair, and worked his lips up for a good spit.

"Now, what the heck kind of thing do you call that?"

Laughing at something said inside, Smoke Jensen stepped out of the house and walked directly to the curious lawman. "That's a quick release lynch pin, to let the team get away from the wagon in time."

"Time for what?" the sandy-haired peace officer fired back.

"Come along with me and you'll see," Smoke promised.

At the rear of the buckboard, eleven wooden cases of dynamite, from Lawrence Tucker's private powder magazine, were being carefully loaded into the wagon. Baskets and barrels of scrap metal from the blacksmithy and sheds of the ranch were being emptied around and over the explosives, except for the one in the middle. It had its top off, and several sticks of sixty percent dynamite were missing.

"You buildin' a bombshell?" the seasoned Ranger asked.

"I thought you'd figure it out right quick," Smoke praised him. "When we get done, this will be like the largest exploding cannon shell in the world."

"How come that one case is open?"

"We get to that one last. After the wagon is in position for what I want it to do. That's the primer that's going to set off all the rest."

"Gol-ly, Mr. Jensen, I ain't never seen anythin' quite like this."

"Those on the receiving end will wish they had never seen this one."

"I want everyone to get a good night's rest," Jeff announced as he joined Smoke at the wagon. "We leave for the B-Bar-H at first light." To Smoke, he invited, "Time for another cup of coffee?"

Smoke Jensen cut his eyes skyward. "If I do, my eyes will turn brown. I'm going to grab a few winks."

"Sleep well," Jeff offered.

"You know it's funny, but I never do the night before a big fight," Smoke responded on his way to the bunkhouse.

Twenty-two

Smoke Jensen saw at once that the time they had taken to prepare for the attack on the B-Bar-H had a double edge. It had given Benton-Howell the opportunity to strengthen his defenses. Instead of penetrating the outer ring of hastily made revetments on the north, they had to go around to the east, because of reinforcements who now patrolled where none had been before. It took some doing, and cost several hours to move slowly enough not to reveal the presence of their force of some twenty-five men and the wagon. Smoke oversaw the operation with patience and good humor.

"Look at it this way," he advised a grumbling ranch hand from the Tucker spread. "The longer goes by without an attack on the B-Bar-H, the more restless and bored those second- and third-rate gunhands are going to get. When we do hit, it will shock them right out of their boots."

"When do we hit them, then?"

"Tonight, well after dark, when all of them are relaxed and off their edge. The big thing is to get a hole cut in the outer defenses, wide enough to drive the wagon through without being detected."

"We have enough shovels along," Jeff York added, as

he rode up beside the buckboard being driven by Smoke Jensen. "Should go fast."

"That is if they aren't as thick around there as on the north," a gloomy Ranger commented.

"Ralph, you always look on the dark side," Jeff snapped.

"He has a point," Smoke Jensen injected. "Even if Benton-Howell doesn't have enough reinforcements now to cover the whole perimeter, we'll have to get rid of those on the east without making a sound. Knives and 'hawks if you've got them," he concluded through the scant opening between grimly straight lips.

Darkness had come an hour before and Pearly Cousins had given strict instructions to the gunmen who had accompanied him not to light up a smoke during their time on watch. It was hard enough seeing before the moon rose, let alone to be blinded by the flare of a lucifer. He yawned and stirred in his saddle. Pearly had been up late the night before, and had only five hours sleep in the past two days. We're stretched too thin, Pearly thought to himself. Best be checking on the lookouts along the east side of the wall. Some of them aren't wrapped all too tight.

Pearly didn't find the rider at the northeast corner. "Must be patrolin'," he muttered aloud. He turned south.

Close to where he expected to find two of the eight men guarding this side of the defenses jawing instead of doing their work, he came upon a riderless horse. That was something Pearly hadn't expected. It ignited the first suspicions.

"Lupe, you takin' a leak, or what?" Pearly asked in a muted voice.

When he received no answer, Pearly edged his horse forward and caught up the reins of the abandoned mount. Then he started inward to seek the negligent sentry. He did not go far before he dimly saw a huddled form on the ground. The black silhouette of a big Mexican sombrero two feet from the body identified it as Lupe. His alarms jangling now, Pearly dismounted and crouched beside the unmoving man.

Pearly rolled Lupe onto his back. Pearly saw that Lupe's throat had been slit from ear to ear. Stealthy motion caught Pearly's eyes, as a huge human figure rose from the brush directly in front of him. He heard a soft *swish* a moment before the tomahawk in the hand of Smoke Jensen split Pearly's skull to his jawbone.

Smoke wrenched his 'hawk free and cleaned it on the dead outlaw's shirt front. He tucked it back behind his belt, and set off for the spot he judged to be directly in line with the ranch house. When he reached the place, he found the other night stalkers there ahead of him.

"Had an extra one to take care of," he explained. "We had better get started."

Taking turns at the dirt barrier, the lawmen spent only half an hour opening a space wide enough to admit the buckboard. Smoke drove, while Jeff led the mountain man's roan stallion. The Arizona Rangers and ranch hands formed a crescent-shaped line to right and left.

A mile inside the outer defenses, Smoke called a halt. "Time to set the primer charge," he announced tightly.

With that accomplished, the posse started up again. Smoke had allowed enough fuse for what he thought ap-

proximated twenty minutes. He would light it a moment
before they topped the rise to the east of the house. Then
he would set the team in a gallop, and make ready for
the rest of the plan. If it didn't work the way he expected,
if the fuse burned too quickly, then he would never know
it.

"Good luck," Jeff York said tightly thirty minutes later,
as the lawmen dropped back to let the wagon take the
lead.

Smoke Jensen lit the fuse, and slapped the reins lightly
on the rumps of the wheelers. The team dug in, the sixteen hooves of the draft animals pounded the ground with
increasing speed. They crested the steep swale, and the
velocity increased. Smoke snapped the reins again. He
stood upright now, a small rope wrapped around his
gloved left hand. The rumbling of the buckboard's wheels
drowned out the sound of the mounts of the lawmen with
him.

Closer loomed the mounded dirt that formed the inner
fortifications. Smoke Jensen drove straight at the parapet.
Flame lanced at the wagon from half a dozen places.
Still Smoke remained upright, swaying with the erratic
motion of the heavily laden buckboard. The vehicle ca-
reened onward. Closer, ever closer . . . the blackness of
the hastily erected defenses filled Smoke's field of vision. He pulled slightly on the cord in his left hand, felt
the lynch pin loosen. Any time now . . . any . . .

NOW!

Smoke dropped the reins and yanked the lynch pin. It
came free, and the horses, undirected now, curved from
the mass before them, the tongue carried between their
churning bodies. Smoke jumped free and rolled in the

tall grass. Suddenly Jeff York swerved in close at the side of Smoke Jensen. He trailed the reins of Smoke's roan. Without breaking stride, Jeff flashed past. Smoke readied himself and leaped for the saddle horn. He caught it and swung atop his rutching stallion.

Immediately they all curved away and outward from the barrier. Five seconds later, the wagon struck the solid wall of dirt with a thunderous crash. A heartbeat later it exploded with a roar that came from the end of the world.

Waiting for an attack that might or might not come had started to get on his nerves. Geoffrey Benton-Howell paced the thick oriental rug in his study, hands clasped behind his back. His eyes cut frequently to the crystal decanter of brandy on the sideboard that formed part of a wall of bookshelves. No, that wouldn't do, he thought forcefully.

This was no night to get lost in the heady fumes of the grape. Not any night was fit for tippling until that offensive son of a bitch, Smoke Jensen, had been hunted down and eliminated. Nearly a week had passed since Jensen and the Rangers had cleared out Socorro. It did little to improve his outlook to know that the town had filled up once again with eager fast guns. Most of the Rangers had disappeared, and the remainder had forted up in the jail. He needed to get those new men involved in a search for Jensen. Benton-Howell sighed heavily, almost a gasp, and crossed to the door.

He leaned through the opening and called down the hall to the large sitting room. "Miguel, I need you in here for a moment."

When Miguel Selleres entered the paneled study, Benton-Howell had arranged his thoughts in order. Selleres likewise declined any liquor. He seated himself in a large, horsehair-stuffed leather chair and rested elbows on the arms. He steepled his long fingers and spoke over them.

"So, you have grown tired of waiting, *amigo?*"

"Just so. I want you to take two of the better gunmen and ride into Socorro. Organize that rabble, and set them off hunting for Smoke Jensen."

"I thought we had agreed to make him come to us here."

"We did. Only I don't think it is working."

Suddenly, as though to put the lie to Benton-Howell's pronouncement, a ragged volley of gunfire broke out at the dirt barricade that surrounded the house and barn. There followed a moment of silence, then a violent crash of splintering wood. Then the darkness washed away in a wall of sheer whiteness. The sound of the explosion, like a thunderclap directly overhead, came a second later. The shockwave blew every window on that side of the building inward.

It knocked books from the shelves and set the brandy decanter to dancing. Stunned to immobility, the two plotters stared at each other. Fighting for words, Benton-Howell got control of his voice first.

"They're attacking! Take charge of the men. There's no time to head for town. We have to stop them."

"Someone else can go, Stalker perhaps, and bring the others back. They could hit the Rangers in the rear."

"It's half a day in and the same back," Benton-Howell reminded. "By then we could all be dead."

"Or worse, on the way to jail," Miguel Selleres riposted.

Shuddering, Benton-Howell dismissed such weakening visions and began to organize the defenses. "Get torches lit; the men can't see which way to shoot. Are the sandbags in place around the outer walls?"

"Yes, since yesterday. Both floors."

"Have men at every window. Bolt the doors."

Sparks from the fuses in single sticks of dynamite began to make twinkling trails through the black of night. The blasts began to rout men caught in the open yard. Some bolted for the covered passageway that led to the well nearest the house. They made it without incident, only to be forced to cringe on the ground when holes began to appear in the wooden walls, as hot lead cracked through at chest level.

Sharp blasts illuminated the yard, as the dynamite began to explode. Their flashes strobed the action of the disoriented outlaws in the ranch yard. Two went down, shot through the chest, and a screech of agony came from another who had caught a short round in the groin. With a muffled curse, Miguel Selleres rushed from the room to bring order out of the chaos.

Fully a third of the defenders had been knocked off their feet by the tremendous explosion, Smoke Jensen noted as he and Jeff rode through the breach created in the parapet. Dust and the acrid odor of dynamite smoke still hung in the air. Jeff pointed to the rubble of scattered earth.

"If they'd used gabions, that wouldn't have worked," the Arizona Ranger said.

"What are those?"

"Sort of tubelike baskets, made of reeds or thin tree branches; they're used in building fortifications." Jeff looked sort of embarrassed. "I learned that from General Crook, when I scouted for the army."

Smoke grunted. "Good thing the one who built this didn't know it."

Bullets cracked past Smoke and Jeff, and they saw that some of those not effected by the blast had recovered enough to offer resistance. One of the Tucker hands yelped, and clapped a hand to a profusely bleeding wound in his right arm. The shooter didn't have time to celebrate his victory. Smoke Jensen put a .44 round in his ear, and sent him, brainless, onto the outlaw level of Hell.

Suddenly a pack of dogs charged into the yard from a run behind the house. One launched itself and sank fangs into the leg of an Arizona Ranger. The lawman screamed as the teeth savaged him. He swung with the barrel of his revolver. It made a hollow sound when it struck the flat, triangular head of the bristling mastiff.

That had no effect on his grip though. He hung on, his body weight sagging downward, ripping his fangs through tender flesh. Tallpockets Granger whirled in his saddle and shot the vicious monster through the head. It fell away with a whimper and twitched violently on the ground. Another of the beasts, crazed by the explosive blasts, leaped on the back of one of the hired guns. His shrieks could be heard until the huge dog reached his throat. h'

"Keep clear of them," Smoke called out. "They'll do us more good than harm."

Smoke pulled a fused stick of dynamite from his saddlebag and lit it from a cigar clinched in his teeth. He hurled it toward the house. It hit the window frame and bounced off. A moment later it went off with a blinding flash and roar.

More quickly followed from the Arizona Rangers. Two more of the savage dogs died in attempts to attack strangers among the outlaw defenders. Smoke rounded the house and found himself facing two hard cases with six-guns cocked and ready. His right hand dropped to the curved butt-grips of his .44 Colt. One of the gunslingers fired before Smoke finished his draw.

His bullet cut a hot trail along Smoke's left side, below the rib cage. Then Smoke had his Peacemaker clear and in action. It bucked sharply, and he emptied the saddle of the second outlaw. Hammer back and another sharp recoil as the .44 belched. It spat hot lead that ended the ambitions of a would-be giant-killer. Smoke chucked another stick of explosives through a window and spun away.

The blast, muffled somewhat, blew out two walls of the kitchen. Plaster dust and powder smoke made a heavy fog that was all too easy for the hard-pressed gunhawks to hide in. Smoke knew that the noise they had made would soon attract the larger portion of the gunslick army from their outer defenses. He had taken that into consideration in his plans. Now, he decided, would be the time to pull out. He worked the thin leather glove off his right hand and put thumb and forefinger between his lips.

He whistled shrilly and headed at once for the gap

blown in the defenses. The Arizona Rangers and Tucker ranch hands streamed behind him. Only a few random shots followed them. That and the shrill, patently hysterical curses of Geoffrey Benton-Howell.

In the cold, hard light of dawn, Geoffrey Benton-Howell and Miguel Selleres surveyed the damage. Every window in the house had been blown out again. Two walls of the kitchen had been scattered over the ranch yard, and the second-floor extension sagged precariously over what remained. Food had to be prepared in the bunkhouse and the outdoor rock-lined fire pits. Those of the hired guns who remained, shivered in the chill, early morning air as they waited in line for coffee, beans, and fatback.

Half an hour later, as the partners accepted plates of food from the grizzled range cook, a patrol sent out at first light returned.

"Then Rangers blew holes in the barricades in half a dozen places on their way out," Charlie Bascomb, who had led them, reported. "Any time they want, they can pour through on us like water through a sieve."

"Damn him to eternal hell!" Benton-Howell blurted. "It's the doing of Smoke Jensen, you can be certain of that."

"*¡Oye, amigo! No te dejes poner los verdes.* He is only a man," Miguel Selleres jokingly told his partner.

"I am *not* letting him pull the wool over my eyes," Benton-Howell snapped angrily. "You know as well as I what that man has done to us. It's not natural, not . . . human! We started this project off with him waiting a lynch mob in the Socorro jail. Now he has nearly destroyed my home."

"What do you propose?" Selleres prompted.

Benton-Howell considered that a while. "It's obvious that the ranch is not secure enough. There are ample gunmen waiting in Socorro to assist us. If we move the Tuckers into town, Smoke Jensen will hear of it. We can draw him out and make him fight on ground of our choosing."

Selleres played the devil's advocate. "What if he's waiting for us on the way?"

Benton-Howell shaped his plan aloud. "We'll take everyone from here, form a screen of protection around us and our hostages. Once we reach town, we'll be safe enough. You'll see."

Walt Reardon met the raiding party when Smoke Jensen brought the men back to the Tucker ranch. His grim expression alerted Smoke to possible new problems. He and Jeff met with the ex-gunfighter in the kitchen over coffee and sweet rolls.

Walt chomped on a yeasty cinnamon roll, and washed it down with a long swallow of Arbuckle's Arabica before revealing what brought him to the ranch. "Something big is building up in town." Walt cut his eyes to Jeff. "The Rangers you left me have been overpowered one by one, and completely disappeared. Socorro's runnin' chock-a-block with ne'er-do-wells and gunslingers. Somethin' big's cookin', I can feel it in my bones."

"Any ideas?" Smoke prompted. "We did a fair job of rattling Benton-Howell and his gunhands on the ranch."

He looked at the table, chagrined by the admission he had to make. "We were too outnumbered to make a push to get the Tuckers out."

Walt shook his head. "I got this feelin' somethin' big is comin' on. If nothin' else, we need to find those missing Rangers."

Smoke Jensen came to his boots, thumbs hooked in the front of his cartridge belt. "I agree. Cuchillo Negro's warriors are needed to guard the ranch, so I suggest we take the Rangers we have on hand, any hands who volunteer, and head for Socorro."

Twenty-three

Clear, sharp eyes, undimmed by long afternoons and nights of drinking and carousing in the saloons of Socorro, first spotted the large plume of dust that rose from the horses of the Rangers and ranch hands. It took little time to realize that trouble rode toward town. Even so, the alert gunhawk placed on lookout on the north edge of Socorro waited until he could count heads, make certain who and how much trouble was headed his way. Then he sent one of the hungover wannabes to report his findings.

"Go to the Exchange Hotel and tell Mr. Benton-Howell that twenty-three men are headed this way. Tell him Smoke Jensen and that Ranger are in the lead."

The two-bit gunslick ambled away, while he held his head with one hand and licked dry lips, wishing for a little hair of the dog—no, wolf—that had bit him the night before. He found the lordly Englishman in the saloon of the Exchange, which gave him an excuse to get a drink.

First he had to report, which he did, cringing a little from the expression of wrath that grew on Benton-Howell's' face. When he delivered the message, he turned toward the bar. "No drinking. Not today," Benton-Howell declared imperiously. "Every man must be sober for what is sure to come." He turned to Quint Stalker, who sat at a table drinking coffee, which he had surreptitiously laced with rum in defiance of the orders of the big boss.

"Quinten, I want you to deliver a message to Smoke Jensen. Under a flag of truce, naturally."

"Sure, Boss. What do you want to say?"

Benton-Howell told him and sent the gang leader on his way. On the slow ride to the edge of town, Quint Stalker tied a strip of white petticoat to the barrel of his Winchester. He had torn it from the undergarment of a soiled dove he had encountered on the street. He reached the city limits only a minute before Smoke and the posse thundered up to the wooden bridge that crossed the dry creek. Quint hoisted his white flag, and showed himself in the middle of the road.

"I got a message for Smoke Jensen," he called out.

Smoke edged forward on his roan stallion. "Spit it out."

"Mr. Benton-Howell done told me to tell you that he's turned Miz Tucker an' her brats over to Miguel Selleres. *Señor* Selleres has orders to kill them slowly, starting with the youngest kid, if you don't give yourself up within one hour."

Anger flared in Smoke's chest. He dare not risk the lives of the Tuckers further, yet he had no intention of providing target practice for a bunch of second-rate *pistoleros*. He had to buy some time.

"Do you know what happened in the Middle Ages when a messenger brought bad news?" he asked Stalker.

"No, what?"

"They killed him."

Stalker blanched. "Now, look, I'm under a flag of truce. You got no call to kill me. It ain't fair," he ended with a nervous titter.

"Very little is in this life," Smoke returned.

Stalker knew enough about the gunfighter business to know Jensen wanted something, a deal, a way out. "You got that right. What are you after, Jensen?"

A bleak smile answered him for a long moment, and Quint Stalker felt a chill as the icy gray eyes of Smoke Jensen bored into him. "Time. I didn't expect to find the Tuckers here. need to rethink things."

Sensing he had regained the upper hand, Stalker snapped, "You've got an hour, that's what The Man said."

"I need more than that. Make it two hours. Tell Benton-Howell that if I see the Tucker family, alive and well, after that, I'll come in alone."

"No tricks?"

"Your boss has all the aces, Stalker," Smoke Jensen replied in a disarming tone.

"I'll see what I can do." Smirking, Stalker turned on one boot heel. Then he threw over his shoulder, "If you hear a gunshot an hour from now, you'll know Mr. Benton-Howell has rejected your terms."

"Damn! What do we do now?" Jeff York exploded.

"It's a rigged deck, the way I see it," Smoke told him bluntly. "It's too obvious to mention what will happen, if I go in there alone. If I don't go in, the Tuckers will die. Benton-Howell is a desperate man."

"I can believe that," Jeff allowed. "He has to see that

his scheme is falling apart. Even if he gets you, there's no way he can bring it off."

"My thoughts, too, Jeff. So, here's what we'll do," Smoke offered. Without hesitation he laid out his plans.

Ten minutes went by before Tallpockets Granger walked his mount down the main street of Socorro, a white shirt tied to the muzzle of his rifle. He stopped outside the Exchange Hotel and called out for Quint Stalker. When Quint appeared, Tallpockets waved the white flag over his head to make it clear that he was under truce. Then he leaned forward and spoke eye to eye with Stalker.

"Smoke Jensen wants to talk to you again. He says he wants to spell out the manner of his surrender."

"I'll be right with you." Stalker returned to the hotel, to walk back out in less than half a minute. "The Boss says that's all right with him."

They rode together to the edge of town. There, Stalker threw a look of contempt at Smoke Jensen and spoke in a crisp tone of command. "Mr. Benton-Howell said you were in no position to set terms. But he agreed to listen this time. What is it you have in mind?"

"I've decided to turn myself in. Provided that the Tuckers are unharmed. And I want to see them riding away from town, alone, or no deal. They go free before I reach the center of town. And no back-shooting, or the rest of my friends here will take Socorro apart, regardless of what happens to me or the Tuckers. Benton-Howell and Selleres will hang, and there won't be a one of those two-bit *pistoleros* left alive."

Anger rose to choke Stalker, so that he spluttered when he snapped, "That's bluster, Jensen, and you know it. You must be gettin' old. Old and yellow, deep down in your core, or you'd not be runnin' yer mouth instead of your gun."

Fire replaced the ice in the eyes of Smoke Jensen. "You want to try me now?"

Quint Stalker hesitated a moment, and Smoke Jensen thought, *gotcha!* "Another time. I'll take what you said to the Boss, and we'll see." He turned his mount and rode away.

Fifteen minutes later, he returned. "Mr. Benton-Howell agrees," Quint Stalker shouted across the dry creek. "I'm to accompany you to the jail to see there are no tricks . . . from either side."

"How noble of you," Smoke responded sarcastically.

Stalker looked hurt. "I insisted on it. I admire you for this, Jensen, and I wanted to make sure there was no hanky-panky on either side."

Quint Stalker's words raised Jensen's assessment of the outlaw leader. He shrugged and cut his eyes to Jeff, "You know what to do." To Stalker, "Let's get on with it." Smoke eased his roan onto the bridge.

From that first step, Smoke felt his gut tighten with sour tension. At each step the horses took, a spot between his shoulder blades grew warmer and tingled with anticipation of a bullet to rend and tear his flesh and end his life. Not one to fear death, the mountain man still had a healthy regard for living. By the end of the first block, with not a hard case in sight, Smoke began to gauge each building as the possible spot from which the assassin's bullet would come.

Beside him, Quint Stalker appeared to be equally apprehensive. His eyes cut from side to side, suspicion deeply planted on his face. Sweat popped out on his brow, and he licked his lips continuously. Smoke suspicioned that Stalker's palms oozed moisture inside the black leather gloves.

"Don't you trust your masters?" Smoke taunted, partly to break his own chain of anxiety.

"Of course—come to think of it, not a hell of a lot. It's me that's the target out here, not them."

"Good thinking, Stalker."

Another block further along, Stalker nodded toward the balcony of the Exchange Hotel. "Over there."

Smoke cut his eyes to three tiny figures standing there. Jimmy, Rose, and Tommy Tucker huddled close together, the older boy's arms protectively around the shoulders of his siblings. They had all been crying, and began again at the sight of Smoke Jensen riding in a prisoner.

"Don't let 'em do it to you, Smoke," Jimmy's high, thin voice cut through the dust haze to Smoke's ears.

Smoke gave the boy a short, friendly wave. Lace curtains at a second-floor front window fluttered and drew apart. A Mexican *pistolero* stood beside Martha Tucker, a wicked grin whitening his face under a thick, drooping moustache. Smoke reined in. He jabbed a finger at the hostages and spoke harshly.

"Bring them down here. Now."

Quint Stalker sighed heavily and shrugged. "This is the part makes me uneasy. They don't get loose, until you're locked in jail. The Boss ordered it that way."

Smoke Jensen started a curse, broke if off, knowing it to be futile. If the shooting started now, the Tuckers would die for certain. "Never could abide two-faced bastards like your Benton-Howell," he growled bitterly.

"Truth to tell, I ain't too fond of him, myself," Stalker muttered.

Smoke eyed him thoughtfully. "Ever think of changing sides?" From the light that glowed in Stalker's eyes, Smoke knew that he had planted a seed in fertile soil. "Let's get on with it."

At the jail, without a shot fired, Stalker dismounted, tied off his horse, then drew his six-gun. He covered Smoke while Jensen climbed from the saddle and let himself be led into the office. With Ferdie Biggs no longer among the living, a new jailer had been selected. His smirking grin revealed a missing front tooth and the yellow stain of an inveterate tobacco chewer. Quint Stalker removed Smoke's cartridge belt and twin .44s and tossed them on the desk. Then the jailer revealed his nature to be much like his predecessor.

He took two quick steps forward and solidly punched Smoke Jensen in the ribs. Pain shot through Smoke from the bullet scrapes on both sides, as he rocked with the blows. He caught another pair in the gut, and fought the urge to double over from the effect. Carefully he sucked in fresh air.

"Are you any relation to Ferdie Biggs?" Smoke asked in as calm a voice as he could manage.

"Naw, I ain't no kin of his."

"Funny, there's such a resemblance," Smoke taunted.

Smoke's taunt had the desired effect. With a roar the lout lunged forward again without any caution. Smoke's hard, looping left caught him on the point of his protruding jaw; the gunfighter put all his body behind it. He had the satisfaction of hearing a loud snap and feel the loose wobble of bone before the jailer dropped like a stone.

"Gawdamn!" Stalker blurted.

"He needed that."

Awe filled the eyes of Quint Stalker, as he nodded his head in agreement. "I still gotta lock you up. You know the way."

Down the corridor of the cellblock, Smoke found three of the missing Rangers, locked together in one large cell. No doubt the holding tank for drunks. They all had depression written on their faces.

"In you go," Quint Stalker said with a wink.

He opened the cage, and Smoke joined his three allies. Without further comment, Stalker left the cellblock and the jail and returned to the Exchange Hotel.

Deft, brown fingers worked at the fastenings of the wire basket that enclosed the cork. With it pried open and removed, two thumbs pried the cork until it popped loudly and flew to the ceiling of the men's bar in the Exchange Hotel. A shower of bubbles followed. Laughing, Miguel Selleres turned to the four other men in the room.

"We have much to celebrate, *Señores*. Our good friend, Sheriff Reno, is out of jail and . . . Smoke Jensen is inside!"

"Not to mention we still have the hostages, old boy," Geoffrey Benton-Howell chortled as he presented his glass to be filled.

"More important, the Tuckers will not be released until

the ranch is signed over to the three of us," Dalton Wade crowed.

"They'll not be released even then," Benton-Howell stated quietly, instantly drawing the attention of Sheriff Reno, Dalton Wade, and Miguel Selleres.

"Whatever do you mean by that, Sir Geoffrey?" Dalton Wade asked, concern creasing his brow.

"There's no percentage in leaving behind any living witnesses. Surely you see the wisdom of that, Dalton."

"My word. I'd never given that problem any consideration. Isn't it a bit savage to take the lives of women and children?"

Benton-Howell peered at his partner over the rim of his champagne glass. "We live in brutal times, my friend. We cannot afford to have anyone—outside of ourselves— left to bear tales of how we obtained all this property and the wealth of that gold field in the White Mountains. Oh, yes, I have been assured the transfer will take place as promised. You can see the importance now, can you not? Not even these troublesome Arizona Rangers must escape our little cleanup."

"Yes," Selleres agreed. "Which brings us to what means to use to dispose of Smoke Jensen."

All four men remained silent with their thoughts a moment. Then a beatific smile spread on the face of Benton-Howell.

"I think the most demeaning, humiliating, degrading form of death should be applied to Smoke Jensen. Unfortunately, there is not a single guillotine to be had in this forsaken country. So, I suggest we hang him. How ignoble."

Soft applause came from Dalton Wade and Miguel

Selleres. Sheriff Reno nodded approval. As did Quint Stalker, who had to fight to keep his face rigidly devoid of any expression. The plotters were convinced of the complete defeat of Smoke Jensen, only the outlaw leader felt no surprise when a cacophony of sound blasted into the elegant barroom, followed by the crumbling of stone and brickwork from the direction of the jail.

Following Smoke Jensen's instructions, the Rangers watched until he disappeared into the jail, then drifted off in groups of threes and fours. They made their way out of sight of town at the slow pace of men who had reluctantly admitted their cause to be lost, yet unwilling to leave in a body. The ruse worked, Jeff York realized half an hour later when no pursuit had begun against them.

At that point, Geoffrey Benton-Howell had as yet to pronounce their death sentences along with the rest. After the Rangers departed, Quint Stalker had withdrawn the lookouts, leaving only some of the hungover dregs to keep watch, so that his men could join in the celebration. Before he had returned to the hotel, he noted a number of those who had come bounty hunting, drift off toward more promising fields. He would soon regret that.

Jeff York and six men had no difficulty in slipping unobserved into Socorro. They went directly to the jail, located the cell holding Smoke Jensen and the missing Rangers. They cut short any reunion for the business at hand.

"Get mattresses," Jeff instructed curtly. "Sit down clear of this wall, cover yourselves, and hold your ears."

"Awh, crap, Jeff, you ain't gonna blow us outta here, are you?" one lanky, horse-faced Ranger complained.

"Come up with a better way, and I won't have to," Jeff quipped.

While he spoke, Jeff rigged a bundle of dynamite sticks to the wall, close to the small window, which he figured for the weakest point. With everything in readiness, he lit the fuse and cleared out with his Rangers. The blast reverberated all over town, bounced off the steep walls of the gorge in which the village had been built, punished ears for a quarter mile, and set dogs to howling hysterically.

It didn't do too much for the men in the cell, for that matter. The brick wall within the native fieldstone one pummeled them with chunks that would leave bruises the next day. Even with fingers in ears and mouths open, the pressure was enormous. Two Rangers lost consciousness, and Smoke Jensen discovered he had a bloody nose. A tad bit more dynamite, and they'd all be playing harps for St. Peter, he thought dazedly as the caustic fumes and mortar dust swirled around him. Only indistinctly did he hear the pound of hooves, as Jeff and his volunteers rushed back to extricate them from the jail.

Upright beside Jeff York, Smoke Jensen gestured to the ruined building they had just exited. "We have to get our weapons."

"Already taken care of."

Smoke frowned as the import of that struck him. "Then why in Billy blue hell did you try to turn us into red mush?"

"Thought it might scare hell out of some of these tender feet gunhawks."

"You did a fair job of that on us." Jeff gave a shrug, so Smoke continued, "Give me my rig, and let's go get these bastards who hide behind women and children."

Twenty-four

Geoffrey Benton-Howell had no doubt as to the source of the explosion. He immediately sent Quint Stalker to organize the horde of gunslingers who milled about the streets of Socorro, most of them confused as to what was going on. Miguel Selleres went upstairs at once, to make sure the Tuckers remained secure in the Exchange Hotel. He spoke urgently to the guards outside the door to the room that held the children.

"No one gets in there, none of our own or any lawmen."

"*Sí, Señor Selleres,*" one Sonoran *pistolero* responded respectfully. "Not a soul will get past us."

"See to it." Selleres went on down the hall to where Mrs. Tucker had been kept. "Unlock it," he demanded. Inside, he crossed to a small table where Martha Tucker sat taking her evening meal. He shaped his features to show pleading. "*Señora,* there is going to be a great deal of bloodshed. You can prevent it. Simply sign the ranch over to us . . ." Selleres ended with hands outstretched, palms up in silent appeal.

"I do not believe in fairy-tales, *Señor* Selleres. The moment I sign those papers, myself and my children are dead. On the other hand, I can trust that for now, no stray bullet will strike any of us."

Selleres hardened his face. "Can you trust that we will not kill you outright, rather than let you fall into the hands of Smoke Jensen?"

A chill-ran along Martha's spine. She girded herself for the answer she knew she had to make. "If you are that thoroughly reprehensible, then I can only place my trust in the Lord . . . and Smoke Jensen."

A burst of gunfire from down the street interrupted the hot retort that started from the lips of Miguel Selleres. He turned on one boot heel and started for the door.

Two gun-toting henchmen appeared high up in the windows of the feed mill. The tinkle of broken glass alerted those below. Smoke Jensen went to one knee and snugged the Winchester .44 carbine to his shoulder in one smooth motion. Jeff York raised his Colt, and put a .45 round through the corrugated metal skin of the grain elevator.

It expanded as it went its way, and slammed into flesh an inch above the buckle on the cartridge belt of one hard case. He jolted forward in reaction to his wound, and lurched through the window sash. His startled companion had only a moment to hear the agonized scream, as Smoke Jensen put out his lights for all time with a hot lead snuffer. The sniper's body jerked backward and out of view.

"That was close," Jeff observed.

"They never got off a shot," Smoke reminded him.

Halfway down the next block, four men ranged across

the street. They had a variety of mismatched weapons, which spoke for their lack of expertise. What they lacked in knowledge they made up for in courage—or foolishness. All four entered the dance with blazing six-guns.

Smoke Jensen downed one easily, and heard the nearby crack of a bullet that sailed past his head. He lined his sights on another as two more weapons opened up through windows on the second floor above the general mercantile. He made a quick shot at his target, missed, and swung the muzzle of the Winchester upward. Three rounds levered through the Winchester silenced one of the hidden assassins. From behind Smoke the six-gun of Tallpockets roared and spat flame.

"They ain't gonna do any back-shootin'," the lanky Arizona Ranger remarked casually.

"We have to get to the Exchange Hotel fast," Smoke urged. "Every minute puts the Tuckers in more danger."

"Was I doin' it," Tallpockets drawled, "I'd get me away from here an' come at 'em from behind. Let me an' the boys take care of Main Street."

Smoke smiled broadly. "I appreciate the offer, Tallpockets. And I'll take you up on it. Jeff, Walt, and I will take this alley and come at the hotel from the back door."

"Three of you gonna be enough?" Tallpockets asked, then he looked over the trio indicated, grunted, and answered his own question. "I reckon so."

The street fighting grew fiercer as the outlaw scum and bounty-hungry drifters realized a major push was on against them. The way they saw it, they had to stand their ground; they simply had no way to go and no money to take them there. While they hotted up the battle,

Smoke, Jeff, and Walt darted down an alleyway and turned into the one that paralleled the main street. Three blocks to the hotel, and no way of knowing how many of Benton-Howell's gunhands they would encounter.

They made it only a block, and ran into half a dozen desperate men forted up in the rear of the saddler's shop. Lead flew thick and fast. Smoke Jensen felt a searing pain just below the point of his right shoulder, and cut his eyes to a ragged tear in the cloth of his shirt. Another fraction of an inch, and he'd be dripping blood again. Suddenly one of the defenders showed enough head for a clear shot.

Smoke took it with his old .44. The hat of the hard case flew off as his head snapped back. His eyes glazed as he sagged to the floor. A pair of boot heels could be heard pounding on the floorboards, headed for the front. That slackened the fire enough for Jeff York to dart along the alley, past the shop. From that angle, he poured fire into the back of the saddlery. Smoke and Walt did the same.

A couple of yowls of pain came from the interior. Then the firing lessened. A table, hastily put in place to barricade the back door, slid noisily across the floor. Nervous sounding, a voice called to them.

"That does it. We give up! We're coming out."

Smoke Jensen knew the darkness served as an ally to the dangerous men inside. He set himself and responded, "Come out one at a time. Hands in sight."

"Sure—sure. Don't shoot us, huh?"

A moment later the door opened, and a man's silhouette appeared in the frame. He advanced, hands at shoulder height, palms forward. So far, so good. Another man followed a moment later. When the body of the first to surrender blocked the view, the second man reached forward and yanked a hidden six-gun from the small of his partner's back. He threw a shot in the general direction of Smoke Jensen.

And died for his treachery. Smoke drilled him through the left eye. Bleating his nonexistent innocence, the first man went to his knees. The three lawmen ignored him for the moment, and concentrated on the others. A trio of rounds sped through the doorway, and the others came out so docile that one would think they were in church.

"That's more like it," Jeff York growled.

They quickly trussed up their prisoners and left them for the other Rangers to tend to. Of one accord, Smoke and his companions started off toward the hotel. Smoke found the back door first. He tried it, found it latched, and pondered their problem.

"This isn't going to be as easy as we thought," he advised the others. "If we make any noise going in there, they just might kill Martha and the children."

Whether by chance or design, the beleaguered gunfighters in the streets of Socorro drew back on the Exchange Hotel and the few buildings immediately around it. There they rallied and put up a determined resistance. Without a foolish risk of life, the Arizona Rangers could not expose themselves to make a frontal assault. Gradually it became obvious to everyone that the battle had degenerated into a standoff.

By one-thirty in the morning, only a few of the more aggressive individuals took potshots at their counterparts.

Another problem presented itself, brought to the attention of Smoke Jensen by Walt Reardon.

"We've got more prisoners than places to put them. Blowin' out that wall weren't such a good idea. That drunk tank could hold an easy twenty, twenty-five."

Smoke thought a moment. "Go to the Tinto Range Supply. There should be some barbed wire there. Use all you need to crisscross that opening like a spiderweb. Then put some men to guarding it. Some of the Tucker hands should be fine for that. They aren't getting paid to be shot at. Jeff and I will hold the fort here."

"Mighty interestin' idea. Just might work." Walt scooted out of there.

Within half an hour, prisoners had begun to be shifted from the grain bins of the livery into the holding cell of the jail. The first ones inside stared in stunned disbelief at what appeared to be a gaping hole in the wall.

"C'mon, boys, let's make a break for it," Wink Winkler muttered to those nearest to him. He made a dash for the opening, only to be caught in midair on the all but invisible strands of barbed wire. He howled in agony and thrashed a while, until he realized he only made it worse.

"Never did like that damned stuff," one hard-faced gunman remarked.

"Been more than one war fought over it," another agreed.

"Git me down offa here," Winkler wailed.

"Sure, but it'll smart some."

"You get close to that wire, and I'll blow your head off," came a voice from outside.

"Do something, get me off of here!" Wink Winkler wailed on the verge of hysteria.

"Reckon I could shoot you, to put you out of your misery," the Tucker wrangler suggested.

Morning brought no change in the stalemate. It also did not provide any easy access into the hotel. Smoke Jensen left Jeff York and three Arizona Rangers to watch the back exit to the Exchange Hotel, while he scouted for ideas. He found a possible solution within a block of the two-story structure.

He also received some bad news. Simms, one of the Rangers, came upon Smoke while he was trying to drag a tall ladder out of a litter of barrels and boxes outside the back of a store. The bantam rooster of a lawman announced that he sought Jeff York.

"Jeff's at the Exchange Hotel back door."

"We've got more troubles," Simms replied. "Durin' the night, more of this border scum drifted into town. Seems as how they got us caught between the ones we've corralled, and themselves."

Smoke Jensen gave it only a moment's thought. Using the ladder to scale to the second floor windows at the back of the hotel would have to wait. "When you're surrounded, there's only one thing to do."

"Surrender?" Simms asked doubtfully.

"Where've you been all your life? What we're going to do is attack in both directions at once." Smoke set off immediately to inform Jeff.

Eyes glazed with blood lust, the newcomers to Socorro sensed an easy kill. They moved in on the thin line of

Rangers with weapons in hand. Their shock was complete then, when half of the lawmen turned on them and opened fire, while the remainder yelled chillingly and charged buildings to either side of a large hotel. The rapid-fire crackle of rifles and six-guns drowned out the exclamations of consternation.

Three of the hard cases went down in a hail of bullets. Two ran toward the partial shelter of an alleyway, only to be met with the flat report of a shotgun. A scythe of buck shot kicked them off their boots. Writhing in the dirt, their multiple wounds gradually went numb.

Few among their fellow gunfighters took notice, as the downed gunhawks lost their struggle to hold onto life. After a moment of stunned inactivity, the remaining fast guns released a ragged volley of their own. By then the astonished defenders inside the buildings nearest the Exchange Hotel found themselves overwhelmed by the surprise assault. Smoke Jensen led the way into the dry goods store.

Smoke's .44 barked with authority, as he jumped through a shattered window and pushed aside a mannequin in the display case. It bounced off a rack of dresses, and a member of Quint Stalker's gang used its distracting motion to cover his move to get Smoke Jensen.

Rising up, he swung the muzzle of his Colt into line with Smoke, only to find himself staring down a long, black tunnel to the afterworld. Smoke Jensen fired first. Hot lead released a thunderous pain in the chest of the outlaw, who slammed backward to upend over an island of discounted women's shoes. High-top button creations in uniform black flew in three directions.

When the powder smoke cleared, Smoke Jensen saw

his man lying still in death. "Put some men in place to hold this window," Smoke told the nearest Ranger.

Numbers began to tell. Doing the unexpected had gained the Rangers the dubious shelter of two wooden frame buildings, only to be pinned down by concentrated fire from outside. Several of the lawmen gave fleeting thought to how Benton-Howell's defenders in the hotel must have felt. Smoke Jensen took a quick mental inventory.

It didn't look good. Not counting those who broke through the ring of guns in the hands of the newly arrived hard cases, he could account for only some seven men not wounded or dead among the Rangers. They still faced some thirty or more guns. He had to find a way into the hotel. In memory, the ladder beckoned.

"Can you hold them here?" Smoke asked of Tallpockets.

He received a curt nod. "Don't know how long, but we'll do our best. Jeff an' the other boys should be hittin' 'em from behind soon. What'er you gonna do?"

"Get in that hotel." Not waiting for a response from the Arizona Ranger, Smoke headed for the rear of the shop.

A small loading dock behind the dry goods store could be accessed by three heavy plank steps. Smoke Jensen didn't waste time on them. A small shock ran up his legs when his boots hit the ground. He turned right and soon located the ladder. Fighting a sense of being too late, he lugged the heavy wooden object back to the hotel. Smoke leaned it against the clapboard siding of the hotel under a window. Colt in one hand, he started upward.

When he reached a position below the sash, Smoke

Jensen crouched and removed his hat. He held it in his left hand, while he raised his head and six-gun to peer inside. The room was empty. Smoke suddenly realized that he had been holding his breath. Stale air gusted out of his lungs, and he drew in a fresh draught. He tried the window, but it had been secured by a slide latch.

No time for finesse. Smoke cracked the lower center pane of glass, and reached through to slide the bar out of place. Then he raised up the lower half of the sash. He climbed into the room without incident. He crossed the room in four long strides, and paused at the door.

Smoke strained his keen hearing to gauge the unknown surroundings outside. At first he heard nothing, yet caution urged him to open the door only a crack. His first glance of the hallway showed him some ten gunmen lounging around, worried looks on their faces. Then all hell broke out on the street in front of the hotel.

Twenty-five

Jeff York levered rounds through the Winchester in a blur of speed, as he advanced on the hard cases milling in the street. One of the steadier of the band of thugs placed a round close enough to put Jeff down behind a full watering trough. He hunched forward on his elbows and took aim at one gunhawk's left kneecap. The Winchester bucked, and the man screamed as he went down.

But not out of the fight. His six-gun cracked and brought a shower of splinters from the trough. Stinging pinpricks on his face, told Jeff that the man could definitely shoot. His next round ended the contest with the border ruffian doubled over his perforated intestines. Jeff sought another target.

He had all too many, Jeff reflected on the situation. Enough that they were no longer intimidated by gunfire from the Rangers. They gathered their ranks and actually began to advance. A shirtless ruffian bounded out of the barbershop two doors down from Jeff, and raised a Smith and Wesson American to blast the life from the Arizona Ranger.

Jeff saw him first and put the last round from his Winchester through the small white button, third down on the front of the thug's red, longhandle underwear top. His mouth formed a black oval in his shaving cream-lathered face, and he did a pratfall on the boardwalk. His weapon discharged upward and shattered one square pane of glass in a streetlight. Dead already, he didn't feel the shards that pierced his scalp and chest. Three more popped up seemingly out of nowhere.

Screams of rage reached Jeff's ears a moment before he heard the distinctive yowl of a coyote. The voices of several desert birds joined, then came the thunder of hooves. Jeff York looked behind him to see seven riders, hugging low on the necks of their horses, rumbling toward the center of the fight.

Bands of red and yellow cloth fluttered from the forestocks of three rifles, and he saw the sharp curve of a bow a moment before an arrow flashed overhead and buried its point in the stomach of a would-be gunfighter not five feet from where Jeff lay.

Cuchillo Negro and six of his warriors had come through at a crucial time. They pounded down on the suddenly disorganized outlaws, and brought swift death with them. Several of the wiser among the hirelings of Benton-Howell took off running toward the nearest empty saddle. They took flight in utter panic, leaving all possessions behind. Others chose to fight it out.

They got a poor bargain for it. Hot lead laced the street from both Ranger positions. Black Knife operated his trapdoor Spencer with cool, smooth expertise. Round after round of lethal .56 caliber slugs smacked into flesh. One gunhawk went down with two Apaches swarming over him, knives flashing silver, then crimson in the sunlight.

In that mad, swirling instant, what had been certain

defeat for the Arizona Rangers turned into a promise of victory.

Boot heels thumped along the carpeted upstairs hall in reaction to the rattle of gunfire. Smoke Jensen watched the retreating backs of the hard cases, as they responded to the increased fighting outside. When all but two started down the wide staircase, Smoke Jensen stepped out of the room he had entered moments before and took stock.

A pair of men stood at the door to each of two rooms. Guarding the bosses? Smoke pondered a moment. At the far end, one gunhand was mostly out the door of the balcony that fronted the establishment. Another waited his turn. That meant five guns against Smoke. Six in the worst case. An arrow thudded into the wooden panel of the balcony door with enough force to wrest it from the hand of the youthful outlaw. A moment later he went to his knees, hands clutched to the shaft of the projectile that protruded from his chest.

Only five guns now. Considering who Smoke Jensen suspected had been confined behind those guarded portals, he could not simply leave well enough alone. When he opened up on the gunmen below, they would no doubt kill the hostages at once. He walked up to the Anglo pair guarding the center door.

"Benton-Howell said for me to relieve you two. He needs more guns in the fight downstairs."

Suspicion shined in the eyes of the nearer outlaw. "How'd he tell you that with you up here?"

"Don't you know anything about this place? There's a

brass speaking from the desk connected to every room."
Smoke had noticed the device beside the door as he had
exited, and took the chance that everyone was aware of
them. "He just blew into it, and it whistled in my room.
I answered and got told what to do."

"Yeah. I guess I did see them things. Looked like a
pipe organ behind the counter."

"That's the one. Now go on, before those damned
Rangers get inside the building."

They turned away with a dubious look, then joined the
third white man at the top of the stairs. "I ain't gonna
go out there. Damn Injuns have ridden in," he told them.
"I'll go with you boys."

Once the three were out of sight, Smoke turned his
attention to the two sombrero-wearing *bandidos* at the
other door. He walked up to them, displaying a casual
manner. A smile and his poor and rusty Spanish should
help put them off guard, Smoke reckoned.

"Oye, my Spanish she is not so good," Smoke greeted
in mixed language. "Your *jefe,* he says for me to tell you
that they need more guns—*mas pistolas*—downstairs.
You are to go at once."

"Don Miguel ordered us to stay here, not to leave unless he told us," the burlier of the pair protested in rapid-
fire Spanish.

"¿Como? You speak too fast for me."

"Not too fast for me," a heavy voice rumbled from
the head of the stairs.

A sharp crack of a .44 round from his Merwin and
Hulbert punctuated Quint Stalker's statement. The bullet
burned along the meaty portion of the small of Smoke
Jensen's back. Smoke sprang across the hallway, out of

reach of the two Mexican bandits, and spun to face Stalker.

"I see you got out of jail."

"Damn right, Jensen. You an' me got a score to settle."

"Words are cheap. Let's get to it," Smoke grated, hand on the grip of his pistol.

"I don't think so. Ramon, Xavier, grab him."

For all the girth of Xavier, he moved like a startled cat. As his ham hands closed on the arm of Smoke Jensen, he left his ample belly open to ready attack. Smoke did not overlook it. He drove two hard, fast rights into the swell of gut before him. Xavier grunted and yanked Smoke toward him. By then, Ramon had Smoke's other arm. Smirking, Quint Stalker advanced along the hall. The Merwin and Hulbert drooped indolently in his gunhand, but even with his victim held captive, he took no chances with Smoke Jensen.

When he reached an arm's length from Smoke, Stalker cocked a solid left and drove knuckles into Jensen's face. "Hold him up," Stalker commanded. Another punch to the cheek, and Smoke Jensen went slack in their grasp.

Quint Stalker leered at the apparently dazed Smoke Jensen. "I'm gonna make this last, Jensen. Go real slow, give you a lot of pain . . . before I kill you."

Smoke gasped as he imperceptibly tightened his muscles, positioned now with his weight supported by the Mexican outlaws. His ears caught a distinct sound from outside. "You . . . may not . . . have time, Stalker. Those Apaches still want to get their hands on you."

The word Apaches galvanized Quint Stalker. He turned his attention away from his intended victim to listen to the war whoops that drifted through the open doorway.

Then he saw the dying hard case with the arrow in his chest. Time to move, Smoke Jensen judged. Swiftly shifting his weight, Smoke drove the pointed toe of his boot into Stalker's groin.

A banshee shriek ripped from the throat of Quint Stalker. Following it came a wet, sucking sound, as the hurting outlaw leader fought to pull air into his body and stop the misery. He doubled over until his chin touched his knees. Before the Mexican bandits could react, Smoke kicked Stalker in the face. Then, his feet planted firmly on the carpet runner in the hall, Smoke Jensen flexed powerful muscles in his shoulders and slammed Ramon and Xavier together face to face.

Their foreheads met with a *klonk!,* and Ramon went slack-legged to the floor. Quint Stalker lay twitching on the carpet strip. Smoke Jensen had no desire to trade punches with Quint Stalker, let alone the massive Xavier. He had his .44 halfway out of the holster when Xavier spotted the motion and, still dazed by the ramming, groped for his Mendoza .45 copy. He freed it and fired too soon. The slug zipped between the legs of Smoke Jensen and ploughed into a floorboard. Vibration from the hammer blow partly revived Quint Stalker.

He squinted and blinked his eyes to fuzzily see that Smoke Jensen had his Colt leveled. Smoke fired while Xavier tried desperately to cock his six-gun again. The, slug slammed into Xavier's hip; he staggered and finished cocking. Eyes tearing in pain, he sought to sight in on the insubstantial target of Smoke Jensen.

Eyes fixed on Xavier, Smoke brought his pistol to bear and tripped the trigger. Ramon's hand closed on Smoke's ankle, and he yanked as the hammer fell. The .44 bullet went wide of its intended mark. With his attention now divided between the Mexican bandits, Smoke did not notice Stalker's stealthy, crablike crawl away from the conflict.

His strength rapidly waning, Xavier sent a round over Smoke's left shoulder. Smoke Jensen had had enough of this. His next round shattered Ramon's shoulder, and the grip on his leg released at once. He turned back to Xavier, as the pudgy Sonoran went white-faced and sagged back against the opposite wall. Internal bleeding had sapped him of all his strength. He slithered to a sitting position and sighed regretfully before he passed out.

That's when Quint Stalker regained reason enough to take a shot.

Quint Stalker's bullet cracked past Smoke Jensen's head close enough for the gunfighter to feel its hot breath. One thing he knew for certain, he did not want Stalker to reach the ground floor and bring the news of Smoke's presence in the hotel. Far too many guns waited him down there, and what little element of surprise remained was all Smoke had going for his plan to free the Tuckers. Quint Stalker had already negotiated the top three treads, his weight borne by the banister, over which the outlaw leader had draped himself heavily.

A quick memory check told Smoke that he had emptied his right-hand gun. He holstered it and went for his second .44. The time lapse got Stalker to the upper landing, where he paused, gasped, and looked upward. He was out of sight of Smoke Jensen and glad of it. Determined not to let Stalker get away, Smoke advanced down the hallway toward the head of the stairs.

When he reached his goal, the wooden ball on top of the newel post exploded in a shower of splinters. Several stung and bit into Smoke's cheeks. Ignoring them, he threw a quick shot down the stairwell. Hot lead brought forth a yelp of alarm, when it tugged at the shoulder piece of Stalker's vest. At once, Smoke bounded down four steps.

Stalker fired again and, with his strength returning, retreated downward before he could check the results. There were none, except for a hole in the plaster high over Smoke Jensen's right shoulder. Smoke came after him at once. At the central landing, feet planted squarely on the level, Quint Stalker's bullet caused Smoke Jensen to dive to one side to avoid a mortal wound.

Crying out at this near-triumph, Stalker started off down the final flight of stairs. Smoke Jensen reached the platform seconds behind Quint Stalker. He steadied his arm and took aim. Stalker looked back, spun on a boot heel, and tried again to blast Smoke out of existence. Smoke Jensen fired first.

Smoke's slug took Quint in the chest, to the right of his sternum. The outlaw boss rose on tiptoe and a thin whine came through his lips. He tried to raise his gun barrel . . . and failed. Smoke shot hid in the center of the chest.

Stalker teetered backward and cartwheeled down four treads. His body went slack, and he rolled the rest of the way to the bottom of the staircase. Smoke Jensen was already heading upward. He took the steps two at a time. Excited voices followed him.

"Have the savages gotten in?" Benton-Howell's English accent floated upward.

"Someone has," another voice answered, as he spotted the body of Quint Stalker.

"Then go after them," Benton-Howell commanded.

Half a dozen hard cases started for the stairway. At the same moment, chunks of plaster showered into the room from the wall dividing the hotel from the dry goods store. Another crash drove the heavy metal base of a display rack through the lath. The barrels of rifles and shotguns followed.

A few of the hired guns made instant response, only to be cut down in a hail of lead. Not bound by years of loyalty, the majority saw the inevitable end for their kind, and deserted the cause. They rushed out into the street to surrender, hope filling them that the Indians had ridden on to other depredations.

There the Arizona Rangers began to disarm and handcuff the demoralized mob of shootists. Jeff York detached himself from his men and made for the hotel. Upstairs, Smoke Jensen caught a glimpse of a flat-crowned Cordovan sombrero disappear down the back stairway. Suspecting defeat, he hurried to the first of the two rooms that had been guarded.

He threw open the door . . . and found the stark cubicle empty.

"Selleres has them," Smoke Jensen shouted to Jeff York, when the Arizona Ranger's head topped the stairs. "He went down the back."

Jeff didn't waste time asking if Smoke was sure.

Smoke Jensen rarely made such a statement if he didn't know for certain. Instead, he strode rapidly to where Smoke stood at the top of the back staircase. As he did, Jeff passed two open doors, the rooms behind them gaping emptily.

"We're going after them?" Jeff asked.

"Just you and me. I don't want to frighten Selleres into killing any of them."

They started down, only to find the way blocked by three of Quint Stalker's loyalest men; Vern Draper, Marv Fletcher, and Charlie Bascomb. Bascomb fired first. His bullet cut the air between Smoke and Jeff. Smoke got a slug into the leg of the young gunslinger, and sent him tumbling back down the stairs. That bought Smoke and Jeff half the flight, before a muzzle appeared around the corner of the hallway and sent a bullet winging upward.

Hunkered down, Smoke and Jeff duck-walked uncomfortably down the next five treads. A six-gun blazed in their direction, and Smoke put a round through the wall. A soft grunt answered him. No more shots came, and they made it to the bottom. A quick look showed Charlie Bascomb sprawled on the floorboards of the rear hallway in a pool of blood. He wouldn't be holding them up any more.

"Out back," Smoke prompted.

He made his way cautiously to the open back door. The moment Smoke Jensen's head appeared around the jamb, Vern Draper and Marv Fletcher opened up. Smoke jerked back in time. The slugs whistled down the corridor. Smoke saw that Jeff had wisely flattened himself against the far wall, out of the line of fire.

"We'll lose too much time going around the long way,"

Smoke figured aloud. "Nothing for it but to rush them." At that moment he would have given anything for Walt Reardon's 10 gauge L.C. Smith.

Both he and Jeff took time to reload. Then, with a six-gun in each hand—something Preacher had told Smoke never, ever to do—he crouched low and went through the doorway, his, matched pistols leading him. They blasted alternately in a steady rhythm. From behind he heard Jeff York join the dance. Marv Fletcher cried out and spun to one side, hit by two slugs at the same time. He fell like wet wash. That left only one.

Vern Draper backed up in the direction obviously taken by the fleeing Miguel Selleres and the hostages. He fired repeatedly as he gained what speed he could in his ungainly walk. Beyond him, near the mouth to the alley farthest from the activity around the hotel, Smoke caught sight of Jimmy Tucker's towhead flashing white in a ray of sunlight. Geoffrey Benton-Howell yanked the boy by his collar. Another man, whose identity Smoke Jensen did not know, dragged the other children along. Miguel Selleres roughly shoved Martha Tucker in the desired direction.

Unwilling to risk their lives, Smoke Jensen holstered his right-hand .44 and drew his coffin-handle Bowie. He hefted it and closed fingers around the grips. A swift up and down motion of his arm, and he released the blade. It turned one full time in the air, and buried half its length in the chest of a surprisedVern Draper.

The six-gun fell from numbed fingers, and Vern's eyes bugged at the enormous, hot pain in his chest. Draper went rubber-legged and staggered to one side. Smoke Jensen pushed past him, and only faintly heard the thump of Jeff York's six-gun when it ended the life of the snaggle-toothed outlaw. Smoke started running, with Jeff pounding along behind.

Beyond the fleeing conspirators and their captives, a coach had rumbled into place. The armored carriage of Miguel Selleres.

At the direction of the corrupt *haciendado,* three burly Mexican bandits, who had accompanied the coach, stepped between their leader and the two lawmen. Each wore the wide, floppy sombrero of a *charro,* with bandoliers of ammunition crossed over their chests. Beneath the cartridge belts they wore short, open bolero jackets, white shirts with string ties and lots of lace ruffles. They were large men, but not with puffy fat, yet their bellies protruded over the belts that supported their holsters.

Each had a brace of Mendoza .45s, canted forward so to provide easy reach to a man in the saddle. Their tight trousers, the outer seams trimmed with silver conchos, pegged down to slender tubes where they met the tall boots. They all sported flowing, long, thick moustaches that drooped to their jawlines. Without comment, they swiftly drew their weapons.

Jeff York killed the one opposite him before the *bandido* could squeeze his trigger. Beside him, he heard the steady bang of Smoke's .44. Jeff's target flopped on the ground and raised a cloud of dust. The two Smoke had shot staggered forward a step, fired wildly in the general direction of the lawmen they faced, and then took another bullet each.

Impact turned them inward, facing each other, their

foreheads rebounded off one another, and they spun away, arms hooked together in a macabre do-si-do. Meanwhile, Benton-Howell energetically shoved Jimmy Tucker into the coach. He gestured impatiently to his third partner, Dalton Wade, to pass him the other two children.

By then, Selleres' three bandits had been dispatched. Slowly, the cloud of expended powder began to clear. Miguel Selleres found himself facing Smoke Jensen and Jeff York, smoking Colts in their hands.

"It's over, Selleres. Let your hostages go," Smoke Jensen demanded.

Swiftly, Selleres grabbed Martha Tucker under one arm and laid his wrist tightly across her throat, the muzzle of his Mendoza pressed to the soft flesh behind her chin. "Put up your *pistolas, Señores,* or I will kill her before your eyes."

Twenty-six

The sneer on Miguel Selleres's face portrayed more fear than contempt. "We are leaving here. All is lost, *¿como no?* We'll take the woman and these brats for safe passage. Do not come after us."

"Why not? You'll kill them eventually," Smoke challenged.

Selleres shrugged. *"Que obvio. Pero no es importante para té."*

"It's sure as hell important to the woman and her kids," Jeff York growled.

"Holster your guns or she dies," said Selleres coldly.

Jeff York cut his eyes to Smoke Jensen. Smoke considered only for a brief second, then gave a small nod. Both lawmen slid iron into leather. Miguel Selleres began to back toward the armored coach.

Madness glittered in his eyes. "We're leaving now. But we'll be back. Everyone will be made to pay for what they've done to us. The whole damned world will tremble before us!"

At that moment, Martha Tucker managed to dip her chin low enough to get a mouthful of the arm holding her. She sank her teeth in and ground them.

With a howl of anguish, Miguel Selleres jerked his

head upward in reflexive response to the pain. His grip loosened, Martha opened her mouth and fell to one side. Smoke Jensen drew his left-hand .44

"No, we won't," Smoke Jensen barked, as his bullet popped a hole in the forehead of Miguel Selleres.

The Mendoza Colt dropped from a lifeless hand. Selleres had overlooked one vital requirement. He had not cocked his weapon. Driven by desperation, Dalton Wade made the terrible mistake of unlimbering the age-worn, 5-shot Herington and Richards .38 from its long, soft pouch holster. To do so, he had to release the hand of Tommy Tucker. It did him no good, though. A bullet each from Smoke Jensen and Jeff York struck his chest at the same moment. Screaming, Rose Tucker ran after her little brother. A major transformation had come over Benton-Howell. He sank to his knees, hands upraised in supplication, tears streaming down his full cheeks, face ruddy.

"Please, don't kill me. I don't want to die. None of this was my idea. You—you can't kill me," a sudden hope rising in his quaking body. "I'm a peer of the realm! And, after all, no one important got hurt."

Smoke Jensen turned an icy gaze of utter contempt upon the groveling Englishman. "We'll save you, all right, *Sir* Geoffrey . . . for the hangman. Jeff, go after the Tucker kids."

Once they had been restored to their mother, who wept copiously in relief over the safe resolution of their dangerous situation, Smoke Jensen turned his attention back to Benton-Howell.

"Sir Geoffrey?" His lips curled with contempt. "Well, you're sure not a gentleman, let alone a knightly one. You're a coward, a murderer, and a thief. You're so low

and corrupt, you'd have to reach up to scratch a snake's belly. I said we'd save you for a date with the hangman, but I didn't promise what condition you'd be in for the trial." Smoke undid his cartridge bell. "Put up your hands and defend yourself."

Benton-Howell began to splutter. "Bu—but, I'm—I'm your prisoner, sir. You cannot strike me."

In an eye blink, Smoke Jensen hit him with a right and left to either side of the jaw. Benton-Howell sagged and raised a futile left arm in an attempt to block the next solid punch, which whistled in as a sizzling right jab. He gulped and backpedaled. His shoulders slammed against the heavy side of the coach. Jimmy Tucker's head popped out the door.

"Yaaah-hooo! Kick him between the legs, Smoke."

"James Lee Tucker," Martha admonished, scandalized by her son. "Such language. For shame."

Jimmy didn't look the least repentant. "I mean it, too, Mom."

Left arm still up, Benton-Howell darted his right in under its concealing position. Suddenly Smoke Jensen was there. One hand clinched a lapel as Smoke spun Benton-Howell around. Smoke pulled down the frock coat to reveal a concealed shoulder holster that held a short-barreled .44 Colt Lightning. Jeff stepped in and plucked the weapon from its holster. Smoke swung the frothing-mouthed Benton-Howell around and slammed his head into the armored side of the carriage. It made a solid *thunk.*

Smoke brought his dazed opponent face to face, and went to work on the midsection. Feebly Benton-Howell tried to fend off the blows. Clearly this was not a fight, it was a beating, plain and simple. Every bit of the out-rage and frustration of the last mountain man poured out on the source of it all. Benton-Howell doubled over, his air exhausted, and Smoke Jensen straightened him up with a hard left.

The Englishman's knees buckled and his head drooped. Still Smoke bore in. Blood ran from a cut on the cheek of Benton-Howell, from the corner of his mouth, and the corner of an eye swollen shut by severe battering. At last, Smoke Jensen took control of his anger and eased off. When the red haze left his eyes, he found Benton-Howell on his knees, thoroughly battered and de-feated.

Disgust plain on her face at having witnessed the sav-aging of Benton-Howell, Martha Tucker hugged her chil-dren to her and spoke with unaccustomed chill to Smoke Jensen. "It's over then?"

"Yes. All but the roundup of the trash and, of course, the trial. I've no doubt Benton-Howell will be convicted of ordering your husband's murder. And he *will* hang."

"Yes . . . of course," she responded stiffly. "At least that way it will be done according to law."

Her sudden, inexplicable disapproval stung Smoke Jensen. He started to make some sort of reply, thought better of it, and shrugged. He retrieved his hat from the ground, dusted it off, and indicated the way back toward the hotel with it. Without further comment, Martha Tucker followed, her children clustered at either side.

They had progressed only a third of the way down the alley, when a shot crashed overloud in the confined space, and little Tommy Tucker slammed forward out of the protective circle of his mother's arm. Martha took one stunned look at the spreading red stain on the boy's back, and began to wail hysterically. Young Rose Tucker screamed and dissolved into tears. Jimmy hit the ground.

Smoke Jensen reacted quickly also. He jumped to one side and looked beyond the frozen tableau of the Tuckers to where a wooden-faced Forrest Gore worked the lever of his Winchester in a frantic effort to chamber another round. Smoke's hand dropped to the butt of his .44, and he freed it before the bolt closed on Gore's rifle.

Smoke's arm rose with equal swiftness and steadied only a fraction of a second to allow the hammer to drop. Quickly he slip-thumbed three more rounds. All four struck Forrest Gore in the chest and belly. The Winchester flew to the sky, and Gore jerked and writhed with each impact. A cloud of cloth bits, flesh, and blood made a crimson haze that circled his body. Jeff York turned in time to plunk two more slugs into the child-killer. Then he spun, pistol still smoking, toward Benton-Howell.

"That does it! No waiting for the hangman, damn you. It's your scheming that brought it to this. Now you pay."

"No, Jeff!" Smoke Jensen barked harshly. "Let him sit and sweat and wait for that rope to be put around his neck. That way he'll die a thousand times over."

Jeff York's shoulders sagged. "You're right, Smoke. Sorry, I lost it for a moment."

Martha Tucker drew out of her grief long enough to look up with a face drawn with anguish, and addressed Smoke Jensen with some of her former warmth. "Thank you, Smoke Jensen. Thank you for saving a fine lawman's career and self-esteem. And thank you for avenging my husband and my—my son."

All at once, Smoke Jensen felt as though he had been

the one to take a beating. "I did what I had to do, Martha. Now, we have a lot yet to accomplish."

Martha Tucker had been restored to her ranch. A week had gone by since the Arizona Rangers had cleared the streets of Socorro of saddle tramps and low-class gunfighters. They had ridden away after little Tommy Tucker's funeral. Each one had expressed their deep sympathy for the courageous woman who had lost a husband and son within a month's time. Even Cuchillo Negro and his Apache warriors left small, feather-decorated gifts on the raw earth of the grave. Then they, too, rode off to the west.

That left Smoke Jensen alone at the ranch. He recalled the tension and black grief at the burial of the small boy, and a sensation of relief flooded him as he watched Martha Tucker step from the kitchen, smiling and brushing at the swatch of flour on her forehead in a familiar gesture. She smiled up at him as she approached where he stood with his saddled roan.

"I've put a pie on. I—I sort of hoped that you would stay on, if not with your hands, at least yourself, for a while."

"I really can't, Martha. I'm long over due in returning to my ranch."

"With it in the capable hands of men like Walt and Ty, I see no reason why a few days more would matter."

Smoke sighed. "Truth is, I miss 'em. The High Lonesome, the Sugarloaf, and . . . my wife. It's time I got back to them. Goodbye, and bless you, Martha Tucker. You're a strong woman. Strong even if you were a man."

"Why, I—I take that as the supreme compliment," she said, clearly flustered. Then Martha rose on tiptoe and kissed Smoke lightly on one cheek. "Goodbye, Smoke Jensen. You'll be missed . . . awfully."

Jimmy Tucker rushed forward and hugged Smoke Jensen around the waist. He was too deeply moved for words, but his silent tears spoke it all. That made it even more difficult for Smoke Jensen to take his leave, but he did.

Prying the lad's arms from around him and giving a final tip of his hat to Martha, Smoke swung into the saddle and rode off. He didn't look back until he reached the top of the ridge to the northeast. The backward glance did not last long, for his thoughts had already spanned the miles ahead to his secure nook in the Shining Mountains, the cozy log and stone home on the Sugarloaf, and his beloved Sally.

DANGER, SUSPENSE, INTRIGUE . . .
THE NOVELS OF

NOEL HYND

FALSE FLAGS	(2918-7, $4.50/$5.50)
THE KHRUSHCHEV OBJECTIVE	(2297-2, $4.50/$5.50)
REVENGE	(2529-7, $3.95/$4.95)
THE SANDLER INQUIRY	(3070-3, $4.50/$5.50)
TRUMAN'S SPY	(3309-5, $4.95/$5.95)